THE MINISTER AND THE MASSACRES

THE
MINISTER
AND THE
MASSACRES

Nikolai Tolstoy

Century Hutchinson Ltd
London Melbourne Auckland Johannesburg

© Nikolai Tolstoy 1986

This edition first published in 1986 by Century Hutchinson Ltd,
Brookmount House, 62–65 Chandos Place, London WC2N 4NW

Century Hutchinson Publishing Group (Australia) Pty Ltd
PO Box 496, 16–22 Church Street, Hawthorn, Melbourne, Victoria 3122

Century Hutchinson Group (NZ) Ltd
PO Box 40–086, 32–34 View Road, Glenfield, Auckland 10

Century Hutchinson Group (SA) Pty Ltd
PO Box 337, Bergvlei 2012, South Africa

British Library Cataloguing in Publication Data
Tolstoy, Nikolai
    The minister and the massacres.
    1. World War, 1939–1945   2. Prisoners and prisons
    3. World War, 1939–1945 – Forced repatriation
    I. Title
    940.54'72   D805.A2

ISBN 0-09-164010-5

Photoset by Rowland Phototypesetting Ltd,
Bury St Edmunds, Suffolk
Printed and bound in Great Britain by Anchor Brendon Ltd,
Tiptree, Essex

Contents

Acknowledgements

It is now some twelve years since I first became concerned with the subject-matter of this book, during which time I have visited many countries and consulted large numbers of people. It was a laborious task; but rewarding in more ways than one, and I have gained some valued friends along the way. In such circumstances I will, I fear, inevitably have overlooked in the last-minute compilation of this list the name of more than one generous helper or adviser, for which I hope I will be forgiven. Among surviving participants there were many, Slovene, Croat, Serb, Cossack and British, for whom the events of May and June 1945 represent very painful memories. Though the task was a delicate one, I was pleasurably surprised to find only two people who actually declined to assist me, and among the rest there were those who gave generously of their time over a period of years.

I would accordingly like to record my gratitude to the following: Mr Bozidar Abjanic; the Rt Hon Lord Aldington; Mr G. C. Allies; Dr David Andrews; Dr Georg M. Aschner; Dr Stanislav A. Ausky; Major Hugo Baring; Miss Evelyn Bark; Major P. H. Barre; Mr Daniel Beazer; Miss Nora Beloff; Mr Ladislav J. Bevc; Mr L. Birch; Mr Branko Bokun; Sir Frederic Bolton; Miss Serena Booker; the Rt Hon Lord Boothby; Mr Paul Borstnik; Sir Bernard Braine, MP; the late Major-General H. E. N. Bredin; Mr Gordon Brooke-Shepherd; Captain Philip Brutton; Mr Ronald de Bunsen; the Cabinet Office; Captain P. A. Carr; Mr David Chandler; Lieutenant-Colonel Brian Clark; Colonel John Coldwell-Horstfall; Sir John Colville; Mr John Corsellis; Professor Danijel Crljen; Mr Stevan Curuvija; Mr Roger Custance; the Ministry of Defence; Mr Frank Dejak; Mr Janez Dernulc; Captain Milan Djordjevic; Mr Kenneth Elliott; Mr David Floyd; Lieutenant-Colonel R. L. V. ffrench Blake; Mr Michael Frewer; Mr

D. J. Frogley; Mrs Brenda Fuller; Major the Lord Gibson-Watt; Mr Andrew Gibson-Watt; Count Leopold Goëss; Mr John Gollop; Brigadier Adrian Gore; the late Dr Franc Grum; Hofrath Leopold Guggenberger; Prince Azamat Guirey; Mr Francis Hepburne Scott; Major R. S. V. Howard; Mr A. Hribar; Gillian M. Hughes; Dr Joze Jancar; Professor Jere Jareb; Major F. R. Jephson; Captain D. J. Karakusevic; Major-General R. C. Keightley; Mrs Marija Kelava; Mr M. Kent; Captain R. N. Kingzett; Mr Peter Koltypin; Mr Lev Kopelev; Mr Frank Kozina; Father Vladimir Kozina; Professor Stephen Kresic; Mrs Zdenka Palic-Kusan; Senator Misha Lajovic; Dr Melvin Lasky; Mrs Margot Lawrence; Mr Robert Leigh; Mrs Nina A. Lencek; Major-General P. R. Leuchars; Mrs Marija Ann Levic; Mr V. Ljotic; Captain Earl Lloyd-George of Dwyfor; Mr R. Marcetic; Mr Patrick Martin-Smith; Major J. R. Martin Smith; Lt-Colonel Barry McGrath; Princess Tatiana Metternich; Mrs Liljana Milberg; Mr Jovo Miletic; Lieutenant-Colonel Anthony J. Morris; Captain O. D. Morris; General Sir Horatius Murray; General Sir Geoffrey Musson; the National Trust Archives; Herr Hans Werner Neulen; Mr Nigel Nicolson; Captain David Nockels; Lieutenant-Colonel J. Odling-Smee; Mr Radovan Ojdrovic; Dr Ivo Omrcanin; Mr Ivan Palcic; Lieutenant-Colonel Murphy Palmer; Mr John M. Parry; Mr Ted Pavic; Mr Stevan K. Pavlowitch; Dr Jure Petricevic; Professor Eugene E. Petriwsky; Miss Florence Phillips; Mr Stanislav Plesko; Professor George R. Prpic; Mr Z. R. Prvulovich; the Public Record Office; Mr David Pugh; Mr R. Radcliffe; Mr Miodrag M. Radotic; Mr George Raguz; Lieutenant-Colonel J. D. N. Retallack; the Rev. Malcolm Hart Richards; Mr Hugh Richardson; Mr Richard Roberts; Mr T. K. Hickman Robertson; Major K. F. Rooney; Lieutenant-Colonel Robin Rose Price; Professor Edward J. Rozek; the Royal Artillery Institution; Mr H. Eric Ryall; Mr Mladen Schwarz; Dr Ljubo Sirc; Dr W. Sircus; Miss M. N. Slade (British Red Cross Society); Colonel Donald Smith; Mr Peter Solly-Flood; *The South Slav Journal*; Mr M. S. Stankovic; Professor Norman Stone; Rev. C. W. H. Story; Mr Branko Terzic; Count Ariprand Thurn-Valsassina; Brigadier Christopher Thursby Pelham; Brigadier C. E. Tryon-Wilson; Mr Josip Turkovic; Mr Paul Tvrtkovic; Mr Peter Urbanc; Major Peter Verney; Mr Stanisa R. Vlahovic; Mr and Mrs Dimitrije Vojvodic; Major A. E. F. Waldron; Mr Nigel Watts; Mr Richard Watts; Mr Arnold J. Weight; General Sir James Wilson; Sir John Wilton; Lieutenant-Colonel Denys Worrall; Mr D. T. Wroth; Mr Milan Zajec; Mr Joseph Zelle; Mr P. Zupan.

Lastly I would like to make especial mention of my friend Ernst von Weyhausen, who introduced me to the intricacies of the Apricot computer and Wordstar programme. The extent to which this eased my task would sound too much like hyperbole to bear recapitulation. The finished text owes much to Richard Cohen, who combined infectious enthusiasm with critical perceptiveness.

Photograph credits

Imperial War Museum, 1, 11, 12, 14, 15, 19 and 20
Wilhelm Wadl, *Das Jahr 1945 in Kärnten*, 2
Hofrath Leopold Guggenberger, pp 2–3
Henry Grossman, 10
Dr Franc Grum, 17

Dedicated to
our dear daughter Alexandra
born 14 July 1973

For reasons of authenticity, original spellings and punctuation have been retained in all quotations and extracts.

Preface

Since the publication of my *Victims of Yalta* in 1978 it has become common knowledge that the Western Allies in 1944–7 handed over to Stalin great numbers (more than two million) of refugee Soviet citizens, whom the upheaval of the World War had stranded in Central and Western Europe. The majority of these people were either massacred on arrival or despatched to the notorious death-camps of the Gulag administration. All this took place as the result of an agreement signed by the British, American and Soviet foreign ministers at the Yalta Conference in February 1945. Regrettable or misguided as most people would perhaps now consider the operations, they arose from decisions made at the highest levels and represented official policy of the British and United States Governments.

The task of chronicling that enormous tragedy was laborious, involving extensive research among the voluminous archives released by the British Government and the tracing of innumerable eye-witnesses from all over the globe. Grim though the subject-matter was (one with which I had some personal concern), as a task for research it was not in essentials different from any other historical investigation. My task was to marshal the evidence as comprehensively as possible, and it remained largely for the reader to supply the interpretation and conclusions.

At a very early stage of my investigation, however, I was struck by a glaring anomaly which came increasingly to absorb my attention. The Yalta Agreement related exclusively to Soviet citizens. How had it come about, then, that in May of 1945 the British Army in Austria had surrendered to the Soviets a large number of Cossack officers, together with their families, who had never been Soviet citizens, having emigrated at the time of the Russian Revolution? Most prominent among these was the aged Ataman of the Don Cossacks, Peter Nikolaevich Krasnov, whose melodramatic historical novels written in pre-war emigration had aroused my youthful enthusiasm. He and his most prominent companions were subsequently hanged in Moscow, while the remainder were almost all shot or died in forced-labour camps.

Previous books concerned with the forced repatriation, by the Pole Mackiewicz, the Englishmen Huxley-Blythe and Bethell and the American Epstein, had alluded in passing to this aspect, assuming reasonably enough that it was an accidental outcome of the larger operation being effected at that time in great haste and some confusion. This was to become a semi-official view. In the House of Lords on 17 March 1976, Lord Hankey, a former senior Foreign Office official, expressed his 'very deep regret that in the heat and utter turmoil of the summer of 1945, with 7 million civilians of many nationalities, in addition to all the prisoners-of-war, being repatriated from Germany and Austria in only 20 months, it was impossible for the military authorities, British or American, to weed out all individual cases.' There were 'some sad mistakes'.

Lord Hankey had no direct knowledge of the Cossack tragedy (in conversation with me he expressed great sympathy for their plight), and his view reflects a widespread impression. After examining the relevant British war diaries and talking to soldiers involved, however, I soon came to the conclusion that the 'accident' theory was untenable. First, it was clear that the presence and status of the non-Soviet Cossacks was well-known at all levels within the Fifth Corps, the unit to which they had surrendered at the close of hostilities. Second, *all* orders relating to the handover of the Cossacks emphasized that non-Soviet citizens were to be screened and retained in accordance with policy laid down by the British Government. Given these indisputable facts, how could the surrender of the Tsarist exiles be attributed to an oversight?

It seemed that two versions of the event existed. According to the official record, preserved among War Office files, the non-Soviet Cossacks were ordered to be screened and retained in British custody, and nothing in the files suggests that anything but this took place. Indeed, the official report drawn up a month after the event declared unequivocally that screening *had* taken place. In reality some two or three thousand Tsarist émigrés, holding foreign or League of Nations passports and for the most part dressed in flamboyant Tsarist uniforms, were deceived into travelling to the Soviet lines at Judenburg.

We seem to be inhabiting two different worlds, one fictional and one tragic reality.

Further research revealed that elaborate precautions had been taken to ensure that the Soviets regained this group of their most inveterate enemies in particular, and that equally skilful measures had been adopted to prevent this aspect of the operation from becoming known outside the Fifth Corps. In short, the evidence suggested strongly that the tragedy resulted not from the muddle or oversight that one could so readily envisage in the chaotic circumstances of the time, but was planned and implemented throughout with great care and forethought in deliberate contravention of orders from above.

But if this view were correct, who could have been responsible for flouting undeviatingly clear government instructions in order to perpetrate an atrocity greatly beneficial to the Soviet Government, but of no perceptible advantage to British interests? What was the motive for his or their action? These were questions which I was unable to answer in *Victims of Yalta*, and I was compelled to conclude my investigation with the admission that, 'whether we shall ever know the full story is questionable'.

For the time being matters were left in this unsatisfactory state. Some years later I discovered that Winston Churchill himself, with all the resources of the Cabinet and War Office at his disposal, had been similarly unable to penetrate the secret. In the spring of 1953, disturbed by allegations received from an émigré Cossack general, he had ordered a full enquiry. After an exhaustive search among the files, Brigadier Latham of the Cabinet Office was obliged to confess that 'though we know most of the details of what happened we are at present unable to say why these events took place'.

I seemed to have reached a dead end. I remained deeply dissatisfied, however. A terrible crime had undoubtedly taken place, and exceptional measures appeared to have been adopted to conceal the identity of its perpetrator. A murder requires a murderer, and a conspiracy a conspirator. Somewhere, I felt, there existed a veiled figure who was aware of my fruitless efforts to uncover his identity. Though absorbed in other tasks, I continued on the alert for any clue which might arise.

Two considerations spurred me on. I must freely confess to feeling a strong personal identification with the cause of the Cossacks, alongside whom my grandfather had fought in the Civil War against the Bolsheviks in 1918. Indeed, but for the kindly intervention of an Austrian train guard in the autumn of 1939, my sister Natasha and I might well have been interned in wartime Austria and found ourselves

at the respective ages of eight and ten in the Cossack camp outside
Lienz in 1945. As neither age nor sex was respected by the Cossacks'
persecutors, we too should in that case have been despatched to the
hands of SMERSH at Judenburg. All this is hypothetical, and at this
stage no doubt sounds highly dramatic, but I can only say that I felt
strongly I had a duty to do what I could to expose the identity of the
man responsible for the unauthorised deaths of so many of my
defenceless compatriots.

It was at quite an early stage of my investigation that one name
began to emerge above the rest. On first launching into research for
Victims of Yalta, I had addressed appeals for information to all the
surviving protagonists. The response was fruitful, with one remarkable exception. As Minister Resident in the Mediterranean in 1945,
Harold Macmillan bore responsibility for providing political advice
and decisions in British-occupied Italy and Austria. In view of his
high authority in a region where many thousands of Russians had
fallen into British hands and subsequently been repatriated, he was
an obvious person to consult. At the same time I had no reason to
believe that he had been directly involved in the business with which
I was concerned, since the decision to repatriate Soviet citizens had
been made at Cabinet level. His task, on the face of it, had merely
been to transmit and explain that decision to the Supreme Allied
Commander, Field-Marshal Alexander.

It was with some surprise, therefore, that in April 1974 I received
a curt reply from Mr Macmillan, informing me simply that, 'I am
sorry that I cannot be of help to you.' Though he was clearly under
no obligation to assist every historian approaching him, this refusal
appeared perplexing and, as I was later to learn, unusual. My suspicions were aroused, and his name moved to the forefront of
my concern. I have often wondered since how I might have acted
subsequently had Mr Macmillan invited me to tea to expound on the
chaotic state of Europe following the German surrender, the manifold
responsibilities falling uniquely on his shoulders at that time, and the
deep concern (set out in his diary at the time) he had felt for the plight
of hapless refugees then pouring into Austria. I have to confess that,
my suspicions unaroused, I might never have marked those initial
slight but significant clues which led me eventually to penetrate his
closely-guarded secret.

At the time of the public outcry which greeted the appearance of
Victims of Yalta, I was approached on different occasions by Yugoslav
émigrés, who urged me to write about the parallel plight of thousands

of their compatriots handed over to be slaughtered by Tito at the time of the Cossack tragedy. I was strongly sympathetic to their cause, but had to reply that as the Yugoslavs did not come under the Yalta Agreement, and as my field of study lay largely if not exclusively in Russian affairs, I felt their story should be told by a Yugoslav specialist.

But then it happened that my friend David Floyd wrote an important article on the subject at the end of 1979, published in the magazine *Now!* I read it with detached interest . . . that is, until I came across this quotation from a report by a Foreign Office official: 'The handing over of Slovenes and others by the Eighth Army in Austria to Tito's forces at the end of May was, of course, a ghastly mistake which was rectified as soon as it was reported to headquarters.'

It was the phrase 'a ghastly mistake' which attracted my attention. *Two* 'ghastly mistakes' occurring at the same time and place appeared an improbable coincidence. I saw at once that the Yugoslav tragedy represented not only a subject in itself worthy of study, but one which might open up fresh avenues in an investigation which for some time seemed to have reached a dead end.

Examination of the relevant Foreign Office and War Office files revealed anomalies even greater if possible than those attending on the Cossack handovers. The Cossacks were divided into two categories, Soviet and non-Soviet, repatriable and non-repatriable, which might (but for the evidence I had uncovered) suggest a source of confusion. In the case of the Yugoslavs, however, there existed no ambivalence of any sort. The British and American Governments had throughout maintained a consistent policy that *no* Yugoslav citizens falling into British hands were to be returned against their will. Despite this, thousands had been surreptitiously handed over. Something was very wrong, and it looked as if the twin operations might represent aspects of a single covert exercise. So at least I reasoned.

Gradually the evidence began to accumulate. It soon began to look as if some hand had been at work, altering and removing documents, with the apparent purpose of implicating Field-Marshal Alexander. By this stage, however, the existence of what could only be a deliberate false trail merely provided further evidence of the extraordinary thoroughness with which the real culprit had covered his tracks. Slightly unnerving was the discovery that a crucial public document which I had actually handled had some time after been removed or destroyed.

Then came the moment in an hotel room in Toronto when my friend, the Croatian scholar Dr Jerome Jareb, handed me the copy of Alexander Kirk's revealing report of 14 May 1945. Now I felt I knew who my man was! But the manner in which he deceived not only his Cossack and Yugoslav victims but his own colleagues, at Fifth Corps Headquarters in Austria and Allied Force Headquarters in Naples, the Foreign Office and the Cabinet, was so complex and ingenious that it was still no easy task to unravel the skein of events.

Patiently I built up a circumstantial case which proved, to my satisfaction at least, that Mr Macmillan (as for convenience I shall refer to him, rather than Lord Stockton as he has since become) had himself largely engineered the whole affair. I had published the fresh evidence, such as it was, concerning the Cossacks in my book *Stalin's Secret War* (1981), and on the Yugoslavs in an article in *Encounter* (May 1983).

The case I presented was admittedly circumstantial and speculative, leaving considerable room for differing interpretation even if the salient points appeared clear enough. It also included a number of errors of commission and omission. I would regret what proved to have been a jejunely premature venture more than I do, were it not that publication stimulated anew public interest in the matter. As a result I began to receive a fresh flow of information, some of it of great value. Indeed, I have been led to wonder sometimes whether the best way of researching a book is not to write the book first, and wait for the evidence to come in afterwards.

It would be needlessly pedantic and tedious to the reader were I to specify what is no longer acceptable, in view of the extensive revision which the mass of new material has entailed. The curious or critical may compare for themselves where I went astray. As the story in *The Minister and the Massacres* rests largely, if not entirely, on direct evidence, the element of speculation is now greatly reduced. *Victims of Yalta* on the other hand contains a great deal of matter germane to the forthcoming investigation, particularly in the form of first-hand accounts by participants in the tragedy, many of whom are now sadly dead. I have avoided extensive repetition of this material, first, by employing allusions rather than quotations *in extenso*; second, by introducing fresh eye-witness accounts (often from revealing new angles) descriptive of the same events.

Following publication of my brief survey of the extant evidence in my *Encounter* article came a series of breakthroughs, so dramatic as almost to suggest that fate had chosen this point to intervene. In December 1983 Macmillan himself appeared on television in a series of interviews with Ludovic Kennedy. In one of them he was sharply questioned about his role in the repatriation of the Cossacks, Kennedy laying stress on the consideration that numbers were known not to have been Soviet citizens. In the *Sunday Telegraph* Gordon Brooke-Shepherd commented that Macmillan 'visibly uneasy for a change, repeatedly told his BBC interviewer, Ludovic Kennedy, on Friday evening, that he "was only obeying orders" in authorising the controversial handover, which led to the certain death or imprisonment of most of the individuals involved.'

Macmillan's uncharacteristic discomposure struck others beside Brooke-Shepherd. A prominent member of the Macmillan family had approached the BBC after viewing the original recording, demanding angrily that the entire section of the interview relating to the question of the Cossacks be omitted from the screened version. But this both the producer and Ludovic Kennedy resolutely declined to do.

It was disappointing that issues of crucial importance had not been raised during the interview, and questions I had been putting to Macmillan in correspondence for more than a decade remained unanswered. But at least I had his explanation, which was something. Not long afterwards, in any case, I had the considerable satisfaction of being able to talk face to face with another key figure in the story, whom I had also been unable to meet before. This was Lord Aldington who, as Toby Low, had been Brigadier General Staff to Fifth Corps: the man who signed the orders arranging the handovers of Cossacks and Yugoslavs. For some years after my initial request for an interview in 1974 he continued to insist that he was unable to recall any of the circumstances. This was disappointing since, after Macmillan, he was undoubtedly the most significant surviving participant in the event. Then came an unexpected break-through. In November 1984 I was invited to address the boys at Winchester College on the subject of forced repatriation. It happens that Lord Aldington is Warden of the College, and those parts of my talk which referred to his role in the operation aroused some discussion, leading to the publication of a letter in the College magazine by a member of the staff, Mr Mark Stephenson.

Mr Stephenson objected to the fact that all reference to Lord Aldington had been omitted in the account of my talk published in the College magazine, *The Wykehamist*, and enquired whether this arose from excessive tact or a misguided attempt to censor a valid topic of discussion. 'But', he went on to point out, 'the audience knows that Count Tolstoy discussed them; so do many others, who did not hear the lecture but have been told about it; so your suppression of the facts is futile.'

The anonymous reviewer replied briefly that lack of space had been the relevant factor, adding:

> 'However, we understand that Lord Aldington hopes to visit the College in the course of the half and answer questions arising from Count Tolstoy's lecture.'

Lord Aldington responded shortly afterwards by declaring that he would himself address the boys in order to set the record straight. His memory of events now proved extensive, and his explanation that the tragedies arose not from conspiracy or insensitivity, but purely as a result of administrative confusion and (in the case of the Yugoslavs especially) pardonable failure to appreciate the nature of the fate awaiting them, appeared generally accepted. With regard to the failure to screen the Cossacks, he pointed out that he had taken care to issue elaborate screening orders, which were for some reason disobeyed by officers further down the chain of command.

Lord Aldington's address interested me greatly, though I was disappointed not to have been present to put to him some questions on specific matters of fact which concerned my researches. Fortunately I did not have to wait long for an opportunity. I was at this time conducting a correspondence with Major-General Richard Keightley, Commandant of the Royal Military Academy, who was understandably anxious to clear his father's name of the serious charges I had levelled at him in *Victims of Yalta* and elsewhere. General Keightley had no direct knowledge of the matter, but in view of his concern I suggested we meet for a discussion. At the very least he would have an opportunity to challenge my case and compel me to reconsider the evidence carefully.

This he was happy to do, confessing at the same time his fear that little good could come of it, in view of the fact that he knew no more than any other interested observer. Meanwhile, however, he had been in touch with Lord Aldington, a family friend since the war years, and suggested to him that he was in a far stronger position to enlighten me. This brought about an ironical situation. Lord Aldington, who had over the years persistently declined my requests for an interview, was now obliged to comply, in order not to appear indifferent to the pressing concern of a family friend. Aldington in consequence agreed to join our conference, and so it was that on 8 May 1985, eleven years after my first approach, I was able to put to him questions he alone was in a position to answer.

At first he simply repeated at length the same account he had given to the boys at Winchester, and finally, looking suddenly at his watch, explained that he had a pressing appointment elsewhere. However, I asked him if I could simply put to him some half-dozen questions to which the shortest of replies were necessary; and under Richard Keightley's concerned gaze he agreed. If I had ever had doubts about the investigation I had mounted and the truth of what had happened in 1945, the following few minutes, observing Toby Low's developing reaction to my questions, banished them convincingly.

Other testimonies and documents continued to pour in, until I could feel confident that after twelve years' search I possessed enough information to provide an authoritative account of all the secret aspects of the operation. The evidence on which it is based is presented as fully as possible, so that readers may judge of its value for themselves.

Before proceeding to the story proper I would like to issue an emphatic caution. While I believe that it is at last possible to present a credible account of the events and the circumstances from which they arose, there will always remain a grey area into which no research can ever penetrate. Not even the participants themselves can be expected to recall with total accuracy the emotions they felt at the time, nor the precise degree of their motivation and involvement. While it is possible to establish from correlation of oral and documentary evidence how the screening order relating to the Cossacks was circumvented, for example, we shall never know quite what each officer felt or knew.

In the cases of Field-Marshal Alexander and Generals McCreery and Keightley in particular (all of whom had died before I could interview them), it must be conceded that their involvement or understanding may well have been in some degree greater or less than the evidence indicates. My policy has been to adopt the normal presumption of innocence where suggestion of complicity is lacking. Ultimately the reader must be his or her own judge, the evidence constituting parameters of possibilities rather than fixed delineation of a rounded whole.

Only one major aspect remains as mysterious as when I first launched my investigation, and that is the question of motive. Presumably the only man who can answer that is Macmillan himself, and regrettably he remains the only person who declines to reply to my questions. For the present all that can be done is to eliminate a number of suggested motives, including those advanced by Macmillan himself. Whether Mr Macmillan intends to take the true answer with him to the grave is a matter that only time can tell. Perhaps the appearance of this book will instigate fresh revelations.

There may be those who find it distasteful that Macmillan should have such a terrible charge levelled at him in his declining years, and who wonder what can be gained by resurrecting a tragedy now more than forty years past. To this I can only reply that the event is one of considerable historical importance, which the public is entitled to understand. Moreover Macmillan's is not the only name to have been tarnished by the event, and a misunderstanding of his rôle has led recently to cruelly unjust accusations being levelled at the late Field-Marshal Alexander. Above all, it should be recalled that there are many thousands of people for whom the massacres of 1945 represent a tragedy infinitely greater than that of blemished reputation. The few survivors of the massacres and the victims' surviving relatives, as I learned again and again during harrowing interviews, are convinced that only the emergence of the truth can provide some belated residue of justice.

1

Encounter on the Drava

'In my dealings with the Chetniks I formed a favourable impression of their honesty and sincerity. They were well satisfied that, being in British hands, they would get a square deal.' (Major-General Horatius Murray, commanding Sixth Armoured Division, 3 May 1945)

It was at the beginning of April 1945 that the Allied Armies in Italy launched their final massive assault on German lines in North Italy. General von Vietinghoff's forces were dug in on a 150-mile front stretching from just south of Spezia on the Gulf of Genoa to a point north of Ravenna on the Adriatic coast. In his Order of the Day Field-Marshal Harold Alexander, Supreme Allied Commander in the Mediterranean (SACMED), assured his armies that, 'The German forces are now very groggy, and only need one mighty punch to knock them out for good. The moment has now come for us to take the field for the last battle which will end the war in Europe.'

The 'mighty punch' began on 9 April, when General Richard McCreery's Eighth Army delivered a colossal bombardment against the fortified lines of the German Tenth Army, whose left flank rested on the Adriatic. Even for veterans of El Alamein, Anzio and Monte Cassino the scale of the onslaught appeared spectacular. Preparations had been going forward for two and a half months, with enormous army dumps being prepared behind the Anglo-American lines for the day when improved weather would permit the long-awaited final advance.

Geoffrey Cox, an intelligence officer with General Freyburg's New Zealand Division, recalls the moment the bombardment began at 1520 hours on the ninth:

We prepared our ears for the guns, but before we heard them the patch
of the stop-bank ahead seemed to be lifted in the air. Black earth, grey
smoke, yellow dust, red and ochre flames suddenly rose along its edge.
Then, and then only, came the sound of the guns, roaring and baying
and clamouring one after another, until the whole eastern horizon was
solid sound. Overhead shells raced, with all their multitudinous sounds
– twenty-five pounders slithering, or tearing past like a long curtain being
ripped in two; the 4.5 and 5.5 churning their way through the air, as if
they were whole trains being driven at speed, invisibly above our heads
and hurtling down on the bank. Sometimes the noise would seem to get
harsher, as if the sky were a vast steel shutter, being hauled down on to
the enemy as a shopkeeper hauls his down to cover his shop door before
he goes home. It seemed impossible that all this noise could come from
something invisible, and you looked up as if expecting to see the hazed
sky streaked and torn by passing shells, as artists show them in comic
cartoons. But there was nothing there but the haze and the circling planes,
far up, coming round to dive . . .

I've no doubt that it felt like the end of the world to the Germans
crouching in the stop-bank. It did not take much imagination to picture
them there in their holes, sweating, smoking when they could get the
chance, crouching and bent, with the wounded being helped out one by
one, and the dead lying crumpled and bent like the living, at the bottom
of their slit trenches. You had to search in your mind, and remember the
concentration camps and the gas chambers, and above all remember that
if it wasn't them it would have been us, to stifle in your soul the knowledge
of this line of murder being drawn across the sunny green plains on an
April afternoon.[1]

The devastation proved as effective as was intended. By eight o'clock
the New Zealanders were across the River Senio and pushing north.
During the fortnight that followed, Alexander's 'mighty punch'
drove forward across successive river-lines covering the German
front. Von Vietinghoff threw in his last reserves, but to no avail. By
21 April the American Second Corps and Polish Second Corps had
fought their way into Bologna, while the Eighth Indian Division had
moved swiftly past Ferrara and reached the Po. It was now all up
with the Germans in Italy. By the last week of April their armies
were in headlong retreat, streaming northwards for the Brenner Pass
and eastwards up the Udine-Villach gap. On 29 April General von
Vietinghoff signed articles of surrender for all forces under his command, an agreement which became effective on 2 May.

The impending collapse of the German front in North Italy at last
permitted immediate consideration of the attainment of a major

Allied strategic objective, which the Germans' dogged stand had up to now relegated to the realms of speculative discussion. Until 1918 the city of Trieste on the Adriatic had been the major port of the Austro-Hungarian Empire. After the downfall of the Central Powers at the end of the Great War, it had been awarded by the victorious Entente to their ally Italy. However, the city's population included a sizeable minority of Slovenes and Croats, in consequence of which it had also been unsuccessfully claimed by the newly-created King-dom of Yugoslavia – a claim which in 1945 Marshal Tito had the declared intention of exacting, following the collapse of Fascist Italy and withdrawal of the German Army. The British, however, were determined to prevent what they regarded as these 'extreme Yugoslav claims'.[2]

Up to the middle of April an active policy decision on the post-war fate of Trieste and the surrounding region of Venezia Giulia had had to remain shelved. It was quite possible that Tito would reach the city first, and clearly the ultimate decision rested in large degree, whatever the diplomatic rights and wrongs, on the military *status quo* at the close of hostilities. But by 24 April German resistance beyond the Po was seen to be on the point of total collapse, and a swift breakthrough of the Allied armies towards Trieste was clearly immi-nent. Tito's forces, in contrast, were being held up before Fiume by stiff German resistance covering the withdrawal of General von Löhr's Army Group E from Yugoslavia into Austria.

On the twenty-fifth the Chiefs of Staff received detailed plans of Alexander's proposed thrust for Trieste. After a brief delay, during which Churchill consulted with the newly-appointed United States President Truman, Alexander was authorised on 28 April to advance his right flank across the Piave to forestall Tito in seizing Trieste. No time was wasted in implementing this instruction, and four days later (2 May) the New Zealand Ninth Brigade succeeded in breaking through into the disputed city – only to find that Partisans had also been fighting their way in from the eastern outskirts since the previous day. Between them they succeeded in overcoming the surviving German garrison, and then both sides settled down to an uneasy confrontation that seemed all too likely to break out into a new blaze flaring up from the embers of the old. The Partisans behaved with a provocative truculence which required all the Eighth Army's tact and discipline to counter peacefully.

It was at this tense juncture that the New Zealanders came to learn that not every Yugoslav was a Communist, and that there existed units other than those bearing the Red Star of the Partisan brigades. On the morning of 2 May Geoffrey Cox received a message from a signals officer concerning some Yugoslavs who wished to surrender to Freyburg's Division. 'They aren't very clear about what they are,' ran the puzzled report, 'but they are certain that they're not on Tito's side.' Cox instructed a delegation to be sent on to him.

> At lunchtime an ancient green bus drove up filled with grey-bearded and moustachioed soldiers in a uniform we had not seen before, grey with eagle badges. One introduced himself as a brigadier in the Royal Yugoslav Army. With an insistent cheerfulness he explained in French the situation along the Isonzo. They would be willing to be interned if they could keep their arms. All they wanted was a chance to use these arms in the coming war of Britain and America against Communism.

Cox's reply that there wasn't going to be any war against Russia was received with incredulity, and his flat statement that the men's surrender could only be accepted if they gave up all their arms caused considerable consternation. However, Cox decided reluctantly that it was his job to try to sort out the matter, and set off in his jeep, the Yugoslavs' bus following behind, to visit their encampment. The Royalists were drawn up between the villages of Cormons and Mosse, just off the Udine-Gorizia road. As he passed through their lines, Cox noted their surprisingly high state of morale and discipline.

> I must record that they looked excellent soldiers, tall, marching with disciplined ease. They were fully equipped with automatic weapons – including some Bren guns and Spandaus. They were mostly young men, some only boys. They looked fresh, well fed, well equipped – in short like an army which has received ample help, not like a partisan band.

A young British officer present, who shared the socialist views of many of his contemporaries, formed a similarly sympathetic view: 'I had come to look on them as Fascists: whereas these people, or at least all the rank and file, were peasant and worker types, kindly and cheerful, and anything but a collection of mercenary thugs.'

In Mosse, Cox was taken to a whitewashed house where the Royalists' commander, General Damjanovic, had his headquarters. Damjanovic, 'a tall, pale, bespectacled man', explained his forces' predicament with the aid of a map. They had made a fighting withdrawal before the advance of the Communist Partisans.

'We want only one thing,' he declared emphatically; 'that you let us fight on your side against Communism. We want only to fight the Russians.'

'But we are not going to fight the Russians,' Cox stressed again. 'They are our allies.'

The Royalist Yugoslavs, many of whom had allowed their hair to grow long in consequence of an oath not to shave or cut their hair until King Peter II returned to Belgrade, shook their heads and murmured sceptically, 'You will see, you will see.'

By now Cox had learned to his relief that orders had arrived for Damjanovic's surrender to be organised by the Sixth Armoured Division. All that remained for the New Zealanders was to negotiate a cease-fire between the Royalists and their Partisan opponents. This done he took his departure, leaving the Sixth Armoured Division to arrange for the disposal of the surrendered Yugoslavs.[3]

Damjanovic's force consisted of some 12,000 men, accompanied by a large number of camp followers, chiefly women and children. Damjanovic had been *chef de cabinet* to General Nedic, ruler of the German puppet-state in Serbia. At the same time he was the principal confidant in the administration of the Royalist resistance leader, General Mihailovic. In October 1944, as the war moved towards an Allied victory, Mihailovic ordered Damjanovic to withdraw towards Bosnia with units loyal to the King. Then, the following March, Mihailovic appointed him commander of Chetnik and Serbian Volunteer Corps troops in the Ljubljana Gap.[4] Finally, towards the end of April, Damjanovic began withdrawing westwards in order to link up with Allied troops advancing into Venezia Giulia. To avoid any harmful effect on morale, the troops were told that they were being deployed on the line of the Tagliamento, which would constitute the new post-war frontier of Slovenia.

Hotly pursued by a large force of Partisans, the Royalists crossed the Isonzo at Gorizia, destroying the bridge behind them (one wretched Croat sapper blew himself up in the process). Here they prepared to defend themselves until they could explain their position to the British – preferably before the British received a different version from the Partisans. Shortly afterwards there ensued the negotiations already described. Surrender terms having been accepted, arrangements were being made for the Royalists' withdrawal to safety within the Sixth Armoured Divisional area when a new danger arose. On 4 May a British unit threw a Bailey Bridge across the river, thus unwittingly supplying the Partisan commander with the means of crossing the Isonzo and attacking the retreating Royalists. This the British refused to allow, and a detachment of the Welsh Guards blocked the Communists' advance while their would-be victims were hastily shepherded to the rear.[5]

Damjanovic's force, which for the time being had been permitted to retain its arms for self-defence against Partisan attacks, was directed in the first instance to Palmanova, south of Udine. Before this the commander of the Sixth Armoured Division, Major-General Horatius Murray, had called on Damjanovic at his headquarters in Cormons. He explained that his 'orders were to disarm them before moving them to another area away from Tito's troops', but nevertheless found some difficulty in allaying Royalist fears.

> They were [he reported] very much concerned with their ultimate fate. They feared that we might hand them over to Tito, in which case they were quite clear what their fate would be. They foresaw mass executions, which might or might not be true. I was advised that applications had been made by Tito to the British Government from time to time for the extradition of his opponents, all of which had been refused. The Chetniks were speaking with sincerity when they implored me to ensure that they should not be handed over to Tito.

So far as the immediate future was concerned, General Murray was able to provide satisfactory assurances. That very day he had received Eighth Army Instruction No. 1465, which laid down that 'Chetniks, troops of Mihailovitch and other dissident Yugoslavs will be regarded as surrendered personnel and will be treated accordingly. The ultimate disposal of these personnel will be decided on Government levels.'[6]

Despite this assurance of immediate safety, General Murray was clearly concerned that the decision arrived at 'on Government levels' should be in accordance with the laws of war and humanity, and went on to note that,

> The Chetnik delegates are agreeing to being disarmed and to be interned peacefully on the assumption that they will not subsequently be handed over to Tito. Personally I cannot imagine the British Government would ever agree to such a suggestion, but I was not in a position to give the required assurance . . . In my dealings with the Chetniks I formed a favourable impression of their honesty and sincerity. They were well satisfied that, being in British hands, they would get a square deal.

Later, General Murray recalled that his troops 'cooperated splendidly to bring . . . about [the safe disposal of the Chetniks at Palmanova].

In any case they took strong exception to the methods the Communists used to seize control of that part of Europe.'[7]

Though at the time he had no means of knowing it, General Murray's confidence that the British Government would not contemplate despatching the surrendered Chetniks back to Tito was justified. Questions relating to the status and treatment of anti-Titoist Yugoslavs falling into the hands of Alexander's forces had first been raised by the British Ambassador in Belgrade, Ralph Stevenson. On 27 April he sent a telegram (no. 215) to Harold Macmillan (Resident Minister at Field-Marshal Alexander's headquarters outside Naples), and to the Foreign Office in London. He pointed out that large numbers of anti-Partisan units were profiting by the withdrawal of German Army Groups D and E to evacuate themselves north-eastwards out of Yugoslavia, and were hence likely to fall into the hands of Allied Forces advancing upon Trieste in the near future:

> An urgent decision is therefore required on the attitude to be adopted by ourselves when the commanders of these troops offer their services to the Allied commanders in North Eastern Italy. Three courses are possible:
> (a) They should be used as auxiliary troops;
> (b) They should be handed over to the Yugoslav Army;
> (c) They should be disarmed and placed in refugee camps.

Of the three alternatives, Stevenson considered that:

> Course (a) is out of the question in view both of our relations with Yugoslav Government and proven collaboration of these forces.
> Course (b) as a general policy is inconsistent with traditional claim to asylum of political refugees at the close of a civil war.
> Course (c) seems to me to be most reasonable solution of this thorny matter.[8]

Next day (28 April) Sir Orme Sargent, Deputy Permanent Under-Secretary at the Foreign Office, sent a copy of Stevenson's recommendations to the Prime Minister, together with additional comments of his own:

> We had hoped that these anti-Partisan forces in north-west Yugoslavia might, without any assistance from us, prevent Tito from entering Venezia Giulia and Trieste in advance of our troops.
>   Instead of doing this it now looks as though these Partisans will offer their services to the Allied Commanders which is much more awkward.
>   I do not see how we could justify collaboration with these troops who

hitherto have openly collaborated with the Germans. I suspect that they are the Croatian police called Ustachi, maintained by the puppet Croatian Government and Slovenian White Guards. I doubt whether they include Michaelovitch's forces which when last heard of were bottled up in South Bosnia.

Sargent's conclusion was that 'I am afraid we must agree to the course proposed in paragraph 5(c) of Stevenson's telegram . . . Whatever is decided will have to be cleared with the Americans.'[9]

Sargent also accepted that the units in question should be disarmed and held in refugee camps.

Churchill proved to be in full agreement with the course suggested, replying on 29 April to the effect that, 'There is no doubt that . . . [Stevenson's] para. 5 (c), i.e. that they should be disarmed and placed in refugee camps, is the only possible solution. You should inform the State Department accordingly, as from the Foreign Office. It is no good worrying Mr. Eden with this.'[10] (Foreign Secretary Anthony Eden was at that time attending the United Nations Conference at San Francisco.)

The policy now being settled as far as the British Government was concerned, the Foreign Office notified the United States Government of the proposed policy measure.[11] Meanwhile Alexander Kirk, United States Political Adviser to Alexander at AFHQ, had become disturbed by a proposal made by 'British G1 section' that surrendering dissident Yugoslav troops 'should be turned over to Tito for disposition in order that we might not have responsibility for them as displaced persons'. On 1 May, the date of this proposal, he telegraphed the State Department for instructions, recommending strongly on his own account 'that while such personnel should not be permitted to fight alongside Allied troops, they should be disarmed and disposed of as though they were prisoners of war'.

On 2 May United States Acting Secretary of State Joseph C. Grew replied, endorsing Kirk's suggestion and informing him that the British Government had independently arrived at the same conclusion:

The Department approves your position regarding anti-Partisan Yugoslav troops in Venezia Giulia, which may now be amplified in the light of a report and recommendation sent by your British colleague [Harold Macmillan] to the Foreign Office, and shown to us by the Embassy here . . .

We agree that the troops in question who wish to surrender to American or British commanders in northeast Italy should be disarmed and placed in base camps for investigation; that those wishing to return to Yugoslavia as individuals should be permitted to do so; and that all others should be removed to refugee camps; and that those against whom there is evidence of war crimes should be handled as such. We are communicating these views to the British Embassy, and since they are in substantial agreement with the position of the Foreign Office we understand that Ambassador Stevenson will be instructed to inform the Yugoslav Government accordingly. This telegram is being repeated to Patterson [US Ambassador in Belgrade] for his information and for use in replying to any inquiry on the subject which he may receive from the Yugoslav authorities.[12]

Action had been swift and concerted. Within one week of Ambassador Stevenson's raising the issue with Macmillan and the Foreign Office the British and American Governments had issued a ruling, and on 3 May Macmillan was able to inform the Foreign Office that Alexander had ordered Fifteenth Army Group to treat all surrendering anti–Tito troops 'as disarmed hostile troops', whose 'ultimate disposal will be treated on a governmental level'.[13] It was that same day, by coincidence, that General Murray reported the surrender of Damjanovic's Chetniks at Cormons, who were accordingly interned at Palmanova.

The policy, so far as the British and American Governments were concerned, was to remain unchanged. A week later a Member of Parliament, Lieutenant-Colonel Sir Thomas Moore, was officially informed in response to his enquiry in the House of Commons that, 'any anti–Tito Yugoslav Forces which surrendered to, or are captured by the 8th Army should be disarmed and interned'.[14] Nearly a year after that (12 April 1946) the Deputy Adjutant-General, Brigadier J. L. C. Napier, confirmed that, 'It is against the existing policy of H.M. Government to repatriate any [Croatian] subject against his or her wishes except in the case of War Criminals, where a prima facie case has to be submitted and approved by H.M. Government and the U.S. Government.'[15]

This ruling received ready acceptance at Allied Force Headquarters (AFHQ) in Italy, where Field-Marshal Alexander, Supreme Allied Commander in the Mediterranean (SACMED), had recently become acquainted with the predicament of those Yugoslavs who believed they had reason to fear the newly-dominant Communist regime of Marshal Tito. Tito's Military Mission had requested the immediate return of all liberated Yugoslav prisoners of war, but as the majority were officers captured during the brief campaign following the

German invasion in April 1941, they tended to be strongly Royalist in outlook and so reluctant to return. Alexander at once objected, notifying SHAEF and the War Office that he would 'accept only those Jugoslav Generals who of their own free will elect to join Tito and return to Jugoslavia'. This was because he feared 'that anxiety on part of Jugoslav Military Mission to return all by air means that they want them back in Jugoslavia for disciplinary reasons . . .'

Alexander's reaction was reported by his political adviser, Harold Macmillan, to the Foreign Office, whose comment was that, 'The line taken by AFHQ is clearly right, and in keeping with our views in analogous cases.'

An official noted also that:

> The Soviet Govt insist on the return to Russia of all their nationals & so far as red Russians are concerned we have done nothing to oppose them.
>   The I.R.C.C. [International Red Cross Committee], having heard that certain Italian prisoners of war in India & the Middle East have expressed the wish not to return to Italy, at least at present, have written us expressing the view that the Geneva Convention, in spirit, if not in letter, is opposed to the return of prisoners of war to their native land if there is reason to believe that they may be victimised.[16]

Thus it can be seen that any misgivings General Murray might have held with regard to Allied policy towards surrendering anti-Communist Yugoslavs were groundless. By 3 May 1945 the British and American Governments had informed their respective Political Advisers at AFHQ, Macmillan and Kirk, that *no* dissident Yugoslavs were to be handed over to Tito's forces against their will, and Field-Marshal Alexander had transmuted this decision into Eighth Army Instruction No. 1465. It was in consequence of this that General Damjanovic's 12,000 troops were transported to safety in the British camp at Palmanova.

There was little time to reflect on the matter, however. With the surrender of German forces in Italy, Anglo-American forces were anxious to push northwards into Austria as swiftly as possible. Germany was on the point of collapse, and the victorious Allies were determined to have their forces advanced as far to the east as possible at the moment when hostilities ceased. Soviet forces advancing from Vienna and the Hungarian frontier were nearing Graz in south-eastern Austria, and threatening to beat British forces into the southern Austrian province of Carinthia.

German forces facing Alexander's had ceased fighting, but the passes into Austria were clogged by thousands of retreating troops, with accompanying tanks, artillery and transport vehicles. General Richard ('Dreary Dick') McCreery ordered advance units of his Eighth Army to make their way as swiftly as possible through all obstacles, not halting until they encountered advancing Red Army units as deep within Austrian territory as possible.

Another matter of grave concern was Tito's threat to occupy a large part of southern Austria, and incorporate it into his planned Greater Yugoslavia. Just as he had revived tenuous claims to Trieste and Venezia Giulia, so also he planned to use the presence of a Slovenian element in southern Carinthia as a pretext for annexation. Advancing over the Austro-Yugoslav frontier on the Karavanke Mountains, Communist Partisan units overran Austrian territory up to and beyond the line of the River Drava. Though officially styling themselves the Third Yugoslav Army, to the local inhabitants whether of German or Slovenian ethnic origin they appeared as little more than lawless banditti. But with the German surrender there was no one to halt the Yugoslav advance except the approaching British Eighth Army.

It was therefore with intense relief that the population of Carinthia greeted the arrival of the first British troops to enter the provincial capital. At 10.30 on the morning of 8 May (the date of the overall German surrender), armoured cars from an advance unit of General Charles Keightley's Fifth Corps drove into the main square of Klagenfurt – only to find that Yugoslav Partisans were also ensconced in the city. Shortly afterwards General Keightley and his staff arrived and established Main Corps Headquarters in the town hall (*Rathaus*), an imposing building fronting Klagenfurt's tree-lined main square, whose principal feature appropriately was a massive statuary of Hercules with his spiked club beating back a truculent-looking dragon.

The dragon's intentions became swiftly apparent. As Nigel Nicolson, Intelligence Officer for the First Guards Brigade, noted at length at the time, Partisan pretensions veered from the menacing to the absurd:

They showed at first considerable tact in steering clear of the British zone of operations, even asking our permission to move their battalions from place to place south of the river, but it soon became evident that after they had built up their armies in Carinthia, they intended to adopt a far more ambitious policy. Scarcely before we realised their object, trainloads of partisans were arriving in Klagenfurt, sections and platoons were established in every village, pro-Tito political meetings were being held under our very eyes, propaganda leaflets distributed, and the civilian population looted and intimidated. The crisis came with the posting of a proclamation throughout the region, of which the operative clauses ran as follows:

'The Yugo-Slav army has entered Carinthia in order to clean the land once and for all time of Nazi criminals, and guarantee the Slovenian and Austrian population a truly popular democracy, freedom and prosperity in the new, victorious and powerful Great Yugo-Slavia.

'We hereby make known that throughout the whole of liberated Carinthia military authority of the Yugo-Slav army has been established. The population and all branches of the administration are to extend every help to our army and to obey unconditionally all published decrees.'

Carinthia, in fact, had already been annexed to Yugo-Slavia, and British military government in the province over-ridden. There could be no other interpretation of this unfortunate document. It was followed up by similar announcements by the Belgrade radio, which explained that the basis of the claim was the presence of a persecuted Slovene minority in Carinthia, and the time had now come for their liberation . . .

As the Yugo-Slav proclamation was posted virtually side by side with AMG [Allied Military Government] notices saying that we were 'paving the way for a free and independent Austria', even the British genius for compromise found itself a bit strained. A firmer policy in our relations with Tito was immediately ordered. The proclamation was removed by us from every building not actually occupied by his troops: we were to impede Tito activities by every device short of shooting: we were to report most exactly every movement and every incident: all threatened civilians were to be taken into protective custody: on no account were we to help the partisans with petrol, food or ammunition. In short, we were to hold the ring while the matter was argued out in Belgrade by Marshals Alexander and Tito, and avoid any incidents on the spot which might prejudice their discussions. Discourage, delay, check, obstruct – but nothing more. If Tito's troops insisted on passing through our road blocks they must eventually be allowed to do so.

It was not at all easy to carry out these orders, and much depended on the junior leaders, the section and platoon commanders, who were continually being faced by problems which required the most tactful handling. Thanks entirely to their good sense, no fighting ever openly broke out between us. The same cannot be said of Tito's junior leaders, uneducated, fiery peasant boys, veterans of the most savage campaigns, inspired by the words of 'our glorious leader', and determined to enjoy some of the fruits of their hard-won victory. They were responsible for much of what occurred . . .

One of the few points in our favour was that the rank and file of Tito's army were extraordinarily simple men when separated from their officers. It was then an easy matter to persuade them to surrender their loot, to stop fiddling with German equipment, to remove themselves from any place where they were not wanted. A single tank or a platoon of infantry would often scare them away by their mere presence: a Sherman 'broken down' astride a railway track was sufficient to hold up a Tito train for a whole day. They would act in a manner typical of Balkan peasantry, childish and acquisitive and sometimes even humble. They removed, for instance, all the mediaeval weapons and armour from the Klagenfurt Museum, and when found playing with them in a barracks, they obediently trundled the lot back to the Museum in a wheelbarrow. On another occasion they borrowed an Austrian girl, and returned her to home *virginem intactam* two days later.[17]

Andrew Gibson-Watt, then a youthful lieutenant in the Welsh Guards, recalls that the men of his platoon were for the most part extreme left-wing Socialists from Tonypandy and other mining towns in South Wales. But personal observation of the behaviour of the Yugoslav Partisans turned them ferociously anti-Tito overnight, and in no time at all they were spoiling for a fight should matters come to blows.[18]

However, despite their inflated wartime reputation as fearless guerrilla fighters, direct military action was not the Partisans' forte. As events were shortly to show, they were less a disciplined army than a horde of licensed executioners. And it was their intended victims who provided a problem as taxing to the administrative capacity of Fifth Corps staff as were Tito's followers to their diplomatic talents. To quote Nigel Nicolson again:

There seemed to be no limit to the number of nationalities which appealed to us for our protection. The Germans wanted to be safe-guarded against Tito, the Cossacks against the Bulgarians, the Chetniks against the Croats, the White Russians against the Red Russians, the Austrians against the Slovenes, the Hungarians against everyone else, and vice versa throughout the list. This part of Austria, being one of the last places to be liberated, had indeed become the sump of Europe. Not only was it the last refuge of Nazi war-criminals, but of comparatively inoffensive peoples fleeing from the Russians and Tito, unwanted and all but persecuted wherever they went. In the British and Americans lay their only hope of salvation. So it was that even before the armistice, whole nations were on the move into Austria from the east and from the south, and we were faced immediately on arrival with the problems of settling them somewhere apart from one another, disarming them, feeding them, and composing their political differences, before any thought could be given to their repatriation.

As early as 11 May, the day Tito openly laid claim to Carinthia, the first mass of refugees from Yugoslavia arrived at the River Drava, after having crossed the Yugoslav-Austrian frontier. It fell to the Grenadier Guards to accept their surrender next morning, and the bemusement of the Guardsmen when faced with this extraordinarily heterogeneous group – fugitives from a civil war of which they had barely heard – is understandable. They comprised, as Nigel Nicolson reported, 'a Corps which surrendered to us en masse, under the command of a German Oberst von Seeler. The Corps was made up of 10,000 Germans, 13,000 Slovenes, 4,000 Serbs and 4,000 White Russians, together with hundreds of horses and thousands of women and children.'

As it is the fate of these people which forms a principal theme of this book, it is necessary to understand who they were and what had caused them to flee in such desperation from their own country. These questions will be pursued in the next chapter.

2

The Flight of a Nation

'There is no doubt . . . that they [the anti-Partisan Yugoslav forces] should be disarmed and placed in refugee camps, [it] is the only solution.' (Winston Churchill to Sir Orme Sargent, Deputy Under-Secretary at the Foreign Office, 29 April 1945)

News of the German surrender on all fronts came over the radio just as advance units of the British Sixth Armoured Division were driving over the Predil Pass from Italy into Austria, setting foot for the first time on the soil of the defeated Third Reich. A scorching sun shone down on the enormous column of tanks and lorries as it wound above steep alpine gorges, disappearing at times into long cool tunnels and emerging again into burning daylight. At the Austrian frontier post some wit had erected a large mailed fist, the divisional emblem. Its thumb, controlled by an electrical device, moved cheerily up and down in the familiar 'thumbs-up' gesture. For Britain the hard-fought struggle was over, and the local Austrian population also appeared relieved that the end had come. Neat, well-kept farms set amid lush pastures and blossoming orchards spoke of a coming time of peace and contentment.[1]

But just as one world was being reborn another was sliding to its destruction. Fifty miles to the south-east of Villach, the first Austrian town to be entered by British occupation forces, lies the city of Ljubljana, capital of the northern Yugoslav province of Slovenia. There the same May sun shone down on scenes of terror and despair, as a whole nation found itself threatened with extinction. The white, blue and red tricolour of independent Slovenia hung from public buildings everywhere, but for how many hours longer no one knew.

The flag of Nazi Germany also drooped despondently from a solid yellow-painted, neo-classical building at the north-east corner of

Congress Square. This was the Kazina, where German military Government headquarters was living out the last hours of its existence. Two years earlier it had housed the Italian occupation authorities; now within days it might expect visits from yet another conquering army. The drone of enemy bombers was rarely absent, and it no longer required the keenest of ears to detect the approaching rumble of artillery fire.

It was on the afternoon of Monday, 7 May that a staff car sped past the Ursulinska Church and Zvezda Park in the centre of Ljubljana, and drew up before the Kazina. Out sprang a Russian officer and dashed up the steps. He was Colonel Anatoly Ivanovich Rogozhin, formerly serving the Emperor Nicholas II and now, twenty-seven years after the death of his imperial master, commanding the *Russkii Corpus*, last surviving unit of the old Russian Imperial Army. The very existence of such a formation at the end of World War Two appears a remarkable anachronism, whose peculiar position of danger Rogozhin now found understandable difficulty in explaining to General Reisler, commander of the Ljubljana military district.

To the visitor being ushered into the General's office the atmosphere of impending disintegration was no novel sensation. After the Russian Revolution he had served with forces vainly striving to overthrow the Bolshevik dictatorship. After the disastrous culmination of the Russian Civil War, the remnant of Baron Wrangel's defeated White Army was extricated by the British and French navies from the Crimea. Some 135,000 staunchly anti-Bolshevik Russian troops were transported to Gallipoli, and then interned on the island of Lemnos. After suffering terrible privations and the ravages of typhus and dysentery, the majority of refugees had succeeded in making their way to various countries in Europe. Before embarking on this diaspora, they were told by Wrangel that the immediate battle with the Bolsheviks might be over, but the struggle would now take on a different form. In their scattered refuges the Russians kept in touch with their central command based in Paris, and all energies were to be devoted to the day when the international and Russian internal political situations would permit a resumption of the crusade against godless Bolshevism.

Several Balkan states accorded a warm welcome to their Slav brothers, most prominent among them being the newly-created Kingdom of Yugoslavia. There King Alexander received not only a large body of distressed refugees, but also two complete divisions which in reorganised form set up a regular military establishment, with its own cadet corps, artillery school and other administrative units. Yugoslav hospitality and generosity were warmly reciprocated by the exiles, and when in April 1941 Germany and her allies invaded Yugoslavia, the commanders of the White Russian para-military organisation (among them Colonel Rogozhin, commanding the Guards Cossack Division) hastened to offer their services to the Yugoslav High Command. However, the country's speedy collapse in the face of overwhelming German superiority and the ferocious Blitzkrieg on Belgrade precluded the Russians' participation in the campaign.

After the German invasion of Russia, the Yugoslav Communist Party under the leadership of Josip Broz Tito joined gathering resistance against the occupying Germans and Italians. Their principal efforts, however, were directed against the great majority of Yugoslav citizens who were as determinedly hostile to Communism as they were to Nazism. An obvious and immediate target was the émigré Russian community, against whom Stalin's espionage services had been waging war for a generation. It was not long before several hundred Russians had been indiscriminately massacred by Communist Partisans, and families living in the countryside had been obliged to take refuge in Belgrade and other large cities.

Threatened with continuing attack and the likelihood of ultimate extermination, White Russian leaders appealed to the German military authorities for permission to arm and protect themselves from attack. It was in this way that the *Russkii Corpus* came into existence. An essential condition of its formation, accepted by the German military authorities, was that it should be used solely in the common struggle against Communism, and under no circumstances against the Western Allies.[2] Under German auspices it was deployed to guard communications and vulnerable key points from sabotage and guerilla attack. Finally, when in late 1944 the war reached Yugoslavia, the *Corpus* became a regular combatant unit engaged on the front, where on several occasions it enjoyed the satisfaction of resuming battle against the Red Army.

Casualties had been heavy, however, and of some 12,000 men enrolled in June 1944 there remained by May 1945 a bare 3,500. A week earlier their commander, General Steifon, had suddenly died of a heart attack, and his successor Colonel Rogozhin was faced with the daunting task of saving his men from capture or liquidation by Tito's Partisans.[3]

It was this predicament that Rogozhin had to try to explain to the diehard German General Reisler, commander of the Ljubljana military district. A general capitulation of the German armed forces was clearly imminent, Rogozhin pointed out (it had in fact already been signed by General Jodl at Rheims early that morning), and it was his duty to preserve the White Russians from falling into the hands of the Communists.

'There can be no talk of any capitulation,' replied Reisler sternly. 'We are staying here. The fight goes on.'

But next day Reisler had vanished, and Rogozhin was informed that Germany would surrender on all fronts at 4 a.m. the following morning. All Axis forces were being evacuated as swiftly as possible towards Austria: they were to cross the Karavanke Mountains by the Loibl Pass, and make for the town of Klagenfurt in Carinthia. Rogozhin was placed in overall command of all non-German units engaged in the retreat. These were three regiments of Serbian Royalist volunteers, commanded by Lieutenant-Colonel Tatalovic; a body of Slovenian Home Guard (Domobranci) under General Krenner; and the 500-strong Regiment Varyag, composed mostly of former Soviet Russians and belonging to the so-called 'Vlasov' Army of Russians serving with the German armed forces.

All had good reason to dread falling into the hands of the Communists, but the Serbian Colonel Tatalovic raised a consideration which was swiftly coming to dominate thinking among the commanders of the stricken anti-Communist units. What would be the attitude of the Anglo-American forces towards a body of men commanded by an officer in German-supplied uniform? This was the position of Rogozhin and his men, whereas the Serbs wore the uniform of King Peter II, an Allied sovereign. However, this was not the time to argue over such niceties; all that mattered was to cross the mountains as swiftly as possible to gain the relative safety of Austria. By late afternoon on the ninth the column set out northwards from Ljubljana, the trucks of the *Russkii Corpus* following immediately on the heels of a German motorised unit whose task was to prevent any attempt by Tito's Partisans to cut the escape route.[4]

The evacuation had begun; but this was not exclusively a military withdrawal, nor did mortal danger menace only the departing troops. Throughout all Slovenia alarm and despair swiftly gripped the civilian population. They knew only too well what would be their fate once the Communists seized control of the province.

The Slovenes were a small but proud people, with a population of about one and three-quarter million. The majority were small farmers and peasants, staunchly Roman Catholic and for the most part peacefully inclined, in contrast to their warlike Croatian and Serbian neighbours to the south. Until the creation of the state of Yugoslavia they had no political connection with the Serbs and Croats, and over the centuries had constituted part of the civilisation of Western Europe, with a strong tradition of attachment to constitutional and juridical liberties. Nevertheless, unlike the Croats they had for the most part accepted with enthusiasm their absorption into the Yugoslav state, and were largely loyal to the Karageorgevich dynasty.

Following the Nazi occupation, Slovenia had been partitioned between Germany and her allies Italy and Hungary. Hitler ordered Upper Carniola to be thoroughly Germanicised, in the process of which some 50,000 Slovenes died in Nazi camps. The persecution was so inhuman that even the governor of the Italian-occupied sector complained that 'the German treatment of the population is actually worse than cruel. Armed robberies and killings occur every day. Churches and convents are looted and closed.' Slovene resistance to the occupying forces was correspondingly fierce, and large numbers of Germans and Italians were killed by different resistance groups.[5]

With the outbreak of war between Germany and the Soviet Union, a new and horrific dimension was added to the sufferings of the Slovenian population as the Communist Liberation Front launched its own civil war within the province. Until the German invasion of Russia, it has to be remembered, the Yugoslav Communist Party had actively opposed participation in the 'imperialist war' being waged by the Western plutocracies against Nazi Germany. After 22 June 1941 they reversed this attitude, though throughout their actions made it plain that their struggle was being directed more in Soviet interests than those of their own country.[6] The Party's priority was the destruction of all opposition among the people so as to be prepared for a revolutionary takeover once the occupying powers should be removed by the turning tide of the war. Their methods were not over-scrupulous, recalling Lenin's recommendation that Communists should 'wade up to the knees in filth, if need be, crawling on our bellies through dirt and dung to Communism, then in this fight we shall win . . .'[7]

From the outset straightforward terrorism was practised against the civilian population. On 4 December 1941 Slovenian Communist Partisans murdered Fanus Emer, a prominent resistance leader, after luring him into a trap.[8] Similar episodes multiplied, and in the period 1941–2 it has been calculated that well over 2,000 victims were immolated. At times the aim appears to have been one of creating a general atmosphere of terror, as when in the early summer of 1942 sixteen gypsies (including two babies) were indiscriminately massacred at Sodrazika. Generally, however, the policy was specifically designed to terrorise the population into support for the Partisans. On 13 May 1942, for example, Partisan killers tortured then stabbed to death the Zavodnik family (father, son and twenty-eight-year-old daughter) at Bistrica in the Mirenska Valley. A few days later they visited a similar fate on the Uharniks in Mirna; this time the daughter was only fourteen. On 3 June a young pregnant schoolteacher, Ivanka Novak, was savagely beaten to death as an act of vengeance for the flight of her husband to Ljubljana.[9]

These were no random incidents of 'mindless acts' of indiscriminate violence, but a settled policy of coercing the population into acceptance of Communist domination of the resistance movement. Of this the people were well aware. The most prominent Slovenian Communist was Politburo member Edvard Kardelj, a puritanical Marxist 'theoretician' whose fanaticism disturbed even Fitzroy Maclean's sympathy for the Partisans' cause. Later he wrote:

Perhaps the most important of all [Tito's associates] was Edo Kardelj, a small, stocky, pale-skinned, black-haired Slovene in the early thirties, with steel-rimmed spectacles and a neat little dark moustache, looking like a provincial schoolmaster, which, as it happened, was what he was. He, I found, was the theoretician of the Party, the expert Marxist dialectician.

There were a lot of questions about the theory and practice of Communism that I had always wanted an answer to. Now was my opportunity. Kardelj knew all the answers. He was a fascinating man to talk to. You could never catch him out or make him angry. He was perfectly frank, perfectly logical, perfectly calm and unruffled. Muddle; murder; distortion; deception. It was quite true. Such things happened under Communism, even might be an intentional part of Communist policy. But it would be worth it in the long run. The end would justify the means. Some day they would get their way; some day their difficulties would disappear; their enemies would be eliminated; the people educated; and a Communist millennium make the world a happier and a better place. Then the need for strong measures would disappear. He might not live to see this happen. But he was quite ready, as they all were, not only to die himself but to sacrifice everybody and everything that was near and dear to him to the cause which he had chosen, to liquidate anybody who stood in his way. Such sacrifices, such liquidations, would be for the greater good of humanity. What worthier cause could there be? And he looked at me steadily and amiably through his spectacles.[10]

In September 1941 Kardelj issued a manifesto threatening all who resisted the Party with liquidation. This was no idle boast. He was to claim publicly that, exactly two years later, 'in four days in September 1943 seven thousand of the White Guard traitors were actually erased from Slovenian soil'. After 700 National Guardsmen, who surrendered under amnesty at Turjak Castle on the nineteenth of the month, had been massacred (many after being tortured),[11] Kardelj remarked exultantly to a colleague: 'That ought to demoralise them!'[12]

Documents which later fell into the hands of anti-Communist forces proved that the Party was indeed implementing a policy based on the avowed use of terror. Order no. 80 of the 'Ljubo Sercer' Partisan Battalion informs a priest, acting as go-between, that unless eight named villagers 'surrender with arms, the hostages in our camp will be executed'. In the following year (1943) the same battalion commander, Politkomisar Novak, required (Order no. 416) that all conscripts should be closely interrogated regarding their understanding of the principles of Marxism. Part of the order read:

All those who do not know much about the history of Communism and show no interest must be liquidated. So far statistics show that 95% of young conscripts from 15 December [1942] until now [3 February 1943] have deserted, and this must not be allowed to happen again. These liquidations must be carried out very discreetly, and you will be held responsible if people get wind of them.

Lists of opponents destined for liquidation were compiled which eventually totalled tens of thousands of names. Captured during military operations, some of these lists were published in the Slovenian Catholic press arousing great perturbation among the intended victims and their families.[13] This was the purpose of the whole policy.

Even after 22 June 1941 there were several occasions of collaboration between the Partisans and the occupying powers; at times sinister, at others venial – or virtually inevitable – given the circumstances of life in an occupied state.[14] A consistent theme, however, runs through all these transactions. To the Partisans, the destruction of non-Marxist elements in Slovenia took precedence over operations against the occupying forces. In December 1943, for example, a large

force of Partisans attacked the town of Kocevje, which was held by
a small but determined garrison of National Guards, together with
some German troops. Despite the most desperate assaults the Partisans were unable to break through the defence, and finally resorted
to the despatch of an envoy with an offer of terms. The note was
preserved and later published. It read:

> To the Germans in the town of Kocevje:
> Take away the arms of the Slovenian Domobranci [National Guards],
> place them on wagons, and send them across the bridge to us. If you
> will do that, we will grant you an *Amnesty* and you will be able to stay
> alive.

It was with the anti-Communist Slovenians they sought a reckoning,
and not the Germans.[15]

Apart from overt terrorist attacks on the Slovenian population,
whom the Communists rightly suspected of being overwhelmingly
hostile to their ideology, the Partisans operated a policy which would
have gratified the shade of Machiavelli. Towards the end of 1943 the
Party issued an instruction to its members advising them on how to
infiltrate and serve in German, quisling and Chetnik formations in
order to promote Partisan objectives. It also stressed the necessity of
ascribing all attacks and sabotage against the occupying forces to
the anti-Communist resistance, so that ensuing reprisals should be
blamed on them.[16] This confirmed a long-standing practice, remarkable for its ingenuity and effectiveness, if not for its morality or
patriotism. Hit-and-run attacks on German or Italian forces in selected
localities deliberately courted brutal reprisals against the local inhabitants, who in turn were induced to harbour resentment against
Chetniks or other nationalist resistance forces credited with the action.
Frequently the enemy destroyed whole villages, leaving the young
men (prime targets in any reprisal operation) scant choice but to take
to the mountains, where the Partisans were waiting to recruit them
into their ranks.[17]

Inevitably, this resulted at times in the Royalist and nationalist
resistance's harbouring its strength and proffering a less active front
against the occupier. As a Serbian businessman had earlier reported on
arrival in Istanbul, 'Mihailovic [the Royalist leader] is only defending
himself, because for him the protection of the people is uppermost;
while for the Communists the most important thing is the defence of
the Soviet regime imperilled by German Panzer divisions.' Mihailovic

was proved right in his fears; the Germans were swift to introduce reprisal measures on a barbaric scale.[18]

The Italian response to Partisan attacks was to withdraw to the larger towns and keep their heads down behind strong perimeter defences, leaving the rural population to survive the Partisan terror as best it could. A radical change in the situation came in September 1943, when Italy surrendered to the Allies. The Partisans (who, unlike their Chetnik rivals, appear to have received advance warning of the capitulation) seized the opportunity to possess themselves of vast quantities of modern weapons held in Italian garrison arsenals, frequently with the collaboration of Communist sympathisers among the troops. In this way the Partisans became all at once a formidable military force, which they had not been before. Tanks and artillery, handed over to them by the Italians, continued to be operated by Italian soldiers who swiftly transferred their loyalties from the Fascist to the Partisan cause. Thus, at the siege of Turjak in the same month, the defences were breached by Italian heavy artillery, tanks and armoured cars operated by troops still in Italian uniform.[19]

The simmering civil war, which up to now had consisted largely of isolated acts of terrorism, appeared on the point of developing into a bloodbath. Lacking even the threadbare 'protection' of the Italian authorities in the towns, the Slovenian population at large had no alternative but to look to its own defences.

During their time of occupation the Italians had permitted the organisation of village guard units, *Vaska Straza*, which possessed little capacity beyond that of observation and directing appeals to the dilatory Italian police and military. With the Italian surrender, the German Seventy-first Alpine Division moved swiftly to occupy Ljubljana. Large numbers of village guards and other Slovenes, terrified by the wave of Partisan atrocities and in particular by the massacre of prisoners at Turjak, had crowded into the city. General Raapke, the German commander, ordered them as well as the Italian garrison in the capital to be disarmed.

It was at this juncture that the German authorities were approached by the Mayor of Ljubljana, General Leon Rupnik, a veteran of the old Austro-Hungarian Army, who was widely respected by the Slovenian population and who at this time represented the only functioning civil authority. Explaining that Slovenia was in a state of civil war, he pointed out that their mutual interests would be best served by permitting the non-Communist population to defend itself against the enemy. The Germans were only too anxious to exclude themselves from this imbroglio, and after brief discussions agreed not only to rearm the village guards but also to permit Slovenia a large degree of autonomy. On 22 September General Rupnik was sworn in as Chief of the Administration for Ljubljana Province, which became for internal purposes an autonomous state flying the Slovenian flag and employing the Slovenian language in all its transactions. The village guards were reformed into a regular militia, designated the Slovenian Home Guard (Domobranci).[20]

Naturally this involved a fair degree of co-operation with the German authorities, which Titoist propaganda was swift to exploit. While this collaboration undoubtedly constitutes a relevant factor, which was to influence British attitudes at a later date, it should be seen in perspective. International law accepts that civil authorities in occupied territory should continue their functions in accordance with laws in force. In occupied France and the Channel Islands police and judicial authorities continued to maintain internal order, even though it could be argued that this ultimately lent aid to the occupying power. The alternative, of course, is to oblige the enemy to impose order through martial law. With an occupying power like Nazi Germany and a tiny country like Slovenia, this was at best to contemplate the most cruel oppression (in Upper Carniola alone 50,000 Slovenes had been killed by the Germans and an equal number abducted to forced labour in Germany). At worst it could have resulted in genocide – a prospect only too congenial to the occupying power.[21]

Armed for the first time on a level with the Partisans, the Slovenian Home Guard (Domobranci) swiftly gained an ascendancy over their adversaries. Villages and towns were effectively protected, and the war was for the first time prosecuted vigorously in regions hitherto accepted as Partisan territory. Within a year the Partisans were everywhere on the run and conceding defeat, despite the influx in January 1944 of 'a very large tonnage' of British supplies.

An experienced and shrewd British officer, Lieutenant-Colonel Peter Moore, returned to Italy in February 1945 and immediately drew up a revealing report of the situation. He had previously been attached to Slovenian Partisan Headquarters over the winter of 1944–5. After stressing the poor morale of the Communist rank-and-file (despite their excellent British equipment), Moore went on to note the dispiriting failure of successive Partisan operations, generally owing to their 'passive attitude' – the more inexcusable in view of recent intensification of Allied air strikes against German communications. Though their activities had been 'magnificent' in the past, the Slovenian Partisans had 'now ceased to be an asset and . . . become a liability'.

Summing up the results of his four months' observation, Moore concluded that:

> The Slovene Pzns have lost interest in fighting the Germans as such and are conserving their forces for:
> (i) The capture of Ljubljana, and liquidation of the White Guard [i.e. Domobranci] after the defeat of Germany . . .
> (ii) The occupation of Trieste and all NE Italy up to the Tagliamento to permit a 'fait accompli' at the peace conference
> (iii) The occupation of Klagenfurt and Villach . . .

In marked contrast to the poor morale and performance of the Communists was the state of the Domobranci, who 'although they are 100% collaborationist . . . [have] paradoxically improved out of all knowledge in the past 6 months and it is now unlikely that after the withdrawal of the main German forces 7 [Partisan] Corps will be able to take Ljubljana and put down the White Guard without considerable assistance from Croat JANL [Communist] formations, which would however be decisive.'[22]

However high their morale, it had become clear in the first week of May 1945 not only to the Domobranci but the majority of Slovenians that the 'liquidation' projected by the prescient Colonel Moore was drawing horribly close. Fearful of being cut off by Red Army units of Marshal Tolbukhin's Third Ukrainian Front to the north-east, and with Bulgarian, Romanian and Yugoslav Partisan forces pressing hard on their flanks, Germany Army Groups E and F were making a hasty withdrawal from Greece and Yugoslavia northwards to Austria. All those who had reason to dread the anticipated bloodbath had no option but to leave their country in the wake of the German retreat. Clearly the end of Germany was also in sight, and there was all the more reason to ensure that when the final collapse came they should fall into the hands of the civilised British and Americans, rather than those of their persecutors and their Soviet allies.

Already on 1 May a large force of Serbian and Slovene Chetniks under the command of General Miodrag Damjanovic had crossed the Italian frontier at Gorizia and made contact with advance units of the British Eighth Army. They were accompanied by several thousand civilian refugees. Their surrender at Cormons to units of the

British Eighth Army and internment at Palmanova have already been described in the last chapter.[23]

In the first week of May 1945 the streets of Ljubljana became packed with refugees from the countryside, mostly small farmers and peasants travelling in horse-drawn carts packed with whatever could be hastily assembled of their household goods. On Saturday the fifth news spread that the defence units, the Domobranci, who had so successfully kept the Communists at bay for nearly two years, were preparing to withdraw across the mountains into Austrian Carinthia. A huge crowd gathered at the railway station, preparing to board the 4 p.m. train for Jesenice. There – all being well – it would be possible to take another through the Rosenbach Tunnel and on to Villach in Austria. Four o'clock came, but no train arrived.

After some time an announcement was broadcast that the train would not depart until six o'clock. At five the platform gates were opened, and the crowd surged forward and crammed into the passenger carriages. Finally at six o'clock the engine whistle shrieked, and the train began to roll slowly out of the station. Every minute of delay suggested some unforeseen check; the frontier was sixty kilometres away, while fifty kilometres to the south Partisan forces were said to be entering the town of Kocevje preparatory to the final dash for the capital.

The train crawled with what appeared preternatural slowness through the rich Slovenian countryside. Rumours abounded in the cramped carriages; were there Communists among the railwaymen? After two hours the train had only reached Kranj, a bare twenty-five miles from Ljubljana. Now conductors moved along the train, announcing that it would not after all leave for Jesenice that evening. The passengers descended to spend the night in a nearby air-raid shelter, uncertain what the next day would bring.

At early dawn the sleepless refugees streamed back to the station, only to be informed by the booking clerk that 'trains to Jesenice are no longer running'. The crowd remained rooted to the platform; where could they go now? Shortly afterwards the official reappeared to announce the coming departure of a train for Trzic. A buzz of discussion arose; at Trzic the line ended before the towering range of the Karavanke Mountains. Beyond lay Austria, but the only way over was by ascent on foot, traversing the mountains by the Loibl Pass tunnel. But needs must when the Devil drives, and half an hour later the passengers boarded the train.

Once in Trzic they alighted, and set off on the military highroad leading up to the Loibl Pass. It was a beautiful spring day, with the sun blazing down on the trudging column. Few took in the delights of lush meadows and towering, snow-covered crags. They tramped on in silence, a single concerted hope engrossing all their thoughts: would they reach the tunnel in time? The only sounds were the clatter of horses' hooves as they struggled forward under their burdens, the squeaking of cart wheels, and the changing roar of truck engines struggling with the increasing gradient. The enormous serpentine column was gathering with every weary step as vehicles came streaming up the highroad from the south. Interspersed among the fugitives could be seen the lorries, tanks, armoured cars and horse-drawn artillery of General von Löhr's retreating Wehrmacht forces.

After several hours of marching the foremost travellers arrived before the two stone obelisks marking the entrance of the tunnel through the Loibl Pass. Before long a huge crowd of desperate refugees was crouched around on the slopes, gazing in mute desperation at their only threshold of escape. For the opening was guarded by armed sentries of the German frontier police, who drove civilians off the road in order to wave through retreating columns of the Wehrmacht's once-proud Army Group E. A group of the vast crowd, more energetic or desperate than the rest, began to clamber up the heights above, intending to try the hazards of scaling the Ljubelj Peak.

Few could refrain from glancing fearfully southwards. Scarcely a family there remained unmarked by Partisan atrocities. Among the crowd was Vladimir Kozina, the son of a peasant farmer from the Ribnice Valley, with his two sisters Draga and Milka. The gale of revolution had snatched him from his final studies for the priesthood at the Ljubljana Seminary. In the little churchyard of St Mark at Zapotok lay the grave of his elder brother Frank, riddled with Partisan bullets after resolutely declining to join their cause. There too were the bodies of his parents, hacked to death one dark night in August 1942, together with that of his eldest brother John, a paralysed cripple since childhood, shot through the forehead at point-blank range. Vladimir and his sisters, alerted by horrified village neighbours, had come upon the bloodstained scene in the cellar of their home. Like all around them, the Kozinas had no need to guess what would be their fate if ever they fell into the hands of Tito's troops. And now, not far off, a rattle of machine-gun fire crackled and echoed among the cliffs. An agitated murmur ran through the crowd: the Partisans were approaching!

Back in Ljubljana panic gripped the entire population. Afterwards survivors recalled the doom-laden atmosphere; a whole people was conscious that only days – perhaps hours – lay between them and their engulfment by the revolutionary tide. The night of the 7–8 May was deathly still in the capital. As one witness recorded:

> Silence. A strange silence, full of sounds. From the highway, stretching into the distance, was borne the squeaking of wheels, the monotonous droning of lorries, the clattering of tanks, the sonorous hubbub of retreating detachments and fugitives, and the agitated barking of dogs. And yet all was still. The stillness before the storm.
>
> Thousands of people were fleeing, tens of thousands, hundreds of thousands. All were intermingled there, soldiers, ammunition trucks, Red Cross lorries, columns of fugitives. They travelled on foot, journeying on through the mountain passes towards the River Drava, towards Austria.
>
> The dawn of the 8th May broke. The human stream flowed on through the city. Someone was praying. Drivers crossed themselves and urged on their horses.
>
> The city slept, or pretended to be sleeping . . . On the outskirts, there, at Studenec, something was burning, and the glow reddened the sky, but there was no gunfire. It had stopped the evening before.

These were the recollections of a young White Russian woman, attached to one of the émigré units. She was among the multitude who had good reason to fear falling into the hands of the Partisans. Ariana Delianich never forgot the bewilderment and fear of those last days when all around the whole apparatus of ordered society was being swept away in a tide of blood. Human relations took on a new and stark immediacy when from hour to hour none knew whether the final separation might not come.

> I was uneasy in my heart. My nephew was leaving with the regiment, my sister's only son . . . In recent months serving under the same banner he had come to be closer and dearer to me than before. It was hard to be separated from him, departing for the unknown – harder even than when he had been at the front. There it had been a soldier's duty, but here one sensed – treachery.
>
> No sooner had we emerged from the city than we were instantly caught up in the unceasing flow of refugees. In front of us were two regiments of Serbian Volunteers, and behind – Slovenian Domobranci under the command of Major Vuk Rupnik, son of the General. Throughout all that mass of fleeing people one saw pallid faces with a suppressed longing in their eyes.

Limping onwards, I overheard a soldier in the front rank of transports. A snub-nosed, freckled boy from 'over there', from 'under the Soviet heel', as he put it, grumbled in nasal tones: 'Why are we running from those dirty dogs? And why are we giving up everything without a fight? How many times have we smashed them to pieces in our battles? Look what strength we've got! Let's gather ourselves into a fist and smash their red nose . . .'

Yes. Only yesterday all were set for the struggle, seeing only one way out of the battle – victory or death. But today they were gradually being transformed into a grey, purposeless mass.

The straggling column wound on along the highway northwards to Kranj; tanks, lorries, artillery, and horse-drawn wagons hemmed in by a swelling crowd of Slovenian refugees, pushing prams and carts, and bearing what they had been able to snatch of precious household belongings. From the hills on either side an occasional rocket flared up, to indicate where companies of Domobranci mountain troops were keeping the surrounding slopes free of Partisans. On the grass beside the road lay scattered piles of small-arms, abandoned for the most part by German troops whose war was now over. Many were retrieved by the White Russians, Serbs and Slovenes, who felt their struggle to be but opening on to a fresh and still more dangerous phase.

After miles of exhausting marching, continually spurred on by thoughts of what would befall those left behind, they began to climb the steep ascent to the Loibl Pass. Many ignored the zigzag windings of the mountain road, preferring to scramble straight up as best they might, supporting themselves with sticks, and clinging on to prickly bushes. As the front of the column neared the darkened entrance to the tunnel, a sense of panic gripped the crowd. The Partisans were awaiting them in the darkness, machine-guns trained on the entrance! The Austrian frontier beyond, up to the River Drava, was already in Communist hands! There was no rumour too frightening for acceptance. Only the day before – so it was said – Partisans had captured a German hospital train travelling from Celje for the safety of the frontier at Maribor. At the railway station at Pragersko they removed a thousand wounded patients and medical staff, slaughtered them indiscriminately and threw the corpses into nearby anti-tank ditches.

On the road to the Loibl Pass groups of German soldiers, so recently the Slovenes' formidable protectors, were now for the most part hopelessly drunk on pillaged Slovenian *hruskovec* (slivovitz) and *jabolcnik* (apple brandy). A broiling sun continued to burn down on the stricken crowd, broken almost to exhaustion by the forced march along the stony highroad. Still, at least the way was clear. After the initial attempt by German sentries to deny the throng of civilian refugees access to the Loibl tunnel, a group of Slovenian Chetniks had opened fire on them and cleared the escape route.

Among the multilingual throng, none felt more helpless and doomed than the Russians. For the second time in a generation they had seen their world collapse about them and were compelled once again to flee for their lives. In 1920, though, the world had sympathised with their plight, the British and French fleets had been there to rescue them, and a haven lay ahead among their hospitable fellow-Orthodox in Yugoslavia. Now they were the last scattered remnants of the emigrated White Army, hounded by their inveterate enemies, and escaping – where?

What had spread as flying rumour among the crowds straggling up the mountain road now reached Colonel Anatoly Rogozhin as indisputable fact at the temporary headquarters of the *Russkii Corpus*, in the village of St Anna at the foot of the pass. An urgent report arrived from his German superior, Colonel von Seeler, announcing that severe fighting had been taking place to the north all that day: the Partisans were making desperate efforts to cut the line of retreat. Von Seeler himself was directing operations against them, and urgently required support from Rogozhin's infantry. The Russian Colonel at once gave orders for the Fifth Regiment and two battalions of the Fourth to press forward, while he himself set off to investigate.

Meanwhile a daring group of Slovenian Domobranci had entered the tunnel and signalled back that all was for the moment clear. The crowd began pressing forward into the dark interior. Inside was pitch-black, in blinding contrast to the brilliant sunshine outside. The wave of refugees pushed on into the heart of the mountain, along the underground highway constructed by the toil of German slave-labour during the Occupation.

'The journey seemed endless to us,' recalled Ariana Delianich.

The vault and walls of the tunnel had not been faced. Subterranean water flowed everywhere around us. We made our way almost up to the knees in liquid, squelching, sliding mud. People and horses slithered about and fell. Vehicles became stuck and sank down; people were compelled to drag them forward, throwing overcoats, rifles or even fully-packed suitcases under the wheels – anything that came to hand. In the pitch darkness electric torches gleamed like glow-worms . . . Many were obliged to use ordinary cigarette-lighters and matches. Grumbles in all imaginable languages, curses, the snorting of horses, at times their shrill neighing resounding along the vaulted roof; all were repeated in echoes and mingled with the general hubbub. Someone, somewhere, fired a gun. At once everyone froze, but then moved onwards with renewed strength and effort, driven from the rear. Those on foot, for the most part old people, women and children, caught up and seated themselves in the overloaded transport wagons.

Far above them another column of refugees, prevented earlier from entering the Loibl Tunnel, had made a painful ascent over the summit of the mountain range. Mrs Nina Lencek, then a twenty-one-year-old university student from Ljubljana who had become separated from her parents in the long march, recalls that: 'Finally we came to the top of the Pass, and there was the road down. On the other side I remember there was still snow on the ground, and we were so tired and exhausted we just lay on that cold snow to rest a little bit.'

At long last the head of the column re-emerged into the sunlight, and exhausted refugees flung themselves down on the grass on either side of the road. The sun blazed down, birds sang, and a snatch of rainbow glittered in the spray of a nearby waterfall. Even the vegetation was more lush on the Austrian side of the mountains, and despite the continuing threat of danger a feeling of elation gripped many among the emerging crowd. The long ordeal in the darkness appeared like a traversing of the Valley of the Shadow of Death. 'It seemed, in this wonderful region, that the majestic, glittering word LIFE shone out and resounded on all sides.' As they resumed their march down the precipitous winding defile, snow-covered crags towering high on either side, people began to joke and laugh, soldiers relaxed their former air of harassed vigilance, and an extraordinary atmosphere of hope and confidence took hold. They were entering Austria; the Partisans and Red Army seemed far behind, and very soon they would be encountering the British and American armies.

The news grew better hour by hour. Driving ahead of his advance regiments, Colonel Rogozhin came upon von Seeler's headquarters in the village of Unterbergen. The German commander explained that there was no longer any need for the Russians to fight. Partisan armour had indeed tried to cut off their retreat at the passage of the River Drava just ahead, but four Wehrmacht tiger tanks together with the émigré Russian mounted unit 'Edelweiss' had smashed their way through during the night, seizing the crucial bridge which the enemy had fortunately failed to destroy in time. Now there was no obstacle between them and the British headquarters in Klagenfurt! At long last they were safe.

'We shan't be giving up our arms,' cried Serbian soldiers of Colonel Tatalovic's Chetnik regiments gleefully. 'On the contrary. We'll rest a little at Klagenfurt, receive new uniforms, ammunition, fresh weapons – and then back to Yugoslavia to thrash the Titoists!'

As they approached the Drava through spring meadows yellow with dandelions, they encountered the first long-awaited English soldiers. Two tanks of the Grenadier Guards were drawn up near the bridge, before which the bodies and weapons of the defeated Partisans lay still. After a brief exchange with Colonel von Seeler, some British officers approached Rogozhin. One of his officers, Lieutenant Raevsky, scion of one of Imperial Russia's greatest military families, spoke fluent English and acted as interpreter. The Englishmen proved to be extremely polite and welcoming, but could not restrain their astonishment when they found they were dealing with a Tsarist military unit. Understandably, they had no idea that Russian forces existed apart from those of their Red Army allies.

It was agreed that the formal surrender should take place the next morning (12 May). All military units – Russians, Serbs, Slovenes – were to pass across the bridge over the Drava, piling their arms on the further side. This inevitable aspect of the surrender caused momentary anguish among many of the troops. A Don Cossack was heard to growl that life without arms was scarcely worth living – why, a Cossack without a weapon was naked! But the cheery guardsmen conducted only the most perfunctory search, and for the moment a large number of small-arms, ammunition, and even hand grenades remained secreted by their owners. Watching his regiments defile past the ever-growing heap of weapons, Colonel Rogozhin felt a mounting melancholy. He knew he was witnessing the last parade of the *Russkii Corpus* as a fighting unit.[24]

Jovo Miletic, then a twenty-one-year-old corporal in the Serbian Volunteers (Chetniks), recalls the day that also saw the end of their hopes for a free Yugoslavia:

We met two English tanks before we reached the River Drava. They came towards us as we were streaming around them. We were armed and so were they, but the meeting was silent. The cupolas were open, they looked very cool, we were glad to see them. Hardly any of us knew any English (it was not a subject that was taught in our schools before the war!), and we carried on towards the bridge across the Drava. On this side of the bridge there were a lot of Germans with their tanks, camping and in no hurry to cross the Drava even though the capitulation of Germany had been signed. Against all that stationary force a single English soldier guarded the bridge which we crossed. Soon after that we were told by our superiors to lay down our arms, which we did. We laid them at the side of the road, such a mixture of arms of every make no other military corps in the world could have had. On marching on we soon noticed a group of Tito's partisans armed with machine guns amongst English soldiers at the gate of a large house, looking at us with sardonic smiles and listening to our singing. We were singing so as not to cry.

Others present detected different sentiments among the British troops. Mrs Lencek remembers, 'there were some British soldiers – young, they were – I saw compassion in their faces, and they gave us cakes and biscuits, especially to the children and older people. They were standing there; they could not do anything, but they were standing there feeling compassion.'

The flow of troops and civilians moved on as directed by gesturing British troops along the highroad leading north towards Klagenfurt. For many there came a sudden surge of panic as they encountered groups of Communist Partisans, who jeered malevolently and scrambled to plunder the arms they had been unable to seize in battle. A motor-car adorned with a large red star and streaming Communist Yugoslav flag roared past, and shortly afterwards they saw what appeared to be a Soviet tank. Many felt renewed misgivings. So far from being safely in British hands it seemed to them that the victorious 'Allies' were intermingled; and with the Partisans operating on 'home ground', might not their demands preponderate?

This impression was corroborated as individual groups of Partisans sprang up into wagons, robbing the helpless passengers of their watches and few remaining valuables, and contemptuously tearing crucifixes from their necks. Minutes afterwards, however, uniformed motorcyclists roared past in a cloud of dust. 'The English!' shrieked the marauders in alarm, fleeing in disorder to the neighbouring hills.

Eventually the refugee column was directed to a road on the left which led them to a huge level area of pasture and ploughed land by the little village of Viktring, and it was here that English soldiers indicated that the refugees should set up camp. In no time at all lines were marked out, signs and markers erected, rows of tents started up, and improvised shelters created by wagons and carts. By the evening of 13 May it was thought some 35,000 people had gathered in the Viktring field. A British officer present noted that, 'At one time this column stretched for some ten miles along the rd to Viktring, together with their horses and lorries, supplies and women.'[25]

John Corsellis, a young volunteer with the Friends' Ambulance Unit, who arrived a few days after the refugees' arrival to help administer the camp, provided this description in a letter home to his mother:

> . . . it is on the edge of a widish plain, and consists of a large field surrounded on three sides by small streams and further large fields and then rapidly climbing pine covered hills on one side, the latter developing into quite respectable mountains. On one side also is a large and attractive monastery planned around three courtyards and beyond that up a hill a textile factory, which during the war was turned into an aero-engine parts factory and is now occupied by some 600 of the refugees – mainly women and children.
>
> The vast bulk of the refugees live in the open in the above-mentioned field, using for shelter what material they can find – some have tents made from sacking, gas capes, overcoats and blankets, some have shacks made of wood and bark, some live in their carts with some material stretched over the top. When I arrived [on 18 May], they all had their horses inside the camp and as there were over 400 horses [this was in the civilians' camp; there were many more in the area occupied by the troops] you can imagine what the ground was soon like. The horses of course always got the best accommodation: some had even got roofs made of boards. When it was dry things were not too bad, but this district is particularly liable to sudden storms with heavy rain and then the place was liable to become a sea of mud.

It was an extraordinarily colourful and varied scene. There were the neat picket-lines of Colonel Rogozhin's *Russkii Corpus*, with the white, blue and red tricolour of Imperial Russia drooping from their flagpole above. There too were Colonel Tatalovic's three regiments of Serbian Volunteers, brimful of optimism and assuring one and all that, after a brief period of recuperation, the British would send them on to a rendezvous in Italy with their young king preparatory to marching triumphantly back into a Yugoslavia purged of atheistic Communism. For were they not soldiers of an Allied army? Less sanguine were the feelings of General Krenner's 12,000 Slovenian Domobranci. For them national and personal survival had inevitably involved co-operation with the German occupation forces – and how would the British look on that? But such fears were for the moment allayed by the friendly attitude of the British soldiers they encountered.

That night the general feeling was one of relief, and confidence in the future. As dusk came on, campfires were lit and meals prepared. Children ran in and out of shelters improvised from blankets stretched between the wagon-rows, while mothers once again set up home with what was left of clothes and utensils snatched up in panic-stricken moments before their flight. From the military cantonments arose the solemn strains of evening prayer, sung variously by Orthodox Russians, Serbs and Montenegrins, and by Catholic Slovenes and Croats. Elsewhere were heard shouts in German or Hungarian, or a still more improbable linguistic medley where small Romanian and French SS units found themselves camped side by side.

Everyone was alone with his or her thoughts. Mrs Lencek's memory is of a poignant sense of total isolation:

'At least we knew we were safe. That was all that mattered. But there was another aspect, which I at least felt very keenly. We were not only refugees from our country, but also exiles from society. We were nobody. We had lost our identity, whoever we were. We were just DP number so-and-so.'

Ara Delianich was unable to sleep that night. It was her birthday, the strangest she had known in an unsettled life since her distant sunlit childhood by the Black Sea in pre-revolutionary Sebastopol. She lay on her back beside her wagon, staring up at the night sky with its glittering array of watching stars. Occasionally a shooting-star traced a flaring plunge and vanished. Where to? What would become of all these thousands of forsaken people, driven by 'the gale of the world' to this remote green corner? The previous day someone had declared that they were all to be shipped off to perform twenty years' forced labour in Madagascar. How crazy! And why Madagascar, where surely only black men lived?

There had been worse camps and worse times than this. In 1920, at Gallipoli, Lemnos . . . The firm tread of a patrol of Grenadier Guardsmen passed by the other side of the line of wagons. From the camp perimeter gleamed the protective headlights of British tanks. 'Highway robbery!' a red-moustached British officer had contemptuously termed those Partisan depredations on the road to Viktring. Yes, perhaps they would all sail to Madagascar, and live in the hot sun with the negroes . . .[26]

3

The Coming of the Cossacks

'The English value and respect their adversaries, and under no circumstances act injuriously towards prisoners-of-war. The war is over. Victors and vanquished must beat their swords into ploughshares and set swiftly about building up a peaceful life.' (Major-General Robert Arbuthnott, commanding the Seventy-eighth Infantry Division, VE Day 1945)

While the First Guards Brigade was receiving the surrender of the fugitives from Yugoslavia who had made the perilous crossing of the Loibl Pass, other units of the Fifth Corps found themselves incurring similar problems with large bodies of Cossacks.

On 10 May Major Henry Howard of the First King's Royal Rifle Corps was visited in his camp by General von Pannwitz, who had arrived to arrange the surrender of the Fifteenth Cossack Cavalry Corps. This was a force of anti-Communist Cossacks serving in the Wehrmacht for the purpose (as they saw it) of liberating Russia from Stalin's dictatorship. In 1943 a training camp had been established at Mlava in the Ukraine, where all Cossacks in German service were to be organised into a fully-fledged fighting unit. Most of the officers were German or Austrian cavalrymen of distinguished noble and military ancestry, and from its earliest days the Corps command also included a substantial number of White Russian émigrés from Belgrade, Paris or Berlin, who welcomed the opportunity to renew their struggle against the Bolsheviks.

After initial surprise at occasional characteristic displays of independence, von Pannwitz and his officers became impressed by the Cossacks' specialised military skills. Colonel Alexander von Bosse, a Russian-speaker of Baltic origin, was placed in charge of training. He noted that:

the Cossacks far surpassed the German personnel in taking advantage of terrain and in the art of camouflage. Thus, for example, after each rush the Cossacks always rolled a few yards to the side into a previously selected position and so escaped enemy observation. It was not necessary to teach them to dig in, as they did so instinctively. Internal discipline was good, but external discipline was somewhat below German standards. Saluting was practised and improved. Sand table exercises were of great interest to platoon and section leaders. Here the Cossacks displayed a wealth of ideas aimed at deception and trickery, infiltrating and ambushing, that would have provided any German sand table course with valuable suggestions for improvements . . . Demolition exercises were especially enjoyed by the Cossacks.

A great attraction for recruits was the organisation of religious services, an Orthodox chaplain being attached to every regiment. Many of those educated in the Soviet Union, who had not been baptised and received eccentric first names such as 'May', 'Tractor', 'October', or 'Ninel' ('Lenin' backwards), were now baptised, received traditional Russian Christian names, and were issued with crucifixes. As for entertainment:

Choral singing and Cossack dances, preferably with rather than without vodka, were the favourite evening amusements in the camp. On Sundays and holidays the men executed the famous 'Dzhigitovka' riding feats amidst enthusiastic applause and loud cheering. Parties given by the various units ended in drunken orgies which had to be supervised and kept in check by details appointed for this purpose in advance, especially whenever indiscriminate shooting began, which, although all a part of the game, met with scant sympathy on the part of the German officers and garrison headquarters. However, no accidents occurred.

Discipline too was applied in the traditional Cossack manner:

Judging by our standards, the Cossack commanders inflicted very severe punishments. The usual one was three days' confinement in a dark cell on a bread and water diet. The commander of the 5th Don Regiment even had men flogged, but he was nonetheless very popular and never spoke of his men except as 'his children'.

This was the celebrated Colonel Kononov, who also maintained among his entourage his personal executioner, a ferocious half-Cossack half-Greek who sported gold ear-rings.

In September 1943 the Cossack Corps was ordered to entrain for

Yugoslavia, where their special skills in guerilla warfare were to be pitted against those of Tito's Partisans. There was considerable disappointment that they were not to fight, as they had been led to expect, against their old foes in the Soviet Union. However, fighting is what a Cossack is bred for, and at least their enemies would be Reds. By the end of the month they had arrived in Croatia, where they were assigned the task of protecting rail and road connections between Zagreb and Belgrade. Though new to the country and unfamiliar with mountainous terrain, the Cossacks soon proved more than a match for the much-vaunted Partisans. They were particularly skilful at laying and avoiding ambushes, at launching unexpected raids far from their lines, and at keeping the enemy (who had hitherto operated with considerable impunity against German units) permanently on the qui vive.

> While on mounted duty the Cossacks would habitually fire from horse-back with submachine-guns into corn fields in order to draw the enemy's fire, or the advance guard would suddenly wheel about at some woods, a corn field or a village and gallop back. If no shots were fired it could reasonably be assumed that the area was clear of the enemy.

So redoubtable did the Cossacks' reputation become that it was not long before Tito's Partisans were driven to panic simply by rumours of their approach. For those who lingered long enough to witness the spectacle, it could be an unnerving sight to see a squadron of apparently riderless Cossack ponies charging home at the gallop – it being Cossack practice to swing down and come in firing from under their horses' bellies.

The experience of a Croatian schoolgirl at this time illustrates the effect the very name 'Cossack' had upon Tito's followers. In September 1944 Marija Ann Levic was thirteen years old, when the Partisans came to occupy her home town in Croatia. Her father and two elder brothers had already escaped, but Marija's mother and four children were arrested. About a month later the Communist authorities learned of the flight of their menfolk, and the family was taken away by train under armed guard, allegedly to be handed across enemy lines to the Croatian Army.

Eventually the railway track came to an end in open fields. The Partisan guards made the prisoners descend, telling them they and two other families with them were to leave the road ahead and march instead through the forest towards Croatian lines. This forest was in fact a notorious place of execution employed by the Partisans, and Marija's mother refused to move into the darkness under the trees. Crying out that if they wanted to shoot them they could do it in the open, she threw down their cases and sat down among her children on the road.

What their guards would have done next the family never found out, for at that moment a pale-faced Partisan came running out of the forest, crying out in terror, 'The Cossacks are coming! The Cossacks are coming!' Without a word or a pause the Partisans took to their heels and ran 'like chickens'. Shortly afterwards a Cossack patrol came trotting up, and the abandoned prisoners were taken on a horse-drawn wagon to safety in the nearby town of Banovo Jaruga, which was occupied by anti-Communist Croatians. Later Marija learned that the fleeing Partisans had borne the panic aroused by the Cossack name to her home town, which was instantly abandoned by its Titoist garrison. When the Cossacks entered the abandoned place they released twenty-two citizens, lying under a death sentence which the Partisans had fled too swiftly to execute.[1]

In theory the Cossacks were acting in part at least as allies of Germany's client state in Croatia. In fact, however, they sympathised strongly with their Serbian fellow-Orthodox, whose churches were on occasion pillaged or destroyed by the Catholic Croatian Ustashe. Eventually the Cossacks entered into an unofficial 'non-aggression pact' with the Serbian Chetniks of General Mihailovic, despite the fact that he was at the same time warring against their German masters. Such anomalous arrangements became possible because the German officers in the Corps had become profoundly sympathetic towards the Cossack people and cause, and for the most part deeply regretted Hitler's besotted determination to reduce all Russians to a nation of slaves.

In the spring of 1945 the Fifteenth Cossack Cavalry Corps achieved its longed-for aim of encountering the Red Army in the field. Operating on the left flank of the German armies in northern Croatia, they fought with despairing heroism against Soviet and Bulgarian units, repelling the enemy again and again and inflicting heavy casualties. Finally, when news of the German surrender came over the radio, General von Pannwitz managed to extricate his force from the front and make a forced march westwards. At the same time as the Slovenian exodus through the Loibl Pass, described in the last chapter, was occurring the two divisions of the Cossack Corps crossed over into Austria some sixty kilometres to the east, at Lavamünd.[2] From there they advanced swiftly to meet the nearest British unit, to whom they surrendered in the manner already described.

On 11 May the Cossacks piled their arms in a field just outside Völkermarkt, then continued their march to points indicated by the British where they were to set up camp. At first they were all within the area administered by General Murray's Sixth Armoured Division, but a week or so later most units of the Fifteenth Cossack Cavalry Corps were moved to the area controlled by the neighbouring Forty-sixth Infantry Division, commanded by the New Zealand Major-General Steven Weir. Despite their relief at thus being extricated from falling into the hands of Stalin's or Tito's forces, the senior German commanders entertained serious misgivings as to British intentions for their future. When General von Pannwitz asked Major Charles Villiers, an SOE (Special Operations Executive) officer who was interrogating him, to intercede at Fifth Corps Headquarters, Villiers was told by the Brigadier General Staff (Toby Low) that no promises of any kind could be made, and that for the moment the Cossacks must sit tight in their encampments until a decision was arrived at.

As the war ground to a halt the Fifteenth Cossack Cavalry Corps was one of two major Cossack units to fall into the hands of the Fifth Corps of the British Eighth Army. Allied military intelligence had been aware since the end of 1944 of the presence of another body, a so-called 'Cossack Division', in Northern Italy. SOE agents had reported some fierce brushes between the Cossacks and local Italian resistance groups, but otherwise little appeared to be known of them.

In the last week of the war, when Eighth Army units were making their final push to Trieste and northwards into Austria, it was feared that these Cossacks might attempt isolated resistance. On 6 May Lieutenant-Colonel Alec Malcolm of the Eighth Argyll and Sutherland Highlanders received orders to advance up the Tagliamento to the small town of Tolmezzo in the Carnian Alps, where the Cossacks were reported to be quartered. There was an ironical side to the coming encounter, since the Scottish Highlanders in Britain had in past centuries played a similar role to that of the Cossacks in Imperial Russia. However, the Argylls arrived in fighting order at Tolmezzo only to find that the Cossacks had decamped – 'probably back into Austria'.

That the Cossacks had removed themselves over the mountains into Austria proved to be true. On 8 May a small Cossack delegation arrived at Tolmezzo in a car bearing a white flag. By now the British

Thirty-sixth Infantry Brigade had established its headquarters in the building occupied by the Cossack leadership a week earlier. Present at Brigade Headquarters was the Divisional Commander, Major-General Robert Arbuthnott, who received the newcomers with courteous attentiveness. There were three in the party: the tall, distinguished-looking General Vasiliev, formerly serving in the Russian Imperial Guards; young Nikolai Krasnov, close relative of one of Russia's most celebrated Civil War leaders, General Peter Krasnov; and Olga Rotova, a White Russian émigré from Yugoslavia. Olga had learned English when working there for the Standard Oil Company, and it was she who now acted as interpretress.

Ushered into General Arbuthnott's office, General Vasiliev (speaking through Olga Rotova) began to explain the position of the 'Kazachi Stan', as their settlement was known. Their sole quarrel was with the Bolsheviks, with whom they hoped to resume fighting as soon as possible. Arbuthnott made no direct reply to this ambitious request, explaining that the first necessity was for the Cossacks to be disarmed.

'Do you regard the Cossack formation as prisoners of war?' enquired General Vasiliev.

'No,' replied Arbuthnott. 'Prisoners of war are those taken in battle; we regard you as having given yourselves up voluntarily.' He went on to explain that the British respected an honourable adversary, and that it was never their policy to treat prisoners harshly. The war was over; it was time to beat swords into ploughshares and rebuild a peaceful world.

At this point another senior British officer entered the room. This was Brigadier Geoffrey Musson, commander of the Thirty-sixth Infantry Brigade, who appeared more familiar than his superior with the Cossacks' predicament. He confirmed that immediate disarmament was required, explaining that he would visit the Cossack camp next morning to settle matters. Arrangements being for the moment satisfactorily concluded, Arbuthnott ushered his visitors into an adjoining room and offered them a snack lunch after their journey.

Food was brought in, and Arbuthnott turned to more relaxed conversation. Clearly intrigued by the appearance of the youthful Nikolai Krasnov among a group of men intent on reviving a civil war now over for a quarter of a century, he asked him a number of questions about his background. Nikolai explained that he had emigrated as a child with his parents from Russia after the Revolution, and had lived thereafter in Yugoslavia. Having completed his military training he joined the royal army and was captured by the Germans during the invasion of 1941. The Germans invited him on release to join a volunteer unit in their army serving in North Africa, but he declined to fight against the British, Russia's ally in the Great War. Together with his father and 'grandfather' (in fact cousin), the famous Ataman Krasnov, he had joined his compatriots in the Kazachi Stan.

General Arbuthnott was greatly struck by the fact that none of his Russian visitors was a Soviet citizen, nor could they be said to have done anything material to aid the enemy cause. But there was no further time for reflection, as Brigadier Musson returned to announce that the armed escort for the Cossack delegation was waiting to accompany them back over the Plöckenpass. Pressing presents of tea, sugar, chocolate and cigarettes upon Olga, Arbuthnott followed his visitors down into the street to where their car was waiting.

Before departing, Olga could not resist asking the General what was his personal view of 'the Bolsheviks'.

'None too good,' replied Arbuthnott emphatically. 'But for the present they are our allies.'

'But how can you trust them,' ventured Olga boldly, 'knowing as you do of their policy of destabilising British India, even during the present war?'

'True,' replied the other laconically. 'But for all that they are at present our allies, if not our friends.'[3]

The delegation returned to Cossack headquarters at Kötschach at 9.30 that evening, and hastened to report all that had occurred to Nikolai Krasnov's 'grandfather'. Old General Peter Nikolaevich Krasnov was a remarkable figure, regarded with veneration by the Cossacks. Born in 1869 of an old Don Cossack family, he was seventy-six at the time of these events. In the Great War he had commanded a cavalry corps on the Eastern Front with great distinction. A convinced monarchist and upholder of the historic traditions of the Cossack nations, he had been in command of the Third Cavalry Corps, instructed by Kerensky in October 1917 to suppress the Bolshevik coup in Petrograd. However, his troops fraternised with Soviet sailors, Kerensky fled, and Krasnov himself withdrew to the Cossack territories in the south of Russia. There he was elected Ataman (leader) of the Don Cossacks, and raised the standard of revolt against the Bolsheviks until his resignation early in 1919. Afterwards in emigration he wrote a number of polemical novels attacking the Soviets, and after the war broke out co-operated with other prominent White Russians in promulgating anti-Soviet propaganda.[4] Finally, as the war drew to a close, he travelled to Italy and joined his fellow-Cossacks at Tolmezzo in February 1945.[5]

Despite the friendly reception accorded the Cossack delegates by the British generals at Tolmezzo, General Krasnov felt some misgivings. Having at least in form collaborated with the enemy, the Cossacks might not be regarded with overmuch sympathy by their captors. It was necessary to make their peculiar position quite clear to the British military authorities.

After his departure from southern Russia in 1919, Krasnov had served for a time under the White General Yudenich on the Petrograd front at the time when the emergent Baltic States were fighting to repel a Bolshevik invasion. The British were assisting the ill-armed Balts, and attached to the Baltic *Landeswehr* was a young officer seconded from the Irish Guards: Major Harold Alexander. Krasnov knew him at that time, and it appeared a fortunate chance that it was his old acquaintance, holder of the Tsarist Order of St Anne, who now commanded the Allied armies into whose hands he and his comrades had fallen.

Krasnov at once sat down to compose a letter to the Field-Marshal, setting out the circumstances under which these scattered fugitives from Bolshevik terror had come to find themselves in a place so remote from their own country. In it, 'He reminded him how they had fought together against the Communists during the Russian Civil War and requested that the British troops under his command protect the Cossack land from the Soviets and transmit to his government the request that all of them be accorded political asylum as stateless refugees.'[6]

The last two words were those which bore unique significance in the context in which the Cossacks now found themselves. Sentiment in wartime is rarely a plentiful commodity, but the British at least were certain to be rigorous in implementing the provisions of international law. The Cossacks would be content with almost any fate, other than that of being sent back to the Soviet Union. For those who were Soviet citizens there was always the unpleasant awareness that the Soviet Government was certain to request their return. But for the White Russian émigrés like the Krasnovs, General Vasiliev and Olga Rotova there could be no question of being 'sent back'. They had never lived in the Soviet Union, having for the most part escaped in British and French warships in 1919 and 1920, when the Red Army finally established control over southern Russia. Since then they had lived the life of exiles in Belgrade, Munich, Paris, Berlin. They had thus never been Soviet citizens, and were either stateless, bearing League of Nations passports ('Nansen certificates'), or had become citizens of the countries in which they had settled. Virtually all under the age of twenty-five had actually been born abroad.

The German-appointed Ataman of the Kazachi Stan, General Domanov, was a former Red Army officer. But the majority, that is to say some sixty-eight per cent (the estimate is based on Cossack field returns) of his fellow-officers were old émigrés.[7] As there were 2,756 officers registered on the staff roll,[8] this amounts to some 1,800 men who were not Soviet citizens. In addition to these one must include an unknown number of other ranks, and a sizeable proportion of the women and children. It seems that among the 25,000 or so Cossacks surrendering to the Thirty-sixth Infantry Brigade there must have been 3,000 or more who were not Soviet citizens.

Neither General Krasnov nor any other old émigré was seeking to extricate himself from sharing whatever fate attended those of their comrades who were in the equivocal position of being Soviet citizens. At least, no trace of an attempt to do so has survived among the voluminous Cossack and British sources. Rather, the implication appears to have been that old and new émigrés were so inextricably intermingled that they should all be regarded as stateless refugees. Krasnov's letter was passed up to General Arbuthnott's Divisional Headquarters, but for the moment no reply was forthcoming.

The morning after the Cossack delegation's return from Tolmezzo, Brigadier Musson and his staff arrived at Kötschach inside the Austrian frontier to confer with Domanov and the other Cossack leaders. The atmosphere once again was amicable and understanding, and it was agreed that the Cossacks should proceed on their way northwards to set up camp in the valley of the Drau near the little town of Lienz. The main Cossack camp was established around a former Wehrmacht barracks at Peggetz, east of Lienz. Further downstream between Oberdrauburg and Dellach there was another camp for some 4,000 Caucasians, who were commanded by a distinguished Tsarist and Civil War émigré general, Sultan Kelich Ghirey. The whole valley was hemmed in by lofty, snow-covered mountains, but otherwise there was little to prevent the Cossacks and Caucasians from wandering where they chose. The camps were administered and guarded by the Eighth Battalion Argyll and Sutherland Highlanders and the Sixth Royal West Kents.

A week after the settlement of the Cossacks at Lienz they were joined by another distinguished veteran of the Civil War, the Kuban Cossack leader Andrei Shkuro, together with 1,400 men of his Cossack training regiment. Shkuro's courageous exploits in the Great War and subsequent Civil War had endeared him not only to the Cossacks but also to the British, allies of the Whites against the Bolsheviks. On 2 June 1919 King George V honoured him with the Companionship of the Bath, whose cross he still wore on his uniform alongside others awarded by King George's cousin, the Emperor Nicholas II.

Despite the fact that the able-bodied Cossacks were organised into regiments bearing historic Cossack names, the Kazachi Stan presented a very different appearance from that formidable fighting force, the Fifteenth Cossack Cavalry Corps, which was at this time being held by the British some miles to the east. About a third or even half their number were not fighting men, and the camp at Peggetz rang with the cries of children playing and women preparing meals. To help them organise their existence, Lieutenant-Colonel Malcolm deputed a youthful Welsh officer, Major 'Rusty' Davies, to take charge. Davies found this task challenging but enjoyable. He could not speak a word of Russian, and so chose as his aide and interpreter a young Captain Butlerov, an émigré from Paris. Butlerov, as his name suggests, was descended from a famous Irish Jacobite family, whose ancestors in the eighteenth century had been driven by revolution at home to serve abroad in the ranks of a foreign army. It happened, too, that his grandmother was English and consequently he spoke the language fluently.

Davies, young and enthusiastic, soon made himself at home among the Cossacks, helping them to organise sanitary arrangements and schools for the children, and launched a camp newspaper. No one knew how long they might be there, and it was necessary to act as if their stay might be a long one. During the next few weeks Davies became particularly friendly with his part-English companion Butlerov, and soon learned much about the traditional Cossack way of life. Butlerov also taught him to ride, and together they would move about the camp, observing the peaceful scene in the beautiful Alpine valley. Supremely adaptable, and accustomed for centuries to living off the land, the Cossacks had in no time re-established 'Cossack land' on Austrian soil. There were groups of men undergoing military drill, children chanting out their lessons, priests conducting church choirs through the intensely moving cadences of the

Russian Orthodox liturgy; while in the open fields young Cossacks showed off the feats of the world-famous *dzhigitovka* – spearing tent-pegs from horseback, seizing handkerchiefs from the ground with their teeth at full gallop, or standing upright on the saddle in a formation canter – to Davies's never-failing astonishment.

The atmosphere of a timeless Russian past seemed transported to this remote locality. Davies and his fellow-officers of the Eighth Argylls were profoundly struck by the extraordinarily cosmopolitan background of many of their charges. Several thousand of them had after all passed the previous quarter-century in different countries of Western Europe. Among the officers, French and German were heard almost as often as Russian. Their professions, too, had been as varied. There were schoolmasters from Paris, taxi-drivers from Brussels, restaurant-owners from Munich, journalists from Belgrade. Shkuro had for a time even earned his living as a trick-rider in a travelling German circus; it seems likely that he is the only Companion of the Bath to have done so.

The 'British connection', though not so prevalent, was still strong. Apart from Butlerov and Olga Rotova, Davies found that a number spoke fluent English. There was even a White Russian who had served for many years in the British Hong Kong police, whose exemplary actions on one occasion had earned him the Military Cross.

At first Davies, who for four eventful years had heard nothing of the Soviet Union but what percolated through sympathetic wartime Allied propaganda, found it hard to understand why the Cossacks expressed continual horror at the thought of ever having to return to that country. The Cossacks in turn were baffled by the Welshman's complacent view of conditions within the Soviet Union. One day matters were clarified a little for Davies at least, when a group of Cossacks brought up to him an old lady. 'That's what they did to me,' she explained calmly, holding out her hands. Her fingernails had been torn out by the roots.

After the hardships of their previous life, the Cossacks were content for the most part to enjoy their new, peaceful existence. Under a warm May sun life was more than tolerable in the barracks and tents of Peggetz. Misgivings were confined largely to some of the senior officers. General Domanov in particular seemed consistently dispirited. For Krasnov, Shkuro, Vasiliev and the others prospects appeared promising enough. Their old allies the British would in due course decide on a suitable place for them to settle – with any luck in the empty spaces of some overseas British colony. Domanov's position was perhaps less assured, for he was a former Soviet citizen, a major in the Red Army, taken prisoner by the Germans. Under Soviet law he had already earned himself a death sentence by 'allowing himself' to be taken prisoner; but far worse than this was his subsequent service in what was officially at any rate a unit of the Wehrmacht. The Soviets must already be well aware of his existence, and would doubtless soon be demanding his return. It seemed unlikely that the British would make any great bones about handing him over.

On 18 May, a week after the Cossacks' arrival in the Drautal, the British divisional commander, Major-General Arbuthnott, toured the camp. His manner was easy and affable, he appeared pleased with the evidence of good order all around, took especial interest in the cadets' school which had been established for Cossack boys, and ordered a general increase in rations. To most Cossacks this visit portended nothing but good, but some of the more experienced officers began to suffer misgivings. For as yet no reply had arrived to General Krasnov's appeal to Field-Marshal Alexander, written over a week earlier. Krasnov sat down to pen another letter in which once again he set out the Cossacks' predicament, reminded the Field-Marshal of their common service in the White cause under General Yudenich, and requested asylum somewhere in the free West for the homeless wanderers. Major Davies took charge of the letter, which he passed on to Colonel Malcolm. From Battalion Head-quarters in Lienz it was passed on to Brigade in Oberdrauburg, from there to Division, ending up at the Fifth Corps Headquarters in Klagenfurt.[9]

For the refugees fortunate enough to gain the safety of British-occupied Austria during those last chaotic closing days of the war, the fortnight following VE Day was a time of intense relief, accompanied by an uneasy undertone of apprehension. There was little fear that they would fall once again into the hands of their enemies, once the British Army had shown it would stand firm against Tito's ill-disciplined Partisans.

It is true that the manner of the first British officer General von Pannwitz had encountered at the time of his surrender had been distinctly cold, even harsh, despite the fact that they had last met at a house-party on the Bismarcks' East Prussian estate. Major Charles Villiers was unlikely to view the Cossacks' plight with sympathy, for he had served in Yugoslavia with SOE, becoming a close personal friend of Marshal Tito. But the attitude of British Army officers serving with the regular forces was in the main strongly sympathetic, once they had come to understand the realities of the situation.

Count Leopold Goëss then commanded the Second Battalion of the Sixth Terek Cossack Regiment, and remembers the fairly typical change in attitude which followed his surrender:

My unit was rearguard in the retreat from Croatia to the Austrian border during the period 8 to 11 May 1945. After having refused repeated demands by Tito's troops for our surrender, we reached the Austrian border near Unterdrauburg on the night of 11 May. There the bridge was already occupied by Bulgarian troops. We tried next the possibility of crossing the Drau river at Lavamünd but the Bulgarians on the other bank were quicker. And now the situation became more and more serious, as we were not prepared to surrender to the Bulgarians, and the latter began preparing an attack supported by tanks.

By chance there turned up an Australian P.O.W. whom I asked to go and try to find some British troops and tell the commanding officer that there was a Cossack regiment prepared to surrender to them but not to the Bulgarians. And really after about 2 hours a jeep turned up with two British officers, one of whom being Brigadier Scott (I can't remember which regiment). [They were, as will be seen shortly, Brigadier T. P. D. Scott, commanding Thirty-eighth (Irish) Infantry Brigade, and Lieutenant-Colonel Murphy Palmer of the Royal Irish Fusiliers.]

He told me and my Regimental Commander that we had immediately to surrender to the Bulgarians, and that he had nothing more to tell us. I answered that our surrender to the Bulgarians would mean our certain death, and that we would certainly not go that way. Brigadier Scott became rather furious, saying that the Bulgarians were their allies and so on, but finally agreed to go and see the Bulgarian commander about the problem. Returning after about 30 minutes, he told us that after we had laid down our arms on the field where we were preparing for our defence, they would give us free passage to the next British troops. Knowing the Bulgarians better I didn't accept the proposal, and Brigadier Scott turned away furiously and went off.

But after some time he came back, telling me that he had to excuse his allies who really seemed to be crooks, as they were already preparing to make us prisoners after we had put away our arms. After having told me that he would show us how a British officer sticks to his word he went off, and in about two hours a lorry with a platoon of British soldiers turned up to be our safeguard for the night. And in the morning an officer arrived and said that now we could lay down our arms and follow him: a British regiment would help us through the Bulgarian lines. And so we marched over 4 miles escorted by British tanks into the British occupied zone.

The officer in charge of the escort was Lieutenant-Colonel Murphy Palmer, commanding the Royal Irish Fusiliers, who has kindly provided me with an account of their journey. As it was interrupted by an incident of considerable significance, I give the story in his own words:

I assembled a truck-load of Fusiliers and Pat [Scott] and I drove over the bridge and up to where the battle was going on. We ran into a Cossack picket but fortunately it did not open fire as we should have been sitting targets. At the top of the hill there was a large open plain and as far as one could see there was nothing but horses, soldiers, waggons and all the impedimenta of a cavalry brigade of 5,000 men. We drove on through the middle of them eventually arriving at a large farmhouse and yard and this we assumed would be the headquarters of the Cossack regiment. Pat and I got out and walked round to the front of the house where we saw a Cossack with two lovely hunters with ordinary saddles, followed by an Irish Red Setter dog. Someone ran into the house presumably to tell the German officers that we had arrived. A young German officer [Count Goëss, whose account has just been quoted] came out, bowed in the usual way and spoke most perfect English. We asked if he commanded the regiment. He said that he did not but that he was the Staff Officer. The regiment was commanded by Prince zu Salm. He told us that the Prince was having his lunch so we told him that the Prince should come out at once. The Prince came out and saluted and said that he was prepared to surrender. The Staff Officer was an Austrian Count and when I remarked on his good English he told us that he had been at Oxford just before the war. I told the Prince that his men should be disarmed and put all arms in a heap at the back of the building and that this heap would be guarded. I asked him where he had got such lovely horses and he told me that he had bought them in Dublin at the [1937] Horse Show and that the dog had been given to him by a girlfriend he had in Dublin!

Pat Scott told me that he had to go as he was urgently required at another problem spot. He told me that it was my duty to get these people back to our 8th Army area as best I could. I realized that I was now in fairly big trouble as we had to go down the hill, over the bridge and through the Bulgarians who were now firmly ensconced in the village. I decided that the only thing to do was to go in the middle of the night when the Bulgarians would all be drunk and so busy with the local ladies that they would be unlikely to interfere with us. I told the Prince to have his men ready to march at 3 a.m. and I ordered him to give me twelve horses on which I mounted twelve New Zealanders [recently liberated prisoners-of-war] who said that they would be only too willing to help as I was in a mess.

We started off at the appointed time and the whole thing went really

quite well; one of my company of Fusiliers was holding the bridge and
the others were scattered about in the column keeping the whole thing
on the move. We went plodding on at 2 or 3 m.p.h. until about 11 a.m.
I went in front in the jeep and the Prince rode behind me. At 11 a.m. the
Prince sent the Staff Officer to tell me that they wanted to stop and cook
a meal. I said that on no account was this to happen as I realised that the
Russians must have been getting nearer and nearer, and as the column
was about 5–8 miles long, I was thinking of my own company of Fusiliers
who were acting as rear-guard only just clear of Lavamund. However,
the Prince told me that his men had eaten very little food and were not
able to go on marching – so they just stopped and I could not do anything
about it. They jumped over the local ditches collecting timber. There
were fires going for miles along the road and they were cooking whatever
there was to eat.

In the middle of all this, General Sir Charles Keightley arrived on the
scene and he asked me why I had let them stop. I explained that it had
not been my idea and that I could not help it. He was none too pleased
and told me to get going as quickly as possible as he did not want the
Russians to get hold of the whole column. General Keightley went away
then and the Cossacks consumed their meal quickly – we set off on our
way. We arrived back in 8th Army area some time in the late afternoon
[of 12 May] where we were met and the Cossacks were directed into a
large space which had been marked out for them.

Next Colonel Palmer directed his Adjutant, Captain Brian Clark, to
escort Prince zu Salm to the headquarters of the Fifteenth Cossack
Cavalry Corps where he was to receive his final instructions. Today
Captain (now Lieutenant-Colonel) Clark vividly recalls a confusing
jeep journey along unknown roads. Their route was littered with
empty cartridge-cases, detritus of a war still scarcely over, and three
times they were obliged to halt to allow Clark's driver and the Prince
to repair a punctured tyre. Eventually they found von Pannwitz's
Headquarters, where matters were arranged to mutual satisfaction.

A few days later Brian Clark was on duty at Regimental Headquarters in the village of St Andrä, when General von Pannwitz made
an unexpected appearance. Colonel Palmer was out on a tour of his
companies, and so it was to Captain Clark that von Pannwitz expressed his gratitude for the chivalrous manner in which British
forces had accepted the surrender of the Cossacks. Today Colonels
Palmer and Clark are emphatic that they and General Keightley
considered the surrender as having been arranged under honourable
conditions, within the terms of the Geneva Convention on prisoners
of war.

The Cossacks were safe for the present, though their ultimate fate remained unknown. Without any possibility of returning to their homes, at least for the moment, where could they go? Rumours abounded in their camps, ranging from optimistic conjectures that the British would soon learn the hard way what were Stalin's and Tito's true intentions towards the democracies, and consequently recruit Cossacks, Chetniks, Domobranci and others into anti-Bolshevik units for a new war; to asseverations that whole national groupings would be found new homes in African or other colonies of Britain's huge Empire, or that they would be permitted to volunteer for service with the Allies in the Far East.

On the whole, however, the feeling was one of confidence. The 'English gentleman' was in Eastern European folklore a figure recognised by all as one of unimpeachable honour and attachment to civilised decencies. This picture was fully confirmed by the comportment of British troops of all ranks with whom the Russian and Yugoslav interned units came in contact. Historic links of friendship between the British and their Cossack allies of 1919, and with the Royal Yugoslav Army which in April 1941 had sacrificed itself in a futile but valiant effort to save British armies operating in Greece, had been forged too long to be lightly set aside now.

They had in any case received categorical assurances of decent, fair and humane treatment at the time of their surrender; treatment they had every right to expect under the terms of the Geneva Convention. As Nikolai Krasnov, who had received such assurances from General Arbuthnott himself, reflected:

Not one of us for one second dreamed of mistrusting the word of an English general. How could we dare not to believe a King's officer, occupying such a lofty position! . . . People relaxed. They felt themselves to be in the lap of good fortune, knowing how many of our compatriots could not go back to their own country, occupied as it was by the Soviets. Their fate was to us both obvious and clear.

I recall fragmentary conversations between old émigrés and the forever mistrustful, forever 'on the alert', former Soviet citizens. As the first to have escaped, with what warmth did they reassure those who had been let down so often by fate and deceived by their fellow-humans that before us lay the quiet life of ordinary citizens – that is to say, of emigrants in territory occupied by the armies of the great, civilised, monarchist power, joined by ties of blood to our Russian dynasty!

I remember that secret, scarcely heard whisper, that if anything bad was coming to anyone, then assuredly it would not be to the old émigrés,

who had acquired in their twenty-five years of wandering or settled
existence rights of citizenship in the free world.[10]

Good or bad, the fate of all the Cossack prisoners was being decided
at this time by men in Klagenfurt and Caserta, Belgrade and Moscow.
The 'secret, scarcely heard whisper' circulating at Cossack Headquarters in Lienz and in the neighbouring camp at Peggetz had hit
the mark closely enough. In the eyes of the British Government a
great gulf in status lay between those Cossacks who were Soviet
citizens, and those old émigrés who held European or League of
Nations passports. There was no ambiguity in the official attitude,
but in view of what was to follow it is necessary to establish the
position as it stood in May 1945.

Despite initial objections by Winston Churchill, the British Cabinet
had decided on 4 September 1944 to accede to pressing Soviet requests
for the return of all Soviet citizens liberated in the West 'irrespective
of whether the men wish to return or not'. On 16 October at
the Tolstoy Conference in Moscow, Eden informed a suspicious
Molotov that this was indeed to be the basis of British policy. Then,
on 10 February 1945 at the Yalta Conference in the Crimea, the
foreign ministers of Britain, the United States and the Soviet Union
signed an agreement providing for the return to their respective
countries of liberated prisoners of war. The text of the agreement
included no allusion to the use of force, to which the Americans at
the war's end were not yet fully committed. But the British were
bound by their prior Cabinet decision and promise given at the
Tolstoy Conference, and by May 1945 had already despatched home
several thousand Russians who had fallen into their hands during the
Italian campaign and the invasion of France. Several had committed
suicide in terror at the knowledge of what awaited them in their
homeland, while scores had been massacred on disembarkment at
Murmansk and Odessa.

There was good reason, therefore, to expect that those Cossacks
who were Soviet citizens would in due course be sent back to the
Soviet Union. Indeed, according to accepted British Government
policy the matter would appear to have been already decided. Despite
this, however, there was one potential hitch. AFHQ was an Allied
command, and any political decision required the Americans' concur-
rence. The attitude of the United States towards the issue of forcible
repatriation was throughout ambivalent, and at times reluctant or
even hostile. Though the Foreign Office regularly cited the Yalta

Agreement as supplying authority for the use of force, the United States took the text more literally and based its policy on compromise and pragmatic considerations.

The State Department had fought an abortive rearguard action to incorporate into the Yalta Agreement clauses favourable to the rights of Soviet prisoners of war under international law. The accepted interpretation of the Geneva Convention (privately acknowledged but in practice flouted by the British Foreign Office) laid down uniform as the significant factor in establishing a prisoner's status. Specifically, this meant that Russian auxiliaries in German service were entitled to claim all the protection due to German soldiers, and in particular that they could not be forcibly despatched to ill-treatment in a third country – the Soviet Union. An important consideration here was the fear that the German authorities might well retaliate against American prisoners in their keeping, if they discovered that the Americans were pursuing a policy which involved subjecting Wehrmacht soldiers to brutality. This factor disappeared with the defeat of Germany, but the proponents of legality in the State Department and US Army continued to attach great importance to the principle.[11]

The result was an unsatisfactory compromise, with forcible repatriation conceded at one point in principle and its application ignored or denied at another, resulting in a general state of confusion which permitted some major scenes of gratuitous brutality alongside stiff resistance to the policy from soldiers and diplomats at all levels. Thus Alexander Kirk, US Political Adviser at AFHQ, was informed in December 1944 that, 'The policy adopted by the United States Government in this connection is that all claimants to Soviet nationality will be released to the Soviet Government irrespective of whether they wish to be so released.' Despite this Kirk, who strongly disapproved of the policy, wrote again in August 1945 to request a ruling from the State Department on this very issue![12]

Two significant points may be singled out from all the confusion surrounding United States policy. First, despite the firm wording of the directive just quoted, any *application* of force to compel repatriation was instantly followed by vigorous protests and much soul-searching at all levels. Second, the United States (unlike Great Britain) never at any time contemplated, let alone effected, any sort of brutality towards women and children. All in all the attitude of the United States appears to have been coloured by the fact that they knew nothing of those massacres of returned Russians by Soviet security forces which had from an early date been reported in detail to the Foreign Office. Accordingly it was some time before the full implications of the use of force in repatriating Russians became appreciated in Washington.

Any decision arrived at by AFHQ concerning the forcible repatriation of Soviet citizens among the Cossacks might therefore expect American consent in principle, but obstructive qualifications, resistance and even opposition should the application of force become necessary on any large scale.

Finally we come to the old émigrés among the Cossacks. As has been seen, the majority of the officers at Lienz were White Russians who had emigrated during the Revolution and Civil War in 1917–20. They had never lived in the Soviet Union, and could not therefore be Soviet citizens. At no time did the Soviets themselves claim them as such, and they could not of course legally be repatriated to a country to which they did not belong. A number, in any case, had long before 1945 taken out citizenship of various Western European countries.

Ruthless as it undoubtedly was in its attitude towards Soviet citizens in British captivity, the Foreign Office never at any time considered extending the principle of forced repatriation to White Russians. The Yalta Agreement referred specifically to 'Soviet citizens', and rigorous screening was applied whenever it was suspected that a batch of prisoners might include citizens of countries conquered by the Soviet Union during and after 1940, or people who had emigrated before the extension of Soviet rule over the whole of Russia in 1920.

The distinction was one which had been familiar to the British political adviser at AFHQ, Harold Macmillan, since the previous summer. On 27 July 1944, long before it could have been expected that the Cossacks would fall into British hands, Macmillan asked the Foreign Office to supply him with 'a full definition . . . of policy to be pursued towards Russians of all kinds who fall into British hands in this theatre'. In his telegram he presumed that 'men of Russian nationality who are not Soviet citizens' and 'civilians and women of Russian nationality who are not Soviet citizens will be screened' and retained in appropriate camps, while 'male Soviet nationals who fall into our hands . . . will be repatriated to Russia . . .' The Foreign Office replied on 5 August, confirming that, pending a final ruling, 'existing procedure should be followed and any difficulties which arise should be reported'.

Invited at the end of the following January to comment on a preliminary text of the Yalta Agreement on exchange of prisoners of war, Macmillan emphasised that, 'Above all there must be a clear definition of the word "Citizen" used in Russian draft in order not to prejudice the status of individuals who may be affected by post-war territorial adjustments.' Finally, on 19 February 1945, he received the authoritative ruling he had requested: 'The line which we have taken and which you should follow is that all persons who are Soviet citizens under British law must be repatriated and that any person who is not (repeat not) a Soviet citizen under British law must not (repeat not) be sent back to the Soviet Union unless he expressly desires to be so.'[13]

Thus there was no possibility of a misunderstanding, and on 6 May AFHQ [Allied Force Headquarters in Naples] passed down to the Fifth Corps a clear 'definition of Soviet citizen'. In any dealings with the Cossacks during the following weeks it was this definition which was cited as binding in orders.[14]

Four days after this, on 10 May, Keightley received a message from Marshal Tolbukhin, commander of the nearest Soviet troops to the north-east, inviting him and his senior officers to confer on matters affecting their day-to-day relations. Keightley and his staff travelled up that afternoon from Klagenfurt to Voitsberg, a town inside the Soviet zone of occupation, on the road to Graz. Many topics were discussed, the principal one being the setting up of a temporary demarcation line between the British and Soviet zones. Following ancient custom, the Soviet officers plied their guests lavishly with vodka. The British naturally suspected an intention of influencing their decisions, but matters were agreed to mutual satisfaction – indeed, with much bonhomie.

Among subsidiary matters raised was that of the thousands of Russians – liberated prisoners of war and slave-workers, chiefly – who had fallen or might fall into British hands. There was also the question of the Cossacks, who were believed to have surrendered to the British. The Soviets were most anxious to have them all returned promptly: were the British prepared to oblige? Keightley acknowledged that 'we have some', continuing with a non-committal acknowledgement that all would undoubtedly be arranged in accordance with existing agreements between their respective governments.

After this General Keightley's party took their leave, with mutual expressions of goodwill and desire for co-operation. By the time they returned to Klagenfurt, however, their heads were swimming from the effects of over-generous Soviet hospitality, and the General and his staff plunged into the waters of the Wörthersee in order to sober themselves up. Despite the mutual protestations of goodwill, Keightley was annoyed by his first experience of Soviet intransigence and truculence, and at that evening's staff conference declared that 'never again' would he go to visit them.[15]

Next day the General sent his chief administrative officer, Brigadier C. E. (Teddy) Tryon-Wilson, to discuss the administrative problem of the huge masses of refugees hourly arriving in the British zone. Tryon-Wilson arrived at Voitsberg between 10.30 and 11 a.m., to be greeted with the same effusive hospitality afforded Keightley's party the day before. A long table was set out in an open field, laden with food and drink. Behind each officer's seat stood a smart Red Army girl, whose duty was to ensure that no one's glass remain empty for a moment. The senior Soviet officer present proposed a succession of toasts, and it was at once clear that he proposed to subject Tryon-Wilson to the same treatment accorded his commanding officer the day before. But by the fifteenth glass the Red Army man tacitly conceded he had met his match and opted at last to settle down to business.

Without further delay he explained that Marshal Tolbukhin was aware that large bodies of Cossacks were now within British-occupied Austria, and that it was essential they be handed over as soon as possible. Tryon-Wilson agreed to pass on this request, adding though that orders received from AFHQ made it clear that only Soviet citizens could be handed over. He went on to explain the definition of Soviet citizenship as laid down by the Eighth Army five days earlier. In reply the Soviet officer handed him a document, which he said contained a list of men whom they were extremely anxious to have handed over to them.

His head reeling, Tryon-Wilson set off for Klagenfurt at about three o'clock. On the way back he glanced at the paper he had been given. It consisted of a typewritten list, in which he was startled to see picked out in capital letters the names of the most prominent Tsarist émigré generals and colonels held by the Thirty-sixth Infantry Brigade at Lienz. Like everyone else on the Fifth Corps staff, he was perfectly familiar with the particular position of the old émigrés. He had read the Eighth Army screening order of 6 May, knew of General Arbuthnott's interview with General Vasiliev on the eighth, and was aware of the appeal which General Krasnov had asked to be forwarded to Field-Marshal Alexander. Most prominent

on the list in Tryon-Wilson's eyes were the names of Generals
Krasnov and Shkuro.

His mind in a whirl, Tryon-Wilson's first action, like that of his
superiors the day before, was to plunge into the Wörthersee to clear
his head. Recovered, he went to General Keightley's Headquarters
in his operations caravan near the lake to report on his mission.
Keightley listened intently, as did his Chief of Staff (BGS) Toby
Low. When Tryon-Wilson came to the demand for the return of the
Cossacks and produced his list, Keightley exclaimed angrily, 'Over
my dead body!' The surrender of General Shkuro to troops of the
Fifty-sixth Recce Regiment at Rennsweg, just north of Spittal, had
taken place the previous afternoon, while General Keightley was in
Voitsberg conferring with the Soviets. Already his colourful charac-
ter, and above all the fact that he had been decorated by King George
V, made him a personality regarded with sympathy and interest. It
was when he saw Shkuro's name alongside that of Krasnov that
Keightley snorted, 'You just can't do that sort of thing!' Fortunately
Keightley's orders made it plain that he was not empowered to 'do
that sort of thing' even were he so inclined – which he most
vehemently was not.

It was next morning (12 May) that Keightley learned from Brigadier Scott of his acceptance of the surrender of Prince zu Salm's
Regiment and other units of the Fifteenth Cossack Cavalry Corps
east of Klagenfurt. Keightley expressed some displeasure, explaining
that strictly speaking the Cossacks should have surrendered to the
Soviets. Scott retorted with some heat that, 'I thought it would be a
damn bad show if they were. I'd accepted their surrender and given
my word. I got very hot under the collar about it.' Keightley told
Scott of the implications of the Yalta Agreement, but nevertheless
ordered him to escort the Cossacks behind British lines. He was in
no position to answer for what might be decided by higher authority
with regard to the Cossacks' ultimate fate.[16] But now that their
surrender had been accepted by the Eighth Army he considered
himself in honour bound to protect them, motoring on as has been
seen to order Colonel Palmer to ensure their safe disposal behind
British lines.

4

Enter Harold Macmillan

'. . . any person who is not (repeat not) a Soviet citizen under British law must not (repeat not) be sent back to the Soviet Union unless he expressly desires to be so.' (Foreign Office telegram to Harold Macmillan, Minister Resident in the Mediterranean, 19 February 1945)

It was a far cry from the large military caravan, with its sophisticated radio transmission system, which comprised General Keightley's lakeside headquarters by the Wörthersee, to the splendid setting of Field–Marshal Alexander's Allied Force headquarters outside Naples. In January 1944 AFHQ had established its offices in the former royal palace of Caserta. It was a grandiose building, with ample accommodation even for the enormous staff which AFHQ had acquired since its inception in North Africa. There were installed not only the military entourage of the Supreme Allied Commander in the Mediterranean (SACMED), but also the offices of his American and British political advisers, Alexander Kirk and Harold Macmillan.

In view of the central role played by Macmillan in the coming story, it would be as well to recollect something of the man and the elevated point of his career which he had reached in the latter days of the war. He was delighted with his office's new setting, which bore resemblances to his father-in-law's mansion at Chatsworth. As he recorded in his diary:

> The house (built about 1760) is larger, I believe, than Versailles. There are four courts, 3,000 or more rooms and so on. The garden leads up the hillside and is filled with fountains, statues, watercourses, etc.

Macmillan's office was of gratifying splendour, and filled with mementoes of an earlier occupation:

My room at Caserta is at last ready, with rugs, and some pictures from the palace – Marat [presumably Murat], Mme Mère, Joachim Bonaparte in a sea battle, etc., etc. They make splendid furniture and to some extent help the acoustics. My room is forty-five feet long – twenty-four feet wide, with a big window as well. It is magnificent![1]

Harold Macmillan was (and is) by any standard a remarkable man. It was his grandfather, Daniel, who left his humble house in Scotland to found the famous publishing house of Macmillan. Daniel's son Maurice married an American girl, a connection of which Harold Macmillan was to avail himself when winning over a suspicious Eisenhower on his arrival in Algiers in January 1943. Harold, grandson of the founder, was born in 1894. He went up to Eton as a scholar, and was an exhibitioner at Balliol College, Oxford (of which University he is now Chancellor). Regarded by his fellow-undergraduates as a somewhat otherworldly, ineffectual idealist, he continued to fulfil his academic promise by emerging with First Class Honours. Like most young men of his generation, his education was interrupted by the Great War, in which he served with great gallantry in the Grenadier Guards, being wounded three times.

After the war he travelled to Canada as ADC to the Governor-General, the ninth Duke of Devonshire, whose daughter Dorothy he married in 1920. Though undoubtedly a love match, the alliance reflected Macmillan's oddly ambivalent relationship with the English aristocracy. In the contemporary novels of John Buchan and plays of James Barrie recurs a formidable character, the 'Scotsman on the make'. Proud of his humble yet, by virtue of their Scottishness, 'classless' origins, he has energy and intellect enough eventually to ensure him a secure niche in an otherwise exclusive British aristocratic establishment. The complex character of the rising Harold Macmillan reflected in some degree facets of this fictional figure.

At an early stage Macmillan consciously assumed many of the outward traits of the archetypal Edwardian noble landowner: the languid manner and careless drawl, faintly old-fashioned appearance and mildly eccentric air of bewilderment in face of the alien bustle of twentieth-century life. To Robert Murphy, his American colleague in 1943, 'Macmillan – in dignity, voice, manners, dress, and personality – was and still is almost the American popular image of an English gentleman.'[2] This was the Basil Radford and Naunton Wayne type of Englishman, dear to Hollywood film producers of the time, whom Murphy distinguished from more reserved and perhaps genuinely typical Englishmen of the same class among the top brass at AFHQ. It was a role Macmillan clearly enjoyed and had been at some pains to acquire. Shooting one day with his brother-in-law, the present Duke of Devonshire, he noticed the picturesquely worn appearance of the Duke's favourite old tweed jacket, and seized the first opportunity of borrowing one of similarly homespun character in exchange for his own impeccably tailored London tweeds.

While he emulated a class whose instinctive self-confidence was so enviably effortless, Macmillan sustained no unavailing ambition to become absorbed into an order whose hereditary status and wealth rested on bases inaccessible to the younger son even of a successful publisher. At Chatsworth and Lismore he counted for little, and was himself awed and bored by the social round of the great Whig aristocracy. Not until the close of his life, when the old order had in any case become drastically reduced in wealth and prestige, did he venture to join their ranks by claiming an earldom.

Within the prevailingly philistine ambience of the English landed magnates Harold Macmillan sensed himself, by virtue of his scholarship and intelligence, to be a man apart; one who, in due course, would by his abilities compel recognition even from those haughty patricians he simultaneously admired and scorned. In manner he was awkward and diffident, wrote a worthy but uninspired book entitled *The Middle Way*, and joined that group of Conservatives (he had become Member of Parliament for Stockton-on-Tees in 1924) whose role was to provide a cautious rebellion against the old party order on respectable issues such as employment and appeasement. In 1932 he visited Moscow, where he encountered Malcolm Muggeridge at the Opera House (Stalin was attending a gala performance). Muggeridge recorded at the time: 'In our box was a man called Macmillan, a Conservative Member of Parliament belonging to the Young Men's Christian Association group. He knew my father. He seemed pretty hopeless about British politics, and had all sorts of good views about national planning and what not.'[3]

It was the outbreak of World War Two that was to provide Macmillan with the opportunity to display his real talents for industry, diplomacy and leadership, so long concealed behind the series of masks he assumed to shield a complex personality from the outside world. After proving himself by capable work at the Ministry of Supply and the Colonial Office, he was unexpectedly chosen by Churchill at the end of 1942 to occupy an entirely new and extraordinarily demanding post of crucial importance in the prosecution of the war. As Macmillan himself recorded in his memoirs:

> There should be a Minister at Allied Force headquarters, now set up in Algiers. He would be of Cabinet rank, though not a member of the War Cabinet. He would be entitled to report direct to the Prime Minister. His status would be roughly parallel to that of the Minister of State in Cairo. But there was an important difference. The Middle East was a purely British concern, and all executive power was in the hands of the British military and civil authorities. In North Africa, the command was American. The headquarters were staffed equally by British and American officers, but the American general [Eisenhower] held the final responsibility, subject only to the Combined Chiefs of Staff in Washington. A Minister of State, therefore, although his rank would be similar to that of the Ministers now operating in Cairo [R. G. Casey] or in British West Africa [Lord Swinton], must depend on the influence that he could exert upon the Supreme Allied Commander.[4]

The task was a daunting one, but Macmillan was fully equal to the challenge. With an ill-defined role, a minuscule staff, and gigantic responsibilities, Macmillan's tact, energy and diplomatic skill swiftly won him the recognition and affection of Eisenhower and his British successors as Supreme Allied Commander, Generals Henry ('Jumbo') Wilson and Harold Alexander ('Alex').

It was with the latter he developed a particularly close working relationship. Six months after his arrival at AFHQ, Macmillan noted of Alex in his diary that, 'He is really a first-class man. The more I see of him, the more I like him. I am very flattered, because I have been elected a member of his Mess, to go and live or eat whenever I like both here and throughout the campaign. That is a high honour.' Not long after he noted again that, 'He is really a remarkable character – his simplicity, modesty and firmness make up a most charming and impressive whole. Like so many men of his responsibilities, he is dependent on a simple but complete faith in the certainty of victory and the guidance of Providence.'[5] It may be suspected that for Macmillan's euphemistic 'Providence' Alexander would have preferred the old-fashioned term 'God'. A devout Christian, he wore beneath his battledress throughout his campaigns a wooden crucifix, which is now preserved at the headquarters of the Irish Guards.[6]

By the end of the war, even Macmillan's world-weary outlook had become affected by Alexander's buoyant nobility and altruism.

On 29 April 1945 Macmillan was at Assisi when he learned of the surrender of the German armies in Italy:

> I am delighted, especially for Alex's sake, that his triumphant battle (there are now 100,000 prisoners) has been followed by the surrender of the armies opposed to him. It is a complete vindication of his strategical and tactical dispositions . . . Hitler has lasted twenty years – with all his power for evil, his strength, his boasting. St Francis did not seem to have much power, but here in this lovely city one realises the immense strength and permanence of goodness – a rather comforting thought.[7]

Towards his American colleagues, however, Macmillan seems to have nurtured some of those ambivalent attitudes with which he had regarded the great pre-war aristocracy. Eisenhower, Bedell Smith, Mark Clark and other senior US generals were talented and likeable men, with whom he worked well; but the increasing preponderance of American power jarred at times. Just as he had known himself to be undoubtedly cleverer than his wife's grand relations, so he now consoled himself privately with the Americans' cultural backwardness. 'These Americans represent the new Roman Empire,' he is said to have explained to some impressionable British officers, 'and we English, like the Greeks of old, must teach them how to make it go.' For relaxation he read Gibbon and Macaulay (then considered esoteric literature), 'But of course the Americans do not read – or at any rate comprehend – history.'[8]

Possibly in order to combat unconscious feelings of inferiority, Macmillan assumed an outward air of cynicism and donnish intellectuality while in his diaries recording his sense of superiority. This, at least, is how it may appear. Like many lesser men he adopted roles behind which he could face the exigencies of public life. Some were genuine reflections of the man within: his industry, intelligence and charm. Others were consciously or unconsciously in some degree false: the forward-looking Tory 'rebel' of his inter-war years, the jaded, world-weary old gentleman of his Prime Ministerial period. Only in old age and retirement, all ambitions achieved, did he settle comfortably into the latter role. His earlier radicalism may have been based on pessimism and ambition rather than conviction. As the political commentator James Margach recalled:

> During the thirties he was so sickened with his own Conservative Party that he not only resigned the party whip – in effect putting himself beyond the pale – but on the testimony of Attlee, never a romancer, he was on

the point of joining the Labour Party. 'Talks were going on, I knew about them. Know what that would have meant? Macmillan would have been leader of the Labour Party, not me.'[9]

To Macmillan his time as Minister Resident with AFHQ was an unexpected culmination of his ambitions. Recently he declared that this was the most historic moment of his life, supervising as he was the vast array of Allied interests throughout the Mediterranean, and mingling on equal or superior terms with kings, presidents, prime ministers, field-marshals, chiefs of staff, and the like. Events which he played a key part in influencing included the pacification of French North Africa, the surrender of Italy, the saving of Greece from Communist insurgence and the final capitulation of the German Army in North Italy. Sir Robert Bruce Lockhart, who met him soon after his final return to England, noted the change these great responsibilities had wrought in him:

> Harold may yet succeed Winston. He has grown more in stature during the war than anyone. I have known him now, off and on, for sixteen years. He was always clever, but was shy and diffident, had a clammy handshake and was more like a wet fish than a man. Now he is full of confidence and is not only not afraid to speak but jumps in and speaks brilliantly.[10]

As the spring of 1945 drew on the Minister Resident found himself increasingly preoccupied with the problem of relations with the emergent regime of Marshal Tito in Yugoslavia. On 4 May he noted in his diary that, 'a fresh headache is rapidly developing – Yugoslav armies are advancing into Venezia Giulia and Austria – in a fierce race with the Eighth Army.' Over the ensuing week a continuous series of meetings was held at Caserta to discuss ways of averting the crisis. On 8 May General William Morgan, Alexander's Chief of Staff, flew to Belgrade in an attempt to induce Tito to accept a purely military demarcation line which would allow Alexander the line of communication he required through Venezia Giulia to support his advance units moving into Austria. Morgan returned two days later with no agreement. Tito, to whose struggle for power AFHQ had contributed so much, was insistent that large areas of Italian and Austrian territory infiltrated by his Partisans were to be absorbed into his new Greater Yugoslavia. Telegrams began to fly between Caserta, London and Washington, as Alexander enquired what forces he could count on, were the dispute to lead to armed conflict.

On 7 May Churchill had telegraphed Alexander, asking him to 'Let me know what you are doing in massing forces against this Muscovite tentacle, of which Tito is the crook.'[11] Now, on the twelfth, he received what he later described as 'a most welcome and strong message' from President Truman. The President agreed that any steps necessary should be adopted to effect Tito's withdrawal from the areas he had occupied, and concluded with the apparently uncompromising assertion that, 'If we stand firm on this issue, as we are doing in Poland, we can hope to avoid a host of other similar encroachments.' Another week was to pass, however, before Truman committed himself fully to the use of force in the event of Tito's continuing to prove recalcitrant.[12]

It was at this juncture that Alexander and Macmillan decided that it would be a good idea for the latter to travel up to Venezia Giulia, where he could confer with the two principal commanders on the spot in the disputed area. At 2.10 a.m. on 12 May Macmillan telegraphed the Foreign Office from Caserta: 'At Field Marshal Alexander's suggestion I am making a short visit to 8th Army headquarters and 13th Corps tomorrow in order to put Generals McCreery and Harding fully in the picture. I hope to be back early on morning of May 13th.'[13] At 8 a.m. Macmillan and his assistant Philip Broad flew in a Dakota transport to Treviso, near Venice, where they were met by the Eighth Army commander, General Richard McCreery. The conference lasted for two and a half hours, during which Macmillan, as he recorded:

> summed up the political and military situation; the problems confronting the Field Marshal and H.M.G. and the equivocal and uncertain attitude of the Americans. I had brought all the files, and showed them the most recent and relevant interchange of telegrams from different capitals in the world. I think this did a lot of good from the psychological point of view and put the general and his staff thoroughly 'in the picture'.[14]

After luncheon Macmillan and Broad flew to Monfalcone, where they met General John Harding, commanding the Thirteenth Corps. Harding explained the extraordinarily complex situation in which his troops found themselves. Yugoslav and British troops were inextricably mixed, to the extent even on occasion of sharing the same billets. In the event of hostilities, he would have to begin by reforming his troops behind a defensive line, probably that of the River Isonzo. Harding exuded confidence, asserting that he could 'maintain this uneasy position for several weeks, if necessary, while negotiations proceed and decisions are taken on a governmental level'. Equally, if those negotiations broke down, he 'was convinced that he could force out the Jugoslavs in their present numbers but it would of course entail an operation of importance'.[15] Macmillan in return explained the chancy political situation, then drove to Venice where he spent the night.

As his telegram to the Foreign Office of the previous day makes clear, it was Macmillan's intention to return to Caserta next morning, Sunday 13 May. Instead there was a change of plan – one which was to have far-reaching and tragic effects. Macmillan and his party set out on a gloriously sunny day for the airfield, where once again they embarked in a Dakota. This time they flew northwards over jagged alpine peaks, many still covered in snow. After a short flight they landed at Klagenfurt in Austrian Carinthia. There, as Macmillan records in his diary, 'We were met by General Charles Keightley [Fifth Corps] and some of his staff. This officer, whom I have met from time to time, is an admirable soldier and a very level-headed and sensible man. He is well suited for his difficult and embarrassing task.' At Keightley's headquarters the political and strategic situation was discussed once again.

The position was confused, with the Partisans proving themselves if anything more of a nuisance than in Venezia Giulia. Keightley, like Harding, was confident he could maintain the existing situation as long as was necessary, or until he felt in a strong enough position to clear up the whole area. In the meantime, however, he was not in a position to do much about the 'minor reign of terror' being effected by the undisciplined and bullying Partisans. On the positive side, though, Keightley was glad to be able to report that relations with Soviet troops of Marshal Tolbukhin's army to the north-west were cordial, a temporary line of demarcation having been agreed between their respective forces. This was a reference to the meeting held three days earlier at Voitsberg.

Next was raised the question of Cossacks and Yugoslavs who had surrendered to units of the Fifth Corps within the past few days. What passed at this discussion is crucial to an understanding of all that followed, and in particular to the vexed question of responsibility. Regrettably General Keightley died just before I could interview him. Macmillan, as described earlier, has consistently declined to discuss the matter with me. Lord Aldington, who as Toby Low was Keightley's Brigadier General Staff, informed me in 1975 that he could recall

nothing of the matter. Recently he declared that he was absent from
the meeting between Macmillan and Keightley: 'As far as I recollect
just those two were present.' From the historian's viewpoint this is a
matter of considerable regret, in view of the fact that under normal
circumstances a BGS would inevitably have been in attendance on his
Corps Commander at so important a discussion. Certainly he should
have been carefully briefed on everything that took place.

Fortunately Macmillan has published an account set down in his
diary at the time. The discussion opened with a review of the
problems posed by Tito's troublesome Partisans. Macmillan noted
that, 'We have to look on, more or less helplessly, since our present
plan is *not* to use force and *not* to promote an incident.' Next the
conversation turned to the question of the Yugoslav and Cossack
refugees, a topic which it seems reasonable to suppose was the major
or sole cause of the Minister's unexpectedly extended journey. For
the infiltration of Partisans into Carinthia was a matter well known
to him from the outset, which he originally considered sufficient to
discuss with General McCreery, who bore overall responsibility for
the whole region. There was no exacerbation of the problem that
morning likely to require an unplanned extra visit, whereas the
question of the Cossacks appears as yet to have been unknown to
McCreery and Alexander.

To return to Macmillan's diary entry:

> . . . among the surrendered Germans are about 40,000 Cossacks and
> 'White' Russians, with their wives and children. To hand them over to
> the Russians is condemning them to slavery, torture and probably death.
> To refuse, is deeply to offend the Russians, and incidentally break the
> Yalta agreement. We have decided to hand them over (General Keightley
> is in touch and on good terms with the Russian general on his right), but
> I suggested that the Russians should at the same time give us any British
> prisoners or wounded who may be in his area. The formal procedure is
> that they should go back through Odessa (which I understand means
> great hardship). I hope we can persuade the local Russian to hand them
> over direct (we think he has 1,500–2,000) and save them all this suffering,
> in exchange for the scrupulous adherence to the agreement in handing
> back Russian subjects . . .
>
> To add to the confusion, thousands of so-called Ustashi or Chetniks,
> mostly with wives and children, are fleeing in panic into this area in front
> of the advancing Yugoslavs. These expressions, Ustashi and Chetnik,
> cover anything from guerrilla forces raised by the Germans from Slovenes
> and Croats and Serbs to fight Tito, and armed and maintained by the

Germans – to people who, either because they are Roman Catholics or Conservative in politics, or for whatever cause are out of sympathy with revolutionary Communism and therefore labelled as Fascists or Nazis. (This is a very simple formula, which in a modified form is being tried, I observe in English politics.)[16]

This, then, was the situation when Macmillan flew into Klagenfurt on the morning of 13 May. It seems likely that he made the journey on his own initiative expressly for the purpose of settling the problem of how to treat the Cossacks and Yugoslavs. In his first public account of his role in the affair, a BBC television interview broadcast on 21 December 1984, Macmillan claimed that, 'The Field-Marshal [Alexander] asked me to go up to Klagenfurt to see what was happening.' This is clearly untrue. As we know from Macmillan's telegram to the Foreign Office, Alexander had only suggested that he visit Generals McCreery and Harding. At the time of his departure Macmillan declared his intention of visiting those two commanders and returning 'on morning of May 13th'. Instead of this, he flew up to Klagenfurt and consequently did not return to Naples until 3.30 on the afternoon of the thirteenth.

There can be little doubt, therefore, that something occurred to make Macmillan alter his plans *en route*. He must either have received a request from Keightley to come up and help settle this difficult question, or have learned of it from some other source. Why Macmillan should subsequently wish it to be wrongly thought that he undertook the extra visit at Alexander's behest may in due course become apparent.

In his diary Macmillan makes it clear that he was fully aware of the presence of 'White Russians' among the Cossacks, though he goes on to obfuscate the issue by claiming he believed that they too were covered by the Yalta Agreement. In fact, of course, he must have known of the strict distinction between Soviet and non-Soviet citizens laid down in his instructions from the Foreign Office – instructions which it was his task to transmit to AFHQ. Even had he unaccountably forgotten, Keightley (for whom this was the major issue) would certainly have reminded him.

In his television interview with Ludovic Kennedy, Macmillan chose to drop this claim, admitting that, though he understood the special status of the White Russians perfectly clearly, he had nevertheless decided they should be handed over:

. . . there were about 30,000 Cossacks, who had been recruited by the

Germans . . . Then there were a lot of so-called White Russians who were with the Germans . . . It was harsh in some ways, because no doubt some of these White Russians were people who'd been against the Communist regime for years. Still they were on the Germans' side and working with the Germans, and we hadn't a great . . . you must remember the conditions at the time. Russia was, after all, our great ally; we'd made the agreement and so we carried it out.

Kennedy pressed Macmillan further on the question of White Russians. After all, 'Some of them had never been in Russia. They were children of people who'd come out of Russia in the Revolution.'

Macmillan: 'Well, why were they up there?'
Kennedy: 'They were fighting with the Germans, weren't they?'
Macmillan: 'Yes, they were fighting with the . . . I mean, they weren't . . . we'd been fighting the Germans for six years – they're not friends of ours . . .'
Kennedy: '. . . Russia wasn't their motherland any more, was it?'
Macmillan: 'Well, that was laid down accordingly . . . It was a very strict rule according to the date of their birth, or of leaving Russia. If they'd left between certain dates, they weren't handed over.'

Macmillan was at this point becoming visibly distressed and confused, but that he appreciated the presence of the White Russians and the distinction with regard to citizenship, and went on to recommend the surrender of the Whites, is from his words all too clear. Yet only four years earlier, Macmillan is reported to have denied knowledge of the presence of any White Russians among the Cossacks: 'Well,' he conceded then, 'I suppose it is just possible that some White Russians – like Prince Obolensky whom we knew in Paris – were included, but I knew nothing about it.'

So far as the Cossacks in general were concerned, Macmillan in his interview with Ludovic Kennedy emphasised that he regarded them as 'practically savages', deserving of scant sympathy whatever their fate. (This damning outlook is shared in part by Toby Low: 'I do remember that we weren't best pleased at that time with people who'd been fighting with the Germans . . . you have to remember that.') Whatever his personal views, though, Macmillan disclaims any direct responsibility for the solution which he successfully urged on Keightley. He in his turn was simply obeying orders.

Pressed by Kennedy to explain why he advised Keightley to hand over the refugees 'to slavery, torture and probably death', Macmillan replied, 'It had to be done. We had no power to stop it. And not to do it would have meant they would have not sent back our British prisoners.'

But Kennedy was persistent on the crucial issue: 'Do you know who gave the orders for this?'

Macmillan: 'Well . . . I, no, not re . . . we, er, I suppose the Combined Chiefs of Staff. We had our instructions from them.'
Kennedy: 'The information I have is that they were not in favour of it, and nor was the Foreign Office.'
Macmillan: 'Well, those were our instructions; they sent us round instructions before we went there.'
Kennedy: 'So did the executive order come from General Keightley or . . .?'
Macmillan: 'Oh no, from the Field-Marshal.'
Kennedy: 'From the Field-Marshal.'
Macmillan: 'And to him from the Combined Chiefs.'
Kennedy: 'From Alexander?'
Macmillan: 'But before the crisis, I mean some weeks before, we had our orders what we were to do under the Yalta Agreement.'

What follows was omitted from the screened interview:

Kennedy: 'So it was Alexander's carrying out?'
Macmillan: 'Well, I mean, but not at the moment of crisis, at . . . I mean they'd come back – they'd gone round about a month before.'
Kennedy: 'Yes, I mean, all I was trying to find out, if you remember, is who –'
Macmillan: 'I can't remember exactly; all I do remember is reporting to Alexander.'
Kennedy: 'Reporting what?'
Macmillan: 'Well, that Keightley and I both thought that we had better carry out the agreement. There was nothing else we could do.'[17]

Macmillan's version of events, then, amounts to this. He was sent to Klagenfurt on the direct instructions of Field-Marshal Alexander in order to implement orders emanating from the Combined Chiefs of Staff. These were to the effect that, regardless of their citizenship and status under international law, *all* Cossacks were to be handed over to the Soviets forthwith. Though this meant that Macmillan and Keightley were not themselves responsible for a policy whose implications they merely fulfilled in obedience to orders, they nevertheless approved of what was done on the grounds that they were fulfilling the Yalta Agreement, and more immediately because fulfilment ensured the immediate return of a large number of British prisoners of war liberated by the Red Army in Austria.

It has to be said that each of these claims can be shown to be false. It was not until 20 June (more than seven weeks after Macmillan's visit to Klagenfurt) that the Combined Chiefs of Staff authorised the repatriation of the Cossacks, and then only on the strict proviso that it was Soviet citizens alone who were to be returned. It is unlikely that Field-Marshal Alexander had as yet learned of the existence of the Cossack problem by 12 May. (The Fifth Corps Sitrep message of 14 May to be cited shortly appears to be the first notification AFHQ received of the Cossacks' surrender.) Alexander did not – indeed, for that reason alone could not – order Macmillan to arrange their forced repatriation. In fact he had no idea that Macmillan was to break his journey and fly on to Klagenfurt, and probably first learned of the meeting with Keightley when Macmillan called to report on the evening of his return.

Macmillan's claim that he believed that the old émigrés were covered by the Yalta Agreement is likewise untenable. Keightley and all his staff were familiar with the screening instructions they had received a bare week before – instructions which represented AFHQ's implementation of a definition supplied by Macmillan himself, in accordance with a firm Foreign Office ruling.

Finally, the suggestion that Macmillan effected an agreement with the Soviets which resulted in the speedy return of British prisoners of war is also false. This 'exchange' did not take place. Alexander notified the War Office on 16 May that:

> Exchange of liberated P/W Eighth Army and Russians agreed . . . Understand exchange began 14 May at Gaza from 2,000 [fit?] 250 sick Russians immediately available from Wolfsberg. Movement of others dependent on local commanders ability to loan transport. Area of operational roads congested. Large numbers surrendered personnel supposedly of Russian origin ex German Cossack Division were in Volkersmarkt Area on 12th May. Rumoured that 500 to 1,000 British P/W are inside the Russian lines near Graz. If and when freed will evacuate by air from Klagenfurt.

This message reveals a number of significant facts. First, the 'exchange' of prisoners of war is restricted at this stage to a one-way flow. Not only are no British prisoners reported to be returning from behind Soviet lines, but their very existence is still only 'rumoured'. This situation continued until the end of the month, for it was on 26 May that Alexander further informed the War Office:

Agreement with Russians at Graz [on 26 May] only applies to handover of Soviet citizens in British Zone Austria. No reciprocal guarantee in respect of British ex PW obtained apart from halfhearted promise which so far has not been honoured. Evacuation to Odessa still continuing from this area.

To this the Chiefs of Staff Committee replied on 28 May (four days after orders had been given for the repatriation of the Cossacks, and three days after Macmillan had left AFHQ for good) urging Alexander to demand reciprocity from Marshal Tolbukhin. It was not until 4 June that Alexander was able to report: 'Negotiations . . . beginning today between representative Commander 8th Army and representative Marshal Tolbukhin in Graz to arrange transfer point at Graz or other suitable location in neighbourhood. Will inform you of result when known.' On the same day (4 June) Alexander intervened personally to *halt* forcible repatriation of Cossacks, whose fate had played no part in these negotiations.[18]

These tedious delays arose from general Soviet intransigence and inability to negotiate compromise agreements, rather than from any insidious attempt to strike specific bargains with the Western Allies.[19]

Three days after Macmillan's return from Klagenfurt Alexander possessed no knowledge of any agreement involving an exchange of the Cossacks for liberated British prisoners. Yet in his memoirs Macmillan asserts that the return of the Cossacks and White Russians 'was a great grief to me . . . [but] at least we obtained in exchange some 2,000 prisoners and wounded who were in the area and had been in German hands.'[20] And in his televised interview with Ludovic Kennedy he declared that, 'I do . . . remember reporting to Alexander . . . that Keightley and I both thought that we had better carry out the agreement.'

Now it may be argued (possibly it is this consideration which lies behind Macmillan's words) that though no specific authority had been granted for the repatriation of the Cossacks, they were covered by general rulings already issued arranging for the return of all Soviet citizens under the provisions of the Yalta Agreement. Thus 'AFHQ letter AG 383.7/414 A–O of 9 March 45' made clear that 'it was intention at that date to repatriate to USSR all proved Soviet citizens irrespective of their wishes'. From 22 March thousands of members of the 162nd Turcoman Division, comprising Soviet citizens serving in the Wehrmacht, which surrendered to Allied forces near Padua, were shipped home to Odessa. No special instructions were required for this operation, which was regarded as coming within general guidelines provided in respect of the Yalta Agreement. On 11 May, two days before Macmillan's arrival at Klagenfurt, the Eighth Army notified the Fifth Corps: 'Understand 1789 Russians in Wolfsberg Camp. Request you make every endeavour ensure they are handed over to Russian forces for repatriation at earliest opportunity. This has been agreed on governmental basis between Britain, US and USSR.' Then, on the very day that Macmillan conferred with Keightley, the Fifteenth Army Group despatched a message to the Eighth Army:

> for your action, 'all Russians . . . to be treated in accordance with United States and British instructions previously issued and should be turned over. Request best available estimate earliest source of origin, that is civilians, Russian formations or miscellaneous, since we are obligated to furnish this information to Russian Goverment'.

Even as Keightley spoke with Macmillan his troops were putting this directive into effect. At midday on 13 May Soviet and British officers held a conference at Wolfsberg, during which the topic was raised:

> The Russians had only one source of complaint, that there were still a number of Russian ex-PW in our own German PW camps. The Bde Comd, 38 Bde, stated that instructions had already been given for their repatriation, and by a fortunate chance, at that very moment, a dozen TCVs arrived at the cage – under view of the Russian General – and began loading the Russian PW en route for Graz. He was much impressed.[21]

Despite this Keightley clearly felt for some reason that the power he already possessed to turn over Soviet citizens was inexpedient for his purpose. As will be seen shortly, he was to report next day to General McCreery that he had 'explained [to Macmillan] that I had no power to do this without your authority'. Following discussion with the Soviets, 'I would ask you officially'. The Cossacks, then, were regarded as a special case, quite distinct from the thousands of liberated Soviet prisoners of war and slave labourers on the point of being transported to the Soviet zone of Austria. Why was this? Keightley was anxious to fulfil what he later referred to as Macmillan's 'verbal directive' to deliver the Cossacks, so why could he not have made use of existing orders instructing him that all Soviet citizens in his area 'should be turned over'?

The answer, surely, lies in what Brigadier Tryon-Wilson terms the 'hot potato' exercising Fifth Corps Staff at the time of Macmillan's visit: the fact that a significant number of the most prominent of the Cossacks were not Soviet citizens and hence *not* covered by previous instructions. As Toby Low, Keightley's Chief of Staff, frankly admits: 'amongst them were officers who belonged to what has become known as the White Russian community . . . Some of them were people who were "wanted" by the Soviet Russians.' It was *they* whom the requested special authority was intended to cover; without it the Cossacks could as Soviet citizens have been handed over in accordance with orders already received. And to include the White émigrés in the handover required an order directed specifically at the Cossacks.

A key file quoted earlier, which provided proof of the falsity of Macmillan's assertion that he recommended the return of the Cossacks in exchange for liberated British prisoners, has an intriguing history attached to it. In November 1973 the Ministry of Defence granted me privileged access to inspect it. From it I made extensive notes and was also permitted to take away photocopies of some of the sheets. By February 1977 my book *Victims of Yalta* was nearing completion, and I wrote again to the Ministry to enquire whether I was permitted to refer directly to this file. In reply I was informed that two other files I had seen 'and BM 3928/PW1 [the file in question] have now all been transferred to the Public Records Office and are available to the public in WO class 204, pieces 1593 B and C'. Later still, in 1982, I thought it time to go through the file again, in case it threw a light on Macmillan's involvement in the policy of forcibly repatriating Russians not covered by the Yalta Agreement. To my surprise it was not included in the file numbers given me in 1977, and I wrote to the Defence Ministry to enquire about the anomaly.

After a lengthy investigation, I was informed, 'The reference you quoted (BM 3928/PW1) would appear to be that of a War Office file, and I am at a loss to understand why it should have been allocated to the PRO Class relating to AFHQ records.' Not only this but, as the Defence Ministry official informed me, 'I have been able to establish that the title of BM 3928/PW1 was in fact "POW in South Africa – Military Mission Report No 2".' But when I examined the file in 1974 it most certainly did not bear this title, and was indeed a

War Office file dealing with key questions relating to Russians held by the British in Austria. There is no possibility of error, since I still possess photocopies from the file, bearing the reference BM 3928/PW1. It seems not only that the original file vanished some time between 1974 and 1977, but that its reference number was then transferred to an innocuous file in order to make the disappearance complete.

But for the chance of my having obtained access to it in 1973, evidence refuting Macmillan's claim to have arranged the retrieval of British prisoners of war might not have seen the light of day. And had it remained accessible it could have made embarrassing nonsense of his recent assertion that 'not to do it [send back the Cossacks] would have meant they would have not sent back our British prisoners'.

In fact it is plain that Macmillan's claim that the handover of Cossacks formed part of an arrangement for the exchange of British and Soviet prisoners is a canard. As Brigadier Low recently admitted, there was in reality never anything more than a pious hope that placating the Soviets by delivering up the Cossacks might possibly pay dividends in this respect. It is true that on 1 March 1985 Low told the boys at Winchester College that, as a result of the surrender of the Cossacks, the British prisoners were returned 'much sooner than we had reason to expect'. But when pressed by me on the point in conversation on 8 May of the same year, he conceded at once that the alleged link between the two operations amounted to no more than wishful thinking: 'I think we both [Soviets and British] felt obligated by the Yalta Agreement, and if we didn't play our part they were unlikely to play theirs.'

This is clearly the true picture. Macmillan's claim that he expected a *quid pro quo* from the Soviets is confined to his diary. Had such a proposal existed in reality it would have been mentioned in the subsequent Fifth Corps report to the Eighth Army of 14 May, in McCreery's report to AFHQ, or during Macmillan's interview with General Robertson on his return to Caserta. For, if genuine, it provided the strongest justification of a policy which Macmillan was so anxious to put into effect, and which he himself claims justified what must otherwise appear an insensitively heartless act. No such justification was made, and none of the surviving officers at Corps and Divisional headquarters to whom I spoke recalled hearing anything of the alleged exchange.

Following his lunchtime consultation with Keightley by the Wörthersee, Macmillan flew southwards back to Italy. Meanwhile

Keightley wasted no time in putting into effect the Minister Resident's proposals which, for reasons we can never know for certain, he now felt impelled to fulfil as swiftly and efficiently as possible.

The day after Keightley's visit to the Soviets at Voitsberg on 10 May, at which the demand for the surrender of the Cossacks had been first made, Eighth Army headquarters sent a request to his Chief of Staff, Brigadier Low: 'Army Comd requires to know at once results of conference your Comd and Russians yesterday.'[22]

Despite the urgency of this request, no reference to the possibility of a handover of Cossacks appears to have been received from the Fifth Corps until three days later, during which time Macmillan's visit to Klagenfurt had taken place. On the day after that visit, 14 May, Brigadier Low despatched to General McCreery a lengthy summary report on the situation within the Fifth Corps area, which included this significant passage on the question of the Cossacks:

> on advice Macmillan have today suggested to Soviet General on Tolbu-khin's HQ that Cossacks should be returned to Soviets at once (.) explained that I had no power to do this without your [i.e. McCreery's] authority but would be glad to know Tolbukhin's views and that if they coincided with mine I would ask you officially (.) cannot see any point in keeping this large number Soviet nationals who are clearly great source contention between Soviets and ourselves (.) . . .
> met Lt Gen on Tolbukhin's staff today and after very cordial meeting all arrangements with Soviet and Bulgars confirmed(.) all relations with Soviets most friendly with much interchange whisky and vodka (.)[23]

This version of events contains falsifications which can only have been intended to deceive McCreery and presumably others higher up the chain of command. Keightley and Low had already been informed of 'Tolbukhin's views' on the subject of the Cossacks during their visit to Voitsberg on 10 May, and had received formal confirmation of them through Brigadier Tryon-Wilson on the eleventh. Worse still, Low's report goes out of its way to describe the Cossacks as 'Soviet nationals', though the issue was that so many – particularly the most distinguished figures – were known at Fifth Corps headquarters not to be Soviet citizens, and yet it was they who featured most prominently on the list of those whom the Soviets wished to see handed over.

Since we know that the Soviets had already demanded the Cossacks' return, and Macmillan had issued his 'verbal directive' (as Keightley was to term it in a subsequent report) to comply,

Keightley's exchange with the Soviet general on 14 May concerning the Cossacks must have consisted, *not of an offer to return them should a request be forthcoming, but of compliance with the request already made.*

The fact that this report can only have been drawn up for the purpose of deception appears to indicate that McCreery was not in the secret, being presumably considered by Macmillan, Keightley and Low as likely to disapprove of the plan to include non-Soviet citizens among those to be handed over. Formerly his Chief of Staff, McCreery was known to be a close friend of Alexander's, and to share the chivalrous outlook of his admired chief.

But character alone cannot be sufficient guide to investigation. Is it possible that McCreery was also privy to the secret negotiations whose nature is concealed in the Fifth Corps report of 14 May? In that case we should have to assume that falsifications contained in the report were designed not for the deception of their recipient, but as 'cover' for McCreery as well as Keightley should the matter ever come to be investigated.

One cannot say that this is impossible, but it is certainly improbable. Fifth Corps' prevarications over supplying an account of their negotiations with the Soviets on 10 and 11 May seem to suggest a less-than-active desire to bring the Eighth Army into the picture at an early stage. That Keightley was fully capable of lying about the transaction is a matter of proof. On 18 July he was to provide Lady Limerick of the British Red Cross with categorical assurances that no violence had been employed in repatriating Cossacks, and that no non-Soviet citizens had been knowingly included among them. Of the Yugoslavs he related that all had freely volunteered to return to Yugoslavia until news of a massacre trickled back, whereupon he (Keightley) had instantly halted the entire operation for good. All these statements constituted deliberate falsehoods.[24] As is shown in this and the next chapter, Macmillan too has woven a series of falsehoods around his role in the affair.

McCreery, on the other hand, cannot be shown on any occasion to have resorted to deception over the repatriation issue. In contrast it is clear that he entertained a strong moral objection to the principle of forced repatriation, and to the more inhumane aspects involved at this time in particular. By the end of the year he was himself Commander-in-Chief in British-occupied Austria, when the problem arose once more. But when the Foreign Office pressed him to employ force to return Russian refugees he returned a flat refusal, pointing out that a 'high percentage of Soviet DP consists of women and children against whom the use of force by British soldiers would be contrary to normal British practice'. He was particularly concerned too about the question of citizenship, pointing out that the handovers of May and June affected '58,000 displaced persons who were repatriated as military units and may have included a proportion of men of Russian origin who were not necessarily undisputed Soviet citizens'.[25]

Assuming that McCreery was not party to the scheme to conceal from higher command the Soviet demand for the White Russian generals, it seems inescapable that those responsible for the Fifth Corps report of 14 May counted on Macmillan's confirming its two major falsehoods. The likelihood of his being called upon to do so was no remote chance. For Macmillan's diary reveals that, when he departed from Klagenfurt, he 'flew first to Eighth Army (at Treviso) where we were met by the commanding general, McCreery. A short chat; picked up some sandwiches, etc., and then Philip [Broad] and I took off for Caserta.'

This 'short chat', as an account by Macmillan's American colleague Alexander Kirk shows (it will be quoted shortly), was concerned with the question of repatriation of the Cossacks and Yugoslavs. McCreery's presence at the airport at the moment of Macmillan's transit cannot have arisen from chance, and it is clear that the Minister had arranged for him to be there. As all the major issues must have been covered during their lengthy conference of the previous day, it looks much as if Macmillan sought McCreery out for the exclusive purpose of impressing on him the necessity for handing over the Cossacks. Brigadier Low could not in his report of 14 May have described the Cossacks as exclusively 'Soviet nationals', nor claimed that the Soviets had not yet requested the Cossacks' return, had he not been confident that these points tallied with the account Macmillan had given McCreery the day before.

It seems, therefore, that the discussion held by Macmillan with Fifth Corps headquarters included an agreement to concert moves for the deception of General McCreery. He was to learn simultaneously from the Minister Resident and Brigadier Low that the Soviets had not yet demanded the Cossacks, and that the Cossacks were all Soviet citizens. The purpose was to evade screening orders in force so as to include the Tsarist generals and other old émigré Russians among those returned.

Additional indication of the lengths to which Macmillan was prepared to go to conceal the true nature of the proposed repatriations

lies in reports he drew up immediately after flying back from Austria.
The day after his return from Klagenfurt the Minister Resident sent
the Foreign Office an official report on his two-day mission to
AFHQ's forward zone: 'I returned to Caserta early yesterday afternoon. I visited while I was away General McCreery (Commander of
the 8th Army) and General Harding who is in command of the 13th
Corps at Monfalcone.' An account of his conversations with the two
generals follows, *but no mention at all of the flight to Klagenfurt and the
conference with General Keightley.*[26]

To return to Macmillan's journey. After spending two hours with
Keightley at Klagenfurt, the Minister Resident and his staff returned
by air to Naples, where they arrived about 3.30 in the afternoon.
After reading his latest correspondence and replying to an important
telegram from Churchill concerning the dispute with Tito, Macmillan
drove up to Alexander's lodge at 6.30, had a bath, and changed his
clothes. After that came a pleasant dinner with the Field-Marshal, at
which one presumes Macmillan must have recounted the events of
his flying visit to the Eighth Army. In his television interview with
Ludovic Kennedy Macmillan claimed of this session that, 'all I do
remember is reporting to Alexander . . . that Keightley and I both
thought that we had better carry out the agreement [to send back the
Cossacks and White Russians]. There was nothing else we could do.'

It is impossible to be certain, but in fact it seems unlikely that
Macmillan mentioned the matter at all to Alexander that day. This
at least appears to be the implication of an important document now
to be considered. The evening after Macmillan's return, Monday, 14
May, the American Political Adviser to AFHQ, Alexander C. Kirk,
despatched this 'URGENT' telegram to the Secretary of State in
Washington:

2162, May 14, 11 p.m.
    Situation of surrendered enemy personnel in British Fifth Corps area
has been reported by CG Eighth Army [McCreery] as follows:
    Unmanageable numbers of refugees and prisoners of war are materially
deteriorating [detracting?] from operational capacity of the corps. It is
suggested negotiations be opened with Marshal Tolbukhin for return of
28,000 Cossacks to Russian lines. Alternatives for remainder surrendered
personnel appear to be:
    One. That they be concentrated in area of Radstadt and responsibility
for their final disarmament and guarding be assigned to Twelfth Army
Group. This would facilitate Fifth Corps being prepared for possible
hostilities with Yugoslavs. (See our 2163 of May 14, Midnight)

Two. That a proportion of numbers involved be returned to Italy and concentrated under same arrangements as surrendered personnel of German Army group southwest.

General McCreery has recommended course one as most expeditious. This afternoon General Robertson, Chief Administrative Officer AFHQ requested us to concur in a draft telegram to CG British Eighth Army authorizing him to turn over 28,000 Cossacks (see our 797 of October 16, 1944, Midnight), including women and children to Marshal Tolbukhin, and further instructing him to turn over to Yugoslav Partisans a large number of dissident Yugoslav troops with exception of Chetniks.

General Robertson stated that Macmillan, who talked with CG Eighth Army yesterday, had recommended this course of action. We asked whether the Russians had requested that these Cossacks be turned over to them, and Robertson replied in the negative and added 'but they probably will soon'. We also asked General Robertson what definition he proposed to give to 'Chetniks' and he was very vague on this point. We then stated we could not concur without referring the matter to our Government. CAO expressed disappointment that we did not seem to agree with him on this point but added that he was faced with a grave administrative problem with hundreds of thousands of German POWS on his hands and could not bother at this time about who might or might not be turned over to the Russians and Partisans to be shot. He would have to send his telegram in spite of our non-concurrence.

Department's views would be appreciated urgently.[27]

It appears improbable from Robertson's account, as described by Kirk, that Alexander had as yet been consulted on the matter. For in face of Kirk's unexpectedly resolute opposition to his proposal, Robertson would surely – had he been able to do so – have adduced in its favour the authority of the Field-Marshal, which would have borne greater weight than that of Macmillan. Moreover Alexander's agreement would have entitled Robertson to point out that he was acting according to the orders (or at least in accordance with the wishes) of his Commander-in-Chief. The tone of the discussion reported by Kirk suggests that it was not Robertson who was making his own decision whether or not to despatch the order. Indeed, had Alexander given Robertson an order there would have been no reason for the latter to consult Kirk at all.

Macmillan's diary entry for the day after his return from Austria is brief: 'The last two days were very tiring. So much flying, whizzing, motoring, jeeping and talking, combined with the great heat, are fatiguing. I stayed in bed or lounged in the garden all the day, with a little desultory reading and much dozing. It did me good.'

It seems odd that after so uneventful a day Macmillan should have forgotten to mention his significant discussion with General Robertson. That such a discussion took place appears certain, though whether in person or over the telephone is unknown.

It might at first glance be presumed that Robertson was citing Macmillan at second-hand from the report he had received from Eighth Army that day, which paraphrased Low's Fifth Corps account of Macmillan's recommendation. But Low confines himself to mentioning Macmillan's recommendation that the Cossacks should be returned, and this is also the only repatriation alluded to by McCreery.[28] Yet, as Robertson told Kirk, Macmillan *also* 'recommended' that McCreery be instructed 'to turn over to Yugoslav Partisans a large number of dissident Yugoslav troops with exception of Chetniks'. This additional instruction Robertson must presumably have received directly from Macmillan.

It seems to have been Macmillan's influence that persuaded Robertson to assume authority for action which should properly have been decided by the Supreme Allied Commander. Robertson's authority as Chief Administrative Officer covered a broad perspective, but certainly did not extend to the implementation of major political decisions. A directive reversing existing policy regarding treatment of surrendered Yugoslavs was a markedly political action. That Robertson regarded it as such is indicated by his approach to Kirk.

The reason for not following the normal channels by requesting authorisation from Robertson rather than Alexander may have arisen from the reasonable expectation that the latter would be reluctant to co-operate in such an affair. His negative response to a suggestion that thousands of émigré Cossacks, together with their women and children, should 'be turned over to the Russians and Partisans to be shot' cannot have been difficult to anticipate, and it would have been dangerous to alert him to a project he was likely to obstruct. When Alexander in succeeding days came to raise the question of the Cossacks and Yugoslavs with Eisenhower and the Chiefs of Staff, the only policy he contemplated was that they be transferred to safety in Germany and Italy respectively.

What is certain is that Robertson was deceived by Macmillan on all the crucial issues. He had been given to understand that the Soviets had not yet asked for the Cossacks, 'but they probably will soon'. This represents a deliberate deception, as does the failure to alert Robertson to the fact that the Soviets were demanding the return of non-Soviet citizens. At Voitsberg four days earlier General Keightley had received the Soviet demand for their return, a demand reiterated emphatically the next day in the form of the typewritten list handed to Brigadier Tryon-Wilson. Macmillan had learned about these requests only the day before General Robertson made his unsuccessful approach to Alexander Kirk. They had, however, to remain secret, since their content betrayed the fact that those whom the Soviets were most anxious to acquire were not Soviet citizens, and so excluded from return in instructions laid down by AFHQ. Only in the privacy of his diary did Macmillan acknowledge that White Russians were to be sent back with the Cossacks.

It seems incontrovertible that it was Macmillan who intervened on 13 May to overcome Keightley's revulsion at the idea of surrendering high-ranking officers of the old Russian Imperial Army to certain death at the hands of their enemies; officers whose surrender Keightley and his subordinates had accepted on honourable terms, and for whom as individuals the General felt considerable respect. As existing instructions explicitly forbade the repatriation of this category of prisoner, Macmillan was obliged in addition to persuade Keightley to participate in a subterfuge designed to accomplish their betrayal in defiance of his orders.

For it is clear that, until swayed by Macmillan's authority, Keightley felt neither empowered nor inclined to act in the matter of the Cossacks. Only the day before the Minister's visit he had intervened to ensure the protection of a surrendered Cossack regiment from the pursuing Red Army, reproving Colonel Palmer with some acerbity for not making more haste in evacuating them to safety. Senior officers in the Fifth Corps noted an immediate change in attitude and atmosphere following Macmillan's visit. General Sir Horatius Murray, at the time commander of the Sixth Armoured Division, has written to me stating unequivocally that, 'I put the trouble where we were mainly with Macmillan, Minister of State Mediterranean for Winston Churchill.' It was on 15 May, when General Keightley visited his Divisional headquarters, that Murray learned the Cossacks would be forcibly handed over, and summoned their German officers to issue an unauthorised warning.

Macmillan's visit likewise resulted in a total reversal of established policy towards surrendered Yugoslavs. Up to the time of the Minister's departure from Klagenfurt General Keightley had planned to despatch them to safety in accordance with the AFHQ order of 3 May. As late as 14 May, following an apprehensive petition from Serbs held at Viktring Camp, the First Guards Brigade Sitrep noted that, 'In view of this appeal, priority has been given to the Serbs in the use of RASC transport returning to Italy, and they will be sent to join the other Chetniks at Palmanova.'[29]

Like General Murray, Brigadier Tryon-Wilson, A/Q (Adjutant-Quartermaster) on Keightley's staff, is certain from all he heard and saw that it was Macmillan who impelled Keightley to adopt the course which followed. Before the Minister's visit, the General had expressed disgust in Tryon-Wilson's presence at what he clearly regarded as an impertinent Soviet demand; afterwards in contrast elaborate plans were set in train to ensure maximum compliance with that demand.

Tryon-Wilson's first-hand account is confirmed in broad terms by an authoritative Soviet version of events. General S. M. Shtemenko, in 1945 Deputy Chief of the Soviet General Staff, refers in his memoirs to the surrender of the Tsarist Generals Krasnov and Shkuro briefly thus:

> The Soviet Government then made a firm representation to our allies in the matter of Krasnov, Shkuro, Sultan-Ghirei and other war criminals. The British delayed complying for a little, but then, not placing any great value on the White Guard Generals or their following, placed them in lorries and delivered them into the hands of the Soviet authorities.[30]

Shtemenko's account is valuable for two reasons. First, it confirms that it was the old émigré leaders the Soviets were after, and it was their names which were openly handed to the appropriate British military authority. Shtemenko does not even mention the former Soviet officer, Domanov, who actually commanded the Cossacks. Nikolai Krasnov noted in his memoir the remarkable interest displayed by the Soviets in the senior Tsarist officers after their handover by the British at Judenburg. At the same time, 'It was surprising that Domanov, who played such a big role when we were under the wing of perfidious Albion, counted here for absolutely nothing. None of them was interested in him. It appeared as if he passed quite unnoticed'.[31]

Second, Shtemenko's version makes clear the fact that at first the British felt unable for some reason to comply. Shtemenko's words imply more than the mere delay inevitable before a request can be translated into official acceptance and implementation. In the Red Army delegation of authority has always been reduced to a minimum.

'The British delayed complying' (or 'stalled': the Russian word is *povremenili*) certainly implies a purposive delay, a temporary reluctance to comply. Clearly the brief stalling referred to corresponds with Brigadier Tryon-Wilson's firm citation on 11 May at Red Army headquarters at Voitsberg of the unequivocal screening instructions the Fifth Corps had received from AFHQ five days earlier. For the 'representation' (*predstavlenie*) alluded to by Shtemenko can only be the typewritten demand handed to Tryon-Wilson at Voitsberg. Some time after Tryon-Wilson's journey – the interval covering Macmillan's visit – the British (as Shtemenko makes clear, to the mild surprise of the Soviets) abandoned screening and agreed to hand over the émigré generals. Finally, the fact that Keightley made his offer to hand over the Cossacks on 14 May establishes that the British 'delay in complying' occurred before that date; a chronology which precisely matches Brigadier Tryon-Wilson's account.

An authoritative Yugoslav source likewise confirms awareness that a dramatic change in British policy occurred precisely at the moment of Macmillan's visit to the Fifth Corps. On 10 June 1985 the Belgrade newspaper *Borba* printed an account by the veteran Partisan General Kosta Nadj of his experiences at the end of the war and its immediate aftermath. At that time General Nadj commanded the Yugoslav Third Army, occupying southern Carinthia. Initially (following the unconditional surrender of German forces on 8 May) the British command in Austria had been resolute in declining to hand over to Tito's forces German and accompanying anti-Communist Yugoslav units whose surrender they had accepted. The Chief of Staff of the German Army, General Schmidt-Richberg, subsequently fell into Yugoslav hands and recounted details of his negotiations with the British command. 'According to him, the English were at first ready to meet all their [the Germans'] important requests [to be permitted to surrender to them rather than to Tito]. However the English suddenly altered their policy on 14 May.' The Partisans were subsequently to claim that it was fear of Yugoslav martial prowess which led Keightley to make this abrupt turnabout. From British records we know that this vainglorious delusion bore no basis in fact, and Schmidt-Richberg revealed to his captors that in reality 'the change of attitude in command of the Fifth Corps arose (according to his account, he learned this from the Fifth Corps Chief of Staff) from fresh directives by the Government introduced in the meantime, and that these directives had tied the hands of the Fifth Corps'.

Schmidt-Richberg's concern was with the German Army Group

E as a whole, but there is no doubt that the German commander, von Löhr, included his Yugoslav and Russian auxiliaries in these negotiations. A week earlier von Löhr had directed an urgent appeal to AFHQ, requesting every assistance to prevent 'the danger of a bloody extermination of the Croat people by Tito's forces after the collapse of the military power of the Germans and Croatian formations'.[32] At the time of Schmidt-Richberg's negotiations the Yugoslav and Russian units in Viktring Camp were still under the command of von Löhr's subordinate, Colonel von Seeler. This the context of General Nadj's account demands, since he goes on to make it clear that up to the fourteenth his government had reason to believe the British to be likewise scheming to retain 'Chetnik and Ustashe units'.

The role played by Macmillan now seems clear. The decision to enforce repatriation was a political one; Macmillan was the War Cabinet's highly experienced Political Adviser in the Mediterranean, a man in direct contact with the Prime Minister, Cabinet and Foreign Office. His prestige was immense, and unlikely to be questioned by a general in the field when relating so clearly to matters within his ministerial purview. It was Macmillan who advised Keightley to hand over all the Cossacks, Macmillan who sought out McCreery (during his brief return stop at Treviso on the thirteenth) to back Keightley's request, Macmillan whose authority served to extract an order from General Robertson authorising the handovers, and Macmillan who deliberately concealed what he was doing from the Foreign Office.

It has been seen that it is unlikely, despite his recent claim, that Macmillan informed Alexander of any of these moves when he saw him on the evening of 13 May. Certainly the accounts received from him by McCreery and Robertson were deliberately deceptive. Nor is there compelling reason to suppose that Robertson was aware of anything amiss. It is true that he ignored Kirk's objections and issued the instructions recommended to him by Macmillan; but he may well have thought Macmillan's approval sufficient, both with respect to his high office and in view of the fact that (so he was led to believe) measures were contemplated only against Soviet citizens (already covered by the terms of the Yalta Agreement) and known Ustashi collaborators. Of course, Macmillan *may* have confided further to Robertson, but in the absence of evidence it seems more reasonable to assume that he would have taken care to tell the General no more than was necessary.

There seems to be little question but that it was Macmillan's initiative which prevailed in Klagenfurt. To Keightley he could have acknowledged that existing instructions apparently left no option but to screen the Soviet citizens and retain all the Yugoslavs. Nevertheless there were pressing reasons of state for circumventing those orders. What reasons Macmillan provided there is no certain means of knowing, but they must have been persuasive in the eyes of a not very intellectual or politically aware soldier of middling rank, all of whose energies up to the previous week had been devoted to commanding men in war.

Brigadier Tryon-Wilson has told me that it was generally believed at Fifth Corps headquarters that Macmillan was passing on instructions from the highest political authorities in London. If, as seems likely, this impression derived from Keightley himself, then it presumably represents what Keightley in turn was told by Macmillan. To Tryon-Wilson this certainly appears the most likely explanation. As has been seen, the Yugoslav General Nadj reports that Brigadier Low declared that 'a change of attitude [regarding treatment of Surrendered Enemy Personnel] by 5 Corps command . . . derived from new directives issued in the meantime by the [British] Government, and these directives tied the hands of 5 Corps'.

It was unfortunate for the Cossacks and Yugoslavs that the commanding general into whose hands the chance of war had placed them was, while honest and able in his job, also a man of restricted experience and narrow intellect. Of respectable middle-class upbringing and single-minded military outlook, he lacked something of broader perspectives shared by commanders of the background of Alexander and Arbuthnott. In battle he was a first-rate commanding officer: cool, confident and energetic. To Nigel Nicolson he appeared a *beau sabreur*, tall, authoritative and decisive, as befitted an officer of the Fifth Dragoon Guards.

These excellent qualities could also be displayed in less attractive guise. General Murray found Keightley arrogant and something of a bully if crossed. His knowledge of the world had been entirely confined to soldiering, and shrewd observers sensed that Keightley prided himself on being one of the 'coming men'; a thorough professional, unlike the 'gentlemen' officers of the old school – many of them horse-loving Irishmen and Scotsmen.

A natural sense of fair play made Keightley instinctively averse to betraying prisoners whose surrender he had honourably accepted. Had Macmillan not appeared unexpectedly on the scene he would doubtless have been as glad as any of his subordinate officers to see the Cossacks escape their fate. But once superior authority had intervened, his way was clear. 'We have a job to do; we're not here to philosophise.' It was with such words that he brushed aside Brigadier Patrick Scott's intercession on behalf of the Cossacks. Like Brigadier Musson and Colonel Malcolm in the chain of command below him, his tended to be the rigid viewpoint of 'their's not to reason why'. An intelligent Austrian observer thought him very like 'the worst type of German officer'; and in its ruthless courage, efficiency, ambition and exaltation of the soldier's oath of blind obedience, Keightley's character did indeed display characteristics often associated with a certain type of Prussian officer. And, like all too many of 'the worst type of German officer', he found the path of unthinking submission to authority one that could in unforeseen circumstances lead to terrible things.

But there was nothing vindictive in Keightley's attitude towards the Cossacks – just 'a job to be done' – and it will be seen that when towards the end of May the pressure applied to him began to slacken, he was content to see surviving prisoners in his hands protected from further persecution. In the absence of satisfactory evidence of his motivation he should not be judged too harshly. He adopted a tough approach and dealt brusquely with objections from his subordinates, but probably felt this to be the only way of enforcing a measure regarded with almost unanimous distaste by the whole Corps. It may be that he disliked the policy just as much as they, but felt in view of the overpowering arguments presented by Macmillan that the policy represented a 'cruel necessity' which had to be implemented regardless of normal considerations of humanity. Until five days before their meeting Keightley had been fighting a war in which moral dilemmas balancing smaller sacrifices against greater had been for him an almost daily consideration. Decisions had to be made swiftly and enforced unquestioningly.

What is unlikely is that the initiative for surrendering the Cossacks originated in any way with Keightley. Macmillan claims that Keightley was agreeable to handing over the Cossacks because they represented an impossible administrative problem: 'What were we to do with all these people? Well, actually, we hadn't the physical power to do very much . . .' Toby Low advances the same argument: 'Mr Macmillan was obviously deeply impressed during the visit which he paid to General Keightley on 13 May by the awful conditions in which the relatively small British Army in Austria was working.'

However it is hard to see either the old émigré Cossacks or the Yugoslav refugees as more than a minor nuisance in the smooth running of the Fifth Corps area. It was essential to maintain good relations with Marshal Tolbukhin; but Keightley had no reason to assume that an international crisis would result from his explaining that he lacked authority to hand over two or three thousand Tsarist émigrés. Soviet pressure to alter British Government policy could only be applied at inter-governmental level. There had in any case as yet been no occasion for Soviet irritation: on 13 May their request for the Cossack generals was but two days old and still awaiting a reply. When Toby Low in his Sitrep of 14 May described the Cossacks as 'clearly great source contention between Soviets and ourselves,' he was expressing his own and/or Macmillan's assessment; nothing on the ground had yet taken place to justify such a claim.

It seems equally unlikely that the administrative problem of maintaining the refugees in camps represented so insuperable a problem as to override all considerations of humanity and international law. At this time Keightley was responsible for 278,650 prisoners of war in south-eastern Austria,[33] and the presence or otherwise of some 70,000 Cossacks and Yugoslavs among them can scarcely have represented the critical factor. The General had intervened personally the day before Macmillan's visit to ensure that 5,000 Cossacks came under his control rather than that of the Soviets, and it will be seen shortly that AFHQ was fully capable of dealing with the problem by means other than that of repatriation.

We do not know what reasons were provided by Macmillan for handing over all the Russian and Yugoslav refugees, but it is not difficult to envisage them as compelling. It could have been argued that for high reasons of state, involving the most delicate relations with the Soviet Union, Churchill and the Cabinet had decided on this one occasion to ignore rulings in force and comply with the Soviet request. This would inevitably involve some irregular procedure, even acts not normally regarded as consonant with a soldier's honour. For that reason the fewer people who were in on the secret the better. The proposed victims were traitors to their countries, had done much to assist the Axis war effort, and were in any case responsible for the most atrocious war crimes. Nevertheless uneasy consciences might jib at what was proposed, in consequence of which it would be best to manage the whole affair within the Fifth Corps, without bringing the Eighth Army or AFHQ into the picture.

This reconstruction is not entirely speculative. Three weeks later,

General Arbuthnott, Keightley's divisional officer principally concerned with the Cossack handovers, wrote of the decision to repatriate
them that, 'every aspect of the matter was carefully examined and
the conclusion was reached that for the eventual resettlement of
Europe and the future hope of peace the return of these people to
Russia was not only necessary but desirable'. This can only represent
what Arbuthnott was told by Keightley, and what the Corps Commander had in turn been led to believe by Macmillan. The wording suggests lofty considerations of state far beyond Keightley's
competence to judge, and provides a strong hint of the menacing
prospect held out by Macmillan were his proposition not to be
accepted.

Is it possible (as I myself tentatively suggested in an earlier essay
on the subject) that high reasons of state had indeed prevailed, and
that Macmillan was voicing the views of his superiors in London? A
moment's reflection, however, proves that it cannot be. For it is
Macmillan himself who claims that his orders came directly from
Field-Marshal Alexander, and that those in turn derived from the
Combined Chiefs of Staff. In fact the Chiefs of Staff did not come
to any decision on the subject until the handovers were complete,
and it was not until 20 June that Alexander finally learned of their
decision. The ruling itself, moreover, laid down that *no* Yugoslavs
should be handed over compulsorily, and conceded the return only
of Soviet citizens among the Cossacks. Had Macmillan really received
secret instructions from the Cabinet there would be nothing now to
prevent his saying so – nor any reason for falsely claiming instead
that it was Alexander who gave him the order.

A further important consideration, so Macmillan asserts, was that
the wretched Keightley was simply in no position to resist the
overwhelming might of Tito's aggressive legions, and succumbed to
force majeure. He has stated, 'It was a very difficult situation: we had
only one brigade and there were thousands of them . . . the poor
General Keightley who had the army, he had only one brigade.' This
seems a disparaging underestimate of the resources of the Fifth Corps,
with its armoured division and two infantry divisions – to say nothing
of Brigadier Cooper's independent Seventh Armoured Brigade.
Though war with anyone was the last thing wanted, there can be
little doubt that the Fifth Corps represented the most formidable
fighting unit in the region. Just over a week later the Partisans hastily
decamped from all Carinthia, overawed by a mere hint that the
British might employ force to evict them. Whatever Keightley's

misgivings, they surely related to considerations a little less daunting than those now recalled by Macmillan.

Macmillan's protests in any case look very like an attempt to shift the weight of responsibility on to Keightley's shoulders. Keightley's initial reaction, *before* Macmillan's visit, had after all been to ignore the Soviet demand – despite his 'one brigade'. Keightley's subsequent orders and messages include no allusion to the alleged need to recover British prisoners of war in Soviet hands, and no suggestion that the retention of the Cossacks represented an insoluble logistical problem. Similarly, apprehensions that retaining the Cossacks might exacerbate relations with Tito or Tolbukhin reflected not Keightley's own perception of the situation, but what he took to be political considerations beyond his sphere of responsibility. On the contrary, his messages to the Eighth Army and those passed down within the Fifth Corps emphasise that the decision to resort to forced repatriation resulted from a 'verbal directive' issued by Macmillan, and stemmed from political considerations beyond the competence of a mere Corps Commander to assess.

All things being equal, there can be no doubt that Keightley would have been happy to have rid himself of the trouble of maintaining any sizeable section of the huge body of refugees and prisoners of war for which the Fifth Corps was responsible. But up to 13 May all the evidence shows that for him accepted standards of honour and justice prevailed over relatively minor considerations of administrative convenience.

The facts, after all, speak for themselves. To the Soviet request on 10 May for the return of all Cossacks Keightley had been non-committal, explaining that the matter lay outside his competence to decide. On 11 May he expressed indignation at their impudent (as he saw it) demand for the handover of the Tsarist officers. It is true that he felt no responsibility or sympathy for Cossacks who fell directly into Soviet hands, and reproved Brigadier Scott for not rejecting their surrender. However, once accepted, he felt the responsibility so strongly as to go out of his way to draw into his area a large body of Cossacks who would, but for his intervention, most likely have been caught up by the Red Army without British involvement.

Major Anthony Morris, in 1945 second-in-command of the First Royal Irish Fusiliers, was in no doubts about the general feeling within the Fifth Corps at that time. It was his battalion that accepted the surrender of Prince zu Salm's 5,000 Cossacks on 12 May: a surrender successfully accomplished through the intervention of General Keightley himself.

Today Colonel Morris writes:

> [Brigadier] Pat Scott told me that he had to make the decision to accept the Cossack surrender on his own, as he could not reach higher command apart from Gen Arbuthnott, the Div[isional] Comd, who had told him that, as the man on the spot, he should do what he thought best. I remember that communications were for a short time almost non-existent, and that Pat Scott had to make an instant decision to avoid further bloodshed . . .
>
> He certainly had no idea at the time that the Cossacks would have to be handed over to the Russians under the Yalta agreement. Subsequently he was horrified, as we all were: I heard Gen Arbuthnott expressing the same sentiments and saying that Gen Keightley (5 Corps) shared them. I seem to remember that I heard that Alexander was questioning the deal, with Macmillan, or maybe with his representative, Harold Caccia, but was told to carry out Orders.

Lieutenant-Colonel (now Major-General) H. E. N. Bredin, A/Q on Arbuthnott's staff, learned similarly that Keightley shared Arbuthnott's objection.

With regard to the Yugoslav refugees, assembled for the most part in Viktring Camp, Keightley initially adopted an equally resolute stance. Though they could easily have been prevented from crossing the Drava on 12 May, their surrender was accepted after protracted formal negotiations lasting much of the previous day,[34] and they were shepherded into asylum in their improvised encampment. A strong guard was placed to protect them from harassment or abduction by the Partisans. Until the arrival of General Robertson's executive order of 14 May, resulting from Macmillan's intervention, Keightley continued to plan for their evacuation to safety in Italy.

Keightley was a bluff, dashing serving soldier. Supremely capable in his exacting profession, he shared the average soldier's dislike for and suspicion of politics and politicians. One of the ablest of his divisional commanders, Major-General Horatius Murray, was convinced Keightley had little understanding of the Yalta Agreement, though he was wont to cite it blandly as authority for the tragic events which ensued.

Fortunately Keightley possessed an extremely capable Chief of Staff in the form of the thirty-five-year-old Brigadier Toby Low, whose legal background and political experience made him familiar with wider problems than those of day-to-day soldiering. As BGS he was not only responsible for directing the whole subsequent operation in all its details, but also for negotiating directly with Soviet and Yugoslav representatives. He was not, as was Keightley, a regular soldier. Born in 1914, Low was educated at Winchester and Oxford, and called to the Bar immediately before the outbreak of war in 1939. He had served with distinction in North Africa and Italy, but with the ending of hostilities was contemplating the resumption of peacetime ambitions.

It is uncertain whether he and Harold Macmillan were acquainted at the time of the latter's visit to Klagenfurt on 13 May 1945, but they certainly shared a common ambition. For Low was preparing, as a member of that Conservative Party of which Macmillan was one of the leading luminaries, to contest a seat in the coming general election. Ironically, the July landslide in favour of Labour caused Macmillan to lose his seat at Stockton, while young Toby Low became MP for Blackpool North. But by November Macmillan was back in the House of Commons, where he resumed his steady climb towards the pinnacle of British political power. In January 1957 he became Prime Minister in succession to Anthony Eden, an office he retained until October 1963. Meanwhile his friend Low had also risen to prominence within the party, which indeed he managed as Deputy Chairman during the last four years of Macmillan's premiership. And in the year before Macmillan's retirement Toby Low was raised to the peerage as the first Baron Aldington. Thus, subordinate officer though he was, Brigadier Low was undoubtedly in a strong position to influence his commanding officer when it came to perplexing political and diplomatic issues beyond the normal scope of a straight-forward serving soldier. That he did so is (for what it is worth) the opinion of many of his former colleagues with whom I spoke.

So the scene is set. Fifth Corps' deceptive telegram of 14 May, alleging that the Cossacks consisted solely of Soviet citizens and making no reference to the presence of Yugoslav internees at Viktring and elsewhere, was passed up by the Eighth Army to AFHQ. General Robertson, at Macmillan's instance, responded by issuing the following administrative order:

To:- action 15 Army Group Main Eighth Army . . .
From:- AFHQ cite FHCAO [Field Headquarters Chief Administrative Officer]   FX 75383   14 [May]
1. all Russians should be handed over to Soviet forces at agreed point

of contact est[ablished] by you under local arrangement with Marshal
Tolbukhin's HQ. steps should be taken to ensure that Allied PW held in
Russian area are transferred to us in exchange at same time . . .
3. all surrendered personnel of established Yugoslav nationality who
were serving in German forces should be disarmed and handed over to
Yugoslav forces.[35]

The wording of this order was clearly the subject of careful thought.
The expression 'all Russians' appears intended to skate round any
direct allusion to the Cossacks, with whom (as Robertson's explanation to Kirk makes clear) this order was exclusively concerned. It
also ingeniously includes non-Soviet citizens among those to be
handed over; though in ambivalent phraseology that could always
be explained away should the necessity arise, reflecting Macmillan's
diary reference to 'the agreement in handing back Russian [*sic*] subjects.'

In the same way the expression 'all surrendered personnel of
established Yugoslav nationality who were serving in German forces'
simultaneously precluded sympathy for the intended victims, while
being inclusive enough to apply to virtually all uniformed Yugoslav
refugees. After four years of enemy occupation there was scarcely a
military formation in the country (the Partisans included), which had
not been obliged to compromise itself in some degree by collaboration
with the enemy.

Finally there are the exceptions that prove the rule. Though the
order of 14 May specified that 'all Russians should be handed over',
two 'Russian' units were from an early date arbitrarily excluded from
repatriation. These were Rogozhin's *Russkii Corpus*, last encountered
arriving at Viktring Camp from Yugoslavia, and Shandruk's 10,000-
strong Ukrainian Division. Both were known to include sizeable
proportions of Soviet citizens, yet shortly after the time of
Macmillan's visit they were separated from their fellows due for
repatriation and removed to safety in other camps. Why they were
spared and others of virtually identical background condemned remains mysterious. Here we are concerned not with the reason, but
the fact. The various Russian units' differing fates must have been
decided at the highest Corps level, though no record of this crucial
decision-making process is to be found.

The retention of the Ukrainian Division is particularly significant.
Much sympathy was felt within the Fifth Corps for the Cossacks
(Colonel Morris remembers 'thinking that they could have come

from a British cavalry regiment'). The Ukrainians in contrast had everything going against them. As recently as 10 May they had been engaged in fighting on the Eastern Front, and according to inter-Allied agreement should have been compelled to surrender to the Red Army. The Division had no aristocratic French- and English-speaking officers, and included a large number of Soviet citizens. Above all, it belonged to the most hated body in the German Army: its official title was the *14 Waffen-Grenadier Division der SS 'Galizien'*.

The Soviets had every reason for wishing to lay hands on this unit, and the British no justification for retaining it. Two months later Stalin himself was to demand their surrender. And yet they were not returned. The most likely explanation of this anomaly was that the Ukrainians had taken the sensible precaution of claiming to be a Polish force; Churchill was later informed that 'this body of about 10 thousand personnel surrendered almost intact as a Polish division'. Before their surrender to the British, the Ukrainians had managed to get a message through to General Anders' Polish Corps in Italy. Relations between Britain and the Polish forces in the West were exceptionally delicate at this time, the Poles fearing that they might be compelled to return to a Soviet-occupied homeland. As Churchill was to note, 'We had to be careful about the Polish Army, for if the situation was mishandled there might be a mutiny.'[36] The delivery at this time to the Soviets of a unit claiming Polish loyalties and including many Polish citizens could have had very serious repercussions.[37]

Whatever the reason, it is inconceivable that General Keightley could have taken upon himself to make a major political decision of this kind. If, as is claimed by those who wish to lay the blame for the Cossack handovers at his door, he was the initiator of the operations, how much less scrupulous might he have felt about the delivery of a fighting SS unit? And, by the same token, if the Ukrainians could be silently whisked out of Austria that May, why could the Cossacks not likewise have been (as Field-Marshal Alexander was to order in vain) spirited away to safety? There can be no doubt that the decision to reprieve the Ukrainian SS Division was a political one, involving considerations of weight and complexity. Yet there appears to be no evidence extant to show when and where this decision was made.

It would seem reasonable on *prima facie* grounds to presume that it happened on the occasion when treatment of all 'Russian' units in

British hands was under discussion, and it is not difficult to see why the record of such a transaction might have proved too sensitive for preservation. Neither the Ukrainian Division nor the *Russkii Corpus* is mentioned in Keightley's report of 14 May, though both units had surrendered to the Fifth Corps two days earlier. It would be fruitless to speculate further, though it has to be noted that some forty pages of Macmillan's diary for this period are said to have disappeared.

As early as 16 May orders were given for the extraction of the White Russian *Russkii Corpus* from Viktring Camp, and two days later they were transferred to a new site at Klein St Veit, deeper within the British zone.[38] For some reason it had been decided they, too, were to be exempt from the coming repatriation. The reason for this exemption is unknown, but here the important thing is the fact. Nothing in Robertson's order of 14 May validated excepting Rogozhin and his followers (nor the Galicia Division) from inclusion in the contemplated repatriation, which would seem to imply that the decision had *already* been arrived at. Given the brief period of time involved, it seems virtually certain that the fate of Rogozhin and his men was decided at the conference between Macmillan and Keightley three days before the decision to remove them from Viktring. If so, this aspect of the operations provides revealing evidence just how specific were the terms of that discussion with regard to the categories of Russians to be returned or retained, and hence how fully aware Macmillan was of the distinction between the 'White' (to use his description) and Soviet elements among Russians surrendering to the Fifth Corps.

Thus when Brigadier Low received Robertson's telegram it was already known how to 'decode' it. 'Such-and-such units are to be handed over to the Soviets, this one screened, that one retained' – so the arrangement would have gone. The confident way in which Low set about sorting the sheep from the goats implies that everything which followed had in broad outline already been discussed and decided during Macmillan's visit to the Fifth Corps headquarters. Anything Macmillan said to McCreery on the thirteenth and which Robertson learned on the fourteenth had to tally with the Fifth Corps' own reports to the Eighth Army and AFHQ. And if Field-Marshal Alexander began to concern himself with the problem – as indeed he soon did – then he, too, must be kept from suspecting anything untoward.

5

Stratagems of Deception

'The question of the handing over of the so-called "Chetniks" . . .
looks . . . as though there might have been some kind of slip-up
about the orders referred to . . .' (Sir George Rendel, Southern
Department of the Foreign Office, 27 May 1946)

On 13 May General Keightley at Klagenfurt received (as he was
shortly afterwards to term it) a 'verbal directive from Macmillan to
return all Soviet nationals in Corps area to Soviet forces'. He passed
up a request for confirmation of this directive, which arrived next
day on the desk of General Robertson at AFHQ in Caserta. In
addition Macmillan recommended to Robertson 'further instructing
him [Keightley] to turn over to Yugoslav Partisans a large number
of dissident Yugoslav troops with exception of Chetniks'. Robertson
responded, as was seen at the close of the last chapter, by issuing
an administrative order empowering Keightley to hand over all
'Russians' in his custody, together with all Yugoslavs who had been
serving in the German forces.

Thus from 14 May Keightley possessed unequivocal authority to
effect the immediate handover of his unwanted charges regardless of
their wishes; a handover which in the case of the Cossacks he had
himself urged. Yet a fortnight was to pass before he began their
repatriation, and then only because he succeeded in obtaining a *second*
(much more qualified) authorisation from AFHQ on 25 May. In the
case of the Yugoslavs at Viktring, he was to wait until 24 May before
transporting them across the frontier, again on the authority of a
second (also severely qualified) order elicited from AFHQ.

What is the explanation of this anomaly? Why did Keightley not
implement Robertson's order at once, seeing he had himself requested
it? Why the relatively long and (as Keightley's messages make clear)

irritating delay? With Robertson's unequivocal order in his files, why did he feel obliged to request renewed authority for the handovers? The answer is that Robertson's order was rendered invalid soon after it was issued, following dramatic events crowding the next three days.

Unfortunately no more can be gleaned concerning Robertson's motive in ordering the repatriation of Cossacks and Yugoslavs than is touched on in Kirk's brief account. His was 'a grave administrative problem with hundreds of thousands of German POWS on his hands', whereas Macmillan was concerned (according to his own account) with the fulfilment of the Yalta Agreement and the facilitation of the return of liberated British prisoners. It is understandable that the Chief Administrative Officer should have been concerned with questions of logistics and supply, while the Minister Resident addressed himself to political issues. Nevertheless there are other important considerations implicit in the respective timing of Macmillan's conference with Keightley, and the issuing of Robertson's order a bare twenty-four hours later.

When Macmillan conferred with Keightley on the morning of Sunday, 13 May, the General explained the problems incurred in dealing with Tito's lawless and truculent Partisans, who had arrived in southern Carinthia about the same time as British forces of the Eighth Army. They represented considerable nuisance value, but Keightley felt confident enough to inform Macmillan that, 'it was possible for him to maintain the present uneasy position for the time being until he is strong enough to clear up the whole of his area'. Relations with the Red Army and their Bulgarian auxiliaries were good and, as Macmillan noted, 'no trouble is anticipated here'. Apart from these delicate but ultimately solvable issues, Keightley had to 'deal with nearly 400,000 surrendered or surrendering Germans, not yet disarmed (except as to tanks and guns) who must be shepherded into some place or other, fed and given camps, etc.'

A subsidiary problem was that of the refugees, principally those who had fled from Yugoslavia. They, so Macmillan was informed, amounted to some 40,000 Cossacks and 'thousands of so-called Ustashi or Chetniks, mostly with wives and children . . .' The majority of the latter were the fugitives from Slovenia whose arrival in Viktring Camp I have described in chapter two. Their number was estimated at this time as 21,000. There was also a Croat Division concentrated at Eisenkappel with a complement of 7,000 men and 3,000 accompanying civilians, and elsewhere similar numbers of assorted Hungarians and Ukrainians.[1]

Keightley explained that, 'British and Russian Corps Commanders have had a meeting', at which the boundary line between their zones had been amicably agreed. It was at this session, on 10 May, that the Soviets had requested the return of the Cossacks: a request with which Macmillan gave Keightley a 'verbal directive' to comply.

In his diary entry Macmillan is reticent as to what course he recommended for the 30,000 or so Yugoslav refugees. He expatiates at some length on the undeserved misery of their situation, but makes no mention of any suggestion as to their treatment. Fortunately it is possible to reconstruct the missing evidence from another source. After flying from Klagenfurt at noon, Macmillan touched down at Treviso in North Italy for a short meeting with Eighth Army Commander Richard McCreery. He had already conferred at length with the General the day before, and it seems that this brief consultation at the airfield was most likely arranged at the last minute at Macmillan's instance.

In his diary Macmillan mentions that he and McCreery had 'a short chat', and thanks to Kirk's account of his visit from General Robertson next day we know what was its subject-matter. Robertson, reported Kirk,

> requested us to concur in a draft telegram to CO British Eighth Army authorising him to turn over 28,000 Cossacks . . . including women and children to Marshal Tolbukhin, and further instructing him to turn over to Yugoslav Partisans a large number of dissident Yugoslav troops with exception of Chetniks. *General Robertson stated that Macmillan, who talked with CO Eighth Army yesterday, had recommended this course of action.* (italics inserted)

Though some of the refugees at Viktring Camp were Chetniks, no reference to them as such appears in reports compiled by the Fifth Corps units; and it seems probable that in singling them out as a grouping Macmillan had in mind General Damjanovic's force of 12,000 Chetniks. They, it will be recalled, had surrendered to the Eighth Army in North Italy on 3 May, and been sent under AFHQ instructions to safety at Palmanova. No attempt was made at any time to include them among the Yugoslav citizens later repatriated, and their position was secure throughout. In any case the essential point is that Macmillan's recommendation related exclusively to the 30,000 Yugoslav refugees whom he learned to be in Fifth Corps custody, with or without exceptions.

The motive and justification for this recommendation remain

obscure. As yet no request for their delivery appears to have come
from Tito's side,[2] and Keightley himself failed even to include their
relatively small number among the 'surrendered personnel in this
area whether German, Austrian or Russian' whose removal he was
to urge so vigorously on McCreery the day after Macmillan's visit.
McCreery himself had, following orders from AFHQ, issued a week
earlier his 'Instruction No. 1465' which as we have seen laid down,
'Chetniks, troops of Mihailovitch and other dissident Yugoslavs
. . . will be regarded as surrendered personnel and will be treated
accordingly. The ultimate disposal of these personnel will be decided
on Government levels.'[3]

It is the last sentence which surely provides the key to understanding McCreery's apparent endorsement of Macmillan's instruction;
an endorsement which represents a surprising volte-face from the
position he had held hitherto. It must also explain General Robertson's
preparedness to issue his order of 14 May which, in direct contravention of existing AFHQ rulings (in turn reflecting political directives issued by the Allied Governments), ordered that, 'all surrendered
personality of established Yugoslav nationality who were serving in
German forces should be disarmed and handed over to Yugoslav
forces'. For it was Macmillan who represented the British Government, and whose duty it was to provide political guidance at AFHQ.
When he 'recommended this course of action' to McCreery and
issued his 'verbal directive' to Keightley, they had no reason to
question his authority. Robertson, however, who was in a much
better position to appreciate the political nuances, felt it would be
desirable to obtain confirmatory American consent, and in consequence made his unsuccessful approach to Kirk.

So far as Keightley is concerned, it has been shown that strong
evidence exists suggesting that he felt considerable moral repugnance
to accepting Macmillan's instructions. Macmillan's prestige and arguments (whatever they were) were so powerful that he not only
managed to override Keightley's objections, but (as will be seen)
induced him to engage in deceptions necessary for the policy's implementation which drew him increasingly down into a moral morass
of intrigue and prevarication. Similar arguments presumably prevailed in part over McCreery, though in his case he was also subjected
to deliberate deception. Keightley falsely reported to him that the
Cossacks were all Soviet citizens, and that the Soviets had not yet
requested their return; claims he could not possibly have made had
he thought Macmillan likely to contradict them.

Both McCreery and Robertson appear to have entertained reservations, though on different grounds, when faced with Macmillan's proposal. It could not have appeared necessary to dupe McCreery in the manner described had his whole-hearted assent been anticipated; nor would Robertson have thought it necessary to seek substantiation of the Minister Resident's authority by an appeal to that of his American counterpart, Kirk. More significant still is the fact that, by the time the generals came to back Macmillan's project, their perception of the matter had been altered dramatically by a wholly new consideration which had arisen during the twenty-four-hour interval.

Immediately after Macmillan's departure from Klagenfurt, during the afternoon of Sunday, 13 May the Chief of Staff of German Army Group E arrived at Fifth Corps headquarters. To their consternation Keightley and Low learned from him that the whole of General von Löhr's force, 'consisting of 300,000 Germans and 200,000 Croats', was moving north-westwards from Yugoslavia 'directed towards Volkermarkt Klagenfurt area'. As Tito appeared incapable of halting them, it looked as if this half-million-strong horde, possessing 'sufficient rations for 48 hours', would shortly force its way into the area occupied by the Fifth Corps.[4]

That evening Nigel Nicolson, intelligence officer to the First Guards Brigade, recorded in his daily report, 'Biggest element Croat Ustashi Army, 300,000 strong, now withdrawing across Yugo-Slav frontier, having surrendered to Tito. Croat Guards Corps static at Weinberg D.6990. Slovenes and Serbs mostly conc[entrated] Viktring cage. None of these can be repatriated except to almost certain death at hands of Tito.'[5]

The confusion implicit in this account is understandable. By 13 May the Partisans had largely liquidated opposition within Slovenia, and were spread out along the northern side of the Yugoslav-Austrian frontier, up to and beyond the Drava. That fighting between different national and political groupings within Yugoslavia was continuing was known to the British; but, as Nicolson's report notes, it was generally believed that the principal dissident forces were on the point of surrendering to Tito, if they had not done so already.

The Slovenian Partisans were, however, of negligible military value, largely confining their martial ardour to numerous acts of plunder, rape and massacre inflicted upon the civilian Austrian population. Higher Yugoslav command ordered their temporary withdrawal by 12 May, when they would be reinforced by two divisions of the Fourth Army. Meanwhile this thinly-held cordon was ruptured by the homeward retreat of General von Löhr's undefeated Army Group E. In von Löhr's wake moved the Croatian Army, together with a vast crowd of panic-stricken civilians. The Croatian capital Zagreb was evacuated on 7 and 8 May. Fighting all the way, the Croats pushed northwards through Slovenia until about 13 May they gathered around Dravograd, south of the Austrian frontier. There they found their path blocked by Bulgarian troops forming part of Marshal Tolbukhin's Third Ukrainian Front. Fighting not being the Bulgarians' forte, they consented after negotiations to permit the Croats to pass over the Drava into Austria during 14 and 15 May.[6]

Fifth Corps headquarters regarded this unexpected development with dismay, and on 14 May Keightley's Chief of Staff, Toby Low, requested instructions from the Eighth Army as to how they were to handle the matter:

> personal Army Comd from Corps Comd (.) present situation (.) approx 300000 PW surrendered personnel and refugees in Corps area (.) further 600000 reported moving North to Austria from Yugoslavia (.) I am taking all possible steps to prevent their move along roads but this will NOT completely prevent them as they are short of food and are being harassed (.) should this number materialize food and guard situation will become critical (.) I therefore suggest that all possible steps are taken to dispose soonest of all surrendered personnel in this area whether German Austrian or Russian by moving them to Northern Italy or their homes whichever may be the policy (.)

It was this message which included Macmillan's advice of the previous day that the Soviets be asked to accept the Cossacks. Forwarding this report on through the Fifteenth Army Group, General McCreery added the rider, 'Please ask AFHQ to ask Tito how many enemy he eventually wishes to retain. Suggest Croats become Tito's show.'[7]

Up to this time the British had been accepting on an *ad hoc* basis the surrender of German and anti-Partisan Yugoslav units. This proved a severe blow to the pride of the Partisans, who objected that all enemy troops from Yugoslavia should have surrendered to Tito. A deputation visited Fifth Corps headquarters to register a strong objection to this policy. Keightley patiently explained that he had merely been performing the Yugoslavs' task for them, adding 'that any formation which had wrongly surrendered to the British would be returned to Tito's forces'.[8]

The Chief of Staff of the German Army Group E, General Schmidt-Richberg, was informed of this development by Brigadier

Low, who explained that the Fifth Corps was bound by new orders which had just arrived.[9] It was about this time, too, that he received General Robertson's order, directing that, 'all surrendered personnel of established Yugoslav nationality who were serving in German forces should be disarmed and handed over to Yugoslav forces'.

On 13 May Macmillan's concern had been solely with the 30,000 or so Yugoslav refugees who had surrendered to the Fifth Corps, and it was they whose delivery to Tito he had urged upon Keightley and Robertson. Now this relatively minor problem had become subsumed under the urgent necessity of preventing British-occupied Austria from being swamped by hundreds of thousands of fleeing Croats. It was clearly this consideration which swayed General McCreery, when he suggested, 'Croats become Tito's show'; and Robertson's concern may similarly have been with the scale of the threatened irruption. As he pointed out to Alexander Kirk, 'he was faced with a grave administrative problem with hundreds of thousands of German POWS on his hands and could not bother at this time about who might or might not be turned over to the Russians and Partisans to be shot'.

At nine o'clock that evening (14 May) a Croat liaison officer of Jewish origin, Deutsch-Maceljski, arrived at the British lines with an offer of surrender of two Croatian armies of 100,000 each, together with half a million civilians. A running battle was being waged with the pursuing Yugoslav Eighth Brigade, and already that day the Croats had lost three of their thirty tanks to enemy bazooka shells. Brigadier Patrick Scott, whose Thirty-eighth (Irish) Infantry Brigade stood in the path of the Croats' retreat at once telephoned for instructions to Divisional headquarters, which issued a message to brigade commanders:

> Three hundred thousand Germans and two hundred thousand Croats, the greater part of them armed, are moving across the Jug border, although they have all nominally surrendered to Tito. They have with them only enough rations for 48 hours, and are accompanied by thirty thousand horses and two thousand motor vehicles. Eighth Army have been urgently asked for a decision whether we are to accept the surrender of these forces or oblige them to return to Jugo-Slavia. Pending the decision you will hold them South of the Drava.

As Brigadier Verney, commander of the First Guards Division, noted, this 'gives some idea of the problem'. At the same time he was aware of the plight of 'comparatively inoffensive people fleeing from the Russians or Tito, unwanted and all but persecuted wherever they went'.[10]

To Scott it seemed inconceivable that the already overstrained resources of the Eighth Army could absorb this nation on the march. On receipt of Divisional instructions he immediately issued this uncompromising operations instruction:

> (a) National emigration in progress with the object of surrendering to British Army. Numbers involved about 1 million now approaching Bleiburg incl two Army Corps of approx 100,000 each, armed but short of amn.
> (b) Their surrender has been refused and they are not to cross the old Austrian frontier. They have been so informed and warned we intend to use force of arms to enforce our decision.[11]

The fact was, though, that many of the Croats were already well inside the frontier; poorly equipped but in enormous numbers. Scott decided to resort to bluff:

> Our total resources at Bleiburg at that time was Paul Lunn-Rockliffe's battery, a troop or two of 46th Reconnaissance Regiment, a couple of Armoured cars of 27th Lancers, and two or three tanks. The battery of guns was deployed in the most open place that could be found, in case anyone should overlook this big display of force, and another battery was moved south of the River Drava to support them – just in case.

Fortunately, too, Scott was able to call up some RAF fighters to circle over the crowd menacingly.

Brigadier Scott's headquarters at this time was in the castle of Bleiburg, perched on a hill overlooking a little town of the same name. To the south the peaks of the Karavanke Mountains stood as a jagged barrier between Austria and Yugoslavia. Nearer at hand was a huge open field bounded by low wooded hills. Into this space (which was concealed by a low hill from Bleiburg Castle) was crowded an immense sea of people, estimated at well over 100,000. These were the Croat troops and civilians, who had crossed the frontier at Dravograd hoping to make their way westwards to Klagenfurt. Now, however, they found their way blocked by Brigadier Scott's troops, while large bands of Titoist Partisans had infiltrated the woods on either side and taken up a threatening but as yet inactive stance. The Croatian troops were still armed, and the British attitude an unknown factor. A group of senior Croatian generals was taken

under British escort to confer with Scott in Bleiburg Castle. The
dense throng waited under a burning sun while hour after hour passed
by.

Inside the castle Scott received first the leader of the pursuing
Partisans, Commissar Milan Basta, 'a most determined young man
in his early twenties', as Scott recalled, who was spoiling for a fight
with the ill-armed and demoralised Croats, whose number he had in
fact grossly underestimated. 'It certainly looked as if we were well
situated for a front row in the stalls for the ensuing conflict,' continues
Scott's account. 'I had noticed, with relief, that the walls of the
castle were exceedingly thick, and the approaches to it extremely
difficult!'

As it was, he managed to persuade the suspicious Commissar Basta
that the most acceptable course would be for him (Scott) to persuade
the Croats to disarm and surrender voluntarily. His next interview
was with the unfortunate Croatian commander, General Herencic,
whom Scott and Basta managed to cajole and bully into accepting
these unequivocal terms. Deciding there was no alternative, Herencic
capitulated. By 4.30 on 15 May the independent state of Croatia had
ceased to exist. Hemmed in by Partisans, within twenty-four hours
the would-be Croatian national emigration was to be herded back
across the Drava. But before that happened terrible scenes took place
which can never be forgotten by the Croatian people.

The terms accepted by General Herencic were clear enough, but
transmitting them to the immense throng in Bleiburg fields was a
different matter. In the confusion many units thought that it was the
British to whom they were surrendering, while others with a truer
appreciation of the situation prepared to defend themselves or make
their way into the woods. Most, however, gave up their arms and
ran up white flags. Before long the waiting Commissar Basta found
his time had come. Confident that his intended victims no longer
had the means of defending themselves and that the British intended
to stand back, he gave the long-awaited word to his followers. What
then occurred was a slaughter so terrible that its extent can only be
measured through the experiences of those who lived through it.

Ted Pavich was at the time a twenty-five-year-old former diplomatic courier. He saw the Croatian generals drive to Bleiburg to
negotiate with Brigadier Scott, and later heard the command to lay
down all arms. To the south British tanks flanked the milling crowd,
while Spitfires circled overhead. Suddenly there came a rattle of
machine-gun fire from the woods above. The Partisans were firing

into the crowd, too densely packed for the most part to be able to flee. The slaughter was terrible – too terrible, Pavich recalls, to be able to imagine unless one were there. Men, women and children fell in droves as the Partisans played their machine-guns back and forth across the fields. Before long so many people had been killed that the Partisans ventured down among the survivors, and with evident relish set about beating, kicking and stabbing them to death. Pavich was one of the fortunate ones who escaped the bloody scene, only to be captured later by Partisans and thrown into one of Tito's gaols for the next sixteen years of his life.

George Raguz, who was in another part of the crowd at the time, was then fifteen years old. Together with his family he had fled Tito's reign of terror in Zagreb. At Bleiburg a fortunate chance led them to be standing by a farmhouse on the wooded southern slope over-looking the fields, so that they found themselves above the line of Partisan fire. Below was a crowd so huge that never in his life since has he seen or heard of so large a body gathered in one place. He himself was rooted to the spot with terror. Suddenly he saw a flurry of white flags going up below him. Then firing began from the woods all around. Two hundred metres ahead he saw the bullets cutting swathes through the people, the bodies falling in gathering heaps. Nearby he saw a desperate Croatian officer shoot his two small children, a boy and a girl, his wife, then himself. Subsequently Raguz escaped back across the Drava, only to be caught up in one of the notorious Partisan 'death marches'. Despite all this, he was one of the fortunate few to survive and tell the tale.

A third eye-witness account will suffice to suggest a scene at which imagination baulks. Marija Ann Levic was a fourteen-year-old schoolgirl who, with her parents and younger sister and brothers, fled Zagreb on Sunday, 6 May. A week later they had reached Bleiburg, and found themselves among the tens – possibly hundreds – of thousands of people assembled in the meadows alongside the road that skirts its northern edge. On the second day Marija was with a group detailed to sweep the road clear with branches in preparation for the arrival of the British. That afternoon two or three British Army jeeps roared past, one of them bearing (so Mrs Levic recalls) a cinecamera apparatus.

Next day at sunset she heard the sound of firing. A scene of appalling confusion followed. At first the majority of people, too hemmed in to have any idea of what was happening, pushed this way and that, asking each other what could be going on. But very

soon the word spread that Partisans were firing from the shelter of
the woods into the heart of the crowd. Those Croatian Army units
which had retained their arms tried to push through and attack their
hidden enemies, while panic-stricken civilians strove vainly to move
away from the shooting. Marija found herself gazing in horror at a
man lying before her on the ground, his intestines hanging from a
great open wound in his stomach. He was screaming for someone to
put him out of his agony. Corpses were piling up all around, and
there, too, beside her was a young man lying prone with the whole
of the back of his head blown off. At every moment the nightmare
grew more ghastly. Cattle and horses panicked and, screaming with
fear or pain, dragged wagons and carts over the bodies of the
fallen.

Marija herself was hit by a bullet in the foot, though fortunately
the wound proved to be slight. Her mother was shrieking and
weeping. The most terrifying aspect of the massacre was the fact that
it was taking place under the broad open sky, with no shelter at
all from the hail of machine-gun fire which splattered unceasingly
backwards and forwards across the stampeding crowd. Their
executioners were nowhere to be seen, at least not in this part of the
field. Marija and her family stumbled across a railway line and
managed to make their way to the side of a hut, where they crouched
all night.

Next morning the sun rose on an appalling spectacle. The whole
field was strewn with bodies, most of them lying in blood-spattered
heaps while others moaned and tried to drag themselves towards the
distant trees: trees which in fact concealed their enemies, who were
still shooting randomly on to the field of the dead. How long her
family remained in their precarious refuge Marija found it difficult
to remember. It was probably two days, and certainly when they
plucked up courage to emerge and escape from the scene of carnage
they were weak from starvation. Marija's two brothers had become
separated in the chaos, but eventually the family was reunited and
managed to trudge back into Yugoslavia.

The few British troops who obtained a glimpse of this massive
tragedy shared the horror of the victims. They were for the most
part Irishmen, who were able to sympathise with the plight of a small
Catholic nation, heir to an ancient culture, passing under the harrow.
Abjanic Bozidar, a Croat present in the crowd on 16 May, 'had a
good view of the returning British soldiers who escorted the first
columns. Many appeared shaken and in disarray, almost as if running

from something that was dreaded and terrifying. Some openly sobbed and cried out: "They killed them . . . they killed them all . . . Oh my God, what have we done?"'

Colin Gunner, then a twenty-two-year-old lieutenant in the Royal Irish Fusiliers, recalls with disgust what he and Lieutenant Hogan, the Battalion machine-gun officer, witnessed that day. They were standing by with a Vickers machine-gun,

watching the Ustashi being driven along to death by Tito's troops. The Ustashi were nominally Jugoslavs and had fought on the German side from the beginning. Now with Tito's Communists triumphant they were to be slaughtered, and I mean slaughtered. The column seemed endless as they were driven over the Drau bridge to the Jugoslav side. Men, women, children and babies in arms, all were starving, but kept moving by Tito's men mounted on ponies and carrying the infamous steel-tipped Cossack whip, the Nagaika, one blow of which will split a man's face open. They were using them freely. I was told that some died on the bridge with Father Dan Kelleher, the Regimental Catholic priest, present, and I shut my mind to think what that wonderful man of God said and thought.

Hogan and I watched impassively until a man in field grey crashed down in the gutter at death's door. Hogan ordered two of his gunners to lay him on the bank, then pushed some rum down him. This revived him somewhat, and Hogan exclaimed 'he's not a Jug – he's a bloody German!' So he was, as the Ustashi troops had a number of German NCOs as instructors. Hogan moved very fast now, and a sign was put at the side of the road in German: 'all German soldiers fall out here.' Hogan must have seemed like Christ the Saviour to several as they fell out and were given a drink of water and a Woodbine.

A Jug officer complete with whip clattered up on his pony and screamed at the resting Germans like an hysterical whore. The Germans turned their eyes to Hogan. The Jug then made the mistake of screaming at Hogan, and brandished his whip. Hogan spoke to the gunner behind the Vickers: 'if this bastard lifts that whip – blow him out of that fucking saddle!'

The gunner elevated the Vickers to aim square at the Jug's belly, and put his thumbs on the triggers. More hysterical screams – then the Jug turned his horse and buggered off. Neither Hogan nor he had understood a word of either's language, but a machine-gun at a range of ten feet needed no interpreter. About 80 Germans were collected in this way and sent back to a British cage.

Hogan and I also stood in a farm doorway when a Bulgar [the Bulgarian Army was assisting Tito's operation] came down the hill on a bicycle and fell off. Picking himself up he saw that his very first bicycle had a bent crank. Picking up a German Panzerfaust rocket from the ditch, he was obviously going to use it to straighten the crank. Hogan smiled happily and said 'I think we'll go behind the house.' This we did, and a shattering roar sent pieces of bicycle and bent Bulgar onto the roof tiles . . . Near the bridge was a German machine-gun emplacement with a loaded Spandau mounted on a tripod. We heard with satisfaction that some Balkan [Titoist] bastard had tripped the trigger, and mown down a group of his chums. The mills of God sometimes grind swiftly.

How many people were massacred in the Bleiburg fields on 15 and 16 May is unknown. To this day farmers in ploughing are continually turning up bones, military insignia, bullets and other grim relics of the two days that saw the end of the independent Croatian nation. On 12 May 1985 I attended a ceremony on the site held by Croatian emigrants to commemorate the fortieth anniversary of their tragedy, and spoke with many survivors of the event. The extent of the slaughter is indisputable, and Croats are understandably bitter in their recriminations not only against Tito's men who perpetrated the massacre, but also in criticism of the British military authorities who, they maintain, colluded in the crime by delivering the defenceless refugees over to their inveterate enemies.

The responsibility of Tito's assassins for their actions is inescapable, but it seems unfair to lay major blame on the British Army for what transpired. Though Brigade command must have learned before long from troops in the field something of what had taken place beyond the shoulder of the hill facing Bleiburg Castle, it seems doubtful whether they appreciated at the time anything like the full extent of the killing. 'A desultory clatter of musketry seemed to be going on in various directions, but I think it was only the "heartening" type, so dear to the Yugoslavs,' wrote Brigadier Scott. 'As far as I was able to see, during the next twenty-four hours, all the arrangements in connection with the surrender and evacuation were carried out by the Yugoslavs speedily and efficiently.'

Other British soldiers present shared Scott's failure to appreciate that a major tragedy was taking place in the immediate vicinity. The Sixteenth Durham Light Infantry arrived as reinforcements at the height of the crisis on 15 May, and their commanding officer, Lieutenant-Colonel Denys Worrall, later recalled a dramatic but surprisingly pacific scene:

I immediately put platoon posts and in some cases company posts, along that part of the Drava where they might cross . . . I remember that I went down with my driver in a jeep to look round the posts to make certain that everything was all right. In the evening this tremendous flood of chaps came down the road, some of them mounted. I didn't know what to do! I went up to a chap and eventually persuaded him to get them to sit down, which they did. There were thousands of them: they weren't hostile at all, but they were armed. They just wanted to surrender to us, but our instructions were that they weren't to. Of course, if they'd really taken a dislike to me I couldn't have stopped them at all. Anyway, they agreed to go back and went back into Yugoslavia.

As for the terms of the surrender to Commissar Basta, they, too, seemed reasonable enough in British eyes, even if there were some suspicion that the event might not prove quite so fair as the promises: 'the Croatian Army was to be treated as prisoners of war with the exception of political criminals, who would be tried by Allied courts, while the civil population were to be fed and returned to Croatia by the shortest route.' This account is confirmed in a personal communication to the author from Professor Danijel Crljen, who with General Herencic negotiated the Croatian surrender in Bleiburg Castle. Basta, he reports, concluded the negotiations with these words:

> We request the unconditional surrender of your entire army, within one hour. If you accept, the women and children may return to their homes. The soldiers and officers will stay as prisoners of war. The officers will be taken to Maribor (a small town in Slovenia) where those who committed a crime will be tried. If you do not accept these terms, within fifteen minutes, a general attack will commence and you will no longer have the right to avail yourselves of the International Conventions of the Red Cross.

To Herencic and Crljen this declaration appeared the ultimate in cynical deception, but few British soldiers at the time were in a position to appreciate the realities of the Yugoslav situation. It has to be remembered that Tito's wartime role as heroic ally ensured that the civil war he was waging within Yugoslavia, with all its accompanying atrocities, was quite unknown to the average British officer, whose appreciation of Tito derived largely from laudatory articles in *Eighth Army News* and who had much more pressing claims on his attention than the intricacies of Balkan politics. The idea that an allied power was planning large-scale slaughter, even genocide, of its fellow-citizens would at this stage have appeared a remote contingency indeed. As Brigadier Scott himself put it, 'it would be difficult for the Yugoslavs to murder such a large number, and it was anyway unlikely that they would want to'. Another British officer told an astounded Croat with apparent sincerity, 'that the Croats would have to be extradited to Yugoslavia, but if they were maltreated in any way, they could file complaints with the British Consul in Zagreb'.[12] One may smile at the extent of such naïvete, but it is essential to understand the circumstances that gave rise to it.

What made Brigadier Scott feel there was no alternative to turning back the Croatian exodus was simply the scale of the migration:

> I asked them [the Croat commanders] how they proposed to feed such a vast multitude in a Europe that was already entirely disorganised and extremely hungry. I told them that an emigration such as this was quite out of the question at the moment. They could not possibly be fed whatever part of Europe they went to, and such an emigration could only take place after careful preparation, otherwise the whole party would undoubtedly starve.[13]

He had reason to believe that one and a half million people were approaching British lines – and this was but the vanguard of what amounted to the flight of a nation. As two distinguished Croatian scholars, editing a compilation of eye-witness accounts of the massacres published in 1970, observe:

> It is important to note, however, that if the first 250,000 Croatians who reached Austria had been given the asylum to which they were entitled under the laws of international warfare, hundreds of thousands of other Croatians would have persevered in their efforts to escape the Marxist tyranny that was being imposed upon their native land.[14]

Brigadier Scott felt considerably less sympathy for the Croats than for the Cossacks, whom he admired. As Count Archie Thurn, an Austrian serving on his staff, recalls, the Brigadier branded the former as Nazi sympathisers, and found their generals with whom he negotiated to be shifty, uneducated 'wogs'.

It seems that General Herencic and his staff were indeed of poor quality, and badly let down if not betrayed the unfortunate people they represented. Herencic himself Scott remembered as 'a decent man, very correct and German in his bearing'. But he was no von Pannwitz, who rejected the idea of escape in order to share his Cossacks' sufferings. Herencic, browbeaten by Scott and Basta, meekly told his troops to lay down their arms in a manner so hasty and ambiguous that many were led to believe that it was to the British they were surrendering.[15] He then abandoned his followers to their fate, choosing for himself the easier escape of suicide.

Herencic and his fellow-generals have in consequence been bitterly criticised by Croatian émigrés. A soldier present afterwards suggested, for example:

> What they should have done at this juncture was lead us in an attack upon the British lines and upon any Communist troops that dared to get in our way. Although the English had planes, tanks, and artillery, I think that we could have penetrated their lines in a night attack and fought our way through into the interior of Austria where we would certainly have had a better chance for survival than we had here on the frontier of Slovenia.[16]

Such an action would have been utterly hopeless from a military point of view, though it is true that it could have resulted in no greater slaughter than that which ensued in reality. With hindsight, the best policy would surely have been to press forward *peacefully* through the thinly-held British line. Doubtless Brigadier Scott would not have hesitated to open fire to prevent this, but it is inconceivable that British troops would have continued an indiscriminate slaughter for any length of time.

This suggestion is not entirely speculative. Four days later, on 19 May, another body of 10,000 Croats was reported to be attempting to force the passage of the Drava north of Ferlach. Nigel Nicolson's log book provides a revealing record of British reactions. At 1850 hours the Third Grenadier Guards were ordered 'NOT to let Croats over . . . br[idge] whatever happens'. Ten minutes later an enquiry came back to the First Guards Brigade headquarters: 'If Croats attempt to rush br[idge], are we to fire?' The reply was swift and uncompromising: '*NOT* to fire at Croats if they attempt to rush br[idge]. (If they have women and children.)'

The crisis had been a dramatic tragedy of major proportions, but its impact on the British was brief. It was on the evening of 13 May that the British military authorities became aware of a large-scale movement of Croats, but it was believed they had surrendered to Tito. Not until next day was it appreciated that their arrival across the line of the Drava was imminent, and improvised measures were hastily adopted to head them back. 'This crisis reached its climax on the 15th,' as Brigadier Scott noted in his War Diary. 'All the arrangements in connection with the surrender and evacuation were carried out speedily, efficiently and, as far as could be judged, correctly over the following 24 hours.'[17]

Decisions arrived at and orders issued by AFHQ at this time were deeply affected from 14 to 16 May by what briefly appeared a dangerous crisis. Shortly after the Chief Administrative Officer issued his order for the handover of Russians and Yugoslavs on the evening of 14 May, Alexander's Chief of Staff, General William Morgan, despatched an urgent message on the same subject to SHAEF headquarters in Germany. In it he appealed for permission to transfer refugees and prisoners of war in the Fifth Corps area to Radstadt in the American zone of Austria:

> Refugee and PW situation in 5 Corps area becoming unmanageable and prejudicing operational efficiency of Corps. essential to clear it immediately in view of political situation. earnestly request your assistance by accepting concentration under your control in Radstadt area or elsewhere more convenient to you. information regarding numbers is not definite but total may be about 500,000. if you agree, request detailed arrangements be made directly with unit designated by you and HQ 5 Corps.[18]

Thus Morgan, in contrast to Robertson, contemplated transferring the refugees to SHAEF authority rather than their surrender to the Soviets and Yugoslavs.

Field-Marshal Alexander must have become informed of these developments at an early stage, and at first glance it appears odd that he should have permitted two apparently contradictory proposals to be issued simultaneously from his headquarters. The explanation, it will readily be supposed, lies in the confusion aroused by the unexpected crisis over the Croats, and the parallel but conflicting orders represent disparate responses to the same problem.

For reasons which can have had nothing to do with the arrival of the Croat exodus (since they predated it), Harold Macmillan was anxious to turn the Cossacks and Yugoslav refugees *already in British hands* over to their enemies. He urged this policy on Keightley, and it was his influence which weighed heavily with Robertson when he came to issue his order authorising the measure.

General Morgan's request to SHAEF, on the other hand, looks as if it represented Alexander's preference. It will be seen in due course how weighty is the evidence demonstrating Alexander's revulsion at the idea of turning helpless prisoners 'over to the Russians and Partisans to be shot', and Morgan's plea was soon to be reinforced by a similar personal appeal from the Field-Marshal to Eisenhower.

Morgan shared his chief's moral objection to maltreatment of refugees or surrendered enemy personnel. In August he was to protest vigorously against the proposed forced repatriation of some Soviet citizens still held in British camps in Italy:

> To compel them to accept repatriation would certainly either involve use of force or drive them into committing suicide. The use of force would probably entail driving them into railway coaches at the point of the bayonet and thereafter locking them in, and possibly also handcuffing a number of them.
>
> . . . such treatment, coupled with the knowledge that these unfortunate individuals are being sent to an almost certain death, is quite out of keeping with traditions of democracy and justice as we know them. Furthermore it is most unlikely that the British soldier, knowing the fate to which these people are being committed will be a willing participant in measures required to compel their departure.[19]

As far as the Yugoslavs were concerned the position was clearer still: the British and American Governments had informed the Supreme Allied Commander at the beginning of the month that Allied policy was to retain all Yugoslavs as surrendered enemy personnel. Their ultimate disposal would be decided by the Combined Chiefs of Staff, who had not yet been approached on the matter.

Nevertheless General Robertson would not have issued his order without possessing at least the tacit approval of the Supreme Allied Commander; and it may be asked why, if Alexander's objections to the proposed forced repatriation were as strong on 14 May as they were to prove on the seventeenth, he did not at once countermand the instruction. Its text referred, after all, not to the feared advent of the 200,000 Croats poised on the Drava, but to Yugoslavs already in British hands. The answer appears to be that a misconception of dramatic proportions became briefly current at AFHQ at this time, and that this resulted in a faulty appraisal of the situation.

On 15 May, the day after Robertson transmitted his order requiring the handover of Cossacks and Yugoslavs, Field-Marshal Alexander despatched the following message to the Eighth Army for transmission to Marshal Tito:

> From AFHQ. signed Sacmed cite FHDSC
> Action MACMIS rptd 15 Army Group Main 8 Army
> FX 75902. Top Secret Pass following to Marshal Tito. Quote.
> Commander of Allied troops in Austria reports that approximately 200,000 Jugoslav nationals who were serving in German armed forces

surrendered to him. We should like to turn these over immediately to Marshal Tito's forces and would be grateful if Marshal Tito would agree to instruct his Commanders to accept them and to arrange with GOC Five Corps the rate at which they can be received and handing-over point on Austrian frontier south of Klagenfurt for return to Jugoslavia.

The message was presented to Tito the following day (16 May) by Air Vice Marshal Lee, Alexander's representative with the Yugoslav General Staff. The day after that, 17 May, Tito requested Lee to thank Alexander for his signal, going on to declare that:

> The Marshal is in full agreement with Field Marshal Alexander's proposals and thanks him for them.
> The 200,000 Jugoslavs will be taken over by the 3rd. Army H.Q. who have received instructions to this effect.
> Will you kindly inform us where our delegates for the reception of the prisoners are to meet the delegates appointed by Field Marshal Alexander for the handing over.[20]

At first glance this correspondence appears singularly futile. The overwhelming majority of the 200,000 Yugoslavs (i.e. the Croats) had not surrendered to Keightley, who had given strict instructions that in no circumstances should they be allowed to do so.

On the evening of 16 May the Fifth Corps notified Eighth Army: 'No record of any report by this HQ that 200,000 Yugoslav nationals surrendered to the Fifth Corps. our 0413 of 13 [May] asked permission to accept their surrender but other arrangements successfully made subsequently.' The Eighth Army in turn passed a corrective report up to AFHQ.[21]

The misunderstanding presumably arose from McCreery's report of 14 May, in which he alerted the Fifteenth Army Group to the approach of the 300,000 Germans and 200,000 Croats, explaining that he had issued emergency authorisation to Keightley 'to take over formed bodies and disarm them as they cross the border . . . Please ask AFHQ to ask Tito how many enemy he eventually wishes to retain. Suggest Croats become Tito's show.'[22]

This not only explains Alexander's offer to return the Croats to Tito, but possibly also his brief acquiescence in the last section of Robertson's order of 14 May instructing Eighth Army that: 'all surrendered personnel of established Yugoslav nationality who were serving in German forces should be disarmed and handed over to Yugoslav forces'.

Indeed, it seems unlikely that Robertson or Alexander was apprised at this stage of the distinction between the approaching mass exodus of Croats, and the far smaller body of Yugoslav refugees whose surrender had already been accepted by Fifth Corps at this time. To what extent the misunderstanding represented genuine error, and to what extent deception profiting from it, is hard to assess.

On 14 May Toby Low sent the Fifth Corps message to McCreery urging compliance with Macmillan's recommendation that the Cossacks be returned to the Soviets. Eight lines are devoted to this issue, but there was no reference at all to the Yugoslavs in Viktring Camp and elsewhere within the Corps area. It looks a little as if the omission was deliberate, since the report goes out of its way to list refugees in the Corps area as 'German, Austrian or Russian'.

The only reference at all to anti-Communist Yugoslavs in Low's message is to '600000 ['surrendered personnel and refugees'] reported moving north to Austria from Yugoslavia'; i.e. the retreating German Army Group E, with its accompanying 200,000 Croats. News of their approach had arrived that day.

Thus when Robertson accepted Macmillan's recommendation 'to turn over to Yugoslav Partisans a large number of dissident Yugoslav troops', and in consequence ordered that 'all surrendered personnel of established Yugoslav nationality who were serving in German forces should be disarmed and handed over to Yugoslav forces', it looks much as if he was subject to the same misunderstanding that deceived Alexander at this time. The only Yugoslav refugees of whom he was informed were the 200,000 Croats, and in consequence it was surely they to whom his order was intended to apply. He could scarcely have had in mind those already in Corps custody, who had by then been 'disarmed', and of whose existence he does not appear to have been informed.

As the Croats had not 'surrendered' to the British they could not be 'handed over', and Alexander's offer to Tito was in consequence inoperative. It was to effect this non-existent 'surrender' that Robertson's order seems to have been intended in reality, only to be employed for a very different purpose: that of extraditing thousands of Yugoslavs at Viktring Camp and elsewhere: groupings to which Toby Low had made no allusion in the message to which Robertson's order was the response.

It was a major misconception which led the Supreme Allied Commander and his Chief Administrative Officer to believe that the approaching Croats had actually surrendered to the Fifth Corps. Its effect was predictable. The absorption of 200,000 Croats into the Fifth Corps area could not under any circumstances have been envisaged at the time as a viable policy by AFHQ. Alexander, told that they had actually surrendered to the Fifth Corps, at once offered to return them to Tito. This involved a violation of existing instructions, but as was later pointed out, 'while Supreme Allied Commander of course seeks the advice of his political advisers on all occasions he must reserve unto himself right to decide matters of an urgent military nature as he sees fit'.[23]

The belief that, at a time of maximum difficulty, British troops had involuntarily accepted the surrender of 200,000 ex-enemy troops and refugees must indeed have appeared as a 'matter of an urgent military nature'. On the other hand one could scarcely apply that consideration to the purpose for which Robertson's order was employed in reality: the leisurely handover, at a time when the crisis had passed, of a few thousand refugees peacefully established in British camps.

All this suggests that someone had ingeniously succeeded in eliciting from AFHQ an order of broad general application, employed for a specific and quite other purpose from that for which it was intended.

At Fifth Corps no time was lost in making use of General Robertson's order. Next morning a Partisan Commissar, Hocevar, met Toby Low in conference at headquarters in Klagenfurt. After discussing administrative points at issue between their two armies, they proceeded to the matter currently at issue. As Low reported afterwards:

> Immediately I found out that Lt. Col. Hocevar was in comd of 14 Div as well as old 4 Army tps, I raised the question of the situation around Bleiburg. He stated that he knew of our action there, and was most grateful. His intention was that the Croats should be bottled up in the pass leading into Austria, and later disarmed. He said that the Yugoslav tps facing the Croats near Bleiburg would not be moved south into Yugoslavia, and I said that the Corps Commander had given orders to our tps not to cross the border.
>
> We assumed that the Yugoslavs could deal with Croats in that area and would guard and disarm them. If any of them escaped into Austria we would guard them, disarm them, put them in a camp, and later return them to Yugoslavia. Lt. Col. Hocevar agreed to this.[24]

The story of the tragic events which arose from this agreement must be reserved for a later chapter. By the next day, 16 May, the confrontation at Bleiburg had ended, as the mass of disarmed and

terrified Croats was shepherded back into Yugoslavia. But if the
crisis had passed unexpectedly smoothly on the ground in Austria,
there may have been those at AFHQ in Caserta who found matters
taking a temporarily awkward turn.

It will be recalled that on the afternoon of 14 May General Robertson, following Macmillan's recommendation that he issue an order
covering the forced repatriation of Cossacks and Yugoslavs, had
approached the United States political representative, Alexander C.
Kirk, in the hope that he would lend his authority to the proposed
order. Kirk however refused, to Robertson's disappointment, declaring that he could not concur without referring the matter to
his Government. Despite this, secure in the approval of Harold
Macmillan, Robertson issued his order.

If Robertson really expected Kirk to approve such a move, then
he seems to have had little understanding of the man with whom
he was dealing. Possibly he shared Macmillan's estimate of Kirk's
intellectual powers. To his diary the Minister confided that he had
decided, 'Kirk (who has a purely destructive mind) . . . is a clever,
but strange – even unnatural – man. A millionaire, a dilettante –
and an intellectual snob. But he is kind, generous and occasionally
amusing. He has a mind, but does not apply it to any creative
purpose.'[25]

Kirk was, however, a man of considerable integrity. As George
Kennan, who served with him at the wartime Berlin Embassy,
recalled:

> Unintellectual as he was, his instincts were very sound; and when one
> learned enough to see through the poses and to look for the deeper
> meaning of the quips, he was a good teacher . . . when he left Berlin, it
> may have been Kirk who was in my debt when it came to administration
> of the embassy, but it was I who was in his debt when it came to personal,
> and even political, philosphy.

Kirk had in fact the best of experience when it came to understanding
how totalitarian regimes were likely to deal with their opponents,
for he had also been chargé d'affaires at the Moscow Embassy during
the show trials of the late Thirties.[26]

Now he was horrified by the cold-blooded proposal to hand over
thousands of people 'to the Russians and Partisans to be shot'. Since
the problem first arose he had made clear his opposition to the forced
return of any Russians,[27] and only twelve days before Robertson's

visit he had been informed by the US Acting Secretary of State that it was his Government's policy to compel no one to return to Yugoslavia except proven war criminals.

Kirk at once telegraphed Washington a detailed account of Robertson's visit, requesting instructions as to how he should respond. The Acting Secretary of State, Joseph Grew, replied as follows on the following evening, 15 May:

> We believe that no distinction should be made between Chetniks and other dissident Yugoslav troops (URTEL 2162, May 14) and that our position with respect to anti-Partisan or dissident Yugoslav troops in general, in agreement with that of the British Foreign Office and in accordance with Macmillan's recommendation, is clearly set forth in DEPTEL 424, May 2.
>
> Accordingly your refusal to concur in Robertson's telegram is approved and you are requested to inform SAC [Supreme Allied Commander] that we are strongly of the opinion that such contemplated violation of agreed Anglo-American policy cannot be justified on grounds of administrative expediency.
>
> The Department assumes that the 28,000 Cossacks in question are Soviet nationals and, if so, no objection is seen to delivering them to the Russian forces in accordance with the terms of the Yalta agreement. If any are in the category of persons provided for in Section D of Department's 279 of March 31 [i.e. not Soviet citizens] they should not be repatriated to the Soviet Union unless they affirmatively claim Soviet citizenship.
>
> Grew[28]

Thus the State Department ruled, predictably, that no Yugoslavs should be returned, and that only Soviet citizens among the Cossacks were liable to repatriation. This, as has been seen, was also the British viewpoint and represented official Allied policy.

Kirk wasted no time in transmitting this ruling to the appropriate quarters: to Macmillan himself; to Alexander's Chief of Staff, General William Morgan; to General Robertson; and to the Military Government Section concerned with administering refugee camps. It is not certain precisely when he did this, but it seems unlikely that he delayed matters beyond the morning of 16 May, Grew's message having arrived the night before.[29]

Whether the Supreme Allied Commander (SACMED), Field-Marshal Alexander, was already aware of General Robertson's despatch of the order of the fourteenth empowering the Eighth Army to hand over Yugoslavs and Cossacks is unknown. Now, though, he was alerted and began to display concern in the issue. To understand the basis of his reaction and subsequent actions it is necessary to appreciate something of his character and background.

During the hectic weeks following the German capitulation it was upon his capable shoulders that responsibility for the administration of occupied Austria fell. Though it has been claimed that he lacked the innovatory stratetic genius of a Montgomery or a Patton, Alex nevertheless possessed unique qualities which made him one of the best-loved and most respected commanders of World War Two.

Born in 1891, he came of an old landed family in Northern Ireland which had been ennobled in the eighteenth century. The third son of the fourth Earl of Caledon, he took up that traditional career of the younger sons of peers, the Army. In the Great War he served in the trenches with the Irish Guards, and swiftly acquired a reputation for imperturbability under fire. Indeed, his men believed him to bear a charmed existence (so Winston Churchill used to tell in later years), surreptitiously treading in his footsteps when crossing no-man's-land in order to share his luck.

When the fighting ended he felt disinclined to accept the tedium of peace-time soldiering, and volunteered to join the staff of Lieutenant-Colonel Stephen Tallents, British Commissioner in the Baltic. The Great War was over, but civil war was raging in Russia. The Bolsheviks had unleashed a reign of terror in the Baltic States, whose inhabitants were trying to establish their national independence. Though Germany had officially surrendered, German troops under General von der Goltz were assisting the Balts (many of whom were of German descent) in their resistance. But with the signing of the Treaty of Versailles on 28 June it was time for the dangerous von der Goltz to go. This Tallents swiftly arranged, and it was the twenty-eight-year-old Major Harold Alexander who replaced him as commander of the Baltic Landeswehr, or defence force. It was in part due to his firm leadership that Bolshevik aggression was halted, in recognition of which he received from the White Russian General Yudenich the Tsarist Order of St Anne with Crossed Swords.

When World War Two broke out Alexander had risen to the rank of major-general, and once again his qualities of courage and coolness in the face of adversity made him an invaluable leader in those initial days of disaster. He supervised the evacuation at Dunkirk, where he was among the last to leave the beaches and commanded the rearguard during the withdrawal from Burma. Finally he was rewarded with the supreme command in North Africa, leading to ultimate triumph in Italy.

It is doubtful if Alexander ever had a personal enemy. His charm was irresistible, and he could persuade the most irreconcilable of adversaries to work harmoniously in a team. His American colleagues considered him 'the ablest of British generals in the Mediterranean theatre of war'. General Omar Bradley thought him 'a general's general'. The Chief of the Imperial General Staff, Sir Alan Brooke, declared him 'charming to deal with, always ready to do what was requested of him, never scheming or pulling strings. A soldier of the very highest principles.'

No one admired Alexander with greater enthusiasm than Churchill. What attracted him even more than Alexander's abilities as a leader was his utter integrity. As Churchill's physician, the perceptive Charles Moran, noted:

> Winston was not given to hero-worship of his contemporaries, and I was puzzled at the time by his affectionate admiration for Alex. It seems that Alex had been able to confirm what Winston had always felt about war. It is fashionable, of course, to subscribe to the belief that war is uncivilized, and Winston, like other politicians, had to make concessions to this popular sentiment. But he has an honest mind, and he knows that from the tremendous moment when he escaped from the Boers to the wonderful years of 1940 and 1941 the greatest thrills that he can recall have all been bound up with war.
>
> To him it was a romantic calling, the highest man could embrace, but it was a game for gentlemen, which had to be played according to the rules. What he loved in Alex was that he had justified his own feelings about war, tried them out in the field and made sense of them. Alex had redeemed what was brutal in war, touching the grim business lightly with his glove. In his hands it was still a game for people of quality. He had shown that war could still be made respectable.
>
> There were, of course, plenty of toughs in the Army, whose peace of mind came from a certain vacancy which has always passed for courage; in them freedom from fear was the outcome of the slow working of their minds, the torpor of their imagination. But Winston drew a clear line between Alex's gallant bearing and the blind courage of a man like Gort. 'Dainty', 'jaunty' and 'gay' were the terms he chose for his knight errant as he flitted across the sombre scene. Here Winston's instinct was sound.[30]

Alexander's talents were ideally fitted to preside over the chaos and confusion that were the inevitable consequences of his victory. From bending almost every thought to the dominant problem of defeating the most formidable of enemies, he was suddenly faced with tasks so multifarious and perplexing as to challenge the resolve of the most capable commander.

In Greece troops from his command were assisting the government to defend its precarious existence against Communist insurgents. In Venezia Giulia and Carinthia British-occupied territory had been infiltrated by Marshal Tito's truculent followers, and within a week it seemed that the Anglo-American command might find itself at war with revolutionary Yugoslavia – possibly (so it was briefly feared) – backed by the victorious Red Army. In Austria the zone for which he was responsible bordered on that occupied by Soviet forces, with whom he was obliged to negotiate concerning a still-fluid border. With the war over and soldiers of all ranks aching to get out of uniform and return home, he had to maintain his armies at the highest pitch of military preparedness and morale – if necessary to fight a new and bloody war against Tito, who until the previous week had been lauded as the most gallant of allies.

As if this were not enough, Allied Force headquarters (AFHQ) was ultimately responsible for the sustenance of a civil population in countries whose economies had been largely destroyed by war. Among them, too, swarmed untold hordes of displaced people wandering homeless in the wake of five years of total war. About a million German soldiers had been taken prisoner, who now required feeding and guarding. And there were the refugees pouring in from the east, fleeing in panic before the advancing Communist armies.

Such a man as Alexander was unlikely to condone, let alone initiate, any dishonourable action towards prisoners of war. As his former Chief of Staff and close friend, Field-Marshal Harding, once emphasised to me, Alexander was pre-eminently concerned with what he termed 'the etiquette of war'. Now that Kirk had placed the issue squarely before him, could it really be expected that he would permit the consignment of thousands of surrendered Cossacks and Yugoslavs to what in Macmillan's words was 'slavery, torture and probably death'? For that was undoubtedly what would happen were Robertson's order to be put into effect.

Harold Macmillan must also surely have been deeply disturbed by Kirk's sudden interference. Had all gone as might reasonably have been expected, Robertson's order should have ensured the repatriation of all Cossacks and Yugoslavs within the next few days. Now the tactless Kirk might bring a hornet's nest about his ears. Not only was Alexander fully alerted to the sinister ambiguity of Robertson's order, but in addition the State Department might very likely take up this radical divergence in Allied policy with the Foreign Office in London, which had approved neither of the brutal operations envisaged by the initiators of the measure.

It was seen in the last chapter how Macmillan, following his return from consulting Eighth Army commanders in northern Italy and Austria, sent a report on his mission to the Foreign Office. In it he gave a full account of his meeting with Generals McCreery and Harding, but omitted all mention of his unplanned extended journey to visit Keightley at Klagenfurt. It was that afternoon, 14 May, that General Robertson made his unsuccessful attempt to induce Kirk to add his support to that of Macmillan in ordering the return of Cossacks and Yugoslavs. It seems likely in the circumstances that Robertson would have reported this unexpected (Kirk noted his 'disappointment') rebuff to Macmillan.

Next day Macmillan telegraphed the Foreign Office an account of that meeting with Keightley which had been unaccountably omitted from his original report. Its contents make curious reading: 'I made a brief flying visit to General Keightley at Headquarters 5th Corps at Klagenfurt in Carinthia.' The five ensuing paragraphs summarise Keightley's view of the Fifth Corps' position with regard to the Partisans and the Soviet and Bulgarian armies. One passage alone treats of that matter which Macmillan's diary records as comprising so prominent a part of their discussion, causing Macmillan to call at Treviso for a renewed consultation with McCreery. It reads in its entirety as follows: 'In North [*sic*] Carinthia there is a pocket of some 30 Cossacks including women and children.'[31]

Here the '40,000 Cossacks and White Russians, with their wives and children' of Macmillan's diary entry (written at this very time) have been reduced to thirty, and the fact (also confided to his diary) that 'we have decided to hand them over' is omitted altogether. As for the Yugoslavs, for whom Macmillan expressed such deep sympathy in his diary but whose forced return to the Partisans he had urged on Robertson . . . they receive no mention at all!

The omission can only be deliberate, and designed to prevent the Foreign Office from discovering what was intended. Macmillan had, after all, ten days earlier received instructions from the Foreign Office not to hand over any Yugoslavs. Under any normal circumstances a proposal to reverse existing policy in so dramatic a respect must have been a matter for extensive comment. Many of the Cossacks, as he knew, were not Soviet citizens, and on 5 August 1944 the Foreign

Office had drawn his attention to this specific problem, instructing him at the same time that 'any difficulties which arise should be reported'.

One might ask why Macmillan made the apparently absurd reference to 'thirty' Cossacks, when he might as easily have omitted allusion to them altogether? Could it be he felt that reference to so tiny a number would be unlikely to arouse Foreign Office interest, but at the same time prove if necessary that he had reported their presence? The grotesquely reduced figure could always be ascribed to an error in transmission of the telegram.

The question of the Yugoslav refugees was less readily disposed of. *No* Yugoslavs – so Foreign Office policy laid down – were liable to involuntary return. Were the Foreign Office to learn even of the existence of the refugee population in the Fifth Corps area, it was likely they might draw attention in some way to the ruling, now that its implementation had at last become a practical issue.

Even the 'unflappable' Macmillan may have felt some trepidation during the forty-eight hours of 15 and 16 May. True, the majority of the Cossacks appeared ultimately doomed by the Yalta Agreement, whatever the Field-Marshal's reservations; but every day that passed before their return made it more likely that AFHQ would discover the presence of the Tsarist officers whom the Soviets were anxious above all to acquire, and whose delivery Macmillan had secretly impressed upon Keightley. And now the Bleiburg crisis was over, would not Kirk's interference lead Alexander to revoke an order whose wording made it applicable to Yugoslavs whom it was contrary to Allied policy to repatriate?

Alexander's actions show that he began at once to concern himself with the matter. On 17 May, the day after Kirk's protest, he sent the following firm ruling to General McCreery at the Eighth Army:

> Chetniks and dissident Jugoslavs infiltrating into areas occupied by Allied troops should be treated as disarmed enemy troops and evacuated to British concentration area in Distone. Total numbers including eleven thousand already in Distone believed about thirty five thousand.
>
> Eighth Army will keep Distone informed of approximate numbers being thus evacuated.
>
> Question of final disposal is being taken up by AFHQ.

Next day Alexander Kirk reported the text of this order to the State Department, and assumed thenceforward that there would be no further infringements of Allied policy in this regard.[32]

There was nothing equivocal about Alexander's attitude. The Croats had departed, and the exceptional (though as it turned out, superfluous) offer he had made to Tito could be permanently rescinded. As Kirk was informed later:

> Supreme Allied Commander took his decision because of conditions existing of which he was better aware than [US State] Dept . . . in view of divergent political views expressed to him on subject, by Resident Minister [Macmillan] and ourselves, Supreme Allied Commander suspended transfer of dissident troops as soon as emergency conditions ceased to exist.[33]

It is also clear that Alexander adopted a similarly firm approach to the proposed repatriation of Cossacks. In their case no order comparable to that of 17 May halting the handover of Yugoslavs is to be found in the appropriate files, but a parallel instruction with similar intent must surely have been issued by AFHQ at about the same time. For on 21 May the Eighth Army was to despatch a telegram to AFHQ 'asking for policy re Cossacks',[34] an action scarcely necessary were the order of 14 May regarded as still effective.

Having, as he believed, overruled the dual repatriation order of 14 May, Alexander turned at the same time to the question of finding a permanent solution to the problem of the prisoners. On 14 May his Chief of Staff, General Morgan, had requested SHAEF to accept refugees and prisoners of war from some half a million held in the British zone of Austria. This was at the moment the Croat crisis began to blow up. On 16 May SHAEF headquarters replied, regretting that such a move was impossible in view of similarly chaotic conditions in the American zone of Austria.[35]

Now, however, on the seventeenth Alexander despatched a lengthy personal telegram to his friend General Eisenhower at SHAEF headquarters in Germany, requesting assistance in maintenance and disposal of some 220,000 prisoners held in Austria. There were 109,000 Germans, 46,000 Cossacks, 15,000 Hungarians, 25,000 Croats and 24,000 Slovenes. With the possibility of imminent war with Yugoslavia, Alexander explained that he could not look after these multitudes and function on an efficient military basis at the same time. He had not the resources in Italy to feed them, and their removal southwards would in any case clog up his line of communication into Austria. He could look after the Croat, Slovene, Hungarian and

Austrian prisoners, but implored Eisenhower to receive the Germans and Cossacks into his area. Otherwise, 'The only alternative is that as a matter of operational and administrative necessity I shall be compelled to disband them, which would produce confusion in contiguous German territory under your command.'

Eisenhower, however, foresaw no serious difficulties in acceding to Alexander's request. The 109,000 Germans (who were due to return home anyway) and 46,000 Cossacks represented a more tolerable burden than the half-million refugees mentioned in Morgan's message. He replied to Alexander two days later: 'In order further to assist any possible operations by A.F.H.Q. forces in Austria against Jugoslavs, we are willing to accept the enemy personnel mentioned above in the status of "disarmed enemy forces".' So far as supply was concerned, 'rationing will be the responsibility of German/Austrian authorities using indigenous food stocks.'[36] To Churchill, who had written supporting Alexander's plea, Eisenhower replied on the same day: 'we are already doing everything we can to help out Alexander, including an offer to take over some of the prisoners.'[37]

Thus it can be seen that, despite the appalling logistical problems facing him, Alexander did not at this stage contemplate what others might have considered the tempting alternative of delivering the Yugoslavs and Cossacks to Tito and Stalin. Implicit, too, seems to have been a determination to resist any proposed forced repatriation of the Cossacks, considering he well knew (a point Kirk was obliged to concede) that he was already required to do so under the terms of the Yalta Agreement.

Alexander's real feelings are revealed still more explicitly in a further telegram despatched the same day (17 May) as his appeal to Eisenhower. This time he addressed himself to the Combined Chiefs of Staff. As it was for them to provide him with a directive, he was at pains to stress the humanitarian aspect of the problem – despite the fact that someone had misled him into believing that all the Cossacks had fought against the Allies. The 25,000 refugees commanded by General Domanov in the Drautal around Lienz had never fought anyone, unless some defensive skirmishes against Italian Communist Partisans around Tolmezzo counted as combating the Allies. He wrote:

To assist us in clearing congestion in Southern Austria we urgently require direction regarding final disposal following three classes:-
(a) Approximately 50,000 Cossacks including 11,000 women, children

and old men. These have been part of German armed forces and fighting against Allies.

(b) Chetniks whose numbers are constantly increasing. Present estimate of total 35,000 of which we have already evacuated 11,000 to Italy.

(c) German Croat troops total 25,000.

In each of above cases to return them to their country of origin immediately might be fatal to their health. Request decision as early as possible as to final disposal.[38]

Next day (18 May) the Combined Chiefs of Staff Committee met to consider Alexander's request. Sir Andrew Cunningham, First Sea Lord, suggested that Alexander be instructed to hand over the Cossacks to the Soviets, as 'under the Yalta Agreement, they would in any event have to be repatriated to Russia'. No decision was arrived at, however, and the Foreign Office and War Office were invited to examine Alexander's message 'as a matter of urgency, and to advise on the reply to be sent to Field Marshal Alexander'.

By 26 May the Foreign Office had a carefully-considered reply ready:

(a) *Cossacks.* We agree with the J[oint] S[taff] M[ission] that the Cossacks are covered by the Yalta agreement on the reciprocal repatriation of Soviet citizens and accordingly consider it essential that all of them who are Soviet citizens should be handed over to the Soviet authorities in pursuance of our general policy. If we did not do so in the case of these particular people it would be a breach of the agreement and might look like a change of policy in this matter to which the Soviet Government attach great importance and would be assumed by the Russians to indicate hostile intentions towards them. It might also have very unfortunate reactions upon the Russian treatment of our prisoners of war uncovered by them. We suggest that Field Marshal Alexander should make arrangements with Marshal Tolbukhin for the handing over of the Cossacks across the temporary occupational demarcation line.

(b) *Cetniks.* We agree with the J.S.M. that the Cetniks in Southern Austria should be dealt with in the same way as the Cetniks in Venezia Giulia: that is to say they should not be handed over to Tito's forces or returned to Yugoslavia but should be disarmed and interned, pending a final decision on their disposal by the British and United States Governments. We realise that it may be of some embarrassment to 15th Army Group to arrange for the removal of the large numbers of these Cetniks to Italy; but we could not in present circumstances agree to the Cetnik troops being handed over to Tito. (It is not of course possible at this stage to give any ruling on the final disposal of the Cetniks.)

(c) *Croats.* The Croat troops are, in our opinion, in rather a different position from the Cetniks. They are the armed forces of the Croat puppet state set up by the Germans, and, although we never recognised the establishment of the Croat State, the Croat troops are in effect the regular forces of a quisling government operating under German direction. There would be less justification than in the case of the Cetniks for regarding them as irregular forces who have been taking part in a Yugoslav civil war. We should therefore be in favour of handing the Croat troops in Austria over to Tito's forces. Such a move would certainly please Tito and would show him that in some matters at any rate we are willing to treat him as a regular and responsible Ally. We realise, however, that the United States Government might well not be willing to agree to this rather drastic course, which, as Field Marshal Alexander points out, might be fatal to the health of the Croat troops. If the United States Government do not like our recommendations, we are willing to agree that the Croats be treated in the same way as the Cetniks.

The Chiefs of Staff Committee approved these proposals, which they passed on to the Joint Staff Mission, noting that: 'The Americans might possibly object to a policy of handing over all Croats to Tito, in spite of the fact that 900 had already been transferred. In that case we ought to consider whether Croats should not be treated in the same way as the Cetniks, pending final decision on their disposal.'

Predictably the Americans *did* object, and the Joint Staff Mission in Washington 'Pointed out . . . that there is as yet no agreed policy that collaborationists and members of para-military organisations of Allied Nationality should be handed over to their respective authorities . . .' and 'Drew attention to the fact that it has been agreed between the U.S. and British Governments that anti-partisan Yugoslav forces, specifically including Croatians, Ustachi, and Slovenian White Guard, should be disarmed and placed in refugee camps. State Department agreement to this was reported in Embassy's 3123 of 3 May to Foreign Office.'

At this stage a new factor was introduced as a result of a report from Alexander dated 26 May, announcing that the handover of the Cossacks (who were in any case covered by the Yalta Agreement) was in process of arrangement. By 11 June the Combined Chiefs of Staff were in possession of all the relevant facts, and draft instructions were drawn up. As a result of these lengthy consultations it was not until 20 June that Alexander received an authoritative reply to his enquiry of 17 May:

    1. With regard to NAF 975 [Alexander's enquiry], the action already

taken by you with respect to the transfer of Cossacks overland to Soviet Military authorities as reported in your 0-5659 of 26th May 1945 is approved.

2. It is not possible to give you any decision at this time concerning final disposal of the Chetniks and German Croat troops. This matter is presently under consideration by the U.S. and British Governments. For the time being, however, you will continue to retain such personnel in your custody and to handle them in accordance with existing instructions of the Department of State and British Foreign Office to their respective representatives in Italy [Kirk and Macmillan].[39]

It can be seen that this directive simply confirmed policy made known to Alexander and Macmillan at the beginning of May; viz. that the Soviet citizens among the Cossacks were in no different position from any other Soviet citizens held by Anglo-American forces, and were therefore liable to return regardless of their wishes; and that *no* Yugoslavs (other than those individually indicted of war crimes) were to be returned against their will, despite the fact that it had been learned that 900 Croats had already been sent back (presumably through some administrative error). The position had in fact been clear throughout, and there was no ambiguity at any stage in the rulings.

One might well ask why in that case Alexander troubled to approach the Chiefs of Staff at all. As indicated earlier, the most plausible explanation must be that he hoped for reconsideration of what he deemed to be an inhuman policy. The two Cossack units in his care were military units whose surrender had been honourably accepted by forces under his command. At the time of their surrender, on 12 May, AFHQ had informed the Soviet authorities that 'the disposal of Soviet citizens will continue to be regulated in accordance with the present agreements between the United States, British and Soviet Governments;'[40] i.e. the Yalta Agreement. But rather than allow himself to be compelled to apply that blanket ruling to the specific case of the Cossacks, for whom he felt such strong personal sympathy and whose fate if handed over was so predictable, Alexander would at least oblige the British and American Governments to consider the implications of their ruling.

In practical terms the protracted discussion between the Foreign Office, State Department and Combined Chiefs of Staff was irrelevant to the fate of the Cossacks and Yugoslavs held by the Fifth Corps, since their disposal had been decided long before the Combined Chiefs' ruling of 20 June. What it does make clear, though, is

that the Cossacks were not sent back (as Macmillan now claims) as
the result of a ruling by the Combined Chiefs of Staff. Nor had the
Foreign Office or State Department approved the move. Short of
some secret communication of which no trace has survived, it is
therefore clear that no governmental authority outside AFHQ played
any part in arriving at the decision to repatriate the Cossacks made
at AFHQ in the latter half of May.

Throughout the relevant period the position of the British and
American Governments, and of the Combined Chiefs of Staff (the
only body empowered to issue policy instructions to the Supreme
Allied Commander in the Mediterranean), is absolutely clear, and
stands as follows:

The Cossacks. No instructions for their delivery to the Soviets were
issued to Alexander before 20 June. However, the majority who were
Soviet citizens were held to be liable for return regardless of choice
under the interpretation of the Yalta Agreement. Alexander could,
had he wished, have invoked the Agreement as authority for repatriation without seeking further instructions. But, as we know from
his appeal of 17 May to the Combined Chiefs, Alexander did not so
wish; on the contrary, he thought any proposal to surrender the
Cossacks dishonourable and inhumane (so his singling out the large
number of women and children, and the allusion to handover being
'fatal' to their health clearly imply), and one for which he would not
take direct responsibility. In any case, one vitally important aspect
of the policy remained fixed throughout, and that was that the
Cossacks had to be screened before repatriation in accordance with
rigid criteria of citizenship.

The Yugoslavs. Here again the policy was consistent throughout,
and the Combined Chiefs' policy decision of 20 June accorded with
Alexander's viewpoint. All persons of Yugoslav nationality in British
custody were to be disarmed and placed in refugee camps. Their
forcible repatriation was never at any time contemplated as a viable
Allied policy. During the crisis of 14 to 16 May, when it had seemed
that the resources of the Fifth Corps would be overwhelmed by the
irruption of anything up to one and a half million Croats, Alexander
had approved their expulsion eastwards. But on 17 May, the moment
the danger had passed, he overruled Robertson's instruction of 14
May and issued orders to ensure that no further Yugoslavs were
handed over.

Officially, then, the émigré Cossacks (the 'White Russians' of
Macmillan's diary entry) and Yugoslav refugees should have been

safe from compulsory repatriation. The British and United States Governments declared they could not be handed over against their will, and the Supreme Allied Commander in the Mediterranean issued orders strictly forbidding their forcible return. Anyone wishing to flout those orders would have to proceed very carefully and skilfully indeed.

6

The Surrender of the Yugoslavs

'Do you think it possible we can be betrayed?'
'It is possible.'
'And what then?'
'If the moral and political wisdom of the so-called civilised and Christian West is of such a kind, then God help Europe and the world.'
(Colonel Tatalovic, in response to a Chetnik staff officer's queries, 24 May 1945)

By the middle of May Tito had established sufficient control over the frontier hinterland in Carinthia and Slovenia to prevent any further large-scale influx of refugees into British-occupied Austria. The panic-stricken flight of a large section of the Croat population had been halted by Brigadier Scott, employing a mixture of bluff and force, at Bleiburg. Turned back from the line of the River Drava, up to a quarter of a million Croats found themselves at Tito's mercy. Communist troops and political police set to work perpetrating massacres which in scale exceeded the most terrible atrocities committed during four years of war and occupation. At the same time Tito's gaze was turned covetously towards those thousands of refugees who remained for the moment safely protected by British tanks and guns.

By 15 May the Fifth Corps had more or less succeeded in stabilising a refugee problem which over the previous forty-eight hours had appeared on the point of overwhelming them. The Drava provided an effective demarcation line, and strong measures were adopted to hold back sizeable bodies of Croats desperately striving to break through at this last moment. South of the river Croatian Army units continued fighting for several days, inflicting severe losses on the Partisans. Demoralised and outnumbered, they eventually succumbed and joined their compatriots on the 'death marches', during which tens of thousands of people are known to have been killed. Attempts to force the British lines were foiled 'by removing the decking-boards from one bridge and blowing up another'.[1]

The gates had been firmly closed, but only after thousands of Croats had managed to ensconce themselves within. Large numbers had evaded returning with those of their compatriots who had been turned back at Bleiburg, while others had swarmed across at different points along the frontier. Unknown numbers had gone to ground in the countryside, while the remainder were dispersed in prisoner-of-war camps at Griffen, Rosegg, Klagenfurt, Tamsweg and elsewhere.[2] The Sixth Armoured Division held an estimated 11,000 at this time, with more in the Forty-sixth Infantry Divisional area.[3]

If these people thought they were safe, they were speedily to be disabused of the idea. On the same day that Brigadier Scott turned back the main body of Croats at Bleiburg, Brigadier Low at Corps headquarters had agreed with the Partisan Colonel Hocevar, 'If any of them escaped into Austria we would guard them, disarm them, put them in a camp, and later return them to Yugoslavia'. Colonel Hocevar raised no objection to this proposal, and next day Low notified the Eighth Army, 'agree return Croats to Yugoslavia soonest though until then surrendered Croats in Austria to remain under our control'. At the same time an order was passed down through the Sixth Armoured Division to the First Guards Brigade, indicating clearly that it was not only the Croats against whom moves were contemplated:

> An order was received . . . on which the Bde was told to take no immediate action, that all anti-Tito Yugo-slavs were to be handed back to Tito. Elsewhere, this policy has already been put into force, and the first attempts to hand over Croats did not meet with an unqualified success. In the area of Sittersdorf approx 15,000 Croats were invited to surrender to Tito while our own troops withdrew north of the R. Drau. The latest information was that fighting had broken out between the Croats and Tito's men south of the bridge, and the situation is obscure.[4]

As this report indicates, the immediate period following the British arrival in Austria was one of maximum confusion, with refugees and Partisans penetrating the thinly-held British lines along a broad front. No one knew yet what was to be the outcome of the confrontation between Tito and the Allies, the Partisans were firmly established in

Klagenfurt, and innumerable unpleasant incidents were being hourly reported to headquarters. Only exceptional patience and tact on the part of the British troops prevented the latter from flaring up into dangerous conflicts.

At this chaotic time initial handovers of Croats conducted under the Low-Hocevar agreement were conducted in an *ad hoc* manner, governed generally by local exigencies. In some cases groups were delivered under armed guard direct to Tito's troops, in others they were tricked into pursuing the same fatal journey, while elsewhere the Partisans themselves moved in and took over the cowed prisoners. As no general order had yet been issued by Corps, considerable leeway was permitted troops in the field, which as often as not they employed to the advantage of the fugitives.

In individual cases, as Croats themselves had occasion to recall, British troops frequently acted with their customary humanity, declining to hand over particularly anguished groups or warning the potential victims of the danger in which they stood.[5] Dr Jure Petricevic, now a distinguished agronomist living in Switzerland, found himself among a group of Croats held by an Irish unit. He remembers with gratitude how the soldiers urged them to escape, an opportunity of which he and others took speedy advantage.

As the situation grew daily more stable, preparations were made by Toby Low for a general expulsion of all Croats remaining in the area. On 17 May Alexander had ordered a halt to forced repatriation of Yugoslavs, whatever their ethnic grouping, but that evening an officer was sent out from Corps headquarters to check on the disposition of Croats held by the First Guards Brigade. The Brigade itself was at first unapprised as to what was intended: 'Where shall they go?' enquired Captain Nicolson at 8.30 p.m.

The reply was swift:

> Ref Croats at Rosenbach –
> They will stay there tonight –
> A.m. 18 May a senior Tito offr will report to Bde HQ & be sent on to 2 Coy WG [Welsh Guards] (St Peter) to take over the Croats. Corps will arrange for train or road transport to be sent for their onward routing.

Rosenbach was conveniently near the Yugoslav frontier, and next afternoon, 18 May, the Sixth Armoured Division was informed:

> Corps has ordered that all Croats be sent to area Rosenbach, to entrain for Yugoslavia. Transit camp to be formed W.G. area – not too near

Rosenbach, as the victims are not to be told their destination. Able to take about 5,000 men. The first batch will embuss from Portschach area 0800 hrs tomorrow – Escort & guides to be provided by [1 Guards] Bde. There are about 11,000 Croats all told in the Div area.

Nigel Nicolson, upon whom as intelligence officer to the First Guards Brigade fell the duty of transmitting these orders, recorded deep misgivings in his Sitrep at nine o'clock that evening:

> About 2,000 Croats are being evacuated tomorrow morning from two large camps on the northern shore of the Worther See; the Croats, among whom are many women and children, are being taken in TCVs to the Welsh Gds area, where they will stay in a temporary camp until they are called forward to Rosenbach 0271, where Tito already has his reps ready to collect them. The Croats have been given no warning of their fate, and are being allowed to believe that their destination is not Yugo-Slavia, but Italy, until the actual moment of their handover. The whole business is most unsavoury, and British tps have the utmost distaste in carrying out their orders. At the moment it is not known what higher policy lies behind the decision.

The true destination of the 'victims' continued to be concealed right up to the last moment from British soldiers responsible for the handover operation on the ground, and it was on 19 May that Colonel Robin Rose Price of the Third Welsh Guards commented in his War Diary: 'Lovely day. Evacuation of Croats begin. Order of most sinister duplicity received i.e. to send Croats to their foes i.e. Tits to Yugoslavia under the impression they were to go to Italy. Tit guards on trains hidden in guards van. 2,500 Croats evacuated from station Maria Elend by evening of 19 May.'[6]

Despite Colonel Rose Price's forebodings, first impressions suggested that the fate of the returned prisoners might not be unnaturally harsh. In his evening Sitrep, Nigel Nicolson noted:

> The transfer was efficiently organised both by 3 WG and the Tito Major, the latter showing considerable tact in clearing away all Tito soldiers from the area with the exception of himself. First impressions of the reception accorded to the Croats were definitely good. They were kindly and efficiently handled, and provided with light refreshments before continuing their journey by train into Jugo-Slavia. A Tito representative said that only the war criminals among them would be punished, and the remainder sent to work on their farms. We have every reason to believe that this policy, which accords with previous practice of Tito's men, will be faithfully carried out.

This diplomatic posture was not long sustained, however, and British troops swiftly became aware of the reality of the situation. Among the Third Welsh Guards, the battalion principally responsible for conducting the operations, disgust and resentment were swift to spread to all ranks. The Rev. Malcolm Richards, the battalion chaplain, remarked the intense dislike shared by the whole battalion for their unsoldierly task:

> The British part of the bargain of the Tito withdrawal was the handing over to the Tits the Croats and Chetniks we were holding in custody. This intricate and unwholesome task was accomplished, but not without a good many white lies being told, and an equal number of pangs of conscience being experienced as a result of them. The behaviour of some of the Tito guards was brutal, bloody and unspeakably unpleasant to witness. Guardsman . . . beside himself with rage clobbered one of the Tits smashing him against a tree. He was removed to the M.O. for stitches to his head, and Guardsman . . . was put on a charge for insubordination!! This fracas almost exploded elsewhere and amidst a hubbub of noise and shrieks from some of the women some short time elapsed before conditions were stabilised again. The Croat families were brought to Muhlbach, and were fed on the rumour that they were going to Italy, before being despatched to a nearby railway station and to an uncertain and unsavoury fate at the hands of the Tits. We were only able to continue in this harrowing task by constantly reminding ourselves that former events clearly proved that had the boot been on the other leg, the kick would have been no less savage. Even so, one doesn't think along these lines when passive resistance is ordered against inhuman treatment to men, women and children.

The 'uncertain and unsavoury fate' at which Richards guessed was only too real. Major Hugo Baring was then brigade major to the Sixty-ninth Infantry Brigade. About this time he was instructed to hand over a party described to him as 'Ustashi' – the notorious Croatian Fascists. In fact they were a bedraggled group of terrified-looking refugees dressed for the most part in rags, a large proportion of whom were women and children. The party was handed over to a waiting Partisan band on the frontier in the mountains. The Communists marched their prisoners behind some nearby rocks, and it was then that Major Baring 'heard the machine-gunning begin'. As a result he declined to escort any further parties.

About the same time Lieutenant Philip Brutton of the Third Welsh Guards was ordered . . .

to hand over about a hundred members of the former Croat government together with their wives and children to a Tito colonel at the Austrian end of the Ljubljana tunnel. They had been driven in a convoy of 3-ton trucks from Vienna and then transferred to the train which was waiting for them in order to take them on their long, unlit journey to Yugoslavia. Two weeks later I heard that they had been put in an hotel and then put up against the garden wall after lunch and mowed down with machine gun fire. One man escaped: he had been in the lavatory and was overlooked in the last and no doubt hasty search of the place before the butchery. He escaped over the mountains, told the tale and was retained, this time, as a refugee, his family being buried in the fields.

In his diary on 18 May Brutton described the 'extradition of Chetnicks and Croats' as 'most nauseating'.

Mr John M. Parry recalls the operation with similar distaste:

I was a platoon-commander in the 1st Battalion Welch Regt. (6 Armoured Division) on the borders of Austria (Carinthia) and Yugoslavia when the war finished. Several thousand Ustashi (families, priests, non-combatants & combatants) surrendered to us – rather than to Tito – to be *honourably* treated by the respected British as P.O.W.s. Had we not accepted them, then they were going to fight to the death.

Weeks later, we were shocked & amazed to receive them back again with instructions to entrain them in cattle-trucks at the nearby village of Maria Elend to proceed to concentration camps in Yugoslavia. They were packed – jammed tight – in the appalling heat. The men (when they had been informed by the Slav-speaking engine driver of their destination) fought to get hold of our weapons and pleaded on their knees for us to shoot them!! This wasn't a military action (soldier to soldier) – it was beyond our belief and comprehension!!

To this day Parry feels deep anger at being compelled to participate in so unsoldierly an action; one which he feels committed him and his men to a war crime comparable to those perpetrated by the enemy:

Under these conditions – even knowing that the Ustashi had committed atrocities & massacres – when and where does legal military obedience & discipline begin and when does conscience and humanitarian beliefs prevail?

With whom does the crime of 'War Criminality' apply? With the instigator? With the perpetrator? With the intermediaries? It would appear to me that if a country or countries 'win' a war then similar actions are *not* crimes!! In my case:- Tito & Macmillan were the 'winners' so that (at that time) all their directions and actions were legally approved. What bloody nonsense is that? What measure of civilisation is in that sort of thinking?

About 5,000 Croats were handed over at this time by the Welsh Guards, and several thousand more despatched in the same way by other units. To surviving Croatian victims the whole episode understandably appears as one of unspeakable treachery, but even they were able on occasion to appreciate the widespread disgust with which most British soldiers regarded the whole business. Croatian sources record the chivalrous behaviour of a British commanding officer at St Stefan, near Wolfsberg. A party of about 3,000 had been directed there when surrendering:

> Only a few of these people were extradited. The lives of the great majority were saved thanks to the clear-sightedness and honesty of the British commander here. He told the Croatians quite frankly that he had orders from higher English authorities to turn all fugitives over to the Partisans. Then he proceeded to drag out the extradition process, repeatedly telling the Croatians that only those individuals who considered themselves soldiers had to be sent back to Yugoslavia . . . The hesitation of the English in carrying out the extradition at this point enabled most of the other Croatian soldiers in this group to transform themselves into civilians, whom the British officer refused to let the Partisans capture.[7]

The overwhelming majority of Croats returned to the Yugoslavs were massacred at Tito's orders. One of the prisoners who was being marched with others past one of the slaughter-sites in the Forest of Brezovica

> became conscious of an abominable stench that polluted the air. As we continued our march through this forest, we came upon piles of human bodies, all completely stripped of clothing. I would estimate that there were between five and ten thousand corpses in this forest. Those that I saw at close range had been shot; bullet holes were plainly visible on many of the bodies.
>
> One of our Partisan guards told us: 'For three hours we were killing them with heavy and light machine guns.'
>
> The corpses lay piled one on top of the other for a distance of about a mile.[8]

Thousands of Croats continued to be passed across the frontier on a daily basis until 24 May. The policy of repatriating them regardless of their wishes originated from General Robertson's order of 14 May, which in turn represented a response to fears aroused by the approach of a major proportion of the Croatian nation on the borders of British-held Austria. On 15 May Field-Marshal Alexander, mistakenly believing that 200,000 had actually surrendered to British forces, offered to return them to Tito. Brigadier Low's agreement with the Partisan Colonel Hocevar for the return of Croats in British hands, arranged on the same day, was therefore conducted in full accordance with AFHQ policy. The directive from which the policy derived was one hastily improvised in response to an unexpected emergency of overwhelming proportions, and is surely not to be criticised in the false perspective of hindsight.

Paradoxically, it is not the agreement which Low concluded with Hocevar on 15 May, but the operations which followed which appear so equivocal. Had Alexander's orders been fulfilled at Fifth Corps level, that agreement would have been cancelled the moment the Bleiburg crisis was over: on 17 May. In that case few or no Croats would have been delivered to Tito, since the handovers did not begin until two days later, on 19 May.

During the forty-eight hour crisis Alexander had been obliged to set aside his political instructions in order to deal with the military emergency. The guide-lines for his treatment of surrendered 'Chetniks and German Croat troops' had been set out by the British and American Governments at the beginning of the month. They were to the effect that the Yugoslavs 'should be disarmed and placed in refugee camps'.

The moment the crisis was over and he learned that the 200,000 Croats had in fact not surrendered to British arms, he at once issued the order quoted in the last chapter, which required all 'Chetniks and dissident Yugoslavs infiltrating' into Fifth Corps area to be evacuated to Italy. From 17 May Alexander no longer envisaged the forcible return of any Yugoslavs from areas for which he held responsibility as Supreme Allied Commander; not, at any rate, until he received fresh instructions from the Combined Chiefs of Staff. Yet, as has just been seen, the repatriation of Croats, arranged on 15 May, did not begin until the nineteenth. How could this have come about? Have we here an example of the 'tidy' military mind, unwilling to abandon an operation once launched? It might just be possible to envisage something of the sort in the case of the Croats, who were members of an enemy army and whose expulsion could perhaps be regarded as a continuation of the Bleiburg operation. But the Low-Hocevar discussion of 15 May was but the first of three such agreements, the last and most inexplicable of which was settled nearly a week after Alexander's prohibition of 17 May.

To return to the sequence of events: on 17 May, the day Alexander forbade any further handovers, Brigadier Low at the Fifth Corps headquarters issued the following order to divisional commanders:

> 0.462 Secret (.) all Jugoslav nationals at present in the Corps area will be handed over to Tito forces as soon as possible (.) these forces will be disarmed immediately but will NOT be told of their destination (.) arrangements for the handover will be coordinated by this HQ in conjunction with [Communist] Jugoslav forces (.) handover will last over a period owing to [logistic] difficulties of Jugoslav acceptance (.) fmns will be responsible for escorting personnel to a selected point notified by this HQ where they will be taken over by Tito forces (.)[9]

A remarkable feature of this Corps order is that it goes far beyond even the freest interpretation of the AFHQ instruction of 14 May, which had in any case been superseded on the seventeenth. The qualification contained in Robertson's order, that only 'personnel of established Yugoslav nationality who were serving in German forces' should be handed over, is omitted in the Fifth Corps operational order, which refers emphatically to 'all Jugoslav nationals' as being liable for return.

The Corps order is signed by Toby Low ('ARW Low BGS'), and so it was to him that I wrote at the beginning of 1983, requesting an explanation. He replied, 'I do not remember that problem arising in my time in Austria. You will remember that I left on 25th or 26th May. I do remember having to stop a force of Yugoslavs trying to overrun part of Carinthia and seize captured materials including tanks, but not any repatriation.' Fortunately his memory had recovered within less than a year, however, when he came to be questioned in a BBC television documentary based on an article I wrote, 'The Klagenfurt Conspiracy', in *Encounter* in May 1983.

Asked why he widened his orders to include thousands of Yugoslavs who had not 'served in the German forces', Low replied, 'I don't think there was any *widening*. I think there was a – a – just a – perhaps as you'd say – a – hurried and loose use of language. It was *not* meant to go further than "all Yugoslav nationals in uniform who have been fighting with the Germans".' The interviewer, apparently satisfied with this reply, pressed him no further.

The truth is that, by removing the qualification in its order of the same day, the Fifth Corps was enabled to include the 17,000 Slovenes and 4,000 Serbian Chetniks held at Viktring among those to be handed over. There can be no doubt that this was its purpose, and in addition the operation was intended to be accomplished with maximum haste. Next day, 18 May, Nigel Nicolson learned from the Sixth Armoured Divisional headquarters, 'Div will try to get the remainder of Slovenes and Serbs from Viktring cage today – within the next twelve hours – either in transport arranged by Div or on foot towards Yugoslavia.'

This scheme proved unrealistic in the short term, since the railway route through the Rosenbach tunnel was about to be put to capacity use by daily trainloads of returning Croats. Later that afternoon Nicolson was informed of a change of plan: 'There are about 11,000 Croats all told in the Div area. Serbs and Slovenes will go the same way when all Croats have been dealt with.'[10]

Low's order of 17 May is remarkable in that it is phrased so as to include in the repatriation thousands of people excluded under the AFHQ authority received at the Fifth Corps three days earlier. It was also issued in despite of Alexander's order of the same day to the Eighth Army, requiring all 'Chetniks and dissident Yugoslavs' to be evacuated to Italy. Finally, and perhaps most inexplicable of all, the Fifth Corps Chief of Staff took this decision, not in response to a Yugoslav request, but in advance of it.

It was Tito's former colleague, Milovan Djilas, who remarked in 1980, 'To be quite frank with you – we didn't at all understand why the British insisted on returning these people' ('Chetniks and Chetnik sympathisers').[11]

Whatever the reason, this is certainly what appears to have happened. For it was not until two days later, on the evening of 19 May, that a Yugoslav Partisan, Colonel Ivanovic, arrived at Keightley's headquarters in Klagenfurt to negotiate the addition of Serbs and Slovenes to the Croats whose repatriation Low had already agreed with Hocevar on the fifteenth. There he consulted with Toby Low, and together they drew up an agreement. The first four clauses dealt with the evacuation by Yugoslav troops of all Austrian territory. For over a week armed bands of Partisans had infested the British-occupied zone of Austria, which Tito hoped to annex. They had committed innumerable crimes of pillage, rape and murder, antagonising not only the inhabitants but also the previously sympathetic British Army. Now it was agreed by Ivanovic that all Partisan forces would be withdrawn 'south of Yugoslav–Austrian border as shown on 250,000 map by 1900 hours 21 May at the latest'.

This section of the agreement concluded, 'After the withdrawal
as in para 1, the military boundary between Yugoslav forces and
5 Corps will be the Yugoslav-Austrian border as shown on 250,000
map.'

The second part of the agreement dealt with the *Return of Yugoslav
Nationals*, and read as follows:

> 5 Corps will return all Yugoslav Nationals now in the Corps area who
> had been fighting in uniform with the Germans and their camp followers.
> These include:
>> Ustachi
>> Domobrons
>> Cetniks
>> Nedics
>> White Guards
>> total approximately 18,585
>> of whom 3,010 already evacuated to 4 Yugoslav Army.
> Further evacuation would be:
>> 10,000 to 4 Yugoslav Army as already arranged via Rosenbach.
>> 5,500 approx to 3 Yugoslav Army via Bleiburg or Lava-
> mund . . .[12]

In this executive order Brigadier Low altered his earlier reference to
'all Jugoslav nationals' to one which (so he claims today) more
accurately reflected the wording of Robertson's authorisation. But
whereas Robertson referred exclusively to the surrender of Yugoslavs
'who were serving in German forces', Low's definition is phrased so
as to continue to embrace 'all Jugoslav nationals', who had been
'fighting in uniform with the Germans' could be (indeed was) used
to cover anyone in any uniform who had fought against the Germans'
enemies, i.e. Tito's Partisans. Thus Chetniks in the uniform of the
Royal Yugoslav Army, who would not have come under Robertson's
definition, were included in Low's.

Then again the reference to 'their camp followers' extended the
definition to cover thousands of civilians as well. It did not arise from
oversight or loose phraseology. That morning an enquiry had come
up through Sixth Armoured Divisional headquarters, '6,000 Civilian
Slovenes – are they to be handed over to Tito?' At two o'clock
Division had replied with the ruling, 'If civilians can be classed
as "Camp followers" then they can accompany their soldiery to
Yugo-Slavia. N.B. A camp follower is "one who is dependent upon
the soldiery for his livelihood".'[13]

The Yugoslav General Kosta Nadj, then commanding the Third Army on the Austrian frontier, has recently provided a Yugoslav version of these negotiations. The Yugoslav delegation, he recounts, arrived at:

> the shore of the Wörthersee, where General Keightley's headquarters were established in a luxuriously furnished caravan. Colonel Ivanovic made a firm declaration that he was prepared to resort to a fresh conflict if it proved necessary to assert his rights ['to the handing over of Chetnik and Ustashe units']. Keightley promised Ivanovic and Leontic suitably close collaboration. It was then that General Keightley and Ivanovic worked out and signed an agreement that 'all quislings from Yugoslavia must without exception be handed over to the forces of Marshal Tito': even those who had surrendered to the Allies were to be returned.[14]

There appears to be no reason to doubt the accuracy of this account. Ivanovic's belief that the British capitulated through abject fear of Yugoslav arms is plausible enough. He may well have made such a threat, and presumed it effective. But the fact is that everything Low conceded at their meeting had been decided at least two days earlier. What is interesting is the confirmation that Low's plan to hand over Chetniks and Slovenes as well as Croats does not appear to have originated in a Yugoslav request. Ivanovic on the nineteenth felt the necessity to demand by threats that which had already been settled by Low on the seventeenth.

This 'widening' of categories liable to return in the case of the Yugoslavs parallels the decision taken at the same time to set aside screening arrangements for the Cossacks, and serves to confirm that the Fifth Corps, in its enthusiasm for repatriating the maximum number of fugitives, was prepared to go to extraordinary lengths in exceeding, ignoring or disobeying orders.

A final point may be noted in connection with this agreement. Within the Fifth Corps it was put about that the two topics of the Low-Ivanovic agreement were related. As Nigel Nicolson noted at the time, 'As all the world now knows, Tito agreed to withdraw his partisans from Carinthia on 21st May . . . As our contribution to the agreement, it was decided to hand back to Tito all the Yugo-Slav prisoners in our hands who were unfavourable to his cause.' As a result of this, many soldiers became reluctantly reconciled to participating in what might otherwise have appeared an unjustifiably inhumane operation.

In fact the rumour was false, as the repatriation had nothing to do with the withdrawal of Tito's followers from Carinthia. It will be seen later how strong is the evidence that the Partisans' retreat resulted from *force majeure* and nothing else. For the moment it may suffice to recall that Low had decided on the repatriation at least two days before the agreement, and that the Partisan delegates arrived on the nineteenth in ignorance that such an arrangement had been made. Today Low appears confused in his memory on this score. To me he asserted that 'it's false' that there was any sort of deal; 'my recollection is that it was absolutely nothing to do with it'. Yet to the writer Nora Beloff he stated equally categorically in December 1983 that there *had* been a deal, and that returning the prisoners was the only way – regrettable but inevitable – of ejecting Tito's forces from Carinthia.[15]

Low's memory also appears to have played him false on another significant issue. In an address to the boys at Winchester College on 1 March 1985 he made this point:

> I was asked in a BBC interview . . . whether I would have issued the same orders (and that means whether General Keightley would have issued the same orders) to return the Yugoslavs to Yugoslavia if we had known they were going to be murdered. I replied at once, '*of course not*'. We would have had to find some other way of organising several tens of thousands of armed Yugoslavs in German uniform plus their followers in another part of Austria.

In fact the evidence shows that, so far from concealing their intentions, the Partisan officers who negotiated with Low made no bones about the fact that their purpose in recovering the refugees was to wreak vengeance on them. General Kosta Nadj, commander of the Yugoslav Third Army, whose account of negotiations for the 'handing over of Chetnik and Ustashe units' has already been referred to, recalls that 'the allies did not for one moment question our rights in punishing our quislings for their war crimes'; which surely means that this purpose was implicit in the negotiation. In referring to the Low-Ivanovic agreement which followed, Nadj describes the entire body of refugees in British hands as 'all quislings from Yugoslavia'.

The first stage of the operation, the handover of Croats, lasted from 19 to 24 May. There appear to be no examples of force being employed to compel their return, as virtually all fell for the ruse leading them to believe they were travelling to Italy. As a result there is no sure means of knowing what impression reports of these handovers made at the Eighth Army headquarters.

On the other hand it is evident that the Fifth Corps was anxious to avoid any incident that might draw attention to what was taking place. Mrs Zdenka Palic-Kusan was at the time a young girl among the refugees who fled Zagreb on 6 May. The group of seven or eight hundred refugees among whom she found herself arrived about 10 or 11 May at the village of Krumpendorf, on the edge of the Wörthersee. They were exhausted and hungry. There was no food to be had in the village:

so for the next 5 or 6 days we were condemned to starve, living on some scanty rations of a few beans each, vitamin or calcium pills, which some Red Cross vehicle spilled onto the road. They saved our lives.

The place where we were staying was situated further from the lake and next to the main road. On the other side of the road there was a small country railway station of Krumpendorf which stands even today . . .

Beyond the station there was a vast slope of terrain on which another refugee group established themselves before our arrival: they were *all* army people: soldiers and officers, Ustashe and Domobrans. They camped there under tents, about 200–300 metres away from us separated from us by the road. Beyond their camp was the lake. There must have been about 1000 people . . .

Some time in the middle of May both encampments were suddenly surrounded by Partisans, and everyone feared the worst. On the third day of this 'siege' the Partisans mysteriously melted away, and the civilian group decided to send emissaries to British headquarters in Klagenfurt, in the hope of negotiating asylum. British military police permitted a delegation of three to set out. They consisted of two officers and a priest. Their expedition lasted from 8 a.m. until 8 p.m., and it was only unremitting persistence that at last gained them admission to some hard-pressed officer (probably from Allied Military Government) in the Rathaus.

They returned at last to the camp, uncertain whether their mission had been successful or not. No one slept that night, and early next morning they were disturbed by the sound of trucks in the nearby military camp. Zdenka and her sister ran to see what was happening. Overjoyed, the Croatian and Domobran soldiers were being driven off in British lorries in the direction of Klagenfurt. On being asked what was their destination, they replied happily that they were off to a proper military camp under British administration. The operation lasted the whole of that day.

That evening came the turn of the civilians. Zdenka and her

companions were put on to a goods train, which then set off into the night. They felt they were being taken to the Partisans, but for them the story had a happy ending. They were taken to a DP camp in Italy, where they remained safe from repatriation. The soldiers on the other hand, as they learned afterwards, had followed that grim route through the Rosenbach tunnel leading to massacres at Jesenice and Kranj, and for the survivors the terrible 'death marches'.[16]

Zdenka Kusan never discovered the motive behind the reprieve, which she understood to be unique. Corps had ordered that 'all Croats' be returned, and yet a pertinacious plea had saved them. All that can be said is that this provides another example of the curious way in which the Fifth Corps Staff tended to back down hurriedly on their illicit operation, whenever challenged in a manner likely to arouse undue or inappropriate attention.

The handovers of Croats took place after Field-Marshal Alexander's order of 17 May, laying down that all Yugoslavs should be retained as SEP (Surrendered Enemy Personnel) until their fate was settled at governmental level. They formed but the prelude to still larger and equally tragic operations whereby the Serbian Chetniks and Slovenian Domobranci were delivered into the hands of their enemies. On 24 May the Fifth Corps War Diary noted laconically, 'Handover of Croats completed. Handover of Serbs began.'

The Croats had in many ways represented a special case. Croatia had been Germany's ally throughout the war, and her army had served the Axis cause. The Ustashi were known to have committed appalling atrocities against the Serbs, especially at the time of their assertion of independence. The attempted flight of a large part of their nation into Austria during the second and third weeks of May 1945 was on a scale which the British military authorities could not contemplate accepting.

It appears to have been as a direct response to this unmanageable migration that General Robertson issued an order on 14 May to the effect that 'all surrendered personnel of established Yugoslav nationality who were serving in German forces' must be handed over to the Yugoslavs. He was referring principally, if not exclusively, to the Croats, and assured Alexander Kirk that the repatriation was planned 'with exception of Chetniks'. Finally, in the mistaken belief that the Croats had actually surrendered to the Eighth Army, Field-Marshal Alexander sent a message to Tito, offering 'to turn these over immediately to Marshal Tito's forces'.

Thus when General McCreery on 17 May received Alexander's new order, requiring him to evacuate 'Chetniks and dissident Yugoslavs' to Italy, he appears to have felt that this did not prohibit the continuing expulsion of the remaining Croats within the Fifth Corps area. It is possible, too, that he was influenced by the fact that the duped Croats made no attempt to resist return. How much if anything he knew of the methods employed to induce them to go back, there is no means of knowing. But it is surely significant that on the only occasion a body of Croats voiced a determined objection at headquarters, that of the group including Zdenka Kusan, they were summarily reprieved and provision made for their removal from the area within twenty-four hours.

Very different from the official attitude towards the Croats was the view held at all levels with regard to the refugees, principally Serbs and Slovenes, settled since 12 May in the great camp at Viktring, south of Klagenfurt. Their origins and arrival were described in chapter two. As Brigadier Verney, commanding the First Guards Brigade, recalled:

> We formed a huge camp in an open space and collected what we estimated to be about 48,000 people with their cattle, sheep, old folk and young children. The camp was run by a German Corps Staff assisted by a Russian Corps Staff, and it went well as they all understood that the motto of the camp, coined by me, was 'no obedience, no food'. It was supervised by an ordinary British Captain with no special experience and it went very well.

The camp inmates were only too content to establish themselves in their improvised home, maintaining internal discipline which required little or no British intervention. It was ominous activities by Tito's Partisans that called for a vigilant British military presence around the camp perimeter. Already on the evening of 12 May 'a Tito lorry drove very fast down the rd and opened fire with a fusillade of small arms onto a group of German offrs sitting on the bank'. Two days later it was reported:

> The Yugo-slavs have been showing considerable interest in the big PW camp at Viktring. A couple of lorries, with twenty men in each, were cruising this morning up and down the perimeter road outside the camp, as though they were making a careful recce of its layout. Later this evening, a handful of Tito's men were actually found inside the cage, and stated when challenged that they were merely looking for a suitable

German vehicle to take away with them. The presence of three armoured cars on the confines of the camp suggested that their intentions might be more sinister, and a group of D[erbyshire] Y[eomanry] was despatched to tail them.

On 20 May Viktring Camp contained 10,170 Slovene troops and 2,426 Serbian Chetniks (including six Red Cross sisters). Separately quartered nearby were the Slovene civilian refugees: 2,450 men, 3,000 women and 550 children. All in all, the Viktring complex housed nearly 19,000 souls.[17]

Rumours had proliferated during the ten days since the fugitives' arrival. On the one hand it was thought inconceivable that the British, who had accepted their surrender, could be planning to betray them to the Partisans. For long years during the war the population of Slovenia and Serbia had awaited the coming of the Anglo-American liberation forces with eager longing. In the Great War the Serbs had fought with outstanding gallantry on the Allied side, and in 1941 they had answered Britain's appeal by renouncing the pact with Nazi Germany. The consequences had been terrible, but they never doubted there would be an ultimate Allied victory nor that the Allies would see it was in their interest to sustain European cultural, religious and political institutions against the barbaric advance of eastern totalitarianism. Apart from fighting gallantly against the common enemy, Serbian Chetniks (and Slovenian Domobranci) had frequently risked their lives in rescuing and protecting British and American airmen downed over Yugoslav territory.[18]

Though Tito was Britain's ally, it was noteworthy that British troops had acted firmly to prevent Partisan atrocities perpetrated on the defenceless refugees, and had frequently expressed open disgust at the behaviour of Tito's undisciplined troops. The exact whereabouts of General Damjanovic's surrendered Chetniks was still unknown to the inmates of Viktring, but it seemed certain that the British had taken them under their protection. Petitions had been sent to Brigadier Verney by Colonel Tatalovic, commander of the three Chetnik regiments, and Dr Joze Basaj, President of the National Committee of Slovenia. Tatalovic requested that he and his men be permitted to rejoin General Damjanovic in Italy; while Dr Basaj explained that the Slovenian National Army had never collaborated with the Germans, and had fought only for the protection and liberation of their homeland.[19]

Nigel Nicolson, who received the petitions, noted shortly afterwards:

> The only point on which they were unanimous was in their fear that we should return them to Tito, and this was unfortunately exactly what we intended to do. They were not told of our intentions till they saw for themselves the Tito guards boarding their train. We allowed them to remain at Viktring in blissful ignorance and under only nominal guard, for the huge size of the camp ruled out the question of any attempt to wire them in or keep them under the constant supervision of our patrols. It was a sight one had not seen since the early films of the Goldrush. Whole Slovenian villages, their horses and their children (the horses getting the pick of any available accommodation), lay closely packed on a wide stretch of rolling park-land. While the womenfolk remained behind with their babes and cooking-pots, the soldiers would be paraded by their nationalities, and marched about in huge battalions to the beat of a Balkan band. It was not a pleasant task to break up their domesticity, to slaughter their horses for food, and send away their families into a sterner captivity. But we had pledged our word to Tito, and the reception given to them by his men encouraged us to hope that their fate would not be too harsh.

That these last words represented pious hope rather than conviction Nigel Nicolson freely confesses today. Indeed, the outspoken reference in his Sitrep of 18 May to the whole business as 'most unsavoury' had led to a reprimand, and his removal from the task of supervising the operation.

Toby Low, as has been seen, had signed the agreement with Colonel Ivanovic after their conference on 19 May, at which he had taken upon himself to agree to the delivery of all Yugoslavs, whatever their ethnic grouping, age or sex, to be delivered to Tito. His decision, negotiations and agreement had all been conducted in defiance of Alexander's order of 17 May, and in the absence of any authority from the Eighth Army.

Intimations of what was happening soon reached Eighth Army headquarters, and on 21 May McCreery despatched this message to AFHQ:

> Many urgent questions constantly arising concerning treatment of various nationals both members of armed forces and others. Matters constantly complicated by claims of diplomatic privilege members of armed forces or civilians, etcetera.
>
> Consider it essential proper principles are consolidated so that action

can be taken at which present problems can be cleared and principles laid down.

If possible, representative should stay at this HQ as advisor on unforseen problems.[20]

Next day, 22 May, Alexander replied, 'Policy decisions on questions indicated your U 128 of 21 May now being considered this HQ. You will be informed immediately and on receipt you will be in position to consider whether you still need representative as requested.'[21]

If the interpretation of events so far is correct, this response should have aroused consternation at the Fifth Corps headquarters. Alexander's wishes had already been made known through his firm prohibition of 17 May on the repatriation of Yugoslavs. It should have seemed improbable, to say the least, that he would act now to reverse that decision. On the contrary, a fresh ruling would doubtless confirm existing AFHQ policy in a manner impossible to ignore further.

Low's reaction was swift. No sooner was he informed of this unchancy development than he raised the matter with the Eighth Army, emphasising both the necessity of acceptance of the policy he advocated, and the need for an instant decision. Eighth Army once again passed the message on to AFHQ:

> From: Main Eighth Army
> To: AFHQ . . .
> Personal to Gen Macleod. ref 77268 of 17 [Alexander's order prohibiting handovers]. negotiations by 5 Corps with 3 and 4 Jugoslav Armies provide for all military personnel to be handed back to Jugoslavia and considerable numbers have already been handed back approx 50000 still in 5 Corps Area. this considered in accordance with AFHQ FX 75383 dated 14 [Robertson's order to surrender Yugoslavs to Tito]. consider essential this arrangement continues and that all Jugoslav military handed over to Jugoslavs. Dep comd 3 Jugoslav army has now raised question of return all Jugoslav nationals incl ex PW internees slave workers and other displaced persons incl Chetniks. request immediate authority for all these categories to be returned as decision required this evening. consider policy should be for all nationals ie persons born within pre 1939 frontier of an allied country to be handed over to ally concerned except only such as are required for offences against British. For 5 Corps. take no action ref your 0500 dated 20 pending AFHQ reply to this signal.[22]

The implications of this message are unmistakable, and reveal in exemplary manner the differing outlooks of the Fifth Corps and the Eighth Army respectively. McCreery's information about conditions within the Fifth Corps area, which derived from Keightley's head-quarters, contains serious deficiencies and distortions. No distinction had been made between the Croats on the one hand, and Serbs and Slovenes on the other. All are lumped together under the specious designation 'Jugoslav military'. The purpose of this deception is explicit: operations so far conducted are justified on the basis of Robertson's order 'AFHQ FX 75383 dated 14'; an order which was restricted in application to 'Yugoslavs who were serving in German forces', i.e. the Croats.

Low explains that in consequence of that order he has committed the Fifth Corps in negotiations with the Third and Fourth Yugoslav armies to provide 'for all military personnel to be handed back to Yugoslavs'. In fact, as has been seen, the terms of the agreement had been very much more comprehensive: *all* Yugoslavs, including civilians, were to be handed over, and preliminary instructions to that effect had been issued to the Sixth Armoured Division before the Low-Ivanovic meeting had taken place.

Yet four days later, on 23 May, the Eighth Army learns from the Fifth Corps that Colonel Ivanovic 'has *now* [italics inserted] raised question of return all Jugoslav nationals . . . including Chetniks'. But all this had already been settled (including specific mention of 'Chetniks') in the agreement of 19 May! The purpose of pretending it to be a novel issue is explicit: 'request immediate authority for all these categories to be returned as decision required this evening'. Speed was what was regarded as essential, though nothing exists in the Fifth Corps files to suggest why this should be so – except AFHQ's announcement of the previous day that it was on the point of issuing a definitive ruling which would very likely tie the hands of the Fifth Corps in the matter.

The last sentence of the Eighth Army message of 23 May also shows that none of Low's preparations (brought to completion that very day) for the repatriation of refugees in Viktring had so far received any authorisation from McCreery.

AFHQ replied as promptly as requested, informing the Eighth Army on the same day:

Cipher. Top Secret. Serial 6604.
To: Action: Main 8 Army.
Info: 15 Army Gp Main 5 Corps. Distone.
From: AFHQ cite FHGAB FX80836 23rd.
Ref Main 8 Army A4113 of 23 May (4278).

Agree that all Jugoslav nationals in Eighth Army area should be returned by you to Jugoslavs unless this involves use of force in which case they should be dealt with in accordance with AFHQ 77268 of 17.[23]

No sooner had the Eighth Army received this telegram from General Macleod at AFHQ than another arrived from Alexander himself. In it the Field-Marshal replied in detail to McCreery's previous request for a ruling on Yugoslav repatriation. A precise date, 25 May, was appointed for the arrival of a staff officer from AFHQ, who would be empowered to discuss policy proposals now set out in detail:

> This supersedes FX 79968 of 22 May [cited above]. In accordance your request contained U 128 representation this Headquarters will arrive yours 25 May for discussion policy on lines suggested as follows.
> Para 1. No Jugoslavs who have come into the hands of Allied Troops will be returned direct to Jugoslavia or handed over to Jugoslav Troops against their will.
> Para 2. Para 1 includes Chetniks, Ustashi, Croats, Slovenes and miscellaneous refugees and dissident civilians including women and children.
> Para 3. All above will be moved to suitable concentration areas and screened.
> Para 4. As a result of screening all will be divided into 2 classes. Class A: those who have borne arms against Tito and who will therefore be treated as POW or surrendered enemy personnel. These are G-I responsibility. Class B. All others. These will be treated as displaced persons. Those in Italy are an ALCOM [Allied Control Commission] responsibility. Those in Austria become an ALCOM responsibility as soon as passed over the Italo-Austrian frontier by 5 or 8 Army as appropriate.
> Para 5. CCS [Combined Chiefs of Staff] are being asked for disposal instructions for persons in Class A.
> Para 6. Persons in Class B will be accommodated initially in ALCOM and UNRRA [United Nations Relief and Rehabilitation Administration] displaced persons camps in Italy and at Phillipeville Camp.[24]

These proposals were clearly intended as detailed clarification of the policy already set out by Alexander in his preceding message of 17 May, in which he laid down that 'Chetniks and dissident Yugoslavs' should be evacuated to Italy. That this was its intention is confirmed by the interpretation placed upon it by the United States political representative at Caserta. Alexander Kirk's account, which he sent that evening to the State Department, reads as follows:

AFHQ is today informing field commanders that its policy with regard to disposition (re our 2232, May 18, mid) of Yugoslavs in North Italy and Austria provides that collaborators with enemy are to be moved to a center where they will receive treatment as prisoners of war or surrendered enemy personnel.

CCS [Combined Chiefs of Staff] will be requested for instructions as to final disposition. Dissident Yugos will be sent to displaced persons center. Under no circumstances will Yugos who are in custody of Allied troops be returned to Yugo. To prevent further infiltration southern Austrian border and western boundary of Venezia Giulia will be closed to all Yugos.[25]

Nevertheless, Alexander's policy outline was not an executive order. It was Macleod's instruction that McCreery passed on to the Fifth Corps as operative,[26] which ruled that all Yugoslavs should be returned except where this would involve the use of force. (Its text establishes, incidentally, that the Fifth Corps was in receipt of Alexander's order of 17 May, ordering the retention of infiltrating Yugoslavs).

Though the text of Macleod's order appears to envisage the return of most Yugoslavs within the Fifth Corps area, there is no reason to suppose McCreery regarded it as representing a radical departure from Alexander's order of 17 May (whose major provision, prohibition of the use of force, it cited as remaining in effect), or the proposals contained in his message of 23 May. At any rate, it seems unlikely that he would have acted in flagrant contravention of Alexander's wishes, in view of the fact that the latter's representative was due to arrive at Eighth Army headquarters within two days. Next day Alexander confirmed that 'our representative will proceed Udine for discussion'.[27]

No record of any unpleasantness incurred in handing over of Croatian military personnel, not even of any resistance, had as yet reached the Eighth Army. No doubt McCreery felt, all things being equal, that it would be an excellent thing if the refugees crowded into Austria were to overcome their fears and return home.

Alexander's order of 17 May was in accordance with the humane traditions of the British Army and, as has been seen, the idea of driving defenceless people to an uncertain fate was regarded with distaste by most British soldiers. Nevertheless that hastily-promulgated order (which Alexander himself now wished to clarify) contained one obvious illogicality. For in effect it actually prohibited the refugees from returning to their homeland, which it might be presumed an unknown number would wish to do now the initial panic was over. Yet all of them, so Alexander had ordered, should be transported to Italy.

Now it was proposed they should be permitted – persuaded, if possible – to take the more logical course of returning home; *provided*, that is, they were not compelled to do so. So far from envisaging widespread resistance to such a move, McCreery was concerned to retain those whom the British might in due course wish to punish. Those who objected to return would travel to Italy as planned.

No record of the proposed discussion or its outcome appears to have survived in the appropriate files, but there seems to be little doubt that it took place. On 23 May the Sixth Armoured Divisional headquarters learned that the Army Commander was 'expected to visit the Div either tomorrow or next day'. His visit would last a brief forty-five minutes, during which he wished to see Brigadier Verney and Colonel Rose Price: the officers most closely concerned with questions concerning Viktring Camp and the proposed handovers. In fact he arrived on the morning of Friday the twenty-fifth.[28]

In view of the brief period allowed for his visit, and the fact that it coincided with the date arranged for the visit of Alexander's representative, it is unlikely to have been chance that brought the General that morning to Viktring Camp. His purpose, most likely, was to assess for himself the morale and attitudes of the refugees before formulating the policy put forward by Alexander. The spectacle that greeted him must in that case have been profoundly reassuring, had he any doubts about Keightley and Low's motive in wishing to encourage the prisoners to return home, rather than become an unnecessary burden on Allied resources in Italy.

A convoy of Serbian Volunteers was to leave that day. There was an atmosphere of rejoicing, and families from the neighbouring civilian camp had gathered as on the previous day to wave excited farewells to their menfolk, with whom they would shortly be reunited 'in Italy'. True, it was that day a rumour first arose that all might not be as fair as it appeared, but the man responsible was angrily reproved by General Krenner, the Slovenian commander, for spreading alarmist news and provoking hostile feelings towards the British.[29] There was nothing here to suggest reluctance to return, and much to the contrary. McCreery knew that Yugoslavia was the Serbs' destination, but had no means of discovering what *they* believed: unless, that is, Keightley (who accompanied him) chose to enlighten him.

The General's inspection was more perfunctory than average. It was pouring with rain, and in the neighbouring camp for civilians a Red Cross nurse noted afterwards in her diary, 'only time he got out of his car was to walk through mud to shake hands with me. Great thrill [Eighth Army] newspaper bloke chased me afterwards.'

There is a strong possibility, therefore, that Keightley and Alexander's representative from AFHQ (assuming him to have been there) departed for Italy well satisfied that for the present at least there was no need to make elaborate provision at Distone for the reception of large numbers of refugees.

This suggestion is confessedly speculative so far as General McCreery is concerned. We simply do not know how far the truth was brought to his attention. All that can be said with certainty is that people with a much better chance than McCreery for assessing the facts failed to discover what was happening under their noses. The Assistant Commissioner on the Staff of Military Government in Austria spent the week in which the Serbs and Slovenes were evacuated working in their camp. Eventually an account brought by an escaped prisoner persuaded him that a grim fate awaited those returned on the other side of the Yugoslav frontier, and as will be seen shortly this caused him to raise strong objection to the policy. What he never appears to have discovered, despite his actually living among them, was the deception tactic which led the victims to believe they were going to Italy.

The ensnaring of the prisoners required little ingenuity and scant precautions. Few if any of the Serbian and Slovene officers spoke more than a smattering of English, though they understood enough to be reassured by reiterated promises 'on the word of a British officer' that they really were travelling to Italy, and would not be delivered to the Partisans. McCreery's visit came when the operation was only in its second day, and universal optimism and faith in the British prevailed throughout the camp.

There is much that in all likelihood will never be known, but the broad outlines are well established. Alexander's attitude was consistent throughout. From 17 May, when he prohibited the return of 'dissident Yugoslavs', he never contemplated any violation of the principle that people for whom he was responsible should be delivered to their enemies against their will. Nothing is recorded to have occurred in the month of May which could have led him to believe his instructions were being flouted. Though the evidence is less conclusive in McCreery's case, it seems reasonable to conclude that he shared his friend the Field-Marshal's outlook, and had no reason to believe that the orders he transmitted were being evaded or disobeyed.

Brigadier Low, on the other hand, to whom Keightley had granted the 'remit' to supervise the Yugoslav operations, can be shown beyond doubt to have engaged in elaborate deceptions, both of his superiors and the refugees in his charge. He had decided to return them even before his discussion with the Partisan commissar, and made arrangements to do so in defiance of standing orders. The 'authority' under which he finally came to act was not intended for the purpose to which he applied it, and was only obtained as the result of serious misrepresentations of the facts. Finally, the operation itself was effected by methods which it seems fair to say few if any other officers in the Corps would have contemplated initiating, and which disgusted all who were compelled to put them into effect.

It is only fair to add, however, that the motive for his acting in such a manner must have been an extraordinary one. What it was remains obscure. All that can be said for certain is that it is hard to see how it could have had anything to do with the military or administrative concerns of the Fifth Corps, since from 17 May, orders deriving from AFHQ provided for the refugees' speedy removal from the Corps area.

It was as a result of these complex machinations that on the afternoon of 23 May the Sixth Armoured Divisional headquarters came to transmit the 'Scheme for evac of Serbs & Croats tomorrow'. In Viktring Camp the British Commandant handed the Slovenian, Serbian and Croatian commanders a 'Movement Order'. This announced, 'All Croat troops, and All Serbian troops less 50 men at present in Viktring Camp will move to new Area tomorrow, 24th May.'[30] The Commandant explained further to the Slovenian and Chetnik senior officers that they and all their followers were to be transported to Italy to join General Damjanovic. As has been seen, the camp was filled with rejoicing as the news swiftly spread.

Next day, by what appeared propitious chance, was the feast day of the Slavic apostles, Saints Cyril and Methodius. The first group to be despatched consisted of a thousand Serbian Chetniks, headed by Colonel Tatalovic and his staff. Early next morning they rose briskly, struck their tents, and assembled for the customary morning prayer. Mr Z. R. Prvulovich was at that time a subaltern in the

Chetnik troops of the Royal Yugoslav Army cross the Tagliamento into Northern Italy on 3 May 1945, seeking British protection from pursuing Communist Partisans.

The end of Tito's dream of a 'Greater Yugoslavia': Communist Partisans leaving the Karfreitstrasse, Klagenfurt, with their plunder on 19 May 1945, following the Anglo-American ultimatum. 'The great bluff was over,' as the Sixth Armoured Division war diary recorded that evening.

General (former Red Army Major) Timophey Domanoc, Cossack officers and men of the *Kazachi Stan,* the Cossack settlement established by the Germans in North Italy, pictured in German Army photographs taken at the time of their withdrawal into Austria in the first week of May 1945. After the Cossacks' surrender to the Soviets at the beginning of June, most of the Bactrian camels (*far left*) were slaughtered for food.

The forest of Kocevski Rog, where the majority of the 26,000 refugees handed over to Tito by British military authorities in Austria were massacred. This photograph shows trees planted after the limestone cave was filled in by Yugoslav authorities.

КРАСНОВ
АГ-994
1953 г.

Photograph (*above*) from the Gulag pass of Nikolai Krasnov who, despite having left Russia as a baby in 1918, was handed over to the Soviets by British troops on 29 May 1945. As a non-Soviet citizen, he was eventually released under Krushchev's amnesty of 25 September 1955.

The author talking with General V.N. Naumenko, Ataman of the Kuban Cossacks during the Russian Civil War, at the Tolstoy Foundation, New York, in 1979.

Second Regiment of Yugoslav Volunteers, and recalls the scene vividly:

Already six o'clock! Time was flying. Looking forward to the promising future was enough to transfer us into a world of unearthly reality. The regiment was lined up and the elderly padre, Father Zika Bogdanovich, was reading the prayers, asking God's blessing for our journey. His mellow ringing words mingled with the rain and its rebounding noise. The rain was sliding down our cheeks but we hardly noticed it; our minds and hearts were elsewhere, lost in prayer and dedication. Wonderful is the power of prayer; particularly when coupled with deep thanksgiving and devotion.

The starting point was not very far away. Orderly and dignified, we passed by the Chetnik contingent and a sizeable band of the Ustashi. This preliminary assembly-point was soon left behind as we moved to our proper *rendez-vous*. Unit after unit moved along the muddy lane and across the soggy fields. Once again we lined up, this time in depth. As it happened, my regiment was the very first; and how glad we all were. Indeed, we considered it the greatest privilege to head the column of our decimated forces. As we had arrived long before the appointed hour we settled down to wait for the British. By the time they arrived we were getting somewhat impatient: soaked to the skin, we were anxious to move off. The British soldiers searched us quickly but efficiently, all the while remaining cold and expressionless; but they held their hands on their pistols when not otherwise engaged. (Several of my friends told me later that a few British soldiers had secretly expressed pity but at the same time they had mistaken it for mere friendship). While the search was in progress, trucks kept arriving and lining up along the marked lines. Much to our surprise, there seemed to be no particular hurry.

Eventually loading started and this again seemed to take ages. The required numbers were taken, no more and no less and so to the last. Our whole regiment was safely loaded. Those vehicles which we did obtain, as promised last night, were used for the conveyance of our meagre stores, excessive luggage and everything else that was deemed worth taking along. We even had our own motorcyclists, quite a number of them too. They all were very proud, serious and dignified, though some of them somewhat unsteady on their machines, given to them by the Allies!

Nina Lencek recalls joining the families of the departing men, who came from the neighbouring civilian camp to cheer them on their way: 'We all went, because every Domobran boy had a mother, father, brother, sister, fiancée there. They all came over to bid them goodbye. We were all there, seeing them off.' Her father, mother and sister were also among those who travelled with the first convoy. Though unconnected with the military they wanted to take an early opportunity of preparing a new home in Italy, Nina's mother being Italian.

As his men scrambled abroad, twenty-five to a lorry, Colonel Tatalovic approached the British officer in charge.

'Major, where are we going?' he asked.

'To join your army in Italy,' came the reply.

'Word of honour?' persisted Tatalovic.

'Word of honour!' replied the Englishman breezily.

Reassured, Tatalovic climbed into the lorry.[31]

Vladimir Ljotic, education officer in the Second Regiment of Serbian Volunteers, remembers that day with particular vividness. Indeed, he is one of the few who survived to do so. Like everyone else, he trusted implicitly in British assurances that they were travelling to join their comrades in Italy. As the convoy of lorries moved eastwards along the Rosental under the shadow of the Karavanke range there was nothing in the attitude of their escorts to excite suspicion: 'The convoy often had to stop at cross roads. Our men were leaving their vehicles to relieve themselves, or to chat with friends in neighbouring trucks. The British escorts were totally unconcerned. Often, when the convoy suddenly moved on, our men had to sprint in order to regain their vehicles!'

It was not until they arrived at the little railway station of Maria Elend at the foot of the mountains which divide Austria from Yugoslavia that Ljotic became suspicious of British intentions. A strong detachment of troops surrounded them as they alighted; the men bore rifles with fixed bayonets, and there were tanks and armoured cars standing menacingly on the perimeter. A train pulled into the station as they descended, and a Serbian officer from the first truck came up to Ljotic's group, exclaiming in agitated tones that he had seen Partisans descending from the train and concealing themselves in the station building.

Ljotic's fears were mounting at every moment. A local inhabitant loitering nearby was asked where the lines led. He replied that they led in the direction from which they came, to Klagenfurt, and in the other — into Yugoslavia. But what of the direct line onwards, past Villach to Tarvisio in Italy? Ah, that line had been out of service since the First World War. As for the train waiting in the station, that had just arrived from Yugoslavia.

There was little time to reflect on these sinister implications. The prisoners were marched swiftly past the station and made to mount into cattle-trucks, sixty or so to a truck. As Ljotic recalls, 'As all this time I was with a close friend of mine, a lieutenant and a platoon commander, on his prompting I . . . tried to join the officers' coach, but as I had no insignia of an officer on my uniform I was stopped by a British soldier and sent to the cattle-truck.' British troops closed the doors after them, followed by a group of railway men who wired up the bolts from the outside. Vladimir Ljotic, watching everything through the narrow truck window, tried to engage the men in conversation, but they remained mute and passed on. Next moment, however, a further group of railway employees in blue overalls came by. They proved more responsive, and as they were Carinthian Slovenes were able to understand Ljotic's questions.

'Where are they taking us?'

'To Ljubljana,' came the grim reply.

'And what are they going to do with us?'

For an answer the man pointed his index finger at the side of his head. His companion angrily put his finger to his lips, and the party moved on.

'Soon after,' Ljotic recalls, 'the British unlocked the door of our vehicle and some dozen Croats in civilian clothing, among them a woman with a baby in her arms, were crammed into an already overcrowded truck. Now for those who were not already seated there was standing room only.'

At this point the engine-driver appeared, a red star on his cap, and mounted the locomotive. The engine whistle shrieked, and the train began to move. A torrential downpour of rain came on, but Ljotic was still able to view the station from his peephole. Now he saw the sight he had dreaded. The doors of the station office flew open, and a band of about thirty Partisans armed with submachine-guns dashed out and flung themselves into the solitary passenger wagon which the British, preserving military etiquette to the last, had reserved for Colonel Tatalovic and his officers. Ljotic was now to appreciate what a fortunate chance had prevented his joining them.

It was just before this that Tatalovic spoke to one of his staff officers, M. S. Stankovic, who recalls that the conversation went much as follows.

'What do you think of all this?' Tatalovic enquired.

'Not very hopeful.'

'Do you think it possible we can be betrayed?'

'It is possible.'

'And what then?'

'If the moral and political wisdom of the so-called civilised and Christian West is of such a kind, then God help Europe and the world.'

The moment of betrayal had arrived. Miodrag Radotic was one of the few officers who subsequently escaped, and remembers the scene vividly:

> I was the last to enter [the passenger wagon] and I found an empty seat in the corner, close to the window. Across from me were Vasiljevic, Boza Najdanovic and his wife. She was pregnant. The window-pane was broken and the drops of rain were falling into the car. I stood up and tried to cover the window with my raincoat, and I saw something that petrified me. I was only able to stammer – partisans. My friend Milovan looked through the window and turned white like a bedsheet. From the railroad station the partisans, with guns in their hands, were running towards the passenger car.

An officer with a dozen Partisans entered the carriage.

> By this time [Vladimir Ljotic informed me] I was more than clear in my mind that we had been betrayed and handed over to Tito's Communists. At this precise moment a single thought was fixed in my mind: not for a moment could I remain with the Communists on board. No matter what – I must escape! The window through which I was observing the station scene was barred, as all the windows on these cattle trucks normally were. I turned round; as if by a miracle the window diagonally opposite was without bars. I made my way across, stepping over sprawled men. The train was gathering speed. Soon the tunnel would be reached. There was not a second to waste.
>
> I grabbed the bar normally used to slide open the truck door, pulled myself up and, thrusting my legs first through the window, threw myself out of the truck. All I heard during this swift movement was someone yelling, 'Don't be a fool! You'll get killed!' I knew the risk, but I didn't even look where I was jumping; whether a bridge, a ravine or a river were coming. I knew I must get out of that train. I did not even fall over, I just lightly touched the ground with my fingers and sprang upright again.
>
> Then, knowing that the officers' coach with the Partisans in it was coming, I flattened myself down by the embankment and stayed in that position until the train disappeared. Then I ran and hid myself among bushes overlooking the railway track. I was actually saved by the heavy downpour, for from my hiding-place I saw about 200 metres to my right

a pair of British soldiers still guarding the blockaded area, but with their rainhoods on they could only see straight ahead.

I stayed in this place for about two hours, expecting that our 3rd and 4th Regiments would be brought to Maria Elend also, for their move was scheduled for noon. However, it was soon apparent that this would not be the case. From my vantage point I saw that the British contingent was recalling its sentries and tanks. Within an hour Maria Elend was a ghost station without a soul in sight.

Vladimir Ljotic set off to find somewhere to spend the night. Passing himself off as a French workman making his way home, he found a farmer who allowed him to pass the night in his hay barn. Next day (25 May) he made up his mind to return to Viktring Camp to issue a general warning to its inmates, then arrange with friends to flee to some safer asylum. After several hair's breadth escapes, he returned to Viktring late on the evening of the twenty-sixth.

There he found the camp emptied of his fellow-Serbs, all of whom had departed in the transports. However, he met a Slovenian friend, Miran Pirih, who told him cheerfully that it was the Slovenes' turn to leave for Italy next morning. Ljotic at once told him the terrible truth, and asked to be taken to a senior Slovenian officer.

They woke up their Regimental Commander, Major Vuk Rupnik, and I was called in. I again repeated my story. Major Rupnik and his wife, who was with him, were very friendly and understanding. The next day, 27 May, early in the morning, I was taken to a lorry cab, where I found some 3–4 persons. As far as I recall now, only one was a civilian; the others were senior Slovenian officers. They did not introduce themselves, but as I heard later one of them was the Domobranci commander, General Krener. I was put in the middle and given a map of the region to show on it the way we were transported, which I did. After some more detailed questioning, I repeated what I already said to Major Rupnik, that my story was entirely true, but I did not want to be confronted with the British. After my experience, I had lost faith in them. I was convinced that they would again hand me over to the Partisans. This time especially, in order to silence a material witness of their complicity in a crime. Then I was released. My reception by these people was not particularly friendly, but they never indicated that they disbelieved me. Anyhow the same day my story was entirely confirmed by another witness, Lieutenant Djordje Jovanovic, who escaped from Jesenice in Yugoslavia and arrived at Viktring during the night of 26–27 May 1945.

While Krener and his colleagues agonised over the possibility that they might be being betrayed by the British, accounts of the reports brought by Ljotic and Jovanovic began to reach the mess of the Third Battalion Welsh Guards at Rosegg. Quite by chance it was the day after Vladimir Ljotic provided me with this account of his escape that I called on a neighbour across the border in Oxfordshire. In 1945 Sir Frederic Bolton had been a young captain commanding No. 1 Company of the Third Welsh Guards. Freshly arrived the day before from Italy, it was he who was detailed to supervise the first day's entrainment of the Serbian Volunteers at Maria Elend, and whose men Ljotic had so narrowly succeeded in evading.

Did the Chetniks know where they were going?

> No, they didn't, and this really was the beginning of the unpleasant bit about it. Because they said to us, 'Where are you sending us?' And I was forced to say that it was none of my business, and my orders were to get them on the train . . . They kept on saying, 'Where were they going to go?' and I went on saying, 'As far as I'm concerned, you're getting on the train, and that's the end of it.' At some stage or other they produced the fearful expression of, 'All right, an Englishman's word is his bond, so we will do what we're told.' The thing really began to get unpleasant, because by that time we knew that as soon as they were in the cattle-trucks and the doors were locked, all the Tito troops emerged from behind the station and ran up and down the train shouting with glee. All the wretched Chetniks looked out of the carriages and screamed.

Captain Bolton returned to Rosegg that night, and next day it was the turn of another company to undertake the operation at Maria Elend. Their commanding officer, Charles Brodie Knight, reported that evening that he had had to open fire on the prisoners. Clearly the Chetniks were beginning to smell a rat.

> What was the turning point [Sir Frederic went on] was, after about the third day of it, someone appeared who had been in the first lot we sent over, and said, 'Look, you do know what's happening, don't you? As soon as the train leaves here, it goes through the tunnel which you can see up the end there, comes out of the mountains the other side into Yugoslavia, and everyone is marched out and shot.'

This horrifying news swiftly spread among the different companies. Brigadier Christopher Thursby Pelham, then commanding No. 2 Company, remembers the universal indignation it aroused among his fellow-officers. Captain Bolton was particularly disgusted, having witnessed the obscene gloating of 'the red-starred little men' around the trainload of Chetniks, and went to his colonel, Robin Rose Price, saying firmly, 'Look, this is something we really cannot go on doing. This is so totally distasteful that we are not going on doing it.'

Bolton's protest at once confirmed Rose Price's fears concerning what he had in any case always considered a despicable policy. 'He said, "I couldn't agree with you more. I will go and see that it's stopped." What I do know is that, either that day or next day, he represented to the Brigadier that the Battalion wasn't going to do any more; and as far as I know that was the end of our involvement.'

This was Bolton's impression, but Colonel Rose Price thinks it unlikely that he did go to the Brigadier. 'He would simply have told me to go away and get on with it, so there would have been very little point.' Though nobody approved what was happening (Rose Price detested it), there could be no question of actually refusing to obey an order. All that could be done was to express strong objection, and try to ensure that no troops repeated this particular operation more often than was absolutely necessary.

The Welsh Guards formed part of General Murray's Sixth Armoured Division. It will be recalled that Murray had displayed great sympathy for the Cossacks in his charge, and went to considerable lengths to allow them to escape. It may seem odd, therefore, that he apparently seems to have made no initial effort to extend similar sympathy towards the Yugoslav refugees in Viktring Camp. Sir Frederic Bolton's memories may help to clarify a view that was fairly widespread at the time:

> I had no reason to think that they [the Chetniks] were going to be treated badly. Whereas the other two companies that were dealing with the White Russians and handing them over to the Russians had every reason to think that. My vague recollection now is that when we, the two companies doing the Chetnik-Yugoslav business, complained in the mess as to what we had been put through, we were told to run away and play. It was nothing to the unpleasantness the other two companies had had.

So far as the Chetniks were concerned, Bolton's initial reaction had been:

> They're going back, and they probably won't be particularly well treated. There was no reason to think they were going to be beaten up. After all, in those days, Stalin was beastly to the White Russians and the Nazis were beastly to everyone. Apart from that, we didn't expect anyone else to behave unpleasantly at all. Why should we have expected the Partisans

to behave in this sort of way? They'd been fighting with the Allies – with us – and we didn't behave like that; and we hadn't actually seen them – we'd never fought alongside them – so we had no reason to think that's the way they behave . . . we never behaved like this on our side, and therefore you didn't expect your Allies to behave like that.

What swiftly opened his eyes was the attitude of the Partisans which, once witnessed, made clear their intentions towards the helpless prisoners. One thing Sir Frederic remembers is that the revulsion he came to feel for the treatment accorded the Chetniks was shared by all his men. This impression is confirmed by the experience of one of his brother-officers. Lieutenant Andrew Gibson-Watt commanded a platoon lining part of the road along which the column of prisoners was driven before arriving at Maria Elend. In consequence they witnessed none of the more sinister events which so swiftly alerted Captain Bolton. Nevertheless the whole idea of lying and tricking helpless men and women who had relied on the honour of the British Army aroused great disgust among the guardsmen. On returning to quarters, Gibson-Watt was approached by his sergeant, who enquired whether they were to be allotted the same duty next day. On receiving a negative reply, Sergeant Garrison remarked respectfully but emphatically, 'That's just as well, sir, as they wouldn't do it.'

It has to be remembered, too, that it had been falsely put about by the Fifth Corps that the return of the refugees formed part of a 'deal', ensuring the departure of Tito's troops from Carinthia. Whether this aspect influenced General Murray, who seems uncharacteristically to have made no recorded objection to the operation, is now uncertain. In response to my enquiry regarding this point, he replied in August 1984:

> I never personally got involved in the repatriation of the Yugoslavs – I do not know to what extent my staff became involved. So I am afraid I cannot help you, much as I appreciate the importance of the work you are doing . . . I am afraid I am now in hospital – almost completely immobile with arthritis, and somewhat blind.

In any other case one might regard with suspicion a divisional commander's claim not to have been apprised of what his staff was arranging. But in view of Murray's proven sympathy for the Chetniks it seems possible that Fifth Corps policy was 'nodded through' at Sixth Armoured Division headquarters without attracting sufficient notice for the hard-pressed Murray to intervene.

It soon became known that the worst fears of Colonel Tatalovic and his men were justified. Ten days later a Serbian Partisan lieutenant, horrified by all he had seen, was to desert his unit and flee into Italy. There he recounted to Yugoslav exiles his experiences as a member of the unit responsible for the reception of the repatriates. As can be seen in his account, there was a secret British unit actually operating on Yugoslav soil which, if it did not actually participate in the massacres which followed, was acting in close collaboration with Tito's executioners:

Report made at Rome on 25.6.1945; by Branislav Todorovic, born at Belgrade, 33 years of age, Orthodox, before the war a student of technology. He is a lieutenant of the Partisans (or National Liberation Army), never convicted, unmarried, without any property.

Having fled from the N.L. Army, he reached Italy and made the following statement:

'Before arriving at Rosenbach [on the Austrian side of the Karavanke Mountains] I was serving at Jesenice. There on the 24th May, 1945 I received an order to move. The order came from the Brigade Chief of Staff, whose name I do not know. The order was verbal, at about 6 p.m. He told me to prepare to go to Rosenbach, that we might contact the English, from whom we were to receive some prisoners. Together we went to the town of Jesenice, on the staff of 26th Dalmatian Division; while the battalion went to Kranjska Gora to take up a position on the frontier in the greatest secrecy and without the knowledge of the Allies, for we had already been ordered to be always ready to attack. At the staff at Jesenice I was present at a conversation between the Chief of Staff of the Brigade and Captain Slavko Savic, o.c. the battalion. Capt. Savic on that occasion asked whom we were to attack and the other replied "But everyone knows. Whom else but our glorious allies?" Also the political commissars told the troops that we should attack the English, if they would not give up Istria, Carinthia and Trieste.

'I knew that some representatives of our army had been at Rosenbach for several days and had taken over from the English about 800 prisoners, Yugoslav citizens who had fled from the partisans and belonged to the Yugoslav Army in the Homeland, the Domobranci, the Ustashe or the Slovene 'White Guards' (as the partisans called them), and also some non-combatant relatives of these prisoners.

'That same day, the 24th May, I went by a special train of 2 wagons and an engine to Rosenbach, with the Brigade Chief of Staff and an officer of the 26th Division. There we found Captain Dominko, from Makarska, deputy O.C. of a brigade of the 26th Division, an interpreter, two officers and a female partisan who was in charge of the health of the company at

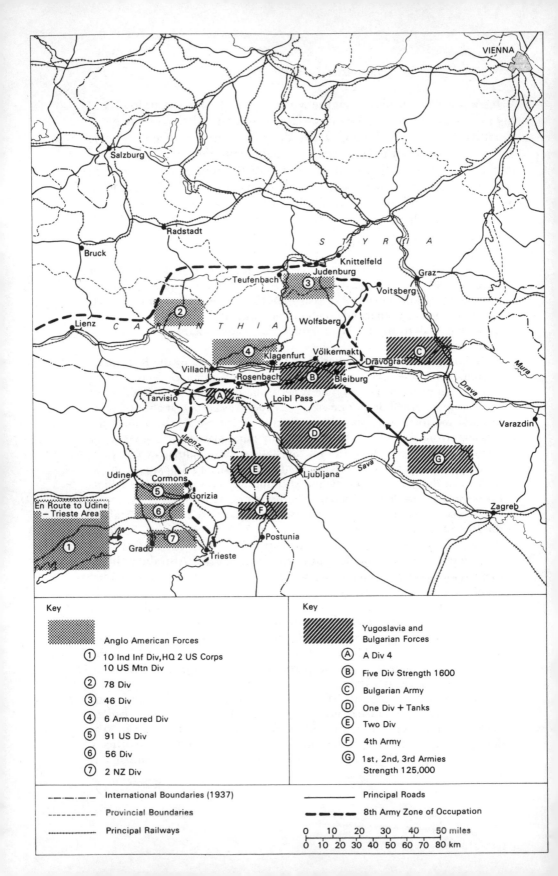

VIENNA

Salzburg

Radstadt

Bruck

Lienz

Teufenbach

Knittelfeld

Judenburg

③

Graz

Voitsberg

Wolfsberg

C A R I N T H I A

②

④

Klagenfurt

Völkermakt

Drävograd

Ⓒ

Villach

Rosenbach

Ⓑ

Bleiburg

Tarvisio

Ⓐ

Loibl Pass

Ⓓ

Isonzo

Ⓔ

Varazdin

Udine

Cormons

⑤

Gorizia

Ljubljana

Sava

Drava

Mura

Ⓖ

En Route to Udine
– Trieste Area

⑥

Ⓕ

①

⑦

Postunia

Zagreb

Grado

Trieste

S T Y R I A

Key

	Anglo American Forces
①	10 Ind Inf Div, HQ 2 US Corps 10 US Mtn Div
②	78 Div
③	46 Div
④	6 Armoured Div
⑤	91 US Div
⑥	56 Div
⑦	2 NZ Div

Key

	Yugoslavia and Bulgarian Forces
Ⓐ	A Div 4
Ⓑ	Five Div Strength 1600
Ⓒ	Bulgarian Army
Ⓓ	One Div + Tanks
Ⓔ	Two Div
Ⓕ	4th Army
Ⓖ	1st, 2nd, 3rd Armies Strength 125,000

—·—·— International Boundaries (1937)

--------- Provincial Boundaries

·········· Principal Railways

———— Principal Roads

▬▬▬ 8th Army Zone of Occupation

0   10   20   30   40   50 miles
0 10 20 30 40 50 60 70 80 km

the station and who was about to be transferred. Her name was Anica Popovic, nicknamed 'Luka', from Vukovar. That night, about 10 or 11, Capt. Dominko introduced us to the English Lieutenant Lakhed [Lockheed], liaison officer, of a unit called '6 Special Force'. This officer told us that at 10 o'clock next day there would be ready a train of 30 wagons and 2 wagons for officers which would pick up 1,500 prisoners at Maria Elend. That evening Capt. Dominko told us that an Ustasa Minister had been sent into the country on an earlier transport; and he showed us a gold watch which he said that he had taken from the latter. The woman also showed us a portfolio full of money and a smaller bag full of watches, rings, etc., which she said that she had taken from prisoners, and she told us that we could do the same without fear of anybody.

'The next day the train arrived a bit late and we entrained half a company of the 3rd battalion, which was [at] Hrusica at the other end of the tunnel, on Yugoslav territory. We did this secretly, so that the prisoners should not know that they were being taken back to Yugoslavia; for the English had told them that they would go to Italy. When we came to St. Maria Elend our soldiers hid in the station and remained hidden until the prisoners were entrained and locked into their wagons. The English saw to the entrainment. When our soldiers emerged, there was a panic amongst the prisoners, who looked terrified and astonished. Some of them shouted "hurray for the English. Don't hand us over to them. They'll kill us, etc." The train moved off and in 15 minutes we were at Rosenbach station, where there were our soldiers who surrounded the train. There were also some English, who had placed some guards there.

'From Rosenbach we went on to Hrusica. The Brigade Chief of Staff went with us; and Captain 'Rasa' (a partisan nickname – his real name I don't know); the O.C. 3rd battalion, Capt. Brale (also a nickname); the commissar of the battalions, whose name I don't know; two Slovene officers of the 14th Division; and the officers of company mentioned. When we got to Hrusica, a whole battalion (the 3rd), at the order of the O.C. who had telephoned, surrounded the train. The O.C. 3rd battalion (Brale) then said to me "Commander, now you too will have something to do." I did not understand what I had to do. But there had been talk in the train about removing the heads of certain people who were to be butchered. As I feared that he was referring to that, I made no answer, so that later I might sham stupid, as though I knew nothing of the business. All the partisan officers went to the two wagons containing the officer prisoners. From the latter and from the other ranks they selected 54, mostly officers, and told them to get ready and come along. Our officers told each they were to slaughter these men. They took them first to the battalion staff where they searched and plundered them and divided the loot among themselves. I was present and witnessed it. They then beat them with sticks so violently that they all collapsed on the ground.

They then waited for darkness and then took the prisoners several hundred metres away into a wood and there disputed as to who should do the butchering. Who did it I don't know, for I made myself scarce in order not to have a hand in it. I fancy that they all shared in the slaughter. I made my way to a labour detachment and there supped and could hear screams and wailing and some revolver shots. The cooks who gave me my supper said nothing, as I did; but their expressions showed how they hated the whole thing.

'All those officer-murderers returned singing. Amongst them was a certain Mile, a Serbian, O.C. the machine-gun company of the 3rd battalion, a favourite of the C.O. He had done most in the way of butchery. To verify what had happened I went up and found 54 bodies which some soldiers were then burying. I saw pools of blood and one corpse that had been knifed, but I reckon that the rest had been knifed also, for I only heard two or three revolver shots and there were 54 dead.

'The prisoners remaining in the train were meanwhile mercilessly plundered by the soldiers. I remember that on the way from St. Maria Elend to Rosenbach 14 chetniks committed suicide in the train and that at Rosenbach, in the presence of the English whom I summoned, we took the bodies out of the train and buried them near the station. I do not remember exactly where, for we had to hurry on with the train.

'From Hrusica the train went on to Jesenice. At Hrusica the train was boarded by the Youth company of 1st Vojvodina brigade, composed of boys from 10 to 16 years. These boys were scattered amongst the wagons, and all the time as we went along I heard shooting, and heavy firing at that, as though a battle had been going on. When we reached the bridge over the Save I saw them throwing corpses out of the moving train, some of which fell in the river and some on the bank.

'At Jesenice the prisoners were got out of the train in a desperate condition and marched to a camp about 3 kilometres away. About 10 per cent were separated into one group and the rest into another. I asked the camp guards the reason for this and was told that the larger group was to be liquidated first. It was dark when I left the camp. I heard machine-gun firing and the camp guard who was acting as my guide said "Eh, they're killing them." He was angry that he had no share in it. "My God," he said, "if only you weren't here and I were there sharing the loot. Now I shall get nothing, as I have to go with you."

'I returned that night, with a special train of wagons and an engine, to Rosenbach and on the way made up my mind not to make the journey again but at all costs to get away. Actually I did twice accompany transports to Hrusica. Thereafter I did not go beyond Rosenbach; for, when I told Lt. Lakhed what was being done with the prisoners, he helped me and arranged with my C.O. that I should stay with him, on the ground that a liaison officer should not go so far from his duty station.

'On every transport after that – and there were 16 of them – the corpses of suicides were found. On the request of the English these were removed from the train at Rosenbach and buried. I asked the English to do this, so that they might see the real state of affairs and that my statements about the treatment of the prisoners was true. I was never again present at any butchery or killing, but I heard about it from my soldiers or soldiers of the companies employed on the job and I know that the same events were repeated on the other transports as on the first. Only the numbers differed. Sometimes more were killed, sometimes less. And those not killed were condemned to labour camps and to heavy labour without proper food, so that I don't think they will last long.

'On the 3rd June I arranged supper for the English. I thought that I should be the only partisan present. But as a big transport of prisoners was arranged for next day, there came the officers who had been at the killings, all except the Brigade Chief of Staff. Of the English Capt. Brown was at supper and 2 captains from the regiment at St. Jakob, also Lt. Lakhed and Lt. Gelbajt (? Galbraith). By a special train late that night arrived the assistant commissar and the commissar of the 3rd battalion, a Montenegrin whose name I don't know. That evening I got into close relations with the English. On that account I became suspect to the partisans. Next day I was summoned by telephone and told to report at the staff at once. I knew what that meant. Accordingly, I fled into Italy.'

This account was published in an émigré newspaper in the United States and not long after was brought to the attention of the Foreign Office. J. M. Addis of the Southern Department minuted on 3 September 1945: 'Todorovic's account has the ring of truth and its general tenor is confirmed by other reports which we have seen. There is little doubt that there was an extensive and indiscriminate slaughter of the Yugoslav quisling troops; and it is distressing to reflect that they were passed across the frontier by British troops.'[32]

Every day for the ensuing week these grim events were repeated. On 25 May, the second day of the operation, Nigel Nicolson noted laconically in his log book:

1. Train ready in Stn.
2. 1650 Serbs marching to Stn. at Maria Elend.
3. There may be trouble since local inhabitants informed Serbs of their true destination. 3 W.[elsh] G.[uards] are taking precautions.
4. Suggest moving Transit Camp nearer the Stn. for the future.
5. Corps L.O. says:–

(a) 15000 more likely to be evacuated via Maria Elend during the next few days.

(b) that proposed evacuation of all Yugoslavs via Klagenfurt is 'not on' owing to the Gradient of the line.

(c) that he says evacuation could be speeded up so far as trains are concerned.

6. 80–90 are at present being loaded into each cattle truck. This is too many.

They were no illusions over the likely fate of the repatriates; they were all 'en route for the slaughter-house', as a Partisan officer at Maria Elend made clear to the British military escort. By now the news was reaching the steadily-depleting camp at Viktring. The day Vladimir Ljotic arrived back at Viktring with his terrible news, a 'movement order' had been issued by the camp commandant to the Slovenian, Croat and Serb commanders, informing them that, 'All Croat, Serbian Chetnik, Slovenian Chetnik, and 600 Slovenian Home Army personnel will be moved from this camp to new area tomorrow, 27 May.'[33] But despite Ljotic's account General Franc Krenner, commander of the Slovenian National Army, was disinclined to believe that the British could have behaved in the treacherous manner implied, and gave strict orders that alarmist rumours were to be suppressed. It is possible that we have here another explanation of the different attitudes displayed by the British military command towards the Cossacks and the Yugoslavs. General von Pannwitz was a man of the highest personal qualities, who deliberately chose to accompany his Cossacks to certain death. The Slovenian General Krenner, in marked contrast, was a man remarkable only for extreme ineptitude and cowardice. A man of more forthright character might have done something to impress on the not unsympathetic British the terrible danger under which his people lay.

Next day, 27 May, 3,000 Slovenes were handed over through the Rosenbach tunnel, and that night three Serbian officers arrived back at the camp with similar stories to that of Ljotic. Once again Krenner rebuked them strongly for scaremongering, but this time was himself sufficiently alarmed to set off for the Sixth Armoured Divisional HQ in Klagenfurt to seek clarification. After a three-hour wait in an ante-chamber, he was seen by an adjutant, who presented him with an order written in German 'From Major-General Murray, Commander of the 6 British Armoured Division, to General Krener, of the Slovenian Militia', explaining that orders had been received to send the fugitive Yugoslavs to an unknown destination. As a soldier he had to obey his orders, and he trusted that General Krenner would in turn do the same.

Slovenian accounts present Krenner in a poor light, slow to recognise what was happening, and when he finally did come to understand, anxious only to save his own skin. Nevertheless even he expressed grave suspicions when faced with this equivocal document. When the British officer reassured him that their destination was Palmanova, Krenner pointed out that trains were not running to Tarvisio, and that on a suggested alternative route all the bridges were down. The Englishman shrugged his shoulders, lamely conjecturing that Krenner's information was inaccurate.

On 29 May Dr Joze Basaj, President of the National Committee of Slovenia, received further eye-witness evidence that Yugoslavia was the true destination of the transports. He

> immediately went to see the British commander Lieutenant General Kcightley in Celovec [Klagenfurt] to find out what was going on. After considerable waiting he was eventually admitted to Keightley's presence where Keightley indignantly denied that anything like the handing over of refugees occurred and threatened with severe punishment all who might spread such rumors.[34]

After Krenner's return to Viktring he found most senior members of the Slovenian Committee as reluctant as himself to believe that the gathering quantity of gloomy reports were based on anything but irresponsible speculation and rumour-mongering. It was not until the thirtieth that he sent his chauffeur to Bleiburg (now also employed as a staging-post in the handovers) on a reconnaissance mission. The chauffeur, Franc Sega, returned with the horrifying news that Bleiburg was swarming with Partisans, who were taking over groups of Slovenian Home Guardsmen from their British escorts.

As soon as he heard this, General Krenner hastily changed into civilian clothes and left the camp. At 12.45 next morning Nigel Nicolson's log book recorded, 'General i/c Slovenes missing in his green Adler coupé.' Before that, at 9 a.m. Chetnik and Domobran officers informed their men that it was now known for certain that the British had delivered all their comrades over to Tito for slaughter, released them from their military duties, and advised them to don civilian clothes and disappear. Large numbers dispersed at once, while many others, confused or stunned by the dreadful news, stayed where they were. If the British were in league with the Communists, where was there now to flee?

Terrible reports were flying in from every quarter. The previous day (29 May) the Cossack officers had been offered up to SMERSH at Judenburg, and it was learned that all the other Cossacks were doomed too. At Klein St Veit Colonel Rogozhin, unaware of the quirk of British policy which had spared him, lived in hourly expectancy of a summons for his *Russkii Corpus* to share the Cossacks' fate. Unaware, too, that the tragedy at Viktring was already several days old, he requested the enterprising Ara Delianich to drive to Viktring with a warning. Her account of the journey provides a unique first-hand view of the tragic events occurring all over British-occupied Austria at this time. It was an apocalyptic scene of desolation and inhumanity.

Already Ara had been over to Lienz, to the doomed Cossacks' camp at Peggetz, and witnessed the departure of their officers for the 'conference' at Oberdrauburg. At Spittal on 29 May she arrived just at the moment Andrei Shkuro was being bundled into a car by his British captors, preparatory to being delivered to the Soviets at Judenburg. With him were his aides, several of whom Ara recognised as fellow White Russians from Belgrade. The old Cossack General was protesting vigorously, pointing out that he held the English Order of the Bath.

'Give me a revolver!' she heard him cry; 'I do not fear death, but I do not want to fall alive into the hands of the Red swine!'

At dawn on the thirtieth Ara set off again in her Opel, this time southwards. A grim vision greeted her and her companions:

> We arrived at Klagenfurt at eight o'clock in the morning. On both sides of the road, tethered in their improvised horse lines among the broad pastures, stood thousands of horses. They neighed continually, stretching out their necks. Emaciated, feeble, suffering from dysentery brought on by their provender (newly-mown clover) they dropped like flies. Their corpses, terribly blown up by the heat, as it appeared, lay day and night among the living. Over them swarmed black clouds of insects. In the sky above kites circled around.
>
> With piteous neighs the horses replied to the barking of dogs. The English had built a huge cage, into which their soldiers drove dogs taken from the Germans, fine shepherd dogs and Dobermans. They yelped and barked, tearing about in this pen, fighting among each other to the death. They were fed and watered once a day, being given bloody chunks of meat from the dead horses. Later they were practically all shot.

Apart from a couple of halts on the road to have our papers checked, all went smoothly. We skirted Klagenfurt through side streets. On the road to Viktring three large lorries with trailers passed us, their tarpaulin covers removed. Within sat people in the bright green rags of Soviet prisoners of war, with similarly greenish, dazed faces. Above them fluttered red dusters and handkerchiefs with the inscriptions: 'We are happy to be travelling on the road to the Motherland and our beloved Leader'; 'Long live the saviour of Europe, Generalissimo Stalin'; 'To thee, Father of Peoples, our greeting!' and other prepared slogans.

These wretched people, snatched from slavery in German camps, were setting out across country to another slavery. Later we encountered similar returning convoys of former *Ostarbeiter* [Workers from the East]. Some sang, others wept. The Western Allies were painstakingly transporting these masses in an attempt to clear them out of Germany and Austria as swiftly as possible. Now we found ourselves taking the ill-boding road for the field of Viktring. In only one section of it stood the wagons, home-made tents and huts sheltering fugitive Slovenian citizens. The field appeared to have been swept clean. Driving from the road on to the open space, we could see a group of two hundred Slovenian Domobranci in their bluish uniforms. They were standing in front of ten lorries and as many small tanks, on the sides of which sat English soldiers carrying automatic weapons. A little way off was drawn up a rank of motorcyclists in black berets.

Before our eyes there was unfolding the final act of this dreadful tragedy. The English, having already handed over all the Serbian Volunteers and the greater part of the Domobranci, were despatching the wounded and sick to Tito's justice. Around them were gathering those same sombre soldiers in English uniforms such as we saw at Lienz . . . Those who were able to shift for themselves climbed into the vehicles. No attention was paid to the groans and shrieks of others, lying on stretchers, their limbs amputated or in plaster, many blinded, who were shoved roughly into the trucks. The attitude towards them was indistinguishable from that manifested towards the horses in their horse-lines and the dogs in their pens.

We approached and stood beside a small group of German officers, who were literally struck dumb with horror at what they saw happening before them. Near me on a stretcher lay the young Domobran Yanko Otsvirk, my brother's friend, who had lost his eyesight at the time of the withdrawal: the cart in which he was travelling was hit by an Italian grenade which exploded and destroyed his eyesight. The bandage half concealing his youthful features, with two bright spots of blood seeping through from his eyesockets, and the convulsive gripping of his hands on his chest, told of those physical and moral sufferings which he was undergoing. Two English soldiers picked him up and tossed him head over heels into the truck. A prolonged scream of agony from the invalid pierced the air.

Blows from rifle-butts drove nurses, doctors and hospital orderlies into the lorries. Girls clutched at the hands of their executioners, prayed for mercy, seized onto the edge of the trucks, and were pushed back. One fell, and the English soldiers began kicking her.

A little further on, on a rise leading towards the highway, stood eight Domobranci officers. Their faces were ashen-grey, with empty, leaden gaze. It appeared as if these living corpses had already departed this world, and that only their lifeless bodies submitted to the commands of their persecutors. Among them was the famous Yugoslav Air Force hero, Colonel M-k.

Behind the backs of the Germans I quietly went up to M-k in deadly earnest and, suppressing my agitation and grasping him carefully by the hand, said: 'Colonel! You know me – I can help you to escape. At the third house from the corner on the right-hand side of the street you will find our Opel. Soon no one will be able to see it from here. Go there, without drawing attention to yourself. Sit in the car and wait. We will drive you away.'

The Colonel did not turn round. His eyes slid round to my face. I felt how the muscles of his hand trembled in response to my greeting. His reply was scarcely audible:

'My soldiers and officers have already been sent to their deaths this morning. Now they are taking the wounded, my brave brothers-in-arms. I will not abandon these people. I am guilty . . . they wanted to flee, but I dissuaded them, trusting in these monsters' humanity. Tell everyone who knows me that I am going peacefully to my death. I don't want to live on as a betrayer.'

An English sergeant, standing nearby and noticing our conversation, suddenly bellowed out, swearing in the most obscene manner,

'Clear off, Nazi swine! What are you doing here? D'you want us to send you Germans where we're sending this lot?'

The German officers swiftly stepped back, turned round and almost sprinted down the slope to the road. The Colonel turned round to me, crossed me in the Catholic fashion, and got into the lorry. At that moment a shot rang out, a second, and an ensuing ragged volley.

A one-legged invalid on crutches was racing across the field, skipping and zigzagging just like a hunted hare. Thrusting away the ground from beneath him with his supports, with great leaps the wretched man was racing to conceal himself in the forest.

The English soldiers knelt down and opened fire on him with their rifles. They were roaring with laughter. They were enjoying themselves. Obviously in the enjoyment of their 'game' they were not shooting at his body but below his feet, raising clouds of dust and earth with their bullets. That scoundrel who had shouted at me and Colonel M-k snatched up from his chest a submachine gun and let fly a burst of fire at the cripple's stomach.

People have told me about the terrible scream given off by a shot hare. I have never been hunting, feeling an insuperable repugnance to killing living beings for sport. But I shall never forget the cripple's screams as he collapsed on the ground.

The beaten folk in the lorries uttered a howl. A German girl, a nurse standing quite near me, fell down in a faint. The lorry motors started up, and they moved out onto the road. Before and behind them trundled tanks. From the last truck I could see waving the pale hand of Colonel M-k.

Standing in the distance, the Slovenian refugees, with heads lowered, dragged themselves slowly back to their improvised households. Austrians from houses bordering the field hurried back through their garden gates, whispering to one another. Lieutenant Sh. gave me a sign and moved in the direction of our car. It was dangerous to stay alone in the field with the English. I followed, but paused and looked back. On this trampled earth, by this same forest, among the damped-down campfires of Viktring, lay the lifeless body of the invalid and his broken crutches.[35]

The picture is not a pleasant one. Regrettably, there is no reason to discredit this account and every reason to believe it to be a reliable testimony set down by a patently honest and accurate witness. Nina Lencek also witnessed the violence employed once deception proved ineffective:

They were forced to get into the trucks. We felt as if they were cattle being sent to the slaughterhouse; that was exactly the feeling we had . . . Some were resigned, others were forced on to the trucks; they were roughing them up with rifle-butts. I remember – now it comes back to me – crying, people shouting 'goodbye!', screaming. It was heart-breaking. There was terrible sadness: every family had lost sons, their fathers, their loved ones, who were being returned.

Under ordinary circumstances the British soldier is as humane and chivalrous as his brutal trade permits, and there were many among the suffering Cossacks and Yugoslavs at this time who had grudging reason to pay tribute to those qualities. But higher command at Fifth Corps had made an insidiously determined effort to instil in troops conducting the operation a belief that the majority of those being handed over were war criminals and traitors, Balkan bandits who were receiving no more than their deserts. The victims were de-humanised, and their resistance to return could be regarded but as further evidence of their contumacy and guilt. As German officers watching had reason to know, when the command structure becomes perverted by inhumane purposes, it is not long before the corruption spreads below.

On the day Ara Delianich visited Viktring 3,000 Slovenes were evacuated. Next day, 31 May, saw the last sweep of military personnel within the camp. Many of these were mingled among civilians in the neighbouring camp, where they had sought refuge after the general warning issued by their officers on the previous morning. They were sifted out and despatched to Tito's forces via Bleiburg. They comprised a total of some 1,950 Slovenes and fifty Croats. A despairing fatalism gripped many, now aware of the horrific fate meted out to those of their comrades who had already departed. As they left, they explained to those left behind: 'If God wishes this ultimate sacrifice of us, we too will go where our brothers and friends have gone. We're ready even to die for the truth.'[36]

These tragic events at Viktring Camp and elsewhere aroused wide-spread horror and revulsion even before the full extent of the ensuing slaughter had become known. Had German officers been indicted for conducting a similar operation, there can be no doubt that they would have stood inculpated of a major war crime.

It would be wrong, however, to end this chapter leaving major blame apportioned to soldiers who were obeying what were for most unpalatable orders. Deceits practised by shamefaced subalterns on trusting Serbs and Slovenes were paralleled at a much higher level. In an earlier chapter it was seen how General Robertson's order of 14 May was directed at the tens of thousands of Croats pouring across the Drava in mid-May. That crisis was over within forty-eight hours of its inception, but Robertson's order was retained as improvised justification for handing back to the Partisans Croats whose surrender had been accepted by British troops.

By 24 May the Croats had for the most part departed, and the order of 14 May was employed in yet another context: to return Slovenian soldiers and civilians, and those Chetniks whom General Robertson had himself specifically excluded from the terms of his instruction. The label 'Croatian', tarnished as it was by the country's collaboration with Germany, provided valuable camouflage for an operation which by the end of May was ingeniously extended to cover Serbian Chetniks who had fought loyally as Britain's allies, and Serbian Domobranci who had at peril of their lives rescued and protected Allied airmen.

On 19 May the Foreign Office received a curious account of the situation in Austria from Macmillan's assistant, Philip Broad. Broad – 'a clever, amusing man', Macmillan thought him – was the Resident Minister's expert on Yugoslav affairs, having been previously Counsellor at the Embassy to the Yugoslav Government, and Macmillan's representative in Bari.[37] The relevant part of his telegram is as follows:

> 200,000 Croat troops have surrendered to Marshal Tito in Bleiburg area and a further 35,000 in Wildenstein area south east of Klagenfurt. These surrenders, together with 36,000 Quisling Yugoslavs already in British hands, should account for practically the whole Croat army and will accordingly release Yugoslav divisions for other tasks.[38]

The '36,000 Quisling Yugoslavs already in British hands', whom Broad specifies as forming part of the Croatian Army, is in fact an allusion to the Serbian Chetniks and Slovenes held at Viktring. One wonders how a man of Broad's deep experience of Yugoslav affairs could have arrived at such a misconception. Less than a week earlier, after all, he had accompanied Harold Macmillan to Klagenfurt, where the huge mass of refugees assembled in Viktring fields had formed a major topic of their discussion with General Keightley.

It was a misconception that was to prove persistent. Ten days later, on 29 May, Broad in another telegram to the Foreign Office made reference to 'trains from Yugoslavia which are repatriating Croatian prisoners'.[39] In fact it was as early as 24 May that the Fifth Corps War Diary recorded, 'Handover of Croats completed'. On 28 and 29 May it was Slovenes who were being returned to Yugoslavia at the rate of 3,000 a day. Finally, when the Foreign Office came to conduct an investigation into the manner in which the repatriation had taken place in violation of instructions sent to the Resident Minister at the beginning of May, it received this abbreviated and inaccurate version of events: Fifth Corps, so it was learned, had 'agreed to hand over Croats to Yugoslavia and 900 Croats were transferred on the 24th May'.[40] It seems that 'Croat' was a term of wide-ranging utility at the Resident Minister's office.

7

The Pit of Kocevje

'We Marxists . . . always knew . . . that socialism cannot be "introduced", that it emerges in the course of the most tense, the most
sharp – to the point of frenzy and despair – class struggle and civil
war, that between capitalism and socialism there lies the long period
of "birth pangs", that violence is always the midwife of the old
society, that to the transition-period from the bourgeois to the
socialist society there corresponds a special state (that is, a system of
organised violence against a certain class), namely the dictatorship of
the proletariat.' (V. I. Lenin, *Collected Works*, xxxv, p. 192)

Among the Domobranci paraded on the morning of 29 May was a
twenty-year-old Slovenian lad named Milan Zajec. Like many other
village boys in his neighbourhood he had joined the Home Guards
in 1943 in response to Partisan atrocities in his locality. At the
beginning of May his unit had been defending the town of Kocevje,
south of Ljubljana. After a stiff fight lasting most of the morning of
2 May, it was discovered that the German detachment on their flank
had decamped without warning, and the Slovenian troops were
forced to withdraw to the capital. Assigned temporary guard duty
on a hospital train (the patients, as they learned later, were massacred
almost to a man by the Communists), they found themselves not
long afterwards caught up in the general retreat of Slovenian troops
and civilians across the Loibl Pass. In this way Zajec found himself
settled with thousands of other refugees in the great camp at Viktring.

For five days the camp had been emptying fast as thousands of its
inmates departed 'for Italy'. Now it was Milan's turn. After the
customary morning prayer, his company with their horses travelled
in a column of trucks accompanied by tanks and jeeps to the station
at Rosenbach. Suspicions were suddenly aroused by the sight of a
group of Partisans making off into the woods, and by widespread

plundering on the part of their British guards. 'You have no right to take my watch,' complained a Slovenian officer. 'If I don't, Tito will,' the soldier replied bluntly, but returning the watch. Before anyone could reflect on these ominous words, the escorting troops drove the prisoners into the boxcars of a waiting train, locking the doors behind them.

Now, as on previous operations, the British guards withdrew, to be replaced by previously-concealed Partisans. Milan could see everything which passed by means of a small hand-mirror, which he held out of an aperture. Threats and curses came from all sides, and an exultant voice could be heard to declare, 'Now we shall kill everybody!' During the journey in the long tunnel under the Kara-vanke Mountains Partisan assailants broke into wagons, looting what property remained after the attentions of the British, and beating all who objected. At the first stop on the Yugoslav side these attacks were renewed, after which the train proceeded without stopping until it reached the town of Kranj at about two o'clock in the morning.

At Kranj Station the Slovenians found that the authorities had assembled a large mob, who were permitted to stone and beat the cowering prisoners as they descended and were marched off in column to a nearby camp. There the commandant delivered a threat-ening harangue: if anyone attempted to conceal property on his person he would be shot. That this was no idle threat was evinced by twenty or so corpses littering the ground; but clearly even this was not considered sufficient warning, and a youth was paraded before the prisoners. He was a seventeen-year-old boy from Ljubljana named Polde Koman, known to many present. The commandant declared that Koman had secreted a revolver; upon which a guard stepped up to the prisoner and smashed in his front teeth with a pistol-barrel. 'Lie down!' came the command. Koman obeyed, and was instantly shot dead with a submachine-gun. At first the comman-dant ordered the corpse to be thrown into the latrine, but then relented and permitted it to be buried in open ground.

The whole of that day (30 May) groups of Partisans invaded the camp at intervals, interrogating the prisoners and, in many cases, avenging local grievances. Milan Zajec was fortunate in evading attack, but saw many terrible beatings which left people half-dead with shirts stiff with blackened blood. Unconscious, they had buckets of water thrown over them to revive them for a further bout. Next day, 31 May, a car arrived with a delegation of high-ranking commissars who supervised further lengthy interrogations. In the same camp were five of Milan's elder brothers, including twins. When opportunity offered they gathered together, comforting the young man as best they could. Comfort was also provided by a group of priests who, concealed in civilian attire, moved cautiously about the camp, hearing confessions and granting absolution.

On 1 June the camp inmates travelled by train and on foot to St Vid, on the outskirts of Ljubljana. There the Communists had taken over a large seminary building for their own purposes. This seminary had already acquired a sinister reputation among the population, but for Milan and his companions it was to be a brief stopping-place. That afternoon they were moved into Ljubljana and took their places on another train. Rumours abounded in the cramped confines of the box-cars. Were they bound for Russian concentration camps? But the train began to move on tracks leading south-eastwards, towards Kocevje, where Milan had been stationed with his Domobranci unit only a month ago. Now some people began to declare that they were all about to be killed. The bridge was down over the Ljubljanica river just outside the city, and the prisoners were compelled to descend and cross by a footbridge. As at Kranj, a dense mob had been assembled. They were gratified by the sight of the Home Guardsmen being savagely beaten yet again as they scrambled into a train waiting on the further bank.

The prisoners were confined in this train until the evening, when at six o'clock they heard the familiar sound of the angelus bells ringing out from churches in the countryside around. All prayed fervently. Then, at dusk, the train shuddered and lurched forward on its journey. By a calculation of the units present (mostly Slovenian Domobranci, with a small party of Serbian Chetniks and another of Croatian Home Guards), Milan Zajec reckoned that there were about 2,000 people on board. Trundling slowly through the darkness, the train did not reach the town of Kocevje until the first light of dawn next morning.

The wagon doors were unbolted, and the prisoners descended, blinking in the grey daylight, on to the platform. They found themselves surrounded by thousands of armed Partisans. Formed up four abreast, the captives were marched up the street to the high school which, like most public buildings in the new Yugoslavia, had already found a new purpose. It was crammed with people, even to the attics, where men desperate for air in the crush were knocking bricks out of the walls. Among the milling crowd striving to gain a gulp of the only 'food' provided – pine-needles boiled in water – Milan glimpsed three of his brothers.

Their stay in the high school was not long, however. Milan was among a group of about 200 taken to another large building nearby, formerly housing the local branch of the athletics association 'Sokol'. As they peered about them, bewildered, someone spotted on their right an ominous sight: a pile of clothes spattered with what looked like bloodstains. On the left was a pile of two-foot lengths of wire. Hustled forward by Partisan guards, each man had his hands bound tightly behind his back with this wire, and was then strapped arm by arm to a companion. In some cases, where another was missing, the bound couple was shackled to a third captive.

As soon as this was accomplished, a lorry was backed up to the entrance, and the trussed prisoners were pushed up an improvised log ramp into the back of the vehicle. Six trucks in turn took on their loads, twenty or more prisoners to each consignment. In the rear truck Milan caught a glimpse of his three brothers (the fourth they had left with the main body in the high school, and the fifth was fortunate in never reaching Kocevje). The twins were wired together, and the third to another man.

The convoy moved out on to the highway. To Milan, who had so recently performed his military duties in the neighbourhood, it was familiar countryside. Through Rudnik, Salka Vas, Zeljne: they were travelling north-eastwards up to the huge mountain forest of Kocevski Rog. They had gone about fifteen or twenty kilometres and were passing already among the darkened firs of the forest fringes when another lorry passed them, travelling in the direction from which they had come. Piled in the back was a heap of uniforms. Shortly afterwards a prisoner began to sing a familiar hymn. Silenced by blows from the guards' bludgeons, he joined the rest in recitation of prayers, which were tolerated.

Soon from ahead of them within the forest came disturbing sounds. First they heard the thud of a heavy explosion, followed shortly afterwards by the unmistakable rattle of machine-gun fire. Next came a terrible screaming, accompanied by peals of raucous laughter. There was no time for reflection, for now they had left the road and pulled up in a large clearing. Kicked out in heaps on to the ground, the men had their laces cut and shoes removed.

As Milan and his companion struggled to their feet, they witnessed a scene which might have been taken from a mediaeval representation of the torments of hell. Close beside them was a young prisoner from a previous consignment. Naked, with his hands tied behind his back, he was covered from head to foot with gashes and stab-wounds.

More slashes were being inflicted even at that moment by a fanatical Partisan. From a bare three paces' distance, Zajec saw to his horror that both the boy's eyes had already been gouged out, and blood was seeping from the hollow sockets. The Partisan, ignoring everything else around him, relentlessly sawed away with his knife at what was left intact of his victim's flesh.

The newly-arrived prisoners were formed up into a column and driven forward. Their guards derived amusement from continually making them crouch down and get up. Owing to the wire biting into their wrists and arms, this could only be achieved with considerable difficulty and intolerable pain; but if they were slow to obey they were at once beaten or hacked with the short, crooked knives which the Partisans bore for the purpose. After some hundred yards of this torture the column was halted.

By this time Milan's hands had lost all sensation of feeling, as the wire had bitten through his wrists to the bone. The prisoners' bonds were temporarily unfastened, and they were ordered to strip naked. Despite threats and blows, Zajec clung to the cotton drawers he wore under his trousers. When he left home to join the Domobranci, his mother had tied about his neck a medallion of the Virgin. 'Always keep this on you, Milan,' she had urged, 'and our Holy Mother will protect you.' When he first fell into the hands of the Communists, he had managed to conceal it in a tuck of his underpants, and he was determined whatever befell not to be parted from it. Fortunately the guards overlooked this in the haste of their operations.

Now they were all driven forward in haste, plunging through jagged thornbushes between triple ranks of Communists. The inner line lashed them on with blows from their cudgels, while the outer ranks stood guard with rifles in case by some mischance the half-conscious prisoners suddenly turned on their tormentors. They were careering down a slope when there was a cry of 'halt!' From behind the stumbling figures ahead of him Milan glimpsed for the first time what his enemies had planned for them. Before them in the ground gaped the black entrance to a huge underground pit, in area about the size of a small house. It was all happening so quickly he had scarcely time to register the fact.

Just in front of Zajec a man fell, shot dead, by the edge of the chasm. Two Partisans started forward and began rolling the body over the side into the pit. Another shrieked out a command to Zajec to halt, but ignoring it he rushed on and sprang over the body in his way. Bullets flew all round him, but he plunged unscathed down into the darkness. He had landed on an untold seething mass of naked bodies. All about him he could hear people crying, moaning, praying. Zajec himself prayed for death. The circle of sky above was shadowed by sheaves of falling bodies, plummeting on to the heap around. It was a scene of unimaginable horror. Zajec shrieked out in vain to the Partisans above, 'Kill me! Kill me!'

As his eyes became accustomed to the gloom, he was aware of another man lying at the hollowed edge of the cavern, protected by a projecting overhang, who was calling to him. By now Zajec had two or three bodies lying across him, and he was resigned to dying as soon as possible within the swiftly-accumulating heap. However, the sight of one living, friendly face was enough to recover the urge to survive, and he dragged himself out from under the bodies and across to the side. Both men were still bound, and Zajec set to work untying his comrade's wired wrists with his teeth. Eventually, despite having his front teeth badly broken, he was successful. His companion was so enfeebled that some time passed before Zajec himself could be untied.

The two men lay back, exhausted, against the rock. If they thought there was to be any respite, however, they were mistaken. Soon afterwards a small round object dropped into the centre of the cave, followed by another and another. There followed a series of blinding flashes and shattering explosions, the noise being increased a hundred-fold within the enclosed confines of the subterranean cavern. The Partisans were ensuring the efficacy of their work by lobbing in hand grenades, interspersing them with sporadic bursts of machine-gun fire at point-blank range into the still writhing mass of naked bodies.

Ignoring the pain from his splintered teeth, Zajec set to work untying as many as he could of those who appeared still by some miracle to have life in them. He estimates that he managed to free in this way upwards of a hundred Slovenian Domobranci, who lay propped by the cavern wall. This slow and painful procedure continued all that day, with fresh corpses being added continually to the mass already there. All that sustained them in this hour was their religious faith. 'Lord forgive them, for they know not what they do!' Zajec heard one mortally-wounded victim cry, on first being tumbled in – so loudly and clearly that the Communists above heard him. Their response was to hurl in a further succession of grenades, and spray the general area with submachine-gun fire. Still the man survived. Zajec called softly to him during a lull to join the group of survivors by the side, but he was bleeding profusely, and died slowly and helplessly in the open area.

So passed Saturday, 2 June 1945. About eighty men, most of them dreadfully wounded and losing quantities of blood, were still hanging on to life. But the night was in its own way as hellish as the day. No more victims arrived, but the soft thuds and ensuing detonation of grenades shattered the darkness, as fresh units of Partisans whiled away the long hours of guard duty. Next day, Sunday, passed in the same way as the previous one, with an unceasing succession of bodies hurtling down, followed by grenades and bullets. The moaning and crying continued unabated too, as explosions tore the bodies into a bloodied mess. Zajec and his comrade were protected from the blast and ricochetting splinters by a small spur of rock. Haunted by a continual fear that the guards might decide to descend and finish off by hand anyone surviving, they managed to drag six or seven corpses before them as an improvised rampart. Few of the others survived long. Many had multiple injuries sustained as they were dashed in their fall against the rocky sides of the pit. Continual loss of blood, lack of food or water, and the effects of lying naked in the freezing subterranean cold at night ensured that few were alive next morning.

The first two and a half days saw a virtually unceasing rain of bodies descending into the cavern. At midday on Monday, 4 June there was a pause of about half an hour, but then the process continued as before, with the usual sporadic bombings throughout the following night. On the morning of the fourth day Zajec and his friend began to talk of the possibility of escape. But how? That they had survived at all appeared miraculous, and how could they possibly scramble out in their enfeebled state, let alone get past the guards present in such numbers, and so evidently on the alert? There were at this stage five survivors strong enough to stand upright, and one or two began to express impatience: they would clamber out now. To Zajec this seemed madness; he might well die where he was, but to raise one's head above the rim (assuming it were possible) was to invite instant death. He resolved to wait.

One desperate comrade set himself to scale the overhanging side, and to everyone's astonishment succeeded eventually in painfully dragging himself up and over the edge. A sudden feeling of elation gripped those below. If he could escape, then why not all? The elation was short-lived. From above came a gruff exchange of questions and answers. No shot rang out, but a moment later the body of their friend was hurled down, stabbed to death by the Partisans' knives. Lying back in the darkness, Zajec saw an exultant Partisan step to the edge and peer down. The sunlight was shining full on his face; the man was grinning so broadly that Zajec could see he had but one tooth in his mouth.

Not long after came a mysterious sound from above. There was a noise of people apparently digging. Then came a prolonged pause and silence, followed abruptly by a tremendous explosion, vastly more shattering than anything that had passed before. Four more followed in succession; the overhanging edges of the chasm mouth disintegrated and crashed down on to the coagulated mass of bodies, now scores of corpses deep. The Partisans were dynamiting the sides of the cave in order to ensure that no one else survived below. What was quite extraordinary, Zajec recalls now, was that after the thunder of the explosions and crashing rocks had died away he could *still* hear groans and sobs from all around. That Zajec and his three companions survived was due to their being sheltered in their narrow recess. Around them lay the many bodies of those rescued earlier at the cost of so much effort and pain – all dead.

As a result of the dynamiting the entrance to the hollow was now greatly enlarged, and into it the Communists began flinging smoke-bombs. This was painful to the eyes and frightening, but served no evident purpose. Perhaps the Partisans were simply using up the allowance of explosives with which they had been so liberally supplied by their allies.

By that evening Zajec had spent four days in the pit of Kocevje. Since they first were handed over to the Partisans they had received minimal food and drink, and now he had survived nearly a hundred hours without sustenance. He was afflicted by an overwhelming desire to vomit, but with nothing in his stomach could only retch painfully. That evening (Tuesday) he fainted and lay unconscious all night long.

By next morning two of his surviving comrades were dead, and one alone besides him remained. The fifth day of their ordeal had begun, and from an early hour the alternating rain of bodies and grenades began yet again. Near Milan Zajec lay three victims more horribly mangled than most; falling rocks had crushed in their chests and left their bodies lacerated and unidentifiable. Zajec's companion, a man forty years older than himself, muttered that it was vital to eat something if they were to continue to survive. In the underwear of one of the corpses by them they had found a small penknife, and with it Zajec cut out sections of flesh from one of the bodies and proffered them to the other. His friend managed to get down five pieces of meat, but Zajec himself found his mouth had become so dry that he was unable to swallow anything after the first morsel. Despite this, it was his companion who appeared to grow weaker.

Looking about them, the two men had become increasingly absorbed by the possibilities of a tree which lay toppled within the pit. When the cave had been mined the previous day the tree had slid down and lay with its trunk projecting over the edge. To those below it represented a ladder to freedom. But the extraordinarily unrelenting efforts of the Partisans to ensure that no one survived made them at the same time preternaturally suspicious. What if the tree were booby-trapped? It was precisely the sort of precaution or malicious deception they might be expected to adopt. Why otherwise would they have allowed it to remain? Determined not to fall into their trap, Zajec made a succession of unavailing attempts to scale the rocky side. But whereas before the sides had been rough enough to offer precarious footholds, the dynamiting had left them relatively smooth. It proved a hopeless venture.

All that day sheaves of bodies fell as before, screaming down into the abyss. Further dynamiting took place, perhaps to ensure space for the seemingly endless numbers being butchered. The prolonged echoes which reverberated round and round the narrow place were excruciatingly painful to the ears. So far from becoming accustomed to the horror, Zajec found it still harder to bear. The thousands of bodies were beginning to decay, and the stench and flies grew ever more intolerable. The concentration of so much suffering in one small space was unbearable enough, but as the torture continued each day, doubling, trebling, quadrupling, it grew overpowering. As the enfeebled victims, many still wired together, sought to struggle from beneath the encumbering bodies of their dead comrades, they shrieked out incoherently, coughing up blood and calling upon patron saints or absent loved ones. Groups of priests kept up their prayers as long as their breath allowed. For Zajec there was also the thought that there, somewhere deep down in that pullulating shambles, lay his four brothers.

The evening of the fifth day was drawing to a close, and he resolved at last to make an attempt to escape. Death was drawing ever closer to him. To be shot while escaping would only briefly anticipate what must in any case shortly be a certain end. He clambered over the shifting sea of dead and dying, and began to scramble slowly and painfully up the fallen tree. His head was filled with a resonant buzzing; at the time he thought it came from somewhere around him, but later realised it must have been the lingering effect of the explosions.

As he emerged into the fresh air of the forest he could not for a while really believe that he was no longer in the pit. The first thing he saw was the moon, in its first quarter, gleaming brightly down. The next object his eyes lighted upon, however, recalled him to reality. It was a body, dangling head downwards from a nearby tree. Fortunately there appeared to be no guards in the vicinity. Zajec set off as fast as his gravely weakened constitution would allow, plunging into the safety of a nearby valley and trudging on all night to put as much distance as possible between himself and the scene of his ordeal. He longed to throw himself down and sleep, but in his ears he could hear an insistent voice, which repeated at each moment of temptation, 'Keep going, Milan, keep going; you must not sleep.' So, pausing only to suck up dew from the long grass, he stumbled on till daybreak.

He knew he was still not safe, and trudged blindly on for most of the next day. For nearly a week his only food had been that single morsel of human flesh forced upon him in his despair, and some bunches of grass. It seemed the ultimate cruelty that, after surviving all the horrors of the pit, it appeared he must succumb to starvation in the open countryside. For even his tough spirit could achieve no more; not one step further could he go. He stumbled to a halt . . . and there, not three paces before him, he saw a patch of wild strawberries growing thickly together as if piled on a dish, in the midst of an open glade. Not one strawberry had he seen in his day's march, and not one was he to see thereafter.

The fruit revived him considerably, and he found himself able to resume his journey. He was in a deplorable state; his leg was badly infected by poisoning from the wire shackles, and he was infested with lice from the rags given him when the Partisans at Kranj had stripped him of his uniform. By the evening he came to the outskirts of the village of Koblerje, near the railway line which had transported him and his 2,000 comrades to Kocevje a week before. But Koblerje was full of Partisans, and Zajec was obliged to hide in the woods outside. Fortunately he came upon an old, overgrown well, and not even the rat he found lurking within could prevent him at long last from drinking his fill.

Night came on, and he ventured to approach a villager he saw passing near. The old woman took pity on him, and gave him an egg, some milk and a potato. The last his throat was still too constricted to get down, but he felt some enfeebled sense of recovery. Shortly after that his wild appearance (he was clad only in shirt and underpants, both stiff with dried blood, was limping and emaciated, and bore a week-old beard) sent a young girl fleeing in fear back to the village. This in turn frightened him, and he felt impelled once more to seek refuge in the forest. Eventually he learned of another village, Otaoice, whose inhabitants were known to be stalwartly anti-Communist.

Otaoice was some ten kilometres away, and he found his strength fast waning; too fast, he felt, to last the journey. Still, Otaoice was also on the railway line, and this he followed northwards, pausing from time to time to lick the metal track in desperate but unavailing effort to alleviate the pangs of thirst which now tortured him more severely than ever. He found himself once again unable to move one more step. He collapsed to the ground and, to his horror, found his body starting to shake uncontrollably. During his five days in the pit he had marked this as an unfailing symptom of impending death. It was two o'clock in the morning, and he felt himself to be nearing the end of his strength. Starting up, he looked about him desperately, and was greatly surprised to find himself standing before a house he had not noticed a moment earlier.

A light came on at a window that instant, and Zajec lurched forward and knocked at the pane. A woman looked out and asked him who he was. 'I am a Home Guardsman, who has escaped from the massacre in Kocevski Rog,' confessed Zajec. The woman was suspicious, accusing him of being a Partisan. The penalty for harbouring one of the fugitives was terrible: as everyone knew, detection or betrayal would result in the destruction of one's home and death. But eventually Zajec's pleas and his pitiable condition persuaded the woman of the truth of his story, and she burst into tears. Overcome likewise, Zajec fainted; to find himself moments later being helped upstairs to an attic bedroom. He collapsed on the bed and slept for ten hours.

When he finally awoke it was midday. The kindly woman revived him with a glass of spirits, confessing as she did so she had been convinced for a time that he was dead. Zajec stayed in the woman's home, in a secret hideout especially prepared for such a purpose, for five days. It was then she came to him in a state of agitation with the news that Communists were on their way to search the village. The old woman gave him some clothes and food and escorted him back to the forest, both of them bearing farm implements to explain their journey.

Much refreshed by his rest, Milan made his way to another village, where a relative lived. Afraid for both their sakes to live in her home, he constructed a small shelter out of rocks with a straw roof concealed by pine branches nearby in the forest. He lived in this manner like a hunted animal for nearly a year. The village was frequently visited by detachments from OZNA, the state political police, who searched every house and interrogated the inhabitants. Communist patrols from time to time passed near Zajec's improvised retreat, and on one awkward occasion he was within inches of discovery. But he had supplied himself with a revolver and hand-grenade and was resolved to sell his life dearly, rather than fall into the hands of enemies whose methods of dealing with those they disfavoured he had more reason than any to know.

Eventually Zajec learned through a friend, a priest from Ljubljana, of the existence of a secret route used for smuggling fugitives out of Yugoslavia into Italy. On 6 April 1946 he escaped across the frontier to Gorizia. There he was interrogated by an officer from Allied Military Government, a Captain Bentley, to whom he recounted the whole of his extraordinary story. Captain Bentley was in this way the first Englishman to learn what actions had been performed in his country's name during the days of May and June 1945.

Bentley gave Zajec a pass (still in his possession) to go to a refugee camp at Udine. He stayed in Italy until December 1947, when he migrated to Argentina. The events of his ordeal were burned into his memory, every detail of each of those five days in the pit at Kocevje being as fresh in recollection today as forty years ago. Nor can he forget his brothers Stane, Nace, Tone and Joze who remained behind in the forest charnel-house. Yet another brother, Janez, had been murdered by the Communists in 1944. But despite the sufferings and betrayal, his is a profoundly gentle, kindly, unembittered personality, providing the impression of a man possessed of great reserves of spiritual strength. He, however, is unshakably convinced that his life was saved on successive occasions by the power of the medallion of Our Lady given him by his mother.

'I am as sure as I am sitting here,' he told me; 'for no one else could have helped me in that place.'

It would be a bold person who doubted him.

Milan's sufferings seem remote from Harold Macmillan's ornate

salon in the Palace of Caserta. But great interests of state affect very
ordinary people, and it would surely be inappropriate to analyse
complex diplomatic and military issues without pausing to consider
for a space the fate of those whom they were to affect so deeply.
There is, moreover, reason to believe that peculiar circumstances
attending the slaughter at Kocevje may have reflected not merely the
brutality of its perpetrators, but also the interests of those whose
decisions were ultimately responsible for the event.

One of the most remarkable factors about the Kocevje massacre
was the extent of the precautions taken by the Yugoslav Communist
Government to ensure that no one escaped to tell the tale. It seems
unlikely that this policy arose solely from that wanton cruelty which
was one of the most salient characteristics of the new order. It appears
to have been a matter of policy to ensure that the silent glade in
Kocevski Rog should preserve its secret. Yet, despite the extraordinarily elaborate precautions adopted, Milan Zajec was not the only
person to survive and bear witness to the tens of thousands slaughtered.

Frank Dejak was another twenty-year-old among the Domobranci
at Viktring. His story was one familiar enough to Slovenians of the
time. His mother, a widow, kept a small bar and grocery. When he
was eighteen, at the time of the Italian capitulation, he and other
village boys had been kidnapped and forced to serve in the ranks of
Tito's Partisans. He escaped once, but was recaptured, and continued
with the Communists until May 1944, when he slipped away to
Ljubljana and joined the Domobranci. At the beginning of May he
was with a unit defending his home town of Ribnica, between
Ljubljana and Kocevje; then, with the coming collapse of the
Slovenian state, he and his brothers and sisters joined the stream of
fugitives who crossed the frontier and passed into the hands of the
British on 12 May.

At the end of the month he, too, was despatched by the British
authorities 'to Palmanova'; that is, into the hands of the Partisans at
Rosenbach Station. At Jesenice, on the Yugoslav side of the tunnel, he
saw a dozen British soldiers (presumably members of the undercover
'Sixth Special Force') engaged in assisting the Communists to handle
the consignment of prisoners. Their first stay was for four days at
the concentration camp at Kranj, where officers and NCOs were
screened and segregated, and all were stripped of personal property.

Next they were shifted to the by now notorious diocesan high
school building at St Vid. Milan Zajec had spent only a few hours

there before travelling on towards Kocevje, but it seems that the liquidation operation had become clogged already by the huge numbers involved, and Dejak spent nearly a week at St Vid. He was witness to the continual ferocious beatings – with rifle-butts, sticks and belts – with which their gaolers paid off old scores. Fortunately no one recognised him, and he escaped relatively lightly. He was among a group of about 500 crammed into the seminary chapel, so tightly that they had to remain upright day and night. The only food was a bowl of watery vegetable soup served once a day. The heat was intense, at no time was any water supplied, and prisoners were collapsing all around. Only two or three times in four days were they permitted to go to the washroom to relieve themselves.

What neither Zajec nor Dejak knew was that the St Vid seminary had served as a posting-centre for the Yugoslav holocaust even before the arrival of the inmates of the camp at Viktring. Dimitrije Vojvodic, a Serbian Chetnik, recalls his stay in the St Vid concentration camp in the days immediately following the liberation. He had fought for the Yugoslav and Allied cause throughout the war, being severely wounded in battle both against the Italians and Germans, and was promptly arrested by the Communists after their victory. In the second half of May he found himself among some 5,000 Serbian Chetniks and between 12,000 and 15,000 Croats and Slovenes held in St Vid. The yards and buildings were littered with the corpses of victims killed at random by their Communist guards.

About the beginning of the third week in May a commissar announced that the prison was to be evacuated next day, as a fresh consignment of prisoners would be arriving from Austria. Next day Vojvodic and the others were wired together in pairs and driven away in columns of trucks. They were being transported, so they were told, to another concentration camp at Celje. In fact they were taken up into the Kamnik Mountains south of the Austrian frontier, to a place where there was a series of large anti-tank trenches. There the 30,000 or so prisoners from St Vid were slaughtered by machine-gun squads, Vojvodic was among the mass of men herded up to the pits, and saw eighty priests, singing a hymn as they died, cut down in a swathe before him. He himself fortunately managed to undo his bonds and slip away into the forest, preferring a swift death while escaping to lying wounded and suffocating in the trench. Of those he encountered, Vojvodic estimated that nearly thirty escaped at that time. He himself travelled by night through the forests, until on 26 May he crossed over to the British lines. He was fortunate in being brought before a humane officer who, after listening to his account of events over the frontier, arranged for him to be placed safely in a DP camp near Salzburg.

That this massacre took place by night as well as day, and that a number of prisoners succeeded in escaping, suggest that the operation was conducted in great haste. This confirms what is already known from the British records, namely that it was on 19 May that Brigadier Toby Low informed the Partisan Colonel Ivanovic that '5 Corps will return all Yugoslav nationals now in the Corps area', 10,000 of whom were to be handed over at Rosenbach for transfer to St Vid. It was to clear the camp for these that the men imprisoned with Vojvodic were massacred.

To return to Frank Dejak: on 8 June, a week after Milan Zajec, he left St Vid on the route taken now by thousands before him, through Ljubljana to Kocevje. They arrived at Kocevje Station at one o'clock in the morning, but had to stay locked in their boxcars until daylight. At about 5 a.m. they descended and were driven into the Kocevje high school building. Dejak estimated that there were about 800 in their group. Those to whom he spoke were confident that nothing too dreadful was likely to happen to them. A trial before a People's Court, six months perhaps in prison – it was hard to believe that worse was in prospect. The streets and buildings of Kocevje were as familiar to Dejak as those of his home town of Ribnica, a mere eighteen kilometres away.

From the high school building they were marched to the former blind people's home, where all 800 were crowded on to the first floor. Then they descended again, ten by ten, to be paraded in pairs in a small room, where guards wired their hands behind their backs and tied couples together by their arms. In the truck outside they were compelled to kneel down with heads bent, so as not to be able to know where they were going. But, like Milan Zajec, Dejak had spent some time on police duties in the surrounding countryside, and was able to detect the route. Concealment of the locality of the place of killing was clearly an important aspect of the operation. After leaving Zeljne and entering the forest, the truck suddenly slowed down and drove round twice in a tight circle. The guards then asked the prisoners if they could identify a small church on a hill nearby. Dejak knew it to be the church of St Anne, but remained silent with the others. Evidently the guards wished to be satisfied that the manoeuvre had confused the prisoners, and perhaps it was this consideration that led them to indulge in prolonged beatings and kickings of the heads of the kneeling prisoners.

Now they turned off into the clearing where the massacre was to take place. Their shoelaces were cut away and their shoes removed before they were pushed out on to the ground. Then they were marched barefoot for about ten minutes towards the pit. It was the morning of Saturday, 9 June, and the sun shone warmly down on the dappled green of the forest floor. The men were halted, untied, and compelled to strip off their clothes. The majority were stark naked, but Dejak, like Milan Zajec before him, managed to retain his underpants. Again they were marched swiftly another couple of hundred yards (Dejak noted that their path had led them in a curve back to within two or three hundred yards of the road) to the mouth of the pit. Throughout their short march the prisoners were subjected to ferocious beatings, many being battered to death and left where they fell. Afterwards he saw these corpses hurled into the pit.

At the edge of the precipice a guard halted Dejak and ordered him to look him straight in the eye. A swift interrogation followed, which Dejak realised later was designed solely to check whether he had any gold teeth. For in the pit itself were many men whose jaws were broken and bloodied where their teeth had been wrenched out. He possessed no such prize, and the Partisan raised and cocked his gun. Dejak did not wait for the shot but hurled himself over the edge of the pit. Four days had passed since Milan Zajec had made his momentous escape, and the level of corpses had continued to rise as the daily consignments from St Vid came in.

The Communist's gun went off as Dejak leaped, and Dejak felt a bullet tear through the side of his leg. He fell heavily on to the mass of bodies, and for a moment was unable to see anything in the darkness. Then, as his eyes swiftly became accustomed to the gloom, he was aware of some badly wounded men lying by the side, who called to him to crawl across before further bodies fell on him. He did so, and so was able to survey the scene from the relative safety of the edge. The rim of the cave was about fifteen metres above him; how far down it extended there was no longer any means of knowing.

By midday Dejak had recovered sufficiently to assess his position. By now some 6,000 bodies had accumulated in the chasm, of whom about a dozen remained alive, crouching by the edge. There was talk of escape, as the men eyed the knotted roots of a tree projecting some five metres up from the side, surviving from one of the periodic dynamitings witnessed by Milan Zajec, during his five days' stay. At another point there was also a small tree trunk, about ten inches in diameter. That night, about midnight, Dejak scaled this natural ladder without great difficulty and made his way towards the forest. This was presumably the same tree by which Milan Zajec had made his escape.

Over to the right he could see a large fire blazing, at which were gathered about twenty Communist soldiers. Pausing momentarily to recover his strength, Dejak began cautiously moving off under the trees. There was a waxing moon and it was not difficult to find his way, accustomed as he had become to the darkness. Unfortunately he trod on a dry twig, which snapped loudly. Shouts of 'Halt!' came from the sentries, and Dejak froze. Fortunately the guards by their bright fire could distinguish little in the surrounding gloom, and evidently decided that some animal had disturbed their vigil. Their heads turned one by one back to the blaze.

Dejak crawled carefully away for a couple of hundred yards, then made off as swiftly as he could. He walked all that night and the next day, dressed only in his underpants, with his feet wrapped in a shirt taken from one of the bodies. Helped by a village woman he met on the way, he trudged on, plagued by hallucinations that he was surrounded by Partisans. At one point he collapsed for two hours in a faint. Eventually he recovered and reached home. To his alarm his house was deserted except for the family dog, who greeted him ecstatically. He went to bed, full of dread that his mother might have been abducted or compelled to flee her home by the Communists. But at five o'clock in the morning she returned, overjoyed to find her lost son returned. He told her of his terrible experiences, impressing on her the need never to reveal that he was a survivor of the Kocevje massacre.

After two or three weeks lying up in his home, Dejak felt obliged to seek a safer refuge. For almost three years he lived in different places of concealment. During the first six months he was in too weakened a state from the beatings he had received to consider escaping, and after that he and those around him were deluded by hopes that within a short spell of time Tito's primitive dictatorship would be toppled. Eventually he escaped over the mountains to Austria, arriving there on 22 May 1948.

Later Dejak learned that the Communists had somehow discovered that he had escaped, and consequently subjected his mother to a six-months' trial, before sentencing her to three years in gaol. Harsh conditions of confinement caused a breakdown in her health, and she was released after nearly two years. What struck the Dejaks as strange was the inordinate interest taken in Frank's escape from the pit at Kocevje. Hundreds of thousands of people had been massacred by the Communists all over Yugoslavia after their seizure of power, most of them without any attempt at concealment. Yet time and again Mrs Dejak was visited by high-ranking officers from OZNA, asking repeatedly for details of her son's story. They were clearly desperately concerned to recover him; it will be seen what may have been the significance of this obsessive concern with the particular crime of Kocevje.

To the Communist authorities it must have appeared incredible that anyone could have survived the massacre, and indeed when one considers the survivors' accounts it seems miraculous. Apart from Zajec and Dejak only one other man is known to have escaped and lived to tell the tale. I spoke to him also, and though his story confirms many of the details of the others, the event is so extraordinary, and so important to an understanding of the mysterious conspiracy at Klagenfurt, of which the slaughter at Kocevje was the result, that it is necessary to conclude this chapter by hearing Frank Kozina's version of events.

Kozina (not to be confused with the Kozina whose death is mentioned on p. 27: both Frank and Kozina are common names in Slovenia) was slightly older than the other two escapers, being just twenty-four at the time. His home was in the same district as Dejak's, near Ribnica, where he worked as a labourer on his father's small farm. In 1942 the Italian occupation authorities had removed him to a concentration camp in Italy, from which he only returned in May 1943. Almost immediately afterwards he was abducted by Communist Partisans and obliged to serve with them against his own people. But their effectiveness as a fighting force proved derisory, and his superiors took care that any risk of being harmed by the enemy should be slight. Eventually he ran away home, and in January 1944 joined the Domobranci. He spent some time on patrol duty, guarding trains on the Ljubljana railway line, then for the last three or four weeks of the war was serving in Kocevje along with Milan Zajec and one of Milan's brothers.

When the collapse of Slovenia began, at the beginning of May, Kozina's unit departed northwards, intending to cross by train over the frontier to Austria. But the railway lines were clogged with others similarly fleeing, and they finally found themselves stuck in a line of engines, carriages and trucks which stretched for perhaps twenty kilometres. At Lesce they abandoned their train and set off on foot

over the Karavanke Mountains. Partisan snipers from time to time
opened fire at them, but were swiftly chased away by escorting
Domobran units.

On crossing the Drava they were received by British troops who,
as other Slovenian refugees experienced, immediately set about strip-
ping them of what valuables took their fancy. To Frank Kozina this
was a moment of disillusionment: throughout the war it had been a
matter of pride that Britain was Yugoslavia's steadfast ally, and
that whatever other armies did the British invariably behaved 'like
gentlemen'. But in the camp at Viktring he found morale high, with
everyone eager to return home and do battle with the despised
Partisans.

Then came the welcome news of the transfer to Palmanova, and
on 29 May he was among the party which included Milan Zajec
handed over to the Communists at Maria Elend Station. A deep
fatalism descended on Kozina and those around him when they
realised they had been betrayed. With no possibility of escape or
refuge, it seemed better to die swiftly. At Kranj he was present at
the murder of young Polde Koman, also witnessed by Milan Zajec.
Kozina, who knew Koman, was among the party detailed to bury
him in a corner of the compound.

Next morning another batch of about 2,000 prisoners arrived from
Viktring. The crush in the camp was tremendous. A remarkable
aspect of the whole episode was the extent to which familiar faces
were continually appearing, a factor understandable among so small
a nation as the Slovenes. Kozina knew many of his fellow-prisoners;
the fresh consignment included teenage brothers from his own
village.

After three days Kozina's section of the Viktring-Kocevje human
pipeline was able to move on, and travelled the next stage to the
seminary building at St Vid. There he was confined in the chapel.
By this time visits to the washroom had become an unbearable ordeal,
as Partisans were lying in wait there to beat the prisoners almost
senseless. Teams of interrogators arrived, and once again Kozina saw
faces he knew. One captain had sat two places from him in school,
but possibly from charitable motives affected not to recognise him.
Then came a strip search. No sooner was Kozina undressed than his
interrogator set about him, lashing him with the buckle end of a
heavy belt, and kicking him in the chest with his boots. The other
prisoners were suffering likewise, and the whole area was awash with
blood. In such a place death did not seem so terrible. Kozina was

young and had no one dependent on him; but he felt pity for an older man nearby, Anton Zidar, who had a pregnant wife waiting at home with two or three children.

But Frank Kozina was young and strong and did not, like so many others, die at St Vid. On the afternoon of 8 June he was taken by train to Kocevje. Journey and arrival were accompanied by yet further brutal beatings; Kozina had lost count of how many times this had happened. In the cattle-truck on the way to Kocevje he caught sight of some young friends staring longingly out of the barred window. To him this was foolishness: better to have done with it all than undergo further suffering before the inevitable end.

Next came the wiring in pairs; men were fainting from the stifling heat in the overcrowded rooms, their hands and arms turning blue as the twisted wire bit into their flesh and prevented circulation. Thrust into the waiting trucks, they were compelled like those before them to kneel and bow their heads. Guards crouched at each corner to ensure that no one glanced up to recognise their route. As prisoners in other convoys had experienced, the trucks turned around twice as they neared their destination, and the men were asked whether they knew where they were. On this occasion they could hear bursts of gunfire a little way off.

'No one said anything,' Frank Kozina recalls. 'We started praying. Before we prayed in whispers, but now we prayed aloud. We knew the people we were dealing with, what they were capable of, and we knew we were finished.'

Kozina was last off his truck. The first sight he saw, as his shoelaces were being slashed and his shoes removed, was a group of Partisan executioners. They were equipped with a remarkable collection of improvised instruments designed for killing and maiming: axes, pitchforks, jagged knives fastened to poles. Among the killers Kozina suddenly recognised a man who had been with him on a Partisan officers' course held on the Slovenian-Serbian border in 1943. He felt a moment of fear, but the man turned away with an unmistakable look of shame on his face.

Brought to the edge of the chasm, Kozina was untied from his partner and compelled to strip to his underwear. He, like Dejak, was to owe his life to the fact that the haste of the operation left him untied. He was thrust further towards the brim. He recognised his executioner, a man named Karel Francu from the village next door to home. Despite this, Francu looked him straight in the face and asked him to give his name and place of birth. Kozina at once guessed his purpose; at one side he had glimpsed an ammunition box filled with gold teeth, watches and rings. The Partisans wasted no time in despoiling their prisoners: the box was swimming in blood from smashed jaws and severed fingers.

Levelling a shiny new revolver, Francu ordered him to squat down. As he did so the gun roared in Kozina's face. He felt a burning pain across his scalp and instinctively jumped backwards into the abyss. By a fortunate chance the bullet had passed through his hair, grazing the side of his head without inflicting serious injury. As he spun over he grabbed at the bole of a tree lying against the side of the cave, checking his fall a little as he slithered down. Unfortunately his heel was dashed against a sharp projecting rock, which cut through to the bone. He could see the bone through the gash in his flesh. Now he found himself scrambling across the thousands of dead bodies which had been accumulating over the past ten days of killing. Within two hours of death the corpses began to putrefy, the skin appeared slippery and partially detached from the flesh beneath, and a watery secretion oozed out where it was broken. A dense cloud of flies covered the shifting mass. It was bitterly cold. From behind him in the darkness Kozina heard a weak voice urging him to pull himself to the side before the Communists began throwing in bombs. Crawling back, he found a man lying on the edge of the pile of naked bodies. Nearby was another survivor, whose voice Kozina recognised as that of a young student he had known. This boy had already been four or five days in the pit. By next morning he was dead. It was this night, however, which saw the escape of Frank Dejak. He had been in the same truck as Kozina, but neither knew of the other's survival within the gloomy vault.

Frank Kozina managed to drag clothes from the dead to keep himself from the intense cold, and found a damp patch of stone on the side which he licked from time to time in an effort to stave off increasing thirst. By next morning (10 June) he found himself among a group of about a dozen survivors who had succeeded in dragging themselves to the edge. In despair someone suggested that there might be a tunnel somewhere at the side, and some time was spent in dragging aside bodies in this hopeless search.

As the second day wore on Kozina began to think they must all starve to death, trapped as they clearly were. The sides of the hole were higher than a telegraph pole, though the bodies lay piled ten or more feet deep on the cavern floor. Then came the dynamite explosions Milan Zajec had experienced the previous week. Kozina thought this time his end really had come, as the unexpected blasts left him momentarily shaken and stunned. But once the shattering echoes and great cloud of dust had died away, he saw that the explosion might be set to their advantage, since at certain points the overhanging edges had collapsed on to the bodies beneath, leaving sections of the banks less impassable. The tree down which he had fallen now stood away from the edge, its base upheld by the deep layer of corpses settling about it. The survivors resolved to escape that night. They were possessed by fear that the Partisans might drench them all with petrol and incinerate them.

That night, about two o'clock, they began a concerted effort to climb out at a point rendered less precipitous by the explosions. The first man, Karel Turk, became stuck when halfway up, but a superhuman effort on the part of Frank Kozina, pushing him up from below, enabled him to scramble over the lip. Exhausted, he staggered back, but was soon at work helping up the next man, Janko Sveter. Between them they managed to lodge Sveter on a precarious foothold about halfway up, but there his enfeebled frame left him impotently hanging. Those below urged Turk to go and search for a branch or section of wire from the pile where prisoners were unbound. But before anything could be done the rock face collapsed in a heap of boulders on to the group waiting below, crushing most of the men. Sveter just managed to grip hold and draw himself up to safety.

There was nothing to be done for the mangled dead and dying, and Kozina himself, a man of considerable strength and endurance, finally managed to scale the side. Assisted by Turk, he pulled himself out on to the grass. The first glimmering of dawn was appearing in the clearing, and there was no time to be lost. Together he, Turk and Sveter set off through the forest, suffering frightening mirages of Partisan tanks recurring at intervals. They walked for almost two days and nights until they reached temporary safety at the Kozina home, after which Frank's comrades separated and went their several ways.

Not long afterwards Kozina came across Frank Dejak, who had been thrown into the pit in the same truckload and escaped a night earlier than he. Together they lay hidden in various refuges for nearly three years. During that time, however, they rarely spoke of the pit of Kocevje, so terrible was the memory. When they did so, it was only when they felt temporarily secure enough to allude to their terrifying experience.

Eventually, aided by enterprising sympathisers, Kozina escaped to the safety of Italy. Only later did he appreciate just how fortunate was his escape. Janko Sveter was later drowned – accidentally, some held, though others laid his death at the door of the dreaded OZNA. Karel Turk was less fortunate. He was picked up and thrown in gaol on some fanciful charge. Repeated interrogations eventually elicited the fact that he was a survivor of the Kocevje massacre.* He was taken back to Kocevje and crucified by the edge of the pit.

The accounts of the three survivors Zajec, Dejak and Kozina are confirmed by a young Partisan, who later defected and set down an account of his experiences in 1953. He was a member of the Eleventh Dalmatian Brigade, which had taken part in Tito's 'capture' of Trieste. On or about 25 May, the day after the Fifth Corps began the mass handovers, his unit was to provide a group of picked men to guard a company of sixty or seventy executioners, commanded by a Captain Nikola Marsic. On 26 May they went to St Vid, where the executioners entered the compound and committed the atrocities already recounted. Nearly a thousand prisoners were taken out next day and slaughtered in a large pit excavated in the countryside just outside Ljubljana.

On the twenty-eighth the executioners and their escort were sent to Kocevje. The young Partisan recalls:

> Our job was to guard the prisoners until trucks arrived to take them away from this place, . . . then to load them on to these trucks. During the eight days that we remained at Kocevje, ten or more trains came in on the rail line every twenty-four hours. Each of these trains was composed of between ten and twenty boxcars, all well nailed up and sealed, and loaded with prisoners. The captives came from Ljubljana and other places. Most were men, but there were some women among them. These . . . females were subjected to mass rape as soon as they were brought to the building which we were guarding. There were also many fifteen- or sixteen-year-old boys among the prisoners. I know that the blond-haired Slovene captain saved one of these boys from being shot, probably because he was acquainted with him or his family.
>
> There were more Croats than Slovenes among the prisoners with whom I came in contact. Also there were some Serbian Chetniks brought here. I do not know to what units they belonged. We heard that during our eight-day stay thirty to forty thousand prisoners were slaughtered in two nearby mountain ravines.
>
> On the eighth day . . . a dance was arranged to honour and amuse the 'execution company'. Women were brought for them, and the men

---

* A woman confined in the same prison who knew Turk learned of his subsequent fate, and later recounted it to Frank Kozina.

swaggered around boasting that they had 'liquidated' thirty to forty thousand people during the past eight days. I judge from the number of prisoners I saw taken out of the building we were guarding that there must have been more than thirty thousand victims. Since we shipped more than twenty railroad car loads of clothes from this place, it would appear that this estimate is not too far off the mark. I saw only about ten or fifteen women among the captives, but there were certainly more who were murdered there. Naturally, I did not see every arrival, since I was not on duty all the time. I know that the women were not stripped of their clothes in the vicinity of the building where we were stationed, but were conducted fully clothed to the place of execution. They were dishonoured again in the ravines close to their final destinations . . .

There were about two hundred boys between fourteen and sixteen years old who wore the uniforms of the Ustasha youth. All of these boys were killed, except for the one spared by the Slovene captain. They kept saying they were innocent of any wrong doing. Many of them cried like the women.

The day on which the final massacre took place was a Saturday [9 June?]; five or six high-ranking Communist officers visited the military building where the prisoners were housed before execution on this day . . . These . . . officers had come to check on how we had packed up the uniforms and valuables of the victims . . .

The inspecting commission spent hardly half an hour in our building. From here they went to the forest to see the mass graves in the ravines. I was told they had come to Kocevje to see how the killings had been carried out and to make sure that all visible signs of the massacres, that is the ravines into which the bodies had been thrown, were covered up. Before they left Kocevje we heard several loud explosions in the forest. We assumed that bombs or dynamite had been used to topple masses of rocks on to the . . . corpses . . .

On Sunday morning at seven o'clock, the 'exterminator company' left by train for a vacation at Lake Bled. I didn't know this at the time, but learned it only much later when these killers rejoined their old companies, which had been sent to Macedonia in the meantime. They told me that as a reward for the massacres they had committed at Kocevje they had received twelve days' vacation on the island of Bled, where they were lodged in a former luxury hotel. They received good food, went swimming, had sail boats at their disposal and saw plays performed for their special benefit every evening by a group of amateur actors provided by the Headquarters of their Division (the Twenty-Sixth Dalmatian Division). In addition, all of the 'exterminators' received two or three decorations from the Tito Government, along with gold watches, cameras and other presents of value.

From Tito's point of view these medals had been well earned. The strain of those days took its toll of even these picked stalwarts: 'I heard that some of them became epileptic later on – perhaps the so-called "partizanska bolest" (Partisan sickness), from which they suffered, was a form of nervous breakdown.'[1] This indeed seems likely; in the Soviet Union the MVD maintained a special sanatorium for officers who were suffering the strain of excessive 'interrogation' duties. As an MVD officer confessed, 'It's been statistically proved that three years' work in the operational organs is enough to turn a man into a chronic neurasthenic.' Regular symptoms were impotence and drug-addiction, principally to morphia and cocaine.[2]

Another Partisan involved in similar duties confirms this account, adding interesting details:

> I do not know exactly how many trainloads of prisoners arrived during the seven or eight days that we remained at Kocevje. Usually these prisoner trains pulled in to the station either late in the evening or just before dawn. The Communist authorities did not want the civilian population of the town to know what was going on. From ten to twenty boxcars were included in each train and the prisoners arrived completely exhausted and almost starved to death. They knew what was in store for them but they were too tired and dispirited to care . . .
>
> I had to escort the prisoners from the train to the barracks and to their final place of detention. Since I did this just one day, I can only guess the number of prisoners who were brought to Kocevje to be slaughtered. From other people who were there, I gathered that as many as twenty thousand may have been butchered. A special company of hardened Marxists was formed for the purpose of carrying out the mass executions. A certain Albert Stambuk was the Assistant Commissar of this unit.[3]

After the mass executions were over, the mouth of the cave was completely dynamited and filled in. It is likely that many of the last victims were still alive when this happened. Afterwards young larches were planted on the site, in the same way that the Soviets attempted to conceal the scene of their crime at Katyn. Today the whole region is a forbidden area, but a few years ago a Slovenian émigré on a visit to his homeland made his way to the site and took a number of photographs. They show the younger larches standing in clear contrast to the indigenous birch, spruce and larch *in situ* at the time of the slaughter. The spot where the cave entrance lay is still clearly indicated by a shallow depression, where subsidence must have taken place after the original filling-in. On the trees around the visitor saw signs that surviving relatives continue to risk their lives in calling to commemorate the fallen. Candle-stubs remained standing on surrounding boulders, a rosary hung from a tree, and crosses had been cut on tree-trunks, together with the initials NSD – *Nasha Slovenska Domobranska*, 'Our Slovenian Domobranci'.

Today, the dictatorship finds it is no longer possible to preserve total public silence about the tragedy. Recently the Yugoslav historian Dusan Biber wrote an article (18 October 1984) published in *Knjizevni Listi*, in which he drew attention to the increasing interest in the subject displayed by Yugoslav émigrés and Western scholars.

Next, in an article attacked by government spokesmen, a young Slovenian woman writer, Spomenka Hribar, referring to 'the victims from [Kocevski] Rog', declared:

> We have to open our history. But the key to this door lies not in searching for the guilty one, but in a thorough analysis of the historical path of the nation during that epoch. But if we never learn – as a nation – to mourn *all* our victims, we shall never find this key.
>
> A clear and courageous conscience would be capable not only of admitting to the crime as a crime, but also that these mass graves, wherever they may be, should become hallowed ground accessible to view, if exhumation and decent reburial, appropriate to our civilization and culture, remain impossible. Not because they were Domobranci, but because they were people. The dead are dead, and nothing else can be done for them . . .
>
> In the centre of Ljubljana, in its heart, an obelisk should be erected crying to high heaven the tragedy of a small nation . . . There should be a simple inscription upon this obelisk: 'They died for their country.'[4]

It seems unlikely that any such act of national retribution will occur so long as the present government continues in power. On 20 May 1985 an official ceremony was held at Poljana, the nearest town over the frontier from Bleiburg, from where so many thousands of victims were handed over by the British. Highlight of the occasion was a speech by a high-ranking Slovenian government official, Stane Dolanc. After references to 'Tito's strategy and tactics', which crushed German military might single-handed, came references to the 'new social order . . . which many did not like . . . They did not succeed because political meddlers could not overcome the sincerity and intelligence of the people's masses.' Dolanc continued, 'What should we say, to those who today, forty years later, interpret all these events, tearing them out of the context of the then military, political and other conditions, individual happenings, certainly among them some very tragic, and try to prove the inhumanity of our Revolution?'

The answer, the orator explained, lay in a forthright rejection of 'the so-called "national reconciliation". This is not only retrogressive, it is a wrong mentality from the historical point of view, without mentioning simple human logic. We shall never agree to a conciliation between revolution and counter-revolution . . . We are being attacked although none of our nations has ever been more free than now and has ever seen such a development in the economy, culture and other fields as during the last forty years.'[5]

It was at Kocevje that the majority of prisoners from Viktring Camp delivered by the British to the Communists were massacred.[6] As the victims' accounts indicate, OZNA resources were stretched to the limits to effect so massive a slaughter within such a short time, and the human pipeline passing from Viktring to Kocevje became clogged at the transit-camps in Skofje Loka, Kranj and St Vid. Speed was clearly regarded as essential if the operation were to be completed as efficiently and, above all, as secretly as possible. In consequence Toby Low was obliged to arrange for a secondary route, passing via Bleiburg in the British zone of Austria to Celje and Maribor in Yugoslavia. This journey led to a place of execution fully as terrible as the pit of Kocevje.

Janez Dernulc was among the second load of Domobranci who left Viktring for Bleiburg on 28 May. His commanding officer had told him they were bound for Italy, and it was with a feeling of elation that he climbed up into his truck. But it was not long before he began to entertain misgivings. Instead of travelling westwards towards Tarvisio, they appeared to be moving east. At Bleiburg they received a rude shock when they were turned over to the waiting Partisans and taken by train over the frontier to Dravograd. (There was a British liaison officer stationed in Dravograd to ensure that all went as it should.[7] It seems improbable, to say the least, that he was unaware of the torture and massacre in the town at this time of hundreds of Chetniks delivered by his superiors from Bleiburg.)[8] At Slovenjgradec, four stations down the line, they spent the night in a school. There they were separated into categories, and suffered ferocious beatings (which Dernulc himself fortunately escaped) in the washrooms.

Next morning they were taken in trucks to the village of Mislinja. The road and railway beyond the village were blocked, so they were made to descend and march the rest of the way to Celje. Many times the prisoners asked their Partisan escorts what was to happen to them. The guards, who probably knew no more than they, made reassuring responses; but Dernulc reflected on the reign of terror the Partisans had been practising in Slovenia for over two years, and knew that they would receive no mercy from such an enemy. The long march, in columns four abreast, lasted through the ensuing night, which enabled Dernulc and a friend to abscond into the darkness. After a number of narrow escapes, he succeeded in making his way a couple of months later to the safety of Italy.

Dernulc was a lucky man. It was a comrade who whispered, 'Now or never: jump!' But for that, he feels, he would have stayed with the column. Reports have gradually emerged since about the fate of his companions, and of all the others despatched by the same route. Accompanied by the usual beatings and occasional murders, monotonous to describe but horrible enough to imagine, their journey continued to a concentration camp at Teharje, seven kilometres east of Celje. There they were subjected to continual floggings and tortures, while the Communists plundered and interrogated them. About eighty officers were segregated and taken into a yard by the barracks. As a survivor recalled: 'Their hands were tied behind their backs and each one's head was one complete bloody wound. They had been so disfigured by the blows that they were impossible to recognise. Their jaws were battered, their teeth and jaws broken, and blood flowed from their mouths.' They were machine-gunned *en masse* and their bodies thrown into a nearby anti-tank ditch. Presumably because there was no natural ravine capable of accommodating huge numbers of bodies, the massacre at Teharje was much more drawn out than that of Kocevje.

> Each evening for 5 weeks they drove up 8 to 10 big trucks and stacked the tied guardsmen on them. They piled them aboard like cordwood. The victims were already half-dead. They tortured them so much that coming from these covered trucks were heard the actual animal, lunatic sounds of the insane. The Red escorts were jumping on these tortured bodies. This scene recurred each night until they had driven all of them away.

The former prisoner from whose account this is drawn eventually discovered the destination of the departed prisoners:

> For a change we sometimes had to cart earth also. From somewhere they pulled out a broken-down German supply wagon. Up to 30 of us would

get around the wagon; some of us pulled, others pushed, but nevertheless it went very slowly because we didn't have any strength. We loaded 3 cubic meters of earth, pulled it uphill, then down again into the valley. This was done many times.

Towards the end of July, we set off with this wagon to the southern side of the camp . . . we were loading earth and carting it to the left side of the main entrance where there had originally been a small ravine; this area was now all dug up and the earth turned over. To this plain we had carted probably more than 200 cubic meters of earth. When we stepped on this area, we had the feeling that everything was over water. The ground gave way so that one's foot sank up to the ankle into something soft and rotten which had been covered by at least 2 inches of dirt. Nobody dared to dig to see what it was underground that made the ground move in such an odd way as if it were alive. We also didn't dare to ask, but we all knew that we were walking over the bodies of the murdered, because there was such a stench in that area that it was hard to bear.

The witness from the description just quoted was released on 18 August, as for some reason the handful left alive by that stage was pardoned and released. Despite this, it is clear that the Communist organisers were as concerned as their colleagues at Kocevje that news of the massacres should not leak out: 'Before they handed out the releases to us, a Communist said to us: "You will now be released to freedom. But – if anyone utters a single word about what he saw and experienced, we will come and shoot him at home."' A group of ten who had escaped earlier and were recaptured were done to death in peculiarly brutal fashion. However, as at Kocevje, there were two or three who escaped miraculously from the pits themselves.[9]

The number of refugees received from the British military authorities in Austria and liquidated at Tito's orders far exceeded the number of Polish officers murdered in the notorious Katyn massacre. On 1 June 1945 the Fifth Corps reported to the Fifteenth Army Group: 'Evacuation of respective nationals to Russians and Jugoslavs continued. 26,339 Jugoslav nationals have now been evacuated from Corps area.' This was broken down as follows: 12,196 Croats, 5,480 Serbs, 8,263 Slovenes, and 400 Montenegrins.[10] These figures may have been considerably underestimated. Slovenian émigré sources, for example, calculate their contingent as having comprised nearly 10,000 Domobranci, accompanied by several hundred civilians.[11] Today Slovenian émigrés in the United States are engaged in a determined effort to publish as nearly exhaustive as possible a memorial list of their compatriots killed in this and other wartime atrocities. So far two volumes of the *Bela Knijga* have appeared, with another in preparation.

These massacres, carefully planned and implemented on a colossal scale, must by any standard be regarded as one of the most significant factors in Tito's post-war pacification of the country. Understandably, the subject is not considered one suitable for public airing by the present Yugoslav Government. What is much less explicable is the silence on the subject practised by so many Western historians writing about Tito's wartime career and subsequent seizure of power. A respected British scholar, Phyllis Auty, worked during the early part of the war in the BBC Yugoslav Section, and afterwards with the Political Intelligence Centre, Middle East, in 1943–44. She conducted extensive researches both in Yugoslavia and abroad for her well-received biography of Tito, and was even granted an audience with the Marshal himself, who 'answered all questions frankly and fully without hesitation or evasion, giving the impression that he was content to let his record stand up to any examination'.

Auty's account of the 1945 massacres is as follows: 'Known collaborators – and Rankovic's intelligence system had been collecting dossiers throughout the war – were routed out, many were tried, some were killed.'[12] This is an oddly inadequate description of a holocaust which, in the proportion of the population to have suffered, was fully equivalent to the worst comparable atrocities of a particularly inhumane war. Yugoslavs free to discuss the subject tend to adopt a less detached viewpoint. Milovan Djilas was at the time a senior member of Tito's Politburo, and one of his most favoured collaborators. Though at the time not directly involved in the major killings, he has made clear on different occasions his subsequent disgust and indignation. He writes:

> Along with the Germans, our enemies who collaborated with the invaders or bound their destiny to the fascist powers – the Chetniks, the Ustashi, Home Guards, and the Slovenian Home Guards – also laid down their arms. Some of these groups got through to the British in Austria, who turned them over to us. All were killed, except for women and young people who were under eighteen years of age – so we were told at the time in Montenegro, and so I later heard from those who had taken part in these senseless acts of wrathful retribution.
>
> These killings were sheer frenzy. How many victims were there? According to what I heard in passing from a few officials involved in that settling of scores, the number exceeds twenty thousand – though it must

certainly be under thirty thousand, including all three of the groups just cited. They were killed separately, each group on the territory where they had been taken prisoner. A year or two later, there was grumbling in the Slovenian Central Committee that they had trouble with the peasants from those areas, because underground rivers were casting up bodies. They also said that piles of corpses were heaving up as they rotted in shallow mass graves, so that the very earth seemed to breathe.

This last detail might appear to be an exaggeration, but is substantiated by first-hand testimony. Stanislav Plesko, for example, was one of the Domobranci handed over by Keightley and Low on 28 May, who spent nearly a fortnight in the notorious transit camp at St Vid. There he suffered the same tortures and starvation as the others, until about 19 June he was fortunate enough to escape being butchered there or at Kocevje by escaping over the wire. He was on the run for three years, before escaping to Austria.

During the first weeks of his flight he was hiding for a while near Brezje, where many of the wounded Domobranci had been taken from St Vid to be killed. There was a heatwave at the time and, as he has recently explained:

> there was such a stench that the people couldn't stand it. They didn't know what it was, but it was something terrible . . . There was a big storm, and the waters rose, bursting the cement sealing the mass grave. The drinking water in Ljubljana was poisoned, polluted. After that the authorities got German prisoners to pull all the bodies out of the grave and transport them into the bush several hundred metres away. There they reburied them; and after *that* they killed all the Germans, except one who escaped and related the story.

Apart from acknowledging that the massacres undoubtedly took place, Djilas was also concerned about the question of responsibility:

> Who issued the order for this extermination? Who signed it? I don't know. It is my belief that a written order didn't exist. Given the power structure and the chain of command, no one could have carried out such a major undertaking without approval from the top. An atmosphere of revenge prevailed. The Central Committee did not decide that. And what if it had? Doubtless the Central Committee would have gone along with those in power. There was never any voting anyway. And I would have agreed – perhaps with some reservation which would not have threatened my revolutionary resolve, my adherence to the party, and my solidarity with the leadership. As if there were no justice, truth, and mercy outside

the ideology, the party, and an aroused people, and outside us leaders as their essence! We never spoke of it either in the Central Committee or privately among ourselves. Once in a rambling conversation – after the clash with the Soviet leadership in 1948, of course – I mentioned that we had gone too far then, because among the executed also were some fleeing for ideological reasons alone.

Tito retorted immediately, as if he had long since come to a final, though hardly comforting, conclusion: 'We put an end to it once and for all! Anyway, given the kind of courts that we had . . .'[13]

In Viktring Church today may be seen an inscribed memorial set up by exiles from America:

IN HONOREM B. MARIAE VIRGINIS
PROFVGI EX SLOVENIAE, FRATRVM
MEMORES HINC IN MANVS INIMICORVM
A.D. MCMXLV TRADITORVM.
DE TRANSOCEANIS TERRIS RENOVATIONI
HVIVS TEMPLI PARTEM GRATI TRIBVERVNT.

One day, it is not to be doubted, an obelisk will be raised not only in the centre of Ljubljana but above the grave of the fallen in the glade at Kocevje. There, if true justice is done, it will bear the name not only of Josip Broz (Tito), but those of his principal British collaborators, without whose secretive aid the tragedy would never have taken place.

8

The Surrender of the Cossacks

'Germagen Rodionoff was evacuated yesterday with the Cossack officers. He is not a Russian subject and has been living in Paris for 15 years. Apparently he is a teacher. His family is in France, and it would appear that he has been put in the Cossack camp by mistake. May we have your advice. It seems highly probable that there are a large number of persons in the Cossack camp who are not of Russian [i.e. Soviet] origin. What is the position regarding these people?' (Lieutenant-Colonel Alec Malcolm, commanding the Eighth Argyll and Sutherland Highlanders, to Brigadier Geoffrey Musson, 29 May 1945)

While messages were flying between Caserta, London and Washington in May and June of 1945, events on the ground in Austria were pursuing their own course in ways which were far from reflecting decisions being made on high. Indeed, the central problem of this mysterious and tragic history lies in the discrepancy between the events themselves and the documents which purport to implement or describe them. At times it appears as if they relate to two distinct worlds; whether or in what degree the discrepancy arises from muddle, error or intent will it is hoped be seen in due course.

As the Combined Chiefs of Staff deliberated the fate of Yugoslavs and Cossacks held by the Fifth Corps in Austria, they learned on 26 May that Alexander had authorised 'the transfer of Cossacks overland to Soviet military authorities'. The Combined Chiefs in due course indicated their approval of this move, the Cossacks' fate having already been decided in principle at the Yalta Conference along with that of all other captured or liberated Soviet citizens. In the case of the Yugoslavs, however, the ruling was emphatic and unambiguous:

no Yugoslavs were to be returned against their will, 'despite the fact that 900 had already been transferred'.

It will be recalled how Domanov's Cossacks, the Kazachi Stan, had withdrawn from Tolmezzo in North Italy over the mountains into Austria, where they surrendered to troops of the British Thirty-sixth Infantry Brigade, commanded by Brigadier Geoffrey Musson. These Cossacks, accompanied by some 4,000 Caucasian refugees under the command of the former Tsarist General Sultan Kelich-Ghirei, were directed to settle for the present in the valley of the Drau, in a fifteen-mile area stretching from Lienz to Oberdrauburg. The battalion responsible for the maintenance and guarding of the settlement, the Eighth Argyll and Sutherland Highlanders, was provided with no indication of the length of the Cossacks' stay, and the camp administration was established to last if necessary for an indefinite period while the powers-that-be arrived at a decision over the Cossacks' ultimate destination.

To Major 'Rusty' Davies, the youthful officer placed in charge of the settlement, it seems in retrospect as if matters continued on an unchanging level for months on end, so absorbing was his task. With its families, schools, newspaper, religious services and sporting activities, the Cossack camp's requirements were more those of a country town than a prisoner-of-war camp. The settlement was self-policing and almost entirely lacking in any sort of physical perimeter. Generals Krasnov, Domanov, Shkuro and other senior Cossack officers were quartered in the town of Lienz, alongside Colonel Malcolm and his officers. Individual Cossacks would wander off if they chose down the valley or into Lienz, and there was no practical means of preventing small-scale escapes – a problem which did not arise, since there appeared to be nothing to escape from or to.

Naturally there was much discussion among the Cossacks as to their ultimate destination. Some imagined that room would be found for them somewhere in the limitless open spaces of the British Empire, where a Cossack land would be established in all its traditional purity. It would be far from their beloved steppes, but also safe from the ubiquitous attentions of the NKVD (as the KGB was then known). Rusty Davies, frequently questioned on this all-absorbing topic, could only reply truthfully that he knew no more than they did, and was as dependent on orders as everyone else.

Davies's commanding officer, Colonel Malcolm, knew no more than Davies. He was a brave and efficient officer, but four years of

fighting had left him with little time, even had he the interest, for
the study of politics. So far as the Russians were concerned, however,
he was strongly affected by a consideration from which few Englishmen were at that time entirely immune. As he recalled to me in 1978:

> The events at Lienz took place less than 3 *weeks* after 6 *years* of war. One's
> reaction to events then was very different to what it is now after 33 years
> of peace.
>   Secondly I agree strongly . . . that we were attuned to be friendly to
> Russia, not only because of left wing propaganda but also, more practi-
> cally, because Russia had fought with the greatest gallantry in Europe for
> 2 years about, and without her efforts we would never have set foot in
> Europe and probably would have lost the war. She was our vital ally and
> you cannot reverse your mental outlook in 3 weeks.

This did not mean that Malcolm regarded the Cossacks with hostility,
but as inevitable casualties of war – and perhaps not altogether
deserving ones at that. Their ultimate fate was no concern of his, his
task being the straightforward administrative one of seeing his charges
properly fed and disciplined. Until he received further instructions
this was what he would do to the best of his ability.

While the Cossacks at Lienz and elsewhere set about establishing
improvised homes in barracks and tents, their fate was a matter of
urgent discussion at Klagenfurt and Caserta. On 13 May Macmillan
flew in to Corps headquarters, providing Keightley with a 'verbal
directive' for the repatriation of all Cossacks, including White émigrés
not covered by the Yalta Agreement. That day and the next, having
concerted the scheme with the Fifth Corps, he deceived the Eighth
Army and AFHQ commands by pretending that all the Cossacks
were Soviet citizens and concealing the fact that the Soviets had
on the tenth and eleventh demanded their return. From General
Robertson he extracted an order authorising the Eighth Army to
return 'all Russians' held in their area.

It was at this point that operations designed to fulfil the Soviet
demand received an awkward check. On the seventeenth Field-
Marshal Alexander took up the cause of the Cossacks with the
Combined Chiefs of Staff and General Eisenhower. The terms of the
Yalta Agreement could not be evaded with regard to the return of
Soviet citizens, but procrastination and special pleading might yet
protect them from their intended fate. With the Supreme Allied
Commander's attention alerted to the Cossacks' predicament, it was
no longer possible to make use of Robertson's order and hand the

Cossacks swiftly over to their enemies with no awkward questions asked about delicate matters like citizenship. At any rate Robertson's order, as a subsequent message by Keightley makes clear, was no longer considered operative. The AFHQ order of 25 May eventually employed as authority for the operation was virtually indistinguishable in its provisions from that sent out by General Robertson on the fourteenth, again indicating that the earlier order was regarded as lapsed.

The pretext originally advanced by Keightley as necessitating the Cossacks' delivery to the Soviets was the pressing one of overcrowding within his Corps area. Yet preparations proceeded at a leisurely pace, long outlasting the early crisis, and it was not until the end of the month that they were driven across the zonal frontier.

In view of the provisions of the Yalta Agreement, it might be thought that, strictly speaking, Alexander had no choice but to return so large a body of Soviet citizens to their country of origin. It is improbable that he would have regarded the matter in this light. The Cossacks for the most part comprised serving units of the Wehrmacht, who had surrendered to the Eighth Army under the normal honourable terms. Under accepted interpretation of the Geneva Convention they had a right to be treated no differently from other prisoners of war, and their involuntary transfer to be maltreated by a third power would have constituted a gross infringement of the Convention.

Alexander is in any case unlikely to have issued his appeal to the Combined Chiefs on the Cossacks' behalf while simultaneously accepting provision for their forced surrender to the Soviets. Nevertheless preparations within the Fifth Corps for the repatriation operation had begun in anticipation of orders as yet uncontemplated at AFHQ.

The Cossacks in the Drau Valley around Lienz were held within the Seventy-eighth Infantry Divisional area, with the component Thirty-sixth Infantry Brigade immediately responsible. The Brigadier, Geoffrey Musson, first learned of what was planned on or about 20 May, as we learn from the Thirty-sixth Infantry Brigade War Diary: 'It was agreed at the Yalta conference that all Soviet nationals found in territories occupied by the Allies should be returned to the USSR. This fact was made known to Commander 36 Inf Bde about 20 May 45'.

Next morning a conference was held by General Keightley at the Fifth Corps HQ, at which divisional commanders were informed of the decision to repatriate Soviet citizens held within their areas. The Cossacks and Caucasians were to be transported by train in cattle-trucks, together with their belongings: 'The ratio of humans to horses to carts is approx 10:3:1. A train composed of 21 cattle trucks and 9 flats (assuming 50 humans or 8 horses per truck and 4 carts per flat) will carry 350 humans, 112 horses and 36 carts.'[1]

Apart from the logistics of the operation, the question of the large number of non-Soviet citizens held by the Thirty-sixth Infantry Brigade was raised. Since reference to the Yalta Conference decision was concerned exclusively with 'Soviet nationals', how were these others to be treated? Under pressure from perplexed battalion, brigade and divisional commanders, it was impossible for Corps headquarters to avoid facing up to this problem: 'Various cases have recently been referred to this HQ in which doubt has been raised as to whether certain formations and groups should be treated as Soviet Nationals in so far as their return to the Soviet Union direct from 5 Corps is concerned.' From the Thirty-sixth Infantry Brigade report on the subsequent operation we learn in confirmation of this that: 'Even before it was known that they were to be returned, they [the Cossacks] made frequent petitions, in interview and in writing, that some other course [than delivery to the Soviets] should be adopted with them.'[2] These petitions included that handed over by General Peter Krasnov soon after the Cossacks' arrival in Austria in the second week of May.

In response to these persistent enquiries Toby Low, Brigadier General Staff (BGS) to General Keightley at Fifth Corps HQ, issued a 'Definition of Russian Nationals' sent out to divisional HQs immediately after the Corps conference on 21 May. This elaborated a rather confused general ruling, which inexplicably excluded Colonel Rogozhin's *Russkii Corpus* from return, and went on to lay down that:

> Following will be treated as Soviet Nationals:
> ATAMAN Group
> 15 Cossack Cav Corps (incl Cossacks and Calmucks)
> res units of Lt-Gen Chkouro
> Caucasians (incl Mussulmen).

This list is oddly selective and ambivalent. The descriptions are for the most part ambiguous or inaccurate, and make no reference at all to the major groupings of Domanov's Cossacks at Lienz, beyond singling out for no appreciable reason Shkuro's 1,200 men from a total of 25,000 or so. In view of the fact that the Fifth Corps possessed accurate returns for the different Cossack units, it is possible that the confusion and ambiguity were deliberate, being intended to prevent too close examination of the constituent groupings.

However that may be, the overall position should have been clear:

> Individual cases will NOT be considered unless particularly pressed. In these cases and in the case of appeals by further [presumably Cossack] units or formations, the following directive will apply:
> (a) Any individual now in our hands who, at the time of joining the German Forces or joining a fmn fighting with the German Forces, was living within the 1938 body of USSR, will be treated as a Soviet National for the purposes of transfer.
> (b) Any individual although of Russian blood who, prior to joining the German Forces, had not been in USSR since 1930, will not until further orders be treated as a Soviet National.
> (c) In all cases of doubt, the individual will be treated as a Soviet National.[3]

There was thus on the face of it no question of handing over any of the old émigrés, except where in individual cases there was difficulty in establishing credentials. This was likely to be the case more rarely than might be supposed today, since in wartime Europe people clung with desperate tenacity to their identification papers; without them they could only with extreme difficulty travel on public transport, receive rations, be allocated lodgings, etc.; in addition papers were regularly inspected by the Gestapo and, subsequently, the British military occupation authorities.[4] Captain A. P. Judge, who in the course of his duties as an intelligence officer with the Thirty-sixth Infantry Brigade had to sift whole refugee camps, was much struck by this factor. In one refugee camp he visited he

> spent a whole day going through their documents and their backgrounds. There were 120 persons all told, men, women and children and they split down into 19 different nationalities, including a Czech national of Turkish extraction! The largest single group were White Russians from France and Belgium, carrying the appropriate *carte d'identité* and *permis de séjour*, etc. etc. One I remember well had worked in Rumania for the Red Cross and still carried a letter of commendation from a Capt. Mackenzie for services rendered to Russian refugees in 1919–20.

This, then, was the position at Fifth Corps headquarters on 21 May.

Though no operational instruction for the handover of the Cossacks had yet been received from AFHQ, authorisation was anticipated on the general grounds that as Soviet citizens the Cossacks would be covered by the Yalta Agreement. At the same time the presence of a substantial number of prominent non-Soviet citizens among them was known to all at Fifth Corps. Brigadier Tryon-Wilson says it was a frequent topic of conversation among Corps staff throughout this time. Toby Low makes no bones about it: he and his colleagues were throughout familiar with the vital distinction.

As he recalls, the Cossack

> divisions also included Russians who had not either served in the Russian Army or been in Russia in the last 15 years . . . amongst them were officers who belonged to what has become known as the White Russian community . . . Some of them were people who were 'wanted' by the Soviet Russians [an allusion to the list brought by Brigadier Tryon-Wilson from Voitsberg on 11 May] . . . a distinction was clearly drawn between the two classes of people in the orders that were issued.

As soon as news broke that the return of the Cossacks was envisaged, vigorous objection was raised by the commander of the Seventy-eighth Infantry Division, whose duty it would be to transmit the order. This was Major-General (afterwards Viscount) Robert Arbuthnott, heir to an ancient Scottish noble family. Toby Low remembers Arbuthnott protesting hotly that 'we should be no party to this affair'. He 'disliked sending any of them back – he thought it just as wrong to send a Soviet Cossack back as to send a non-Soviet Cossack back. Because he said that they had both been fighting for the Germans, and they're just going to be killed.'

In view of General Robertson's order of 14 May instructing the Eighth Army that 'all Russians should be handed over to Soviet forces,' it might seem that the Fifth Corps was left with no room for manoeuvre. The loose expression 'all Russians', looks suspiciously like a covert device intended to evade screening in fulfilment of Macmillan's 'verbal directive' instructing Keightley to repatriate not only 'Cossacks' but also non-Soviet '"White" Russians'.

This first protest by General Arbuthnott, together with others in connection with the Yugoslavs held at Viktring, reached Eighth Army headquarters. On 21 May the Eighth Army sent a message to AFHQ, already cited with reference to the Yugoslavs, requesting the despatch of 'a representative who can lay down principles and answer specific questions' regarding matters of citizenship.

The situation at Fifth Corps headquarters on 21 May was markedly ambivalent. At the conference held that morning divisional commanders were told that measures were afoot for the Cossacks' handover. During the same day General de Fonblanque from the Fifth Corps staff met Soviet officers, with whom he opened preliminary talks regarding transport arrangements for the forthcoming move.[5] The handover itself had been agreed in principle by General Keightley a week earlier: as Brigadier Tryon-Wilson says of de Fonblanque's meeting, 'that's when all the loose ends were tied up'.

Yet it was also that day (21 May) that Eighth Army headquarters, apparently unaware of these moves, applied to AFHQ 'asking for policy re Cossacks'. The application itself appears to have disappeared from the files,[6] but its existence suggests that Eighth Army headquarters did not regard itself as empowered to hand over the Cossacks at this time.

Whether or not this was so, Alexander's reply was unequivocal. Next day, 22 May, he replied to the Eighth Army: 'Policy decisions on questions your U 128 of 21 May now being considered this HQ. You will be informed immediately and on receipt you will be in position to consider whether you still need representative as requested.' At the same time he issued the following directive:

1. all who are Soviet citizens and who can be handed over to Russians without use of force should [be] returned direct by Eighth Army.
2. any others should be evacuated to 12 Army Group [under SHAEF control].
3. definition of Soviet citizen is given in AFHQ letter CR/3491/G1-British of 6 May addressed to 15 Army Group and Main Eighth Army, ref your A 4073 of 21 May asking for policy re Cossacks.[7]

The intention of Alexander's order is further clarified by an account of it provided by his American political adviser, Alexander Kirk, which he telegraphed to the State Department at midnight on 24 May:

AFHQ instructed Brit Eighth Army that Cossacks who are Soviet citizens and who can be handed over to Russians without use of force should be sent back direct by Eighth Army. All others should be evacuated to Twelfth Army Group.

Final disposition of such persons is to be in accordance with Crimea agreement. Eighth Army has been instructed under Brit law that all persons who are Sov citizens will be repatriated but any person who is

not a Sov citizen under Brit law will not be sent back to Sov Union unless
he expresses a desire to do so. Under Brit law Sov citizens are those who
come from places within boundaries of Sov Union as established before
outbreak of present war. Those coming from territories west of such
boundaries have Polish or Baltic state citizenship unless there is evidence
that they acquired Sov citizenship by voluntary act.[8]

This AFHQ ruling arose from Alexander's request of 17 May to
General Eisenhower, in which he had requested the General to accept
the Cossacks under SHAEF command. On 21 May Eisenhower had
notified Alexander:

> as result of meeting with Generals Macleod and Eberle we understand
> the enemy personnel urgently required to be moved . . . consist of a
> maximum of 150,000 surrendered enemy of which approximately 105,000
> are Germans . . . and 45,000 are Cossacks still fully armed . . . the
> Cossacks may be expected to move more or less as organised bodies
> intact . . . Accompanying the Cossacks are an estimated additional 11,000
> camp followers (women, children and old men). until these persons can
> be segregated and properly disposed of as displaced persons they should
> be accorded the same treatment as the forces they accompany.[9]

Next day, 22 May, Alexander's Chief of Staff, Lieutenant-General
William Morgan, despatched this ruling to General McCreery at the
Eighth Army headquarters:

> Secret. Personal for General McCreery from General Morgan.
> Reference telephone conversation with my M.A. 1800B hrs, this evening.
> One. SHAEF movements into 5 Corps area should be arranged between
> 15 Army Group and 12 Army Group in accordance with advice 8 Army.
> Gruenther [Alexander's chief US staff officer] is arranging.
> Two. You have authority to pass Cossacks direct to Russians provided
> force has not repeat not to be used.[10]

The Eighth Army and Fifth Corps were accordingly instructed to
begin arrangements for the Cossacks' peaceful evacuation from the
Fifth Corps area:

> Route designated for movement is Lienz-Vipiteno-Innsbruck. Desire
> arrangements for movement over portion this route in your sector be
> made directly with Eighth Army. 3 US Army is dealing directly with
> representative 15 Army Gp now at 5 Corps HQ on details of movement.
> For Eighth Army. When details of movement worked out deal directly
> with 5 Army movement over portion route that sector. For Lt Col Gerrett

5 Corps. Keep Eighth Army informed plans for movement to enable prompt movement arrangements to be made with 5 Army. Include in your daily sitreps numbers moved.[11]

These messages are quoted in full in order to make it clear that on 22 May Alexander had every intention of clearing the Fifth Corps area of all Cossacks. Had his orders been fulfilled all would have departed with maximum speed to the American and Soviet zones. Yet, as we shall now see, the Fifth Corps went to remarkable lengths in order to frustrate the planned operation. Whatever Keightley's and Low's motives in so doing, one thing remains clear. Administrative convenience or expediency cannot have been among them, since it goes without saying that *fulfilment* of Alexander's instructions would have solved the problem overnight.

Despite this Toby Low was determined, come what may, that force would be used. His concern was not to be rid of the Cossacks, but to ensure their delivery to the Soviets. The day after receiving Alexander's ruling, he sent this strongly-worded request to the Eighth Army headquarters:

As a result of verbal directive from Macmillan to Corps Comd at recent meeting we have undertaken to return all Soviet nationals in Corps area to Soviet forces. Macmillan mentioned no proviso about use of force and we have issued instructions that force may be used if absolutely necessary. Consider quite impossible to guarantee to return Cossacks and so honour our verbal agreement with Soviet forces unless we are allowed free hand in this matter. Consider therefore may be necessary to use force to move Cossacks at all from present area. Longer they remain at present area more likely force will have to be used. Request you confirm our freedom of action in this.[12]

This plea is remarkably revealing. The failure even to mention Macmillan's claim that the purpose of the pledge was to recover in exchange British prisoners of war liberated by Soviet forces suggests, to say the least, that it was not a very pressing consideration in the eyes of the soldiers most closely concerned.

There are several incongruities implicit in Low's request which are difficult to explain at face value. On 14 May Keightley informed McCreery that Macmillan had advised him to hand over the Cossacks to the Red Army. He agreed with the suggestion, he reported but replied that he could do nothing without orders from his superior officers. Eleven days later, he turns this procedure on its head. Now it turns out that it was Macmillan's orders which were binding, and the military who must adjust their policy accordingly. As Keightley could have no discernible interest in preferring to force the Cossacks across to the Soviet zone, rather than turn them peacefully over to the Americans, it seems that it was Macmillan's wishes rather than his own that he was expressing.

The implication seems clear that Macmillan's 'advice' had in reality amounted to an instruction, which for some reason Keightley found compelling. Had the Minister thought to authorise the use of force, Keightley seems to be saying, there would be no need for him now to be seeking further authority. That circumstances at the time of Macmillan's visit led Keightley to regard Macmillan's advice as tantamount to an order is understandable, even if we do not know what were the factors in Macmillan's recommendation which swayed the Corps Commander. What is more difficult to comprehend is why he should have continued ten days later to regard it as so binding as to impel him to contest and even ignore later orders from AFHQ: orders which, for aught he knew, might have been approved by the Minister Resident.

The impression aroused by these exchanges is that Keightley was for some reason deeply concerned to urge Macmillan's policy against that adopted by Alexander. It looks, too, as if Keightley continued to be kept *au courant* with Macmillan's wishes. There was no practical inhibition on direct communication between the Minister and the General, since the Fifth Corps was linked by direct radio transmission to AFHQ.[13] Could it have been coincidence that Macmillan returned from his three-day visit to England on the afternoon of 22 May, the day AFHQ issued its 'no force' order; and that it was next day in defiance of that order that Low fulfilled the 'verbal directive from Macmillan', which (as he argued) by pledging the return of all Cossacks made force obligatory?

This suggestion may be regarded as excessively speculative. But it is Keightley's *continuing* advocacy of Macmillan's policy which surely requires explanation. It is less the persistent resistance to measures insisted upon by Alexander from AFHQ which surprises, than his otherwise inexplicable desire to pursue an alternative so unnecessarily detrimental to the well-being of his Corps.

Instead of taking prompt steps to fulfil his orders of 22 May, which would have had the effect of ridding the area of all Cossacks in a speedy and orderly manner, he went out of his way to ensure that the operation was conducted under conditions of maximum stress and danger, greatly taxing to the administrative resources, morale, and even safety of his troops. From the moment it became known that repatriation to the Soviet zone was under contemplation, protests arose from all ranks. General Arbuthnott of the Seventy-eighth Division objected in the most vigorous terms the moment he learned what was afoot, repeating his protests on two successive occasions. General Murray of the Sixth Armoured Division made his disgust so plain that Keightley was compelled to remove large numbers of Cossacks from his area. Lieutenant-Colonel 'Bala' Bredin, who as A/Q to the Seventy-eighth Division was responsible for assessing the morale of troops, reported widespread revulsion throughout the other ranks. 'This isn't what we fought the war for, sir!' was a recurring complaint. Nor were these the reactions from his men that so capable a general as Keightley normally goes out of his way to arouse.

It was not just the troops' moral welfare that was endangered by his gratuitous insistence on the use of force. In the event the Cossacks' resistance proved unexpectedly to be more in the spirit of Tolstoy or Gandhi than their own warlike tradition. This was scarcely the reaction to be anticipated from men of their legendary martial qualities. It was not until 27 May that disarmament of the Cossacks took place, an operation of necessity very rough-and-ready and largely reliant on Cossack co-operation. A thorough search was in the circumstances impossible, and it was Cossack good faith rather than British efficiency which ensured the absence of firearms. As a Fifth Corps report noted afterwards:

> Disarmament was completed without incident on 27 May. Subsequent searchings of camps showed that the majority of weapons were handed in; isolated instances occurred later of Cossacks and Caucasians who had escaped from their camps still being in possession of firearms when they were encountered by our patrols. There is little doubt that the officers of both forces did all they could to ensure compliance with the disarmament orders issued to them by the British battalions concerned.

Brigadier Musson's order of the day on the eve of the operation clearly envisaged it as one which could easily get out of hand, putting the lives of British troops seriously at risk: 'Be firm. Remember that quick and determined action taken immediately may save many incidents and lives in the future. If it is necessary to open fire you

will do so and you must regard this duty as an operation of war'. He
concluded by stressing that:

(a) Personal arms will be carried by all ranks at all times,
(b) Officers will have an escort,
(c) No one will go about alone.

Next day Musson reiterated the dangers facing troops engaged in an
operation whose implementation was so potentially hazardous and
outcome so unpredictable: 'Above all else try to avoid casualties to
yourselves, your officers and your comrades. This will be achieved
if you are always on your guard.'[14]

But before the handover operations it was impossible to know
what arms still lay concealed among the tens of thousands of formidable warriors camped at the foot of mountains providing ideal cover
for the guerrilla warfare at which they excelled. Their predicament
desperate, fighting could have lasted for days or weeks, causing
severe casualties among British troops. Yet this was the risk Keightley
went out of his way to encounter, when by mere acceptance of orders
he could instead have seen the Cossacks peacefully entrained for
Radstadt!

Clearly Keightley wished for none of these things, but nonetheless
was influenced by overriding considerations which impelled him to
incur predictably severe risks. However, it can at least be said that
there was nothing secretive about his approach; at least, not in respect
of the operation as a whole. Despite the flat prohibition on the use
of force contained in the order of 22 May, he applied for the ruling
to be overturned. Seemingly confident of a favourable reply, he made
his agreement with the Soviets and undertook operational measures
in anticipation of a speedy reversal of Alexander's policy.

That Keightley preferred forced repatriation of Cossacks via Judenburg to peaceful evacuation to Radstadt seems inexplicable in terms
of the interests of his Corps. There is another remarkable anomaly
implicit in his message to the Fifth Corps of 23 May.

As General Musson stresses today, the Thirty-sixth Infantry Brigade lacked resources for enforcing screening procedure laid down in
the AFHQ directive of 6 May and the operational order of 22
May. In addition, screening on the spot would have the effect of
prematurely alerting the Cossacks to what was afoot. Whether or
not it was possible in reality will be considered shortly. But there
is no question that the problem greatly exercised the divisional

commander responsible, and that he put the matter forcefully to his Corps Commander.

Brigadier Low was at pains to raise one major operational hazard with AFHQ: that of the use of force. But why did he not raise this other equally essential consideration at the same time? The answer, inescapably, is that he withheld mention of it as a matter of considered policy. No message concerning the Cossacks emanating from his headquarters to the Eighth Army had yet alluded to the known presence of large numbers of non-Soviet citizens among them, despite the fact that they represented a major consideration at Fifth Corps headquarters. But to talk of the need for large-scale screening at this stage would of necessity reveal for the first time the fact that the Cossack camp included large numbers of people not liable for repatriation.

Next, Keightley took a step which is perhaps more revelatory of his true intentions than any other. The AFHQ order of 22 May had laid down that the Cossacks could be returned to the Soviets without the use of force, and went on to repeat the instruction of 6 May that strict screening was obligatory in accordance with the official definition issued on 6 May. On 23 May Keightley replied with a request to be permitted to use force.

Now, on 25 May, he belatedly took up the question of screening. As the order of 22 May did not call for a reply on this issue, it looks as if the Fifteenth Army Group had requested a reassurance before delivering fresh instructions. The reassurance duly arrived, but makes disturbing reading in view of Toby Low's frank admission that the Cossacks

> included Russians who had not either served in the Russian Army or been in Russia in the last 15 years . . . amongst them were officers who belonged to what has become known as the White Russian community . . . Some of them were people who were "wanted" by the Soviet Russians.

Lieutenant-Colonel Gerrett, the Fifteenth Army Group officer attached to Fifth Corps headquarters to supervise the evacuation of Germans and Cossacks to the Americans, reported to his headquarters:

> 5 Corps confirm that approx 42000 Cossacks to be handed over to Russians are Soviet citizens within the definition of cited AFHQ letter.

Any not eligible for transfer to Russians will be included in surrendered personnel [evacuated to the US zone].[15]

If no other evidence existed, this message alone would prove that the old émigrés were deliberately included among the Soviet citizens returned, and that this aspect of the operation was withheld from higher authority. The report was clearly intended to reassure the Fifteenth Army Group that the main body of Cossacks consisted in its entirety of Soviet citizens. The reference to 'any not eligible' is specious: as will be seen, no screening took place, and so far as is known no Cossacks were evacuated at that time to Radstadt.

Following this assurance that non-Soviet citizens would be screened and evacuated to safety, the Eighth Army transmitted this message on the same day, 25 May:

A 4152 Top Secret (.) ref this HQ A4149 dated 25 (.) Ruling now received 15 Army Gp (.) all Soviet Citizens including arrestable categories will be treated as surrendered personnel and will therefore be handed over to Russians (.) For 5 Corps (.) please take action accordingly (.) No further Soviet Citizens to be evacuated.[16]

Here at last was what it is evident the Fifth Corps Staff had been angling for. At the same time this successful manoeuvre in no way reflected Corps concerns or interests. From the point of view of the Fifth Corps Alexander's order of 22 May should have provided the perfect answer to their problem. Within days every Cossack could have been evacuated peacefully from the area. It is true that in that case the Soviets would only have received that minuscule proportion of the Cossacks who were both Soviet citizens and desired to return to the Soviet Union. But that was scarcely Keightley's problem. It was for AFHQ to concern itself with larger political issues of that nature, rather (so it might be thought) than a mere Corps commander in the field.

What was the precise intention of the Fifteenth Army Group order is hard to envisage. It clearly represents a considerable concession in the direction of Keightley's wishes, since it lays down that all Soviet citizens are to be returned and none evacuated. A cynic might plausibly suggest that it authorises the use of force in all but name. Since Keightley's request for permission to use force remains unanswered it could be regarded as tacitly conceded.

As there is no means of ascertaining what was known of the Cossacks at AFHQ, it is impossible to say what degree of reluctance to return on their part was envisaged, nor what corresponding pressures might be regarded as reasonable. But the failure to provide a direct acknowledgment of Keightley's request for permission to use force does not suggest any great commitment to the prospect, nor is it likely that any excessive violence on the scale actually employed was envisaged. But Alexander's attitude is best assessed by an overall review of his actions.

The Field-Marshal's intervention follows a clear pattern of advance and recession which could effectively be plotted on a graph. The moment the related problems of Cossacks and Yugoslav prisoners were brought to his attention, his Chief of Staff, General Morgan, transmitted a request to SHAEF to accept the 'refugees and PW' in the Fifth Corps area. On 17 May Alexander himself intervened to launch his appeals on the Cossacks' and Yugoslavs' behalf to the Chiefs of Staff and General Eisenhower. He simultaneously issued an order forbidding the return of Yugoslavs and made it clear, the evidence suggests, that General Robertson's order of 14 May ordering the Cossacks' return was no longer to be regarded as effective. At the same time the Yugoslavs were ordered to be evacuated to Italy. Following Eisenhower's agreement on 19 May to absorb the Cossacks within his command, Alexander similarly issued an order on 22 May arranging for their evacuation to safety at Radstadt.

Thus by 22 May, so far as Alexander was concerned, the position of both Cossacks and Yugoslavs must have appeared secure. Their forced repatriation was prohibited, and within days both groupings would be removed far from Red Army and Yugoslav lines.

Despite this Toby Low at Fifth Corps issued an order on 17 May for the return of 'all Jugoslav nationals at present in the Corps area'; and on 21 May a senior officer from the Fifth Corps discussed with Soviet representatives the 'transport and handover of Cossacks'. One is left with the overriding impression that Keightley and Low were acting in confident expectation of an imminent reversal of the Supreme Allied Commander's policy in these matters, though they made no attempt at this time to respond to his intervention.

It was not until 23 May that Keightley took up the question with his superiors: not with a request for an alteration of the policy, but with a blunt announcement that he had that day made a binding agreement with the Soviets to return all Cossacks. In addition he had sanctioned the use of force to fulfil this arrangement, a sanction for which he demanded confirmation from AFHQ. On the same day AFHQ was likewise informed that an agreement had already been made to hand over all Yugoslav 'military personnel'. Concealing the fact that the agreement in fact included 'their camp followers', it was urged that they too (under the heading of prisoners of war, displaced persons, etc.) should be subject to compulsory return.

In response to these peremptory demands Alexander promptly reversed his policy, conceding on 23 May that Yugoslavs could be returned provided no force were employed. On 25 May he similarly conceded that all Soviet citizens should be handed over, while continuing to draw the line at any overt authorisation of the use of force.

Alexander's sudden climb-down is remarkable. One may detect how grudging and reluctant was the shift in policy even in the laconic phraseology of the orders. That relating to the Yugoslavs dwells on the continued prohibition of force, while Keightley's demand for its use against the Cossacks receives no direct acknowledgment. The impression received with regard to the Cossacks is that Alexander felt newly constrained to concede the principle of the Yalta Agreement, but trusted to the soldiers to employ measures consonant with the humane and honourable traditions of the British Army. This was not such an implausible delusion as hindsight might suggest. At this very time SHAEF and AFHQ were between them transferring more than 20,000 displaced Soviet refugees a day to the Soviet zone, and so far no unpleasant circumstances had been reported.[17]

All in all the succession of events appears extraordinary. What could have brought the Fifth Corps to believe it possessed *carte blanche* to proceed against its prisoners: not in absence of orders, but *in despite* of them? And what brought about Alexander's sudden change of mind, reluctant but real, on 23 May?

Neither in the case of the Cossacks nor in that of the Yugoslavs was any reference made to considerations affecting the interests of the Fifth Corps or the Eighth Army. None could be made, since the declared purpose of Alexander's orders was to evacuate their unwanted charges as swiftly as possible. In fact the declared motive was in both instances entirely political, and hence extraneous to the concerns of the military. In the case of the Yugoslavs the Eighth Army request announced that it considered all nationals of Allied countries ought to be returned to their country of birth. Such a proposal might have featured appropriately on the agenda of a meeting of foreign ministers, or profitably have occupied a session of the United Nations. It was scarcely the immediate concern of Keightley or McCreery.

As for the Cossacks, the *only* reason given for their return was that Macmillan had ordered it ten days earlier. Keightley's wording makes it clear that it was this, and not the order Macmillan extracted from General Robertson the next day, which bound him. It was on 14 May that Keightley 'on advice Macmillan . . . today suggested to Soviet General on Tolbukhins HQ that Cossacks should be returned to Soviets at once', and only the following morning that Robertson's order arrived at the Fifth Corps headquarters.[18] In short, the only motives advanced for the repatriation were political, and the only authority for proceeding with it that supplied by Harold Macmillan's 'verbal directive'.

It is this, surely, that explains both the belated (23 May) demand for Alexander to endorse Fifth Corps policy, and his surprisingly submissive response. For Macmillan had left for England on 19 May, returning on the afternoon of the twenty-second. He spent that evening with the Field-Marshal, and it was on the following day that the requests for a change in policy came from the Fifth Corps. It looks a little as if the Fifth Corps Staff delayed applying for fresh instructions until the return of the Resident Minister. It was after all his policy they declared themselves to be fulfilling, and to him that Alexander would have looked for confirmation or consultation.

It is intrinsically likely that he did so. By the time of Macmillan's evening visit to Alexander on 22 May, the policy the Minister advocated on 13 May had come to be overruled. Macmillan himself asserts unequivocally that he believed the return of the Cossacks essential, and has never wavered from that viewpoint. Given ample opportunity for consultation it is hard to believe that he did not, in face of the Field-Marshal's opposition, continue to press his policy.

Exactly what the Minister said to the Field-Marshal only he can tell. As he has consistently declined all requests to speak on the subject, it may be that we shall never know the answer. It seems certain it would have been a very persuasive argument that brought the Field-Marshal to accept a point of view his every action reveals he regarded with repugnance. Equally, it is hard to see what it can have been. At the time of Macmillan's return the Foreign Office had as yet provided no ruling on the Cossacks,[19] and never consented to the repatriation of Yugoslavs.

It might nevertheless appear tempting to conjecture that it was during his visit to England that Macmillan received instructions which he relayed to Alexander on his return, thus bringing about the change in policy which ensued. Perhaps loyalty restrains him from revealing a secret communication from some powerful member of the Government? There is no evidence for this, nor does it seem likely. In his television interview with Ludovic Kennedy, Macmillan was at pains to stress that it was Alexander who gave him the order to send back the Cossacks. That happens to be untrue, but scarcely indicates an exaggerated delicacy in such matters.

It seems more likely that Macmillan for reasons only he can explain never spoke of the Cossacks at all while in England. The day he arrived, Saturday, 19 May, Macmillan drove straight to Chequers. There he remained closeted with the Prime Minister until the early hours of the morning. Churchill was in expansive mood, and eager to learn all the Minister Resident's news. In Macmillan's own words: 'After dinner, a short film, and then a lot of talk (till about 2 a.m.) about Tito. I did my best to explain to P.M. the whole position, as we saw it at A.F.H.Q., and all the various problems which we had to face locally.' Macmillan stayed the night, and did not leave for home until the following afternoon.

Among 'all the various problems which we had to face locally', Macmillan appears to have omitted mention of the Cossacks. He might have thought it one that would appeal to Churchill's marked love of the picturesque and romantic, particularly in view of his ardent championing of the Cossacks' cause during the Russian Civil War. Churchill's speeches urging support for the Whites in 1919, declared Lord Robert Cecil in the House of Commons, gave him a mental picture of Churchill 'riding at the head of Cossacks making a triumphant entry into Moscow'.[20]

There would be little remarkable about Macmillan's reticence, in view of all the great issues that were discussed – but for the fact that it was at this very time that Churchill was brooding over the Cossacks whose fate now hung in the balance. On the day Macmillan arrived at Chequers, Churchill had received a message from Eisenhower, informing him of Alexander's request that SHAEF should take over the Cossacks held by the Eighth Army, and explaining that he had agreed to do so.

What memories their name conjured up we do not know, but there is no doubt that he pondered the matter. Next day he found time during all the talk with his visitor to send an enquiry to General Ismay, his Chief of Staff: 'Could I have a further report on the 45,000 Cossacks, of whom General Eisenhower speaks in his SCAF.399. How did they come in their present plight? Did they fight against us?'[21]

The concluding queries perhaps betray a sympathetic viewpoint: it seems intrinsically likely that the Prime Minister would have shared Alexander's outlook. In the following month he was to speak to Alexander on this question, expressing 'great apprehension as to future of all those peoples who refused to return to their native countries because of opposition to political regimes', and going on to urge Alexander 'to be particularly careful to see to it that no force was used to persuade anyone to return to his native country'. Alexander responded within a month by prohibiting forcible repatriation altogether, an action arousing considerable indignation at the Foreign Office, where it was held with some justification that he had exceeded his powers.[22]

Whether Churchill had held or expressed such views in May is conjectural. What is more pertinent to the present enquiry is that he felt the necessity to direct the question to Ismay at all. For there, seated opposite him, was Alexander's closest colleague: a man more likely perhaps than any to know the answer. Not only were the Cossacks held within the region covered by Macmillan's ministerial responsibility, but he had himself flown into Austria a week before: a fact he could scarcely have avoided mentioning during the prolonged discussion of Tito's designs in that region. Did Churchill never think to ask Macmillan the question whose answer it took Ismay a fortnight's labour to unearth?

One would be inclined to dismiss this curious aberration, did it not call to mind another example of the Minister Resident's unusual reticence concerning this particular subject. Five days earlier, following his return from Klagenfurt, Macmillan reported to the Foreign Office that Keightley had informed him of the presence of 'a pocket of some 30 Cossacks including women and children'. To his diary, however, he confided that they totalled 40,000, together with accompanying wives and children.

There was it seems much misinformation about. As will be seen in chapter ten, Alexander on 5 June is reported by a credible eye-witness to have laid the blame for the return of the Cossacks at Eden's door. There is no reason to doubt the sincerity of his belief, but equally little reason to doubt that he was seriously misinformed. There exists no evidence that the Foreign Secretary intervened in the matter at any stage. Rather, it was around this time that Eden expressed annoyance with Macmillan for exceeding his powers by 'interfering with Italian and Balkan affairs', claiming, too, that Macmillan 'usurped functions' properly exercised by the Foreign Office.[23] So far as the Cossacks were concerned, there would in any case be no motive for Eden's concealing his intervention. Rigid implementation of the Yalta provisions for enforced repatriation of Soviet citizens was a policy he pursued harshly, unimaginatively – and openly.

It has to be conceded that there are frustrating gaps in the evidence, for which no amount of speculation provides a satisfactory substitute. Despite this, the outlines seem clear:

1. On 13 May Macmillan provided Keightley with a 'verbal directive' to return all the Cossacks, despite the fact that he knew they included prominent non-Soviet officers. He also 'recommended' the return of the Yugoslavs.

2. Thereafter Keightley proceeded with preparations for the handovers, confidently ignoring all orders to the contrary emanating from AFHQ, and consistently deceiving his superiors over the non-Soviet status of many Cossacks. As Macmillan was familiar with this factor, Keightley must have had reason to feel confident that it would be excluded from the report the Minister gave the Field-Marshal on the evening of his return to AFHQ.

3. Despite this, Keightley did not feel in a position to undertake the operations themselves without further orders, and for these he delayed application until the moment of Macmillan's return from London.[24]

So far as the Fifth Corps was concerned, Macmillan's was the policy adopted throughout, and the only effect of Alexander's intervention was to delay operations until he could be brought to change his mind. Preparations, however, continued as if Alexander's orders were never issued. 14 May was almost certainly the day Keightley agreed with the 'Soviet General on Tolbukhin's HQ' (in the circumstances, more likely than not from the NKVD or SMERSH) that all Cossacks – the émigré generals and officers included – would be handed over. By 20 May news of the intended handover had reached the Thirty-sixth Infantry Brigade headquarters. On the twenty-first an officer from the Fifth Corps conferred with Soviet functionaries, and arrangements were confirmed at a further meeting held on 23 May at Wolfsberg in the British zone.

Keightley's actions show that he was bent on using force whatever his instructions. On the morning of the day (22 May) he received the AFHQ order prohibiting its use he held a Corps conference in Klagenfurt, at which he announced that 'Div[isions] will be prepared to shoot at Cossacks to enforce the evacuation plan'. It is, however, noteworthy that knowledge of the intention to employ force to ensure the return of all Cossacks in despite of the AFHQ order of 22 May – above all those the Soviets were most desirous of acquiring – was confined to a very small number of initiates. As late as 24 May an Eighth Army administrative instruction continued to note that 'with regard to the Russians all who are Soviet citizens and can be returned without the use of force will be returned direct; any others will be returned through 12 Army Gp (SHAEF)'.[25]

However at the Fifth Corps headquarters, where it was impossible to conceal the fact that the use of force was contemplated, it was put about that authority for its employment was essential in order to *effect* screening, not evade it. As Brigadier Tryon-Wilson recalls:

> It was entirely on the basis, which was perfectly straightforward, that how the devil could one carry out the instruction of dividing individuals into sectors in such an integrated operation such as the Cossacks were, without a certain amount of force being necessary? Because apart from there being women and children, apart from there being men, there were troops as well . . . you could not separate them without a possible degree of force . . . just to divide them into their proper sectors for screening.

On 24 May a Fifth Corps staff officer met a Soviet representative inside the British zone at Wolfsberg. There 'Russians agreed to accept Cossacks from 6 Brit Armd Div and 78 Div areas by train at Judenberg and those from 46 Div by march route at Voitsberg'.

On the same day (24 May) the Fifth Corps issued an operational order for the

Return of Cossacks to Soviet forces

This letter sets out the provisional plan for the move of Cossacks from the British to the Soviet area as agreed by Chief of Staff 57 Soviet Army and GSO.1 5 Corps on 24 May.

1. *Definition*
   Throughout this letter the term 'Cossacks' is taken to mean those tps of Soviet nationality incl their Camp followers and German cadre who have fought with or co-operated with the enemy.
   For definition of Soviet nationals see this HQ letter 405/G dated 21 May.

2. *Disarming and Segregation*
   On 28 May
   (a) all Cossack tps wll be completely disarmed
   (b) all possible action will be taken to round up and confine either all or part of the Cossack forces in div areas.
   (c) the offrs will be segregated from the other ranks and placed in

confinement. German offrs will be separated from Cossack offrs. All will be disarmed.

3. *Move of offrs*

(a) Fmns will move the offrs in MT [motorised transport] under strong guard to arrive at Voitsberg B.6454 as soon after midday as possible on 29 May

(b) At Voitsberg Soviet guards will take the place of British guards and the offrs still in British MT (incl British dvrs) will proceed to a camp South of Graz under Soviet guards and with Soviet guides. The MT will then return to fmns.

(c) It is of the utmost importance that all the offrs and particularly senior comds are rounded up and that none are allowed to escape. The Soviet forces consider this as being of the highest importance and will probably regard the safe delivery of the offrs as a test of British good faith.'[26]

The wording of this order unmistakably envisages the use of maximum force necessary to compel return. In addition, despite the statutory reference to the definition of Soviet nationals, it is abundantly clear that the operation is to be directed *primarily* towards rounding up and handing over 'all the offrs and particularly senior comds . . .' All this was conducted in anticipation of the Fifteenth Army Group authorisation, which did not take place until the next day, 25 May.

With the anticipated ruling from the Fifteenth Army Group in his possession at last, Low (on Keightley's behalf) was enabled to proceed without further delay to implement the agreement he had arranged with the Soviets on the twenty-fourth. On 27 May he issued an executive order entitled 'Hand over of Cossacks', instructing divisional commanders to put into effect at once his 'provisional plan' of the twenty-fourth. The proposal to hand over those Cossacks who were Soviet citizens came as no surprise to divisional and brigade commanders, who had known for at least a week that such an event was in prospect. However, there were two aspects of Brigadier Low's instructions which the divisional commanders to whom they were confided found unpalatable.

Though the provisional plan of 24 May included a preamble stating that it was intended to apply only to Soviet citizens, and drawing attention to screening regulations, it was clear from what followed that this was casuistry. The injunction that 'all the offrs and particularly senior comds are rounded up and that none are [*sic*] allowed to escape' was clearly directed primarily at Krasnov, Shkuro, Kelich-

Ghirei and other White officers gathered at Lienz. That this was the order's intention was at once appreciated by the commander affected, Major-General Arbuthnott of the Seventy-eighth Infantry Division.

Arbuthnott had already objected twice in the most vigorous terms to the idea of returning any Cossacks to what all sensed to be certain death. This was on the occasions Brigadier Tryon-Wilson transmitted to him the Corps instructions of 21 and 24 May. Arbuthnott's protests are also remembered by Brigadier Low, and by Major-General H. E. N. ('Bala') Bredin, then A/Q on Arbuthnott's staff.

So far as the Tsarist officers were concerned, though, nothing could be easier than for Arbuthnott to test the validity of his orders by taking literally the provisions for screening which they contained. At one point Brigadier Tryon-Wilson remembers his grumbling, 'How the hell are we supposed to conduct the screening?' which implies that at this stage he still believed the screening provisions genuine. It was Brigadier Tryon-Wilson who took him the operational order to proceed with the forcible repatriation, which was to include the 'senior commanders', all but two of whom were former Tsarist generals. Arbuthnott understood that screening provisions stipulated in his written instructions were to be set aside, and was furious. As a fellow-cavalryman he admired and liked the Cossacks, and declined to obey an order he regarded as wholly dishonourable.

Tryon-Wilson (who liked it no better) was obliged to report back to General Keightley, telling him, 'now you'll have to see him, sir, and tell him yourself.'

Keightley, who was by now fully persuaded of the necessity of the policy, groaned and muttered, 'Oh God, it is very difficult. All right, I'll tell him.'

He thereupon summoned Arbuthnott to Corps headquarters and gave him a flat order which the latter felt he could no longer disobey. Arbuthnott departed, appalled by the task with which he had been entrusted. Tryon-Wilson saw him emerge from the General's caravan in a high state of indignation: 'Buthy came out, swearing and grumbling like hell.'

Today Toby Low denies that there was any intention to abandon screening, and insists he understood throughout that it would take place, expecting his references to the procedure in orders to be effective. When Arbuthnott objected, he asserts today, 'I reassured him in my order of the 21st, I remember. We said, you will hand them back according to the Yalta Agreement: these people will go back, and those people won't.'

How then, I asked him, did it come about that nevertheless screening did not take place, and the Tsarist officers were handed over? Low replied that conditions on the ground made screening impractical, and so the Corps provisions came of necessity to be overlooked.

> Something happened from the 27th onwards. I *understand* what happened was that conditions in the forward area became such that screening was not possible . . . My case is that conditions in the forward area were such that it simply wasn't practical to screen. I gave orders expecting people to screen. It's not the first order I gave to a staff officer which proved uncarryable out.

Low's suggestion that commanders in the field unilaterally decided (without troubling to inform him) to set aside screening for purely pragmatic reasons is flatly contradicted by the evidence. The general with direct responsibility under Arbuthnott for all Cossacks and Caucasians held in the Drau Valley was Brigadier Geoffrey Musson. While agreeing that his Brigade possessed no adequate facilities for screening so large a body of men, he denies that this consideration had anything to do with its failure to take place. He was given a clear order by General Arbuthnott to ignore the screening clauses in his orders. More than this, he was instructed not to allow the battalion commanders entrusted with the entrainment of the Cossacks to know even of the possibility of screening.

> I have absolutely no doubt [Musson (now General Sir Geoffrey) recorded recently], that General Arbuthnott knew that no screening was being done in my area. He was quite adamant that all officers must be collected and moved to Spittal. I am certain that 'All officers must go' did not originate from him. He said that the Russians were insisting on it and it is most unlikely that he had any communication with them. This must have been at Corps or higher level and I presume that he must have been told it by General Keightley . . .
>
> The overriding impression that I had then, and still have, is that all the officers had to be sent to the East. All discussions that I had with superior commanders and their staffs confirmed this and I was told on more than one occasion that the order had come from Field Marshal Alexander's headquarters and was H.M. Government policy . . .
>
> I certainly did not conceal from General Arbuthnott that no screening was being done by Colonels Malcolm and Odling-Smee or by anyone else in my area. He was fully aware of it. In fact the plan for

the collection of the officers and their journey to Spittal precluded it.

One thing was certain, Musson sensed, and that was that Arbuthnott 'was under tremendous pressure, I'm sure'. He made no attempt to disguise his distaste for the whole operation, expressing deep sympathy for the 'poor devils' of Cossacks.

General Musson's account is borne out in turn by his battalion commanders, Colonels Malcolm and Odling-Smee, who confirm that at no time did they ever hear of provisions for screening. As Colonel Odling-Smee wrote to me recently, 'I think I can say for certain I never received or saw any order in writing quoting the terms of the Yalta agreement. I did not appreciate the difference between Soviet Nationals and those we called Russians.' When reproached at the moment of handover by an eighty-two-year-old émigré officer, he felt shame and bewilderment, but had no idea the old gentleman belonged to a category whom the written Corps orders were emphatic in excluding from return. General Kelich-Ghirei, the Caucasians' veteran Tsarist commander, had dined regularly in Odling-Smee's mess. Colonel Barry McGrath, then commanding D company of the Fifth Buffs, confirms that, 'I remember no screening of the Caucasian soldiers and families who were camped in nearby fields and who we were ordered to send to the Soviet Forces by train and road. A most distasteful task which was performed with firmness but as humanely as possible.'

Indeed, the first time Colonels Malcolm and Odling-Smee learned of the existence of the screening order was when I came to inform them. When I put this evidence to Low, he expressed bafflement: 'I don't understand this statement you've made that Brigadier Musson and others were told orally not to carry out written orders. That I find very odd.'

So, if Low ordered Arbuthnott to institute screening, and yet Arbuthnott ordered Musson to ignore it, did that mean that it was Arbuthnott who, for reasons known only to himself, unilaterally set aside the order?

'That's right,' Low conceded.

The matter was becoming increasingly puzzling. For according to Low's own account Arbuthnott had protested vigorously against the idea of returning any Cossacks at all. Why in that case should he go straight back to his headquarters and give Musson an entirely unauthorised command to ignore screening provisions that would at least have saved the old émigrés?

'Come off it! Come off it!' Toby Low retorted: 'it was three or four days later.' Ultimately, he concluded, 'you either believe me or you don't.'

Major-General H. E. N. ('Bala') Bredin, then A/Q on the Seventy-eighth Division staff, regards the suggestion that Arbuthnott uni-laterally set aside the screening order with incredulity. He is today emphatic that, 'as far as I knew, everybody was supposed to be sent back to the Russians . . . and that we – particularly when we knew what was going on – we were all trying to find some way of saving the officers. If we'd known that there was a "let-out", we would have said that everybody was not entitled to go to Russia, and fudged it that way . . . As soon as somebody said, "well, look here, the only answer is to open the camp gates and tell the people that they were open and they'd better go", then that was done in several places. Well, if there'd been a more or less legal "let-out", we would have used that "let-out" rather than have to do something which we thought was probably being illegal.' As for General Arbuthnott, 'he was what you might call a very humane chap, and somebody who would give anybody the benefit of the doubt. I can't see him just slurring over this thing and sending everybody back, if it was not necessary . . . He certainly protested . . . he certainly went and saw Keightley; I don't think he got any change out of him.'

The apparently irreconcilable contradictions in Low's version of events may perhaps be attributed to a lapse in memory. The above conversation took place on 8 May 1985. Eleven years earlier, when I first approached him on the subject, Low informed me, 'During the time when I was in Austria up to about May 29th there were a great many difficult questions and I do not remember myself being involved in any matters concerning the Cossack Divisions.' That was in June 1974. In September of that year, replying to a further enquiry, he repeated that he was 'afraid the truth is that my recollection remains as deficient as I stated in my letter of 25th June.' Today Low's view is robustly emphatic: 'We may have been naïve,' he says, 'but we were not in the business of deceit.'

General Arbuthnott was deeply resentful at being compelled to participate in what he regarded as a further act of betrayal, described in divisional orders as a 'deception plan'. About 23 or 24 May General Peter Krasnov sent a second letter to his old acquaintance Alexander, drawing attention once again to the Cossacks' plight, emphasising that he and many others were not Soviet citizens and were conse-quently owed protection as refugees in international law. He con-cluded by requesting an interview with the Field-Marshal. As

Brigadier Tryon-Wilson recalls, this letter like its predecessor reached Fifth Corps headquarters but went no further.

Fifth Corps headquarters was concerned to prevent any discovery by the Cossacks of British intentions towards them. It would be unpleasant were resistance to take place, and contingency plans were drawn up that it was hoped would prove sufficient to overawe them. Cossack men, women and children could be shot and killed, bludgeoned into insensibility with rifle-butts and pickaxe helves, or merely be lined up before a firing-squad or provided with a demonstration of the destructive power of a 'Wasp' flame-thrower.

A still more serious potential obstacle to the successful implementation of the operation was the fear that British officers and men in units detailed to perform this unpleasant task might feel themselves to be engaged in a dirty business; indeed, in words that so many were to employ, 'this was not what we fought the war for'. And even more dangerous than a general revulsion against employing violence against defenceless men (still less the thousands of women, children and babies against whom the Fifth Corps' plans were in large part directed) was the likelihood that émigré officers, speaking fluent English, French or German, would draw attention to the fact that people who were not Soviet citizens were being handed over to their Bolshevik foes. One did not need to be a specialist in Soviet history to guess at their likely fate, nor an expert in international law to realise that such an action was morally and legally indefensible. The fact that the Fifth Corps was so insistent on concealing the existence of screening provisions from officers and men below the level of Brigade in itself proves that protest or even disobedience were considered a likely contingency.

Already numerous petitions and enquiries on this score had been passed up to Corps HQ, not only from the Cossacks themselves but also from British troops in the Thirty-sixth Infantry Brigade responsible for them. It was among Cossack officers that the highest proportion of non-Soviet citizens was to be found, and it was they above all whom the Soviets wished to get into their hands. It was they, too, who alone possessed the linguistic capacity to convey their peculiar predicament to the British. If only the officers could be somehow detached in a body from their followers, and handed over swiftly before they appreciated what was intended!

In the context of this fear, Krasnov's letter was utilised to further a skilful deception ploy. So the old man wished to meet Alexander? Very well, let him do so – and bring all his fellow-officers with him!

Accordingly Arbuthnott, to his disgust, was required to issue an invitation to the Cossack officers to attend a conference with the Field-Marshal on 29 May. Once embarked in motorised transport, they could be hustled across the inter-zonal boundary into the waiting hands of SMERSH. There would be no dangerous protests, since there would be no apparent occasion for protest; not at least until it was too late.

Toby Low denies that this stratagem was conceived at his headquarters. The most he did, he claims now, was to suggest that the Cossacks' (and Yugoslavs') destination be concealed from them. Despite this it appears certain that the deceptions employed were not left to divisional and brigade commanders to improvise. Brigadier K. C. ('Ted') Cooper, commanding the independent Seventh Armoured Brigade, recalled informing Cossacks in his care that they were to travel to 'a new camp'. In fact they were driven south to allay any suspicions they might have nurtured, and then suddenly northwards at speed to the Soviets at Judenburg. There was no question of this deception being devised by Brigadier Cooper himself:

> It was all planned; we all had conferences and that sort of thing – we'd give our ideas at Corps, and work it out . . . I remember some of those meetings when we thrashed it out. It was very detailed in the end; it had to be so that the timing was correct.

Of the deception of Krasnov and the others, General Musson writes to me that it 'was not initiated by me . . . my belief is that the deception was designed to ensure that all officers in my area should be returned.' As it was the Corps order of 24 May which stressed 'the utmost importance that all the offrs and particularly senior comds are rounded up', and it was this that the false invitation to meet Alexander was designed to ensure, so it is intrinsically probable that the deception originated with Corps HQ.

It was on the morning of 26 May that Geoffrey Musson summoned his battalion commanders to a conference at Brigade headquarters at Oberdrauburg. There he informed them that the Cossacks were to be sent home. To guard against the danger of disorder in the camp, the officers were to be separated from the rest by means of the 'deception tactic'. A feeling of disgust arose among those present. The instinctive respect for discipline forged in hard years of war could not obscure the fact that the 'deception plan' involved telling a direct lie to men who trusted in their honour; a lie moreover designed to lure the victims unsuspectingly to an atrocious fate.

Colonel Malcolm returned to Lienz, where he in turn summoned his company commanders and explained Brigade orders. The further down the chain of command the order passed, the more unpalatable it appeared. To Major Rusty Davies, the young Welshman entrusted with the task of looking after the Cossacks, the role required of him appeared quite insupportable. He had come to know and like his Cossack charges, and they in turn reposed great faith and affection in him. How could he be party to an act so treacherous and dishonourable? Greatly disturbed, he blurted out a request to be relieved of his post as liaison officer with the Cossacks. To this, however, Colonel Malcolm returned a firm refusal. For it was the very trust which the Cossacks placed in Davies that would ensure the success of the plan. Equally, his replacement at this juncture might in itself arouse suspicion. Davies was given a direct order to obey, which he found no way of avoiding.

Neither Musson, Malcolm nor Davies enjoyed for a moment what they were doing. But, as they were informed, Field-Marshal Alexander had authorised the plan, and he in turn had received his instructions from Winston Churchill himself. That being so, it was not for men far down in the chain of command to question the validity of orders, whose full implications they had in any case no means of assessing. The true responsibility must lie with those who initiated the operation, rather than those who simply fulfilled their orders. Such were the considerations which passed through the minds of the officers concerned – considerations which so many German officers had been obliged to face in the recent war, and which would before long come under judicial scrutiny at the Nuremberg Tribunal.

On the evening of 27 May, Major Davies appeared at General Domanov's headquarters in Lienz and, speaking through the interpreter, his friend Captain Butlerov, explained that next day all Cossacks were to travel to Oberdrauburg to be addressed by Field-Marshal Alexander. A hubbub of discussion ensued, in which the prevailing feelings were those of relief and excitement. To General Krasnov, indeed, the move appeared remarkably fortuitous. It had been only two or three days earlier, following a visit by the British Divisional Commander, General Arbuthnott, to the Cossack camp that he had written his second appeal to Field-Marshal Alexander. Here, it seemed, was the reply – swifter than could have been imagined!

Other Cossacks, who knew nothing of this fortuitous circumstance, were suspicious. Butlerov in particular took Davies on one side after the meeting, and asked him whether any deceit lay behind the order? Davies's reassurances only partially satisfied him, and he concluded by putting the question to him categorically: 'Look, you're a soldier and must obey orders. But I hope you are also a friend. As you know, I have a wife and child in Peggetz Camp. Will you give me your word as an officer and a gentleman that we will all be back in the camp by this evening?'

'Of course I do,' Davies replied firmly – a reassurance repeated by other British officers when approached by English-speaking Cossacks.

The deception was successful. With the exception of one or two who slipped away, all officers (many of them in Tsarist uniforms with Imperial decorations) appeared on parade next day to enter the trucks taking them to their long-anticipated meeting with the Field-Marshal. To wives and comrades they explained that they would be back that evening without fail. The long column then set off down the valley to Oberdrauburg. What happened there has been described to me by Mr A. P. Judge, then an intelligence officer attached to the Thirty-sixth Infantry Brigade:

> On that day . . . a beautiful spring day . . . Brigadier Musson asked me to interpret at a meeting with the Cossack Division Commander, as instructions had been received from 8 Army as to the disposal of the formation . . . The meeting took place in what I took to be an ordinary farmhouse, beside the main road. An Austrian man and woman were standing nearby and I assumed they were the farmer and his wife. The Cossack vehicles were lined up along the road and Cossack officers were in the process of de-bussing. There was no attempt to address them or hold a 'conference'; within a few minutes of our arriving, we made our way up an outside staircase to an upstairs room, Brig. Musson, Gen. Domanov, the latter's French-speaking chief of staff and myself. I took the French-speaking officer to be the chief of staff from his age and the fact he spoke French and, as I learned a few minutes later, an émigré who had been living in Paris. I do not think it can have been Lt. Butlerov, whom you describe as 'young . . . with a wife and child in Peggetz Camp', whereas the other officer had a wife and daughter living in Paris and did not speak English, because he addressed me in French.
>
> I cannot recall Brig. Musson's exact words but . . . [his speech] was certainly very brief and forthright and I had no difficulty in putting it straight into French, speaking to the chief of staff. He turned and translated to Gen. Domanov, who replied with a few words in Russian, which were relayed to me in French. These I have never forgotten. They were, *'Je*

suis soldat, je comprends.' Brig. Musson got up and left. As I made to follow, the chief of staff, obviously agitated, asked me if I could get a message to his wife in Paris, to say what was happening to them. Gen. Domanov remained outwardly impassive. We re-emerged into the sunlit farmyard, where de-bussing was still in progress. I recall so clearly, just before we went up into the farmhouse, seeing a very elderly Russian officer, who had difficulty getting out of the motorcoach, doubtless hampered by his long Imperial Army sword. He was dressed in Imperial Army uniform of royal blue tunic, dark blue trousers with a broad red stripe and service dress cap, royal blue with a red band. My last sight of him was climbing back into the coach, still with some difficulty. His sword must have been taken away because I think it was his sword I saw there with the Czar Nicholas II cipher on the blade.

This last figure was without doubt the seventy-six-year-old General Peter Krasnov, and the sabre one presented to him by the Emperor himself during the Great War. As will be seen, it was confiscated for a particular purpose, while the General and other Cossack officers were driven on to a wired camp at Spittal. There they were held for the night (about a dozen managed to commit suicide by hanging themselves from electric light flexes or slashing their wrists and throats with broken glass), before being handed over next day (29 May) to waiting NKVD agents at Judenburg, just inside the Soviet demarcation line.

Few British soldiers harboured any illusions as to the likely fate awaiting the Cossacks once they fell into Soviet hands. But all that was to happen in a world of which they knew little, and remote from their sphere of moral responsibility. What did trouble many in varying degree was the subterfuge employed to lure these unsuspecting men to their deaths. If a soldier is shorn of his honour, then what is there left but the uniformed bandit? The war had been fought in a very real sense as a moral crusade, and cold-blooded treachery was the attribute of the defeated Nazis. Gradually men became conscious of what they had lent their hands to. Major Davies has suffered regular nightmares ever since that day. Brigadier Musson has written that he 'feels great distress over this horrible business', emphasising though that 'my own conscience is perfectly clear'. To Captain Butlerov, Major Davies's émigré friend from Paris, he offered the chance of staying behind to assist as a liaison officer. Butlerov resolutely declined, declaring himself bound in honour to accompany his comrades whatever their destination. Musson's respect was aroused, though whether he reflected on the differing standards of honour practised here by a British and a Russian officer I did not care to enquire.

The anger of British soldiers employed in the operations being conducted all over the Fifth Corps area at this time was so widespread that one or two examples must suffice to illustrate it. Captain David Nockels writes to me:

At the time of this dreadful event . . . I was a Lieut. commanding C. Troop R.H.A. [Royal Horse Artillery] with 229 Battery, Anti-Tank R.A. in 46 Division, stationed at Wieting, Austria. We were given custody of a Regt. or so of mounted Cossacks, whom we had to search for knives & any weaponry they might have had. Needless to say the most dangerous items proved to be penknives & the like. And these were handed over quite happily. I was amazed at how happy they were to be with us. They put on horse riding displays for us, and their own remarkable dancing. We loved it, particularly their singing.

They convinced us that they intended joining our forces in the Far East in the struggle against Japan. It was some weeks later toward the end of May, beginning of June 1945, that we were instructed to remove all their horses & gear, & the following day a convoy of 3-ton lorries started taking these splendid fellows to Judenburg.

My troop Sergt. went with the first convoy, and on his return he related to me what happened. He was white with anger & wept when he told of some of the prisoners leaping off the bridge to try & escape the Russian guards. Some of them were boys of not more than 13 or 14 years, through the age range to quite elderly men.

The attitude of [our] other ranks was one of disdain towards the[ir] officers. It was apparent that in our eyes we had let them down – we had cheated the Cossacks. We officers of course knew no more than any of the men, but at that time some of the men were as close to mutiny as any I had ever seen. The position was extremely distasteful and unstable.

My troop were then given the nightly task of combing the hillsides for renegade Cossacks whom local farmers had said were raiding their homesteads for food etc. Needless to say we did not come across any Cossacks – and if we had, I doubt very much we should have taken them into custody!

For the first time in my life I was made to feel ashamed of being British. But the whole business served to colour my views on politics and politicians.

Colin Gunner of the Royal Irish Fusiliers, a unit which had accepted the surrender of part of General von Pannwitz's Corps, expressed similar views:

I am only grateful that my own Regiment was spared the filthy task of handing them over, if only for the fact that we should have faced that dread of all good regiments – mutiny. A friend of mine in one of those units [the Lancashire Fusiliers] ordered to carry it out told me that he 'never knew how many ways people could commit suicide,' and that his Major turned his back on his Colonel, remarking 'I won't do it: court-martial me if you wish.' This was a political decision resisted at all levels of army command, and I will not have it said that it was a stain on the colours of brave regiments. Even now the full story has never come out, but God have mercy on him who died with the decision on his conscience.

Major R. S. V. Howard, serving in the same regiment as Colin Gunner, expresses the sympathetic view of the Cossacks shared by almost all British troops who came in contact with them at that time:

As for the Cossacks – well, we had never seen men like these. They were remarkably cheerful, gave no trouble, and in turn we allowed them to move freely around their vast meadow and to water the horses twice daily. We marvelled at their horsemanship as they went at full gallop down to a nearby stream. Whether they all returned I do not know!

If disgust at betraying men like these was prevalent, it is not hard to imagine the soldiers' feelings when it is recalled that the operation also involved widespread brutality inflicted upon thousands of women and children. Mr L. Birch, then serving with the Royal Inniskilling Fusiliers, writes:

I had seen within the camp area [at Peggetz] large black flags hanging and hastily written posters saying 'we would rather die of starvation here than return to U.S.S.R.' 'Please let us live in peace.' etc. At this time neither I or those soldiers I was with were fully aware of the implications of what was about to happen.

One day we were ordered to make a sweep into the Valley and deter anybody from leaving the camp area – this was the start of the repatriations. During the day we came across several small groups carrying pitiful bundles – men, women and the odd child. It was my bitter experience this day to have a woman stand before me, pull her dress open at the breast saying 'Bitte schushen' ['please shoot me'] – she was one of a party of half a dozen. I told her to go and pointed to the mountains and safety. I have often wondered if any of these ever made it to freedom they sought. Most of the lads taking part in this operation felt certain revulsion as to what was taking place.

News of the increasing disquiet among officers and men of the Argylls, Buffs, Kensingtons and other units involved came to the ears of their superiors at Seventy-eighth Divisional HQ, and a remarkable directive was distributed next day. It read:

> 1. Many offrs and OR in the Army are aware that the Allies have made extensive use of cover and deception plans in sp of factual ops.
> 2. It is of the highest importance that no unauthorised disclosure of Allied practice on this and kindred subjects should be made in any form whatever, even now that hostilities have ceased. This applies equally to methods used in specific ops as to gen policy. Any knowledge of the subject will continue to be treated as TOP SECRET.
> 3. Fmns and units will therefore ensure that this order is brought to the notice of all who are concerned. As it is obviously undesirable to arouse undue comment, its circulation should be strictly limited to those who have had knowledge of deception methods. The actual method of publication is left to the discretion of fmn/unit comds.[27]

As Captain Judge recalls:

> Perhaps because of the order from HQ 78 Division to which you refer that there should be no comment or discussion on the handover of the Cossacks, I can recall absolutely no references nor even casual conversation of this sad affair subsequently, as if no one wished to remember.

Despite the meretricious argument put forward in the order, few officers failed to see a clear distinction between subterfuges designed to mislead an enemy in battle, and the employment of straightforward lying in peacetime as a means of conniving at mass murder.

Though there exists voluminous evidence (some of it attested by the Cossack victims) that most soldiers regarded the operation with varying degrees of shame and disgust, there is little evidence that British soldiers in the Drau Valley at this time were actually prepared to disobey orders. Elsewhere in 1945 and 1946 in Germany and Austria there were cases of high-spirited officers who resolutely declined to participate in similar though far less brutal operations.[28]

One must, however, avoid the dangers of hindsight. Few at that time were in any position to form a balanced judgement of the confusing *mélange* of events taking place so soon after long years of war. Colonel John Coldwell-Horstfall, then commanding officer of the Second Irish Rifles ('not directly involved with the Cossacks') points out that:

there is one warning about this tragedy. The mythology is multiplying, and I have been quite amazed by what has been written in the press, radio or T.V. In my view much of this is rich with remorse in hindsight and bears no relation whatever either to the truth or to the feelings of those involved at the time.

To put matters in perspective our soldiers had been fighting a particularly bloody war, and when the German Army in Italy finally surrendered they soon found themselves mixed up with a murderous Balkan rabble, hanging on the wings like jackals and killing and looting indiscriminately.

In rather similar vein, Sir John Wilton, then commanding D Company of the Royal Irish Fusiliers north of Lavamünd, writes:

I think you should beware of attributing today's attitudes more generally to the British troops in the area at the time. Those directly involved felt the emotional pressures, at any rate after the event. Those (like myself and my troops) a few miles away knew only that some Cossacks (and others) who were being repatriated had until the cease-fire been wearing German uniforms and fighting on the German side. After two years of more or less continuous campaigning in Tunisia, Sicily and Italy we were not feeling particularly sympathetic towards the enemy, and the apparition of the first wraiths in striped concentration camp uniforms on the streets of Wolfsberg as we drove in there did nothing to make us feel more so.

Perhaps a more general view was that of Hugh Richardson, a gunner in the Forty-sixth Infantry Division whose unit was detailed to escort Cossacks on their way to the handover point at Judenburg:

I believe the view has been expressed that we should have refused to repatriate the Cossacks, knowing their likely fate. I think our attitude was that, though we were sorry for them, they must face the consequences of choosing the losing side in war. Anyway, to refuse to comply with orders would have been mutiny, would it not?

These views provide a corrective to the idea that there was any unanimity of opinion among British troops in Austria at that time. All varied according to temperament, experience and understanding. Few people had any conception that the regimes of Stalin and Tito were on a par with the defeated Nazis for cruelty and oppression. Above all there was relief that the war was over, little opportunity for reflection or discussion, and no possibility of comprehending more than a small part of the enormous tragedy taking place around them. For the most part, too, a gulf separated those who were actually compelled to participate in or witness acts hitherto ascribed to the enemy alone, and those who heard of it at second-hand.

Fortunately the evidence is not restricted to *ex post facto* recollections. Four days after the worst operations at Lienz had been completed, General Arbuthnott noted 'that to many the task was most distasteful and there were some who even doubted the necessity for it'.

The attitude of the troops had, however, little bearing on the conduct of operations. The Allied war crimes tribunal passing judgement on German war crimes established as the basis of its proceedings the provision that obedience to orders does not excuse flagrantly inhumane actions. It is generally held that responsibility in such cases must be related to seniority in the chain of command, and it is to the command that we must now look for an explanation of the most serious violation of British and international law; one which if practised by German officers or political leaders would without question have been accepted as an indictable war crime.

What, then, is one to make of Toby Low's claim concerning screening of the prisoners? He maintains that the decision not to implement the screening process laid down in orders resulted from purely local considerations of the operation's impracticality, which he could appreciate though he neither authorised them nor was even aware of their existence. Thus it was purely as a result of administrative difficulties that the old émigrés were included among those repatriated. However, let us see first how matters appeared to his colleagues at the time.

General Arbuthnott was the officer on whom the responsibility for screening would have devolved, and his strong objection to its abandonment suggests that he thought its implementation perfectly feasible, even if administratively taxing. But the fact is that practical considerations did not enter into the matter. Screening did not take place only because it would have alerted the White officers to the plan to hand them over with the rest. This General Musson accepts, and writes, 'The crucial time was on or before 28 May and no screening was practicable within the Brigade area in view of the very clear orders to me that all officers were to be despatched from my area.'

But for this consideration there seems little doubt that screening would have represented a perfectly straightforward operation, well within the capacity of the Eighth Army to conduct. The camp at Spittal, where the Cossack officers spent the night of 28/29 May on their way to the NKVD at Judenburg, had just been vacated by the 10,000 men of the Ukrainian Division. Though comprising a sizeable proportion of Soviet citizens, they had been transported to a camp near Rimini in Italy, where they were eventually screened. Operations of this sort were being undertaken throughout the region without causing a collapse of the military administration. Captain Judge, whose principal task it was at this time to conduct screening operations for the Thirty-sixth Infantry Brigade, is in no doubt about the matter: 'I am surprised that the handover of the Cossacks should have been done with no attempt at screening . . . It must initially have been rough and ready but . . . many genuine cases could have been easily established and the proportion would certainly have given food for thought.'

Identical views were expressed to the author by General Sir Horatius Murray, who as commander of the Sixth Armoured Division was faced with a similar problem further east; and by Major-General Bredin, then A/Q with particular responsibility for such matters on Arbuthnott's staff. The harassed twenty-five-year-old Major Davies, in the midst of the chaos unleashed in Peggetz Camp on 1 June by the first mass round-up of Cossacks, actually conducted extensive improvised 'screening' on his own initiative once he was forcibly made aware of the presence of large numbers of non-Soviet prisoners, probably saving several hundred lives in the process. For many years after he used to receive Christmas cards from some of these grateful survivors, scattered for the most part in DP camps.

Above all, nothing would have been easier than to have screened the Cossack officers once they had been separated from their followers and held in the wired camp at Spittal. In fact the deception tactic which brought them there itself represented an effective screening ploy . . . screening designed not to protect them from repatriation, but to guarantee their delivery to the Soviets. The Thirty-sixth Infantry Brigade order number sixteen of 27 May makes the purpose of the operation plain enough: 'Commandant Spittal Camp will arrange facilities for Intelligence Officer 36 Inf Bde to check nominal rolls of [Cossack] Officers on their arrival in the Camp. It is essential that this is done without delay in order that a search may be made for absentees.'[29]

Remarkable precautions were adopted to ensure that Krasnov and other identified senior Cossack officers were among those consigned to the hands of SMERSH at Judenburg. On 26 May a Russian woman

outside Lienz overheard British officers discussing the coming operation – a discussion in which the names of Krasnov and Shkuro
received ominous emphasis. When Major Davies on the evening of
27 May informed Captain Butlerov of the morrow's 'conference', he
added (doubtless under instruction): 'And . . . do not neglect to
notify General Krasnov. The Commander is particularly interested
in meeting him.' Next morning, about midday, 'there appeared at
General Domanov's hotel a tall English general, who again repeated
Major Davies's order, adding: "Please do not forget to convey my
request to old Krasnov. I beg this of you most urgently."' And when
they finally arrived at Judenburg, a general of the NKVD approached
Krasnov's lorry, eagerly asking for him by name.

Quite clearly Krasnov was a marked man. Still more remarkable
is the case of the redoubtable General Andrei Shkuro, former Ataman
of the Kuban Cossacks. At the time of his surrender to the British
on 10 May he had been described·as the 'old Cossack Gen. Shkuro,
who had fought under Denikin'. Later in the month he wrote twice
to Brigadier Musson to explain his position as a White émigré, and
the Thirty-sixth Infantry Brigade's War Diary includes the following:
'Note: for description of the Cossack forces in general, and of General
Shkuro's part in the organisation in particular, see the two letters
written by him to Commander 36 Inf Bde and forwarded to 78 Div
under 36 Inf Bde letters 129/G dated 23 and 24 May.' The letters
have unfortunately 'gone missing' from the Seventy-eighth Infantry
Division War Diary, but it is clear that someone feared that an elderly
officer who had been raised to the Companionship of the Bath by
King George V might arouse undue interest and even sympathy at
Lienz once his coming fate became known. At 3 a.m. on the night
of 26/27 May a British officer came to his quarters with guards, and
spirited him away in advance of all the other Cossack officers, to
await their arrival under close confinement at Spittal. He was not
released until the column of trucks set off for Judenburg on the
twenty–ninth, where he was greeted by the Soviets with as much
glee and obvious expectation as Krasnov.

The whole episode can only imply that Shkuro, too, had been
singled out carefully for return, and that elaborate precautions were
taken to prevent his drawing dangerously ostentatious attention to
his émigré status and high British decoration, or making any attempt
to escape the fate arranged for him. It must be for this reason that
the operation was carefully obscured in the subsequent Brigade report
of 3 July: 'General Shkuro . . . had been sent to Spittal two days

earlier [than the other officers], as the move of his Regiment was then complete.' In fact his Regiment's move had been completed a week before his night-time abduction, and there was no more reason to move him from the camp than any other Cossack commander. It is clear that the report was intended to lull the suspicions of anyone from above Fifth Corps level who might choose to investigate what had been going on.[30]

The Fifth Corps itself was well aware of the exceptional measures being taken to ensure delivery of Krasnov and Shkuro in accordance with the Soviet request of 11 May. In General Arbuthnott's War Diary a note for GSO1 at Fifth Corps records:

Ref Gen Shkuro's sword.
This not to be handed over to Russians yet.
78 Div will hold and ask for further instrs from 5 Corps. Other offrs swords to be handed over as previously arranged.[31]

At Fifth Corps headquarters Brigadier Tryon-Wilson remembers seeing General Krasnov's magnificent sabre (presented to him by the Emperor Nicholas II) in the hands of Major-General de Fonblanque, Toby Low's successor as BGS. The ultimate destination of these prized mementoes was the MVD (political police) museum at the Lubianka Prison in Moscow.[32]

All in all there can be little doubt that the failure to screen the Cossacks in the Fifth Corps area was an act of deliberate policy. If its practicality had been the real issue, one may ask why then did General Keightley not raise the point in his messages to the Eighth Army on 21 and 23 May? He stressed the impracticality of repatriation unless AFHQ were prepared to reverse its ruling on the use of force. Why did he not at the same time point out that the stipulated screening also represented a major problem, and request resources to enforce it?

Three days after the delivery of the Cossack officers at Judenburg across the zonal boundary, it was the turn of the Cossack other ranks and their thousands of women and children to be handed over. I have described the bloody events of 1 and 2 June in my book *Victims of Yalta*, and will not repeat them at length here. Having discovered the betrayal of their officers and the fact that the British were working hand-in-glove with the Soviets to bring about their destruction, a crowd of several thousand assembled in the central area of their camp at Peggetz on the morning of 1 June. A religious service was organised, with priests presiding from an improvised stand in the centre. Called upon by Major Davies to desist and enter the lorries waiting to transport them into nearby cattle-trucks, they organised passive resistance. The young men formed up with linked arms on the perimeter of the crowd, while the women, children and old people were hemmed inside the circle.

Major Davies saw no alternative to sending in platoons of soldiers armed with rifles and pick-helves, who battered their way into the densely-packed mob and hived off a section of the people, who were then manhandled into lorries and taken to the waiting train. At the sight of this the crowd panicked. They knew where the train was bound for, and what lay in wait for them at its destination. Many present had experience of the death-camps of Gulag and the torture-cells of the NKVD. In Davies's own words:

> As individuals on the outskirts of the group were pulled away, the remainder compressed themselves into a still tighter body, and as panic gripped them started clambering over each other in frantic efforts to get away from the soldiers. The result was a pyramid of hysterical, screaming human beings, under which a number of people were trapped. The soldiers made frantic efforts to split this mass in order to try to save the lives of these persons pinned underneath, and pick helves and rifle butts were used on arms and legs to force individuals to loosen their hold. When we eventually cleared this group, we discovered that one man and one woman [had] suffocated. Every person of this group had to be forcibly carried on to the trucks.

Worse – much worse – was to follow. As the crowd saw that the British would press on, whatever the suffering and violence involved, the whole crowd surged away until they piled up against a fence to the east. There many people were crushed or suffocated to death, until the fence gave way and they spilled over into the field beyond. As Colonel Malcolm reported afterwards, several Cossacks were wounded by British bayonets; one was shot dead. Those who suffered most were the small children, of whom there were a great number. A young mother saw a soldier who 'snatched a child from its mother and wanted to throw it into a lorry. The mother caught hold of the child's leg, and they each pulled in opposite directions. Afterwards I saw that the mother was no longer holding the child and that the child had been dashed against the side of the lorry.'

How many people died that day is unknown, but the number

certainly runs into scores. Apart from those killed during the mass panic, many others were shot by the British while trying to flee to the woods. Still more, driven frantic with fear, died by their own hands. Perhaps the most horrifying sight was that discovered by Major Davies that evening, when all had temporarily calmed down. In a woodland glade lay five bodies. Four were those of a mother and her three children, the youngest of whom was a baby girl just one year old. They had each been shot in the back. Some way off sprawled a man's corpse; beside him lay a revolver, with which he had shot himself through the head. It was this scene which brought home to Davies more than anything the fear which gripped the Cossacks at the thought of returning to the Soviet Union. For there could be only one way of interpreting the tragedy: the father had killed all his family one by one. He had then walked a little way off and put an end to his own sufferings.

To the Cossacks the British troops appeared as brutal and unfeeling as the Soviet guards to whom they were being delivered. In fact the men of the Argylls may have been brutal on this occasion, but they were far from unfeeling. Dr Pinching, MO to the Battalion, saw the tough second-in-command, Major Leask, openly weeping. Major Davies was found by an English-speaking Cossack woman, Olga Rotova, in a terrible state of distress.

'I'm a British officer!' he cried out to her. 'I can't go on watching unarmed people – women and children – being beaten like this! I can't authorise any more violence, I can't any more, I can't!'

The Rev Kenneth Tyson, chaplain to the Battalion, told me that many men came to him afterwards, bewildered and distressed by their unnatural task. 'They could not believe that this was what they had been fighting the war for. They were repelled by the whole business.'

There seems to be little doubt that this dreadful day's work arose in large part as a direct result of the prior separation of the officers from the remainder of the Cossacks. Suddenly deprived of any leadership, they fell prey to mass panic. That Sunday (3 June) Kenneth Tyson took for his sermon the text from Mark 6, 34: 'And Jesus, when he came out, saw much people, and was moved with compassion toward them, because they were as sheep not having a shepherd.' How far things might have gone differently had the officers been there to instil some discipline into their followers is impossible to know. What can be said is that no scenes of bloodshed and fear on a scale remotely approaching this took place anywhere else in the Fifth Corps area, where thousands of other Cossacks were being entrained for the Soviet Union at the same time.

The open treachery, lying and disregard of rights of citizenship in international law employed by Musson and his troops also played a major part in arousing the mass fear that so appalled Davies, Tyson and others present. From genial and sympathetic 'gentlemen', their loyal allies in the Great War, the British appeared all at once utterly brutal and treacherous. Knowing nothing of the extraordinary machinations passing behind the scenes in Klagenfurt and Caserta, the Cossacks had no reason to disbelieve what they were assured by their persecutors: that their admired Field-Marshal Alexander was the architect of all their sufferings, and had sold them to the Bolsheviks.

In so far as the panic and chaos in Peggetz Camp on 1 June was the unintended but predictable result of the 'deception tactic' necessary to lure Generals Krasnov and Shkuro to their deaths, much of the responsibility must lie on the shoulders of those shadowy figures behind the scenes who devised it. Certainly it would be a harsh moralist who laid it all at the door of Colonel Malcolm or Major Davies.

So far consideration of the extradition of the Cossacks has been confined to Domanov's Cossacks and accompanying Caucasians held by General Arbuthnott's Seventy-eighth Infantry Division in the Drau Valley. It will not have been forgotten, though, that the British also held another equally large formation, the Fifteenth Cossack Cavalry Corps of General von Pannwitz, which had retreated from Yugoslavia and surrendered to troops of Major-General Horatius Murray's Sixth Armoured Division just after the cessation of hostilities. Von Pannwitz and his men were also destined for transfer to the Soviets, and in the order following the Corps conference of 21 May the '15 Cossack Cav Corps' was among those ordered to 'be treated as Soviet Nationals', i.e. *en bloc*, without screening.

General 'Nap' Murray was a remarkable and much-loved officer, who had little time for commanders who believed their duty to consist in nothing more than transmitting orders. 'Under such circumstances why have generals at all?' he was to comment later. He had brushed with the peremptory Keightley in the past, and if anyone was likely to object to becoming involved in what could be regarded as a major war crime it was he. Arbuthnott, who was far from being a rebel, had protested vigorously against his covert instructions. Murray, there was every reason to believe, would go much further than mere protest. Indeed, his stand was made plain from a very early stage.

On 3 May he had expressed strong views in his report concerning the surrender of Damjanovic's Chetniks at Cormons. Troops under his command had accepted von Pannwitz's surrender under the normal terms, and he felt strongly about this too. About 15 May, two days after Harold Macmillan's unexpected flight into Klagenfurt, General Murray learned that the return of the Cossacks had been decided upon. His reaction was to summon the German officers of the Cossacks. Addressing them in fluent German, he informed them frankly of the danger.

'It is true to say that I said, "Look here",' General Murray told the author thirty years later; '"you want to examine your position, and you must make it clear to the people down below that you're in some danger. I have every reason to believe that you may have to go back to Russia." There was a slight pause then, and they couldn't get out of that room quick enough!'

During the week that followed, Murray 'made no attempt to establish exactly how my orders were interpreted. In fact the looser and the more nebulous they were, it seemed to me, possibly the better . . . all I know is, we lost the hell of a lot of men!' As the month drew on he sensed the ring was closing on the Cossacks, but remained resolved to co-operate minimally or not at all with any orders he regarded as clearly dishonourable. His uncompromising views were well known to Keightley and Low, who realised there was no possibility of persuading Murray to accept the conspiratorial scheme imposed upon the reluctant Arbuthnott at that time. 'But, funnily enough, I never got orders – if I'd got orders like that, I wouldn't have obeyed them! And I'm astonished that Arbuthnott sat down under them . . . And then to have the conference that was never going to take place is something I thought *absolutely unbelievable.*'

Keightley was shrewd enough not to attempt to foist off such a scheme on the fiery Murray. 'I had a row with Keightley: he was a bully, and he was rather apt to take short cuts. He didn't get any change out of my outfit, in the sense that he got it out of Arbuthnott. That Arbuthnott stooped to such a level, which I wouldn't have thought any British officer would ever do!' Keightley, as a result of their earlier difference, 'knew that I was unlikely to be a very helpful subordinate in this way . . . You see, old Charles Keightley marched about the place talking about the Yalta Agreement, but it doesn't seem to me as if he had the slightest idea of what it meant! . . . To go and intervene in the way that Arbuthnott did and carry out an operation such as he did – we wouldn't – we wouldn't have done it, I'm absolutely certain. We certainly didn't in the event.'

That this was how General Murray really thought and acted at the time was confirmed to me by Brigadier Clive Usher, who was placed in charge of the whole operation, and by Colonels Henry Howard and Robin Rose Price, whose battalions were principally involved. Murray was not even concerned with the problem of distinctions of citizenship, such as temporarily disturbed General Arbuthnott. The Fifteenth Cossack Cavalry Corps was listed by name in the order for return, which specified them at the same time as 'Soviet nationals'. To hand the German officers over to the Soviets for liquidation was obviously a gross infringement of the Geneva Convention, and they were warned at once of what was in the offing. For the rest of the Cossacks, General Murray was quite happy to see them disappear too; and in fact several thousand melted away into the surrounding countryside.

Faced with these blunt indications that General Murray would not co-operate in any operations involving excessive brutality or use of force, General Keightley made no attempt to enforce his orders within the Sixth Armoured Divisional area. Instead, the day after the Corps conference of 21 May, the whole of the Fifteenth Cossack Cavalry Corps except for one Brigade was hastily transferred from Murray's area to that controlled by the Forty-sixth Infantry Division.[33] The transfer included General von Pannwitz, whom the Soviet authorities were so anxious to lay hands on, and whom they later hanged in Moscow. The pretext given for this move was that of congestion within the Sixth Armoured Division's region, but as the evacuation of all Cossacks was planned for a bare week later it would be hard to believe that this was the real reason for so troublesome a move.

There is in fact no doubt that this sudden move was designed to place the bulk of the Cossacks under the control of a less recalcitrant commander than General Murray, one unlikely to look too suspiciously between the lines of his orders. Brigadier Tryon-Wilson, who as Corps A/Q was closely involved in the location of personnel, is convinced that this was the purpose. General Murray's officers characteristically made no bones about making the matter public knowledge. Count Leopold Goëss was then commanding the Second Battalion of the Sixth Terek Cossack Regiment. He wrote to me recently to point out:

The Cossack Corps became concentrated during the second half of May in the so-called Gortschitztal, with the staff in Mühlen. At this time I acted as liaison officer between General v. Pannwitz and the British. One evening, returning to Mühlen, a British officer stopped my car and said: 'You know I'm not allowed to speak with you (non-fraternization). I only want to inform you that tonight Scottish troops will take over from us, and that means something.' I informed my Regimental Commander, who immediately prepared to bring away the German personnel, and went back to the Corps staff where a visit of a Scottish Brigadier was already announced for the next morning.

There I interpreted the order, reading roughly as follows: General von Pannwitz has 30 Minutes to pack and be ready for transport. The German officers and other personnel gather there and there, the Russian officers and noncommissioned officers take over the command of their people, and so on. That was the beginning of their way to Judenburg and the so-called 'repatriation'. There was no difference made between Soviet citizens, citizens of other nations, or Germans.

The only plausible explanation for the glaring discrepancy in Divisional reactions to Corps commands must surely be that Keightley knew that he had no means of enforcing his order where it was seriously challenged. It seems inconceivable that, had his orders come down from McCreery and Alexander, he would not have called Murray to order. Murray was too good a soldier to disobey an outright command – as he himself says, 'that would be insubordination' – however far he was prepared to take advantage of imprecise instructions. Those whom he permitted to escape included the senior German commanding officer, Colonel Wagner. (In his log book, Nigel Nicolson, Intelligence Officer to Guards Brigade, recorded openly on 27 May that 'Gen. Wagner knows his destination'.) Murray was left to interpret his orders as loosely as he chose. Like General Arbuthnott, he had been informed of the provision that, 'It is of the utmost importance that all the offrs and particularly senior comds are rounded up and that none are [sic] allowed to escape.' Yet Murray received no reproof for allowing the escape of Colonel Wagner, who had been openly warned of his impending fate by Brigadier Usher.

General von Pannwitz himself declined to avail himself of any opportunity to escape, being resolved upon sharing the fate of his beloved Cossacks. Edward Leigh, then a subaltern in the Second/Fifth Leicester Regiment, vividly recalls the last parade of the Fifteenth Cossack Cavalry Corps:

A beautiful crisp early morning in May 1945 just above a village called Mühlen in those lovely hills on the borders of Styria and Carinthia northeast of Klagenfurt. At a crossing of two tracks stood a group of officers including their corps commander (? von Pannwitz) mounted on fine cavalry chargers. Sitting on chairs a few women, one middle-aged, blonde, very dignified in white starched nurse's uniform with a red cross on her bosom. No one spoke or smiled. Then the thud of horses' hooves muffled on the narrow unmetalled track, and for what seemed hours the Cossack Corps rode past its commander at a walk. [Mr M. Kent, also present as an interpreter, noted in his diary that it took 'from 8 [to] about 1 o'clock – thousand upon thousand']. Two by two, stiffening as they approached, loose reined, hands resting on the horses' withers. Their faces totally expressionless, everything so quiet that the jingle of their equipment seemed to ring out. The scene had an unreal dreamlike quality. Then the carts & field kitchens creaking and the hospital carts, red crosses on their caravan covers, nurses walking beside them. Except that the uniforms were a dirty greenish grey and that everyone was unarmed I could have been with Nicholas Rostov in 1805 – those were his peasants.

Not long before Leigh had met 'one of their staff officers in the local *gasthaus* and dined and drank with him – a quiet, well read and humorous man. He told me, and I am sure that it was the truth, that he was a younger son of a landlord family, had escaped from Russia in 1920 and ended up in Paris where he had lived till 1941. Then he had volunteered to fight on the Russian front.'

The hidden figure or figures who pushed through the handover of Krasnov, Shkuro and other White officers, whose names they had received from the Soviets on 11 May, knew themselves to be riding a tiger. The executive order from the Fifteenth Army Group of 25 May had conceded no authority to employ unusual violence to compel the repatriation of Soviet Cossacks, and had categorically ordered the screening of all non-Soviet citizens. Despite these instructions they devised an extraordinarily elaborate scheme designed for the specific purpose of including the émigré Cossacks, veteran opponents of Bolshevism, for surrender to the NKVD and SMERSH at Judenburg. All written orders were carefully phrased to make it appear as if screening was intended to be effected. General Krasnov's appeals to Alexander were destroyed at Fifth Corps HQ, and the dangerously flamboyant General Shkuro was actually snatched from camp and held in secret confinement for thirty-six hours following letters in which he drew attention to the question of his citizenship. The complexity and risks of the operation are in themselves testimony to the importance the handing over bore to those who planned it.

The spurious orders to screen included in all orders down to Brigade level were not intended for the deception of the officers to whom they were delivered. The only possible motive for their inclusion was to mislead anyone inspecting them subsequently. Were that to happen it would have to be presumed that the Fifth Corps had genuinely intended screening to take place, but in the event, in Toby Low's words, 'the screening process simply did not take place, and could not take place, because of conditions in the area'. What happened could be laid at the door of the local commanders – certainly not of the Fifth Corps Staff.

On 7 June General Arbuthnott issued a remarkable message to all units under his command. It included the following passages:

> At the virtual conclusion of the transfer of the Caucasian and Cossack communities from the Lienz area to the Soviet Military Authorities at Judenburg I would like to express to all ranks who took part in this operation my appreciation of the way in which this duty was performed.
>
> I am fully aware that to many the task was most distasteful and that there were some who even doubted the necessity for it. I would like everyone to know that I was not unmindful of these sentiments. However, all can rest assured that every aspect of the matter was carefully examined and that the conclusion was reached that for the eventual resettlement of Europe and the future hopes of peace the return of these people to Russia was not only necessary but desirable.[34]

This attribution of necessity to high-flown but vague demands of *raison d'état* reflects what Keightley impressed upon Arbuthnott, and presumably what Keightley had himself been instructed in his turn. For the Sixth Armoured Division was likewise told that it was 'of great political importance that [Cossack] PW should be delivered to Russians complete'.[35]

It was a view unlikely to have occurred spontaneously to either soldier, neither of whom claimed any insight into political matters. As we have seen, General Murray was convinced that Keightley did not even understand what the Yalta Agreement was about, let alone more delicate diplomatic considerations. These nebulous references to the higher statecraft bear the ring of a politician's justification, plausible but imprecise. Particularly interesting is the fact that orders emanating from the Fifth Corps never on any occasion made reference to the one consideration which must have influenced even the most conscience-stricken British soldier in Austria at that time. This was the factor which Macmillan tells us formed his prime motivation in agreeing to the return of the Cossacks: the exchange of liberated British prisoners of war.

9

The Old Émigrés Return Home

'The Russians were particularly keen on the return of the officers, many of whom were Tsarist émigrés . . . During the journeys the Cossacks were offering the troops almost anything they possessed and imploring them to shoot them, as they fully realised what awaited them at the other end.' (Lieutenant-Colonel M. C. Pulford, officer commanding Second Lancashire Fusiliers, May 1945)

Those who despatched the Cossacks and Yugoslavs to their enemies nurtured no illusions as to their likely fate. General Robertson, issuing the order used to justify the secret handovers, confessed that he 'could not bother at this time about who might or might not be turned over to the Russians and Partisans to be shot'. At the time he arranged the handover of the Cossacks and White Russians, Harold Macmillan noted without apparent regret that, 'To hand them over to the Russians is condemning them to slavery, torture and probably death.'

The harsh treatment inflicted by the Soviet regime on the hundreds of thousands of its citizens returned under the terms of the Yalta Agreement is today sufficiently well known. In this chapter my concern is specifically with the fate of the old émigrés among the Cossacks, those whom no interpretation of the Agreement could envisage as liable for involuntary 'return'.

After being rushed from the cage at Spittal to the Soviet lines at Judenburg, the Cossack officers were placed in custody under guard by troops of Marshal Tolbukhin's army. Just across the bridge over the River Mur (where some Cossacks had taken the opportunity of hurling themselves to their deaths) was a huge concrete steel mill. Its machinery had already been dismantled and removed by the Soviets, and a large chamber within the empty structure, 250 metres by 50, was now employed as a temporary prison for the Cossack officers.

Red Army officers, agog with curiosity, came to visit them. For the wretched Domanov and other former Soviet citizens they displayed nothing but contempt; they were traitors to their Motherland. But for the White officers, veterans of the Civil War who had never acknowledged Soviet power, they displayed marked politeness and respect. They were especially delighted at encountering in person the legendary Shkuro, whose racy reminiscences of their old battles in 1919, interlarded with an inimitable range of foul language, brought him a circle of admiring listeners. What the Soviet officers could not understand, however, was how the British had come to include their old allies among those returned. Their commanding officer, General Dolmatov, expressed great astonishment at finding Tsarist officers among the prisoners.

Shortly afterwards arrived a body of interrogators from SMERSH, who were rather less gentlemanly in their attitude. However, they, too, appeared surprised that the British had made so uncalled-for a concession.

'Surname, Christian name, patronymic, date and place of birth? Where were you living before 1939?' asked one Chekist, stopping before one of the old émigrés, who was one of the few to survive to recount his experiences.

'I named a town in the Balkans. He stopped writing and glanced up at me:

'Then you're an emigrant? You're not liable for repatriation. Comrade Stalin did not claim the old emigrants. Why are you here?'

'They handed me over by means of a trick. I was never a Soviet citizen. I am a Bulgarian citizen.'

The Cossack felt a brief moment of rising hope, to be dashed by his interrogator's next words:

'You're not liable for repatriation, but once you end up here you don't get out again. I myself worked in Germany, but now I have returned against my wishes.'

A few days later, when the Cossacks had been moved to a fresh transit-point, the same old emigrant encountered identical incredulity from a SMERSH investigator:

'Émigré? You're not liable for repatriation, but once in our hands you don't get out of here!'[1]

That the lower echelons of the SMERSH team were ignorant of the secret agreement including old émigrés in the handover may suggest that up to the last minute their superiors were by no means confident that the British really would make so remarkable a concession – one for which the Soviets were offering no *quid pro quo*. They must have been aware of the covert nature of the operation, and of some of the consequent risks being taken by their British colleagues.

A group of SMERSH officers who came to watch the departure of the Tsarist generals on the next stage of their journey were at once contemptuous of British duplicity and puzzled by their motivation. A few months later one of them was to defect to the Americans in Vienna, and later recalled his 'glimpse of a piece of history':

> 'They're a grant lot, the English,' laughed the lieutenant-colonel. 'They give Shkuro their decoration, called after some saints, Michael and George, I think it was. Now, if you please, they're quite happy to deliver him to our door.' All our chaps who were standing near began to laugh.

One of the group later mused over a puzzling aspect of the deal.

> One evening when I was looking through the list of Cossack officers, before they were dispatched to Moscow (we received these lists from our investigation branch), I went over the whole affair in my own mind. How could the British have done this? Perhaps it was the work of their socialists, who, after all, were also in the government. But Churchill, the Prime Minister! You could hardly call him a socialist! . . . Yes indeed, there was a lot I couldn't understand.[2]

Many of the Cossacks got no further than the Judenburg steel-mill. British troops across the river heard repeated bursts of small-arms fire during the next few days. They were able to guess at what survivors' accounts now confirm:

> Under the roar of the factory engines shootings continued day and night. On the right of the highroad, opposite the factory, was a workmen's settlement. Some of them (former Communists) managed to gain entry to the factory where they saw and heard much. One day the inhabitants of this settlement, as well as those in the town, were astonished: the factory had begun to operate! Smoke was rising from the factory chimneys, but all the workers remained unsummoned at home. Every gaze was turned towards what was happening in the factory. Scouts were sent out. Their report was regarded as absurd and incredible, and nobody believed it: the Soviets were cremating the Cossacks . . . However, they swiftly came to accept it as soon as work began again for the settlement, and after the whole town was oppressed by the stench of burning human flesh.
>
> The factory was 'working' for five and a half days. After this came the last detachments of Cossacks (it was 15 July 1945), and Russian girls

formerly working in the district were summoned to the factory. Their task was to 'scour the factory of Cossack parasites'. This was the expression used by one of the Soviet officers.[3]

For the most distinguished of the old émigrés, those Tsarist generals whom the Fifth Corps had taken such particular precautions to inveigle into their trap, a special fate was reserved. First an English officer presented the Soviet colonel with a carefully-compiled list of the people being handed over. Then, even as the leading Cossack generals were descending from their vehicle after crossing the bridge at Judenburg, a senior Red Army officer approached, calling out, 'Who in this group is General Peter Krasnov?'

The old Ataman identifying himself, he and his companions were at once separated from the other Cossack officers. With General Krasnov were his cousins General Semeon Nikolaevich and Colonel Nikolai Nikolaevich Krasnov, and the latter's young son, also Nikolai Nikolaevich. It was young Nikolai who miraculously survived to re-emerge years later in the West, where he wrote the memoirs from which this account is in part drawn. Accompanying the four Krasnovs were Generals Shkuro, Vasiliev, Solamakhin, Domanov, and Sultan-Ghirei, and old General Krasnov's aide-de-camp, Colonel Morgunov. Of these only Domanov was a Soviet citizen. Treated for the most part with respectful politeness by their Red Army guards, they were confined in the former factory office. There they were joined by General Helmut von Pannwitz, who was resolved to stay with his faithful Cossacks to the end.

A little while afterwards a Red Army captain entered to request Generals Krasnov and Shkuro to visit the Soviet general commanding in the Judenburg district. As they were leaving the room, Shkuro cynically contrasted the attitude of their declared enemy with that of those treacherous friends who had presented him with one of their highest decorations, and with equal equanimity had since arranged his coming murder.

'Very likely it will be pleasanter talking with "our people" than with "those others".'

The Soviet General Dolmatov proved to be the best type of Red Army officer. In his mess was assembled a group of his colonels, who greeted the White commanders with studied courtesy. It turned out that they had been fighting in 1918 and 1919 on opposite sides of the same front. At once reminiscences were exchanged in lively manner, all reflections of a political nature being studiously avoided.

As the conversation drew to a close, Dolmatov declared with evident sincerity:

'I would like to think that you both are not distressed at the prospect of returning to the Motherland. Believe me, the war has changed many things. Soviet power is no longer something to fear. You, as I am told, are travelling to Moscow. They won't hold you long there. They'll talk to you, find out what they need, and send you away. You'll meet many old friends, recall old times and live out your own lives in the Motherland. Good luck!'

Throughout their brief period in the hands of the Red Army the White officers received the same courteous treatment. Dolmatov's feelings reflected a sentiment widely held in the Red Army at this time. After the unparalleled victory over Hitler's hordes a feeling of euphoria swept across the whole Russian population. All the unparalleled sacrifices and dauntless heroism could not have been for nothing, and the new world promised in official propaganda must now surely have arrived! Stalin sensed this new mood and dreaded it: now that the external enemy was miraculously defeated, he would have to turn once again on the infinitely more feared internal foe – the Russian people.

From time to time the prisoners received callers of a different stamp from the gentlemanly officers and friendly men of the Judenburg garrison. Nikolai Krasnov (the source of the account which follows) recalled: 'We were called upon by silent visitors – officers – agents of Soviet counter-intelligence: SMERSH and the military branch of the NKVD. They entered the room, took us in with a glance, as if counting heads, and went away, shutting the door firmly behind them.'

These in turn were replaced by another distinguished, highly-decorated army general, whose name they did not learn. He talked much with General Krasnov, appearing intensely interested in all the old Don Ataman had to say on the situation in their country. Repeating Dolmatov's assurances of honourable treatment and a new future for the post-war Soviet Union, he went on to enquire of Krasnov how he envisaged developments. Deeply impressed by what he had seen of the Red Army, Krasnov thought for a few moments, then declared:

'The future of Russia is a great one! Of that I have no doubt. The Russian people are immovable as a fortress. They are forged in steel. They have endured not just a single tragedy, nor just a single yoke. The future lies with the people, and not with the government.

Regimes come and go, and Soviet power will pass. Neros are born and vanish. Not the USSR, but Russia will deservedly regain her honourable place in the world.'

The Soviet general was visibly struck by these words, on which he stood reflecting, untroubled by the presence of a number of other Red Army officers. Then, as he turned to leave, he asked suddenly whether among the 'gentlemen' present there were any Soviet people. Domanov and another ex-Red Army man reluctantly acknowledged themselves. The General gazed sternly at them, then said:

'See here . . . these people, whom we call "Whites", in 1918 and thereabouts fought against us with arms and propaganda. Openly. They held to their ludicrous reactionary ideology. They are our enemies, but to some extent I can understand them. The Soviet Union nurtured you, made you what you are, gave you a position, and how did you repay her? Well, as it happens they'll be talking about all that with you in Moscow. You haven't got long to wait!'

With which he departed abruptly.

Not long afterwards the whole party was driven in lorries to Graz, where their guards were replaced by SMERSH officers. It looked as though someone had taken note of Shkuro's excessive popularity among the regular troops. After a night in prison, they travelled to a SMERSH operational base at Baden-bei-Wien, where they were photographed and subjected to that repetitive questioning to which the Soviet security services are traditionally addicted. Old General Krasnov was questioned at length about his career as a novelist; young Nikolai was surprised at the interrogators' familiarity with the General's works.

On 4 June the party was flown to Moscow. At the airport they were transferred to prison vans – marked 'Bread' on the outside, to mislead Western journalists – which drove them at speed through the streets to another large prison. Guided along endless corridors past rows and rows of cells, Nikolai Krasnov was eventually thrust into a recess smaller than a telephone kiosk, in which he could neither sit nor stand. It was a strange homecoming to the country he had left within a few months of his birth, and which he could not even remember. He was in the Lubianka Gaol, headquarters of the NKVD.

The acoustics of a solitary cell were new to me, but the deep and deathly silence was broken from time to time by a heart-rending scream, the animal-like howl of a tortured or dying being. I asked myself whether it was real or a trick, relayed through a microphone hidden somewhere in a recess of the box . . . I winced at a terrible shriek which – it seemed to me – rang out almost from within my own cell. It was a woman's scream:

'Kill me, you devils, but let me breathe! Aaaah!'

I felt as if my hair stood on end. My heart froze. In the years that followed I often seemed to hear that woman's scream. For then I knew nothing of the fate of my wife and mother, or of any of the wives and mothers of our officers.

Everything in the building was calculated, whether deliberately or not, to induce in its involuntary inmates a surrealist state of alienation. The innumerable identical corridors, the deadly silence, the bizarre regulations and purposeless rituals – all these were enough in themselves to affect a prisoner's mental equilibrium:

We passed through corridors. Not once was there a turning. Doors. Doors. More corridors. It seemed to me that they were conducting me through a labyrinth in order to destroy my sense of direction. It is possible that we traversed the same route more than once, but everything was so monotonous and featureless that I had no means of knowing.

Finally Nikolai was shown into a room where he was stripped and searched with extraordinary minuteness from head to foot. Dissatisfied even with this, a supervising colonel of the MVD (Ministry of Internal Affairs) drove his finger unexpectedly up the young man's rectum, elegantly wiping it afterwards on his own handkerchief. Satisfied at last, the colonel ordered the guards to dress Krasnov in his uniform, 'and take him at once to "him"'.

Once again they passed through the succession of passages and ascended an unknown number of storeys in a silent lift, until Krasnov found himself unexpectedly taken down a richly-carpeted passage and ushered into a large, luxuriously-furnished chamber. With a pang of anguish and delight, he found himself standing before his father. But before they could exchange more than a few words, father and son were taken on through a high doorway into an even larger hall, carpeted in deep-piled Bokhara, whose walls were decorated with a three-yard-high portrait of Stalin, and another of his security chief, Lavrenty Beria. In the far depths of the room, the Krasnovs saw before them, seated at a magnificent writing-table, a general in the uniform of the MVD. 'Merkulov!' came a whisper from behind their backs. So this was the mysterious 'him' whom Nikolai was to see!

Every Russian, Red or White, knew the name of the dreaded Minister of State Security, second only to Beria in the Soviet hierarchy of terror.

Vsevolod Nikolaevich Merkulov had risen to power in December 1938, after Beria replaced Yezhov as head of the NKVD. He had been a student with Beria at Baku at the time of the Revolution, and who continued to entrust him with commissions of great importance. In 1940 he travelled to Berlin as colleague-cum-watchdog with Molotov during the latter's discussions with Stalin's former ally, Hitler. In the same year he and Beria implemented Stalin's decision to massacre the Polish officers at Katyn, and in 1941 it was he who organised the mass deportation of citizens from the occupied Baltic States. After the shift in alliances, when Hitler's invasion threw Stalin into the arms of Britain, Merkulov was responsible for arranging for British engineers to destroy the Baku oil wells in the event of the victorious German Army's conquering the Caucasus. Now, as his ensuing words were clearly to imply, he had assumed control of the delicate negotiations with the British resulting in the secret surrender of the Tsarist veterans.[4]

Merkulov evidently attached great symbolic importance to the capture of the famous Civil War generals, and though normally far from loquacious could not resist the temptation on this occasion of unburdening himself before two victims who were unlikely to live to repeat the tale. In view of this, his words are of great significance, and worth repeating from Nikolai Krasnov's detailed memoir. As will be seen shortly, there are strong reasons for accepting the accuracy of his account:

> The General remained silent. We did not stir. Then he slowly raised his great head and examined us boldly and openly, just as people examine the exhibits at a waxworks exhibition. The officer stood like a statue just behind us.
>
> 'Have some tea and a bite to eat, "gentlemen" Krasnov!' Merkulov suddenly said in a sharp voice. 'And provide them with cigarettes.'
>
> An obliging hand set out an open packet of Kazbek cigarettes on our little table. The officer went out.
>
> Once again there was silence. A long drawn-out silence. Merkulov was clearly waiting for us to take our tea. A tray appeared with the steaming drink, deliciously bitter to smell. An attractive service. On the plates everything was *comme il faut*, as my father liked to say.
>
> 'Go ahead!' ordered the General. There were just the three of us. 'Don't be shy, "gentlemen"! Eat up and drink your tea,' continued Merkulov,

rising to his feet. 'It is not often we have tea-parties in the Lubianka. Only for special guests!'

A peculiar smile appeared on his face, quite masking his intentions.

'When you've finished eating, I shall tell you something. They have probably already told you who I am. I am – Merkulov, one of your future – well, let's say it – bosses!'

There was a pause. The General walked backwards and forwards by his desk, softly and smoothly swaying at the hips and turning lithely on his heel.

'How was your journey? You weren't air-sick?' (What was that, a hint at Shkuro?) 'Has anything upset you? Is there anything you need?'

And not waiting for a reply, swiftly, as if it were no concern to him, Merkulov addressed himself directly to Father:

'Why don't you smoke, Krasnov, and why not drink your tea? It seems to me that you're not very chatty or friendly! I've a feeling that by this silence you are trying to conceal your agitation, your fear; but there's no need for concern. At least, not in this room. Look, when they summon you before the interrogator, I advise you to speak only the truth and find an answer to every question, otherwise – we shall have to string you up.'

Merkulov laughed softly.

'Do you know how they hang people here? First of all slowly, by easy stages – even not too painfully, but afterwards . . . Haven't you read the detailed accounts of such interrogations in Ataman Krasnov's books?'

My fingers grew cold. In my temples a pulse beat out a furious 'tom-tom'. My heart beat so loudly that the noise might have been heard by Merkulov, standing at his desk a bare ten metres away. My father was silent. His face was pale but perfectly composed. I envied him.

'Don't hope for freedom,' continued the General; 'you're not children! However, should you not be obstinate, all formalities will be concluded easily, you will sign something-or-other, you will serve a couple of years in ITL [the corrective labour camps] and there you will become accustomed to our way of life – you'll find it a delightful part of the world. Then, perhaps, we'll let you go. You'll live.'

Again a pause.

'There it is, Colonel Krasnov, choose between telling the truth and staying alive, or refusal and death. Don't think I'm scaring you. On the contrary! Why, Peter Nikolaevich, Semeon Nikolaevich and you – are our old acquaintances! In 1920 you managed to slip like quicksilver out of our hands, but now – it is we who hold all the cards. You're not getting away . . .'

He took several steps back and forth. His hands were clasped behind his back, and he twiddled his crossed fingers. I could not help noticing that a ring flashed on one of them.

'So, Colonel, shall we have a little talk?'

'I have nothing to talk to you about!' my father replied sharply.

'What do you mean by "nothing"?' laughed the Chekist quietly. 'Agreement is worth more than money, Krasnov. Your past doesn't interest us. We know all about that. But there are certain small details about your recent activities which it would do no harm to hear from your lips.'

'I've nothing to tell you! I don't understand what all this procrastination is about. Finish the whole business now. A bullet in the back of the neck and . . .'

'Oh, no, "Mister" Krasnov.' Merkulov smiled crookedly as he lowered himself into an armchair. 'Things are not as simple as that. Just think. A bullet in the back of the neck, and that's all? Nonsense, Your Excellency. You'll have to work. There's plenty of time before you get in your coffin. Time enough before you fertilise the ground. But first you will work for the good of the Motherland! A spot of timber-felling, a spell in the mines with water up to your belt. You will spend time, my dear, up by the 70th parallel. That'll be interesting. "You'll see life", as we say. You don't know "our" language. You don't know the camp slang which has sprung up in the Polar region. You'll be hearing it. . . . You'll walk with macaroni legs,' the General roared with laughter. 'But you'll work. Hunger will keep you at it.'

We sat silent. My head buzzed. The palms of my hands were sweating from impotent rage.

'We've got to build, Colonel Krasnov! And where shall we find the hands? There's no great profit from the gallows and the "blindfold". Times have changed. We shoot people only rarely. We need hands that work, that don't need paying. We've waited twenty-five years for this joyful meeting with you. You émigrés have had quite long enough deluding your young people abroad.'

Merkulov was a little out of breath after his monologue. A thick vein stood out on his forehead. His eyes became sharp with spite and hatred.

'You're scared? What of? Scared of work? But what is the point of all this? You don't believe a word I say, and I don't believe any of yours. To me you are a White bandit, and to you I am Red scum. However, we Reds are on top now. So it was in 1920, and so it is now. Power is with us. We don't flatter ourselves with the hope that we'll manage to re-educate Krasnov and convert him into an obedient Soviet sheep; you'll never be smitten with love for us. But we'll make you work for Communism, build it up, and that will provide the greater moral satisfaction.'

Merkulov fell silent, fixing his eyes expectantly on Father.

'Why all this long introduction?' replied Father in a tired voice. 'I understand everything perfectly without explanations, General. I am quite aware how hopeless is our position. I and my son are soldiers. We have both fought. We have both looked Death in the face. It makes no difference to us on which parallel, the seventieth or the hundredth, he sweeps his scythe. I only kick myself for one thing: why did we trust the English? However, my head will be off . . .'

'Ah! If it were only death!' sneered Merkulov. 'You can drop those resounding words about "a soldier's death". That's outdated claptrap. Death came past you without even noticing you. But that you trusted the English – that was true stupidity. They are a nation of shopkeepers. They will sell their best friends without blinking an eyelid. Their policy is prostitution! Their Foreign Office is a brothel, in which sits a premier – a great diplomatic "madam". They trade in other people's lives and their own conscience.

'As for us, we don't trust them, Colonel. That's why we took the reins into our own hands. They don't know that we have them checkmated and now we have made them dance to our tune, like the last pawn. Sooner or later there will come the battle between the Communist bear and the Western bulldog. There will be no mercy for our sugared, honeyed, grovelling, fawning allies! They'll fly away to the Devil's mother with all their kings, with all their traditions, lords, castles, heralds, Orders of the Bath and Garters and white wigs.

'Under the lash of the bear's paw there'll remain nothing of all those who cherish the hope that their gold will rule the world. Our healthy, socially strong, young idea – the idea of Lenin and Stalin – will conquer. That's how it'll be, Colonel!'

Merkulov stood up and, concluding these last words, crashed the side of his hand sharply on to the table.

After a similar tirade delivered to Nikolai Krasnov, Merkulov dismissed the prisoners. Nikolai saw his father once again, in October of that year, and then no more. The Colonel, like his son, was sent to one of the northern labour camps where the terrible conditions killed him even more swiftly than Merkulov had anticipated.

This verbatim account of the interview with Merkulov is, like all reported conversations, a dramatic reconstruction from memory. However, despite its melodramatic content, there are compelling reasons for accepting it as accurate in essential details. When Nikolai Krasnov came to write the memoir from which these excerpts are drawn, he noted, 'Despite the fact that eleven years have elapsed, this meeting with Merkulov and everything he said made such an indelible impression on my memory that I believe I have reproduced it exactly as it happened. I may have omitted some things, but I have added nothing.'

This total recall was not due solely to the exceptional nature of what had passed, nor to the years of solitary suffering which burned all he had undergone into his consciousness. Immediately after this unnerving interview Nikolai was parted from his father and taken down to the Lubianka bath-house, where to his delight he found the old Ataman, Peter Krasnov. The General was resigned to his coming end, but avowed his confidence that his nephew, young and fit, would somehow win through and return to 'our own people' in the West. He then went on to impose a sacred duty on the young man:

> If you do survive, fulfil this testament of mine. Describe everything you experience, what you see or hear, whom you meet. Describe it as it was. Don't exaggerate the bad. Don't paint in false colours. Do not depreciate what is good . . . Do not lie. Write only the truth . . . Keep your eyes wide open. Here, under these circumstances, you will have no chance to write, not even brief notes, so use your mind as a notebook, as a camera. This is important, gravely important. From Lienz to the end of your journey of sufferings, remember it all. The world must learn the truth about what has happened and what is happening, from the betrayal and treachery to – the end.[5]

Nikolai solemnly vowed and, by what can only appear as a miracle, fulfilled his vow as his 'grandfather' had foretold. After more than ten years in forced-labour camps, where he underwent experiences more harrowing even than Merkulov's gloating account could have led him to believe, he was among that tiny number of surviving old émigrés amnestied by Khrushchev, and permitted to return to the West. Just after Christmas 1955 he was set free in Berlin, and made his way at once to a cousin in Sweden. There he sat down and did not cease from writing until he had completed his story, exactly as required by the old novelist-general.

> Today [he concluded] is January 28, 1956. It is a month today since I came to freedom, to the free world, in Stockholm. In that month I wrote this memoir. I wrote frantically every night. It seemed to me that every extra day distancing me from that boundary landmark, painted red and white and crowned with the five-pointed star, might wipe from memory or introduce new impressions into the mental notebook I had compiled in the USSR. Today I completed my book. I do not know when or under what circumstances it will appear, nor who will publish it; but I have kept my promise given to Grandfather in the basement bath-room of the Lubyanka Prison.[6]

A year later the book was published in Russian by an émigré publishing house in San Francisco, but though it was widely read by Russians, and appeared in an inaccurate English translation in New York in 1960, it aroused no interest in the world at large. Not long after completing his task the author, his health ruined by years of appalling suffering, died suddenly in the Argentine.

It might have seemed to Krasnov and those around him that all had been to little avail, but the old General was surely right. The *book* had survived, so preserving an indestructible testimony. Above all, it preserved the extraordinary colloquy with Minister of State Security Merkulov.

Merkulov's rantings, as reported by Krasnov, epitomise much that is endemic in Soviet thinking. There is the bullying tone, the undisguised relish in cruelty, and the obligatory grandiloquent boasts of the invincibility of Soviet power, which can be paralleled almost word for word in comparable declamations of the period. We can also detect a love of deception for its own sake, of the delights of hoodwinking clever or sanctimonious persons in authority. Then again, a tacit admission of inferiority runs through the whole harangue in face of the superior culture of old Russia and Western Europe; compensated by vindictive sarcasm and a genuinely chiliastic sense of destructive rejuvenation.[7]

In the same month that the Krasnovs were interviewed by Merkulov, the Polish resistance leader Zbygniew Stypulkowski was being interrogated by one of his underlings, a Major Tikhonov, in another part of the building. The tone and content of Tikhonov's threats were remarkably similar to those of his superior. 'When we came to discuss my probable sentence,' wrote Stypulkowski, 'Tikhonov said it was easy enough to part with one's life, but not so easy to face life-long internment in the Siberian *lagry* (camps).' His interrogator went on to remark contemptuously:

> What are you waiting for? For an armed conflict of Russia with Great Britain and the U.S.A.? That is only an illusion. Before we reach that stage you will be watching events from the other world. Besides, there never will be a war with Great Britain – we'll finish her in another way. Once our foot is on India's threshold she won't budge . . . What can Great Britain do in such circumstances? She is a colossus which we can help to die naturally.[8]

A recurrent theme in Merkulov's train of thought is the treachery and duplicity of the Soviet Union's British ally. Gratification, bemusement and contempt are intermingled in his assessment. If

Merkulov's reactions reflect those of the rest of the Soviet leadership it is clear that, whatever the motive for the British handover, the action had aroused neither gratitude nor incentive for reciprocity, but merely contempt and mistrust. Nothing in his words intimates that the British received any compensatory concession in return for their remarkable compliance.

Despite the victory of the Bolsheviks, the pathetic life of the Whites in emigration, and the fact that the Krasnovs now lay entirely at his mercy, Merkulov was still possessed by the most virulent resentment of what he saw as their pretensions to superior culture and civility. This was perhaps one of the motives which made the Soviet leadership so extraordinarily determined to destroy what to outsiders must have appeared an utterly negligible threat.

Perhaps the most fascinating point in Merkulov's monologue is that in which he makes allusion to the British public figure who had betrayed the Whites into his power. What makes the glancing reference so suggestive is the strong likelihood that Merkulov would have known the identity of his mysterious opposite number conducting secret negotiations on the British side. On 4 June, the date of the interview in the Lubianka, the covert arrangement to include old émigrés in the handover of Soviet citizens was just three weeks old. That it was Merkulov who summoned the Krasnovs in order to crow over their discomfiture must mean that it was he who was ultimately in control, on the Soviet side, of the exceptionally delicate and important negotiations conducted behind the backs of the British and American Governments and their military authorities in the Mediterranean. As few people as possible would have been let into the secret, and he made it plain that he was *au fait* with everything that had passed – even to the petition drawn up in French by General Krasnov in the Kensingtons' cage at Spittal. The Soviet security apparatus was undoubtedly exceedingly well informed of everything pertaining to the surrender of the Cossacks. As a former SMERSH officer explained: 'our NKVD agents . . . had been with Krasnov for a long time. They had played the parts of anti-Soviet Cossack officers who had gone over to the Germans and were handed over to us along with the others.'[9]

That Merkulov's phraseology was accurately recalled by Krasnov seems likely. The latter had no reason to associate the British Foreign Office with his betrayal, since the Cossacks knew nothing of the provisions of the Yalta Agreement and so far as they considered the matter at all presumed that the order for their repatriation had been ordered by Churchill and transmitted by Alexander through the normal military channels.[10]

Equally, there is no likelihood that Merkulov was indulging in a general tirade against the Foreign Office as author of the Yalta Agreement, into which he subsumed the related issue of the return of White émigrés. The official British standpoint on the necessity for screening repatriated Russians was undeviating throughout, as Soviet representatives at all levels were continually reminded when attempting to overreach their legitimate authority. Equally, if the deliberate inclusion of White émigrés among the Cossacks handed over in Austria resulted from an *ad hoc* military arrangement by the Fifth Corps or the Eighth Army, there would be no reason for Merkulov to bring the Foreign Office's 'madam' into the picture at all.

To Merkulov the distinction between the two operations, the one authorised and the other prohibited by the British Government, was unmistakable. Moreover, his reference to the buying and selling of 'their own friends' could have no application to the return of Soviet citizens under the Yalta Agreement. In no context could Merkulov have conceived of Britain's sustaining any sense of obligation towards liberated Soviet prisoners, many of whom had served in the German armed forces. Nor would he have envisaged their handover as a betrayal, since they were being returned to the State to whom their loyalty was due.

Merkulov's words suggest that he knew the old émigrés to have been 'sold' by an influential figure linked to the Foreign Office. His reference to this unnamed personality is curious. 'Their Foreign Office [the words are in English in the text] is a brothel, in which sits [or presides] a [or 'the'] "premier", a great diplomatic "madam".' At first glance this could be taken as an allusion to the Foreign Secretary, Anthony Eden. There are, however, good reasons for rejecting such a conclusion. First, it is on the face of things unlikely that Eden could have played any part in the secret arrangement to surrender the White Russians. On 13 April he had flown to the United States to attend President Roosevelt's funeral and take part in discussions at the San Francisco Conference. He did not return to England until 17 May, three days after the conspiracy had been put into effect at Klagenfurt.[11] Second, it is inconceivable that Merkulov could have been so ignorant of the British Foreign Secretary's correct style as to use the term 'premier' to describe him. Formalities of protocol are in general dear to the Soviet heart. In this case Merkulov had played an important role in arranging Churchill and Eden's wartime visits to the Soviet Union, and would have had frequent occasion to register the correct usage. Alternatively, were Merkulov employing a designation of general meaning, one might expect a term like *nachalnik, khozyain*: 'chief', 'boss'.

There is no article in Russian, so 'premier' could signify either 'a' or 'the' premier. The Russian word 'premier' has two distinct meanings, both corresponding to foreign usages. It means, first, 'premier', 'prime minister'; and, second, a leading or 'star' actor. Merkulov's contemptuous allusion, in view of the conventional inappropriateness of the term, suggests that he was indulging in a slighting pun at the expense of a functionary whose role he regarded in a despicable light.

In the overall context of Merkulov's tirade it looks as if he envisaged the anonymous organiser of the Whites' surrender as something of an effete *poseur* (in Soviet eyes, of course), 'a leading actor'. In selling the Whites down the river, he and his collaborators had gone further than simply co-operating with legitimate Soviet interests or fulfilling diplomatic obligations; they had 'traded away their own consciences'. It is possible, too, that the imagery of the brothel implies that the corruption with which Merkulov invests his picture of the 'premier' and his colleagues included a sexual aspect – an element which the NKVD was never slow to exploit. Finally, the passage employing metaphors drawn from chess may indicate that Merkulov considered his coup to have resulted less from a favourable response to a forceful demand, than from a series of skilful deceptions, resulting in an arrangement by no means to Britain's ultimate advantage.

Young Nikolai Krasnov survived his ordeal, thanks to his youth and good health. None of the others of the élite group flown to Moscow was so fortunate. His father died in one of the northern camps a few months later. On 17 January 1947 *Pravda* announced that a military court had tried and sentenced the following 'agents of German Intelligence, leaders of armed White Guard units during the period of the Civil War, Ataman P. N. Krasnov, Lieutenant-General of the White Army A. G. Shkuro, the commander of the "Wild Division" – Major-General of the White Army Prince Klich Sultan-Ghirey, Major-General of the White Army S. N. Krasnov, and Major-General of the White Army T. I. Domanov, and also the German Army General of the SS Helmuth von Pannwitz . . .'[12]

For reasons best known to themselves the Soviets had converted Domanov from a major in the Red Army to a general in the White, and also falsely made General von Pannwitz an officer in the SS. The long delay between the officers' arrival in Moscow at the beginning of June and their execution eighteen months later was doubtless due to the prolonged interrogation they would have undergone. Interesting allusions in a recent Soviet publication reveal, for example, that General Peter Krasnov was closely questioned concerning his activities at the time he endeavoured to suppress the original Bolshevik coup against Kerensky in 1917.[13]

The six generals were executed by hanging in the courtyard of the Lefortovo Prison in Moscow, presumably by the drawn-out process described so graphically by Merkulov.

The generals reserved for this special treatment had been separated from their fellow-officers shortly after their arrival at the Judenburg steel-mill. The remainder were carefully searched and interrogated, surprise being continually registered at the presence of the old émigrés. Not long after their arrival the British delivered truckloads of Cossack womenfolk, who were clamouring anxiously for husbands, brothers, fathers, sons. At night NKVD agents would appear from time to time seeking specific officers. These were taken out and not seen again. Daily consignments of groups of seven to eight hundred were removed and set off for the east. The trainloads started with batches of women and children, who were at once separated for ever from their menfolk.

During the journey from Judenburg to Graz Red Army and NKVD troops entered the wagons, plundering and beating up individual Cossacks. At Graz the prisoners were discharged into a huge wired transit-camp, where once again they had to provide full details of personal particulars. There were many suicides among those whose imagination too vividly pictured their coming fate. Watch-towers were situated at intervals round the perimeter, from which guards fired without warning at anyone approaching the wire. British troops delivering batches of Cossacks witnessed drunken sentries loosing off submachine-guns at random into the dense crowd below. An old émigré officer saw a boy of seven or eight shot dead in front of his mother; he had crossed unwittingly into a forbidden zone to relieve himself. The sentry came down, threw the small body to the ground in front of the distraught mother, and gave her a stern reprimand for permitting the boy to stray. The corpse was taken away, the mother being prevented from attending the burial.

In the centre of the transit camp at Graz was a disused underground air-raid shelter, employed now by the NKVD as death row for people who for one reason or another were to be taken no further. Every day batches of prisoners were removed to an unknown destination. Rumours abounded in the camp, but the departed prisoners' ultimate fate remained a mystery.

As the time came for each section to continue its eastward journey, the prisoners were driven to a waiting train and locked into wired cattle-wagons, fifty-four to fifty-six to a truck. At every halt NKVD guards sprang out and lined each side of the track, while others came up the line banging with wooden mallets at the sides of the trucks to ensure that no one had succeeded in loosening a plank. For the prisoners, jammed upright against the sides, these continual sudden blows were extremely painful, but their cries of protest only excited bellows of laughter from the guards outside.

The trains trundled through Hungary and Rumania, countries devastated by war and now being absorbed into socialism. Amid their fears the émigrés could not help feeling shame at the sight of returning Soviet servicemen weighed under by mountains of lumber looted from peasant homes in capitalist eastern Europe. Eventually, after four to five days' journey, the prisoners arrived at another large transit camp on the Soviet-Rumanian frontier. There they were crudely disinfected and had their heads shaved by teams of German prisoners.

Afterwards they were made to sit in columns of up to three or four hundred, ten yards apart, surrounded by Chekist machine-gunners. The old émigré N. Bezkaravainy, who later returned to the West and set down a detailed description of his ordeal, recalled how they were then addressed by a tall, thickset colonel.

'Comrades! I have come from NKVD headquarters in Moscow to keep you informed. I presume you would all like to know what they say? Comrades! I will not conceal the fact that you are bound for the Urals.'

Emboldened by this relatively courteous approach, Bezkaravainy called out, 'It's simple enough – we're off to Siberia!'

The burly Chekist answered calmly, 'Siberia is also in the Soviet Union. Yes, that's where you're going. We don't want to separate you from your families. When you get to the place arranged for you, write to your families, write and invite them to join you, and we will try to bring them to you at once.'

Bezkaravainy stood up and asked permission to speak.

'Carry on,' replied the colonel.

'What is the position of those people not liable for repatriation, who arrived here through an error?'

An unpleasant smile flickered on the officer's face, as he enquired, 'Are you an old emigrant?'

'Yes,' replied the Cossack, seized by a sudden start of irrational hope. 'Yes, I am an emigrant and a Bulgarian citizen.'

The colonel's good humour increased:

'Whether that's so or not, you fought against us and must, like all prisoners of war, serve your sentence; afterwards, if the Bulgarian Government asks for you, we'll hand you back.'

'But will the Bulgarian Government be informed that I am here?'

The colonel glanced down at him, shrugged and moved on.

The last stage of the journey took place in the manner to which the prisoners were now accustomed, in stifling, overcrowded wagons, where the prisoners gasped night and day for a breath of air or drink of water. It was notable that precautions were taken to prevent the local population from witnessing their passage. Trains would halt all day on the open steppe, in order to pass through centres of population at night-time. Next to Bezkaravainy was a Cossack of his acquaintance, who spent his waking hours praying and gazing at a photograph of his daughter.

It was through incompetence rather than malice that the prisoners were increasingly tortured by pangs of thirst. Their principal diet was scraps of salt fish, after which they received a sparse ration of dirty water issued in a rusty bucket. It was not long before even this meagre ration ran out, and Bezkaravainy goes on to describe the anguish which followed:

> People sat with gaping mouths, breathing with difficulty in the absence of sufficient air and from desperate thirst. Sweat trickled from naked bodies. Tongues swelled up and became so stiff that they could scarcely move within the mouth. Everyone took on a brutalised, horrifying appearance, and began to cry out: 'Water!' Suddenly, as if by a signal, all got up and began drumming on the sides of the wagon with mugs and tins, shrieking: 'Water! Why are you torturing us?'

The noise from some 4,500 prisoners confined in fifty wagons was incredible. The guards, somewhat unnerved, reacted in the only way known to them, jumping down and training machine-guns on the train. But their shouted threats were drowned by the mounting cacophony. Thirst had maddened the prisoners beyond reason. They were struggling for any opening they could see, gasping for breath and crying for water. Growing ever more desperate, groups began smashing at the sides with empty water-drums and wresting at the barbed wire on the windows. A Kuban Cossack managed to thrust his head through the barbed wire, gulping at the warm air outside. To shouted threats that he would be shot if he did not withdraw, he yelled despairing defiance. A volley of shots rang out, and he fell back, struck in the head.

This wounding had some effect, and people fell silent in the truck, gazing down at the body at their feet.

> A threatening murmur broke the silence.
> 'Torturers! Murderers!' And once again we recalled the English with hatred and with curses, as authors of all our misery. I never once heard the Americans or any of the other Allies cursed in this way. All hatred, all hostility and threats, were directed at the English.

Now the Chekists began opening up some of the older wagons, which they feared might not survive the battering from within, and fired random volleys inside. From Bezkaravainy's wagon the wounded Cossack was dragged out and executed with a bullet through the head on the grass by the railway track.

Water was still not forthcoming until, by what to the desperate Cossacks appeared a miracle, a shower of rain came on. There was a frantic struggle to extend mugs, hands, heads past the barbed wire, and Bezkaravainy never forgot the blessed feeling of those drops of rain which fell momentarily on his upturned face. Eventually, four hours later, a new engine arrived with a sparse supply of water – eighteen litres to be divided among each group of ninety people.

This appalling journey continued for what seemed like several weeks. From time to time groups of NKVD men would enter a wagon to conduct searches. These involved the beating and plundering of the weakened prisoners, who had almost entirely lost the use of their legs from crouching in cramped conditions for weeks on end. The ordeal continued unabated until on 10 August the train arrived at its destination, the town of Osinniki in Central Siberia. Terrible as it had been, this two months' journey formed the prelude to more dreadful sufferings.[14]

The Cossacks were for the most part distributed in a series of camps of the Gulag administration in Central Siberia.[15] Another old émigré, formerly an officer in von Pannwitz's Fifteenth Cossack Cavalry Corps, recalled how at his camp (Prokopevsk) all Soviet citizens were removed in January 1946, leaving the White officers segregated at their work. Later they were joined by a contingent of

German prisoners of war, and conditions were so harsh that an average of ten people died each day over the winter. Bezkaravainy writes:

> Those who died were buried naked. The people deputed to conduct the burials were picked up at two o'clock in the morning and supplied with spades, pickaxes and stretchers, on which they placed the frozen bodies of the dead. They had to carry them 3–4 kilometres across the snow in a frost of 30–35 degrees or worse. During the journey the frozen corpses would slide off the stretchers. Each stretcher bore three corpses and was carried by six men, stumbling through snow up to their knees. A tally with the identification number of each dead man was attached to a finger of his left hand. From the middle of 1947 they began being buried in old underclothes, and from 1951 they were interred in coffins made from plank-ends.
>
> Once arrived at the cemetery (an unenclosed area on the hillside), they began to dig the graves. The ground was frozen to a depth of one-and-a-half to two metres – not even a crowbar or pick could get through it. How many bitter, hard trials did we undergo while scratching out these graves half a metre deep and a few metres wide! It took 3–4 hours to complete one of these so-called burials before one could return to the camp. I spent about two months on this duty.

Another grim addition to an already intolerable daily round was provided by the arrival of NKVD special interrogation units. Cossack officers were hauled out at six o'clock in the evening to answer the customary pointless questions for hours on end. At five in the morning they were released, to commence the day's work an hour later. These interrogations were regularly accompanied by savage beatings alternating with spells of standing in isolation outdoors in the freezing darkness. Many Cossack officers were removed after these questionings and never seen again.

By the autumn of 1948 between 1,500 and 2,000 Cossack officers taken by the British from Lienz and handed over to the NKVD had been reduced in number to 250. Practically all who died succumbed as a result of the harsh working and living conditions, while those removed by the NKVD had virtually all gone to their execution. Four or five had been released and for some reason permitted to live as 'free citizens' in the region.

By 13 October seventy-eight old émigrés were taken from the camp in a convoy of lorries escorted by guards with machine-guns and dogs. The NKVD sergeant in charge gave a simple instruction,

regularly repeated thereafter: 'A step to the right, a step to the left –
I shall consider that an attempt to escape, and will open fire without
warning.'

Their destination was a large prison at Kuznetsk. From their place
of confinement they were summoned one by one before a senior
Chekist, who gravely informed them that under Article 58, section
4 of the penal code they were now sentenced to twenty-five years in
the 'special camps'. One of the prisoners simply burst out laughing
when told, explaining that faced with such a sentence one could only
laugh.[16]

The Cossack officers' new destination was the notorious labour
camp complex of Karaganda in Kazakhstan, where by 1949 virtually
all the old émigrés were held. Their segregation emphasises once
more that they comprised a special category in Soviet eyes. Their
task, as a survivor recalled later, was one of back-breaking endurance:

> I worked at first in a stone-quarry, and then the team to which I belonged
> was transferred to construction work. There I worked at the extraction
> of clay; for the digging they provided ten barrows on average, which in
> the course of a single day had to be completely filled with clay – that is,
> about four and a half cubic metres of clay, which had to be heaved up
> out of a hole three to four metres deep. At this work I came down to 48
> kilogrammes [7 stone 5 pounds] in weight (I am 182 centimetres [5 feet
> 10 inches] tall).

To the prisoners, half-starved, worked to their limits, and succumbing daily to appalling ill-treatment, the outside world ceased to
exist. It was ludicrous to suppose that anyone could survive his
twenty-five-year term of servitude, even if that really were the limit.
Their wives and children, also handed over by the British at Lienz,
were presumably held in similar camps somewhere in the endless
deserts and snowfields of Gulag, unlikely to survive long the cruel
conditions and vicious attentions of NKVD guards and camp criminals. Even that tiny handful who through some whim of the administration had been released was obliged to live permanently within the
same inhospitable region.

But the outside world had changed. On 5 March 1953 the Father
of Peoples died in his *dacha* at Kuntsevo. A shudder ran through the
Soviet system, from which it has yet to recover. Even the camp
guards appeared momentarily unnerved, wondering whether their
world was coming to an end. By the end of the year Khrushchev and
his allies within the Politburo felt strong enough to strike at Beria,

head of the NKVD. His execution was announced in *Pravda* on 25 December. Also shot was Beria's deputy and right-hand man, V. N. Merkulov; both were accused of having worked against the Revolution from its outset, in collusion with British Intelligence.[17]

In order to strengthen his power base within the country, Khrushchev decided to reduce drastically the enormous slave-labour force, amounting perhaps to twenty million or more people, on which the Soviet economy had in large part depended for the previous two decades. On 17 September 1955 an 'Amnesty Decree' was eventually issued by the Supreme Soviet, ending punitive measures against those people who had voluntarily or involuntarily lent aid to the Germans during the war.[18]

Measures had been put in hand before that. In August 1954 lists of prisoners in Gulag camps claiming foreign citizenship were ordered to be drawn up. On 21 September most of the surviving White émigré Cossack officers were assembled in a special camp at Churubai-Nura, forty-five kilometres from Karaganda. There they were informed that those possessing relatives living abroad would be permitted to travel to be with them. They were questioned once again about their circumstances, and were asked in addition where they planned to go and who were the relatives to whom they would apply. This concern with the matter of the relatives may suggest that the Soviet Government's motive in permitting these émigrés to leave arose at least in part from a desire to avoid embarrassing pressures such relatives might apply on their respective governments, at a time when Khrushchev was seeking to project a more civilised image at home and abroad.

Not long after their transfer the old émigré prisoners were allowed much milder treatment and fed better preparatory to departing for the West. For the most part they were finally permitted to go in the latter half of 1955 and the spring of 1956.[19] One of those who was released, Colonel Alexander Protopopov, drew up in 1957 a list of the survivors. Eleven stayed in the Soviet Union, either through choice (five went to the old Don Cossack territory) or because they were stateless and so did not possess foreign citizenship. Twelve went to Soviet-occupied Rumania and Bulgaria, and to Titoist Yugoslavia. Finally, thirty-one actually re-emerged into different countries of Western Europe.[20]

There may have been one or two others unaccounted for, but it is clear that in all not more than some three score old émigrés from among the Cossack officers survived out of the thousand and more secretly handed over by the British at Judenburg: roughly five per cent. There appears to have been no trace of the unknown number of women, children, civilians and other ranks included in the total Cossack handover. The survival rate of the women, children and old people is likely to have been small, and it may well be that all died.

Those officers who did return to the West were for the most part broken in health and utterly destitute. The handover of the Cossacks in 1945 had been concealed from the press and was entirely unknown to the Western public at large. There was no likelihood of the story's becoming at all widely known, nor if it were of its obtaining any credence. Incoherent accusations made by shabby, excitable foreigners could only excite sympathy or derision. And yet the presence of the returned old émigrés was potentially explosive. Their comrades who had escaped repatriation could naturally testify to their fate, but that was not the same thing as the first-hand evidence of men who had themselves undergone this entirely illegal and unauthorised ill-treatment. It is quite possible that, had they fallen into the right hands, they could have taken legal proceedings which, whether successful or not, would have aroused the most embarrassing enquiries.

That this did not happen was due mostly to the pathetic circumstances of the homeless refugees, and also to the fact that the conspiracy which had sent them back to the Soviets was still so closely-guarded a secret as to be known only to its organisers. The old émigrés were simply unaware that their return had been contrary to British policy, and could not therefore exploit the one aspect which might have done untold damage to their hidden persecutors.

Nevertheless enquiries were directed to the authorities. On 17 July 1947 an enquiry from a Mrs Tiashelnikov was forwarded by Major Tufton Beamish, MP, to the Foreign Office. Presumably a relative of one of the Cossacks returned, she was enquiring 'regarding the whereabouts and possibly to secure the return of the people repatriated to the USSR'. The Foreign Office made enquiries of the War Office. By November a report outlining events in Austria in May and June 1945 was received from HQ British troops in Austria, which declared among other things, 'That everything possible was done at this period to prevent non-Soviet Nationals being included with those to be evacuated.' This aspect was stressed – there is no reason to believe with anything other than good faith – in the Foreign Office reply to Major Beamish, which went on to regret that there was no possible way of tracing prisoners within the Soviet Union.[21]

So the matter appears to have rested for some years, aired only in émigré publications perused for the most part exclusively by émigrés. Then, on 28 February 1953, the émigré Cossack Major-General Ivan Polyakov wrote to the British Prime Minister, Winston Churchill, who had entered on his second term of office. In a well-written, temperate and accurate account of events at Lienz, Polyakov appealed to the Prime Minister to look into the matter, which in the number of people involved exceeded the well-publicised massacre of Polish officers at Katyn. Not long before, Polyakov pointed out, an article on the subject had appeared in a Dutch daily newspaper: 'German newspapers pointedly remarked that the accusations came not from former enemies but from a Western ally, and voiced the opinion that atrocities should be investigated regardless of who perpetrated them, especially in the case of Lienz where there are hundreds of witnesses easily available.'

In his letter Polyakov strongly emphasised the fact that many were not Soviet citizens. Citing the prominent examples of Krasnov and Shkuro, he went on:

> Neither had ever been a Soviet citizen. Like thousands of other Cossacks they had left Russia in November 1920, and since that date had lived in foreign countries. General Shkuro was a Yugoslav citizen . . . The Kremlin rulers made it clear to their subjects that the Western Democracies had delivered to the Soviet authorities every person they wanted. Not only deserters from the Red Army, but also anti-Communist leaders who thirty years ago tried to save Russia from Communism. Russian officers and soldiers who had never been members of the Red Army nor Soviet citizens. Even Russians born in foreign countries.

The General concluded with a polite but vigorous request for an enquiry 'to establish the true offenders . . .'

This may well have been the first occasion that Churchill was made aware that large numbers of non-Soviet citizens had been handed over. He was clearly disturbed by the allegation, and on 27 April the head of the Northern Department of the Foreign Office, Henry Hohler, wrote to the Under-Secretary of State at the War Office outlining the allegations made by General Polyakov:

> Her Majesty's Embassy, Washington have been instructed to send a non-committal acknowledgment, but in case the matter is pursued or raised in Parliament Sir Winston Churchill desires to be in possession of all the available facts.
> It is believed that the men referred to were members of the Pannwitz

Cossack Corps, which fought in the German army under the title XVth S.S. Cossack Corps and that their repatriation was carried out under an agreement signed in Vienna on the 23rd of May, 1945 between General Alexander and the Soviet authorities, which derived its authority from the Yalta Agreement. No copy of the agreement signed by General Alexander exists in the Foreign Office archives, and Sir Winston Churchill will accordingly be grateful if he may be furnished with a copy of its text, together with any additional relevant information.

On 19 May Brigadier H. B. Latham of the Cabinet Office replied to explain that, after a careful search of the appropriate records, 'We have so far been unable to trace a copy of any agreement signed by General Alexander authorising this repatriation.' The file[22] contains no further developments, and it appears that Churchill had to rest content with this rather unsatisfactory outcome of the enquiry.

The failure to find the text of Alexander's agreement is scarcely surprising, in view of the fact that it never existed. The Field-Marshal was not in Vienna on 23 May 1945, and the date bears no obvious relationship to the succession of orders concerning the Cossacks passing between AFHQ and the Eighth Army at that time. As this is the first time this canard appears to have been aired, it looks as if someone with close access to the Prime Minister, someone whom presumably he would expect to have direct knowledge of the matter, had proffered this false information. The intention was apparently twofold: first, to identify the largely non-combatant Cossacks at Lienz with von Pannwitz's fighting Corps, and to claim falsely in turn that they formed part of the SS; and second, to place responsibility for the handovers squarely on the shoulders of Field-Marshal Alexander.

These enquiries were pursued in the absence of the Cossacks, who were still toiling and dying in Soviet forced-labour camps. After the trickle of surviving old émigrés had been permitted by Khrushchev to return to Western Europe in 1955–57, a group of fourteen of them, headed by Colonel Alexander Protopopov, and describing themselves as the 'Union of Cossack Officers emigrated in 1920 who returned from the Soviet concentration camps in 1956/7', petitioned Queen Elizabeth II for assistance. In reply they received the customary polite acknowledgment, and there the matter might have rested but for the sympathetic interest of an English journalist, Peter Huxley-Blythe.

After correspondence and discussion, Huxley-Blythe arranged for a more detailed petition to be drawn up, in the following terms:

Petition

We, the undersigned, are Cossacks who fought against Communism in Russia from November, 1917, until 1920. In December, 1920, we were forced to emigrate with the Army of General Wrangel to Yugoslavia. There King Alexander received us warmly, finding work for all the soldiers and granting generous pensions to the aged.

In October, 1944, we were again forced to leave our homes, our second homeland of Yugoslavia, fleeing before the Communists to find refuge in Lienz, Austria. There we were arrested by British troops and handed over to the Red Army at Judenburg, Austria, on the 29th May, 1945.

We were arrested on the orders of General Alexander of the 8th British Army while the extradition to the Red Army was organised by Lieut. Colonel Malcolm and Major Davies. When we were arrested they gave us their word of honour that we would not be handed over to the Red Army, In spite of this we were extradited. Those who did not go voluntarily or tried to escape were either shot or beaten with rifles. British soldiers searched us and took our watches, money, and other valuables.

On May 28, 1945, at 6:00 p.m. we learnt that we were to be handed over to the Soviets. We lodged a formal protest and produced our documents to prove to Lieut. Colonel Malcolm that we were old émigrés. He told us that we could show our documents to Joseph Stalin. Following this we immediately wrote letters to King George VI of England, to the British commander, to King Peter of Yugoslavia, and to His Holiness Pope Pius XII and gave these letters to Lieut. Colonel Malcolm. No answers were received.

Early in the morning of May 29, 1945, we were rounded up and transported from Lienz to Judenburg under armed guard. We were, upon arrival, handed over to the Red Army. General Dolmatov then took charge of us. He told us that he was astonished the British had extradited old émigrés as the Soviets had only demanded that the Western Allies extradite those persons who had been Soviet citizens.

As a result of our extradition we were all sentenced to 11–12 years in prison camps in Siberia, where we were forced to undertake the hardest work. Now we are old, ill, and unable to work for our living.

We therefore entreat Her Majesty the Queen of England and the British Government, who were responsible for our misfortunes, to grant us sufficient compensation for those lost 11–12 years we spent in Soviet prison camps.

This request was accompanied by a separate letter from Captain Anatol Petrovsky, which emphasised still more pointedly the illegality of the operation; though Petrovsky, like his fellows, naturally imagined that it was the British Government which had ordained the handover.

I am a Russian émigré [he began] and a former fighter against Communism in the ranks of the White Army in 1919–1920.

After the defeat of the White Army in the Crimea I was forced to leave my Motherland – Russia – and enter the Kingdom of Yugoslavia where I lived, studied, worked and served until April, 1941, i.e. the capitulation of Yugoslavia.

On May 28, 1945 . . . I was betrayed and handed over to the Soviet frontier forces of the M.V.D. . . .

From 1945 to 1956 I was kept in various Soviet concentration camps, having been condemned, without trial, to a term of 10 to 26 years' imprisonment. [Due to] The long years of suffering and separation from my relatives, being held as a criminal in the mines of Siberia, Vorkuta, and other places, I have lost my strength and health. As a result I am unable to undertake any real work and am forced to live as a displaced person, receiving only token support from the town hall.

Taking into consideration the fact that I was handed over to the Soviets, an illegal action, as the British Military Command knew I was not a Soviet citizen, I feel justified in applying to and requesting that Her Britannic Majesty, Queen Elizabeth II, grant me material aid to compensate for the years of Soviet imprisonment, 1945–56, and so recompense me for loss of health and allow me to live out my remaining years without facing starvation.

Here at long last was the damning evidence concealed for so long from the British Government. Contrary to instructions issued beforehand and reports compiled afterwards, the old émigrés *had* knowingly been surrendered to the Soviets. It was Churchill who had arranged the rescue of Petrovsky and his comrades from Bolshevik vengeance in 1920, and Churchill who in July 1945 'urged Alexander to be particularly careful to see to it that no force was used to persuade anyone to return to his native country.' Much more recently the same issue of principle had arisen at the close of the Korean War. In 1952 Churchill wrote to Eden, declaring, 'It is a matter of honour to us not to force a non-Communist prisoner of war to go back, to be murdered in Communist China. This is not a matter of argument, but one of the fundamental principles for which we fight and, if necessary, die.'[23] How would Churchill feel were he, six years later, to learn the truth concerning the extraordinary act of betrayal secretly executed in the name of his government, but contrary to all his inclinations and instructions?

Regrettably, though we may readily guess, we shall never know what Churchill's reaction would have been. For by 1958 he was no longer Prime Minister. It was his successor who received the surviving Cossacks' petition; a man who, by a quirk of historical chance, had in 1945 been still closer to the forgotten operations which brought about such untold suffering and misery. He, however, saw events in an altogether different light. It was the former Minister Resident in the Mediterranean, the Right Honourable Harold Macmillan, who now occupied Number Ten, Downing Street. What we do know is that the letters were passed by the Prime Minister to the Foreign Office, from whom the Cossacks learned: 'A thorough examination of the facts led to the conclusion that no action could be taken to assist the persons named in your letter.'[24]

10

The Arrival of the Field-Marshal

'Camp in high spirits, 'cos F.M. said they wouldn't be sent back Yugo'. (Diary of Jane Balding, Red Cross nurse in Viktring Camp, 4 June 1945)

The repatriation operations which sent tens of thousands of Cossacks and Yugoslavs to their deaths at the end of May and beginning of June 1945 were conducted under conditions of maximum haste and secrecy. The extensive use of violence and deception had not been authorised by higher authority, and the return of non-Soviet émigré Russians had been expressly forbidden in all instructions emanating from AFHQ and the Eighth Army. Troops in the field swiftly grew resentful of their unsoldierly task, and dangerous questions were beginning to be pressed concerning the issue of citizenship and rumours of massacres across the Yugoslav frontier. How long might it be before these awkward topics reached the ears of General McCreery or Field-Marshal Alexander? Speed was of the essence if Macmillan's commitment were to be satisfactorily fulfilled.

At least the return of the Serbian and Slovene military and para-military units had passed off without a hitch. Unable to believe that their British friends and (in the case of the Chetniks) allies would betray them to Tito, with whom the British had a week earlier been on the point of war, they trusted implicitly in the good faith of British officers who assured them they were travelling to join their comrades in North Italy.

The fate of the Yugoslav military personnel in Viktring Camp was without doubt cruel, shameful and unnecessary. However, those at Fifth Corps headquarters responsible for the operation were now preparing to initiate a deed of violence if possible still more terrible in its implications. It will be recalled that the stream of panic-stricken refugees fleeing through the Loibl-Pass tunnel before Tito sealed the frontier included large numbers of civilian refugees. At Viktring they had been sifted from the para-military units and placed in a camp about a mile away. On 20 May they constituted 2,450 men, 3,000 women and 550 children: a total of 6,000.

Now it was planned to deliver all these defenceless people over to the killing ground. On 23 May an order had been extracted from AFHQ which conceded 'that all Jugoslav nationals in Eighth Army area should be returned by you to Jugoslavs unless this involves use of force'; otherwise they were to be evacuated to join their compatriots at Distone in Italy. At first the order had been effectively implemented by the ingenious method of assuring prisoners entering the transports 'on the word of a British officer' that they were travelling to Italy. On the night of 26 May a Serbian Chetnik returned to camp with a first-hand account of their true destination and fate at the hands of the Partisans, and this news spread swiftly, causing deep concern both to the threatened Yugoslavs and British officers responsible for the transportation. It was no longer possible to evade the implications of the Field-Marshal's directive by resort to deception.

The Fifth Corps' reaction to stiffening Slovenian resistance was to disobey AFHQ's restriction on the use of force, and henceforward violence was employed to whatever degree was found necessary to enforce compliance with orders. On 28 May Slovenian Domobranci who objected to entering the transports were informed by a British officer that he would use force should they continue to disobey. On the same day the Slovenian commander, General Krenner, visited the headquarters of the Sixth Armoured Division in Klagenfurt, where he was handed a written instruction confirming that General Murray had received orders to employ force against recalcitrants. On 30 May scenes of violence took place in Viktring Camp, resulting in considerable brutality.

Whatever the motives for returning military and para-military personnel held at Viktring, it is hard to see why those responsible for this policy felt impelled to go on to include the civilians. It certainly cannot have been because the Fifth Corps lacked facilities to look after so relatively small a number; nor could it have seemed likely that Tito's troops (now safely behind the Karavanke range) would resort to arms in an attempt to recover them. In the absence of any other obvious motive, it seems possible that those who were so flagrantly prepared to disobey AFHQ's orders of 17 and 23 May, flouting the Supreme Allied Commander's emphatically reiterated instructions that no one should be unwillingly repatriated, feared that the survival of any witnesses might bring the nature of their activities into the open. The only effective way of silencing the civilians was to include them for return to Tito, who as was known had effective ways of removing such inconvenient people from circulation. For whatever reason, it was decided that evacuation of the civilian refugees would commence on 1 June, the day after the departure of the last major batch of Domobranci.

The camp for civilians at Viktring had since 19 May been under the command of an officer from Allied Military Government – AMGOT. This was Major P. H. Barre, a thirty-eight-year-old Canadian seconded from the Royal Montreal Regiment. On VE Day he had found himself at Ferrara, whence he moved up into Austria with the occupying forces. At Klagenfurt he was ordered to go down to sort out what was reported to be a huge conglomeration of refugees at Viktring. Assigned a young Austrian Luftwaffe officer as driver and interpreter, he drove over to see what was happening.

> We went down there [he explained recently to me] and we saw this group. We didn't know who they were, and we made enquiries. They had walked over the Karavanke Mountains with their horses and cattle and sheep and bicycles and roller-skates and whatever else. They were in family groups: the wagon, horses, tethered to their group, with their father, mother, and all the children and aunts and uncles around the wagon. They were all mixed up, because although they came from Ljubljana and around there, they were not all necessarily acquainted with one another. They got acquainted there. My job – I was alone at that moment – my job was 'what do I do with all these people?'

Barre's first move was to organise a camp committee, whose president was a highly-respected Slovene doctor, Valentin Mersol, who had studied at Johns Hopkins University, and consequently spoke English. Between them they soon had the camp running remarkably efficiently. Barre managed to procure Army water-purifiers to provide drinking-water from a stream running through the centre of the enclosure, organised a hospital in a neighbouring golf club, billeting where necessary in houses of the local Austrians, and detailed an unarmed camp police to maintain order. This proved scarcely necessary, as he found the Slovenes hard-working and co-operative people only too anxious to assist their sympathetic commandant. They in turn organised their own schools, run by their nuns and priests.

Shortly afterwards Barre was joined by an energetic Red Cross nurse, Jane Balding. The task Barre and she faced was a daunting one, though by no means unusual at that chaotic time. On 23 May Jane noted in her diary:

> Went out to new camp at Viktring . . . amazing sight 6,000 odd men, women & children encamped in open on one side & 11,000 soldiers on other [these were the Chetniks, Domobranci and others, whose repatriation was to begin the next morning]. All fugitives from Tito. Tanks & armed British guards all round as Tito's mob threaten to massacre them all. Like some fantastic film . . . Nearby factory . . . houses most of children & mothers, took small baby to civilian hospital in Clagenfurt . . . chased round all afternoon trying to lay on milk for camp.

Though it was the end of May, appalling weather made conditions in the camp very unpleasant. On 24 May, she records, 'Pelted with rain all night; was afraid I'd find camp washed out.' Jane found Major Barre a 'grand sort', and travelled around with him, raiding former Nazi offices for paper for the Slovene schoolchildren and begging linen for the medical hut. On 25 May, '500 more refugees arrived last night at our camp. Wish I had seen them – mostly men in full uniform on horseback, behind came women (? camp followers) mostly in bare feet!'

John Corsellis, a young volunteer with the Friends' (Quaker) Ambulance Unit who arrived in the camp the day after Jane Balding, shared her high estimate of Barre's character. As he wrote to his mother at the time:

> At the Slovene camp the British workers number four: two Red Cross women, a French-Canadian major i/c and myself. One Red Cross woman [Jane Balding] is a parson's sister and a mixture of North Country and Irish, has a biggish heart but is pretty impossible in every other way – very full of herself and how she does things, with a nurse's outlook, etc., etc. [it is only fair to note that Jane Balding's diary includes some mild reflections on Corsellis's capability!] but the other [Florence Phillips] is Scotch, has imagination and ability and should be easy to work with. The major [Barre] is a charming and self-effacing man, who is very patient with the refugees, does his best for them and certainly does not try to 'manage' his staff.

On the twenty-sixth came the first murmur that something sinister was taking place in the neighbouring military camp, and Jane Balding recorded in her diary learning of 'awful tales of returned refugees being murdered in tunnels; main question seems to be, do they return to be murdered or stay here & starve or die of pneumonia if they are not under cover soon. Incessant pelting spring rains – camp one huge swamp.' But as yet Jane Balding and Major Barre could not bring themselves to believe that the refugees really were being sent back to Yugoslavia to be slaughtered. On the twenty-eighth Jane noted, 'camp thinning out; Chetniks (troops) being taken off to P.O.W. cage'. By this she presumably meant the Yugoslav Royalist camp at Distone in Italy, to which the Chetniks were told they were going.

Major Barre, instead of simply attempting to suppress alarmist reports, endeavoured on every occasion to ensure that those who claimed inside knowledge of what was occurring should be permitted an open hearing: better this than gossip proliferating. He himself continued to reject the notion that his British colleagues were capable of luring the refugees to their deaths, and when on 29 May he was asked outright whether this was the case, replied indignantly, 'Do you think that the British could really do something like that?'

Nevertheless he was sufficiently disturbed by the persistence of the rumours to make enquiries among his British colleagues and superiors. They, too, had received alarming reports, but could neither confirm nor deny them.

By Wednesday, 30 May the Domobranci command was completely persuaded of the accuracy of reports of British betrayal and Partisan atrocities brought back by Ljotic (whose dramatic escape from the train was described in chapter six) and others. The news was swift to reach the neighbouring civilian camp. Mrs Nina Lencek, then a twenty-one-year-old former student whose parents had volunteered to travel 'to Italy' on the first day of the operation, vividly recalls the atmosphere that prevailed during the last few days of May: 'There was a terrible sadness. Every family had lost their sons, their fathers, their loved ones, who had been returned.'

The stories had become far too consistent to be dismissed any more as idle rumour-mongering, and Jane Balding became extremely concerned with the responsibility imposed upon her by the Red Cross code. The bustling manner which had mildly irritated Corsellis at their first encounter reflected a strong-minded determination once aroused not easily deflected. As Mrs Lencek recalled: 'she had white hair, quite small, very energetic and matter-of-fact. She was running from one tent to another, seeing to it that people were clean, and organised what they needed.' Jane Balding also felt deep sympathy for the pathetic plight of her charges. Mrs Lencek was shortly afterwards transferred to a camp at Spittal, where one day in the barracks she broke down and told Jane of her parents' fate: 'I was crying, and she was crying with me. She was very compassionate.'

Never one to hesitate over what she regarded as a moral principle, Jane instigated drastic action. Her diary entry for 30 May is brief but revealing. Accompanied by John Corsellis, she went 'round camp – ashamed to pass my [refugee] friends – militia almost gone from camp, camp in state – think they've gone back to Tito – Red X resigning in body unless they get lowdown.' Next day Major Barre joined in taking vigorous action to check what was happening, as Jane Balding's diary relates: 'very unhappy atmosphere in camp – much silent weeping – persistent rumours of militia being disarmed & sent back to Tito – must get position clear.' During the afternoon she went with Major Barre and the Slovenian camp leader, Dr Mersol, to tour some hospitals. By five o'clock they were back in Viktring, where sinister tidings awaited them: 'returned to camp – civilians to be removed tomorrow – left Major B. to find out where & why.'

What follows is taken from Dr Mersol's account, substantiated by Major Barre. At his improvised headquarters office in Viktring, Barre found awaiting him an order to repair to the headquarters of the neighbouring military camp, where he would receive instructions concerning the forced repatriation of civilian refugees from Viktring. Major Barre did not conceal the nature of his message from Dr Mersol, whose outrage could not be restrained.

'Well, well!' he exclaimed; 'it is true, isn't it, Major Barre, that the British are sending our people to their deaths in Yugoslavia?'

Barre turned pale. He was suddenly faced with the reality of what he had been able to dismiss hitherto as idle talk among a large body of men starved of information. He had come to like and respect the people entrusted to his care, and judged by their desperate aversion to returning home that they had good reason to fear ill-treatment at the hands of Tito's regime. He came to a swift decision.

Turning to Mersol, Barre requested him to accompany him to the military camp. Lieutenant Ames, the camp commandant, ordered Mersol to wait outside his office. Barre, however, insisted that the presence of the president of the Slovenian civilians' committee was essential, and they both entered. Shrugging, Ames pointed to a message lying on his desk.

'I have orders,' he explained abruptly, 'to bus 2,700 Slovenian refugees. They will leave the camp tomorrow, June 1st. 1,500 of them will be transported to the station in Bleiburg; 1,200 go to Rosenbach. People must be ready for departure by 5 a.m. Trucks will drive them to the depot for boarding the trains.'

Before the deeply troubled Barre could reply, Dr Mersol broke in with an indignant appeal:

'The British have repatriated the Slovenian refugees to Yugoslavia. They handed them over to the Communists, who, as our reports tell us, are slaughtering them. Your present orders prove to me that Domobranci have indeed been sent to Yugoslavia, and this in spite of your word of honour and of the promises that they would be sent to Italy. Up to this moment, I could not believe that the British, whom we Slovenes hold in such high esteem, whose protection we sought, whose shot-down pilots we rescued during the last war . . . I myself have saved the lives of many British soldiers during World War I, offering help and medical assistance . . . I could not believe that the British would be capable of committing such a crime, of betraying their friends who have done no wrong – Slovenes whom you have granted asylum and protection. I could not believe that the British would send these innocent people to their deaths in Yugoslavia. I beg you, Major Barre, do everything in your power to stop further deportations!'

Barre was faced with the same agonising moment of truth encountered by 'Rusty' Davies of the Argylls three days earlier, when he was first informed of the decision to surrender his Cossack charges to the Soviets. There were significant personal differences, however. Davies was a youthful (twenty-five-year-old) temporary officer, snatched by the exigencies of total war from the bank where he worked in a Welsh provincial town. Knowing little or nothing of the international situation, he allowed his compassionate feelings for the Cossacks to be overruled by his innate respect for military discipline, inculcated during hard years of war, and more specifically his regard for the superior judgement and education of his commanding officer.

Barre, on the other hand, was a considerably older and more experienced man. As a member of AMGOT [Allied Military Government of Occupied Territory] his relations with his superiors lacked the intense bonds of loyalty which life in a wartime battalion mess engenders. He was, moreover, a Canadian, and hence able to stand a little aside from considerations influencing British units around him. Finally, whereas Davies had only the Cossacks' evident fears as a guide to their likely fate, Barre like everyone else around Klagenfurt possessed first-hand knowledge of the Partisans' brutality, and in particular of their repeated attempts immediately after the refugees' surrender to assassinate groups within Viktring Camp.

Meanwhile Lieutenant Ames was angrily ordering Dr Mersol to be silent, and not meddle with British Army orders. Turning back to Barre, Ames ordered him to have the required 2,700 civilian refugees paraded at dawn next day for the first consignment. But Barre, horrified by the treachery and cruelty implicit in the order, and indignant at the way he had been kept in the dark until now, declared that he would seek confirmation of the instruction from his superiors at AMGOT in Klagenfurt.

His own car having broken down, Barre borrowed Ames's and set off for Klagenfurt with Mersol beside him. Mersol took advantage of this to press home on the sympathetic Canadian the true nature of what the British intended. The handover involved a clear violation of international law. British officers had repeatedly lied in order to deceive the Chetniks and Domobranci into going peacefully to their deaths, and now they were planning to add to this crime the slaughter of helpless civilians entrusted to their charge. How could the Major lend a hand to such a barbaric act? Barre could not conceal his deep emotional disturbance.

At Klagenfurt they drove up to the Rathaus to consult with Major William Johnson of AMGOT. It was six o'clock in the evening. The interview began with Dr Mersol's repeating his impassioned plea, after which he was requested to leave the room. In an agony of apprehension Mersol waited outside while a clock ticked out half an hour. From Johnson's office came repeated sounds of telephone calls being made and received. Finally Major Barre appeared at the door and ushered the doctor in. Major Johnson offered him a chair. Silence fell on the room for a few moments. Then Major Johnson leaned forward to declare, 'We have decided that the civilians will not be sent to Yugoslavia against their will. Only those who wish to return may go.'

Mersol could hardly believe his ears. At best he had expected long and complex negotiations, yet here, within half an hour, the whole policy had been abruptly reversed! It seemed too good to be true. Fearful lest this might represent some new British act of deception, Mersol stammered out his thanks and began explaining just what would happen to his people should they ever be permitted to reach Tito's extermination camps. Johnson interrupted brusquely, assuring the doctor, 'You don't have to inform me about conditions in

Yugoslavia. I know quite well what's going on there. That's why we have decided to do what I have told you.'

Barre and Mersol returned, exultant, to Viktring. A suspicious Lieutenant Ames had to be placated by the obtention of written confirmation that the entire policy of forced repatriation had been effectively halted, but nothing could now mar Dr Mersol's jubilation. The joyful news quickly spread through the camp, and a notice was posted announcing the end of forced repatriation, and requiring a list of names of volunteers only. As Jane Balding noted in her diary two days later, 'camp has option of returning to Yugoslavia – 150 out of 6,012 were for it, then backed out – persistent rumours of unarmed militia being handed over to Tito.'

This episode is of intrinsic interest, providing as it does a happy example of a large number of refugees being saved from the cruel end to which they had been consigned. Its deeper significance lies in the evidence it provides of a dramatic reversal of policy which took place at Fifth Corps headquarters during the last two days of May.

In the preceding week vigorous objections to repatriating Cossacks by so senior an officer as General Arbuthnott had been flatly rejected at the Fifth Corps. A large body of Cossacks was shifted from the Sixth Armoured Divisional area, seemingly because it was feared that General Murray might decline to be as thorough in rounding them up as was required. Captain Nicolson was severely reprimanded merely for expressing his distaste for the policy of surrendering Yugoslavs to Tito. Up to about 28 or 29 May the forced repatriation operations had been pushed through with maximum – indeed excessive – thoroughness. As has been described, Arbuthnott and Musson were ordered to ignore screening provisions for Cossacks, the notorious 'deception tactics' lured tens of thousands to their deaths, and the Slovene civilians had been added to the category of repatriables. Now, suddenly, the whole atmosphere had changed.

Two days earlier a similarly remarkable example of a radical reversal of the previously rigid policy had occurred in respect of the Cossacks still held by General Horatius Murray's Sixth Armoured Division. Among the officers of the Fifteenth Cossack Cavalry Corps was a number of old émigrés, recruited from Paris and elsewhere during the war. Numerically and in rank they were far less obtrusive than the distinguished group of generals and other officers known to be held by the Seventy-eighth Infantry Division at Lienz. As a result it was not until the eleventh hour, when the Cossacks were being rounded up for handover on 29 May, that Major Henry Howard of the First King's Royal Rifle Corps was approached by a Cossack officer, speaking fluent French, who asked him if it could really be intended to betray a former officer of the Tsar, brought out of Russia in a British warship in 1919, to the Bolsheviks? There were others, too, among his fellow-officers in the same position.

Greatly disturbed, Howard initiated a hasty enquiry which swiftly brought to light an embarrassing contradiction in Brigadier Toby Low's order of 21 May. As the War Diary of the Third Welsh Guards describes it:

> Corps order . . . [contained] a definition of a Soviet Citizen as (amongst other qualifications) someone who has been in the Soviet Union since 1930 . . . Since our order stated definitely that only Soviet Citizens were to be sent back to Russia, but at the same time specifically classed our particular concentration as Soviet Citizens, these two orders were completely at variance since the 50 Cossacks concerned had not been in the Soviet Union since 1920. There was at once a mad rush for telephones, the transport was held, interrogators were rushed to the scene and the answer came back that a reprieve was possible. Interrogation produced the answer expected, namely that the party of 50 were in the non-Soviet Citizen category and amidst, it must be admitted, a general rejoicing they were returned to their cage.

This 'timely reprieve', as Colonel Robin Rose Price went on to note in his War Diary, 'came from 5 Corps.'[1]

Now, on 31 May, at the first objection by a junior Canadian officer in AMGOT, an entire camp of 6,000 people listed for handover in Brigadier Low's order of 19 May was reprieved without argument! As Major Barre says, 'I am quite sure – and I'm speaking now as truthfully as I can – I'm quite sure that Johnson must have had knowledge of the stoppage before he told me. Because I think it came too *easily* . . . I'm sure that Johnson *must* have been advised (I wouldn't say "ordered", because I don't think it would come as an order) – but been advised, "well, all right, drop this matter, this won't happen now." . . . I'm sure it came from much higher.'

'Much higher' ultimately meant the Corps Commander, General Keightley. In practical terms, though, the repatriation operations came under the control of Keightley's Chief of Staff, Toby Low. It was he who issued all the orders originating and establishing the policy, and in fact, as he informed me recently, 'I was given the remit by the Corps Commander to handle the Yugoslav situation . . . I would tell him every day what was happening, though he was not involved.'

But by 29 May, when Colonel Howard made his enquiry concerning the status of White Russians, and on 31 May, when Major Barre protested against the return of Slovene civilians, decisions were no longer being made by Brigadier Low, but by his successor in office. As Low explains, 'On or about May 29th, 1945 I left Austria to return to England to fight a seat in the General Election. Since I won the seat I did not return to Austria afterwards.'[2] The BGS thereafter was Major-General Edward 'Dolly' de Fonblanque. It is hard not to believe that we have here the factor which brought about so sudden and revolutionary a change in policy; a change which, as will shortly be seen, General Keightley made only the feeblest effort to frustrate.

It is interesting to note, however, that it was thought necessary to conceal from higher authority the true reason for this sudden and unintended abandonment of Fifth Corps policy of returning all Yugoslavs regardless of their wishes. On the day of Barre's successful protest, 31 May, AFHQ was informed that the remaining Slovenes at Viktring had discovered what awaited them on the further side of the frontier, and had in consequence refused to obey the order to go. As has been seen, nothing of the sort had happened. Though the Slovenes were indeed fearful of return, the first they learned of the order arranging the evacuation for 1 June was when Barre and Mersol returned from Klagenfurt with the news that it had been withdrawn.

It was not the Slovenes' refusal to return that halted the policy: Slovenes had after all been unsuccessfully refusing to return since 27 May. The true reason, as will now be seen, was quite different, and it was this the hasty retraction of the order and falsified report to AFHQ were clearly designed to conceal.

The sudden decision to drop the policy, and the concealment of the true reason for this volte-face, could scarcely have occurred had there been reason to believe that AFHQ would approve the Fifth Corps' brutal operations. This is surely sufficient refutation of any suggestion that Alexander's order of 23 May authorising the Fifth Corps to return Yugoslav citizens without the use of force was simply a blind, intended to provide cover for an operation he did not care openly to avow.

The secret decision taken on or about 13 May not to return the Ukrainian SS Division and *Russkii Corpus* is indicative of the range and nature of the planning which initiated forced repatriation operations within the Fifth Corps area. The decision not to hand over the Slovenian civilians which halted the operations is still more revealing.

There can be no doubt that the Fifth Corps was deeply committed to the return of all the inmates of Viktring Camp. The same evening (23 May) that authority to deliver the Yugoslavs at Viktring to Tito was obtained from AFHQ, the executive Movement Order was issued in Viktring Camp. During the week that followed exceptional measures were adopted in order to ensure the return of all military personnel, including explicit instructions to employ whatever force might prove necessary.

On the thirty-first the last convoy of Slovenian soldiers departed, and the Camp Commandant issued orders for the evacuation of civilian personnel on the following day. Nevertheless when Major Barre came to lodge his objection, he was surprised to find himself pushing at an open door. It was clear to him that a decision had already been made to abandon the operation, though for what reason he was unaware. Barre was right in his guess: another more influential objection had been lodged that day, which explains Major Johnson's grim comment that he knew quite well what was happening to the prisoners in Yugoslavia, and why the plan for returning the refugees was so suddenly abandoned.

The Assistant Commissioner for Military Government in Austria was John Selby-Bigge, whose headquarters were in the Rathaus in Klagenfurt. The Dowager Lady Falmouth, then also working with the Red Cross, described to me what he told her shortly afterwards. Selby-Bigge himself had frequent occasion to visit Viktring Camp, and his story confirms that the Fifth Corps addressed its deception tactics not only to the returning Chetniks but also the Red Cross. (As late as 28 May Jane Balding was led to believe 'Chetniks (troops) being taken to P.O.W. camp'.)

As Lady Falmouth explained, Selby-Bigge was informed that:

there was this direction from the high command that those [Serbs and Slovenes] who wished to return should go, and quite a large party of them went. They were all delivered over the frontier into Yugoslavia, and a short time after they'd gone one of them came back to say that when they got there they'd all been put up against a wall and shot – or, anyhow, liquidated. This man had escaped and said to his friends: 'now, whatever you do, don't go'. So when the next lot of them were due to go, they refused. There was a good deal of difficulty in the camp. Nobody more was sent. But they [presumably, the Camp Commandant] reported back to the Corps Commander, Keightley, that they didn't want to go.

He [Keightley] saw Selby-Bigge, who was the Red Cross representative, who got on very well with them [the Chetniks], who evidently accepted his advice. [Keightley] said to him that he wanted him to encourage them to go. To which he replied that he didn't think he could, because this report had come back, which appeared to be authentic, and the Red Cross couldn't do that. They couldn't encourage people to do a thing that they didn't want to do, when it was obviously difficult.

Keightley was very insistent, saying it was an order from higher up, and on Selby-Bigge's refusing he said, 'well, this is an order!' To which Selby-Bigge said, 'well, I'm very sorry, sir, but I'm not under your command: I'm an official of the Red Cross, and I'm afraid I can't do this.' So Keightley said, 'very well, you must go', and sent him back to England. To which Selby-Bigge said: 'of course I quite understand. I'll go back and report to my people. I can't do it.' That was the end of the interview. As he went out of the door, Keightley said: 'it's all right, they won't go'. And they didn't.

It was on Thursday, 31 May that the Fifth Corps reported the refusal of the remaining Domobranci to go, and it was probably the previous day that Selby-Bigge held this interview with Keightley. A few weeks later General Keightley was to tell Lady Limerick, the Vice-Chairman of the British Red Cross, 'that he had had a talk with Selby-Bigge, who had evidently spoken rather strongly about the return of Displaced Persons to their countries, when they were not willing to go, and had said that he was recommending the withdrawal of our personnel. General Keightley was very disturbed by this . . .' It was on the evening of 30 May that Jane Balding noted in her diary that the Red Cross would resign in a body unless they received reassurances as to the safety of the Slovenian civilians. This must have been at Selby-Bigge's instructions.

Keightley, as has been seen, promptly backed down when faced by Selby-Bigge's protest. As Nigel Gosling, a Red Cross colleague, noted shortly afterwards:

> I understand that Selby-Bigge took the matter up personally with the Army Commander. I saw him after the interview, and he seemed satisfied. There was in fact an instruction issued (verbally) immediately afterwards that no refugees were to be removed without their consent, so far as M.G. [Military Government] were concerned (Russians and enemy D.P.s are an Army responsibility).

A few weeks after the event Keightley provided his own version of what Fifth Corps policy had involved in an interview recorded by Lady Limerick. It makes curious reading:

I asked him what the position was of all the displaced Russians and Yugoslavs, and he told me that there were two incidents which gave rise to the story. In the first incident, several thousand Cossacks were taken prisoner, but had been for the last 3½ years fighting in the German ranks; they were dressed in German uniform and were taken prisoners of war. With them were some 1,500 or so Russian men, wives and families; they were an armed body moving round in regiments. According to the policy laid down, it was decided to return these people to Russia; there was evidently some protest, as he said they only had to 'shoot twice' and in neither case hit anybody. They were then interviewed and agreed to return to Soviet Territory together with their wives and children. The men went back without any more pressure; the women protested at first under the instigation of their priest, but subsequently followed him into the train, and they all went back together. A British Officer accompanied them into Russian territory and heard the officer in charge of the Soviet forces explaining that they must now be re-educated as Soviet citizens and that they must be prepared to work hard, but that they would in no way be penalised. There was no evidence at all that they had been shot.

I asked whether he knew the Cossacks in question had been from districts overrun by the Germans in their invasion of Russia, or whether they had been living in Central Europe before the War, and were in fact supporters of the old regime. He said that he did not know and it was impossible to find out – he thought some might be, but that the only evidence they had, was that they had been fighting in the German Army, and none to prove that they were White Russians.

In the case of the Yugoslavs, there were a considerable number of Yugoslav Displaced Persons (not soldiers), they were asked if they were prepared to return to Yugoslavia, and expressed themselves quite willing, in fact volunteered and were accordingly sent off by train and lorry. After they crossed a bridge, they were all machine-gunned. On this information being received, no further evacuations to Yugoslavia were made, except where the people expressed themselves anxious and willing to go – in fact, the evacuation of D.P.s there has practically ceased. General Keightley gave me categorical assurance that there were no unwilling people being sent back.[3]

Selby-Bigge's intervention undoubtedly saved hundreds, if not thousands of lives. Its interest to the historian lies also in what it reveals of Keightley's attitude to the forced repatriation of Yugoslavs. So apprehensive was he that the news might leak out, that the whole elaborately-arranged operation was abruptly halted. It is apparent that no one beyond a chosen few was intended to learn even of its existence, and then only when it became absolutely necessary. Selby-Bigge, who was actually working in the camp, only discovered the true nature of what was happening when Ljotic brought back his horrifying first-hand report. That the 6,000 civilians were to be returned had been settled in the instruction of 23 May, agreed with the Yugoslavs that evening, and transmitted as an operational order to the Commandant of Viktring Camp on 31 May. Yet as late as 30 May Nigel Nicolson, intelligence officer to the First Guards Brigade, whose duty it was to arrange transport and escorts, had not been informed of the plan. At nine o'clock that morning he passed a message to Divisional headquarters enquiring, 'Viktring . . . Any policy with regard to civ[ilian]s?'[4]

A number of important points emerge from this episode. It reveals the extreme trepidation with which Keightley regarded any hint that the story might get out, and the haste amounting almost to panic with which he abandoned the project when it came to be openly challenged. Above all, it shows that the agreement with the Yugoslavs could be arbitrarily revoked without exciting the mildest protest, let alone any damaging action. The Slovenes were transported not long afterwards to another camp at Spittal, where they do not appear to have provided an excessive strain on Fifth Corps resources.

In short, it can be seen that Keightley, and not McCreery or Alexander, was master of the situation. He could alter the policy as arbitrarily and suddenly as he chose, the only restriction on his actions being the fear lest others discover what was happening. To the Eighth Army he can only report lamely that the Yugoslavs refuse to leave, which surely represents implicit acceptance of the likelihood that McCreery would regard that as sufficient reason to halt the operation.

But was Keightley in fact the master? Up to about 28 May he had ruthlessly overridden forceful objections by officers as senior as General Arbuthnott. Now, it seems, he must give way before the first obstacle to materialise. Macmillan and Low, the men who respectively authorised and arranged the forced repatriation, were gone. A momentary attempt to bluster Selby-Bigge into compliance, and all was dropped. For all we know, Keightley may not have been reluctant to see the end of a policy to which, in the case of the Cossacks, he had at first vigorously objected. This at least is the view of many of those who knew him most closely at this time.

A secondary and possibly related factor in the unscheduled abandonment of forced repatriation was an event now imminent, which was to put a permanent stop to policies which had come to disgust virtually every soldier compelled to participate in them. On the morning of 1 June it became known at Klagenfurt that the Supreme

Allied Commander was arriving on a tour of inspection in the Corps area. The visit was scheduled for Monday, 4 June, and early on the morning of Sunday an order was hastily passed via the Sixth Armoured Division to Major Barre: 'Hold fast on all evac. into J[ugo]–S[lavia] TFO [till further orders]. (less that of civs this am).'

The civilians referred to were a handful of volunteers for return to Yugoslavia. Next day at Rosenbach Station, so one of their number who defected shortly afterwards recalled, a trained team of Partisan killers was to await 'a big transport of prisoners'. With them were British officers of the Sixth Special Force, whose mysterious role will be examined in chapter twelve.[5] They were presumably disappointed in their expectations.

On the evening of 3 June Major Barre visited Dr Mersol in his quarters and asked him to be at hand next morning, when a distinguished visitor would arrive.

Next day, just after noon, a procession of vehicles drove into the camp compound. The inmates of Viktring were marshalled by their improvised shelters, all spick-and-span for the great occasion. Outside the camp headquarters Major Barre was waiting. By his side were his two assistants, Red Cross nurses Jane Balding and Florence Phillips, and Dr Mersol. Field-Marshal Alexander, accompanied by Eighth Army commander General Richard McCreery, descended from his staff car and approached them. After a brief formal meeting, Major Barre presented Dr Mersol to the Field-Marshal. Earlier he had impressed on the doctor that he was being offered a unique chance to bring the truth home to the Supreme Allied Commander, and that he should make the most of it: 'Doctor, this is your golden opportunity to put in your last plea. Make use of it!'

Alexander shook hands with Mersol, listening with evident interest to what he had to say. Introducing himself, the doctor explained succinctly how he and his compatriots had been obliged to flee in terror across the Karavanke Mountains into Carinthia, where they had given themselves up to the protection of the English. Now the Domobran troops had been forcibly returned and executed without trial by the Titoists.

'Our Domobranci never fought against the Allies,' he concluded; 'On the contrary, they saved your pilots and helped the Allied cause whenever they could. They fought only against the Communists who, in Slovenia and other regions of Yugoslavia, were nothing more than bandits and murderers.'

The Field-Marshal followed these words with what those present took to be intense interest and curiosity.

'How do you know that the soldiers have been killed?' he asked.

'We have been informed by individuals who have escaped and returned across the mountains. They gave us detailed evidence of it.'

Impressed by Mersol's patent sincerity, Alexander asked him about his own circumstances. The doctor showed him on a map the position of his home and the route across the Loibl Pass by which the Slovenian fugitives had fled the rising tide of Communist terror. Alexander then pursued another train of thought. All around him, crouched by their makeshift shelters, were crowds of peasant women and children, their eyes fixed on the man who alone bore power to preserve their lives or consign them to a ghastly end.

'What do the majority of the refugees do for their living?' he enquired.

'Most of them are peasants who left their homes and their land out of fear of being murdered by Communists. I wish to thank you, sir, and the other British authorities for the help and assistance you have given us in the recent past. We ask you to grant us asylum and continuous protection and help. We beg you, please let us stay in Viktring. Do not send us back to Yugoslavia! This would mean torture and certain death for many of us.'

Clearly pained by Mersol's account of the fate of the Domobranci, the Field-Marshal replied, 'Since you do speak English, I will tell you in English: it is unfortunate that I did not know of this before. I am sorry nothing can be done now.'

As far as the surviving civilians were concerned, though, Alexander provided a firm assurance that their safety was henceforth guaranteed: 'As far as I am concerned, you can remain here. Please rest assured that we will help you and your people.'

With that, politely declining Major Barre's offer to conduct him around the camp, Alexander and his party left to lunch at the First Guards Brigade headquarters.

That evening Lieutenant Ames at Viktring received the following written order:

New Army policy respective Yugoslavs effective forthwith
1. No Yugoslavs will be returned to Yugoslavia or handed over to Yugoslav troops against their will.
2. Yugoslavs who bore arms against Tito will be treated as surrendered

personnel and sent to Viktring Camp at disposal. Further instructions awaited.

3. All this personnel will be regarded as displaced personnel ultimately routed via Italy.

4. No evacuation from Viktring, T.F.O. [till further orders].

    4. vi. 1945.

Up to this moment neither Major Barre nor Dr Mersol could be sure whether the reprieve granted to the civilian refugees on 31 May represented a temporary freeze or total reversal of the policy of forced repatriation obtaining hitherto. Now they knew that the 6,000 displaced persons at Viktring, together with thousands of others scattered across British-occupied Austria, were safe.[6]

Jane Balding's diary entry for 4 June conveys some of the exhilaration that swept Viktring after the Field-Marshal's visit. The day before she had gone down with a 'jiffy tummy', but even sickness was dispelled by Alex's legendary charm:

The day – went to camp early – rumour that F.M. Alexander is in Clagenfurt & coming to camp – later told he was not coming – he arrived as we decided to go home to lunch – stood with Major B. to see him go past – he stopped & got out of car to shake hands – talked for about 10 minutes – shook hands again – filmed an' all – I felt better immediately, full of beans in fact – troops moved out of school house in afternoon, camp moved in – sorted rooms out – camp in high spirits, 'cos F.M. said they wouldn't be sent back Yugo.[7]

To Major Barre the Field-Marshal's visit was an important event; but one which also seemed oddly uncalled for.

I could never understand at the time *why* he came [he explained to me later]. I mean, that theatre of war was so vast. Hostilities were over with, of course, but still the winding up was so vast. There were so many more important things . . . that's probably what brought him. He wanted to see – find out for himself . . . As I remember now, the news [of the forced handovers] wasn't new to him. I can honestly say . . . that I would gather that Alexander knew perfectly well what was happening [when he entered Viktring Camp on 4 June], but not wishing to divulge what he knew . . . His attitude was not one of surprise – he didn't come to Viktring, to our camp, not knowing what was going on, I'm convinced of that. . . . Can you imagine for one moment Alexander, in his exalted position, visiting a small camp like our camp?

As AFHQ had been informed on 31 May of the 'refusal' of Slovenes to return (the real refusal had been that of Selby-Bigge and Barre), it seems probable that Alexander had come to see for himself what was happening. Very likely disturbing reports had begun to filter through: we know that in the parallel case of the Cossacks representations had been carried up to the Supreme Allied Commander. It has been suggested by those who privately hold Alexander responsible for the forced repatriation that the term 'new Army policy' implies that he had hitherto accepted, and therefore bore responsibility for, policy obtaining before that date. This is, however, too rigid an inference: the description would be just as applicable were Alexander revoking a violation or unreasonable misapplication of standing orders. Just how much he suspected or had been informed of before his arrival at Viktring will never be known. In the matter of the Cossacks his antagonism had been unyielding to the use of force and, above all, his insistence on the necessity for screening. In the absence of direct evidence, it is possible to conjecture that his view of the Yugoslavs may have been more flexible in some respects, and here a more general consideration may be noted.

Among all levels of British troops there tended to be a distinction drawn between Cossacks and Yugoslavs. Despite the fact that Soviet Russia was now a valued ally, it was recognised that the Cossacks had their own legitimate reasons for hating and fearing the Communists. Their equestrian skills and picturesque appearance aroused admiration, while many of their officers were cultured men of the world from Berlin, Brussels and Paris, who could converse on familiar terms and topics in French, English or German with their British captors. Above all, virtually no one harboured any delusions as to what would be their fate should they ever fall into Soviet hands.

The Yugoslavs, on the other hand, suffered from several disadvantages in comparison. Few even among the officers spoke English, and there was a widespread tendency for the multilingual and often mutually antagonistic national groupings of Serbs, Croats and Slovenes to be regarded (as often as not, good-naturedly) as 'Balkan bandits'. Their history was dismissed as confusing beyond comprehension. The much-publicised wartime atrocities committed by the Ustashe aroused a more than sneaking feeling that the Croats in particular deserved anything within reason they might get. Tito had in contrast been exalted as an Allied hero; and though his Partisans soon came to be regarded with extreme disfavour, few Englishmen could yet be brought to believe that he was capable of cruelty on a scale they freely conceded to Stalin.

It will be appreciated that these are over-simplified generalisations, but I believe they contain a considerable residuum of truth. It is possible, for example, that McCreery, regarded by all who knew him as an honourable and decent man, had none the less understood, approved or authorised something of what had been happening at Viktring. Alternatively, when one recalls the deceits to which the Fifth Corps Staff subjected him in the matter of the Cossacks (the most striking example has yet to be examined), it seems much more likely that he, and Alexander in his turn, was duped likewise in the case of the Yugoslavs.

Though the 'New Army Order' ending involuntary repatriation of Yugoslavs was issued in consequence of Alexander's visit to Viktring, as was seen it had been hurriedly anticipated in Klagenfurt the day before. The Fifth Corps War Diary records: '104 only of about 5000 Slovene civilians in Viktring Camp offered to return to Yugoslavia when allowed to choose under new dispensation.' In view of Keightley's hurried and unwilling climb-down in face of Selby-Bigge's protest, the motive can only have been fear of exposure.

There exists a remarkable parallel to this precautionary measure in the case of the Cossacks, and the one may serve to illuminate the other. 4 June, the day Alexander issued his 'New Army Policy', was also the day that an order came down through the Seventy-eighth Infantry Division requiring screening provisions for Cossacks to be rigidly enforced. The mere existence of such an order would constitute proof that, contrary to all extant orders and subsequent reports, no screening had been conducted before that date. It is perhaps not surprising, therefore, that all trace of it has vanished from the relevant files, particularly in view of the fact that the parallel 'New Army Order' at Viktring is also not to be found in the Eighth Army or Fifth Corps files (its survival is due to the chance that a copy was preserved by Slovenes within the camp and, as a result of a later correspondence, ended up in a Foreign Office file).

There can be no doubt that this belated order to screen Cossacks existed, however. In 1956 Nikolai Krasnov was told by his wife Lili what happened immediately after his departure from Lienz on 28 May 1945:

> My mother and my wife, in the clothes they had on, without even taking any food, decided to avoid forced repatriation by getting away at once

into the Austrian highlands. They took along only some poison in case they should be seized and sent off to the Soviet Union. Neither my mother nor my wife had ever lived in the Soviet Union and were not actually subject to repatriation, but at the time no attention was being paid to such facts – if you were a Russian you were handed over to the Soviets. Mother and Lili preferred death to life behind barbed wire in the East.

Suddenly, on June 4, a new order arrived: All those who had lived outside the limits of the Soviet Union since before 1939 were not subject to repatriation. Such persons were to be considered DPs. Thus it was that a new social class, recognised by all the countries of the world, came into being – the class of Displaced Persons.[8]

Krasnov's account, derived from his wife, is substantiated by events in Peggetz Camp. On 4 June, for example, the émigré General Verdizhy was arrested by troops of the Argylls. Next day, however, he was suddenly reprieved: 'Gen Verdizhy has turned out to be a Jugoslav national and was NOT therefore sent with the Russian party [to Judenburg]'. It was following the major handover operations on 1 and 2 June that Colonel Malcolm at Lienz received the instructions withheld from him on 26 May by Brigadier Musson, and a camp was established nearby at Dölsach for Cossacks proved to be of nationality other than Soviet. It was upon Major Davies that the principal duty of conducting this newly-instituted screening fell, a task he well remembers. Though the improvised order to institute screening on 4 June must have passed through the Thirty-sixth Infantry Brigade headquarters, General Musson says today, 'I don't know anything about it . . . I just wouldn't know, because I had no knowledge that Alexander was coming – I can't help you on that one.' Musson was sent home on a month's leave the day after the new screening order was passed down, and so was absent from the Seventy-eighth Divisional area when Alexander arrived that afternoon.[9]

In Chapter Eight it was described how Cossacks held by the Sixth Armoured Division were taken over by the Forty-sixth Infantry Division soon after the middle of May. The reason, it seems clear, was the expressed hostility of General Murray and many of his troops to the proposed handover of their prisoners to the Soviets. Brigadier Patrick Scott, who had accepted the surrender of Prince zu Salm's Sixth Terek Cossack Regiment on 12 May, had expressed his disgust at the prospect to General Keightley in person. On 17 May Scott's

Thirty-eighth Irish Infantry Brigade was relieved by the Hampshire Brigade. As the Hampshires were not responsible for the terms of surrender Scott had arranged in good faith with Prince zu Salm, they might have been thought to prove less obstructive about handling the transfer to the Soviet zone. But if this was Brigadier Low's expectation, he was sadly misled.

The Reverend C. W. H. Story was at the time of these events Acting Deputy Assistant Chaplain General at Fifth Corps headquarters. As he explained to me:

Then one day I received a phone call from the Rev John Vaughan, Chaplain to the Hampshire Brigade . . . asking if I could help. His men were nearer mutiny than anyone had known before. They had come to him to ask if Chaplains Branch could do something. They were being ordered to force White Russian p.o.w. at bayonet point into transport bound for Russia. The White Russians believed that whatever promises the Soviet High Command were making, they were being sent to death or the salt mines. They were flinging themselves on the ground & screaming for mercy.

I went to find Brigadier Tryon, Brig. A.Q., but only got his assistant, the DAAG, who merely explained that the return of these men was agreed policy & that the Russian Command had promised fair treatment & re-indoctrination. So I rang the Deputy Chaplain-General, the Rev T. M. Layng, at GHQ, CMF [Central Mediterranean Force], Caserta. He became very angry at the news & immediately rang the Chaplain-General, Conor Ll. Hughes, at the War Office.

What happened after that I cannot be certain. The Chaplain-General would not have direct access to the Prime Minister but to the Adjutant General who would have that access.

My memory is that the following day I was told that the telephone wires had been humming & that Churchill himself had given instructions that no man must be repatriated against his will. Who told me, I cannot now say . . .

What I am sure about is that the matter reached the Chaplain-General – i.e. at War Office level. I feel my own H.Q. (V Corps) had been either extremely callous or most unimaginative about this most deplorable matter, the most disgraceful episode I have heard of in the whole war so far as the British Army was concerned. The only redeeming feature that I can see was the anger & disgust of the common soldier, & the promptness, if it can be proved, of Churchill's reaction to the news.

Mr Story adds that 'I am not now in touch with any of the people to whom I spoke at that time (most are no longer alive) except the

Rev John Vaughan. I spoke to him on the phone a few days ago. He says he heard of no orders cancelling any further repatriation of these men, only a publication of the Soviet Command's promise of fair treatment. But that could well be so, as the unfortunate episode was complete so far as his units were concerned within a few hours of his calling me on the phone.'

This protest must in that case have taken place on the eve of the Field-Marshal's visit, by which time the major handovers were complete. Whether or not the Prime Minister had intervened, there can be no question but that Alexander would have been informed at once of his Deputy Chaplain-General's action, and that in consequence he arrived in Austria with some knowledge of what had been happening.

On 5 June, the day after his visit to Viktring, the Field-Marshal visited General Arbuthnott's Seventy-eighth Infantry Division. That afternoon he called for tea at the headquarters of the Thirty-eighth Infantry Brigade at Treffen, outside Villach. The brigadier was Patrick Scott, who three weeks earlier had persuaded the Croats to surrender to Tito. He was, on the other hand, extremely sympathetic to the plight of the Cossacks. An Austrian officer from the Fifteenth Cossack Cavalry Corps, Leopold Goëss, who escaped repatriation at the end of May, recalls being alarmed by a chance encounter with Scott a few weeks later at a racecourse.

> Telling my wife who he was, she wanted to hide somehow; but that was impossible, and I only hoped that he might not recognise me . . . But he did, and said: 'Listen. Don't believe that we couldn't have found you if we really wanted to – but people who have such beautiful horses and dogs as you shouldn't go to Siberia.'

Now, on 5 June at Brigadier Scott's headquarters, a young cousin of Goëss was to witness a remarkable scene. Count Ariprand Thurn was a twenty-year-old Austrian nobleman, whose home was by chance that castle of Bleiburg where Scott had negotiated the Croat surrender with the Partisan leader Basta. Thurn's family had been strongly opposed to the Nazis, some having spent the war in Dachau concentration camp. In the last days of the war he had at considerable risk to himself assisted the escape of a New Zealand lieutenant. His anti-Nazi credentials being impeccable, and being usefully fluent in English and German, he was taken on to Brigadier Scott's staff as a second lieutenant. To the British Count Ariprand became 'Archie' –

'a tall, polite and bewildered boy', as one of his colleagues remembers him. Ordered 'to join the Irish Brigade as interpreter and general dogsbody', he at once became a boon companion to the dashing young Irish officers, on whom his sister Christa's ravishing good looks are said to have inflicted more casualties than the Wehrmacht.

Before the critical days of the Cossack handovers, Count Thurn had witnessed Scott's revulsion at the prospect of handing over officers possessing Yugoslav or French citizenship, and his desperate but unavailing efforts to have Cossacks in his area transferred to the American zone in Germany. Officers at the Thirty-eighth Infantry Brigade shared a conviction that it was the Fifth Corps headquarters that was determined come what may to force through the policy of surrendering all Cossacks to the Soviets, and that no considerations of treatment traditionally accorded prisoners of war or common humanity would be permitted to obstruct that aim. Equally it was understood that Field-Marshal Alexander was deeply sympathetic to the Cossacks' plight.

When the Field-Marshal arrived at Treffen he was entertained by the pipes and drums of the Brigade playing 'Retreat'. 'After watching this for a short while,' Scott wrote later, 'everyone retired to tables under the trees where we had a good old-fashioned blow-out of sticky cakes and strawberries and cream, while the pipes and drums continued their melodies from a nearby field.'

It was just before this session that Archie Thurn, who was present with the rest of the Brigade Staff, witnessed a significant conversation. Scott received Alexander inside Brigade headquarters, a long low building on the edge of the village formerly housing a Protestant Youth Centre. No sooner was the party assembled than Brigadier Scott launched into the affair of the Cossacks, expressing deep indignation at being compelled to participate in so shameful a business, and explaining at some length the attempts he had made to save those held by his command. The Field-Marshal listened intently, and then, when Scott had ceased his tirade, began to express his own equally deeply-felt sympathy for the Cossacks. He recounted how he had fought alongside the Whites in 1919, and had ever since felt warmly attached to them and their cause.

He bitterly resented the fact that the Cossacks had been handed over to the Bolsheviks, who in his view should never have been allowed to overrun half Europe. The betrayal of the Cossacks should not have been permitted to take place at all. But even he, as Supreme Allied Commander, had been powerless to prevent what had occurred in the previous week. The politicians had taken the matter out of his hands, and arranged the whole dirty business. Who these 'politicians' were the Field-Marshal did not specify, but Thurn distinctly remembers his complaining that if Eden had had more backbone that could have saved the Cossacks.

Archie Thurn was surprised by the outspoken nature of the Field-Marshal's comments, though their tenor was shared by all present. To the historian, Thurn's account is of exceptional significance, since it provides unique first-hand evidence of Alexander's views on first learning details of what had been perpetrated against his wishes. Perhaps the most fascinating aspect lies less in what was said (Alexander's views were plain enough from his actions) than in the company among whom they were spoken. For the Field-Marshal was accompanied on his visit by the Eighth Army Commander Richard McCreery, the Fifth Corps Commander Charles Keightley and the Commander of the Seventy-eighth Infantry Division, Robert Arbuthnott. As Patrick Scott remarked, 'for a short time the whole chain of command was represented at our modest headquarters . . .'[10]

Thurn's account is confirmed by other sources. General Sir William Morgan had been Alexander's Chief of Staff at AFHQ at the time of the handovers, and succeeded him as Supreme Allied Commander later in the year. He explained to me that, as soon as news of the treachery and brutality which accompanied the Cossacks' handover began to reach Caserta, Alexander went up to investigate, and was furious when he discovered what had taken place. (Morgan's words gave the impression that this was the major or sole motivation for the visit.) Having put a stop to further operations of the sort, he returned to Naples resolved that on no account would anything like this happen again while he remained Supreme Allied Commander. Thereafter he rejected Foreign Office demands for individual Soviet citizens to be handed over by force, repeatedly expressing to General Morgan his disgust with the whole policy.

General Morgan's testimony is backed by Brigadier C. E. Tryon-Wilson, A/Q on Keightley's staff. He was familiar with most of what passed at headquarters in Klagenfurt, and heard from colleagues on every side of Alexander's anger at the time of his visit on 4 June. It was clear to him that news of the tragedy had come as a recent, shocking revelation to the Field-Marshal.

Major-General Bredin, serving on the Seventy-eighth Infantry Division Staff at the time, recalls General Arbuthnott's fury at the time he originally received orders for the Cossack handovers. Objections from all sides, Arbuthnott explained to him, had been taken right to the top: 'we've tried everyone, even Alex!' Alexander shared Arbuthnott's distaste and indignation, so Bredin learned, but explained that his hands were tied by what had been agreed at Yalta.

That Alexander raised his objections with yet higher authority is attested by Mrs Louise Buchanan. In 1945 she was staying with friends near Alexander's home at Hillsborough, where the Field-Marshal was spending his leave. There he unburdened himself of the many frustrations bedevilling him in the Mediterranean theatre.

'Certainly,' Mrs Buchanan wrote to me, 'the return of . . . the Cossacks was mentioned and I remember being puzzled by hearing that "Alex's" protests were absolutely ignored and how sick and furious it made him. Like Wavell and Tedder, he was something of a romantic in his soldiering, you know. And that is hard to explain in 1980.'

It is intrinsically likely that Alexander raised such an objection, and it would seem that the protests to which Mrs Buchanan refers were delivered between 22 May, up to which date the forcible handover of Cossacks remained prohibited, and 25 May, when Alexander reluctantly empowered the Eighth Army to return them. There is no record of his having despatched any protests at this time to those from whom he received instructions. Indeed, exchanges passing between the Foreign Office and Combined Chiefs of Staff reveal that they only learned of the proposed handovers after the event, to which they gave retrospective approval. The appropriate figure to whom Alexander would have turned in order to have raised such an issue was in any case Macmillan, who was working alongside him at Caserta between 22 and 25 May. Macmillan himself claimed that 'to refuse' the Soviet demand would be to 'break the Yalta agreement'; and this, so Alexander informed the Fifth Corps officers, was the consideration obliging him to proceed with the operation.

Returning to the Field-Marshal's visit to Treffen on 5 June, it is improbable that Scott would have ventured on his outspoken criticism at the gathering of 5 June had he not been aware that the Field-Marshal shared his views. Correspondingly, Alexander himself could not have spoken as forcefully as he did before Generals McCreery, Keightley and Arbuthnott, had he believed they bore direct responsibility for what had occurred. (Archie Thurn does not recall today whether McCreery and Keightley were actually in the room during the discussion. It seems intrinsically likely, and in any case Alexander would certainly not have permitted even implicit criticism of their actions before subordinate officers.) Whatever Alexander had learned of Keightley's and Arbuthnott's roles in the repatriation operations, it seems that he did not in any way regard them as blameworthy. They were not the authors of a policy whose provisions they had enforced in good faith. The brutal treatment of the Cossacks which so sickened him was but the outcome of the policy which, as Keightley explained, could not effectively have been enforced in any other way.

General Arbuthnott was present in the room and joined Alexander in forceful condemnation of what had happened. From Arbuthnott Alexander must swiftly have learned details of the savage scenes of 1 and 2 June at Peggetz. 'Buthy', as a horseman and an aristocrat, felt a strong rapport with the Cossacks, whose camp he had visited on 18 May. Clearly appalled by Arbuthnott's angry account, Alexander decided to intervene directly to ensure that no further disgraceful incidents inadvertently took place.

Just as he took the trouble to see for himself what was happening to the Slovene civilians at Viktring, so now he travelled to a Cossack camp for the same purpose. Major D. J. Frogley was at this time an officer with Allied Military Government, administering a displaced persons camp at Spittal on the Drau. His camp was visited by Field-Marshal Alexander (presumably – though this Major Frogley no longer recalls – accompanied by Arbuthnott as Divisional Commander), who requested the use of his field telephone. Frogley remained outside the room while the call was being made, but afterwards talked with an officer who was present. He learned that Alexander had been speaking to the commandant of a nearby German barracks, giving detailed instructions for the safeguarding of several hundred White Russians from Lienz due to be handed over to the Soviets. As a result of this the Cossacks were returned to Lienz and not handed over.

Major Frogley's account is confirmed by Mr Richard Roberts, who was welfare officer at what must have been the camp in question:

> At this camp [in Spittal] we had a contingent of Cossacks passing through and they left their horse blankets and all sorts of gear and were on orders to entrain for the Russian frontier. No doubt under the rule of Stalin it would be their final ending. The next group that came through the camp

stayed at the camp and were not repatriated. This was on Field-Marshal Alexander's orders.

It is abundantly clear from the way he spoke at Treffen that Alexander exonerated the generals from overall responsibility for what he learned had happened. The brutality committed by troops under Fifth Corps command had ultimately not to be blamed on Keightley. On 23 May he had requested authority to use force as essential for the policy to be effectively implemented, and it was a policy which Alexander had himself been compelled implicitly to accept.

It was the brutality of the operations that outraged Alexander. But what of that hidden operation, which such ingenious precautions had been taken to conceal? Did Alexander learn anything at this time of the secretive inclusion of Generals Krasnov and Shkuro, together with hundreds of other old émigrés, among the Soviet nationals whose return was covered by the Yalta Agreement? It seems certain that he did not. While permission to use force had been openly requested by Toby Low, no hint of the presence of old émigrés among the Cossacks, let alone their illegal handover, had appeared in any communication emanating from the Fifth Corps. On the contrary, Keightley and Low had gone to elaborate lengths to deceive their superiors.

On 14 May, though fully aware of the falsity of the claim, they had stressed to McCreery that all the Cossacks were Soviet citizens, and concealed the Soviet demand for Krasnov, Shkuro and the old émigrés. Again, on 25 May they sent a solemn assurance to the Fifteenth Army Group that 'Cossacks to be handed over to Russians are Soviet citizens within the definition of cited AFHQ letter'. Yet it was on or about that very day that Arbuthnott's objection to inclusion of old émigrés among those to be handed over was overruled by Keightley.

The purpose of these subterfuges can only have been to prevent McCreery and Alexander from discovering the covert operation, and neither is likely to have been provided with an opportunity for learning the truth during his visit. Apart from general considerations of dishonour and disobedience, the Field-Marshal could not under any circumstances have tolerated the insulting deceptions to which he had been subjected by his own subordinates. Even had he thought it impolitic to take overt action with regard to such gross insubordination, it is inconceivable (as senior officers have stressed to me) that he would have recommended Keightley for his subsequent posting as C-in-C of Commonwealth forces operating in the Far East, had it been brought to his notice.

In fact recently-released documents prove (were further proof necessary) the extent of Alexander's indignation at the gratuitous brutality of an operation which he had resisted so vigorously, and the fact that the deliberate inclusion of old émigrés among Cossacks returned was concealed from Keightley's military superiors.

Alexander stayed the night of 5 to 6 June at the Army Commander's house near Nötsch before returning to Caserta. Next day he despatched a liaison officer to the Fifth Corps headquarters, with instructions to investigate the operations. The officer stayed at Klagenfurt from 7 to 8 June, before reporting his findings.

With regard to the Cossacks, he learned

> no details of any incidents during the handover available at Corps. However it is known that incidents did occur, and Corps are obtaining details of these. Reports should be ready in a few days. 78 Div experienced difficulties – their first estimate of 28,000 was eventually found to be only 22,000, the discrepancy being explained by over-indenting for rations. Some ORs [other ranks] also demonstrated on entrainment.

In the case of the Yugoslavs, the officer reported:

> As with the handover of the Cossacks, this operation proved much less difficult than had been anticipated.
>
> From the Cage at Viktring the Jugs were taken in TCVs to Maria Elend or Bleiburg stations. Escorts and guards at the stations were found by 1 Gds Bde. At the stations Jugs were searched for arms, org into their own units (coys and bns) as far as possible, and entrained. Care was taken to segregate Ustachi from Chetniks, and to provide seats for offrs, women and children.
>
> On completion of entrainment, Tito's guard appeared and took over, a signature being obtained from the Jug guard comd.
>
> As far as is known there were no incidents while the personnel were in British hands, but Jug LO reported 3 suicides and 2 wounded, all believed to have taken place on the train. Conduct of Jug guards seen by 5 Corps LO at Maria Elend was exemplary.

After reporting the escapes of the Slovenian General Krenner and an Ustashe commander, it was noted that 'it is not thought that any other Jugs escaped from the British or Jug guards'.[11] Clearly it would not have done to refer to the escapes of Vladimir Ljotic and others who returned with first-hand accounts of what was happening to

Alexander C. Kirk
(*above*), US Political
Advisor at Allied Force
Headquarters,
addressing citizens of
Cassino after the
liberation. Kirk strongly
objected to the
repatriation of
Yugoslavs, but did not
discover until two
months after the event
that his Government's
protest had been
ignored.

Harold Macmillan
(*right*), Minister Resident
in the Mediterranean, in
Rome on 25 May 1945.
On his return home
from Allied Force
Headquarters he had an
audience with the Pope,
with whom he had 'a
long and rather moving
talk'.

Major–General Horatius Murray (*centre*) with Lieutenant–General Sir Richard McCreery, commanding Eighth Army (*right*) at Murray's Sixth Armoured Division Tactical Headquarters at Udine, North Italy, May 1945.

General McCreery (*below*) talking to Major P.H. Barre and Nurse Balding in Viktring Camp for Slovenian refugees, May 1945. Jane Balding wrote of McCreery's visit: 'only time he got out of his car was to walk through the mud to shake hands with me – great thrill – newspaper bloke chased me afterwards.'

Brigadier G.L. Verney (commanding First Guards Brigade), Field-Marshal Sir Harold Alexander, Lieutenant-General Charles Keightley (commanding Fifth Corps), and Major-General Murray (commanding Sixth Armoured Division) visiting Viktring Camp on 4 June 1945.

Viktring Camp (*below*): (*left to right*) Dr Valentin Mersol, Field-Marshal Alexander, General McCreery, Major Barre, Nurse Florence Phillips, Nurse Jane Balding. Dr Mersol, camp leader of the Slovenes, is pleading for the 6,000 civilian refugees not to be repatriated: 'that would mean torture and certain death for many of us.'

Toby Low (*left*), Deputy Chairman of the Conservative Party in 1959, during the Premiership of Harold Macmillan (1957–63). Low was knighted in 1957 and created First Baron Aldington in 1962. In 1945 he had been Chief of Staff to General Keightley, on whose behalf he arranged the repatriation of some 75,000 Cossacks and Yugoslavs.

Lieutenant-General Charles Keightley, commander of the British Fifth Corps in Austria, 1945 (*below left*).

Major-General Robert Arbuthnott, commanding the Seventy-eight Infantry Division. Arbuthnott objected three times to returning Cossacks from his Divisional area before succumbing to pressure from Keightley and Low.

those returned. Nor did there seem any point in gratuitously informing the Field-Marshal's representative of the deception resorted to in
order to lure the Yugoslavs to their deaths. By now, however,
Alexander knew enough to be aware that matters had not proceeded
quite so free from unpleasantness as Fifth Corps staff had assured his
liaison officer and, as the report noted, 'Corps are obtaining details'.

A month later, on 3 July, the staff of the Thirty-sixth Infantry
Brigade produced a detailed report on handover operations undertaken in the Drau Valley. It contained the relevant written orders,
with their explicit stipulation that screening must be carried out in
accordance with the AFHQ definition of Soviet citizenship, and no
one reading them could imagine that any other course was ever
contemplated.

This impression is confirmed at some length in a nine-page summary account of the operations. In it we learn that:

> Included in the figures [of Cossacks held in the Drau Valley] were an
> unknown quantity of displaced persons of nationalities other than Soviet
> . . . Lack of documents and the speed and secrecy with which the
> evacuations had to be carried out made a complete individual check
> impossible. Steps were taken, however, at the time of the evacuations,
> to segregate persons who were obviously of these categories . . . As with
> the Cossacks, there were a number of displaced persons other than Soviet,
> included in the Caucasian forces. Some 200 of these were eventually
> segregated and sent to the appropriate collecting centres.

Next the precautions taken to prevent these non-Soviet citizens from
being knowingly returned are set out in detail:

> 5 Corps letter 405/G dated 21 May 45, of which a copy is attached at
> Appx 'B', provided a guide as to which formations and units were to be
> treated as Soviet Nationals. It is to be noted that although this directive
> stated that individual cases were not to be considered unless particularly
> pressed, such measures as were possible under the conditions prevailing
> at the time, were taken within 36 Inf Bde to ensure that non-Soviet
> nationals were not included among those evacuated to the USSR author-
> ities.

It is stressing the obvious to state that all this is blatantly false.
Whether or not there was a 'lack of documents' cannot have been
known, since no attempt was made at the time to find out. No
authorised steps were taken to segregate 'persons of nationalities
other than Soviet'. No measures 'were taken within 36 Infantry

Brigade to ensure that non-Soviet nationals were not included among those evacuated to the USSR', for the simple reason that officers conducting were told emphatically that all Cossacks without exception must be returned. This is no debatable point: as the commander of the Thirty-sixth Infantry Brigade (Geoffrey Musson) and the battalion commanders directly concerned (Colonels Malcolm and Odling-Smee) confirm, the screening order was not passed down to officers in the field, who remained ignorant of its existence.

Clearly the intention was to deceive. But whom? No one below Brigade level would have an opportunity to see the report. Moving up the chain of command, we arrive at Divisional and Corps head-quarters. But General Arbuthnott at the first and General Keightley at the second had the best of reasons for knowing that the screening order had not been passed on, since it was they who had passed down the secret oral order setting it aside. It seems inescapable that we must look higher still for the person or persons intended to be kept in the dark. These must surely be General McCreery and Field-Marshal Alexander.

The figure who should know the answer to the problem is Brigadier (now General Sir Geoffrey) Musson, whose Brigade report it was. Why, I asked him, had his staff claimed so explicitly that the screening order had been passed on and implemented, when he himself is the first to admit that it was not?

General Musson explained that he was on leave in England at the time the report was compiled. During his absence Colonel Odling-Smee of the Fifth Buffs took temporary charge of the Brigade, and consequently the report would have been compiled under his authority. This factor makes the falsifications if anything still more significant. As the officer in the field responsible for sending back the Caucasians, Odling-Smee had better opportunity than anyone for knowing that the screening order had not reached battalion commanders. By the same token, since he had played no part in the deception (having himself been deceived) he could have no personal motive for distorting the record.

On having his attention drawn to the claim that individual screening had been conducted, General Musson agreed that the statement was false, adding: 'now, that I'm surprised at'. For, as he frankly emphasises, he received 'an order that "the key thing is that all the officers must go". I don't honestly think screening in my area was really ever considered . . . I think the overriding thing of getting all the officers out of the valley and to Spittal overrode all that.'

Re-reading the lengthy report, Musson feels it would have taken a month to compile. On returning from home leave, he recalls, 'I remember Odling-Smee . . . said, "we've had a good deal of work in getting a report on the evacuation of the Cossacks".' He feels certain it must have been requested for a particular purpose: 'There were no routine reports except the War Diaries . . . I'm sure this was a special report.' From its scope and nature Musson is persuaded it 'must have been called for specially . . . I would think that this was after Field-Marshal Alexander's visit, and there was a witch-hunt on, and so they had to report.'

As has been seen, General Musson's explanation is correct. The report includes a number of accounts provided by officers and men involved in the handover operations, many of which detail the brutality and bloodshed involved. On this aspect there is no attempt at a cover-up, and indeed it looks as if it were the extent of the violence that the Field-Marshal wished fully investigated. This there was no disguising, but the handover of the old émigrés remained a skilfully-concealed secret.[12] As General Musson says of orders preserved in War Diaries: 'They're interesting to the historian, but I don't think they stand auditing always;' – a cautionary aphorism that might perhaps with profit be inscribed over the portals of the Public Record Office and the National Archives.

This deliberate falsification of the record is instructive. Were the historian to rely solely on the extensive written record, he could only conclude that Brigadier Musson had passed on Corps orders to screen the Cossacks, and that this had taken place. It is from the unanimous testimony of all concerned that we know the written record was compiled for the purpose of deception.

Who arranged for the insertion of the false claim that Corps screening instructions had been implemented remains mysterious. What it *does* betray, however, is an unmistakable consciousness that the absence of screening arose not (as Toby Low claims) from the pragmatic setting aside of an instruction rendered inoperable by logistical conditions in the field, but reflected a deliberate conspiracy skilfully devised to avoid fulfilling an order which there could be no legitimate motive or practical consideration for circumventing. As General Musson emphasises, Alexander's order to conduct screening was disobeyed primarily in order to ensure that *all* the Cossack officers held at Lienz were handed over to the Soviets.

A whisper of that aspect of the operation which was intended to remain secret reached General McCreery shortly after the event. On 13 June he despatched a message to Keightley:

> 1. Reports have reached this HQ to the effect that in the course of evacuation to Russia of Soviets and displaced personnel considerable hardship has occurred in a number of cases. This has been due to the fact that men, women and children have been included in the parties who are not Soviet nationals as defined in AFHQ letter CR/3491/G1-Br of 6 Mar 45, contents of which were notified to you in this HQ letter of 13 Mar 45.
>
> 2. In certain cases this has resulted in families being broken up, in other cases, women and children were made to travel with their men folk when it would have been advisable to have allowed them to remain.
>
> 3. The Army Commander fully realises the magnitude of the problem and considers that your HQ handled it with great skill and competence in view of the great difficulties involved such as language, numbers to be dealt with, etc. Cases of hardship or irregular repatriation were chiefly due to the impossibility of accurately classifying the inmates of the camps before repatriation commenced.
>
> 4. In view of certain representations which have been made about the hardships which repatriation has caused, the Army Commander wishes to ensure that no repatriation takes place in future of anyone without full classification by the Displaced Persons Branch of AMG. You will apply to AMG for further personnel to undertake the classification of displaced personnel in any camps which are still under Corps control. This is particularly necessary where displaced personnel may still be mixed up with surrendered personnel and is to ensure that no men, women or children are repatriated to the Soviet who are not Soviet citizens.
>
> 5. On no account is any force to be used in connection with any repatriation scheme.[13]

This message makes it clear that McCreery was unaware of the secret instructions to set aside screening in order to effect the return of the senior Cossack generals, and that he had effectively been kept in the dark throughout the operations. It also shows that he was not informed of Keightley's emergency screening order of 4 June, hastily improvised on the eve of Alexander's visit to the Seventy-eighth Divisional area. It seems clear, too, that McCreery shared Alexander's disapproval of the brutality with which the operations had been conducted; and, implicitly, would not have approved them in advance had their nature been made apparent. Knowing nothing of the machinations resulting from Macmillan's visit a month earlier, he could, however, only presume that there had been some unfortunate blunders.

The improvised screening order of 4 June and the 'doctored' Thirty-sixth Infantry Brigade report of 3 July are indicative of the importance Keightley attached to keeping the secret from McCreery and Alexander, and the risks he knew himself to have been running by conducting such a policy. Nevertheless, were all the direct and circumstantial evidence of Macmillan's involvement to be absent, it would appear incredible that Keightley could have been acting of his own volition.

Alexander returned to Caserta disgusted by the brutal treatment troops under his command had inflicted on defenceless prisoners and refugees. He knew nothing of the conspiratorial handover of the White Russians which Macmillan had somehow succeeded in imposing upon Keightley. But he knew enough to feel the stain upon his own honour and that of his armies. He knew that Slovenes and Serbs at Viktring had been sent in thousands to their deaths, as had Cossacks from Lienz and elsewhere. How much he learned of the extent of lying, intimidation and violence employed to effect this end is unknown, but he knew enough. He had heard from Dr Mersol an account of the massacres perpetrated by Tito's executioners at Jesenice and beyond, and the contents of the Thirty-sixth Infantry Brigade's report of 3 July made shameful reading.

It was too late to do anything about the thousands of victims, but what could be done he did. On 4 June he reiterated, this time with effect, his order of 17 May that no Yugoslavs should be compelled to return to Yugoslavia. Similarly he confirmed McCreery's ruling of 13 June that Cossacks and other Soviet citizens, Yalta Agreement or no Yalta Agreement, were safe from forcible repatriation. On 20 August he wrote a personal letter to Field-Marshal Alan Brooke, stating, 'So far I have refused to use force to repatriate Soviet citizens, although I suppose I am not strictly entitled to adopt this attitude – nevertheless, I shall continue with this policy unless I am ordered to do otherwise'.[14] Unless Alexander were lying to his friend, his assertion serves to confirm that the order of 25 May instructing 'all Soviet Citizens' to 'be handed over to Russians' was never intended as a licence for the use of force.

It was not Alexander's way to justify his actions in public, particularly if that exposed others to recrimination or blame. If politicians felt obliged to pursue questionable policies, let that be their affair. What Alexander could not have envisaged was that his silence would

one day permit Macmillan to claim that it was he (Alexander) who
had ordered the handover of the White Russians.

Though Field-Marshal Alexander was horrified and disgusted by
the policy of forced repatriation of Russians and Yugoslavs from
occupied Austria, he could not as a soldier avoid accepting some
degree of personal responsibility for operations conducted by troops
under his command.

It was presumably for this reason that news of the operations was
kept a closely-guarded secret at AFHQ. As a result it was not until
4 August that Alexander Kirk, United States Political Adviser at
Alexander's headquarters, learned what had happened. Kirk was
appalled to discover that his Government's objection to a major policy
change requiring combined Allied approval had been deliberately
flouted, and at once telegraphed the State Department:

> Re our 2162, May 14, 11 p.m. We have just learned that despite our
> informing Chief of Staff [Morgan], Chief Administrative Officer [Robert-
> son], Resident Minister [Macmillan], and G-5 section [Military Govern-
> ment] of Department's views as set forth in Deptel 484, May 15, 7 p.m.,
> the instructions contained in Robertson's draft telegram in which we did
> not concur were carried out. Thus between May 23 and 31 following
> were turned over to Tito: 12196 Croats, 5480 Serbs, 8263 Slovenes, 400
> Monte[ne]grins.
>
> While British field military authorities reported that Tito troops to
> whom these 'anti-Allied Yugos' were handed over accepted them formally
> and correctly, and that no evidence of their subsequent treatment was
> available, Miha Krek, former Deputy Prime Minister of Royal Yugo
> Govt has addressed a letter to SAC [Alexander] requesting that no more
> be turned over to Tito, that those still alive be protected by Allied
> Missions, and enclosed 'eye witness' accounts by escapees of mass murder
> by Tito's forces of hundreds of those surrendered.
>
> We have also seen a telegram from Brit Major Gen Hurray who
> executed Robertson's orders stating that he collected these people together
> and then instructed them to march without giving them any indication
> as to their destination. When they reached their destination and realised
> they were being turned over to Yugo forces some of them attempted to
> escape and a few were fired at by Yugo guards.
>
> If Dept wishes further action taken in matter we will be glad to receive
> instructions.[15]

Nothing appears to be known about the circumstances under which
Kirk acquired this information so long after the event, but some
inferences may be made. It may be that someone at AFHQ had

surreptitiously alerted him to what had been going on, supplying him with at least three separate sets of documents: an accurate report on the dates and numbers of the repatriations, ultimately emanating from the Fifth Corps; Krek's appeal and accompanying document-ation on the transfers; and a copy of General 'Hurray's' telegram. This last must be a misspelling for General Murray, commanding officer of the Sixth Armoured Division. In view of the information it contained (contrasting markedly with the anodyne Fifth Corps 'official' version, referred to at the beginning of Kirk's second para-graph), coupled with General Murray's known antagonism to the policy, it is possible the telegram was despatched (presumably to the Eighth Army) in the form of a protest or objection. Finally, the fact that Kirk apparently received all these documents of disparate origin at about the same time may imply that they were leaked to him by an objector within the command structure at AFHQ.

Acting Secretary of State Joseph Grew replied two days later, on 6 August:

> Please inform Field Marshal Alexander that Dept is unable to understand why upon receipt of Dept's 484 May 15, the instructions contained in Robertson's draft telegram which did not conform to view of British and U.S. Govts and in our opinion could not be justified on grounds of administrative expediency were not repeat not countermanded in time to prevent transfers which, you indicate (urtel 3187, Aug. 4) did not begin until May 23. You should add that we assume that further transfers of such persons to Yugoslav forces have now been halted in accordance with instructions contained in Fan 576, June 20, to Sacmed.[16]

Kirk at once passed on the protest to the Supreme Allied Commander, reporting the results to the State Department on 14 August:

> On receipt of your telegram 719, August 6 we addressed memorandum to Supreme Allied Commander in accordance with Department's instruc-tions. We have today been informed by Deputy Chief of Staff [probably the US Major-General Lowell W. Rooks] on behalf of Supreme Allied Commander that decision to turn over to Tito Yugoslav nationals under reference was made on grounds of military necessity in view of conditions existing at that time. It was stated that Supreme Allied Commander took note of our nonconcurrence and pointed out that the British Resident Minister [Macmillan] had concurred in proposed action but that in any event Supreme Allied Commander took his decision because of conditions existing of which he was better aware than Dept. The communication from Deputy Chief of Staff added that in view of divergent political views

expressed to him on subject, by Resident Minister and ourselves, Supreme Allied Commander suspended transfer of dissident troops as soon as emergency conditions ceased to exist. It was set forth that while Supreme Allied Commander of course seeks the advice of his political advisers on all occasions he must reserve unto himself right to decide matters of an urgent military nature as he sees fit.

In conversation with Alexander this morning he stated to us that he was obliged to receive surrender of almost 1,000,000 Germans in mid-May and could not deal with anti-Tito Yugoslavs as he would have liked. We stated that we had nothing to add to our memorandum under reference except to point out to him again that Resident Minister acted contrary to policy agreed upon after consultation by Department and Foreign Office.[17]

On the face of it nothing could be more explicit than this document. It confirms, to be sure, Macmillan's key role in urging the forced repatriation. But equally it seems to show unequivocally that Alexander, contrary to all the evidence considered so far, both approved and authorised the policy at the moment of its inception. To those desirous of shifting blame on to Alexander, this document has appeared a godsend.[18]

In fact appearances are deceptive. Taken out of context, individual documents can be made to support almost any case. There is of course no reason to suppose that Kirk's summary account of Alexander's statement is anything but accurate. But examination of the context indicates that, while Alexander was prepared to accept overall responsibility for operations occurring within his area of command, he implicitly disclaimed personal involvement in the particular tragedy to which Kirk referred.

Kirk was informed that the repatriations had been ordered 'on grounds of military necessity existing at that time . . . Alexander . . . stated to us that he was obliged to receive surrender of almost 1,000,000 Germans in mid-May and could not deal with anti-Tito Yugoslavs as he would have liked.' Moreover, 'in view of divergent political views expressed to him on subject, by Resident Minister [Macmillan] and ourselves, Supreme Allied Commander suspended transfer of dissident troops as soon as emergency conditions ceased to exist.' The order in question was the telegram sent by Robertson at Macmillan's instance on 14 May.

All these references are clearly to the crisis aroused by the arrival and repulse of the Croatian national exodus on 14 and 15 May, for which Alexander had indeed assumed direct responsibility. It was their overwhelming numbers which, in Alexander's view, made acceptance of their surrender impractical, and he clearly implies that it was numbers which produced the 'emergency conditions' to which he referred in his conversation with Kirk. Immediately the crisis was over, Alexander had indeed 'suspended transfer of dissident troops'. It was on 18 May that Kirk learned that henceforward Alexander had ordered that all Yugoslavs in British custody should be retained, pending 'final disposition'. Next day Tito agreed to evacuate Carinthia, and by the time Serbs and Slovenes from Viktring Camp started being repatriated on 24 May this evacuation was virtually complete. By any reasonable interpretation of events, 'emergency conditions had ceased to exist' *before* the handovers began.

Without being invidiously specific, Alexander accepted personal responsibility for rejection of the Croats' attempt to surrender to the Fifth Corps at Bleiburg, but implicitly *not* for what followed his order of 17 May suspending 'transfer of dissident troops'. (The second suspension, Alexander's 'New Army Order' of 4 June, was concerned with civilians.) Finally, one has to bear in mind the purpose of the reply made on Alexander's behalf. It was intended to gloss over an unfortunate event which could no longer be rectified; not to betray regrettable illegalities, nor draw attention to deep divides over policy matters once existing between Kirk's two British colleagues.

Of course Kirk ought to have noted the discrepancy in the statement, since the reports he had received referred to operations occurring 'between May 23 and 31', following Alexander's successive orders to cease forced repatriation of Yugoslavs. But he knew Alexander and Macmillan intimately, and was well-informed of the former's successive interventions on the Yugoslavs' behalf. Doubtless Kirk knew more than was set down in his brief telegram. It seems he was aware of another version of events: one which corresponded more closely to reality. In his report to the State Department there is no hint of a reflection on the conduct of the Field-Marshal, despite his assumption of responsibility. Instead he concludes emphatically, 'that Resident Minister acted contrary to policy agreed upon after consultation by Department and Foreign Office.'[19]

11

Unravelling a Double Conspiracy

'One evening when I was looking through the lists of Cossack officers, before they were dispatched to Moscow (we received these lists from our investigation branch), I went over the whole affair in my mind. How could the British have done this? . . . Yes indeed, there was a lot I couldn't understand.' (Lieutenant 'A. I. Romanov', SMERSH officer, summer 1945)

It will be seen that the subject-matter of this history falls into two separate though related categories. First, there is the episode of the post-war repatriation, by deceit, force and threat of force, of some 70,000* Cossack and Yugoslav prisoners of war and refugees. The majority of these people, who included thousands of women and children, were either massacred soon after their delivery or died more lingering deaths as a result of inhumane conditions to which they were subjected by their respective governments.

In all probability a precise statistic of the mortality incurred will never be known. The bones of thousands lie beneath the glade in Kocevski Rog, in mass graves outside St Vid, along the route of death-marches stretching from Kranj to Vrsac, or unearthed annually by Austrian ploughs in fields around Bleiburg and the site of the

---

* This figure is a rough total of all Cossacks and Yugoslavs handed over from British camps during May and June 1945. Of these 20 or 30,000 Croats, Serbs and Slovenes, and between 2,000 and 3,000 White Russians, were delivered contrary to the instructions of the British and American Governments. The remainder of the Cossacks were delivered in the absence of instructions. A small proportion of Croats surrendered between 14 and 17 May could be regarded as covered by AFHQ policy in effect during the brief period of the Bleiburg crisis.

Soviet reception camp at Graz. Cossack corpses were scattered in indiscriminate anonymity about the dreary plain of Kemerova Oblast, or immured deep underground in flooded Donbas coal mines. Still more have vanished entirely, tossed out upon the permafrost to be gnawed by wolves the length of the Arctic tundra.

Generals Krasnov, Kelich-Ghirei and Andrei Shkuro, upon whose fate the whole operation had centred, were hanged slowly in the courtyard of the old Lefortovo Prison. Beyond a brief notice in *Pravda* their passing went unnoticed. There was nothing to link their fate with Macmillan's visit to Klagenfurt, nor was it likely they would 'rise again With twenty mortal murders on their crowns'. In the cellars of Lefortovo a crematorium burned day and night, and from the prison roof 'a tall iron chimney rose up . . . emitting continuously a thin smoke' which deposited a light dust over neighbouring buildings.[1] Only Nikolai Krasnov, at the time near to death in a Siblag correctional labour camp outside Mariinsk, preserved imprinted on his memory all that had passed, including the strange interview with Merkulov in Lubianka.

For the space of a generation the tragedy remained virtually unknown outside the immediate circle of those who suffered, and that of their émigré compatriots scattered about the globe. Each June a group of displaced persons gathered at the little cemetery beside Lienz, to chant a *panikhida* over the graves of men and women killed by British troops when attempting to resist this fate. From time to time mothers, widows or sisters of murdered Slovenian farm-boys crept furtively into the forest of Kocevje, to murmur a quick prayer and hang a rosary on one of Tito's newly-planted larches.

Despite the impossibility of conducting investigation inside the Soviet Union or Yugoslavia, the story in its broad outlines is surely too well-attested, internally consistent, and generally corroborated by other historical evidence to be called in question by fair-minded people. Chronicling such events requires industry and persistence in seeking out the evidence upon which the narrative account relies. An element of selection and analytical assessment is also requisite, but for the most part it is the extent and nature of the evidence that persuades us of its truth.

It is when we come to the other main strand of the story that serious difficulties arise. Who on the British side was responsible for an atrocity of such magnitude, what could have been their motives, and how did they succeed in putting it into effect? That the Communist governments of the Soviet Union and Yugoslavia were capable of acts of large-scale barbarism of this type is consistent with much else in their history, and justified by the ideology which motivates their conduct. But how could the British have lent their hands to such a business?

Britain was after all heir to centuries-long ideals of Christian charity, the rule of law, traditions of 'fair play', and upholder of the Hague and Geneva Conventions protecting prisoners of war. In the week these events began she had emerged from a victorious war, one of whose major purposes was the defeat and punishment of an enemy given to perpetrating crimes of a comparable order.

There is an understandable reluctance, in Britain at least, to accept that Englishmen could knowingly have committed such a crime. That a slaughter of major proportions took place, few would now deny, and that it was British troops who sent the victims to their deaths is a matter of historical record. But *how* did it happen? Surely, given the total incompatibility of such an action with the British character and its lack of parallel in recent British history, is it not reasonable to assume that the tragedy arose from any number of understandable, if not wholly excusable, errors of judgement or pragmatic decisions: administrative confusion inevitable in weeks following five chaotic years of total war; the inflexible responses of the military mind when faced with problems beyond routine experience; or perhaps a regrettable but dire need to placate a powerful ally fast becoming a menacing foe?

As all these factors undoubtedly existed at that time in some degree, might it not seem preferable to fit the aberrant event into the broad pattern of things as they are seen to have been, rather than conclude that Macmillan and other Englishmen behaved in a manner wholly uncharacteristic and seemingly inexplicable?

Such a viewpoint, plausible enough as stated, is however foreign to the principles of historiography, and is in essence no different from any other attempt to press facts into the service of a particular theory.[2] General principles are inadequate as a guide to historical truth, and the evidence should be considered on its own merits. Few can be more conscious of the complexity and extent of that evidence than myself, and it may be advisable to pause here and attempt a brief overview of its implications.

The story, as I have attempted to reconstruct it, can be briefly summarised. Harold Macmillan persuaded Keightley to surrender Tsarist officers and Yugoslav fugitives to Stalin and Tito, despite the fact that his instructions from the British and United States

Governments forbade any such action. For this reason the operation had to be kept secret, not only from the governments themselves and from the Supreme Allied Commander at Naples, but also from the British troops in the field who might raise objection to the obvious illegality and inhumanity of what was planned. In the event the subterfuges adopted proved successful, and thousands of people were sent to their deaths whom the Allied Governments had ordered to be protected.

Though Macmillan has claimed that Alexander instructed him to deliver an order that Keightley was eager to fulfil, both claims were shown to be false. Alexander was consistently hostile to the projected operations, while Keightley objected to their implementation until overruled by Macmillan. The soldiers had no recorded or discernible motive for perpetrating an action of this nature, still less for willingly violating their instructions. The only motives for his action provided by Keightley were throughout political, and the only authority that of the Minister Resident. Macmillan, on the other hand, has from the moment of his contemporary diary entry to his 1984 television interview, attempted to exculpate his involvement by a series of demonstrable falsehoods.

If all this be true, then one can only describe what happened as an unscrupulous conspiracy; a conspiracy ingeniously planned and skilfully sustained, whose purpose was to deliver defenceless men, women and children to their enemies, so (in Macmillan's words) 'condemning them to slavery, torture and probably death'. Historical 'conspiracy theories' are in general rightly regarded with scepticism. They tend to supply simplistic explanations for complex events, to be based on selective use of evidence, and even when not strictly refutable represent the less likely of alternative interpretations. All too often they are sustained by motivations extraneous to the issue, ranging from the political (the belief that the French Revolution was engineered by a secret group of Illuminati), to the ingenious (Margaret Murray's theory of the survival of a thriving witch-cult in late mediaeval Britain), and the purely romantic (*The Holy Blood and the Holy Grail*).

On the other hand there exists an equally irrational extreme, which sees only confusion and muddle in historical events: confusion and muddle which on occasion may reflect little more than a reluctance to assimilate a complex range of evidence. In the case of the subject-matter of this book, for example, it is possible to make the illogical assumption that because the material on which it draws is extensive and the necessity for systematic evaluation of those sources overriding, that this in turn reflects a complexity in the events themselves. 'All was in a state of confusion in Austria at that time,' it has been claimed, 'and nobody really knew what was happening.' The premise is true, but the conclusion false. As all the surviving senior officers testify, the issue of screening Cossacks was a simple one, perfectly understood by all officers involved and very much in the forefront of their thinking.

There is also the inevitable question of bias. 'After all, you are a White Russian, and must feel a deep emotional involvement in this history': so an attaché from the Yugoslav Embassy in London recently reminded me. It would be uncandid to deny the imputation; but its inference, I suggested, was inappropriate. It is not the atrocities committed by his and the Soviet Governments that are in dispute; they represent established fact, and it would be hard for prejudice to exaggerate their enormity. What this book is principally concerned with is the question of responsibility on the British side. However deep my sympathy for the victims, it could provide no incentive for knowingly accusing innocent people of being responsible for their sufferings; apart from any other consideration, the effect would be to exculpate those actually responsible. In the absence of any full investigation, this is in fact precisely what has tended to happen. With Macmillan's effacement from the scene, accusations have recently been levelled at Alexander, McCreery, Keightley and Arbuthnott.

Though it is as well to raise the question, the truth is that the question of selectivity arising from bias or other motivation is largely an irrelevancy. As Collingwood remarked:

> no historian, not even the worst, merely copies out his authorities; even if he puts in nothing of his own (which is never really possible), he is always leaving things out, which for one reason or another, he decides that his own work does not need or cannot use. It is he, therefore, and not his authority, that is responsible for what goes on. On that question he is his own master: his thought is to that extent autonomous.
>
> An even clearer exhibition of this autonomy is found in what I have called historical construction. The historian's authorities tell him of this or that phase in a process whose immediate phases they leave undescribed; he then interpolates these phases for himself. His picture of his subject, though it may consist in part of statements directly drawn from his authorities, consists also, and increasingly with every increase in his competence as an historian, of statements reached inferentially from those

according to his own criteria, his own rules of method, and his own canons of relevance. In this part of his work he is never depending on his authorities in the sense of repeating what they tell him; he is relying on his own powers and constituting himself his own authority; while his so-called authorities are now not authorities at all but only evidence.[3]

In this book I have made a conscientious effort to cite the relevant sources, documentary and oral, as fully as possible. The subject is one restricted by time and space, so that there exists greater than average opportunity to attempt comprehensiveness in this respect. But comprehensiveness will always remain an unattainable goal. Even had I been successful (which is unlikely) in unearthing every document and surviving eye-witness concerned with the operations, and cited all of them *in extenso*, this would still only provide a partial picture. For nobody that summer busied himself exclusively with Cossacks and Yugoslavs: Macmillan was concerned with the crisis over Trieste and the coming British general election; Keightley with the ejection of Partisans from Klagenfurt and the establishment of a zonal boundary with Tolbukhin; Colonel Rose Price with his sequestrated ex-enemy Alfa-Romeo; James Wilson with the urgent need for a battalion cricket-ground; Jane Balding with her streaming cold; and Colin Gunner with Betty in the Post Hotel at Villach.

It is not possible for the historian to present a total picture of events, if for no other reason than that such a thing never existed: at least, not for any human observer. But his purpose may still be achieved to all reasonable expectations without aiming at an unattainable goal. The impinging of contingent matters, important or trifling, on a history which (like all histories) has been in part prised from its setting may be as effectively indicated by allusive sketches or occasional scene-setting. The reader's imagination, drawn from a common human experience, enables him to retain a consistent image even while the pattern of a particular succession of events is brought temporarily forward into relief.

To quote Collingwood again:

The historian's picture of his subject, whether that subject be a sequence of events or a past state of things, thus appears as a web of imaginative construction stretched between certain fixed points provided by the statements of his authorities; and if these points are frequent enough and the threads spun from each to the next are constructed with due care, always by the *a priori* imagination and never by merely arbitrary fancy, the whole picture is constantly verified by appeal to these data, and runs little risk of losing touch with the reality which it represents.[4]

In the present case, however, it might well be thought that there is exceptional 'risk of losing touch with the reality'. For we are faced not only by the normal gaps in evidence every historian must attempt to surmount, but also by stratagems practised at the time and since in order to prevent the true story from emerging. There has been in effect a double conspiracy: that perpetrated during the event, designed to prevent the participants (British, Cossack and Yugoslav) from understanding the covert nature of the operation; and that more cautiously conducted since, principally detectable by the abstraction of sensitive documents.

The historian of the recent past does, however, possess one striking advantage over his colleagues concerned with periods further removed in time, whose sole primary materials are surviving documents and artefacts. For the historian of events occurring within the lifespan of contemporaries is in the fortunate position of being able to interrogate the participants themselves. Oral evidence is in itself neither more nor less valid than documentary; both represent the testimony of human minds. But oral and documentary evidence can be checked against each other in a way that documentary evidence alone cannot.

Whatever the nature of his evidence, the historian's purpose is to ask it questions. The skilled student of the more distant past will tease out answers not directly or intentionally revealed by his sources. But for all his skills, ultimately the only replies he can receive are those which chance or design leaves extant within the sources. With a living witness, on the other hand, the historian's source becomes to an extent adaptable to his needs. He may ask fresh questions leading to new answers. In addition he may attempt, with realistic reservations, to assess the personality of the witness, reflecting upon the influence it may have exerted upon his actions at the time or the reliability of his subsequent testimony. This consideration is of little independent historical value, since it is not a readily communicable quality. But it may assist the historian in assessing whether his researches are being conducted on the right tracks, drawing him towards one line of enquiry rather than another. Replies suspected of being deliberately misleading can also prove of use, suggesting clues as to the motive and content of the deception.

Of course the retired general tending his roses in a Somerset garden in 1985 is not the same as the young subaltern fishing by the Wörthersee in 1945. Time and age have shifted opinions and coloured memories.[5] Still, it is my experience in general that memories are surprisingly reliable, even after very long periods of time. There have been many opportunities for extensive cross-checking, rarely with damaging result. I had occasion to interview in connection with a particular event several Cossack and German officers on the one hand, and British officers on the other. Their paths in most cases had converged on that one occasion, and yet the accounts they gave me of conversations thirty years old were remarkably close.

After Brigadier Tryon-Wilson had supplied me with a detailed account of his negotiations with the Soviets at Voitsberg on 11 May, I was dismayed to find a few days later that the chronology of his version seemingly clashed irreconcilably with the contemporary record preserved in the Corps War Diaries. I brought this to his attention, setting out the parallel accounts for comparison. He read my letter through carefully, then telephoned me. 'It seems I'm wrong,' he conceded, 'but I'm afraid that's the way I remember things.' I discovered shame-facedly a few days later that it was I who had blundered, mistaking one meeting for another in the files. Here was a satisfyingly unexpected confirmation of the Brigadier's reliability as a witness.

The purist will object with justice that oral testimony has to undergo a double transformation: the first incurred in the exchange between witness and historian, and the second when the historian in turn blends the account into his written story. This is incontrovertibly true, but at the same time can on occasion provide a further check on the verisimilitude of the finished narrative. For the witness not only supplies the raw material of which the history is composed, but may also judge the validity of the finished product.

One of the most rewarding letters I received after the publication of my *Victims of Yalta* came from an informant of exceptionally wide experience of the events I had described: Czeslaw Jesman, a Polish officer who worked for months with Russian prisoners in British camps, and travelled on ships carrying repatriated Russians to Murmansk and Odessa. After publication of the book he wrote to me: 'all I can say is that in reading it my old chum Shershun [the NKVD officer with whom he dealt], the . . . Ratov [head of the Soviet Military Mission] and many of my distinguished English colleagues sprang up to life as if I saw them yesterday.'

To relive the past, albeit vicariously and with only a subjective

judgement as to the success of the exercise, Collingwood saw as the
historian's prime task:

> If . . . the historian has no direct or empirical knowledge of the facts, and
> no transmitted or testimoniary knowledge of them [as Collingwood
> argued he cannot], what kind of knowledge has he: in other words, what
> must the historian do in order that he may know them?
>
> My historical review of the idea of history has resulted in the emergence
> of an answer to this question: namely, that the historian must re-enact
> the past in his own mind.[6]

In fact it is scarcely possible to exaggerate the importance of oral
evidence in relation to a book like the present. Without it one can
neither relive the past, nor understand the nature of the events
themselves. This was brought strikingly home to me at a lecture I
attended on 16 October 1985 at the School of Slavonic and East
European Studies of the University of London, by which time most
of my researches were completed. The lecturer, Mr Robert Knight,
subjected my earlier brief attempts at investigating what I had termed
'the Klagenfurt Conspiracy' to serious criticism, much of it justified.
He had read through some of the documents accessible in the Public
Record Office, from which a picture emerged of a harassed General
Keightley bundling Cossacks and Yugoslavs over the frontier in
order to rid himself of an intolerable administrative burden. His
action was endorsed by his superior, General McCreery, and probably
tacitly accepted by Alexander.

Above all, in Knight's view, the crucial issue concerning the White
Russians was clear. Since it was not until 14 May, the day *after*
Macmillan's visit, that Keightley wrote to McCreery reporting his
having asked the Soviets whether they would like the Cossacks
returned, it was impossible for Macmillan to have known whether
the White generals were included in the subsequent Soviet reply.
This response Knight believed to have been received no earlier than
21 May, when Soviet and British officers met to confer on the coming
handovers, and when Macmillan was absent in England.

Macmillan's intervention was minimal, Knight explained, amounting to little more than prior endorsement of Keightley's wishes.
Macmillan could not, therefore, have played any major role in the
decision to return the Cossacks, still less have advocated the inclusion
of the White Russian generals.

The handover [he concluded] was a military decision made at a time of crisis and pressure. The responsibility . . . rests with Alexander, McCreery, perhaps [Mark] Clark, Robertson and, above all, Keightley . . . With the exception of the non-Soviet citizens, the handover of the Cossacks was approved (albeit retrospectively) by those responsible at Allied Forces Headquarters in London and Washington . . . In so far as there was any deception within the British command structure, it came from Keightley, perhaps McCreery, and arose from their determination to clear their area of an unwanted burden as soon as possible. There was no Klagenfurt conspiracy.

This appraisal was for the most part consistent with that part of the documentary record examined by Mr Knight, representing a legitimate inference from its contents. Everything was true – except the facts. As I listened I could not help wondering what Brigadier Tryon-Wilson would have made of this version of events, recalling his account of the message he brought to Fifth Corps headquarters on 11 May and Keightley's response. Not caring to introduce an unpleasant note of controversy into the proceedings, I confined myself to asking whether Mr Knight had actually spoken to anyone who had taken part in the operations he described in such detail. His reply was that he had not, nor did he feel that such people could have added anything material to his researches. Academic historians, he explained patiently, deal exclusively in hard facts: that is, documents and printed sources.

This episode is not included from an ungenerous desire to belittle Mr Knight's researches, which were vigorously endorsed by the meeting's chairman, Dr Mark Wheeler, the distinguished historian of modern Yugoslavia. They comprise an exemplary illustration of the extent to which the written record can in extreme cases amount to little more than what publishers of well-researched spy stories term 'faction'. One can sympathise with Mr Knight's predicament in particular, since many of the documents he examined were drawn up for the specific purpose of conveying the misleading impression he received.

But if the record can be effectively perverted or distorted to such an extent, are we entitled to lend any credibility to what passes for historical narrative? History, as historians never tire of stressing, is not a 'pure' or 'exact' science. Nevertheless, provided the researches on which it is based be pursued as comprehensively and analytically as possible, it can achieve a great deal by the application of its own methods. As Professor Harry Hearder has wisely written:

It is surely . . . true that the physicist or the chemist, with his controlled experiment, can establish an exact truth in a sense that a historian never can. Even so, like the other 'social' sciences, history establishes truths, which, in human terms, can be trusted. That Queen Anne is not only dead, but that she died two hundred and fifty-four years ago, is not only a fact which it would be unreasonable to doubt: it is a statistical statement of a much more reliable kind than most statistical statements issuing from boards of directors or government offices. The legal phrase, that a case can be proved 'beyond reasonable doubt' seems to me particularly useful for the historian. The surface facts which we establish from our evidence can usually be proved 'beyond reasonable doubt'. It is only when causal factors, or more general explanations, are considered, that more than one interpretation becomes possible. What caused the French Revolution, or whether the French Revolution succeeded, are matters of interpretation; that Napoleon lost the battle of Waterloo is a matter of fact, and of a fact that has been proved beyond reasonable doubt.[7]

The 'surface facts' of the 'Klagenfurt Conspiracy', as I persist in believing it may legitimately be termed, appear to me to 'prove beyond reasonable doubt':

1. That a conspiracy took place, whose prime aim was (as General Musson emphasises) to co-operate with the Soviet request for the handover of a number of émigré officers.

2. That, despite the Foreign Office's instructions to conduct screening of Russians to be repatriated, Macmillan collaborated with Keightley to prevent its taking place. This is inferred from the fact that the presence of the émigré generals and the Soviet request for their return were known to Keightley two days before his conference with Macmillan, and that Macmillan admits he recommended compliance with the Soviet request. In view of their respective positions, such collaboration can only imply that the initiative came from Macmillan.

3. That administrative concerns local to the Fifth Corps cannot reasonably be ascribed as a motivating factor in Keightley's case, since orders he received on 17 and 22 May would have enabled him to clear his area of Yugoslav and Cossack prisoners without recourse to unauthorised measures.

4. That Field-Marshal Alexander consistently opposed the return of any Cossacks or Yugoslavs, all his actions being designed to prevent such an event.

5. That written orders were falsified within the Fifth Corps to conceal what was intended, and that they were secretly superseded by contradictory oral instructions.

6. That the organisers of these illicit operations were so apprehensive of discovery as to abandon them at the first serious threat of exposure.

7. That Field-Marshal Alexander expressed by his words and actions on 4 and 5 June his anger and disapproval of those aspects of the operations of which he had become aware.

8. That the subsequent report drawn up by the Thirty-sixth Infantry Brigade can only have been intended to deceive Keightley's superiors.

There are many other significant 'fixed points', as has been seen, but these should suffice. There are also considerations of a different nature, tending towards similar conclusions; an obvious example being the fact that the principal personalities whom the evidence indicates as being responsible for the covert operations can be shown to have lied on different occasions; while those on whose testimony evidence of a conspiracy has been based have so far proved truthful and reliable witnesses.

How much Alexander learned of the extent of the deception to which he had fallen prey will probably never be known. Others at the time who should have been ideally placed to investigate the mystery were unable to discover much more than the bare fact of the operations having taken place. On 10 June 1945, less than a week after Field-Marshal Alexander had called a halt to the repatriation operations, Dr Miha Krek, former Deputy Prime Minister of the Yugoslav Government in Exile, wrote from Rome to Sir George Rendel, previously Ambassador to his Government:

My dear Sir George,
I am writing you this letter in bed, to which I am bound after an operation. I am profoundly sorry for disturbing you, but the news I got today was so extraordinary, so horrible, such unthinkable one and unexpected, that I could not resist thinking it was my duty to inform you about.

In the period from May 27th to May 31st the British Military Authorities in Carinthia delivered 11,100 men of the Slovene Home-Guard to Tito Partisan Military Authorities in Yugoslavia. Some of the men were shot immediately after returning on the Yugoslav territory, especially all officers.

From the enclosed report you will see how it all happened. You know, my dear Sir George, that the Slovene Home-Guard were patriotic, nationalistic, pro-Allied and pro-British in their intentions and in their deeds. You know, that many of them were imprisoned by the Germans, who permitted this organization. Many of them were put into German concentration camps, because the Germans repeatedly discovered that under the cover of this organization, the Slovene boys never stopped their continuous work against the Axis forces. The Slovene Home-Guard never fought against any of the Allied Nations. It was just a Home-Guard Police Force, safeguarding the properties and lives of the Slovenian democratic and catholic people from the massacres and attacks of the Tito Communist bands.

Now, after the armistice, the Home-Guard went together with the other Slovenian refugees, who in ten thousands left their homes and tried to find shelter on the Austrian and Italian territory under the protection of the British forces. The British accepted these Slovenian people and promised them every help and protection; but after a few days the British Military Command began to transport the Slovenian boys and men back to Yugoslavia in the hands of Tito military authorities.

As a Slovene, Dr Krek was primarily concerned with his own people. He implored Rendel to take steps to ensure that further transportations ceased, and begged the British Government to intervene within Yugoslavia 'in order to guarantee at least a minimum of liberty and of the Four Freedoms of the United Nations'. The letter was accompanied by a number of first-hand accounts of Titoist atrocities, extracts from which have already been quoted in this book.

Rendel passed Krek's letter on to the Southern Department of the Foreign Office, commenting:

> I imagine that, even if there is a foundation of truth in all this, we should be extremely reluctant to intervene, even if we could do so with any success.
>
> But Dr Krek was one of the best of the 'old dispensation', and his appeal I think deserves at least our serious attention.

On 29 June J. M. Addis of the Southern Department, minuting this correspondence, observed:

> It is true that in the first few days of the Allied occupation of Carinthia, a number of Slovene Domobranci were delivered across the frontier to the troops of Tito. This was contrary to instructions and was stopped as soon as the news was received. The present policy is that such formations as the Domobranci are disarmed and interned by the Allied Forces and held pending further instructions. No Yugoslav is being returned to Yugoslavia against his will.
>
> We do not know the number of Domobranci handed over to Tito but

I doubt whether the figure is as large as 11,100. Nor do we know how they were treated after they were handed over.

However, matters were not permitted to rest here, as on 25 August Major Guy Lloyd, a Member of Parliament who had come to learn of Krek's charges, wrote to the Foreign Office to suggest:

> some kind of investigation and explanation is necessary, if the allegations contained in the letter and report are correct. I would be grateful to hear from you after you have had an opportunity to look into the whole matter. Stories of such terrible atrocities and massacres of political opponents are so prevalent nowadays, that I agree they must be carefully authenticated, but this one is so terrible, and involves so many, I really feel it is impossible to ignore it, without a protest. To a certain extent also, our honour and obligations are at stake, as I think you will see by the letter from Dr Krek.

Lloyd's enquiry necessitated a formal investigation. The War Office was approached for details. While this enquiry was in progress, J. M. Addis, head of the Yugoslav Section of the Foreign Office, became due for promotion. On 21 September he drew up a memorandum for his successor, John Colville (now Sir John), to keep him *au fait* with the problem. In it he set out the facts as already established in this book: the British and American decision to rule out the use of force in returning Yugoslavs; Alexander's consequent directive to that effect; and the ratification of this policy in the telegram sent by the Chiefs of Staff on 20 June to Alexander. Despite this, however:

> We learned incidentally from paragraph 6 of COS (W)917 of May 29th in R9443/G that while the question of principle was still under discussion between A.F.H.Q., the Chiefs of Staff and ourselves, V Corps, a British formation, had 'agreed to hand over Croats to Yugoslavia and 900 Croats were transferred on the 24th May.' We never saw any of the telegrams from the military authorities in Italy reporting this transfer, and I do not yet know whether any instructions were issued at the time by the War Office to suspend such action. Major James of P.W.2 in the War Office is going through the contemporary files and will send over copies of the relevant documents.
> It was not until some time later that we learned that the unfortunate Croats and Slovenians who had been expelled from Carinthia had been extensively slaughtered by Tito's troops after crossing the Yugoslav frontier.

Three weeks earlier Addis had expressed himself more succinctly and forcefully on the subject: 'The handing-over of Slovenes etc. by the 8th Army in Austria to Tito's forces was a ghastly mistake. It was rectified as soon as it was reported to headquarters. But for about a week at the end of May these unfortunate men were passed across the frontier by British troops to be butchered by Tito's Army.'

John Colville was if anything still more outspoken. Urging that 'since the incident was a disgraceful one the War Office should be asked to have enquiries made into the immediate responsibility for handing over to a certain and unpleasant death these unfortunate Croats, while the question of their disposal was still under consideration at a high level,' he went on to note: 'I think we can do no more than admit that a serious blunder did take place and that the story does not reflect well on the officers immediately concerned. It is no use trying to hush up an incident which is indefensible . . .'[8]

Colville was in an advantageous position to understand just how discreditable the events had been. At the time they took place he had been Private Secretary to the Prime Minister, and so had the best of reasons for knowing that the repatriations had not been authorised by the Government. Recently he has recalled:

> In May 1945 I was still at No 10, and I have no recollection of that unhappy event when the Chetniks in Austria were handed back to Tito. Nor did I make any reference to it in my diary and I suspect that we were not informed . . . I agree with you in thinking it improbable that Alex approved the hand-over. It would have been wholly untrue to his form. Whether Harold Macmillan was responsible I doubt if we shall ever know, for I expect the orders were not committed to paper and it seems clear that the C.O.S., the F.O. and No 10 were not informed. But I doubt if General Keightley would have taken such a step without higher authority.[9]

A year after the operations had taken place it was Colville's turn to reply to a second enquiry into what was proving an increasingly embarrassing affair. On 15 May Dr Harold Buxton, Bishop of Gibraltar, wrote to a Member of Parliament, Professor Douglas Savory, enclosing a copy of a letter from his nephew Francis Scott, 'who was serving as an officer in a Border Regiment' – in fact, as Mr Scott informs me today, the Second Lothians and Border Horse. The Bishop was disturbed by his nephew's account, and asked Savory to take up the matter with the Foreign Office.

The relevant part of Scott's letter read as follows:

At the end of the war, I was stationed in Carynthia [at Sittersdorf, so Mr Scott informs me] on the Jugoslav border keeping an eye on Tito. Quite a variety of D.P.s came over of different kinds and a good number of Tito agents trying to persuade the local Slovene population that Carynthia would be better under Jugoslavia than Austria; also a lot of Germans but those who interested me most were the Chetniks. They have come back into the public eye with the trial of Mihailovitch. They were the remnants of the old Jugoslav national army who had gone on fighting the Germans with our support. In the middle of the war, as far as anyone could see under Russian pressure, we transferred our affections to Tito. From then on the Communist Partisans were much more numerous than the Chetniks and better armed. They spent the greater part of their time rounding up and massacring the Chetniks whom Britain had so recently supported with British and Russian arms. This was still in full swing when we arrived. Of course we were not allowed to cross the frontier but large numbers of Chetnik soldiers were among the refugees who came over and there was no doubt that the Tito troops shot any whom they could catch, saying that they had fought for the Germans.

Our orders were to disarm any Chetniks whom we caught crossing the frontier, to take great care that they were not told where they were going, and then to take them back to a different part of the frontier and hand them back unarmed to the Communists from whom they had just escaped. This hardly seemed to most of us to be in accord with the best British principles of fair play but as soldiers we had to obey orders *which we were told emanated from Whitehall* [italics inserted]. I had to interrogate some of the men in question if they spoke German or Italian and where possible I reported that they had useful information and were worth interrogation. I hoped that in this way there was some chance of them not being sent back. They were all certain that they would be shot by the Communists if they were. Those who were handed back begged the British troops to shoot them rather than hand them over.

One well educated officer told me that he had been a professor of Philosophy at Zagreb university and later a Captain in the Army. He gave me accounts, some of which were later cross-checked, of vast massacres of Chetniks and other Royalists by the Communist partisans after the war ended . . .

I hope I don't seem unduly biased but my feelings over these things were shared by the most Socialist members of my squadron and politics as we know them at home have nothing to do with what goes on elsewhere. What I felt most was the action taken by this country in handing over simple people who had acted as they felt was right in the war, some of them as our allies, to a sticky fate when we had the chance to save them.

In a letter to his mother at the time, Scott noted of the Zagreb professor that, 'When I had finished interrogating him – (in Italian!) he opened his ragged coat and begged to be shot rather than put back over the border as he should have been. This is very common and they really mean it.'

The Bishop had himself been deeply concerned at the time with the fate of the Chetniks. Mr M. S. Stankovic, a Chetnik officer who had been handed over from Viktring Camp and subsequently escaped, came to know Dr Buxton after the war:

> He was in Rome at the time of the tragic events in Viktring Camp. Very soon he learned what happened there, and at once rushed to see Field-Marshal Alexander, who was in Caserta. The Bishop protested strongly, and found the Field-Marshal very sympathetic and understanding. He never mentioned Mr Macmillan. But he said something like this: 'it is very difficult to stop it once the Government machine takes a direction.'

Professor Savory passed Dr Buxton's letter to the Foreign Office, and it was arranged that he should himself call and discuss the matter. On 30 May John Colville noted:

> The Bishop of Gibraltar came to see Mr Hayter and myself bringing with him this letter from his nephew and we explained to him quite clearly that the incident to which his nephew referred must have been the surrender in May 1945 of 900 Croats by the British military authorities which ended in their massacre. In spite of this the Bishop went straight home and wrote his letter to *The Times* on the strength of which Professor Savory asked his question in Parliament.
>
> I do not for one moment believe that there is any truth in Mr Francis Scott's allegations. We have made specific enquiries of the military authorities in Vienna who have denied that they have handed over anybody except escaped Prisoners of War and deserters. Judging from what we are told the military authorities are far more likely to err in the direction of favouring the Yugoslav Royalists than in handing them back to Marshal Tito's men. There may of course have been isolated cases which were hushed up and which never got back to Headquarters but there has certainly never been any order from Whitehall of the kind suggested in Mr Francis Scott's irresponsible letter.[10]

Colville clearly knew no more than he told the Bishop, and relied for authority on the peculiar telegram referred to in the Chiefs of Staff report of 29 May, which claimed that the only major handover had been that of 900 Croats on 24 May. This information bears no obvious relation to any operation known to have taken place. 24 May was the day that the first party was despatched from Viktring Camp to the Rosenbach tunnel; it consisted of 450 Croats and 1,000 Serbs. This looks very like disinformation designed to provide a smoke-screen while the camp was hastily evacuated. The Croats would have been the ethnic group to single out, as the Ustashi association with the Nazis had caused the name 'Croat' to become widely associated in British eyes with 'quisling'.

Even the War Office was baffled in its attempts to get to the bottom of the mystery. In 1947, John Corsellis, who had been working with Slovenian refugees in camps for the past two years, opened a correspondence with various officials on the subject of individual Slovenes in Austrian DP camps, who were fearful of being deported to Yugoslavia on what Corsellis suspected to be trumped-up charges of being war criminals. It was at his instance that a Member of Parliament concerned with the refugee problem, Major Tufton Beam-ish, directed an enquiry to the Foreign Office.

Christopher Mayhew, the Parliamentary Under-Secretary, replied on 15 December, denying that any but proven collaborators were being repatriated and concluding:

> I am very much afraid that these unhappy people have been the victims of provocateurs who are constantly trying to drive a wedge between the refugees and their British protectors, since it has been explained to refugees in our zones on many occasions that nobody with a clear conscience need fear lest he be forcibly repatriated. This impression is heightened by the reference to our alleged surrender of 10,000 Slovenes – a canard which has been refuted on more than one occasion, but which reappears with suspicious frequency in allegations purporting to come from displaced persons.

Corsellis, who had been working in the neighbouring camp for civilians at the time of the Viktring handovers, understandably found this reply inadequate. After some further correspondence, he was invited to the Foreign Office on 12 June 1948 to discuss the matter with Evelyn Boothby, the official responsible for displaced persons in the British zone of Austria. Corsellis asked Boothby how the Foreign Office could rest content with the absurd report of the '900 Croats'. Boothby displayed great interest in Corsellis' first-hand account, frankly confessing his own ignorance. What Corsellis alleged might well be true, he conceded, but the telegram cited in the Chiefs of Staff memorandum of 29 May 1945 was all the Foreign Office had to go on.

He did, however, unwittingly let drop one intriguing piece of information. As Corsellis put it shortly afterwards in a letter to a Slovene, Dr France Blatnik:

> You must know [Corsellis had been told] that our troops who were in Austria at the time had a clear-cut purpose: to organise a line of defence in the event of an attack by Tito or the Soviet Union. Therefore they were not prepared for the arrival of these collaborators and also did not care to have much to do with them. Possibly for this reason perhaps their report was here and there inaccurate and the numbers played down.

Thus far the explanation was confessedly based on speculation, but what followed provides a glimpse of an exchange of which one would dearly like to learn more.

> But it [the account of the return of the 900 Croats] is the only report we have. The officers who signed it are now civilians and the War Office cannot search for them in order to report in greater detail on the whole episode. Thus we're tied to what we have. You maintain that over 10,000 were returned. We do not dispute this, but nevertheless the number . . . remains as the official number for us, because we have it in the reports made at that time.[11]

This account makes clear what is in any case intrinsically likely, that the report in question emanated from 'our troops who were in Austria at the time'; i.e. the Fifth Corps. To suppose that the military authorities in Vienna, whom the War Office had consulted, could not have compiled an accurate report on the basis of the Fifth Corps War Diary would be absurd. Instead they claimed that it was no longer possible to investigate the matter, as 'the officers who signed it are now civilians'.

Who were these 'civilians'? The battalion commanders involved, such as Colonel Rose Price of the Third Welsh Guards, were without exception regular officers still in service. The brigade and divisional commanders, Brigadier Verney and General Murray, were likewise regular soldiers readily accessible to the War Office. As for the Corps Commander, General Keightley – he was in 1948 actually in London, serving as Military Secretary to the Secretary of State for War.

The type of report to which the Foreign Office referred would under any normal conditions have been despatched from Corps headquarters by the Brigadier General Staff. On 24 May 1945 this post was as we know held by Toby Low, on whom General Keightley had devolved the whole business of dealing with the Yugoslavs. Can it be coincidence that the one officer in the chain of command who from 1945 had indeed been a civilian was the one whose post makes him the most likely signatory of the report to which the Foreign Office referred?

That the information contained in the report was false is proved by a cursory glance at the War Diary of the Sixth Armoured Division. But was the War Office really incapable of tracing the address of the distinguished Member of Parliament for Blackpool North? The reader must draw his own conclusions, but it looks as if the British Army was firmly declining to accept responsibility for a policy which did not derive from Allied Force Headquarters, and had not been transmitted by regular military channels; particularly when the officer who arranged the operations had long since resigned his commission.

The Fifth Corps telegram reporting that the total number of Yugoslavs repatriated comprised 900 Croats despatched in error on 24 May is no longer to be found in the files. It is one of a number of vanished documents, of which mention has already been made from time to time in this book. Assembled together, a significant pattern becomes detectable. The missing papers include the following:

1. The two-page typewritten Soviet demand for the handover of Generals Krasnov, Shkuro and other old émigré officers, handed by Brigadier Tryon-Wilson to Toby Low at Fifth Corps headquarters in Klagenfurt on 11 May.

2. General Krasnov's two letters to Alexander, written in May.

3. General Shkuro's similar appeals of 23 and 24 May, which reached the Seventy-eighth Infantry Division HQ but subsequently disappeared.

4. The petitions drawn up by General Krasnov in the cage at Spittal on 28 May, signed by all the Cossack officers and passed up to the Seventy-eighth Divisional headquarters by Colonel Bryar of the Kensingtons.

5. The Fifth Corps' copy of Alexander's 'New Army Policy' of 4 June, ending forced repatriation of Yugoslavs.

6. The parallel order of the same day which for the first time made screening of Cossacks effective in the Corps area. This omission is particularly significant, as the order's presence in the War Diaries would have contradicted the assertion in the Thirty-sixth Infantry Brigade's report of 3 July that screening had taken place *before* 4 June.

7. The War Office file BM 3928/PW1, containing details of the internal enquiry into the problem of the Cossacks, following Churchill's request for information on 20 May 1945. This vanished some time between the early part of 1974, when I inspected it, and the beginning of 1977. The file number had been transferred to another file.

8. Most remarkable of all is the disappearance of the entire archive of Macmillan's office at AFHQ from the time it was transferred from Algiers to Caserta in July 1944. On 9 January 1986, I was informed in a letter from the Foreign and Commonwealth Office:

> 'I am sorry to have taken so long to reply to your letter of 12 November about the records of the British Minister-Resident at Caserta in 1945. I can, however, assure you that the delay reflects the extensive search we have made. Unfortunately, I must now tell you that we too have been unable to trace further records following the Minister-Resident's move from Algiers'.

The Public Record Office shortly afterwards expressed similar bafflement, conjecturing only that there could have been 'room for the loss or accidental destruction of files' during subsequent 'weeding'.

Two threads can be detected running through this skein of doctored evidence. First, there was a concerted effort to conceal the fact that the repatriation had been carefully organised contrary to orders. Second, someone appears to have been at great pains to make it appear as if it were Field-Marshal Alexander who was directly responsible for all that happened.

It is hard in this context not to be reminded of the uncompromising claim made recently by the man who actually arranged the deaths of the Yugoslavs and émigré Cossacks. On 21 December 1984 Harold Macmillan emphasised in a television interview with Ludovic Kennedy already referred to that he had merely acted on Alexander's instructions.

'So did the executive order come from General Keightley?' asked Kennedy.

'Oh no,' replied Macmillan; 'from the Field-Marshal . . . and to him from the Combined Chiefs.'

In his diary entry for 13 May 1945, Macmillan provided this account of the Yugoslav refugees held by the Fifth Corps in camps at Viktring and elsewhere:

To add to the confusion, thousands of so-called Ustashi or Chetniks, mostly with wives and children, are fleeing in panic into this area in front of the advancing Yugoslavs. These expressions, Ustashi and Chetnik, cover anything from guerrilla forces raised by the Germans from Slovenes and Croats and Serbs to fight Tito, and armed and maintained by the Germans – to people who, either because they are Roman Catholics or Conservative in politics, or for whatever cause are out of sympathy with revolutionary Communism and therefore labelled as Fascists or Nazis. (This is a very simple formula, which in a modified form is being tried, I observe, in English politics.)

The entry was probably written that same afternoon, during the long flight from Klagenfurt to Caserta.

Despite these reflections, it was no later than the next day that Macmillan 'recommended' to General Robertson a draft telegram to General McCreery 'instructing him to turn over to Yugoslav Partisans a large number of dissident Yugoslav troops with exception of Chetniks' – an exception about which Robertson, doubtless reflecting Macmillan's sentiments, 'was very vague'. Before this telegram was sent, surrendered Yugoslavs had been shepherded to safety at Palmanova. Afterwards, in implementation of Macmillan's recommendation, they were despatched in their thousands to the pit of Kocevje and the anti-tank trenches of Teharje.

Macmillan has explained the exceptional circumstances under which he kept his diary.

> The Diaries were written on odd pieces of paper, notepaper or scribbling paper, whatever was available, in aeroplanes, in waiting rooms, in my own bedroom at night, and occasionally in tents, caravans or huts where I was a guest of one of the commanders. They are necessarily somewhat confused and repetitive. They began as letters to my wife, but soon became a regular daily journal, which I continued to write even when she was able to come out and visit me. I used to send them home to her in the diplomatic bag every two or three weeks, whenever one was available. She preserved them carefully.[12]

Apart from informing Lady Dorothy and preserving a personal record, their ultimate purpose was that of furnishing a future memoir.

The hypocrisy implicit in Macmillan's expressed sympathy for the helpless fugitives appears self-evident. What is much less so is its purpose. In his official report to the Foreign Office Macmillan deliberately withheld any reference to the question of the Yugoslav refugees. Why then, did he go out of his way to parade this concern in a letter to his wife? She could know nothing of the matter one way or the other, and it was unlikely she would ever hear about it. The inappropriateness of the expressions precludes any possibility of an attempt to salve a guilty conscience; that could only be attempted by some form of justification of the action he had taken. Yet the parade of charitable concern is so laboured and its inclusion at the same time so superfluous as to demand explanation.

The answer can only be, surely, that the passage was designed for the purpose it ultimately fulfilled: that of inclusion in the Macmillan memoirs. Its presence there is suggestive. First, it is clear that its purpose was not – at least not explicitly – that of exculpating himself from any involvement in the refugees' handover to Tito. The hand-over itself is nowhere alluded to in Macmillan's memoirs or diaries, and, thanks to the completeness of the slaughters at Kocevje and Teharje, remained unknown except to friendless groups of Yugoslav émigrés.

Nevertheless Macmillan felt that something must be written pre-senting himself as a man sympathetic to the plight of these friendless people, a man of whom it would be unthinkable that he could have wished them a moment's unease, let alone set about to arrange their slaughter. An acute sense of self-preservation, perhaps, rather than a tormented conscience, told him it was just possible that in some unforeseen way the world might yet learn something of what had happened.

Suppose one day a tale came to be told of mass firing-squads across the Yugoslav frontier? Someone might then resurrect a story long buried, of British treachery and Communist savagery. Who should bear the responsibility when searching questions came to be asked? Macmillan had been in Austria and had spoken with Keightley at the time. But, as anyone would see, he had felt only a deep compassion for the refugees' plight – compassion free of any suspicion that tragedy had been looming. Clearly the culprit must be sought elsewhere.

If one thing is clear, it is the extreme care with which Macmillan covered his tracks. We have no record of his reason for unexpectedly flying from Treviso to Klagenfurt on the morning of 13 May; no minutes of his conversations with Keightley and McCreery; no account of his report to Alexander on his return to Naples. In his diary he omits all mention of his communication with General Robertson on 14 May. Small wonder that in the first books to investigate responsibility for the forced repatriations of 1944–47, those by Huxley-Blythe, Epstein and Bethell, one may search the indexes in vain for the name of the man who arranged the grimmest massacres of all. In my own book, *Victims of Yalta*, I could do no more than raise a single tentative query.

The fact of Macmillan's intervention and its effect are clear from the historical record. An additional factor is the considerable element of risk involved. Had Churchill discovered the truth, there can be little doubt that Macmillan's promising career as Conservative politician would have come to an abrupt end. At any rate, this must have appeared as a distinct possibility when Macmillan was busily spinning his web round victims and colleagues alike.

There can be little doubt that the motive which drove Macmillan to plan an operation cruel and dishonourable like no other in British history was one of overriding impulsion. If the inhumanity did not deter him, the risk to his career and reputation must certainly have done. Why did he do it? There are a number of possible explanations.

First, there is Macmillan's own version. He has claimed that the Cossacks were handed over in order to obtain in exchange freed British prisoners of war; in order to display 'scrupulous adherence to the [Yalta] agreement in handing back Russian subjects'; and because the British authorities had no 'means of dealing with them had we refused to do so.' However, 'it was a great grief to me that there was no other course open.'

Sir Michael Cullis, head of the Foreign Office Austrian Section in 1945, remarks of this explanation:

> Macmillan . . . puts forward a number of justifications (when, if valid, a single one might be thought sufficient!) . . . Was the case all that different from the gratuitous surrender in 1940 by Stalin, and by the Vichy Government, of refugees from Nazi Germany? So, at any rate, I recall asking at the time, at the Austrian desk of the Foreign Office, when I learnt – though only after the event – what had been perpetrated.[13]

It may be noted in addition that all three of Macmillan's explanations are demonstrably false. *No* agreement on the overland return of liberated British prisoners was arranged at that time, and a fortnight later we find Alexander complaining that 'no reciprocal guarantee in respect of British ex PW [has been] obtained . . . Evacuation to Odessa still continuing from this area.' In fact there is no reason to believe that on 13 May Keightley yet possessed any specific information regarding British prisoners in the Soviet zone, nor that Macmillan seriously considered the British prisoners at all in this context. For had he done so in any context more emphatic than that of a pious hope that the Soviets might comply should the British prisoners materialise, Keightley must surely have mentioned it as a factor when next day he urged McCreery to comply with Macmillan's advice. He did not.

The inclusion of the White émigrés among those returned, which constituted the major purpose of Macmillan's stratagems, was directly *contrary* to the accepted terms of the Yalta Agreement. Lastly, so far from there being nothing that could have been done with the Cossacks should they not have gone back, we know that it was a mere four days later that Alexander began making arrangements to transfer them to SHAEF territory; a suggestion that evoked unhesitating agreement from Eisenhower.

Whatever the reasons that impelled Macmillan to adopt the course he did, they are shown not to be the ones he has given. Nevertheless he must have had a motive, and an extremely pressing one at that. Some possibilities suggest themselves, most inconsistent with Macmillan's own explanation, but none is satisfactory.

It has been advanced on Macmillan's behalf that the inclusion of the White officers among the returned Cossacks was an improvised sop to the Soviets at a time of enormous problems facing the Fifth Corps. As was argued in an article in *The Spectator* some years ago:

> The signals to Alexander's HQ were buzzing with worries – about the Yugoslav advance into Carinthia from the south, shortage of food, the million-odd POWs and refugees milling around – *and* the fear of trouble from Tolbukhin's Red Army just up the road. These were all real sources of anxiety, as the documentary record shows . . .[14]

But it has been seen that the logistical problem of maintaining the Cossacks was far from being regarded as insuperable, and that the question at issue is in any case that of at most 3,000 or so White émigrés. The irruption of the Yugoslavs could bear no obvious relevance to the retention or otherwise of the White officers. As for the most potent motivation suggested, it is precisely what the documentary record does *not* show. On the attitude of Tolbukhin's army Macmillan's own report is clear. Keightley, he wrote, informed him: 'In the North East contact has been established with the Russians. British and Russian Corps Commanders have had a meeting and agreed upon a temporary line of demarcation between their respective forces. No trouble is anticipated here although the Russians have advanced into what is technically our zone.' Keightley himself reported at the same time to the Eighth Army that 'all relations with Soviets most friendly with much interchange whisky and vodka,' and it was noted at AFHQ that, 'The Russians . . . are scrupulously observing such local arrangements in Styria as are made by our respective commanders.'[15]

This was two days after Brigadier Tryon-Wilson had made it clear to the Soviets at Voitsberg that British provisions for screening would make it impossible for the Fifth Corps to surrender non-Soviet citizens among the Cossacks. As far as he could see they had for the moment accepted his explanation with equanimity, and no protests had followed his visit. General S. M. Shtemenko, Stalin's Deputy Chief of Staff, refers in his memoirs to the surrender of Krasnov, Shkuro and the others, giving no hint that it resulted from military pressure applied by Tolbukhin. Shtemenko would have known if it had, and had no motive for concealing such an example of Allied weakness in face of Soviet strength.

The Yugoslav General Kosta Nadj visited Tolbukhin's headquarters shortly after this, where he encountered not the exultation one might expect from British weakness in face of Soviet armed might, but rather mild bafflement at British complaisance:

> When I was at Tolbukhin's headquarters both Tolbukhin and Voroshilov told me they had no problems with the Allies. General Keightley, the same man who handed over to us the Ustashe administration and some other Ustashe, Chetnik, Domobranci and Slovenian officer-traitors, surrendered to Tolbukhin the seventy-six-year-old Peter Krasnov, one of the leaders of the counter-revolution in the Civil War who, during the Second World War organised the traitorous Cossack cavalry divisions and corps.[16]

While in the Butyrki Prison in Moscow in 1946, Lev Kopelev (the 'Rubin' of Solzhenitsyn's *First Circle*) met one of Krasnov's adjutants. He had been surrendered by the British to the Soviets at Judenburg in the previous year, and gave Kopelev an account of the Cossacks' betrayal. After Kopelev emerged from prison in 1954, he prepared a biographical memoir since published in the West. Recently he informed me that he lent a typewritten copy to a friend, Boris Slutsky, who had been an officer in Tolbukhin's army of occupation in Austria. On reading the outline account of Krasnov's surrender, Slutsky told Kopelev that the event had aroused considerable comment in the Red Army at the time, where it was generally believed that the British had sold the Cossacks to their enemies for a large consignment of vodka.

The charge is without foundation, but still of interest since it suggests that in Soviet military circles the motive for the handover was inexplicable save in terms of gratuitous betrayal, confirming that whatever pressures were being applied by the Soviet authorities, they did not come from the Red Army. Could the story have arisen from tales of copious libations of vodka accompanying the negotiations between Keightley's and Tolbukhin's staffs? In the absence of any known motive for the unexpected British concession, it may have been jocularly presumed that the vodka was all the reward required. It also incidentally confirms that contempt, and not co-operation, was what General Keightley's action aroused among Soviet military men.

Next there is the parallel decision to hand over the Yugoslavs contrary to the instructions of the Allied Governments. The BBC TV programme *The Klagenfurt Affair*, broadcast on 3 January 1984, argued 'that a deal may have been struck with Tito, that the partisans would withdraw from Carinthia if the refugees were handed over'. The notion that there was a secret deal arises from the fact that the Partisans' decision to withdraw from Carinthia and British agreement to hand over Yugoslav refugees were both settled at the same conference. This was the agreement made at Fifth Corps headquarters between the Communist Colonel Ivanovic and Toby Low on 19 May.

Low himself was interviewed during the programme, when he denied that any deal had taken place:

> The important part of that agreement was that Tito's forces voluntarily had agreed with us to withdraw south of the border. They were at the same time claiming Carinthia as part of Yugoslavia, and they were getting out – and that was the important thing about that. In the course of that we also dealt with these limited arrangements for handing over to them and partly arranging for the transport back to Yugoslavia of these large numbers of Croats and also the other names of Yugoslav nationals. The two things went hand in hand because they were both discussed at that meeting.

But the programme's researchers felt the coincidence to be too good to be true and fastened upon the 'deal' as the underlying motivation of the repatriations. Despite his disclaimer, Low did not appear wholly to reject this conclusion. Asked whether there was a bargain on the lines suggested, he reflected, 'No. There was no need to be a bargain. I was under instructions to do what I was concerned with. That, I say, is my recollection. Of course, reading the papers now, it looks as if there may have been a bargain. I do not remember that.'

Whatever the speculations of the *Timewatch* researchers and Low's reservations, a few moments' further investigation would have shown that there was never a 'deal', nor any question of one.

So suspicious and fearful a man as Tito was unlikely to have consented to any 'deal' without provisions ensuring that the other side would hold to its commitments. The Partisan withdrawal from Carinthia was in fact so prompt that on 21 May AFHQ could note: 'Situation in Carinthia has improved considerably in the past 24 hours. All evidence indicates that Tito has issued orders for a general withdrawal of all Jugoslav forces from Carinthia. 3,000 troops estimated to have moved out of Bleiburg-Lavamund area on 19th.' And by 25 May AFHQ noted with satisfaction: 'Jugoslav evacuation of 5 Corps area in Austria now almost complete. Delay in withdrawal is likely to occur only in the case of 1 Brigade which is still engaged in evacuating Croat prisoners from the area Ferlach Kappel.'[17] The handover of Yugoslav refugees, on the other hand, only got into full swing about that time; and the surrender of the Serbs and Slovenes in Viktring Camp (about which Low was being questioned) was not ratified until the evening of 23 May. From Tito's point of view the bargain would have been valueless unless he had some means of enforcing it. Had there really been a secret agreement, the withdrawal of Partisans could have been judiciously spun out to coincide with the final delivery of refugees from Viktring. Finally, when Keightley halted the operation on 31 May, the Yugoslav authorities made no recorded objection to the fact that 6,000 refugees, whom the Fifth Corps had agreed to hand over, were unexpectedly retained.

From the British point of view the existence of such a bargain, honoured so promptly and fully, would have removed all concern over the Carinthian question. In fact AFHQ actions and decisions at this time show that no agreement had been arrived at, and that the Partisans left only because they were given no choice in the matter. Their patience exhausted, the British and American Governments had resolved to eject Tito's units by force, should they not depart of their own accord. By 18 May preparations for Operation Beehive (codeword Hornet) were in full swing, and the Fifth Corps issued the instruction: 'Military control will be secured by capturing or destroying all Tito tps in the Corps area.'[18]

By 19 May, the date of the Low-Ivanovic conference, the Joint Chiefs of Staff were ready for drastic action, notifying Alexander that:

> In the event of a refusal by Marshal Tito to comply with demands of His Majesty's Government and United States Government you will, on instructions from us, eject (using force if necessary) all Jugoslav forces from Southern Austria, Trieste, Gorizia, Montfalcone, Pola and such areas of Venezia Giulia as are necessary in order to secure and protect your lines of communication in Austria.

Tito took the hint, and within a couple of days his rag-tag army was beginning to stream southwards over the Karavanke Mountains. He was probably wise. Yugoslavia could muster some 180,000 troops to put in the field. It was, Allied Intelligence estimated, 'still only a lightly armed force, with very little artillery or mechanised transport. The Jugoslav Air Force is a negligible factor.' Against this AFHQ could draw on some 429,000 battle-hardened troops, with devastating superiority in air, armour and artillery.[19] Should this prove insufficient, Eisenhower was preparing to despatch General Patton with five armoured divisions across the Brenner Pass, the Mediterranean Fleet was steaming into the Adriatic, and General Arnold had several air squadrons ready to move at once into the zone of operations. As Alexander put it on 22 May: 'now we have Tito on the run . . .' Next day Macmillan himself agreed that 'Tito has backed down'.[20]

None of these menacing preparations would have been necessary had it been known that an agreement had already been reached whereby Tito would withdraw gracefully. The facts do not bear out Macmillan's explanation of his actions in 1945, according to which Tito had 'about . . . 80 to 100,000' troops in Carinthia facing a single brigade of the British Army. Understandably, according to this version, 'the British Army wasn't in much of a mood to fight another war, particularly against Tito's partisans who we'd been told had been a splendid support to us against the Germans for years'. In fact, by 13 May this was no longer the case. Three days before his visit to the Eighth Army commanders Macmillan had attended a meeting in Alexander's office, at which the Field-Marshal 'was vehement in his determination not [to] make any further concessions to Tito and at end of meeting he informed us that so far as he was concerned he had lost all patience with Yugoslav dictator and was ready [to] drive him and his forces out of Venezia Giulia if he could get London and Washington to agree'.[21]

In reality the Partisan force never amounted to a quarter of the number claimed by Macmillan and its military capacity was justly regarded within the Fifth Corps as derisory. Of the officers I interviewed, though understandably not anxious for another spell of fighting, none had envisaged any problem in 'booting out the Tits' when the time came. As Brigadier Adrian Gore, then commanding the Sixty-first Infantry Brigade, recalls today:

> my only involvement with the partizans was to ensure that they did not cross the River Drava into Austria at Klagenfurt, & troops under my command were responsible for guarding two bridges over the river & making sure that they stayed on their side of the bridge. To start with they made a lot of threatening noises but no attack ever materialised, and after about a fortnight they withdrew and all was peaceful again.

General Sir James Wilson, then a subaltern in a Greenjacket Battalion under Brigadier Gore's command, remembers with wry amusement the ejection of a band of Partisans occupying the Town Hall (*Rathaus*) of Klagenfurt. On 19 May, the day of the ultimatum, he was ordered by his Colonel to proceed with his company to the square opposite the Town Hall. There, Colonel Fyffe told him, he would find two troops of tanks from the Derbyshire Yeomanry: 'What I was told to say to the Yugoslavs was to congratulate them on their marvellous victories over the Germans . . . and all the rest of it, and to say that . . . we were privileged and proud to provide them with transport down to the Loibl Pass, and that I'd got my Company outside to give them the honours of war.'

Wilson entered the Town Hall at 2 p.m. to explain that his Company would be ready to do the honours at three o'clock sharp. This offer was received, predictably, 'in a fairly frosty sort of way,' and Wilson emerged with no strong hopes of an orderly outcome. By five to three nothing had happened, and Wilson ordered a platoon of Riflemen to be ready to go in, while each tank of the Derbyshire Yeomanry ostentatiously 'put a shell up the spout'. This was quite enough: at one minute to three the dishevelled Titoist garrison emerged at a trot, each clutching a suitcase full of loot, and sprang into the waiting RASC lorries.

In General Wilson's recollection, British troops regarded Tito's followers as 'a complete rabble'; murderous and thieving, but of

minimal fighting potential. There was one other consideration, however, which must be briefly taken into. AFHQ never doubted its
capacity to remove the intruders – provided, of course, the Red Army
did not decide to take a hand in matters.[22] But this was never a
likelihood, which is why Tito knew he had no choice but to back
down. As Djilas, then a member of the Yugoslav Politburo, recalled,
'The Allies threw us out of Trieste and its environs after the Soviet
Central Committee informed us that, after such a terrible war, the
U.S.S.R. could not embark upon another. The world seemed to turn
against us Yugoslavs and we were alone, growing lonelier all the
while.'[23]

The Allies appreciated that Stalin was highly unlikely to engage in
a major confrontation over Trieste, let alone so trivial a matter as the
fate of Slovenian Carinthia. As early as 9 May the United States
Ambassador in Belgrade, Patterson, reported: 'Colonel Lindsay,
Chief of our Military Mission, attended meeting yesterday and told
me Tito impressed him at beginning as most unsure of himself. I
share with my British colleague the view that Tito is not at all
certain of Soviet support on this issue.' The evening (11 May) before
Macmillan left for Klagenfurt he was told by Randolph Churchill 'of
his conversation with Tito several days ago when he called on the
Yugoslav premier to say goodbye. British Prime Minister's son had
impression that Tito . . . was determined to incorporate that city
[Trieste] within the boundaries of Yugoslavia. He was not convinced
however that Tito had the full support of the Russians on Trieste.'
On 26 May British Ambassador Stevenson in Belgrade was able to
confirm the view his American colleague had reported on the ninth:

> My Soviet colleague called on me today at his own request to discuss the
> question of Trieste. I had already had a conversation with him on this
> subject about a week ago. He informed me today that after our previous
> talk he had advised members of Yugoslav Government with whom he
> had spoken to seek a peaceful settlement of the problem . . . I have
> reported this conversation fully because it reinforces my belief that
> although the Soviet is in full sympathy with Yugoslav aspirations she
> will not intervene actively.[24]

There seems to be no alternative to accepting the burden of Toby
Low's own statement, that there was no 'deal' or agreement linking
the evacuation of Carinthia with the disposal of the Yugoslav refugees. This, incidentally, is also the firm conviction of another senior
staff officer at the Fifth Corps, Brigadier Tryon-Wilson.

None of the explanations advanced to explain Harold Macmillan's intervention at Klagenfurt carries conviction, nor is it likely they were believed true at the time. A possible alternative, that he simply advocated a generally placatory attitude towards Stalin and Tito and acted accordingly without hope of specific return, seems incredible when the extraordinary deviousness and personal and political risks of his action are taken into account. There seems little likelihood that Macmillan's advice to Keightley arose from loose pragmatic considerations of appeasing a truculent aggressor.

Today much more is known about the attitude of the Yugoslav regime at the time, largely on account of a full account provided by Milovan Djilas. In 1979 he was interviewed by the writer George Urban. In a fascinating exchange, the dissident Yugoslav former Vice President touched on many aspects of Communist ideology and practice in the Soviet Union and Yugoslavia, among which was the forced repatriations of 1945. What chiefly excited interest at the time of the interview's publication in the magazine *Encounter* was Djilas's outspoken condemnation of the policy. Of greater interest in the present context, however, is his bafflement as to why it took place at all.

Dr Urban began by asking Djilas bluntly whether he thought the forced repatriation of 20,000 to 40,000 Yugoslavs was right.

> No, it wasn't! The great majority of the people the British forced back from Austria were simple peasants. They had no murders on their hands. They had not been Ustashis or Slovenian 'Home Guards'. Their only fear was fear of Communism and the reputation of the Communists. Their sole motivation for leaving the country was panic. If the British had handed over to us 'Quisling' leaders such as Nedic, and police agents who had collaborated with the Nazis in torturing and killing people, or had done it on their own, there could be no question of the morality of the British action. But this is not what they did. They forced back the lot – and this was profoundly wrong.

And what of the sending back to Stalin of much larger numbers of fugitive Russians? Had the British any justification for that?

> I'm ready to concede that the British had a certain *raison d'état* on their side. The Soviet Union was a much-lauded ally whose government the British had for many years considered to be essentially no different from their own – and most of these *were* Soviet citizens. But what the British did not realise, or at any rate didn't mention in their public utterances,

was that the Soviet Union was no *normal*, that is to say, no *legitimate* state by any accepted standard.

The British failed to see that the Soviet state had no independent judiciary, that the MVD and NKVD was the sole law in the land, and that returning these people to the Soviet Union was turning them over to naked terror. It was astonishing that the British, with their fine sense of justice and the administration of law, should have been so thoroughly remiss in examining the sort of justice that was likely to be meted out to the repatriates.

But if the Soviet Union lacked legitimacy, was Djilas's own revolutionary Yugoslav Government legitimate?

Even less so! We were an entirely new, brash, revolutionary force without a properly elected leadership, courts, and all the rest. Indeed, in 1945 we still went about detaining and executing people quite arbitrarily either for political reasons or for anything else we thought was culpable. Our basis of legitimacy was even thinner than that of the Soviet government.

Dr Urban accepted that this view was understandable in 1979. But had it been Djilas's view in 1945, too, that the British had acted wrongly?

To be quite frank with you – we didn't at all understand why the British insisted on returning these people. We believed, in the ideological context prevailing at the time, that the British would have a good deal of sympathy with these refugees, seeing that they had fled Communism. We thought the British would show 'class solidarity' with them, and some of us even feared that they would enlist them for future use against Communist governments, especially our own. Yet, to our great surprise, they did none of these things but delivered them into our hands. This was all the more astonishing because we knew that many Yugoslavs (Croats and others) who found themselves in Britain as prisoners of war were considered quite safe from repatriation.

Pressed further, Djilas could think of no logical reason for the gratuitously obliging attitude of the British authorities.

This was, as I say, truly puzzling; but I tend to ascribe it to the rule of tidy-minded bureaucrats who wanted to tidy their desks and close the files. You see, the 20–30,000 Yugoslavs in Carinthia were a burden to the British. They had to feed them, house them, keep them under control. The simple way out was to force them back to Yugoslavia.

So the British were guilty of a mixture of indifference, lack of political imagination, and plain imbecility?

> Imbecility above all – they ought to have looked at the character of our government, such as it was at the time, and drawn their conclusions. Yes – the British did completely the wrong thing in putting these people back across the border, as we did completely the wrong thing in shooting them all. In *Wartime* I make no secret of my view that these killings were senseless acts of wrathful revenge.

Was Tito himself responsible for authorising the massacres?

> Whether or not Tito had given direct orders no one knows. But certainly he was in favour of a radical solution – for pragmatic reasons, as the British, too, had pragmatic reasons for returning these refugees. Yugoslavia was in a state of chaos and destruction. There was hardly any civil administration. There were no properly constituted courts. There was no way in which the cases of 20–30,000 people could have been reliably investigated. So the easy way out was to have them all shot, and have done with the problem.

Finally, Dr Urban enquired, could the British authorities responsible have reasonably assumed that all the refugees would be massacred on return?

> I think they ought to have had a pretty shrewd idea of what we'd be doing with them. We had a British Military Mission attached to us. Its members could have entertained no doubt as to how the Ustashis and Chetniks were treating us, and how we were treating their captured men and, in fact, anyone we remotely suspected of supporting them. But the British preferred to shut their eyes.[25]

A major point to emerge from this revealing dialogue is Djilas's confessed ignorance of British motivation in the matter. Yet after the detailed negotiations conducted between Brigadier Low and Colonel Ivanovic at Klagenfurt on 19 May (to say nothing of the exchanges which may have led up to them), it seems unlikely on the face of it that Tito had no inkling at least of *professed* British considerations in the matter. But whatever the Marshal knew seems to have been of too delicate a nature to reveal even to the closest of his colleagues.

This remarkable secrecy – for such it appears to be – is paralleled on the Soviet side of the dual operation. General S. M. Shtemenko, in 1945 Deputy Chief of the Soviet General Staff, refers to the surrender of the Tsarist Generals Krasnov and Shkuro briefly in these terms:

> The Soviet Government then made a firm representation to our allies in the matter of Krasnov, Shkuro, Sultan-Ghirei and other war criminals. The British delayed complying for a little, but then, not placing any great value on the White Guard Generals or their following, placed them in lorries and delivered them into the hands of the Soviet authorities.

Shtemenko, like Djilas, can only speculate on the motive for the handover. One moment the British object to surrendering the Whites, the next they agree; why, he does not know, indulging instead in a conventional sarcasm at the expense of the old émigrés. However, it is not hard to guess the reason for his ignorance.

When General Keightley and Brigadier Low negotiated the surrender, they were dealing with what they took to be the Red Army. But, as Shtemenko makes clear, it was the 'Soviet Government' which made the demand; that is, as one would expect in so delicate a political matter as that of the return of the émigré generals, the MVD. Even so high a military authority as Shtemenko was not permitted to know what lay behind the negotiations. The man who *did* know everything was Minister of State Security Merkulov, who spoke in veiled terms to Nikolai Krasnov of some base act of secret treachery, whereby an important British public figure had 'sold' Britain's former friends to the Soviets.

As Djilas also points out, there existed at least in respect of the Yugoslavs strong reasons why the British might have considered *retaining* the Chetnik and Domobranci troops at Viktring. If, as then seemed possible, war were to break out between the Anglo-American forces and those of Tito, the refugees could have proved an extremely useful card to play. At the end of April the Foreign Office had noted that:

> From the narrow, and rather cynical, political point of view, there seem indeed to be certain disadvantages in assisting Tito at all in his present offensive in Bosnia. Tito's advance northwards, however acceptable it may be from the military point of view, nevertheless brings him nearer to the vexed provinces of Venezia Giulia and Carinthia. It would in many respects be convenient if events should develop in such a way that Tito is temporarily held up by the opposition of the Ustashi and White Guard Forces round, say, Ljubljana and Zagreb while the Allied forces from

Italy are enabled to occupy Venezia Giulia and Carinthia in comparative tranquillity.[26]

That opportunity was now past, and certainly the Allies could not directly have sought support from the Croats, whose army had so recently been allied to the enemy, and who were in any case at the moment of Macmillan's visit about to be prevented from entering British-occupied Austria. But the Chetniks and Slovenes represented a very different consideration. The former, as Royalist allies of Britain, could legitimately have been employed as auxiliaries in the event of hostilities. The Slovenian Domobranci, too, could have been of significant use. Until the tide of war had swept across their province they had preserved it from Partisan influence. The population was overwhelmingly hostile to the Communists – more even than before now that the OZNA reign of terror had begun. Had war broken out between Tito and the Allies, there is no question but that AFHQ armour could in a short time have broken through the main passes, and General Arnold's bomber squadrons would swiftly have broken up what concentrations of troops the Yugoslav Army managed to collect. But it was as guerrillas that the Partisans had earned their (possibly inflated, but none the less significant for that) redoubtable reputation, and the Allies cannot have regarded with equanimity the prospect of seeing their infantry entangled in mountain operations where so many of the advantages would lie with the other side. Here the Domobranci, with their superior local knowledge and popularity with the population, could prove very effective allies. This at least was how Tito saw the matter.

Differing attitudes could legitimately have been adopted by the British over this issue. The point is that there were no overriding pressing reasons of policy for surrendering the Viktring refugees, such as might have led Macmillan to feel justified in deceiving his colleagues and disobeying his superiors in order to force through his project. On the contrary, virtually every consideration of morality, public policy, and strategic advantage lay in retaining the anti-Communist Yugoslavs. In the case of the White Russian officers, the absence of any practical advantage to Allied interests is still more striking. Yet it was a matter Macmillan felt to be of such overriding importance that he would undergo any risk to his career and reputation in order to fulfil General Merkulov's demand.

One can understand that, so long as his part in the return of Cossacks and Yugoslavs remained a closely-guarded secret, Macmil-

lan would have no reason to wish it made public. But once it was
established beyond doubt that he had played an important role in
arriving at the decision it is hard to see what purpose there could be
in continuing to conceal his motive. After all, if there really were
strong reasons of *Realpolitik* which influenced his decision it could
only mitigate his awful responsibility were he to reveal them. Yet
this he has repeatedly chosen not to do.

12

A Question of Motive

'I wondered, immediately after the war, at the sustained and active campaign to force the return to the Soviet Union of all Soviet nationals who had been displaced, many of whom refused to return and some of whom even killed themselves when they thought they would be forced to do so . . . During the Paris Peace Conference [1946] I discussed this with a Communist statesman who occasionally spoke more frankly than his colleagues, and he put the Politburo's position and apprehension regarding Soviet displaced persons with one pithy sentence.

"That's the way we got our start!" he said, and of course that was true.' (Walter Bedell Smith, United States Ambassador to Moscow, 1946–49)

There remains much that is unknown about British responsibility for the handover operations. More evidence will undoubtedly appear, some of it perhaps as a result of the publication of this book. British and American records have been combed, and every effort made to track down surviving eye-witnesses. For the present I propose to conclude with a tentative approach from a different angle. Research in Soviet and Yugoslav archives is not permitted but that need not entirely prevent an attempt at a glimpse over the other side of the wall.

Soviet and Yugoslav motives for wishing to regain those fugitives who had slipped through their fingers may appear too obvious to merit discussion. Clearly a simple desire for revenge was an important consideration, but it would be simplistic to suppose it the only one. The part played by the Soviet security and counter-espionage services was not merely the passive one of gratefully receiving the prisoners as they were passed back across the demarcation lines. The far more positive and extensive nature of their role in reality may serve to illuminate pressures and influences so far absent from the discussion.

The historian S. R. Gardiner is said to have attempted to approach the documentation from which he constructed his great history of the English Civil War in much the same spirit with which it was originally compiled; viz., that at any given stage he should not know what would happen next. Only in this way, he held, can the historian begin to understand why men in the past acted as they did. Within its limitations this must surely be a valid exercise. Hindsight is one of the most dangerous pitfalls in historiography, introducing an unconscious element of historical inevitability.

Let us then momentarily attempt to place ourselves in Stalin's shoes at a time when neither the outcome of negotiations nor that of the post-war settlement as a whole could have been foreseen. Fortuitously a precise date proffers itself as a vantage-point. The evidence indicates that it was on 12 May that Macmillan unexpectedly received news of the Soviet demand for the Cossack generals, handed to General Keightley the previous afternoon.

It was in appearance a time when the Soviet Union had reached the apogee of power and military glory; when Stalin appeared as the far-seeing victor of the greatest war in history. After the terrible losses and humiliations of 1941–42 the Red Army had beaten its adversary to a standstill at Stalingrad, then fought back in a campaign of appalling cruelty and gallantry until the Motherland was liberated. From the summer of 1944, Soviet forces had begun to drive the Nazis from Eastern Europe. Germany's allies, Rumania, Bulgaria and Hungary, were knocked out of the war and occupied; Poland, Czechoslovakia and Yugoslavia were liberated; and, finally, after some of the most ferocious fighting of the entire conflict, Berlin fell to Zhukov's troops on 2 May.

As the historian John Erickson has written:

At the close of this gigantic effort put forth by the Red Army – the capture of Berlin, the drive to the Elbe and to the Baltic – the Soviet command reckoned that it had destroyed no less than seventy German infantry divisions, twelve Panzer divisions and eleven motorised divisions: 480,000 German officers and men were tallied as prisoners of war, 1,500 tanks and SP guns captured, plus 10,000 guns and mortars and a massive array of aircraft.[1]

The triumphant juggernaut, nearly seven million men strong and comprising some fifty-five 'all-arms' armies, six tank armies and thirteen air armies, stood in the heart of Europe.

The whole of this enormous war-machine, together with the vast hinterland behind, stretching from the Elbe to the Pacific, was controlled by one man. His lightest whim, however irrational, was obeyed with alacrity by the bravest of his soldiers, the most absurd of his fantasies extolled. A vast proportion of his subjects, amounting perhaps to some twenty million souls, were literally slaves, toiling night and day in conditions of unimaginable misery. Beyond his hugely-swollen empire, acclamation for the Liberator of Europe was well-nigh universal.

It would seemingly take more than a leap of credulity to conceive such a man taking deep concern in the fate of a handful of scattered refugees in far-off Austria, the minuscule rump of that reactionary opposition which the Red Army in its infancy had swept into the dustbin of history.

But such a view, plausible enough in the abstract, is denied by the evidence. In reality the triumphant dictator was as uneasy and fearful as in those dark days of 1941, when the Wehrmacht had in its turn stood at the gates of Moscow. Paradoxically, the moment of victory had brought with it gathering sensations of insecurity as menacing as any Stalin had known.

Complimented by Churchill at the Potsdam Conference on his brilliant achievements, Stalin was to remark modestly (or sardonically): 'Tsar Alexander got to Paris.'[2] If his hearers were privately thankful that history had not in this case repeated itself, so also for a different reason may Stalin have been.

Following the defeat of Napoleon in 1814, when the Russian Army had entered Paris, no sovereign in Europe had received greater acclaim than its saviour, the Emperor Alexander I. The unprecedented triumph of Russian arms proved, however, a poisoned chalice so far as her rulers were concerned. For the soldiers who returned to Russia were not the same men who had set forth on the heels of Napoleon's retreating Grand Army two years earlier. They were heroes filled with justifiable pride in their glorious deeds, exhilarated by experience of independent command and responsibility unknown within the structure of the Empire proper; men burning with patriotic zeal to better their country and bring its civilisation and culture into line with all they had seen in Germany and France. The Emperor's increasingly reactionary determination to place his country back in leading-strings aroused predictable resentment, idealistic conspiratorial circles were formed, and the bubble burst with the abortive Decembrist revolt of 1825. Two factors predominated in the attempted coup: the majority of conspirators were able young army officers, and the ideals motivating them were almost exclusively of foreign (principally French) origin.[3]

Stalin's historical sense was profound if simplistic, and his view of the past was bound up in large part with parallelism of this sort.[4] But though much of what passed through his mind was remote from reality, fear of dangers thronging on the aftermath of victory was realistic enough. There was a widespread feeling that there could be no return to *those* times, and that at last the Soviet Union was emerging on to that sunlit plateau whose imminence had formed so frequent a theme in the pronouncements of both Lenin and Stalin.

On the morning of the day of victory over Germany, a Red Army officer in Moscow reflected on the significance of the occasion as he and his brother-officers saw it:

> What were we hoping for? The past would not return and the dead would not live again. Perhaps we were glad that we would be returning to the peaceful existence of the pre-war years? Hardly! Our great joy that day arose from the fact that we stood at a frontier, a frontier that marked the end of the darkest period of our life, and the beginning of a new, still unknown period. And every one of us was hoping that this new period would fulfil the promise of the rainbow after the storm, would be bright, sunny, happy. If anyone had asked us what we really expected, the majority would have expressed our common feeling very simply: 'To hell with all that was before the war!' And every one of us knew exactly what had been before the war.[5]

Later the same day (four days before Macmillan flew to Klagenfurt) there took place an extraordinary event unprecedented in Moscow since Lenin first assumed his dictatorship. Thousands of Muscovites poured into Comintern Square, crowding before a large building from which the Stars and Stripes flapped desultorily in the spring breeze. It was the United States Embassy and the crowd had gathered there, impelled by some spontaneous impulse, to give expression to elemental feelings of relief and jubilation. Every sign of American life was cheered to the skies, frantic cries of enthusiasm hailed the American flag, and every American the crowd could lay hands on was hoisted aloft and passed joyfully over the people's heads to the outer fringes. It was a cold day, but for over twelve hours, well on into the night, Muscovites continued their rapturous vigil outside the Embassy. Signs of official embarrassment became plain. Police tried to move the crowd on, and a brass band was set up as a rival attraction. But all these efforts were in vain, and the people did not disperse until their enthusiasm was temporarily spent.[6]

One may imagine Stalin's reaction when he learned of this extraordinary event. After a generation of anti-capitalist propaganda and NKVD terror directed against anyone who stepped an inch out of line – *this* should have been unthinkable! But the war had been a great shaker-up of tyrannies – even the victorious one. The Soviet Government was in itself partly to blame; in order to keep up morale when the outcome was still uncertain, official hints had been dropped of better times to come and a forgetting of the past once the Fascist beast was destroyed. Now drastic measures were required to turn the clock back. Sweeping purges, comparable to those of the pre-war period, scythed through the population at large, consigning people to internal exile or prolonged terms in forced labour camps. Within the camps of Gulag itself new precautionary measures were put into effect.[7]

But if a counter-revolution were to take place in the Soviet Union, it would be achieved not by unarmed mobs, however large, but – Stalin knew full well – through a coup staged by dissident elements in the Red Army. It was the Red Army which had saved him from Hitler, but he had never been able to trust it. In 1938, when the crisis over Czechoslovakia had threatened to bring about a European war, Stalin's actions proved that he feared the Red Army even more than the Wehrmacht. After all, the Army alone had the means of destroying that hugely swollen NKVD apparatus whose task it was to preserve the dictator.

Long before VE Day, when it had become clear victory was inevitable, cautious preparations began for the curbing of the soldiers. It was 9 February 1945 that Solzhenitsyn, then a young lieutenant, was arrested by SMERSH agents, removed from his front-line battery and despatched to the Lubyanka Prison in Moscow. His crime was a disrespectful allusion to Stalin in a private letter; for which he was sentenced to eight years in corrective labour camps. It was not just subalterns who were subject to such arbitrary treatment. At the climax of victory, deploying his tanks in the smoking ruins of Berlin on the never-to-be-forgotten 2 May 1945, General Krivoshein of the Second Guards Tank Army came under rigorous investigation. SMERSH had retrieved from the rubble a photograph of Krivoshein standing amicably side by side with the formidable Wehrmacht tank commander, Guderian. Krivoshein was lucky; he was able to explain that the picture was five years old, dating from a previous phase of the war when Nazi and Soviet troops were fighting together against the Poles.[8]

With the war over, Stalin's security organs began a thorough purge of the entire Red Army. At SMERSH headquarters at Baden-bei-Wien a colossal screening operation took place with the aim of uncovering NCOs and officers with 'unreliable' class connections, while a top-level SMERSH commission in Moscow decided the fate of generals and marshals. Thousands of soldiers were demobilised and allotted fates ranging from return home to forced labour in Central Asia. Only at the topmost level of all, where doubtless he glimpsed the Bonapartist shadow of another Tukhachevsky, was there a brief delay before Stalin felt safe to move cautiously against his Deputy Supreme Commander. After a year of newspaper prominence, Marshal Georgi Zhukov was abruptly banished to the obscurity of the Odessa Military District command.[9]

All these measures required cunning, persistence and ruthlessness. But those were Stalin's most marked characteristics; and, as the event proved, the machinery of totalitarian controls created by Lenin and brought to fruition by his successor was capable of crushing any opposition – real, potential or imagined. But in the second week of May nothing could yet be regarded as certain. There was, moreover, a threat of potentially massive proportions which lay outside Stalin's control.

Despite the fact that for over two years Germany ruled over extensive regions of European Russia, Hitler made little effective use of the millions of Russians under his control in advancing his war aims. Determined that such Russians as he would permit to survive should be reduced to the status of slaves, he fiercely rejected the idea of recruiting large-scale anti-Communist Russian forces to fight alongside Wehrmacht units. But inevitably, as the manpower problem increased, Russians, Ukrainians and other nationalities of the Soviet Union became enrolled as auxiliaries, until their roll-call totalled nearly a million men. A significant concession was the raising of Cossack units, such as von Pannwitz's Fifteenth Cossack Cavalry Corps, but it was not until the end of 1944 that an increasingly desperate Himmler decided it was time to play the 'Vlasov card'.

General Andrei Vlasov, an able and courageous Red Army commander, had been captured in the summer of 1942. By the end of the year the Germans had appointed him head of a 'Russian Liberation Committee'; a post which was almost entirely nominal, designed merely to provide a focus of loyalty for those Russians who were assisting the German war effort, and create an illusion of a genuinely independent national opposition to Bolshevism. However, thanks to the protection and help of German officers intelligent enough to see that co-operation with the Russian resistance was probably the only remaining hope for extricating Germany from total defeat, Vlasov's prestige and influence increased among Germans and Russians alike.

Ultimately, during the final months of the Reich's collapse, Himmler agreed to the setting up of an anti-Soviet Russian 'government' and the deployment of authentic Russian fighting units on the Eastern Front. On 14 November 1944 the Committee for the Liberation of the Peoples of Russia (KONR) issued its manifesto after a conference held at the Hradcany Palace in Prague. The Prague Manifesto (as it has become known) called in measured terms for the overthrow of Soviet power, and the establishment of a Russian Government which would respect religious, legal and property rights and abolish all the iniquities of the existing dictatorship. Great stress was laid on the 'national development, self-determination, and state independence' of minority peoples within the bounds of the former Russian state.

Apart from a passing allusion to 'the powers of imperialism, led by the plutocrats of England and the USA' and a demand for 'discontinuation of the war and an honourable peace with Germany', the Manifesto betrayed no hint of subordination to Nazi interests. The programme was one which could only appeal to men of humane and liberal views, and even today exerts considerable influence on Russian opponents of the Soviet regime. The Manifesto was much publicised in Russian-language propaganda, and its catalogue of Soviet crimes and deceptions, together with its advocacy of civilised norms of government, struck responsive or apprehensive chords according to the interests of the recipient. A subsidiary purpose of the programme may have been to alert the advancing Western Allies to the existence of a broadly-based Russian opposition movement sharing their democratic and liberal ideals. It was, of course, a 'signal' that fell entirely on deaf ears, though this was not known to Vlasov or Stalin at the time.

The signatories claimed optimistically:

The successful end of this fight is now ensured:
(a) By the greater experience in struggle than in 1917:
(b) By the existence of growing and organised armed forces – the Russian Army of Liberation, Ukrainian Liberation forces, Cossack troops, and national units;
(c) By the existence of anti-Bolshevik forces behind the Soviet lines;
(d) By the existence of growing opposition forces among the people, the government apparatus, and the army of the USSR.

However appealing the generous political ideals of the Prague Manifesto, the claim that it had a realistic chance of being implemented must appear more than a little ridiculous to the modern reader. However, lacking the advantage of foreknowledge, Stalin may not have found the defiant threat quite so fanciful as we now know it to have been. Evidence of his disquiet is incidentally provided by one of the more bizarre episodes in the story. Soviet interests in wartime Germany lay under the protection of the Japanese Embassy, and it was the Ambassador, General Baron Hiroshi Oshima, who conveyed a vigorous protest from Stalin to the Führer against the levying of the Vlasov units. Hitler valued Oshima's advice, and it seems this was one of the factors which made him so consistently hostile to the idea of a German-sponsored Russian liberation movement.[10]

For the first time since 1920 the Red Army found itself facing a determined Russian opponent in the field. At Orel and on the Dnieper Lieutenant Solzhenitsyn had found himself fighting against Vlasovite Russian units which 'fought more ferociously and tenaciously than the Germans and were extremely hard to overcome'.[11] These were auxiliary detachments of the Wehrmacht, but early in 1945 the KONR 'government' was permitted belatedly to raise its own Russian Liberation Army (ROA). With its two fighting divisions, officers' school, reserve units and air force, the ROA comprised some 50,000 men.[12]

Based at Münsingen in Wurttemberg, the ROA divisions were armed and equipped by the Germans, but bore distinguishing ROA badges with the national emblem of the St Andrew's Cross. Their capacity for frontline combat was successfully put to the test in February 1945, when a small volunteer unit commanded by a former Tsarist officer, Colonel Sakharov, distinguished itself in fierce fighting on the Oder. As a result the First Division ROA was ordered up to the line at the end of March from its advance posting at Cottbus, south-east of Berlin. During the first fortnight of April the Division, commanded by the redoubtable Ukrainian General Buniachenko, made a series of desperate assaults on a Red Army salient near Frankfurt on the Oder. It was a dramatic moment for the KONR movement, which saw the first relatively large-scale warfare between the Red Army and native Russian opponents since the close of the Civil War twenty-five years earlier. Apart from Buniachenko's ground forces, the attacks were supported by aeroplanes of the Vlasov forces' air section bearing the insignia of the St Andrew's Cross. After suffering severe casualties during repeated assaults, Buniachenko decided unilaterally to withdraw from the conflict. This was due partly to resentment at the absence of essential German artillery support, and also because neither he nor Vlasov was prepared to lose sight of their major objective: the preservation of the ROA for the coming struggle against Soviet power.[13]

Buniachenko's Division moved southwards towards Czechoslovakia, a feat which has been compared to the march of Xenophon's ten thousand. Avoiding hostile German units, who were bound to regard them as deserters or worse, they arrived on the outskirts of Prague at the beginning of May. Responding to a plea from his fellow-Slavs of the Czech resistance, Buniachenko stormed into the Bohemian capital at dawn on 7 May, smashing his way through diehard Waffen SS units to seize the aerodrome, radio station and other key points. By now thoroughly disillusioned with the Germans, who he felt had used the KONR purely for their own ends, he called upon all German units in Prague to surrender or be annihilated. By now, however, the predominantly pro-Soviet Czech leadership saw this as an alliance which within days might bring retribution from the advancing Red Army, and repudiated any association with the ROA. By 8–9 May Buniachenko had fought his way out of the ungrateful city and made his way south in an effort to make contact with the US General Patton's armour advancing from the west.

The war was over, and nothing remained but to surrender to the Western Allies, who must surely realise the nature of the Soviet threat and welcome such useful auxiliaries. In those last confused hours Vlasov, Buniachenko and other ROA leaders fell into the hands of the Red Army, while large numbers of their followers succeeded in making their way through American lines, where they were interned. Much the same fate awaited the ROA Second Division, which about the same time had been advancing into Bohemia from the south; though in their case virtually all troops succeeded in getting through to the Americans.[14]

Such was the situation on 12 May, the day Vlasov became a

prisoner of the Soviets. The KONR was defeated, but from the interrogation of prisoners (as well as spies, who had infiltrated the Vlasov movement from its inception)[15] disturbing accounts began to emerge. The 50,000 inadequately armed troops of the two ROA Divisions were of derisory military importance in relation to the colossal array of forces on both sides battling out the final days of the Eastern Front, though they had proved that anti-Soviet exiles could fight with a courage and determination equal to that of any Soviet unit. Buniachenko's First Division and his counterpart General Zverev's Second Division formed but part of what was in theory and to some extent in reality a much more extensive movement.

Other units coming under the KONR umbrella included Rogozhin's *Russkii Corpus* from Yugoslavia and von Pannwitz's and Domanov's Cossacks – all of whom were surrendering to British units advancing into Austria from Italy. Links had also been established with Ukrainian and Caucasian nationalist legions, Nedic's quisling Serbian militia, and even with Mihailovic's Chetniks. There was talk of assembling a Third Force in the Balkans capable of routing Tito's bandits and establishing a redoubt in the mountains of Yugoslavia from which to renew the common struggle against Marxist dictatorship.[16]

Fighting units of the KONR and its sympathisers had displayed martial prowess inferior to none of the participants in World War Two. Their numbers were small and their equipment inadequate, but these failings were due entirely to the short-sighted policy of the German supreme command. The potential for recruitment was enormous. Had Hitler not been entirely obsessed with theories of racial inferiority and the policy of blind destruction of the stronghold of 'Jewish Bolshevism', he could very possibly by the end of 1941 have converted the war on the Eastern Front into a Russian Civil War. During the final months of the war, when desperation led some of his colleagues to turn for help to 'their own' Russians, for a brief spell hopes began to run high. During and after the Prague assembly in November 1944, projects for raising an army of five million from prisoners of war and other Russians held in German-controlled territory began to be discussed.[17]

By this time the Germans had long been driven from Russian soil, but they still held within the territory of the Reich itself huge numbers of Soviet prisoners of war, slave labourers, and refugees. The total is not certain, but must have amounted to between five and a half and six million Soviet citizens.[18] By the time of the German surrender in the second week of May 1945, a sizeable proportion of these people had passed behind Red Army lines. Nevertheless, a great number remained for the moment outside Soviet control, principally in the American and British-occupied zones of Germany and Austria.

Eventually, under the terms of the Yalta Agreement, the British and Americans were to return over two million Soviet citizens to the Soviet Union. Between half a million and a million more are estimated to have evaded return and gone to ground in the West. But could Stalin, three days after the war's end, be certain that the Allies' pledge would be honoured so unreservedly? True, the British had for some time been sending back liberated or captured Soviet citizens by sea to Murmansk and Odessa, and overland through Persia. But that was at a time when they still had need of the Soviet Union in the common struggle against Germany. Perhaps, now Soviet and Anglo-American forces were face to face in the heart of Europe, they might review their commitment. In any case the American approach was highly suspect. So far the United States had not followed the British interpretation of the agreement by consenting to employ force in the case of recalcitrant returners. More sinister still, they had consistently adhered rigidly to the Geneva Convention (to which the Soviet Union was not a signatory), stating clearly that they would not compel the return of 'those who demand to be treated as German prisoners under the Prisoner of War Convention'.[19] This meant that the ROA units which had just surrendered to American forces could claim to be exempt from repatriation under the technical objection that they should be treated as serving members of the German Army.

Everything smacked of conspiracy and double-dealing. The ROA divisions had found ready asylum behind US lines, as had the Cossacks, *Russkii Corpus*, and Shandruk's Ukrainian Division in the British-occupied zone of Austria. When on 12 May General Vlasov had been captured by a Red Army detachment, he was discovered to be under the protection of American troops who appeared to be surreptitiously conducting him to safety behind their lines.[20] With the majority of KONR fighting units in their hands, together with a manpower reserve of two or three million Soviet citizens, the Western Allies were in possession of a very potent weapon indeed should the inevitable confrontation lead to war.

All this may appear unwarranted speculation. How do we know this is the way Stalin would have regarded these developments? Though there can be no direct evidence for Stalin's thinking at this time, there is plenty for the reactions it aroused. The treatment of

Soviet citizens returning from captivity in Europe was based on the premise that it was inevitable that anyone who had experienced life outside the bounds of the socialist state must *ipso facto* have become hostile to Soviet power. The overwhelming majority were quarantined for years in the greatly swollen camp complexes of the Gulag administration. The extremity of Soviet fear in this respect is instanced by the absurd case of prisoners liberated from Auschwitz, who were transported at once to Soviet equivalents around the Arctic circle.[21]

That Stalin further feared the Anglo-American capitalists would recruit Soviet citizens in their custody for use as a fifth column in any future conflict seems *prima facie* likely, given his lively fear of the Germans' blundering attempts to exploit a similar opportunity.[22] However, it is not necessary to rely solely on speculation and analogy.

Immediately after the D-Day landings in June 1944, Allied forces began capturing sizeable numbers of Soviet citizens. They were transported back to Britain and held in army camps. For reasons of prestige the Soviets were unable to admit publicly that alone of all combatant nations it was their citizens who had flocked to join the enemy. Accordingly they affected to regard them as liberated prisoners, and asked the British to treat them as such – while at the same time keeping them securely locked up until the time came for their journey home. Regrettably this face-saving device was inapplicable under British law. If they were merely liberated prisoners they would come under the provisions of British civil law, and so could not be held grouped in units, nor effectively rounded up when the moment came for repatriation. The only solution, as the Home Office explained, was that the Soviet prisoners should come under the provisions of the Allied Forces Act. As members of an Allied unit based on British soil they could then be kept together under Soviet discipline, outside the jurisdiction of British civil law.

To the amazement of the Foreign Office the Soviets objected vigorously to the whole idea, and it was not until the following year that they reluctantly agreed to go through a form of accepting the application of the Allied Forces Act to their citizens in Britain. Even then they consented only after becoming convinced that the prisoners would in reality be kept in wired camps guarded by *British* troops, the Foreign Office hoping for its part 'that the arrangement would never be subjected to scrutiny in a court of law'.

Though the Foreign Office seems to have been no more capable of understanding this particular piece of intransigence than that of any other aspect of Soviet policy, the Soviets had themselves made their reasoning explicit. The Allied Forces Act, they explained, 'would have the effect of organising these people into an armed Allied unit in the United Kingdom which did not conform to the wishes of the Soviet Government'.

So central was this thinking to Soviet policy that it was permitted if necessary seriously to obstruct the Allied war effort. An imaginative scheme developed by SOE for the subversion of hundreds of thousands of Soviet citizens serving in German units fighting in France was effectively vetoed by the official NKVD representative in London, because it would have involved parachuting half-a-dozen armed Soviet prisoners in British hands behind German lines.

The obsessive degree to which Stalin's fears extended is exemplified by a trivial incident at a camp for Russians at Newlands Corner near Guildford. When the head of the Soviet Repatriation Commission, General Ratov, wished to place ten reluctant repatriates under arrest, it was suggested by his British counterpart that he should provide the necessary guards. 'He told me,' Brigadier Firebrace reported afterwards, 'that he did not think that he could do this as his men were not armed and he did not think that the Soviet Government would give permission for them to be armed.'[23] When the prospect of a couple of old .303 rifles in the hands of Soviet personnel abroad could arouse such dismay, it can scarcely be surprising that the presence of the Cossack officer corps at large in Austria appeared as a very serious menace indeed.

The threat could only materialise in the event of the British and Americans adopting an overtly hostile attitude towards the Soviet Union, and that was precisely what Stalin believed he had reason to fear. For some months he had suspected that the Western Allies were manoeuvring to negotiate an agreement with the Germans in order to forestall a Soviet presence in Central Europe. Suspicion turned to genuine alarm when he learned of Alexander's secret negotiations for the separate surrender of German forces in North Italy. On 3 April he wrote anxiously to Roosevelt, claiming, 'what we have at the moment is that the Germans on the Western Front have in fact ceased the war against Britain and America. At the same time they continue the war against Russia, the Ally of Britain and the U.S.A.' Milovan Djilas was witness to Stalin's anxiety to avoid 'frightening' the Anglo-Americans in Yugoslavia and even Bulgaria, and to his fear that the Western navies could in the event of conflict gain immediate control of the Black Sea.[24]

VE Day, far from stilling Soviet fears, brought in its train fresh
grounds for alarm. At the Yalta Conference in February the Zonal
Protocol defining the division of post-war Germany into occupied
zones laid down the boundary of the future Soviet-occupied area as
a line running southwards from Lübeck Bay down to the Czechoslo-
vakian frontier – the same as that obtaining today.[25] But the course
of the final campaign had brought the Anglo-American front line so
far to the east of the agreed boundary that almost half of what now
constitutes Soviet-occupied East Germany lay under the military
occupation of the Western Allies. Eisenhower's forces had also moved
well forward into western Czechoslovakia, a country regarded as
within the Soviet sphere of influence. Only in Austria was the Red
Army in possession of any Anglo-American designated territory – a
small section of what had been designated the British occupation
zone.

Churchill had pressed vigorously for Eisenhower to advance
further still and seize Prague before the Soviets could reach the Czech
capital. After the German collapse he wrote on 12 May to Truman,
urging him to join in retaining the existing demarcation line as a
guarantee of Soviet co-operation. Whether or not Soviet intelligence
was aware of these moves is unknown, but the situation certainly
appeared alarming. As Khrushchev recalled, 'At the very end of the
war Stalin was very worried that the Americans would cross the line
of demarcation in the West. He was doubtful that they would
relinquish the territory which Roosevelt had previously agreed to
give us in Teheran.'[26]

Ironically the single most alarming note in East-West relations
struck at this time was one which in reality bore no sinister conno-
tations. On the morning of 12 May the United States announced
abruptly that Lend-Lease supplies to the Soviet Union would cease
forthwith. Ships already on their way were to be turned back. The
Soviets understandably reacted with anger and apprehension. In fact,
though they were not to know, the offensively abrupt manner of this
change in policy was largely due to over-zealous interpretation of
a presidential memorandum by officials of the Foreign Economic
Administration.[27]

In short, any Soviet appraisal of the political and strategic situation
in the second week of May 1945 must have taken into account the
possibility of a renewed outbreak of war. This time, however, it
would be war, not with the collapsing rump of the Third Reich, but
with the all-powerful United States and her allies – who could,

unprincipled capitalists as they were, call if need be upon the surrendered Wehrmacht to assist them. It was a war, as Stalin confessed at the time to Tito, which the exhausted Soviet Union was in no position to fight.

Despite the overwhelming preponderance of the Red Army in Eastern Europe, the occupied countries retained for a time varying degrees of national independence, and were yet to be totally subjugated to satellite status.[28] The possibility of effective resistance did not appear so hopeless as hindsight may now make it appear. In March the NKVD had kidnapped sixteen prominent Polish resistance leaders, triggering off angry responses in Britain and the United States which Stalin considered of small account compared with the importance of attempting to muzzle the formidable Home Army. Nearer home a virtual civil war was raging in the Ukraine, where, as Khrushchev admitted later, 'we lost thousands of men in a bitter struggle between the Ukrainian nationalists and the forces of Soviet power'. Similarly ferocious guerrilla warfare had broken out in the occupied Baltic States and elsewhere.[29]

Militarily all this amounted to little in face of a seven-million-strong battle-hardened Red Army. But was that army a wholly reliable commodity? The purge Stalin had already begun to unleash on its senior generals makes it clear that he did not think so. For the first time since the Revolution millions of armed Soviet citizens were dispersed far beyond the safety of the frontiers, settling down comfortably among all the evidence of European luxury and liberty so long concealed from sight. Moreover, the potential enemy was no Nazi brigand, whose brutality could be calculated to arouse even the most recalcitrant Russian's resentment, but the much-lauded democracies. Could they fail, in the event of a major conflict, to play the vital 'Vlasov card' Hitler had so rashly thrown away?

There had been an unnerving change in the mood of the Soviet people of late. Victories in the field had provided Soviet man with greatly increased *amour propre*, but paradoxically there had also been a sea-change in the morale of the opponents of the regime. In 1940, during the Finnish war, two British intelligence officers had conducted interrogations among 2,000 Soviet prisoners held by the Finns. Though almost unanimous in their dislike of the Soviet regime, their prevailing outlook was one of resigned hopelessness. The British officers concluded that 'the political value of prisoners of war can be assessed as zero . . . The military value of the prisoners of war is nil . . . Any possibility of using them as a military force can be ruled out.'[30] Yet a bare five years later, with the Soviet Union immeasurably more powerful than in 1940, tens of thousands of Russians were to be found fighting in the ranks of the enemy with a bravery that even the Soviets had to acknowledge.

The propaganda effect the KONR forces had on the Red Army was far more unnerving than their limited military activity. Right up to the last days of the war, when Germany's doom and that of her satellites was clear to see, a regular stream of deserters continued to answer Russian-language appeals to come over to the enemy.[31] Colonel Constantin Wagner, commanding the Second Division of the Fifteenth Cossack Cavalry Corps, has described the arrival of a Red Air Force officer, complete with fighter-plane, who came over to his unit in Yugoslavia within a week of the war's end.

At the time of the German invasion the Soviet Government had hastily ordered the confiscation of all wireless sets in the possession of civilians. In 1944–5, however, millions of Soviet citizens serving in the Red Army had of necessity access to radios capable of picking up daily KONR Russian-language broadcasts, reminding them of the hardships and cruelties of life under Bolshevism, and urging them to come over to join Vlasov's freedom-fighters. Frequently interviews were conducted with recent deserters. Germany played little part in the subject-matter of the programmes; indeed, Stalin was frequently referred to sarcastically as *Vozhd*, 'Leader', 'quite clearly in the derogatory sense of "Fuehrer"'. Perhaps most unpleasant of all was the extensive airing of topics, such as Stalin's murder of Kirov, which the Soviet public was not supposed even to think about.[32]

The Soviet Government had valid reasons for fearing the dangerous potential of the Russian, Ukrainian nationalist, and other dissident troops, if skilfully deployed by the Anglo-Americans. Their sheer number and anti-Soviet fervour might serve to alert the Allied high command to the extent of exploitable dissatisfaction existing both within the Soviet Union and the Red Army in particular. Rightly or wrongly, too, the émigré Tsarist officers appeared especially menacing. One of the most remarkable factors in the whole story is the way in which Soviet prisoners, subjected to a quarter of a century of anti-White propaganda, so readily accepted command by émigré officers from Denikine's and Wrangel's armies. On both sides lessons had been learned. From personal experience the *Osttruppen* (soldiers from the East) knew little of their former masters, but they knew a great deal about the methods of those who had displaced them.

Equally, the Tsarist émigrés had had ample time in which to shed the authoritarian ways of the old Russian Army. Indeed, the younger ones had known nothing but the more liberal atmosphere of European countries in which they had been born or brought up. Citizens of the West, too, the émigrés were for the most part men of the world, speaking French or German in addition to Russian, and so uniquely able to co-operate with and even influence their powerful allies, whether German, British or American.

If the overall prospect appeared ominous, the particular circumstances of the twenty-four hours leading up to the German surrender must have copiously watered the seeds of suspicion. The temporary occupation of Prague by Buniachenko's forces, initially in collaboration with Czech resistance forces, was alarming enough. When taken in conjunction with American moves it appeared laden with menace. On 6 May the American Fifth Corps took Pilsen, and was poised to take Prague also, a mere fifty miles to the east and still well beyond the reach of the nearest Soviet forces. Their commander was General Patton, who was openly chafing to beat the Red Army into Prague. To the surprise of the Soviets, Eisenhower ordered Patton to halt his troops in order to allow Koniev's troops to seize the Czech capital.

During these critical days delegations of Czechs appeared at American headquarters, pleading for an advance before the Soviets could arrive. At the same time envoys from the Vlasov units arrived, requesting and being granted opportunity to surrender to United States forces.[33]

The combined Vlasov presence and the American threat to Prague seemed to confirm the grimmest Soviet forebodings. KONR anti-Soviet forces were withdrawing from the city, to fall almost at once under the protection of advanced armoured units of Patton's Fourth Armoured Division.[34] The war itself was actually over, German forces having surrendered unconditionally on all fronts at Rheims on the morning of 7 May. The news had been broadcast to German troops in Bohemia that evening by Radio Prague. They at once accepted the capitulation and prepared to evacuate the city, leaving it in the hands of the Czechs. Stalin moved swiftly to check this dangerous move. Though the Soviet General Susloparov had been authorised to act as plenipotentiary to the instrument of German surrender, the Soviets unexpectedly announced that they did not after all regard this surrender as valid, insisting that the ceremony should be repeated next day at Karlshorst on the outskirts of Berlin. Further obstructive wrangling over textual minutiae and protocol enabled

Soviet negotiators to postpone the final signing until just before
midnight on the eighth. Meanwhile Koniev ordered the Soviet Thirteenth Army in John Erickson's words, 'to cut loose and make all
speed for Prague, at the same time informing all commanders that
he demanded an advance rate of at least twenty miles per day from
the infantry and 30–35 miles from the tank formations'. They reached
the city in the early hours of 9 May, an objective for which Stalin
had ingeniously prolonged the war by thirty-six hours.[35]

Matters were thus delicately poised when next day, 10 May, a
Soviet officer (presumably from SMERSH, whose concern it was)
on Tolbukhin's staff at Voitsberg in Austria asked the visiting General
Keightley for immediate delivery of the Cossack units in Austria. On
the following day Keightley's staff officer, Brigadier Tryon-Wilson,
learned more precisely whom the Soviets were most anxious to
apprehend. They badly wanted the Cossack generals – household
names among the mass of anti-Soviet Russians – and the élite of
émigré officers accompanying them. The request was accompanied
by a typewritten list of their names, with those of Krasnov, Shkuro
and other leaders singled out in capital letters.

The dismay of General Merkulov at his Lubyanka office in Moscow
can be imagined, when he received news that the British had declared
themselves regretfully unable to comply with this particular request.
Under the Yalta Agreement it was accepted that the bulk of Soviet
Cossacks might in due course be handed over; but the Fifth Corps
was powerless under screening regulations issued by Field-Marshal
Alexander just five days earlier to deliver up non-Soviet citizens.

This Merkulov would have recognised as an objection likely to be
upheld, whatever protests the Soviet Government might make. As
early as June 1944 the Foreign Office had emphasised that compulsory
repatriation applied only to Soviet citizens, whose status was defined
as 'a person born or resident within the pre 1 Sep 39 boundaries of
Russia (who had not acquired another nationality – or a Nanssen pass-
port, which would render the subject Stateless) . . .' Though the
Foreign Office was at all times anxious to oblige the Soviets in everything possible, unscrupulous attempts by the Soviet Repatriation
Commission in Britain to include White émigrés among the repatriates
had been firmly resisted.[36] Clearly neither Brigadier Low nor his immediate superior, General Keightley, was in a position to alter instructions based on government policy. A direct Soviet approach to Fifth
Corps had achieved and could achieve nothing, yet something had to
be done in order to lay hands on these dangerous men.

We know now of course what happened. On 13 May Harold Macmillan flew into Klagenfurt and persuaded Keightley to bend the rules in order secretly to hand over Merkulov's 'wanted men'. When Macmillan left Caserta on the morning of 12 May he informed the Foreign Office he was flying to see McCreery and Harding, and it was only subsequently that he reported he had decided to make the additional journey to talk with Keightley. It seems likely that this extra visit took place, not at Keightley's request, but on the initiative of the Resident Minister. Keightley was indignant at the idea of returning the émigré generals, particularly Shkuro, who was, like himself, a Companion of the Bath. There had been no time for the Soviets to do more than make an official request, and the General's course was bound by regulations which he possessed neither power nor inclination to set aside. He had no means of knowing what would be Macmillan's view, and no obvious motive for wishing to consult him on the matter. It will be recalled, too, that though the question of the repatriations was undoubtedly a prime motive for his visit, Macmillan took considerable care to conceal the fact from the Foreign Office.

From whom could Macmillan have acquired news of the embarrassing SMERSH request, assuming Keightley was not the source? Certainly not from McCreery or anyone at the Eighth Army: we know that McCreery did not receive Keightley's report until the day after Macmillan's visit, and then only in a deliberately distorted form. Equally it seems established beyond reasonable doubt that no one higher up the chain of command – at the Fifteenth Army Group or AFHQ – knew of the request, or would have responded favourably to it had he done so. A curious and seemingly inexplicable factor lies in Toby Low's failure to mention the Soviet requests for the Cossacks on 10 and 11 May in his Sitrep reports to Eighth Army headquarters.

It looks as if news of SMERSH's request for the Cossack generals and its rejection by the Fifth Corps somehow reached Macmillan while he was at the Eighth Army headquarters on 12 May. Possibly the news ultimately emanated directly or indirectly from SMERSH itself. Having failed in a direct approach to Keightley, they (or someone on their behalf) tried this second line of attack. This there would have been little point in doing unless there were reason to feel confident that Macmillan might prove receptive to a suggestion that screening provisions should be set aside. For if Macmillan's likely reaction had been an unknown quantity, there must inevitably have appeared to be a strong risk – indeed, likelihood – that he would feel obliged to insist on implementation of his instructions from the Foreign Office to screen and retain old émigrés. In that case, from SMERSH's point of view the chances of recovering Krasnov and the others would have been dramatically reduced if not altogether quashed, by any action drawing Macmillan gratuitously into the picture.

There are positive indications that SMERSH was deeply involved in the British side of the repatriations, and that links between the British organisers of the covert operation and the Soviet security forces went beyond mere illicit compliance with an official request.

First it has to be noted that General Keightley took the extraordinary step of permitting SMERSH officers into his Corps area in order to assist in supervising repatriation operations. The Rev Kenneth Tyson, Chaplain to the Eighth Argylls, accompanied a patrol at the time of the round-up at Lienz. He informed me that:

> a Soviet official accompanied the party, searching for fugitive Cossacks. He wore khaki uniform but as far as I can remember he carried no badges of rank. He was there ostensibly to act as interpreter, but his English was rather halting & indeed meagre. He was not obtrusive but the general feeling among the soldiers was that he was there to see to it that they conscientiously discharged their task. The Cossacks showed no animosity towards him but the fact is they were, or seemed to be, apathetic, beyond feeling & caring – worn-out physically & emotionally. I do not know who authorised the presence of this Soviet official (not officer) or when he arrived at the Battalion H.Q. I understand that several such officials were carrying out similar duties in the area – wherever search parties were operating – but I have no certain knowledge of this.

Tyson's information was correct. British troops and their Cossack victims have alike testified to the presence of these Soviet 'officials', and to the fact that they were armed and granted licence to join in shooting or beating Cossack prisoners. Today General Musson finds the idea of Soviet officers using firearms while operating within his Brigade area 'outrageous', and their presence inexplicable: 'Surely no one could have permitted it.' In view of the fact that he has no recollection of the matter, and that it would in any case be a matter for intelligence beyond Brigade level, he assumes the introduction of these people must have derived from arrangements made by Corps.

At Spittal a Russian émigré calling at the British Town Major's office found the latter openly overruled and browbeaten by his

Russian 'interpreter'.[37] Major R. S. V. Howard of the Royal Irish Fusiliers recalls that in his area:

a sentry reported that a staff car with what appeared to be officers in it had passed down one of the roads – the Cossacks were in a triangle of three roads – and had stopped. Someone in the car had shouted to the Cossacks in a strange language; the car then passed on. Prince zu Salm [the Cossack commanding officer] came to see me in a state of great agitation and said that some Soviet officers had told his men they would be returned to the USSR. Of course we knew nothing of this, neither were we very concerned: the political implications of such an act were not our affair. I was annoyed that the Soviet officers had managed to cross the River Drau which as we understood it was the boundary between our armies.

Keightley's conduct in thus admitting a SMERSH detachment into his Corps area to supervise operations conducted by units under his command is extraordinary – indeed inexplicable – under any normal operational practice. Today General Musson declares himself mystified as to how such a concession could have been permitted, which in any case could not have been arranged below Corps level. It seems on the other hand unlikely that it would have been approved or condoned by the Army Commander, General McCreery, who later in the same year was to express himself as 'strongly averse to allowing Soviet troops to enter the British zone for the purpose of removing their Nationals by force'.[38] One of Keightley's divisional commanders responsible for returning Cossacks, Major-General Horatius Murray, made it clear that he would decline to admit into his command people he regarded as little better than hired assassins. Keightley backed down without demur, clearly feeling that this was not an aspect of the operation which bore too open an airing.

It will be recalled that the Cossack officers were lured to their deaths on the pretence that they were being invited to a conference with Alexander. This tactic bears the hallmarks of a SMERSH deception. Two months earlier the Soviets had dealt with what they regarded as a parallel threat by an identical approach. In order to destroy effective opposition by the Polish Home Army, SMERSH issued an invitation to sixteen of the most prominent underground leaders to confer with Marshal Zhukov. The Poles fell into the trap, and like General Krasnov and his colleagues found themselves flown, not to the Army Commander's headquarters, but to the Lubyanka Prison in Moscow. Even minor details of the deception tallied. At

Lienz a senior British officer emphasised to a Cossack staff officer, 'do not neglect to notify General Krasnov. The Commander is particularly interested in meeting him.' This echoed the approach of the Soviet officer, who 'was very emphatic that General Niedzwiadek-Okulicki, Commander-in-Chief of the Polish Underground Home Army, who till now had not participated in the talks, should be present at the luncheon-party'.[39]

It can scarcely be coincidence that the leader of the Czech nationalist partisans, Frantisek Urban, fell into the identical trap about the same time.[40] Thus the spring of 1945 saw the heads of the Polish, Czech and Cossack anti-Soviet resistance movements lopped off: a remarkable achievement, and one which it is reasonable to suppose stood high among Soviet priorities.

Further circumstantial evidence of Soviet moves in this respect is to be found in aspects of the simultaneous return of Yugoslavs by the Fifth Corps. A particularly odd factor in the circumstances surrounding this operation lies in Djilas's statement:

> we didn't at all understand why the British insisted on returning these people . . . to our great surprise, they . . . delivered them into our hands. This was all the more astonishing because we knew that many Yugoslavs (Croats and others) who found themselves in Britain [and Germany] as prisoners of war were considered quite safe from repatriation.

The astonishment of the Yugoslav leadership is understandable. When Colonel Ivanovic arrived at the Fifth Corps headquarters to insist on the refugees' return, it was in expectation (as General Nadj's account makes clear) of encountering British intransigence. Instead he found to his evident surprise that all his demands had been conceded in advance by Brigadier Low. As we know from the British documents, Low issued orders for the return of all Yugoslav refugees in anticipation both of Yugoslav demands and of instructions from his own higher command. The return of the Cossacks resulted from Macmillan's 'verbal directive' to Keightley of 13 May; as the Minister is recorded at the same time to have 'recommended' the parallel return of Yugoslavs, it is reasonable to assume that the 'verbal directive' covered them as well. The fates of the Cossacks and Yugoslavs appear implicitly linked in his diary entry of 13 May.

It is important to recall that the Yugoslavs, unlike the Soviets, enjoyed no equivalent of the Yalta Agreement on prisoners of war, which could be invoked to justify requests for the return of reluctant repatriates. They possessed on the contrary striking evidence that the British had no intention of complying with demands of this sort. On 3 May at Cormons Partisan efforts to capture Damjanovic's retreating Chetniks had been frustrated by the intervention of troops of the British Eighth Army, and the Royalist units were shepherded to safety at Palmanova.

It may be in addition that the Yugoslavs were aware that Allied policy had hardened by the end of April to explicit prohibition of forced repatriation of their subjects. Both they and the Soviets were regularly receiving the texts of US diplomatic documents from an unknown source in the State Department, and fellow-travellers within the British Embassy at Belgrade are said on credible authority to have passed secrets to the Communist authorities.[41]

Though Tito was anxious to strike at his fugitive compatriots, he might well have felt that there was little point in inviting a predictable snub by making a demand bound to be rejected. It seems certain that he had made no official request at the time of Macmillan's intervention, since it was three days later (16 May) that Alexander enquired of Tito whether he wished the Croats at Bleiburg to be turned over.

Nevertheless there must have been pressure from somewhere to make Macmillan take the extraordinary risks he did in secretly initiating a policy which he knew his government opposed. His diary entry for the conference at Klagenfurt suggests that he was even more anxious to conceal his part in the repatriation of the Yugoslavs than in that of the Cossacks, as does his remarkable omission of the matter in his subsequent report to the Foreign Office.

Tito's closest colleagues found it incomprehensible that the initiative for the return of escaped Croats, Chetniks and Slovenes should come from the British. Like Generals Shtemenko and Tolbukhin on the Soviet side, they appear not to have been made privy to the more delicate aspects of negotiations conducted at this time.

One explanation of this anomaly which suggests itself is that the demand was made by the Soviets on their protégé's behalf. It would then have been through NKVD or SMERSH channels that the request for the Cossacks was combined with additional secret pressure to include the Yugoslavs. The current crisis boiling up in Carinthia and Venezia Giulia represented a major priority among Stalin's strategic considerations. From the Baltic to the Adriatic the erstwhile Allies faced each other along a temporary demarcation line. Already uneasy undercurrents were stirring, but only at the southern extremity was

there an immediate and real fear of local differences erupting into war
– a war for which (so Stalin admitted to Tito) the Soviet Union was
unprepared.

The confused situation in Carinthia and Slovenia could at any
moment spark off a local conflict between the Partisans and forces
under Alexander's command. Such a conflict, if prolonged, would
inevitably draw in large anti-Communist military forces still in the
field.

Hindsight – in this case influenced by the subsequent triumph
of Partisan arms and establishment of totalitarian dictatorship in
Yugoslavia – can all too easily obscure how matters *appeared* to stand
in the days leading up to 13 May. It is often forgotten that the war
in Yugoslavia did not end until 15 May, and was therefore raging at
the time of Macmillan's visit to Klagenfurt.[42] On 4 May the Croatian
Government (then still in its capital, Zagreb) had despatched an
appeal to AFHQ 'for an intervention of your military force with a
particular regard to the danger threatening a great number of the
population of this country'. AFHQ had no intention of complying
with this appeal, which was communicated to Tito's government
next day.[43] But Zagreb only fell to the Partisans on 8 May; and on
13 May, the date of Macmillan's crucial consultation with Keightley,
the Croatian Army, seventeen divisions and 200,000 men strong,
was still withdrawing in good order towards British lines in the strong
hope of obtaining honourable terms of surrender – a circumstance
regarded with deep suspicion by Partisan leaders.[44]

At the same time General Mihailovic had withdrawn with a force
of some 12,000 Chetniks into the heart of Serbia, where the struggle
of the Yugoslav Civil War was entering its culminating hard-fought
convulsion around Mount Zelengora.[45] Just across the frontier in
North Italy the British were protecting a comparable number of
Chetnik troops who had crossed over to their side. Even after the
dictatorship had been established for over a year, Fitzroy Maclean
found Tito and his senior colleagues convinced that this represented
'an attempt on our part to shield war criminals from justice and to
perpetuate a para-military organisation designed to overthrow them
by force . . . There could be no doubt . . . that they believed that
the politico-military organisation of General Damjanovic had
been formed with the knowledge and approval of His Majesty's
Government and that they were genuinely concerned as to our
motives.'[46]

To the Kremlin this represented almost as alarming a prospect as it did in Belgrade. It required no excess of apprehension to envisage a major resurgence of the Yugoslav Civil War, this time, however, with the crisis over Carinthia and Venezia Giulia drawing in British and American troops on the nationalist side. In October 1944 Stalin had conceded to Churchill the right to a major influence in post-war Yugoslavia:[47] a claim circumstances seemed about to provide the means of realising.

Hindsight, influenced by the Yugoslav-Soviet split of 1948, has all too often been permitted to distort the realities of Tito's relationship to Stalin in 1945. Tito's role among subordinate Communist leaders in Eastern Europe was unique, in that he had led a major resistance movement against Nazi occupation with meagre Soviet assistance. The Red Army offensive had passed only through the northernmost part of the country, leaving the Partisans with a realistic claim to have liberated their own territory. Nevertheless Communist Yugoslavia was in May 1945 a wholly committed member of the Soviet camp, subordinated to the interests of Stalin's long-term strategy. Tito was unreserved in his admiration for the Soviet leader: 'a great man . . . a very great man'. His extreme subservience had enabled him to survive in pre-war Moscow when the rest of the Yugoslav Party was drastically purged; he was 'above all willing to take orders and accept the current party line'.[48] In 1945 his loyalty remained as enthusiastic, if accompanied by burgeoning feelings of pride in his independent achievements. These did not prevent him from willingly accepting material marks of Yugoslavia's subordinate relationship to the centre of World Revolution.

In that part of Yugoslavia temporarily occupied by the Red Army the population suffered ravages little different in degree from those inflicted on enemy-occupied territory. To this Djilas alone raised serious objection, with Tito remaining ineffectually silent in face of Soviet dismissals. How Tito, in face of a very different situation, later came to oust Soviet representatives from his country is another story. In 1945 the Soviets were in ultimate control of the country. 'The actual ruler of Yugoslavia' was the brutish and overbearing Major-General Kiselev of the Soviet Military Mission, who on occasion unabashedly overruled Tito himself in the most trivial matters of Yugoslav domestic concern.[49]

There was in any case one major area of policy where Stalin's and Tito's interests coincided. Over the space of a quarter of a century the Soviet Government had developed the most formidable machinery of police control over its subject populations the world had ever seen.

It was this expertise which was placed at the disposal of Tito, ever acutely apprehensive of insurrection or assassination.

It seems that Tito, despite his remarkable talents as an inspiring military leader, was personally a coward. Djilas noted that 'he conspicuously avoided danger', while attributing this factor to 'an inborn caution' and the realistic need to preserve his person for the good of the cause. From his NKVD representative at wartime Partisan headquarters, however, Stalin would have received a less creditable account. As a former NKVD officer in Moscow recounted after his defection to the West:

> A cipher clerk called Zhukov, who worked in my section, later served with Tito in the partisans during the war, harassing the Germans in the mountains of Yugoslavia. On his return he told me that Tito was timid and a defeatist under fire and walked with a stoop, in constant fear of attack. But after the defeat of the Germans, he was a different man. With his bodyguard round him and the Red Army troops supporting him, Tito marched into Belgrade with his chest out and the air of a conquering hero. Such at least was Zhukov's descrption.[50]

Stalin, whose own physical cowardice appears indisputable,[51] possessed an unerring instinct for exploiting human weaknesses, and knew well how to make use of Tito's failing. When Djilas visited Moscow in 1944 Stalin was at great pains to emphasise how personally vulnerable his leader was to British perfidy:

> He kept stressing that we ought to beware of the [British] Intelligence Service and of English duplicity, especially with regard to Tito's life. 'They were the ones who killed General Sikorski in a plane and then neatly shot down the plane – no proof, no witnesses.'
>
> In the course of the meeting Stalin kept repeating these warnings, which I passed to Tito upon my return and which probably influenced his decision to make his conspiratorial night flight from Vis to Soviet-occupied territory in Rumania on 21 September 1944.

Tito gratefully accepted not only Stalin's advice but more practical assurances of safety. After the liberation of Yugoslavia in 1945 he received from Moscow the present of a bullet-proof Packard, similar to those in use by the Soviet leadership. But though Stalin had good reason to wish to preserve his faithful ally from an assassin's bullet he had another, less altruistic, motive for provoking Tito's lively sense of self-preservation. By emphasising the necessity for an effective security police, Stalin was able to ensure that it was one directly controlled by himself. Yugoslav intelligence officers were taken to the Soviet Union to be trained in MGB schools and, as a former NKVD officer revealed, 'From the very beginning, our Soviet missions had busily recruited Yugoslavs to work directly for Soviet intelligence.' Immediately after the liberation of Belgrade, in November 1944, Stalin sent NKVD Major-General Dmitri N. Shadrin to organise a powerful bodyguard for Tito. It included seven Soviet NKVD men, and 'at first Tito seemed to feel more at home with these Russians than with Yugoslav troops.' Tito felt himself under a deep obligation to Shadrin, whom he showered with autographed photographs and valuable presents.[52]

It is possible that it was the Soviet security forces, NKVD and SMERSH who provided the initiative not only in arranging the repatriations with the British, but even in devising the method by which the massacres were conducted. There is much about the techniques applied in the Kocevje massacre which recalls that perpetrated by the Soviets at Katyn in 1940. Particularly striking in both cases is the ingenious attempt to conceal the site by planting young trees over the area. This was what the NKVD did at Katyn,[53] and visitors to Kocevje in recent years have reported that trees on the massacre-site at Kocevje are of markedly younger growth than those in the surrounding forest. It was not necessary for SMERSH to provide the execution squads, but they may well have acted as expert advisers on the methods employed. An indication of this may be found in a deposition by Dusan Vukovic, in 1945 serving with the Protective Battalion of the Second Partisan Army. He was present at Gospic when 400 of the inhabitants were slaughtered:

> I saw one Ustasha who was skinned alive and then hung on a tree with his own skin. I believe that about four hundred of the citizens of Gospic were murdered, most of them in a very sadistic manner. *Also, I should like to mention that I saw officers attached to a Russian delegation that came to check on the Partisan operations, photographing the bodies in the caves.*[54] (italics inserted)

The majority of the 200,000 or so Croats turned back by the British at Bleiburg in mid-May were killed under conditions of indiscriminate savagery in Tito's notorious death marches. Instead of massacring them on the spot, or at convenient points behind the frontier, the Partisans drove their prisoners in columns through towns and villages far into the interior. Throughout their journey the prisoners were beaten, tortured and killed individually and in batches. These death marches frequently covered hundreds of miles, and extended to weeks or even months in duration.

Joseph Hecimovic, for example, was a captain in the Croatian Army held by the British at a camp at Krumpendorf near Klagenfurt. He was handed over to the Partisans along with 4,000 of his compatriots at the end of May 1945. By the time they reached Kranj on the Slovenian side of the frontier their numbers had been reduced to some 1,500. After a brief moment of escape from the death-camp at St Vid outside Ljubljana, Hecimovic was recaptured and joined a large column of prisoners which was marched on a zigzag journey across Slovenia and Croatia, northwards across the frontier into Hungary, until they ended up at Kovin, on the Danube in eastern Serbia. It was now the end of August, and the handful of survivors had covered some 550 miles.

The death marches have been copiously documented from eye-witness testimonies, principally in the massive collection compiled by two Croatian scholars, John Prcela and Stanko Guldescu. The very number of these first-hand accounts incidentally testifies to the sizeable proportion of prospective victims who escaped – a point of some significance. It is abundantly clear from these that the purpose of this laborious method of killing huge numbers of people (which taxed the endurance of guards as well as victims, making frequently escapes inevitable) was to make the executions and massacres as public and notorious as possible. At the village of Djerajlije, for example, Hecimovic and his comrades found the whole population assembled to conduct an elaborately-staged 'running the gauntlet'. This happened time and again with a regularity which proved it to emanate from central government policy.

As a Serb serving on his village's People's Committee explained:

> One day late in June, 1945, we received an order from above that all inhabitants living at the foot of the Kozara Mountain and around Prosara must assemble at an appointed time at the lumberyard in Podgraci in order to kill the Ustashas. The population of this district had to bring hay-forks, picks, knives, and other weapons with which they could carry out this killing of the Ustashas who were about to be brought to this place. All of them were to be slain, without exceptions and without the expenditure of ammunition.[55]

The purpose of involving so large and widespread a proportion of the population as witnesses and participants in the massacres was presumably to strike fear into the inhabitants of Croatia, to gratify Serbian desires for vengeance for past Ustashe crimes, and perhaps to implicate as much of the population as possible in crimes alienating them permanently from the regime's adversaries.

Whatever the motive, the fact of the deliberate publicity accorded these massacres is abundantly attested. This stands in remarkable contrast to the slaughter of Domobranci and Chetniks handed over by the British from Viktring Camp. There the most lively precautions were taken throughout to prevent any observers from detecting what was to happen to the victims once they left the town of Kocevje for the forest, and to ensure that the prisoners themselves should not recognise their route. Above all stringent measures were adopted to ensure that no prisoner escaped to tell the tale. Jovo Miletic, a Chetnik handed over from Viktring by the British, managed to escape from a column marching between the notorious transit-camps of Kranj and St Vid. During his days on the run he was astonished at the exaggerated extent of measures adopted to recapture escapers: 'Partisans mounted an action to catch them and must have covered an enormous amount of the terrain to prevent them from coming to the borders. Thousands of them were spread as if in an unbroken chain over miles and miles of the country to prevent the escape.'

In the case of the handful that did get away from Kocevje itself, desperate measures were undertaken by the authorities to track them down and, failing that, to punish and silence their relatives. The one escaper known to have fallen again into the hands of OZNA was taken back and crucified by the site of the massacre.

There must have been some reason for this striking contrast between the policy of deliberately publicising the massacres of Croats and other enemies of the regime and the stringent secrecy surrounding the killing of the repatriates from Viktring. The latter was concealed for a specific and significant purpose, which cannot have arisen solely from fear lest the population at large discover the secret. As Tito was markedly indifferent to the reactions of his own people, it seems at the least possible that these exceptional precautions were adopted to protect the identity of those who had collaborated in bringing the massacres about.

On 24 and 25 May Radio Belgrade broadcast an address by Tito 'in which he called for the cessation of all "irresponsible" (i.e. non-official) killing'. It was made known that this was an amnesty in honour of the Marshal's birthday, which was celebrated on 25 May. In fact no amnesty occurred, the killings continued as if there had been no broadcast, and it is evident that Tito's announcement was made for some quite ulterior purpose. The true reason had to be made known to the Partisans, since they were required to pay no attention to it. As one of their number later explained, 'the British and Americans had exerted pressure upon the government in Belgrade to put a halt to the orgy of killing that had followed the English extradition of prisoners'.[56]

Yet no such pressure on the part of the British and Americans is recorded, nor is such a move intrinsically likely. Neither the embassies in Belgrade nor AFHQ were yet aware that Yugoslav prisoners were being extradited, let alone killed. However, there must have been some – presumably propaganda – purpose behind the announcement for it to have been issued at all.

Can it be coincidence that 24 May was also the first day of the handovers from Viktring Camp? The fact that such an 'amnesty' had been publicly announced at the time of the first deliveries of Yugoslav refugees would provide valuable cover at the time or thereafter, should unpleasant stories begin to leak from across the frontier.

The AFHQ order of 23 May, which Low employed as authority for the repatriation, forbade the use of force. As has been seen, he resorted to deceit as an effective alternative, enabling it to be claimed that all the Yugoslavs returned were volunteers fully aware of their destination.[57] If by some mischance reports of maltreatment of repatriated Yugoslavs were to reach the Eighth Army or AFHQ, the 'amnesty' would provide ideal evidence that the Fifth Corps could have had no reason to fear that repatriated Yugoslavs were likely to suffer ill usage. On this view the 'amnesty' was proclaimed, not in response to British and American protests against a slaughter already taking place, but in anticipation of possible reactions to massacres commencing that day.

All record of the successive Soviet demands on 10 and 11 May for the handover of Cossacks and old émigrés has been expunged from the record. Could similarly covert arrangements have been made between Tito and those who arranged to present him with the Viktring prisoners? Inside Yugoslavia a Party orator boasted to an unwilling audience of some 15,000 Croats held in the Celje football stadium in the second half of May: 'All of you who are gathered here are our enemies. We are the bosses now. We have received the permission of the Americans and British both, to do with you as we please.'[58]

The evidence must be assessed on its own value. It is, however, a regrettable fact that the repatriation operations extended beyond merely delivering the refugees over to the Partisans. A special unit, whose activities are still shrouded in secrecy, was entrusted by the Fifth Corps headquarters with the task of co-operating with the Partisans in arranging the safe delivery of Chetniks and Domobranci from Viktring. Its duties included arranging for the concealment of Partisan executioners in the stations at Maria Elend and Rosenbach. Its members were kept fully posted about massacres taking place at the other end of the Rosenbach tunnel, and undertook the concealment of evidence that returning Chetniks were committing suicide in the trains.

In an earlier chapter (cf. pages 163–7) the account was quoted of a Partisan officer, Branislav Todorovic, whose duties took him to Rosenbach, the point of entrainment for returning Yugoslavs. On the evening of 24 May he was ordered 'to go to Rosenbach, that we might contact the English, from whom we were to receive some prisoners . . . That night, about 10 or 11, Capt. Dominko [Todorovic's superior] introduced us to the English Lieutenant Lakhed, liaison officer, of a unit called "6 Special Force". This officer told us that at 10 o'clock next day there would be ready a train of 30 wagons and 2 wagons for officers which would pick up 1,500 prisoners at Maria Elend.' The ruse whereby the prisoners had been told they were going to Italy and should not be prematurely alerted to their true fate was also discussed.

Todorovic was with a party of Partisans who boarded the train at Maria Elend and accompanied the prisoners to Rosenbach, the point of departure for Yugoslavia: 'I remember that on the way from St. Maria Elend to Rosenbach 14 Chetniks committed suicide in the train and that at Rosenbach, in the presence of the English [from 6 Special Force] whom I summoned, we took the bodies out of the train and buried them near the station.'

The survivors travelled through the railway tunnel, and on the other side many were indiscriminately massacred. Todorovic, who was in fact a Royalist sympathiser, was horrified at witnessing these atrocities:

I returned that night, with a special train of wagons and an engine, to Rosenbach and on the way made up my mind not to make the journey again but at all costs to get away. Actually I did twice accompany transports to Hrusica. Thereafter I did not go beyond Rosenbach; for, when I told Lt. Lakhed what was being done with the prisoners, he helped

me and arranged with my CO. that I should stay with him, on the ground
that a liaison officer should not go far from his duty station.

On every transport after that – and there were 16 of them – the corpses
of suicides were found. On the request of the English these were removed
from the train at Rosenbach and buried. I asked the English to do this,
so that they might see the real state of affairs and that my statements
about the treatment of the prisoners were true . . .

On the 3rd June I arranged supper for the English. I thought that I
should be the only Partisan present. But as a big transport of prisoners
was arranged for next day, there came the officers who had been at the
killing, all except the Brigade Chief of Staff. Of the English Capt. Brown
was at supper and 2 captains from the regiment at St Jakob, also Lt.
Lakhed and Lt. Gelbajt (? Galbraith). By a special train late that night
arrived the assistant commissar and the commissar of the 3rd battalion,
a Montenegrin whose name I don't know. That evening I got into close
relations with the English. On that account I became suspect to the
Partisans. Next day I was summoned by telephone and told to report to
the staff [i.e. his superior command] at once. I knew what that meant.
Accordingly, I fled into Italy.

No. Six Special Force Staff Section, the unit entrusted with these
tasks, did not form part of the regular army but was a detachment
of Special Operations Executive (SOE), operating outside the normal
chain of command. Major-General Murray, Divisional Commander
of the area, has since stated bluntly that he knew little about their
activities, which had nothing to do with his fighting division, and
indeed had no time for them: 'The "Sixth" Force had nothing to do
with 6th Armoured Division. It would not be a hand we would have
been prepared to play anyway.'[59]

General Murray is not alone in finding difficulty in establishing
the exact role of the Sixth Special Force at this time. No War Diary
of the unit is available, nor does any reference to it appear (at least,
not after an exhaustive search) in the records of the Fifth Corps or
Eighth Army deposited in the Public Record Office. Some years ago
I interviewed the second-in-command of the unit, Edward Renton,
but regrettably he died before I came to enquire into the implications
of the Yugoslav handovers. Sir Peter Williams, who commanded the
unit until 12 May, identifies the officer whom Todorovic names
quaintly as 'Lakhed', as a Scotsman called Lockheed, or Lockhead.

However, the Sixth Special Force's commanding officer still lives,
and has provided a full statement concerning his unit's role in the
matter of the forced repatriations. He is Sir Charles Villiers, a notable

figure in British public life who was at one time chairman of the British Steel Corporation and (with Toby Low) a director of Sun Life Assurance. In 1944 he had served with the Partisans in Yugoslavia, where his bravery in operations gained him the Military Cross. During this period he earned the personal gratitude and friendship of Tito by assisting his son Zarko Broz, who had lost an arm, in escaping to Italy.

A few years ago a Serbian émigré, Stanisa R. Vlahovic, wrote to Sir Charles to enquire about the role of the Sixth Special Force in regard to the repatriations. Vlahovic's knowledge of the part it was alleged to have been played derived solely from Todorovic's account cited above, and its value was what he wished to establish.

Sir Charles Villiers' reply ran as follows:

No. 6 Special Force Staff Section, which I commanded from the end of the War, was being wound down following V.E. Day and had no connection with or knowledge of the repatriation of Royalist Yugoslavs to which you refer. I attended no conferences on this subject and, indeed, my only connection with the V Corps was through their Intelligence Officer . . .

In answer to your questions:

1. I had no knowledge of and did not advise upon the repatriation of Yugoslavs from Austria and I did not at any time meet General Keightley.

2. I was not aware that forcible repatriation of Royalists was taking place and therefore would have no awareness about any Conventions that such action might infringe.

3. I was, of course, aware that General Keightley had ordered Tito's forces to withdraw from the British zone as I had been working with these forces in Yugoslavia. I had, however, no knowledge of any action he may or may not have taken with regard to the remaining Yugoslav Royalists.

4. No. 6 Special Force had absolutely no connection with or took any action in the rounding up of Royalist Serbs.

5. I did not know that V Corps was responsible for repatriation or that this was taking place, nor did I advise General Keightley on any subject.

Please feel free to publish this letter in any way you may choose.

There is clearly a total discrepancy between the accounts of Todorovic and Sir Charles. Todorovic claimed as a participant that the Sixth Special Force was the unit with which the Partisans collaborated in effecting the handovers; that its officers were intimately concerned with and fully informed about every aspect of the operations, including the massacres; and that members of the unit actually participated in burying the numerous Yugoslav suicides. Sir Charles Villiers, on the other hand, emphatically denies that the Sixth Special Force had any knowledge at all of the repatriations, let alone assisted with their implementation. Which account are we to credit? It might seem that Todorovic is unlikely to have been fully conversant with British military procedure, and may have mistaken the identity of the unit with which he had dealings. In that case, though, it would be hard to see how he ever learned of the existence of the Sixth Special Force, or of the identity of Lieutenant Lockheed.

It has to be said straight away that on one material point Sir Charles Villiers' memory appears to be at fault. He states emphatically that his unit's only connection with the Fifth Corps was through their intelligence officer. But this provides quite a false impression, at least if it be intended to imply that the role of the Sixth Special Force was of no great significance, and that there were no direct consultations on important matters of policy between the Sixth Special Force and Corps headquarters.

On 4 March 1975 I conducted a tape-recorded interview with the late Edward Renton who was, as I have described, Sir Charles Villiers' former second-in-command. In mid-May 1945 the Sixth Special Force was engaged on behalf of the Fifth Corps in negotiating surrender terms with the Fifteenth Cossack Cavalry Corps. Renton vividly recalled the scene, with General von Pannwitz banging the table and imploring Villiers to arrange enrolment of the Cossacks in the British Army. Then, continued Renton, 'while he talked to them, I shot off and rang up Corps Headquarters . . . the really operative person at that time was the BGS, who was Toby Low . . . I rang up the Corps Headquarters, and I said we have here General so-and-so . . . I was instructed on no account to accept the surrender.' It is clear from this that the Sixth Special Force, at least on this significant occasion, worked in close collaboration with Fifth Corps headquarters.

Fortunately there is no need for speculation, and matters need not be left in this unsatisfactory state of unresolvable contradiction. Members of the Sixth Special Force were not permitted to keep diaries, whether official or personal, and so it might be thought that no documents survive to reconcile the conflicting accounts of their responsibilities and actions. Fortunately, however, there exists a record in private hands which enables a satisfactory check to be made. Nigel Nicolson has retained *inter alia* the official Log Book in which he entered hour by hour matters which it was his duty to record and report.

The Log Book contains entries which provide remarkable confirmation of the accuracy of Todorovic's account of his relations with the Sixth Special Force. The first relevant entry fully confirms Renton's account of the Sixth Special Force's closely consultative relationship with Corps HQ. On 2 June, with reference to the repatriation of Yugoslavs, Nicolson reported, 'Lockheed has returned to Corps, leaving a message "There will be the usual evening train at 1800 hrs."' Lockheed is clearly the 'Lieutenant Lakhed' of Todorovic's account.

Then on 4 June the Log Book records: '*Lockheed . . . Has name of informer.*' On 5 June details are supplied which tally exactly with Todorovic's version of his relationship with Lockheed and the Sixth Special Force:

Informer is a 'Royalist' who has been with 'Tits' at Rosenbach the whole time . . .

Lt Lockheed (Corps L.O. [Liaison Officer]) says that . . . His interpreter who was a member of the Tit Rosenbach Coy has now been removed into safety since he was becoming unpopular with his fellow soldiers. This has been accomplished without his Coy knowing that we had anything to do with it.

From another reference it appears that Todorovic had been supplying useful intelligence on Partisan troop movements. It can be seen that Todorovic did not provide Lockheed with the true reason for his seeking refuge from the Partisans, which was according to his own account disgust at the atrocities perpetrated with the assistance of Villiers' unit.

The Sixth Special Force was a small and highly specialised unit, consisting only of six officers and twenty men. Its purpose was the undertaking of delicate tasks outside and largely unknown to the regular military chain of command. Today, for example, Nigel Nicolson writes: 'I've never heard of the 6th Special Force. Probably a hush-hush unit, and we were official, non-secret.'

None of the officers to whom I spoke in the Third Welsh Guards had heard of it either. What was the purpose of this division of duties, whereby the Welsh Guards entrained the prisoners at Maria Elend and sent them three or four miles round the corner to Rosenbach, where the Sixth Special Force took over? Why were the Welsh Guards not entrusted with the whole of this part of the operation? The Sixth

Special Force possessed no special operational facilities which would help from an administrative point of view; their officers do not appear to have been able to speak Serbo-Croat, for example, since Todorovic was there to act as interpreter.

It was the local Divisional Commander, Major-General Murray, who in mid-May had raised such strong objection to returning Cossacks in his charge that the Fifth Corps had been obliged to respond by transferring the majority of Cossacks to the custody of the Forty-sixth Infantry Division, whence they could be repatriated northwards to Judenberg. The repatriation of Yugoslavs could not be covered by this ingenious method, however. The frontier zone between British-occupied Carinthia and Yugoslavia came under the administration of the Sixth Armoured Division. There was no other route by which the refugees could be returned. Worst of all, the battalion controlling the vital Rosenbach tunnel link was the Third Welsh Guards, a unit notoriously averse to participating in dishonourable actions. An 'order of most sinister duplicity' was how Colonel Rose Price had described the order in his War Diary entry of 19 May, 'to send Croats to their foes i.e. Tits'. 'Needless to say I loathed the job,' recalls Captain Richard Kingzett, then signals officer with the battalion. Captain Bolton and other officers too raised strong objection on learning of mere rumours of ill-treatment of those they had sent back. How would they have reacted had they been at Rosenbach and seen the daily batches of suicides disposed of by the Sixth Special Force?

In view of the secrecy of the Sixth Special Force activities, particularly the hasty disposal of the suicides' corpses and Lieutenant Lockheed's concern about the 'informer', one is compelled to suspect that the unit's prime role was that of ensuring concealment from units of the Sixth Armoured Division of atrocities being perpetrated by Partisan bands at the point of handover. For instance, Lockheed possessed a first-hand account of massacres occurring at the other end of the tunnel by about 26 May, but no word of this reached anyone in the Divisional command.

Sir Charles Villiers maintains in the letter I have quoted that his 'only connection with the V Corps was through their Intelligence officer', and implies that he maintained no direct link with Brigadier Low of the Fifth Corps headquarters. If his memory be accurate, we have here a wonderful example of that cool 'stiff upper lip' outlook, which foreigners customarily attribute to the British governing classes. For, as Toby Low himself told me:

Charles Villiers is my closest friend. I was his best man. He shared digs with me at Oxford; I hadn't seen him for five years when he reported to me [at Klagenfurt]. I was in touch with him, but I don't remember exactly the way in which he handled the affair. The thing is we had orders separate from him – separate from our orders – as to how we handle Tito's new regime. He [Villiers] had been flying in and out of 'Tito's land'; he was very much SOE at the time, and kept us informed. He helped us to know who was who.

It is inconceivable that at the time Major Villiers was not fully apprised of the nature of the tasks and duties of his minuscule unit. On the other hand, Todorovic's account and Nigel Nicolson's Log Book make it appear that Lieutenant Lockheed was in temporary command at the Rosenbach transit-point in the last week of May and the first of June. Perhaps Villiers and Renton were at that time temporarily detached from their unit, engaged presumably in some secret mission of which no record has survived. This could account for Sir Charles Villiers' lapse of memory over the role his force played in ensuring the safe delivery of Yugoslavs to the Partisans, and in concealing evidence of the tragic succession of suicides, murders and massacres.

It was an extraordinary period in history. Much was not as it appeared, and many people were absent from their regular duties, engaged in covert activities of which we still know little or nothing. It was at this very time, for example, that Tito himself paid an unexplained visit to northern Yugoslavia, just over the frontier from the British Zone of Occupation in Austria. On 2 June the British Ambassador in Belgrade, Ralph Stevenson, was surprised to learn from Vice-President Kardelj that the Marshal was absent from the capital, incommunicado up in Slovenia.[60]

Perhaps it is best to conclude on a note of mystery, for it cannot be denied that there is much that still remains obscure. It has been seen what strong motives Stalin had for wishing to lay hands on the émigré Cossack officers, and why, too, he should have wished to intervene on Tito's behalf for the recovery of his Chetnik, Domobran and Croat opponents. In face of the unambiguous Allied policy of retaining all these people as legitimate refugees, the Soviet dictator turned to his security services for help.

It was a time when the Soviet Union had many highly-placed hidden helpers in Britain and the United States, as subsequent 'spy scandals' have in particular revealed. Hidden networks were activated, traps were sprung. As Minister of State Security V. N. Merkulov boasted in the Lubianka in the first week of June 1945, with a fine gift for mixed metaphors, 'we took the reins into our own hands. They don't appreciate that we have checkmated them, and now they are forced to dance to our tune, like the last pawn on the board.'

Up to 13 May 1945 there had been no question of any Yugoslavs or non-Soviet Russian nationals being handed over to their enemies. On that day Macmillan flew in unexpectedly to see General Keightley, and the policy was dramatically reversed. This could not be done openly, since the treatment of Surrendered Enemy Personnel was based on unchanged Allied government policy, and was consequently effected through what can only be described as extensive and ingenious subterfuge and conspiracy. Keightley concealed from his superiors the Soviet demand for the Cossacks, as it would have revealed that prominent in the document were the names of Tsarist émigrés. Macmillan on his return journey confirmed this false version of events to General McCreery at Treviso, and withheld from the Foreign Office any mention of the forced repatriation policy he had urged on Keightley. In his diary he compiled a record ingeniously worded to deflect possible future suspicion that he could have played a part in arranging the Keightley handovers.

There exists clear evidence of top-level chicanery at AFHQ, with the destruction, concealment or deliberate misinterpretation of crucial orders. At Fifth Corps level the deception had to be even more Machiavellian. False screening stipulations were inserted in Divisional and Brigade orders with the intention of deceiving the Eighth Army and AFHQ commands into believing they had been operative. At the same time oral orders were issued insisting that screening be set aside. Elaborate precautions were taken to ensure the handover of the men whom the Soviet wanted most, men whom the screening instructions would have saved. The high command was then hoodwinked by the Thirty-sixth Infantry Brigade report of 3 July, which claimed that none of these things had happened.

In the case of the Yugoslavs, Alexander's order of 17 May was ignored, and the confirmatory instruction of 23 May circumvented. A secret unit, the Sixth Special Force, was stationed at the Austrian-Yugoslav frontier to ensure that massacres and suicides were effectively concealed from British regular forces.

These operations continued in force, despite the intense revulsion of British troops compelled to take part, until Alexander discovered what had been happening and put a final end to them on 4 June.

Since then Macmillan has claimed that Alexander, and not he, was responsible for all that happened.

The evidence indicates that it was Harold Macmillan, aided by one or two others, who enabled Stalin and Tito to obtain their ends. With what in any other cause would be regarded as admirable ingenuity, he successfully hoodwinked his own government, his colleague and friend the Field-Marshal, the Commander of the Fifth Corps, and even the soldiers entrusted with the appalling task of despatching some 70,000 men, women and children (in his own words) 'to slavery, torture and probably death'. For their part, Stalin and Tito went to remarkable lengths in ensuring that no victim survived to tell a compromising tale.

Macmillan's motives remain tantalisingly mysterious, and may never be known. The explanations he has given are inadequate and inconsistent, documents have been tampered with and destroyed, and a forty-year cover-up operation of extraordinary ingenuity and persistence had all but concealed a trail which must long ago have been believed to have run safely cold. Perhaps the most disturbing factor, though, concerns not what lay behind the Minister Resident's actions in May 1945, but in what followed. For throughout Macmillan's terms of office as Minister of Defence, Foreign Secretary and Prime Minister, the NKVD (subsequently the KGB) presumably had the best of reasons for knowing the whole of a story which in the West it has taken forty years to unravel.

Notes

CHAPTER ONE

1 Geoffrey Cox, *The Race for Trieste* (London, 1977), p. 73–5.

2 Sir Llewellyn Woodward, *British Foreign Policy in the Second World War* (London, 1962), p. 409. For an able summary of the historical background of the Italian-Yugoslav claims on the former Austrian Adriatic coastline, cf. G. Laffan's report for the Foreign Office dated 5 February 1941, printed by Ivo Omrcanin, *Enigma Tito* (Washington, 1984), pp. 447–55.

3 Cox, op cit., pp. 212–17.

4 Jozo Tomasevich, *The Chetniks* (Stanford, 1975), pp. 421, 442, 449. Mihailovic had long-standing ties of friendship with the family of General Damjanovic, and his choice of Ravna Gora as the place where he unfurled the banner of revolt against the German occupation in May 1941 was in part due to the fact that Damjanovic owned extensive tracts of the ridge (Mark C. Wheeler, *Britain and the War for Yugoslavia, 1940–43* (New York, 1980), p. 72). For the ambivalent position of Nedic and his tentative negotiations with Mihailovic, cf. Walter R. Roberts, *Tito, Mihailovic and the Allies* (New Brunswick, 1973), pp. 257–8.

5 Cox, op. cit., pp. 212–17; Susan Crosland, *Tony Crosland* (London, 1982), pp. 36–7; eye-witness account by the late Lieutenant-Colonel Milivoje Vuksanovic, Chief of Staff to the Dinara Division, kindly supplied by Captain Djordje Karakusevic. I am indebted to Mr Nigel Nicolson, then I.O. to the First Guards Brigade, for lending me his copies of Sitreps and other papers relating to his duties in April–May 1945; also to Mr Paul Borstnik, a member of the small force of Slovenian Chetniks under Damjanovic's command, who provided me with an account of the Chetnik surrender at Cormons. Under the pseudonym 'Dore Sluga' he is the author of a novel based on events in wartime Slovenia, *The Orchard* (Toronto, 1978).

6 WO.170/4183,227. This transmitted Alexander's order of the same day to the Fifteenth Army Group (FO.371/48813,5; WO.170/4185,472). The instruction arose in response to a query dated 29 April from the British Military Mission with the Partisans (ibid., 492).

7 WO.170/4337, 29–30; letter of 23 January 1984 from Sir Horatius Murray to the author. Next day (4 May) General Harding, Commander of the Thirteenth

Corps, asked AFHQ: 'Request approval begin evacuation immediately and instructions for disposal' (WO.170/4184,187; cf. 252).

8 FO.371/48812.

9 PREM.3/495/6, 125–6.

10 Ibid., 124.

11 FO.371/48812.

12 National Archives 740.0011 E.W./5-145; *Foreign Relations of the United States: Diplomatic Papers 1945* (Washington, 1960), v, pp. 1226–7.

13 FO.371/48813, 5.

14 Ibid., 68–79.

15 WO.204/11133, 51A. For an authoritative minute outlining the nature of the prima facie evidence required in such cases, cf. Patrick Dean's note of 5 May 1945 (FO.371/48865).

16 FO.371/48918, 67–74.

17 Documents loaned by Mr Nigel Nicolson. Cf. also Wilhelm Wadl, *Kärntens Weg zur Demokratie im Jahre 1945* (Klagenfurt, 1985), pp. 11–21; idem, *Das Jahr 1945 in Kärnten: Ein Überblick* (Klagenfurt, 1985), p. 39.

18 Information supplied by Mr Andrew Gibson-Watt.

CHAPTER TWO

1 Typescript memoir of Major-General G. L. Verney (p. 141), kindly loaned to me by his son, Major Peter Verney.

2 D. P. Vertepov (ed.), *Русский Корпус на Балканах во время II великой войны* , (New York, 1963), pp. 347–8; cf. General V. G. Naumenko, *Великое Предательство: выдача казаков в Лиенце и других местах 1945–1947*, (New York, 1962–70), ii, p. 26.

3 Vertepov, op. cit., pp. 9–21. For numbers and casualty lists, see pp. 402–5, and for the death of Steifon, p. 349. The role of the *Russische Schützkorps Serbien* is set out by Hans Werner Neulen, *An deutscher Seite: Internationale Freiwillige von Wehrmacht und Waffen-SS* (Munich, 1985), pp. 230–2.

4 Vertepov, op. cit., pp. 355–67.

5 Helga H. Harriman, *Slovenia under Nazi Occupation, 1941–1945* (New York, 1977), pp. 30–52; Charles Zalar, *Yugoslav Communism: A Critical Study* (Washington, 1961), pp. 74–5; Vladimir Kozina, '*Slovenia, the Land of my Joy and my Sorrow*' (Toronto, 1980), pp. 7, 22, 95; Malcolm Muggeridge (ed.), *Ciano's Diary 1939–1943* (London, 1947), p. 334; *Matica Mrtvih: podatki o Slovencih pomorjenih po zločinski Osvobodilni Fronti 1941–1945* (Cleveland, Ohio, 1968–70), iv, pp. 61–4.

6 On 8 February 1942 Montenegrin Partisans declared liberated territory under their control to be an integral part of the USSR (Walter R. Roberts, *Tito, Mihailovic and the Allies, 1941–1945* (New Brunswick, 1973), p. 55).

7 John W. Wheeler-Bennett, *Brest-Litovsk: The Forgotten Peace, March 1918* (London, 1939), p. 260.

8 *Matica Mrtvih*, i, pp. 33–45.

9 Ibid., pp. 46–137; *The Slovenian Tragedy* (Toronto, 1970), pp. 25–30.

10 Fitzroy Maclean, *Eastern Approaches* (London, 1949), pp. 326–7. Kardelj and his equally sinister colleague Rankovic were the only members of the Central

Committee not to keep mistresses (Milovan Djilas, *Wartime* (New York, 1977), p. 93).

11 For the Turjak massacre, cf. *Matica Mrtvih* i, pp. 42–3; ii, pp. 72–91; Kozina, op. cit., pp. 127–31.

12 Djilas, op cit., p. 338.

13 Several of these orders were published in facsimile in the volume *Črne Bukve o Delu Komunistične Osvobodilne Fronte proti Slovenskemu Narodu* (Ljubljana, 1944), pp. 19. 67, 105, etc. Cf. also *The Slovenian Tragedy*, p. 15; *Matica Mrtvih*, i, p. 33; iv, p. 48. Their authenticity has been unconvincingly challenged by official Yugoslav sources, but the general programme of physical liquidation of non-Communist elements in Slovenia is widely acknowledged. For example, the former Partisan officer Tone Svetina writes: 'Quite needlessly many people were murdered whereas at least some attempt should have been made to win them over for the cause . . . people were mysteriously disappearing . . . we ourselves helped to create the White Guard [Domobranci] because we were incapable of treating people as human beings. Many had been on our side for two years, but then the commanders began to overdo it.' (*Ukane* (Ljubljana, 1971), ii. p. 870; iii, p. 55.) Similar atrocities were occurring all over Yugoslavia; 'The peasants were seized by fear because nobody quite knew why "they" were killing, what kind of sin was being punished. Some were saying that they were hitting only at landowners, others that they were purging those going to church too often, and some were even worried for fat people because they were allegedly "bourgeois" and their "Black Friday" had arrived.' (Branko Copic, *Gluvi Barut* (Sarajevo, 1966), p. 94.) I am indebted to Dr Ljubo Sirc for these last two references.

14 Roberts, op. cit., pp. 100–12; Kozina, op. cit., pp. 92–100; *Matica Mrtvih*, i, pp. 33–6.

15 Ibid., iii, pp. 42–5; *Črne Bukve*, p. 65. Tito himself later admitted that he was waging war against the indigenous population 'in Slovenia. This then was civil war. But we did not want to talk about this during the war because it would not have been useful to us.' (Interview in the Zagreb newspaper *Vjesnik* of 24 May 1972; reference kindly supplied by Dr Ljubo Sirc.) Throughout Yugoslavia, noted an American officer attached to Tito in 1943, 'the Partisans . . . placed less emphasis on the fight against the Germans than on preparing for the political struggle at the end of the war' (Roberts, op. cit., p. 153). The same applied to the earlier struggle against the Italians (ibid., p. 56).

16 Jozo Tomasevich, *The Chetniks* (Stanford, 1975), p. 398.

17 Kozina, op. cit., pp. 103–4; *Matica Mrtvih*, i. pp. 27–9; Zalar, op. cit., pp. 80–1; Nora Beloff, *Tito's Flawed Legacy: Yugoslavia & the West: 1939–84* (London, 1985), pp. 75–6.

18 Mark C. Wheeler, *Britain and the War for Yugoslavia, 1940–1943* (New York, 1980), pp. 65, 89. For the motivation behind Mihailovic's cautious policy, cf. Roberts, op. cit., pp. 33–4, 48, 100–2.

19 Kozina, op. cit., pp. 118–20; *Matica Mrtvih*, ii, pp. 57, 62–5; cf. David Martin, *Patriot or Traitor: The Case of General Mihailovich* (Stanford, 1978), pp. 147–8.

20 *Matica Mrtvih*, iii, pp. 23–42.

21 The Germans had seriously contemplated deporting 280,000 Slovenes to Croatia and Serbia, while the General Secretary of the Italian Fascist Party in January

1942 proposed the extermination of the entire nation. (Zalar, op. cit., p. 74; Muggeridge, op. cit., pp. 419–20.)

22 FO.371/48811; cf. *Matica Mrtvih*, iii, pp. 42–52. For Col. Moore's activities with the Partisans, cf. Maclean, op. cit., pp. 318, 425, 470–1. His low estimate of the Slovenian Partisans' fighting capacity was apparently borne out by events. On 17 April 1945 SOE informed the Foreign Office that:

> Throughout the winter and early spring the Yugoslav Partisan forces (in the true sense) in Slovenia have, according to our information, been almost entirely inactive. They have taken no part in interfering with German communications and have failed to exploit the openings made for them by Allied air attacks. It is considered that Allied air support has alone saved them from rout and defeat. (FO.371/48812)

The fact is that Tito was by this stage reserving his strength for armed resistance against possible Anglo–American landings on the Dalmatian coast. The Partisan leader Stane Semic–Daki recalled in a memoir published at Ljubljana in 1972 how his division in mid-1944 was instructed by the commander of Communist forces in Slovenia to disengage from fighting the Germans, 'because it had to rest since it could happen that it would have to march through Gorski Kotar to the sea, should it come to a landing of Anglo–American troops on the Yugoslav coast – the Commander-in-Chief of Yugoslavia, Marshal Tito, being opposed to the opening of a second front on Yugoslav territory.' (Reference kindly supplied by Dr Ljubo Sirc.) For Tito's readiness to fight the British and to obstruct Allied operations against the Germans in Istria, cf. Roberts, op. cit., pp. 265, 285–6.

23 Borivoje M. Karapandzic, *Jugoslovensko krvavo proleće 1945. Titovi Katini i Gulazi* (Cleveland, Ohio, 1976), p. 25; *Matica Mrtvih*, iii, pp. 93–4.

24 A day or so later the Partisans absconded with twenty truckloads of arms surrendered by von Seeler's units by the Drava (WO.170/4404).

25 Nigel Nicolson, Intelligence officer to the First Guards Brigade, noted that von Seeler 'had planned the organisation of his surrender with some care, and the first of his officers to cross the river arrived with marked maps showing how, in the German comd's view, the various nationalities should be disposed. The conc areas he had arranged conflicted severely with the dispositions of our own Bde, and he was ordered to assemble the whole force in a camp at Viktring 2077' (ibid.).

26 Vertepov, op. cit., pp. 355–71; A. I. Delianich, *Вольфсберг-373* (San Francisco, 1975), pp. 1–29; Kozina, op. cit., pp. 172–5, 196–9; *Matica Mrtvih*, iv, pp. 9–14; Karapandzic, op. cit., pp. 25–9; Ingomar Pust, *Titostern über Kärnten 1942–1945: Totgeschwiegene Tragödien* (Klagenfurt, 1984), pp. 197–202; August Walzl, *Kärnten 1945: Vom NS-Regime zur Besatzungsherrschaft im Alpen-Adria-Raum* (Klagenfurt, 1985), pp. 186–7, 334. Some excellent photographs of the withdrawal of the *Russkii Corpus* from Slovenia to Viktring appeared in the Russian émigré journal *Наши Вести* (Monterey, June 1985), p. 25; cf. pp. 17–18.

CHAPTER THREE

1 Information supplied by Mrs Marija Ann Levic.
2 This summary account of the Fifteenth Cossack Cavalry Corps is taken from the account drawn up by Colonel von Bosse in October 1950 for the Historical Division of the Headquarters United States Army, Europe (National Archives,

RG 338, P-064); cf. also Hans Werner Neulen, *An deutscher Seite: Internationale Freiwillige von Wehrmacht und Waffen-SS* (London, 1978) pp. 315–22, 346. In this and following chapters dealing with the treatment of Cossacks in Austria, I have confined myself to outlining material dealt with more fully in *Victims of Yalta* (London, 1977), and generally only provide references to documentary and other evidence not utilised there. For the surrender of the Corps, cf. August Walzl, *Kärnten 1945: Vom NS-Regime zur Besatzungsherrschaft im Alpen-Adria-Raum* (Klagenfurt, 1985), pp. 188–9.

3 This account is taken from the printed eye-witness accounts of Olga Rotova and Nikolai Krasnov (General V. G. Naumenko, *Великое Предательство: выдача казаков в Лиенце и других местах 1945-1947* (New York, 1962–70), ii. pp. 24–28; N. N. Krasnov, *Незабываемое* 1945–1956 (New York, 1959), p. 19. General Musson confirmed to me the tenor of that part of the conversation at which he was present.

4 In November 1944 the US Intelligence agency OSS received from its London Outpost (USSR Unit) three copies of General Krasnov's publication 'Historical Studies on the Don' (photocopy from the National Archives kindly supplied by Dr Stanislav A. Ausky, who is preparing a history of the wartime Cossack movement). It would be interesting to learn more of this Allied intelligence interest in Krasnov – supplied by the NKVD mission in London?

5 For an interesting Soviet account of Krasnov's career, cf. M. K. Kasvinov, *Двадцать три ступени вниз* (Moscow, 1979), p. 69.

6 Naumenko, op. cit., i, p. 140; Peter Huxley-Blythe, *The East Came West* (Caldwell, Ohio, 1964), p. 121. For photographs of the British and Cossacks at Kötschach, cf. Walzl, op. cit., p. 331; Wilhelm Wadl, *Das Jahr 1945 in Kärnten: Ein Überblick* (Klagenfurt, 1985), p. 27.

7 Jozef Mackiewicz, *Kontra* (Paris, 1957), p. 185.

8 Naumenko, op. cit., i, pp. 144–5.

9 Brigadier Tryon-Wilson, then a member of the Fifth Corps staff, heard at the time of the safe arrival of Krasnov's two letters at Corps headquarters.

10 Krasnov, op. cit., pp. 19–20.

11 Thus 118 Russian prisoners at Fort Dix, New Jersey 'insisted upon being treated as German POWs under Geneva Convention' (NA.71162114/1C–744), but were nevertheless forcibly repatriated after four months' discussion and vigorous protest by opponents of the policy (Tolstoy, op. cit., pp. 325–9).

12 Ibid., pp. 88, 337. On 10 February 1947 the US Chiefs of Staff noted that, 'The constant trend of United States policy on forceful repatriation of Soviet citizens has been toward narrowing its scope rather than increasing it' (CAB 88/30, 486).

13 WO.32/11137, 62C, 78A, 388A; WO.32/11119, 230A, 231A.

14 WO.170/4183,487.

15 Information from Brigadier C. E. Tryon-Wilson. Eighth Army War Diary records that on 10 May at Voitsberg was held 'Conference between [British 5] Corps [and Soviet 6 Corps] comds at which boundary was agreed to mutual satisfaction'. (WO.170/4183,187,252,455; WO.170/4184,536).

16 Jerome Jareb and Ivo Omrčanin, 'The end of the Croatian Army at Bleiburg, Austria in May 1945 According to English military documents', *Journal of Croatian Studies* (New York, 1977–8), xviii–xix, pp. 117–9, 157–60; Nicholas Bethell, *The Last Secret: Forcible Repatriation to Russia 1944–7* (London, 1974), p. 84.

CHAPTER FOUR

1 Harold Macmillan, *War Diaries: Politics and War in the Mediterranean January 1943–May 1945* (London, 1984), pp. 373, 492.
2 Robert Murphy, *Diplomat Among Warriors* (London, 1964), p. 206.
3 John Bright-Holmes (ed.), *Like It Was: The Diaries of Malcolm Muggeridge* (London, 1981), p. 20. For an excellent thumbnail sketch of Macmillan's character and development, cf. Anthony Sampson, *Anatomy of Britain* (London, 1962), pp. 322–30.
4 Harold Macmillan, *The Blast of War 1939–1945* (London, 1967), p. 216.
5 Macmillan, *War Diaries*, pp. 123, 152.
6 *Daily Telegraph*, 25 February 1985.
7 Macmillan, *War Diaries*, pp. 746–7.
8 Ibid., p. 150.
9 James Margach, *The Anatomy of Power: An Enquiry into the Personality of Leadership* (London, 1979), p. 32. In 1942 Macmillan regarded 'Socialism as inevitable, with the Conservatives standing, not so much for property, as for private lives' (Harold Nicolson, *Diaries and Letters 1939–1945* (London, 1967), p. 252).
10 Kenneth Young (ed.), *The Diaries of Sir Robert Bruce Lockhart* (London, 1980), pp. 519–20.
11 WO. 106/4059,240.
12 Winston S. Churchill, *Triumph and Tragedy* (London, 1954), pp. 480–7.
13 WO. 106/4059,292.
14 Macmillan, *War Diaries*, pp. 755–6.
15 Ibid., p. 756; WO. 106/4059,340.
16 Macmillan, *War Diaries*, pp. 757–8.
17 I am grateful to Professor Norman Stone for supplying me with a transcript of the BBC 1 programme *Macmillan at War*, broadcast on 21 December 1984.
18 BM.3928/PW1, 18C,18D,19A; WO.204/10126. Admiral Archer, head of the British Military Mission in Moscow, 'was informed by Soviet Repatriation Committee on 27 May that instruction would be issued to stop sending British Officers, soldiers and civilians to Odessa also that henceforth those Allied PWs liberated in Southern Regions would be despatched to Graz to be handed over to Eighth Army'. (FO.371/48819,78–9). On 1 June Alexander reported that 'No British commonwealth PW transferred to us by Marshal Tolbukhin though small parties have come through Russian lines. No known estimate of British commonwealth PW still in Tolbukhin's zone.' Despite this, the Fifteenth Army Group had informed Rear Eighth Army on 29 May that 'it is proposed to move 23000 Russian nationals from various areas to Graz at rate maximum 2200 per day to be handed over to Russian forces. date of commencement move NOT yet firm but likely to be about 5 June.'
   To Eighth Army on the same day Alexander signalled:
   'Information received from troopers places some thousands of liberated Allied PW including British and Americans in adjacent areas of Czechoslovakia majority of whom Russians may be expected to hand over to you at Graz in exchange for Soviet citizens'.
   However the 23,000 'Russian nationals' to be exchanged were prisoners of war and slave labourers held by the US Fifth Army in Italy (together with 14,000 of the same categories in Eighth Army custody), and the order bears no reference

to the Cossacks, whose handover was virtually complete by 4 June. (WO.204/10126; FO.1020/39,11,20.)

19 Malcolm J. Proudfoot, *European Refugees: 1939–52; A Study in Forced Population Movement* (London, 1957), pp. 207–10.

20 Harold Macmillan, *Tides of Fortune: 1945–1955* (London, 1969), p. 17.

21 BM.3928,250A; WO.170/4184,549; WO.204/10126. On 14 May the Forty-sixth Infantry Division War Diary noted that: '2/5 Leics make local agreement with Russians that any Russians in 139 Bde area will be apprehended and returned to Soviet territory' (WO.170/4352; WO.170/4404); cf. the Thirty-eighth Irish Brigade report of 13 May (WO.170/4465). For the repatriation of the 162nd Turcoman Division, cf. my *Victims of Yalta* (London, 1977), pp. 304–6.

22 WO.170/4183.

23 WO.170/4241, Appx J, Folio 22. On 1 March 1985, in an address at Winchester College, Toby Low described this Sitrep as 'a signal which I remember drafting myself the next day' following Macmillan's visit of 13 May.

24 FO.371/51227.

25 FO.371/47910,78; FO.1020/362,23A.

26 WO.106/4059,340.

27 National Archives, 740.00119 Control (Italy)/5–1445.

28 FO.1020/42,86.

29 WO.170/4404.

30 General S. M. Shtemenko, *Генеральный Штаб в годы войны* (Moscow, 1973), ii, p. 450.

31 N. N. Krasnov, *Незабываемое 1945-1956* (New York, 1959), p. 47.

32 WO.204/1596; WO.170/4337; WO.170/4185,453.

33 FO.371/48818,97.

34 D. P. Vertepov, *Русский Корпус на Балканах во время II великой войны* (New York, 1963), pp. 368–9.

35 WO.170/4184,569. The order was passed on by the Eighth Army to the Fifth Corps the next day, 15 May (FO.1020/42,92).

36 Edward J. Rozek, *Allied Wartime Diplomacy: A Pattern in Poland* (New York, 1958), p. 406.

37 *Foreign Relations of the United States, Diplomatic Papers: The Conference of Berlin (The Potsdam Conference)* (Washington, 1960, ii, p. 374; Richard Landwehr, *Fighting for Freedom: The Ukrainian Volunteer Division of the Waffen-SS* (Silver Spring, Maryland, 1985), pp. 198–201; Vsevolod B. Budnyj and Orest S. Slupchynskyj (ed.), *Ukrainian National Army First Ukrainian Division in Italy: Rimini 1945–1947* (New York, 1979), p. 60; Nikolai Tolstoy, *Victims of Yalta* (London, 1977), pp. 256–9. On 13 May, the Sixth Armoured Division reported that the Ukrainian Division was concentrated at Teseldorf.

38 Nigel Nicolson Log Book; Vertepov, op. cit., pp. 379–81.

CHAPTER FIVE

1 Cf. Sixth Armoured Division War Diary for 13 May (WO.170/4337).

2 'To be quite frank with you – we didn't at all understand why the British insisted on returning these people' (George Urban, 'A Conversation with Milovan Djilas', *Encounter* (London, December 1979), liii, p. 41.

3 WO.170/4183,227.

4 WO.170/4185,453; WO.170/4184,590; WO.170/4183,545. Though dated 14 May, the report was issued on the thirteenth (cf. WO.170/4184,697; FO.1020/260).

5 WO.170/4465. Cf. August Walzl, *Kärnten 1945: Vom NS-Regime zur Besatzungsherrschaft im Alpen-Adria-Raum* (Klagenfurt, 1985), pp. 190–2.

6 John Prcela and Stanko Guldescu (eds.), *Operation Slaughterhouse: Eyewitness Accounts of Postwar Massacres In Yugoslavia* (Philadelphia, 1970), pp. 149, 160, 196, 241–2, 253, 303. As late as 11–12 May the advance guard of the Croatian Army was engaged in stiff fighting at Zidani Most, south of Celje (cf. the account by the Army Commander, General Luburic, ibid., pp. 43–71).

7 WO.170/4241, Appx. J, Folio 22; FO.1020/47,87.

8 National Archives 740.00119 (Control) Italy/5–1345 and 1445.

9 WO.170/4185,453; cf. General Kosta Nadj's account in the Belgrade newspaper *Borba*, 10 June 1985.

10 Typescript copy of *The War Experiences of Major General G. L. Verney DSO, MVO 1939–1945*, p. 145, kindly loaned to me by his son, Major Peter Verney.

11 Jerome Jareb and Ivo Omrćanin, 'The end of the Croatian Army at Bleiburg, Austria in May 1945 according to English military documents,' *Journal of Croatian Studies* (New York, 1977–8), xviii–xix, p. 139.

12 Prcela and Guldescu, op. cit., p. 82.

13 *Journal of Croatian Studies*, xviii–xix, p. 169.

14 Prcela and Guldescu, op. cit., p. 92.

15 Nicholas Bethell, *The Last Secret: Forcible Repatriation to Russia 1944–7* (London, 1974), p. 87; Prcela and Guldescu, op. cit., pp. 197–8.

16 Ibid., pp. 192–3.

17 For Brigadier Scott's accounts of events at Bleiburg cf. *Journal of Croatian Studies*, xviii–xix, pp. 166, 123–5, 139–41, 145–6, 165–70; Bethell, op. cit., pp. 84–7. Commissar Basta's account and that of a Croatian negotiator accompanying General Herencic appear in *Operation Slaughterhouse*, pp. 136–55. A revealing article concerning Basta's role appeared in the Belgrade magazine *Nin* (May 1982), pp. 22–4. For an excellent overall view of the Croatian tragedy, cf. Antonio Pitamitz, 'Lo Sterminio dei Croati', *Storia Illustrata* (Milan, June 1984), pp. 54–74; 'Bleiburg: La consegna alle forze di Tito', ibid., pp. 102–5; also Erich Kern, *General von Pannwitz und seine Kosaken* (Oldendorf, 1971), pp. 165–7; Ingomar Pust, *Titostern über Kärnten 1942–1945* (Klagenfurt, 1984), pp. 137–46. For Tito's message of 13 May, ordering the indiscriminate annihilation of retreating Croats, cf. Nora Beloff, *Tito's Flawed Legacy; Yugoslavia & the West: 1939–84* (London, 1985), p. 117.

18 WO.170/4185,451. In his parallel directive of the same day, General Robertson alludes to the fact that the Twelfth Army Group is to be approached 'with request that they accept concentration' of German prisoners of war. The 'refugees' mentioned by Morgan are omitted in this context: presumably because Robertson's order envisaged their despatch, not to the Americans, but to the Soviets and Yugoslavs.

19 FO.371/47904,164.

20 WO.202/319,44,63; WO.170/4184,623. Much confusion has been caused by quoting Alexander's message to Tito out of context. For an unfortunately influential example, cf. the letter by Elisabeth Barker to *The Times* on 11 February 1984 (reprinted by Ivo Omrćanin, *Enigma Tito* (Washington, 1984), p. 245). Miss

Barker erroneously cites the message in a context suggesting that the reference is to the forcible repatriation of Yugoslavs from British camps, whose story formed the exclusive topic of the newspaper correspondence.

21 WO.170/4185,439; WO.170/4184,697.

22 FO.1020/42,87.

23 *Foreign Relations of the United States: Diplomatic Papers 1945* (Washington, 1961), v, p. 1250.

24 The report of Brigadier Low's conference with Colonel Hocevar on the morning of 15 May is to be found in WO.170/4241, Appx J, Folio 25, and the subsequent report to the Eighth Army in Folio 26.

25 Harold Macmillan, *War Diaries: Politics and War in the Mediterranean, January 1943–May 1945* (London, 1984), p. 683.

26 George F. Kennan, *Memoirs 1925–1950* (Boston, 1967), pp. 112–5; Charles E. Bohlen, *Witness to History 1929–1969* (London, 1973), pp. 45, 56.

27 Nikolai Tolstoy, *Victims of Yalta* (London, 1977), pp. 82, 84, 88, 337; Mark R. Elliott, *Pawns of Yalta: Soviet Refugees and America's Role in Their Repatriation* (Chicago, 1982), pp. 107, 110, 247.

28 National Archives 740.00119 Control (Italy)/5-1445 KFC.

29 *Foreign Relations of the United States . . . 1945*, v, p. 1246.

30 John Silverlight, *The Victors' Dilemma: Allied Intervention in the Russian Civil War* (London, 1970), p. 305; Robert Murphy, *Diplomat Among Warriors* (London, 1964), p. 236; Arthur Bryant, *Triumph in the West 1943–1946* (London, 1959), p. 117; Lord Moran, *Winston Churchill: The Struggle for Survival 1940–1965* (London, 1966), pp. 173–4; John Colville, *Footprints in Time* (London, 1976), p. 191.

31 WO.106/4059,341.

32 FO.1020/42,116; National Archives 740.00119 Control Italy/5-1845. The Foreign Office appears to have been apprised of Alexander's order of 17 May halting Yugoslav repatriations. On 18 May J. M. Addis of the Northern Department minuted: 'We are as a matter of fact at present not sending back to Yugoslavia Yugoslavs who don't want to go' (FO.371/48918,171).

33 NA.740.00119 Control (Italy)/8-1445.

34 WO.170/4183,487.

35 WO.170/4185,440.

36 WO.106/4059,372–3; PREM.3/364,751–2.

37 Alfred D. Chandler and Louis Galambos (eds.), *The Papers of Dwight David Eisenhower* (Baltimore, 1978), vi, pp. 67–8; cf. p. 66. On 15 May Robert Murphy had advised SHAEF of the Department of State's strict ruling on the screening of Yugoslavs and retention of dissidents opposed to return (FO.371/48918,177).

38 WO.106/4059,371.

39 The documents concerning Alexander's appeals and the response of the CCOS Committee have been conveniently printed by Ivo Omrcanin, *Dramatis Personae and Finis of The Independent State of Croatia in American and British Documents* (Bryn Mawr, 1983), pp. 44–58.

40 WO.204/1596.
  Note: On 13 April 1945 a telegram was sent to Balkan Air Force Headquarters by SACMED (Alexander), in which appears the following sentence: 'Agree that surrendered Yugoslav "Quisling" forces such as Ustashi, Domobrans, Cetniks, or Slovene White Guards should be handed over forthwith to Tito's Jugoslav forces, but consider that you should avoid as far as possible acceptance of

surrender of such "Quisling" forces by Allied troops' (WO.204/1357). In fact the telegram was addressed (at a time when the Anglo-American armies had yet to cross the Po) exclusively to Allied Forces *inside Yugoslavia*, on whose behalf Balkan Air Force HQ had appealed to AFHQ on 7 April. As the Mission comprised a total of some fifty men (apart from a concentration of technicians at the air force base at Zadar) (FO.371/48812), it is clear that the sole consideration of Alexander's order was the obvious impracticality of accepting any surrender offers within Yugoslavia. A full reading of the appropriate orders would have made the distinction clear enough: on 29 April the British Military Mission enquired what was to be the policy towards 'dissident Jugoslav and quisling forces in Venezia Giulia' should they attempt to surrender to 15 Army Group (WO.170/4185, 492).

CHAPTER SIX

1 Nigel Nicolson papers.
2 John Prcela and Stanko Guldescu (eds.), *Operation Slaughterhouse: Eyewitness Accounts of Postwar Massacres in Yugoslavia* (Philadelphia, 1970), p. 80.
3 Nigel Nicolson papers.
4 WO.170/4241, Appx J, Folio 26; WO.170/4404.
5 Prcela and Guldescu, op. cit., pp. 86. 163–9, 170–2.
6 Nigel Nicolson Log Book; WO.170/4404; WO.170/4982. The Croats at Rosenbach had been gathered from Klagenfurt and elsewhere from 15 May (Prcela and Guldescu, op. cit., p. 80).
7 Ibid., pp. 85–6.
8 Ibid., pp. 494–5. The Partisan General Kosta Nadj, whose 3rd Army was responsible for the fate of the surrendered refugees, recently declared in the Belgrade pornographic weekly *Reporter* that 150,000 opponents of the regime fell into his hands, and that 'naturally in the end we liquidated them' (issue of 6–13 January 1985, p. 26).
9 WO.170/4241, Appx J, Folio 28. On the day before Low's order, 16 May, troops were notified of the coming move 'on which the Bde was told to take no immediate action', though shortly 'all anti-Tito Yugo-Slavs were to be handed back to Tito' (Nigel Nicolson papers).
10 Nigel Nicolson Log Book.
11 George Urban, 'A Conversation with Milovan Djilas', *Encounter* (December 1979), liii, pp. 40–1.
12 WO.170/4241.
13 Nigel Nicolson Log Book.
14 *Borba* (Belgrade, 10 June 1985).
15 Nora Beloff, *Tito's Flawed Legacy: Yugoslavia & the West: 1939–84* (London, 1985), p. 123. Miss Beloff informs me that she kept careful notes of her conversation with Lord Aldington. My own was tape-recorded.
16 Cf. Prcela and Guldescu, op. cit., pp. 84–5. Nigel Nicolson's Log Book includes a cryptic entry at 1325 hrs on 19 May: 'Stop civilian Croats etc.'. For further accounts of the handover of Croats at this time, cf. Ingomar Pust, *Titostern über Kärnten 1942–1945: Totgeschwiegene Tragödien* (Klagenfurt, 1984), pp. 89–117, 219–29; August Walzl, *Kärnten 1945: Vom NS-Regime zur Besatzungsherrschaft im Alpen-Adria-Raum* (Klagenfurt, 1985), pp. 204–17.

17 Typescript memoir of Major-General G. L. Verney, DSO, MVO, kindly loaned to me by his son, Major Peter Verney; WO.170/4404; Nigel Nicolson papers.

18 David Martin, *Patriot or Traitor: The Case of General Mihailovich* (Stanford, 1978), pp. 171–3, 262–333; FO.371/59468.

19 Both petitions are now in the possession of Mr Nigel Nicolson.

20 WO.204/2864.

21 WO.170/4183,917.

22 WO.170/4185,408.

23 WO.170/4185,3986.

24 WO.170/4184,972.

25 NA.740.00119 Control (Italy)/5-2445.

26 FO.1020/2838,10C. On 24 May Allied Military Government announced the imminent evacuation of 100,000 Yugoslav nationals, with the qualification that: 'Slovenes will also be held in Austria except that in the case of extreme necessity they may be evac to Italy subject to the prior approval of this HQ by sig'. (ibid., 8A, 10A).

27 WO.170/4184,1002.

28 Nigel Nicolson Log Book; WO.170/4337; *Eighth Army News* (29 May 1945), p. 4.

29 *Vetrinjska tragedija* (Cleveland, 1960), p. 27.

30 Facsimile in *Bela Knjiga* (Cleveland, Ohio, n.d.), p. 204.

31 Information from Mr M. S. Stankovic, then serving on Colonel Tatalovic's staff.

32 WO.170/4241; FO.371/48920,86–91; Borivoje M. Karapandzic, *Jugoslovensko krvavo prolece 1945. Titovi Katini i Gulazi* (Cleveland, Ohio, 1976), pp. 33–8.

33 Facsimile in *Bela Knjiga*, p. 205.

34 Information supplied by Mr Ladislav J. Bevc, who on 28 May 1945 arrived at Viktring as an emissary from Slovenes held in a camp at Lienz. Following the discovery of the real nature of the British operation, Mr Bevc returned to Lienz on 30 May.

35 A. I. Delianich, *Вольфсберг-373* (San Francisco, 1975), pp. 82–4, 108–13.

36 In addition to the first-hand accounts quoted in the text, this account of the handover of military and paramilitary refugees in Viktring Camp is based on the following sources: Nigel Nicolson papers; FO.371/48825,63–4; WO.170/4241; WO.170/4337; Karapandzic, op. cit., pp. 83–107; *Matica Mrtvih: Podatki o Slovencih Pomorjenih po Zlocinski Osvobodilni Fronti 1941–1945* (Cleveland, Ohio, 1968–70), iv, pp. 9–25; Vladimir Kozina, '*Slovenia, the Land of my Joy and my Sorrow*' (Cleveland, Ohio, 1980), pp. 203–6, 227–38, 261–2; *Vetrinjska tragedija v spomin nesmrtnim junakom, izdanim v Vetrinju od 27.–31. maja 1945 in pomorjenim za velike ideje svobode.* (Cleveland, Ohio, 1960), pp. 19–42; Prcela and Guldescu, op. cit., pp. 84–5, 383; *The Slovenian Tragedy* (Toronto, 1970), pp. 35–7; Ingomar Pust, op. cit., pp. 202–29. The Viktring Movement Orders (of 23 and 26 May) are missing from the relevant War Diaries, but appear in photocopies in the commemorative volume *Bela Knijga* published by Slovenian emigrants in the USA (pp. 204–5).

37 Harold Macmillan, *War Diaries: Politics and War in the Mediterranean January 1943–May 1945* (London, 1984), p. 391.

38 FO.371/48817,64.

39 FO.371/48819,31.

40 FO.371/48920,122.

CHAPTER SEVEN

Note: For this chapter I have relied largely on eye-witness accounts kindly given me by Mr Frank Dejak, Mr Janez Dernulc, Mr Frank Kozina, Mr Stanislav Plesko, Mr Dimitrije Vojvodic, and Mr Milan Zajec.

1 John Prcela and Stanko Guldescu (ed.), *Operation Slaughterhouse: Eyewitness Accounts of Postwar Massacres in Yugoslavia* (Philadelphia, 1970), pp. 370–7.
2 Gregory Klimov, *The Terror Machine: The inside story of the Soviet Administration in Germany* (London, 1953), p. 228.
3 Prcela and Guldescu, op. cit., pp. 380–2.
4 I am grateful to Mr Paul Borstnik for providing me with a full account of this controversy. Cf. also *Die Welt*, 14 January 1985, p. 3; ibid., 15 January 1985, p. 5 (reference kindly supplied by Herr Hans Werner Neulen).
5 *Delo* (Ljubljana, 20 May 1985). I am indebted to Dr Ljubo Sirc and Miss Nora Beloff for supplying me with transcripts of this article.
6 Apart from the eye-witness accounts provided here, I have drawn also on Borivoje M. Karapandzic, *Jugoslovensko krvavo prolece 1945. Titovi Katini i Gulazi* (Cleveland, Ohio, 1976), pp. 39–65; idem, *Kocevje: Tito's bloodiest crime* (Cleveland, Ohio, 1965), pp. 54–77; *Vetrinjska tragedija: v spomin nesmrtnim junakom, izdanim v Vetrinju od 27.–31. maja in pomorjenim za velike ideje svobode* (Cleveland, Ohio, 1960), pp. 59–84. For a further eye-witness account of conditions in the concentration camp at St Vid, cf. Joseph Hecimovic, *In Tito's Death Marches: Testimony on the Massacres of the Croatian War Prisoners and Civilians after World War II* (Chicago, 1961), pp. 36–43.
7 WO.170/4241, Appx J, Folio 29.
8 *Jugoslovensko krvavo prolece 1945*, pp. 170–4.
9 *Vetrinska tragedija*, pp. 84–118; Prcela and Guldescu, op. cit., pp. 369–70; cf. FO.371/48825,74–5.
10 WO.170/4142; *Foreign Relations of the United States: Diplomatic Papers 1945* (Washington, 1967), v, p. 1246. By 29 July 29,972 'Yugoslavs, inc Croats, Serbs, Slovenes' had been returned, with 781 awaiting evacuation (FO.1020/39,88).
11 *Vetrinska tragedija*, p. 41. For a breakdown of Slovenian units handed over and their destinations, see *Bela Knijga*, p. 206.
12 Phyllis Auty, *Tito: A Biography* (London, 1970), p. 265.
13 Milovan Djilas, *Wartime* (New York, 1977), pp. 446–9.

CHAPTER EIGHT

1 WO.170/4388.
2 WO.170/4461.
3 WO.170/4241.
4 Cf. Stanislav Ausky, Предательство и измена: войска генерала Власова в Чехии (San Francisco, 1982), p. 89.
5 WO.170/4241.
6 The AFHQ reply of 22 May refers to 'your A 4073 of 21 May asking for policy re Cossacks'. A careful search has failed to unearth the document referred to. There is an A 4073 in the Eighth Army War Diary (WO.170/4184), but it is dated 16 May and refers to Yugoslav food convoys.
7 FO.1020/42,148; WO.170/4183,487; WO.170/4184,917.

8 National Archives 740.00119 Control (Italy)/5-2445.
9 WO.204/1525; FO.1020/42,122.
10 Ibid., 135.
11 Ibid., 130.
12 Ibid., 141.
13 WO.170/4185,639.
14 WO.170/4461; WO.170/4396.
15 WO.170/4184,1037.
16 WO.170/4183,460.
17 Malcolm Proudfoot, *European Refugees: 1939–52; A Study in Forced Population Movement* (London, 1957), pp. 210–11.
18 FO.1020/42,92.
19 Ivo Omrćanin, *Dramatis Personae and Finis of The Independent State of Croatia* (Bryn Mawr, 1983), pp. 49–50.
20 John Silverlight, *The Victors' Dilemma: Allied Intervention in the Russian Civil War* (London, 1970), p. 286.
21 PREM.3 364/17, 748–50. For Macmillan's visit to England, see Harold Macmillan, *War Diaries: Politics and War in the Mediterranean January 1943–May 1945* (London, 1984), pp. 761–3.
22 NA.800.4016 DP/8–145; FO.371/4910,77.
23 Kenneth Young (ed.), *The Diaries of Sir Robert Bruce Lockhart* (London, 1980), pp. 328, 519–20.
24 Macmillan had originally intended to return a day earlier, on 21 May (NA.00119 Control (Italy)/5-2145), and it was on that day that Keightley first applied for instructions concerning the repatriation of Cossacks.
25 FO.1020/2838,8A.
26 WO.170/4241.
27 WO.170/4388.
28 Cf. the examples (in every sense) of Colonel Alec Wilkinson (Nikolai Tolstoy, *Victims of Yalta* (London, 1977), pp. 341, 354), and Brigadier R. P. Waller (*Gunner Magazine* (February 1979)). I am grateful to Mr F. R. Jephson for supplying the latter reference. Formerly serving with the Brigadier, he adds: 'I have reason to believe that he was "court-martialled for refusing to repatriate Cossacks" but I have no idea of "when" or "where".'
29 WO.170/4396.
30 Tolstoy, op. cit., pp. 268–9.
31 WO.170/4389.
32 Tolstoy, op. cit., pp. 269–70.
33 WO.170/4241.
34 WO.170/4389.
35 WO.170/4404.

CHAPTER NINE

1 A. Petrowsky, *Unvergessener Verrat!* (Munich, 1965), p. 104; General V. G. Naumenko (ed.), *Великое Предательство: выдача Казаков* Ь *Лиенце и других местах* (New York, 1962–70), ii, pp. 242, 246.
2 'A. I. Romanov', *Nights are Longest There: Smersh from the Inside* (London, 1972), pp. 153–5.

3 Naumenko, op. cit., i, pp. 173–5. For an eye-witness account of one killing at Judenburg, cf. N. N. Krasnov, *Незабываемое 1945-1956* (New York, 1959), p. 51.

4 For Merkulov's career and character, cf. Thaddeus Wittlin, *Commissar: The Life and Death of Lavrenty Pavlovich Beria* (London, 1973), pp. 21–3, 38; Victor Kravchenko, *I Chose Freedom: The Personal and Political Life of a Soviet Official* (London, 1947), pp. 280–1, 324; Robert Conquest, *The Great Terror: Stalin's Purge of the Thirties* (London, 1968), p. 465; Vaino Tanner, *The Winter War: Finland Against Russia 1939–1940* (Stanford, 1957), pp. 70–1; Gustav Hilger and Alfred G. Meyer, *The Incompatible Allies: A Memoir-History of German-Soviet Relations 1918–1941* (New York, 1973), p. 322; 'A. I. Romanov', op. cit., pp. 55, 138, 184; David J. Dallin and Boris I. Nicolaevsky, *Forced Labour in Soviet Russia* (London, 1948), p. 269; G. A. Tokaev, *Comrade X* (London, 1956), p. 338; Robert Conquest, *Inside Stalin's Secret Police: NKVD Politics 1936–9* (London, 1985), p. 88.

5 Krasnov, op. cit., pp. 41–84.

6 Ibid., pp. 325–6.

7 It may be remarked – coincidence or not – that similar characteristics represent salient facets of the mind of the common criminal (cf. Alfred Adler, *Problems of Neurosis: A Book of Case-Histories* (London, 1929), pp. 129–30).

8 Z. Stypulkowski, *Invitation to Moscow* (London, 1951), pp. 266, 294. One may also compare the speech made by Merkulov's colleague Abakumov to an audience of SMERSH officers at almost exactly the same time ('A. I. Romanov', op. cit., pp. 237–9).

9 Ibid., p. 154.

10 Cf. Naumenko, op. cit., ii, pp. 36–8.

11 The Rt Hon the Earl of Avon, *The Eden Memoirs: The Reckoning* (London, 1965), pp. 528–37.

12 Quoted in Naumenko, op. cit., ii, pp. 296–7. The report appeared next day in the *New York Times*.

13 M. K. Kasvinov, *Двадцать три ступени вниз* (Moscow, 1979), pp. 41–2.

14 Naumenko, op. cit., ii, pp. 237–66; cf. pp. 302–5.

15 Ibid., pp. 297–9.

16 Solzhenitsyn records another example of this strange reaction (Michael Scammell, *Solzhenitsyn: A Biography* (London, 1985), pp. 174, 178).

17 Wittlin, op cit., pp. 397–401, 407–11.

18 For the text, cf. Naumenko, op. cit., ii, pp. 318–19.

19 Ibid., pp. 303–17. Cf., for the treatment of the Cossacks in Siberia, Edgar M. Wenzel, *So gingen die Kosaken durch die Hölle* (Vienna, 1976), pp. 102–8, 160–6.

20 Naumenko, op. cit., ii, pp. 327–8.

21 FO.371/66347; WO.204/10449; WO.204/10450; FO.1020/504.

22 WO.32/15297. I am grateful to my old friend Michael Brereton for drawing my attention to this file.

23 Nikolai Tolstoy, 'The Klagenfurt Conspiracy: War Crimes & Diplomatic Secrets', *Encounter* (May 1983), lx, p. 24.

24 Peter J. Huxley-Blythe, *The East Came West* (Caldwell, Ohio, 1964), pp. 202–13; Petrovsky, op. cit., pp. 95–104.

CHAPTER TEN

1 Nikolai Tolstoy, *Victims of Yalta* (London, 1977), pp. 245–7, 260–2; WO.170/ 4982.
2 Letter from Lord Aldington to the author, 25 June 1974. Much more recently, on 14 February 1983, Lord Aldington altered the date of his departure to '25th or 26th May'. This is certainly too early.
3 FO.371/51227.
4 The day after Low arranged the return of Slovenian civilians to Tito, Allied Military Government was still led to believe that 'Slovenes will . . . be held in Austria except that in the case of extreme necessity they may be evac to Italy subject to the prior approval of this HQ by sig' (FO.1020/2838,8A).
5 FO.371/48920,90.
6 The foregoing account is based on information kindly supplied by the Dowager Lady Falmouth; Major P. H. Barre and Miss Florence Phillips, a Red Cross nurse in Viktring Camp; also on Nigel Nicolson papers; FO.371/48825,76; Vladimir Kozina, 'Slovenia, The Land of my Joy and my Sorrow' (Toronto, 1980), pp. 228–46; *Vetrinska tragedija* (Cleveland, 1960), pp. 42–58. Alexander's words were repeated next day by Dr Mersol to Mr F. Koleman Waukegan, head of the Viktring Camp police (testimony kindly passed to me by Mr Peter Urbanc). Cf. also FO.120/415,37B.
7 I am grateful to Dr David Andrews for permission to quote from his mother's diaries. On 29 May 1945 *Eighth Army News* carried a picture of General McCreery in conversation with Major Barre and Miss Balding during his inspection of Viktring Camp on 25 May.
8 Krasnov wrote the original version of his memoirs in Sweden immediately following his departure from the Soviet Union in 1955. The account of his wife's experiences appears in an epilogue to the English translation (N. N. Krasnov, Jr, *The Hidden Russia: My Ten Years as a Slave Laborer* (New York, 1960), p. 332).
9 Cf. Tolstoy, op. cit., pp. 263–4, 330; WO.170/4389.
10 Scott's account of Alexander's visit is reprinted by Jerome Jareb and Ivo Omrćanin, 'The end of the Croatian Army at Bleiburg, Austria in May 1945 according to English military documents', *Journal of Croatian Studies* (New York, 1977–8), xviii–xix, pp. 175–6. On 17 July 1947, Major Tufton Beamish, MP, noted: 'When I visited Displaced Persons Camps in Austria I was able to get further information about these [Cossack] deportations which were, I believe, finally stopped on the personal instructions of Field Marshal Lord Alexander' (WO.204/10450).
11 FO.1020/39,22.
12 A puzzling exception is the case of General Shkuro, whose handover is referred to in the report, though not his émigré status. I know of nothing that can explain this anomaly. A possibility might be that someone had mentioned to Alexander the fate of the old Kuban Cossack, and that it was therefore felt necessary to include his name in the report. It would be interesting to learn more of the matter, though it seems doubtful if we ever shall.
13 FO.1020/2838,31A. For subsequent objections by McCreery to the policy of forced repatriation, cf. FO.1020/362,23A.
14 WO.214/63A. On 10 July Alexander directed the Eighth Army to 'hand over to Russians those Cossacks who can be returned without use of force . . .'

(NA.740.00119 Control (Italy)/7-1045). On 22 May Alexander had however declined to intervene when high-handed 'screening' by Soviet officials in a British-run camp in Greece was reported to him, on the grounds that 'reprisal unwise as might react unfavourably on British or American PW in Russian ownership elsewhere where numbers are considerable while yours are small' (WO.204/10126). The numbers were indeed very small and, as has been shown earlier, Alexander regarded the Cossacks as a special case, not liable for barter of this sort.

15 *Foreign Relations of the United States: Diplomatic Papers 1945* (Washington, 1961), v. pp. 1246–7.

16 National Archives, 740.00119 Control (Italy)/8-445.

17 *Foreign Relations of the United States . . . 1945*, v, p. 1250.

18 In a BBC 1 *Timewatch* programme, *The Klagenfurt Affair*, screened on 3 January 1984, it was claimed that 'Alexander . . . overrode instructions from Whitehall and Washington that the Yugoslavs should be screened and only genuine Nazi collaborators handed over to Tito', and that 'their repatriation in defiance of Cabinet instructions was ordered by Lord Alexander' (*The Times*, 3 January 1984; cf. the letter from Mr Timothy Gardam (ibid., 20 January 1984)). This sensational revelation arose when *Timewatch* 'discovered a document . . . which shows that . . . Kirk refused to support the May 14 order.' Some idea of the profundity of Mr Gardam's researches may be gained from the fact that this 'discovery' was quarried (unacknowledged) from page 14 of my article 'The Klagenfurt Conspiracy' (*Encounter*, May, 1983). Another writer, innocently accepting the validity of the *Timewatch* 'researches', went on to draw a parallel between Alexander and Eichmann (George Gale, *Daily Express*, 6 January 1984). Among other conflicting speculations, the BBC version suggested that Alexander's 'New Army Order' of 4 June, which halted repatriation from Viktring, was in fact a plant, designed to deflect suspicion that it was Alexander himself who had engineered the operation. It would in that case have been a singularly ineffective plant, since it is in fact absent from AFHQ files, and only survives because by chance a copy fell into the hands of Dr Krek.

19 On 31 July Alexander's Chief of Staff, General Morgan, sent a reply to Dr Krek's letter which provided a similar version of events to that given to Kirk next month by Alexander. Interestingly, Morgan stated that 'in view of the situation that existed at that time in Austria, they [the Yugoslav refugees] were handed over to the Jugoslav Military Forces in the course of the military operations which were then being conducted in parts of that country by both British and Jugoslav forces.' (FO.371/48825,62). Here the repatriation operation for which AFHQ took direct responsibility is still more clearly identified exclusively with the crisis over the arrival of the Croats before Bleiburg in mid-May. For by the time the evacuations from Viktring Camp began no military operations were being conducted in Austria, and Yugoslav forces had entirely evacuated the area.

CHAPTER ELEVEN

1 Aino Kuusinen, *Before and After Stalin: A Personal Account of Soviet Russia from the 1920s to the 1960s* (London, 1974), pp. 140–1.

2 Isaiah Berlin, 'History and Theory: The Concept of Scientific History', *History and Theory: Studies in the Philosophy of History* (The Hague, 1960), i, pp. 8–9.

3 R. G. Collingwood, *The Idea of History* (Oxford, 1946), pp. 236–7.

4 Ibid., p. 242.

5 For the distinction between testimony and evidence, cf. ibid., pp. 256–7. The opportunity to cross-examine and check the testimony of surviving participants in historical events could be argued in some degree to overcome Popper's objection that historical events cannot be repeated (cf. the discussion by Burleigh Taylor Wilkins, *Has History Any Meaning? A Critique of Popper's Philosophy of History* (Hassocks, Sussex, 1978), pp. 60–9).

6 Collingwood, op. cit., p. 282; cf. Wilkins, op. cit., pp. 50–55.

7 Harry Hearder, *Ideological Commitment and Historical Interpretation* (Cardiff, 1969), p. 10; cf. C. Behan McCullagh, *Justifying historical descriptions* (Cambridge, 1984), pp. 26–7.

8 FO.371/48919; FO.371/48920; FO.371/48930 (documents printed by Ivo Omrćanin, *Dramatis Personae and Finis of The Independent State of Croatia in American and British Documents* (Bryn Mawr, 1983), pp. 70–95.

9 Letter from Sir John Colville to the author of 29 June 1984.

10 FO.371/48920.

11 *Vetrinjska tragedija* (Cleveland, 1960), pp. 133–4; information from Mr John Corsellis. The reference to a figure of '600' Yugoslav collaborators handed over derives presumably from the '900' found in FO minutes.

12 Harold Macmillan, *War Diaries: Politics and War in the Mediterranean, January 1943–May 1945* (London, 1984), p. xvi.

13 *Sunday Telegraph*, 30 December 1984.

14 Christopher Booker, 'Judgment at Klagenfurt', *The Spectator* (17 October 1981), p. 13. Mr Booker was of course arguing from the limited amount of circumstantial evidence available at the time of writing.

15 WO.106/4059,343. Brigadier Patrick Scott, commanding in the most forward area around Wolfsberg, recalled afterwards that, 'We never had a moment's difficulty in our dealings with the Russians; everything was done most correctly and with the minimum waste of time' (Jerome Jareb and Ivo Omrćanin, 'The end of the Croatian Army at Bleiburg, Austria in May 1945 according to English military documents' *Journal of Croatian Studies* (New York, 1977–78), xviii–xix, p. 155).

16 *Borba* (Belgrade, 10 June 1985). Nadj learned nothing of the brief British stalling recorded by General Shtemenko. This could be taken to imply that Tolbukhin no longer regarded it as worthy of mention, in view of the swift British reversal of policy three days after their initial refusal. Alternatively, as I shall suggest, the local Red Army command had been bypassed in these essentially political negotiations by the MVD.

17 WO.106/4059,408,435.

18 WO.170/4337, Appx. D, Folio 2.

19 WO.106/4059,251,317–9,322A,389,408. For the departure of the Partisans from Klagenfurt, cf. Wilhelm Wadl, *Das Jahr 1945 in Kärnten: Ein Überblick* (Klagenfurt, 1985), pp. 42–3.

20 Alfred D. Chandler, Jr. and Louis Galambos (ed.), *The Papers of Dwight David Eisenhower* (Baltimore, 1978), vi, pp. 57–9, 62–5; Geoffrey Cox, *The Race for Trieste* (London, 1977), pp. 249–50; NA.740.00119 Control (Italy)/5–2245, 2345.

21 NA.740/00119 Control (Italy)/5–945.

22 WO.106/4059,311A.

23 Milovan Djilas, *Wartime* (New York, 1977), pp. 449–50. For a perceptive analysis of the factors restraining Stalin from intervening at this time, cf. Cox, op. cit., pp. 258–9.

24 NA.740.00119 Control (Italy)/5-945,1245; WO.106/4059,457A.

25 George Urban, 'A Conversation with Milovan Djilas', *Encounter* (December 1979), pp. 40–2. That the Domobranci were for the most part 'simple peasants' who were 'fundamentally anti-German and pro-Allied' is also the view of Captain F. Waddams, a former liaison officer with the Partisans and British Consul in Ljubljana (Nora Beloff, *Tito's Flawed Legacy; Yugoslavia & the West: 1939–84* (London, 1985), p. 126).

26 FO.371/48811. By 29 April Sir Orme Sargent minuted the Prime Minister that, 'We had hoped that these anti-Partisan forces in north-west Yugoslavia might, without any assistance from us, prevent Tito from entering Venezia Giulia and Trieste in advance of our troops. Instead of doing this it now looks as though these Partisans will offer their services to the Allied Commanders which is much more awkward' (PREM.3/495/6,125).

CHAPTER TWELVE

1 John Erickson, *The Road to Berlin* (London, 1983), pp. 621–2.

2 W. Averell Harriman, *America and Russia in a Changing World* (New York, 1971), p. 44.

3 Cf. Nicholas V. Riasonovsky, *A Parting of Ways: Government and the Educated Public in Russia 1801–1855* (Oxford, 1976), pp. 95–6.

4 Adam B. Ulam, *Stalin: The Man and his Era* (London, 1974), pp. 320–1.

5 Gregory Klimov, *The Terror Machine: The inside story of the Soviet Administration in Germany* (London, 1953), p. 69.

6 Ibid., pp. 71–3; George F. Kennan, *Memoirs 1925–1950* (Boston, 1967), pp. 240–2; John R. Deane, *The Strange Alliance: The Story of American Efforts at Wartime Co-operation with Russia* (London, 1947), pp. 180–1.

7 Ulam, op. cit., pp. 616–18, 633–4; Peter Deriabin and Frank Gibney, *The Secret World* (London, 1959), pp. 63–8; Erickson, op. cit., p. 397.

8 Michael Scammell, *Solzhenitsyn: A Biography* (London, 1985), pp. 142–75; Erickson, op. cit., p. 618.

9 Roy A. Medvedev, *Let History Judge: The Origins and Consequences of Stalinism* (London, 1972), pp. 467–9; 'Romanov', op. cit., pp. 163–9; Otto Preston Chaney Jr., *Zhukov* (Newton Abbot, 1972), pp. 348–51.

10 Stanislav Ausky, *Предательство и измена: войска генерала Власова в Чехии* (San Francisco, 1982), pp. 25–39.

11 Scammell, op. cit., pp. 132–3.

12 Joachim Hoffmann, *Die Geschichte der Wlassow-Armee* (Freiburg, 1984), p. 80.

13 Ibid., pp. 164–92; Ausky, op. cit., pp. 93–103.

14 Hoffmann, op. cit., pp. 193–285; Ausky, op. cit., pp. 104–255.

15 'A. I. Romanov', *Nights are Longest There: Smersh from the Inside* (London, 1972), Ibid., p. 56; p. 127.

16 A. Kazantsev, *Третья Сила: история одной попытки* (Frankfurt, 1974), pp. 351–2; Ausky, op. cit., pp. 37–8, 51–2, 67; Hoffmann, op. cit., p. 205; George Fischer, *Soviet Opposition to Stalin: a case study in world war II* (Harvard, 1952),

pp. 66, 103. The Soviet General Staff believed that the Vlasovites planned to set up a redoubt in the Bavarian Alps, awaiting the outbreak of war between the Soviet Union and her former Allies (S. M. Shtemenko, *Генеральный Штаб в годы войны* (Moscow, 1973), ii, pp. 447–8).

17 Ausky, op. cit., pp. 41, 75.

18 Fischer, op. cit., pp. 108–12; Malcolm J. Proudfoot, *European Refugees: 1939–52: A Study in Forced Population Movement* (London, 1957), pp. 207–20.

19 Nikolai Tolstoy, *Victims of Yalta* (London, 1977), pp. 97–8.

20 Ausky, op. cit., pp. 250–5; Hoffmann, op. cit., pp. 282–3.

21 David J. Dallin and Boris I. Nicolaevsky, *Forced Labour in Soviet Russia* (London, 1948), pp. 281–96; Tolstoy, op. cit., pp. 395–9.

22 Cf. Erickson, op. cit., pp. 92–7, 402–4.

23 Tolstoy, op. cit., pp. 64–7, 100–11.

24 Vojtech Mastny, *Russia's Road to the Cold War: Diplomacy, Warfare and the Politics of Communism, 1941–1945* (New York, 1979), pp. 237, 270–1; A. A. Gromyko et al. (ed.), *Stalin's Correspondence with Churchill, Attlee, Roosevelt and Truman 1941–45* (London, 1958), ii, pp. 200–1, 205–6, 208–10; Milovan Djilas, *Conversations with Stalin* (London, 1962), pp. 70, 107, 141. The Yugoslav Communist leader Vladimir Dedijer is still convinced that the Wolff-Dulles negotiations represented a secret Anglo-American conspiracy against the Soviet Union ('Vladimir Dedijer: Testimonies on the Second World War', *The South Slav Journal* (London, 1979), ii, pt. 2, p. 12).

25 Tony Sharp, *The Wartime Alliance and the Zonal Division of Germany* (Oxford, 1975), pp. 90–119.

26 Winston S. Churchill, *Triumph and Tragedy* (London, 1954), pp. 437, 442–3, 498–9; Strobe Talbott (ed.), *Khrushchev Remembers* (Boston, 1970), p. 221.

27 George C. Herring, Jr, *Aid to Russia 1941–1946: Strategy, Diplomacy, the Origins of the Cold War* (New York, 1973), pp. 180–211.

28 One of the most perceptive wartime analyses of the Soviet Union was that compiled by Ronald Matthews, Moscow correspondent of the Socialist *Daily Herald* from 1942 to 1944. As he noted:

> I cannot help feeling that when the influential review *War and the Working Class* argued in one of last summer's issues that one of the reasons why a delay [in the advance into Eastern Europe] might lead to an outbreak of revolutions all over the Continent such as that which followed the last war, it was not for a moment indulging in an argument *ad hominem*. Far from having its tongue in its cheek as it played on the Western Powers' nerves, I think it was expressing a fear that is probably very real in Moscow ruling circles. The fear, I mean, that the freedom which may be found under any new revolutionary regimes in Europe may put dangerous ideas into the regimented masses of Russia. A Germany, for instance, that went Communist in this way might shift the whole balance of power of world Communism. (CAB.66/64,131)

29 Romuald J. Misiunas and Rein Taagepera, *The Baltic States: Years of Dependence 1940–1980* (London, 1983), pp. 81–91; Talbott, op. cit., pp. 140–1, 217–18; Nikolai Tolstoy, *Stalin's Secret War* (London, 1981), pp. 264–71.

30 Ibid., pp. 150–4.

31 Hoffmann, op. cit., p. 171; Ortwin Buchbender, *Das tönende Erz: Deutsche Propaganda gegen die Rote Armee in Zweiten Weltkrieg* (Stuttgart, 1978), pp. 255–7; Wilfried Strik-Strikfeldt, *Against Stalin and Hitler: Memoirs of the Russian Liberation Movement 1941–5* (London, 1970), p. 195.

32 CAB.66/64,91–2.

33 Dwight D. Eisenhower, *Crusade in Europe* (New York, 1948), pp. 417–18; Robert Murphy, *Diplomat Among Warriors* (London, 1964), pp. 311–13; Nikolai Tolstoy, *Victims of Yalta*, pp. 288–93.

34 Ausky, op. cit., p. 230; Hoffmann, op. cit., pp. 271–4.

35 Mastny, op. cit., pp. 276–9; Erickson, op. cit., pp. 631–40.

36 *Victims of Yalta*, pp. 249–50.

37 WO.170/4461 (report of Sgt Kennedy of the Fifth Buffs); General V. G. Naumenko (ed.), *Великое предательство: выдача Казаков в Лиенце и других местах* (New York, 1962–70), i, p. 208; ii, pp. 35–6; A. I. Delianich, *Вольсфберг-373* (San Francisco, 1975), pp. 84–5. On 28 May BGS Fifth Corps noted in a message to the Eighth Army: 'To assist us with org[anisation] return Russian civilians one Russian LO has been Att own HQ Wolfsberg during past week with our permission'. The Soviets wanted to send a further five officers, but this Keightley opposed (WO.170/4184, 1148). Cf. FO.1020/39,22.

38 FO.371/47910,78.

39 Edward J. Rozek, *Allied Wartime Diplomacy: A Pattern in Poland* (New York, 1958), pp. 370–2; Z. Stypulkowski, *Invitation to Moscow* (London, 1951), pp. 211–32.

40 Unto Parvilahti, *Beria's Gardens: Ten Years' Captivity in Russia and Siberia* (London, 1959), pp. 76, 127–8. The use of spurious invitations of this kind appears to have been standard NKVD practice (cf. Roy A. Medvedev, *On Stalin and Stalinism* (Oxford, 1979), pp. 134–5).

41 Eric L. Pridonoff, *Tito's Yugoslavia* (Washington, 1955), pp. 30–1, 100, 212; Djilas, op. cit., p. 77; Ulam, op. cit., p. 611.

42 Milovan Djilas, *Wartime* (New York, 1977), p. 443.

43 Jerome Jareb and Ivo Omrćanin (eds.), 'Croatian Government's Memorandum to the Allied Headquarters Mediterranean, May 4, 1945', *Journal of Croatian Studies* (New York, 1980), xxi, pp. 120–43.

44 John Prcela and Stanko Guldescu (ed.), *Operation Slaughterhouse: Eyewitness Accounts of Postwar Massacres In Yugoslavia* (Philadelphia, 1970), p. 136.

45 Jozo Tomasevich, *The Chetniks: War and Revolution in Yugoslavia, 1941–1945* (Stanford, 1975), pp. 453–7.

46 'Tito – Maclean Talks in 1947', *The South Slav Journal* (London, 1981/82), iv. pp. 35–6, 39.

47 Mastny, op. cit., pp. 208–10.

48 Walter R. Roberts, *Tito, Mihailovic and the Allies, 1941–1945* (New Brunswick, 1973), p. 163; Fitzroy Maclean, *Eastern Approaches* (London, 1949), p. 519; Phyllis Auty, *Tito: A Biography* (London, 1970), p. 129. Cf. the British Foreign Office estimate expressed as late as November 1947 (Victor Rothwell, *Britain and the Cold War 1941–1947* (London, 1982), p. 395). Nora Beloff conjectures plausibly that becoming an informer ensured Tito's miraculous survival of the Moscow purges (*Tito's Flawed Legacy; Yugoslavia & the West: 1939–84* (London, 1985), pp. 53–5).

49 Djilas, *Conversations with Stalin*, pp. 81–3; Pridonoff, op. cit., pp. 46–7, 101–4.

50 Djilas, *Wartime*, p. 394; Vladimir and Evdokia Petrov, *Empire of Fear* (London, 1956), p. 216. Maclean recalls encountering the NKVD agent who is presumably to be identified with this Zhukov (Maclean, op. cit., p. 435).

51 Tolstoy, *Stalin's Secret War*, pp. 50–7.

52 Djilas, *Conversations with Stalin*, pp. 65, 70–1; idem., *Wartime*, p. 419; Pridonoff, op. cit., p. 120; Petrov and Petrov, op. cit., pp. 215–17; Deriabin, op. cit., p. 211. On 6 March 1944 General Donovan of OSS noted that Partisan detachments were kept under control by 'political commissars', who, 'we further understand, have been trained in Russia'; and on 9 February 1945 Alexander Kirk at AFHQ reported 'under-cover NKVD activity' in Yugoslavia (reports cited by Ivo Omrćanin, *Enigma Tito* (Washington, 1984), pp. 33, 350; NA.740.00119 Control (Italy)/6-445).

53 Louis Fitzgibbon, *Unpitied and Unknown: Katyn . . . Bologoye . . . Dergachi* (London, 1975), pp. 286–7.

54 Prcela and Guldescu, op. cit., p. 461.

55 Joseph Hecimovic, *In Tito's Death Marches* (Chicago, 1961), pp. 54–5; Prcela and Guldescu, op. cit., pp. 534–5.

56 Ibid., pp. 244–5, 297. For 25 May as the official date of Tito's birthday, cf. Djilas, *Wartime*, p. 370. There seems no reason to doubt the two separately-attested accounts of Tito's 'amnesty', which is referred to in passing without any motivation for fabrication.

57 FO.371/51227.

58 Prcela and Guldescu, op. cit., p. 336. The British authorities had known long before this of extensive atrocities being committed by the Yugoslav Communist regime; cf. WO.214/63A; FO.371/48825,74. On 12 April an American diplomat from the Belgrade Embassy reported a conversation held with Yugoslav Vice Premier Kardelj who, after listening to suggestions of a post-war amnesty: 'agreed somewhat reluctantly but was careful to state that the list of traitors and war criminals was large and that a very big job of epuration would have to be done in the still occupied portions of the country and Serb "reaction" eliminated' (NA.860H.00/4-1245).

59 Letter of 20 December 1978 to Mr Stanisa R. Vlahovic.

60 FO.371/48819,136. On 27 May Tito made a speech at Ljubljana, declaring that 'the avenging arm of the people' had dealt with 'the enormous majority of class enemies' (*Josip Broz Tito: Govori i Članci* (Zagreb, 1959), p. 279).

Chronology of Events:

relating to the repatriation of Cossacks and Yugoslavs
from Austria in 1945.

19 February
Foreign Office notifies Macmillan that non-Soviet citizens are not
to be repatriated against their will.

13 March
AFHQ passes down this ruling to Eighth Army and Fifth Corps,
arranging a camp where screening can take place.

29 April
Churchill rules that all surrendering Yugoslavs must be retained in
camps pending a government decision as to their fate.

2 May
AFHQ orders Fifteenth Army Group to implement this ruling.

3 May
12,000 Royalist Yugoslavs surrender to Eighth Army and are
retained in accordance with the AFHQ ruling.

6 May
AFHQ sends Eighth Army a definition of Soviet citizenship.

8 May
Domanov's Cossacks negotiate surrender to General Arbuthnott's
Seventy-eighth Infantry Division.

10 May
General Keightley visits Soviets at Voitsberg, who demand handover of Cossacks.

11 May
Brigadier Tryon-Wilson travels to Voitsberg, and receives Soviet
demand for handover of Tsarist generals and other non-Soviet citizens
among Cossacks.

12 May
Keightley intervenes to protect surrendering Cossacks from falling into Soviet hands.
Refugees from Yugoslavia concentrated at Viktring.

13 May
Macmillan flies in to Klagenfurt and confers with Keightley.

14 May
Fifth Corps learns of approach of 200,000 Croats.
Keightley reports to McCreery that Cossacks are Soviet citizens, and that he has that day suggested their return to a Soviet general.
Macmillan reports to Foreign Office on his mission, omitting all reference to his flight to Austria.
General Robertson at AFHQ responds to Macmillan's intervention by ordering return of 'Russians' and Yugoslavs fighting for the Germans. US Ambassador Kirk objects to latter, as contrary to agreed Allied policy.

15 May
Fifth Corps turns back 200,000 Croats.
Alexander, mistakenly believing that they have surrendered to Eighth Army, offers them to Tito.
Macmillan informs Foreign Office of his visit to Fifth Corps, omitting reference to Yugoslav refugees, and stating that only thirty Cossacks are in Fifth Corps hands.
Keightley informs General Murray of plan to hand over Cossacks.
US State Department orders Kirk to object to Robertson's order of the previous day.

16 May
General Morgan, Alexander's Chief of Staff, suggests that Eisenhower take over the Cossacks.

17 May
The crisis over the Croat irruption ended, AFHQ orders all Yugoslavs to be retained as surrendered enemy personnel.
Alexander asks Eisenhower to accept the Cossacks in SHAEF area, and appeals to the Combined Chiefs of Staff on their and the Yugoslavs' account.
Fifth Corps issues operational instructions for all Yugoslavs to be handed over as soon as possible.

19 May
Brigadier Low at Fifth Corps agrees with Titoist Colonel Ivanovic to hand over all Yugoslavs in Corps area.

Eisenhower agrees to accept Cossacks.

Macmillan flies to London.

20 May

Thirty-sixth Infantry Brigade Commander informed of forthcoming handover of Cossacks.

21 May

SHAEF informs Chiefs of Staff that they will accept Cossacks.

Fifth Corps issues 'definition' of Soviet citizens, and sends representative to Soviets to arrange Cossack repatriation.

Eighth Army asks AFHQ for representative to advise on repatriation.

22 May

Fifteenth Army Group provides Eighth Army with directions for transferring Cossacks to SHAEF.

AFHQ instructs Eighth Army to repatriate Cossacks who will go without use of force; remainder to be transferred as planned to SHAEF.

Fifth Corps orders force to be used against Cossacks resisting handover.

Macmillan returns to AFHQ.

23 May

Fifth Corps requests permission from Eighth Army to return all Yugoslavs.

AFHQ agrees to return of Yugoslavs, provided no force is used. Representative coming to arrange their screening and retention.

Kirk reports to US State Department that AFHQ is retaining all Yugoslavs.

Fifth Corps requests from Eighth Army authority to use force against Cossacks reluctant to return, in order to implement Macmillan's directive.

White Russian General Shkuro writes to Seventy-eighth Infantry Division.

24 May

Handover of Serbs and Slovenes at Viktring begins.

Fifth Corps provisional order issued for Cossack handover, laying stress on importance of handing over all senior officers.

General Shkuro writes again to Seventy-eighth Infantry Division.

25 May

Fifth Corps informs Fifteenth Army Group that all Cossacks to be returned are Soviet citizens.

Eighth Army instructs Fifth Corps that all Soviet citizens are to be repatriated.

26 May

General Shkuro secretly transferred to Spittal in advance of other Cossack officers.

British–Soviet agreement at Graz to hand over Cossacks.

27 May

Fifth Corps operational order to hand over Cossacks.

28 May

Cossack officers at Lienz invited to 'conference'.

Return of non-Soviet Cossacks questioned by Sixth Armoured Division, and at once abandoned by Fifth Corps HQ within their area.

29 May

Cossack officers, the majority of whom are known to be non-Soviet citizens, handed over to Soviets at Judenburg.

30 May

Threatened withdrawal of Red Cross if repatriation of Yugoslavs continues.

31 May

Major Barre questions order to return 6,000 Slovenian civilians, which is at once cancelled by Fifth Corps.

1 June

Major scenes of violence begin as thousands of Cossacks are rounded up in Peggetz Camp for return.

3 June

Alexander reports that no liberated British prisoners of war have yet been received overland from the Soviets in exchange for return of Soviet deportees and prisoners.

4 June

Alexander visits Viktring, and issues 'New Army Order' permanently halting repatriation of Yugoslavs.

Fifth Corps issues secret order initiating screening of Cossacks for the first time in Seventy-eighth Infantry Division area.

5 June

Brigadier Musson of Thirty-sixth Infantry Brigade leaves for England.

Alexander visits Seventy-eighth Infantry Division area.

7 June

Alexander sends liaison officer to Fifth Corps, to investigate hand-overs of Cossacks and Yugoslavs.

13 June

McCreery learns that non-Soviet citizens have been included among Cossacks returned, and orders that henceforward screening be enforced and no force employed.

20 June

Combined Chiefs of Staff confirm that Soviet citizens among the Cossacks may be returned, but that all Yugoslavs should be retained.

4 August

US Ambassador Kirk learns for the first time that the Yugoslavs have been handed over, contrary to Allied policy.

Index

Compiled by Gordon Robinson